THE
BOURNE
ULTIMATUM

ROBERT LUDLUM

THE BOURNE ULTIMATUM

RANDOM HOUSE   NEW YORK

Copyright © 1990 by Robert Ludlum

All rights reserved under International and Pan-American
Copyright Conventions. Published in the United States by
Random House, Inc., New York, and simultaneously in Canada
by Random House of Canada Limited, Toronto.

Library of Congress Cataloging-in-Publication Data
Ludlum, Robert.
  The Bourne ultimatum / by Robert Ludlum —Large print ed.
    p.   cm.
  ISBN 0-679-40043-5 (lg. print)
  1. Large type books. I. Title.
[PS3562.U26B685   1990b]
813'.54—dc20 90-42676

Manufactured in the United States of America

9 8 7 6 5 4 3 2
First Large Print Edition

For Bobbi and Leonard Raichert,

Two Lovely People Who Have Enriched

Our Lives — Our Thanks

Darkness had descended on Manassas, Virginia, the countryside alive with nocturnal undercurrents, as Bourne crept through the woods bordering the estate of General Norman Swayne. Startled birds fluttered out of their black recesses; crows awoke in the trees and cawed their alarms, and then, as if calmed by a foraging co-conspirator, kept silent.

Manassas! The key was here! The key that would unlock the subterranean door that led to Carlos the Jackal, the assassin who wanted only to destroy David Webb and his family. ... Webb! *Get away from me, David!* screamed Jason Bourne in the silence of his mind. *Let me be the killer you cannot be!*

With each scissoring cut into the thick, high wire fence, he understood the inevitable, confirmed by his heavy breathing and the sweat that fell from his hairline. No matter how hard he tried to keep his body in reasonable shape, he was fifty years of age; he could not do with ease what he did thirteen years ago in Paris when, under orders, he had stalked the Jackal. It was something to think about, not dwell upon. There were Marie and his children now—David's wife, David's children—and there was *nothing* he could not do as long as he willed it! David Webb was disappearing from his psyche, only the predator Jason Bourne would remain.

He was *through*! He crawled inside and stood up, instinctively, rapidly checking his equipment with the fingers of both hands. Weapons: an automatic, as well as a CO_2 dart pistol; Zeiss Ikon binoculars; a scabbarded hunting knife. They were all the predator needed, for he was now behind the lines in enemy territory, the enemy that would lead him to Carlos.

Medusa. The bastard battalion from Vietnam, the unlogged, unsanctioned, unacknowledged collection of killers and misfits who roamed the jungles of Southeast Asia directed by Command Saigon, the original death squads who brought

Saigon more intelligence input than all the search-and-destroys put together. Jason Bourne had come out of Medusa with David Webb only a memory—a scholar who had another wife, other children, all slaughtered.

General Norman Swayne had been an elite member of Command Saigon, the sole supplier of the old Medusa. And now there was a *new* Medusa: different, massive, evil incarnate cloaked in contemporary respectability, searching out and destroying whole segments of global economies, all for the benefit of the few, all financed by the profits from a long-ago bastard battalion, unlogged, unacknowledged—nonhistory. This modern Medusa was the bridge to Carlos the Jackal. The assassin would find the principals irresistible as clients, and both camps would demand the death of Jason Bourne. *That* had to happen! And for it to happen, Bourne had to learn the secrets concealed within the grounds belonging to General Swayne, head of all procurements for the Pentagon, a panicked man with a small tattoo on his inner forearm. A Medusan.

Without sound or warning, a black Doberman crashed through the dense foliage, its frenzy in full force. Jason whipped the CO_2 pistol from its nylon holster as the salivating attack dog lunged for his stomach, its teeth bared. He fired into its head; the dart took effect in seconds. He cradled the animal's unconscious body to the ground.

Cut its throat! roared Jason Bourne in silence.

No, countered his other self, David Webb. *Blame the trainer, not the animal.*

Get away from me, David!

THE
BOURNE
ULTIMATUM

The cacophony spun out of control as the crowds swelled through the amusement park in the countryside on the outskirts of Baltimore. The summer night was hot, and nearly everywhere faces and necks were drenched with sweat, except for those screaming as they plunged over the crests of a roller coaster, or shrieking as they plummeted down the narrow, twisting gullies of racing water in torpedo sleds. The garishly colored, manically blinking lights along the midway were joined by the grating sounds of emphatic music metallically erupting out of an excess of loudspeakers—calliopes *presto,* marches *prestissimo.* Pitchmen yelled above the din, nasally hawking their wares in monotonic harangues while erratic explosions in the sky lit up the darkness, sending sprays of myriad fireworks cascading over a small adjacent black lake. Roman candles bright, arcing bursts of fire blinding.

A row of Hit-the-Gong machines drew contorted faces and thick necks bulging with veins as men sought furiously and frequently in frustration to prove their manhood, crashing heavy wooden mallets down on the deceitful planks that too often refused to send the little red balls up to the bells. Across the way, others shrieked with menacing enthusiasm as they crashed their Dodge 'Em carts into the whirling, surrounding vehicles, each collision a triumph of superior aggression, each combatant a momentary movie star who overcomes all odds against him. *Gunfight at O.K. Corral* at 9:27 in the evening in a conflict that meant nothing.

Farther along was a minor monument to sudden death, a shooting gallery that bore little resemblance to the innocent minimum-caliber variety found in state fairs and rural carnivals. Instead, it was a microcosm of the most lethal equipment of modern weaponry. There were mocked-up versions of MAC-10 and Uzi machine pistols, steel-framed missile launchers and antitank bazookas, and, finally, a frightening replica of a flamethrower spewing out harsh, straight beams of light through billowing clouds of dark smoke. And again there were the perspiring faces, continuous beads of sweat rolling over maniacal eyes and down across stretched necks—husbands, wives and children—their features grotesque, twisted out of shape as if each were blasting away at hated enemies— wives, husbands, parents and offspring. All were locked in a never-ending war without meaning—at 9:29 in the evening, in an amusement park whose theme was violence. Unmitigated and unwarranted, man against himself and all his hostilities, the worst, of course, being his fears.

A slender figure, a cane gripped in his right hand, limped past a booth where angry, excited customers were hurling sharp-pointed darts into balloons on which were stenciled the faces of public figures. As the rubber heads exploded the bursts gave rise to fierce arguments for and against the sagging, pinched remnants of political icons and their dart-wielding executioners. The limping man continued down the midway, peering ahead through the maze of strollers as if he were looking for a specific location in a hectic, crowded, unfamiliar part of town. He was dressed casually but neatly in a jacket and sport shirt as though the oppressive heat had no effect on him and the jacket was somehow a requirement. His face was the pleasant face of a middle-aged man, but worn with premature lines and deep shadows under the eyes, all of which was the result more of the life he had led than of the accumulated years. His name was Alexander Conklin, and he was a retired covert operations officer in the Central Intelligence Agency. He was also at this moment apprehensive and consumed with anxiety. He did not wish to be in this place at this hour, and he could not imagine what catastrophic event had taken place that forced him to be there.

He approached the pandemonium of the shooting gallery and suddenly gasped, stopping all movement, his eyes locked on a tall, balding man about his own age with a seersucker jacket slung over his shoulder. *Morris Panov* was walking toward the thunderous counter of the shooting gallery from the opposite direction! *Why?* What had *happened*? Conklin snapped his head around in every direction, his eyes darting toward faces and bodies, instinctively knowing

that he and the psychiatrist were being watched.
It was too late to stop Panov from entering the
inner circle of the meeting ground but perhaps
not too late to get them both out! The retired
intelligence officer reached under his jacket for
the small Beretta automatic that was his constant companion, and lurched rapidly forward,
limping and flailing his cane against the crowd,
smashing kneecaps and prodding stomachs
and breasts and kidneys until the stunned, angry
strollers erupted in successive cries of shock, a
near riot in the making. He then rushed forward,
slamming his frail body into the bewildered doctor and shouting into Panov's face through the
roars of the crowd, "What the hell are *you* doing
here?"

"The same thing I assume *you* are. David, or
should I say *Jason*? That's what the telegram
said."

"It's a *trap*!"

There was a piercing scream overriding the
surrounding melee. Both Conklin and Panov instantly looked over at the shooting gallery only
yards away. An obese woman with a pinched
face had been shot in the throat. The crowd
went into a frenzy. Conklin spun around trying to
see where the shot came from, but the panic

was at full pitch; he saw nothing but rushing figures. He grabbed Panov and propelled him through the screaming, frantic bodies across the midway and again through the strolling crowds to the base of the massive roller coaster at the end of the park, where excited customers were edging toward the booth through the deafening noise.

"My *God*!" yelled Panov. "Was that meant for one of *us*?"

"Maybe . . . maybe not," replied the former intelligence officer breathlessly as sirens and whistles were heard in the distance.

"You said it was a *trap*!"

"Because we both got a crazy telegram from David using a name he hasn't used in five years—*Jason Bourne*! And if I'm not mistaken, your message also said that under *no* condition should we call his house."

"That's right."

"It's a trap. . . . You move better than I do, Mo, so move those legs of yours. Get out of here—run like a son of a bitch and find a telephone. A *pay* phone, nothing traceable!"

"What?"

"Call his house! Tell David to pack up Marie and the kids and get out of there!"

"What?"

"Someone found us, Doctor! Someone looking for Jason Bourne—who's been looking for
him for years and won't stop until he's got him
in his gun sight. . . . You were in charge of
David's messed-up head, and I pulled every rotten string in Washington to get him and Marie
out of Hong Kong alive. . . . The rules were
broken and we were found, Mo. *You* and *me*!
The only officially recorded connections to
Jason Bourne, address and occupation unknown."

"Do you know what you're saying, Alex?"

"You're goddamned right I do. . . . It's Carlos.
Carlos the *Jackal.* Get out of here, Doctor.
Reach your former patient and tell him to disap-
pear!"

"Then what's he to do?"

"I don't have many friends, certainly no one I
trust, but you do. Give him the name of somebody—say, one of your medical buddies who
gets urgent calls from his patients the way I
used to call you. Tell David to reach him or her
when he's secure. Give him a code."

"A *code*?"

"Jesus, Mo, use your *head*! An alias, a Jones
or a Smith—"

"They're rather common names—"

"Then Schicklgruber or Moskowitz, whatever you *like*! Just tell him to let us know where he *is*."

"I understand."

"Now get out of here, and *don't go* home! . . . Take a room at the Brookshire in Baltimore under the name of—Morris, Phillip Morris. I'll meet you there later."

"What are you going to do?"

"Something I hate. . . . Without my cane I'm buying a ticket for this fucking roller coaster. Nobody'll look for a cripple on one of these things. It scares the hell out of me, but it's a logical exit even if I have to stay on the damn thing all night. . . . Now get *out* of here! *Hurry!*"

The station wagon raced south down a back-country road through the hills of New Hampshire toward the Massachusetts border, the driver a long-framed man, his sharp-featured face intense, the muscles of his jaw pulsating, his clear light-blue eyes furious. Beside him sat his strikingly attractive wife, the reddish glow of her auburn hair heightened by the dashboard lights. In her arms was an infant, a baby girl of eight months; in the first backseat was another child, a blond-haired boy of five, asleep under a blanket, a portable guardrail protecting him from sudden stops. The father was David Webb, professor of Oriental studies, but once part of the notorious, unspoken-of Medusa, twice the legend that was Jason Bourne—assassin.

"We knew it had to happen," said Marie St. Jacques Webb, Canadian by birth, economist by profession, savior of David Webb by accident. "It was merely a question of time."

"It's *crazy*!" David whispered so as not to wake the children, his intensity in no way diminished by his whisper. "Everything's buried, maximum archive security and all the rest of that crap! How did anyone *find* Alex and Mo?"

"We don't know, but Alex will start looking. There's no one better than Alex, you said that yourself—"

"He's marked now—he's a dead man," interrupted Webb grimly.

"That's premature, David. 'He's the best there ever was,' those were your words."

"The only time he wasn't was thirteen years ago in Paris."

"Because you were better—"

"No! Because I didn't know who I was, and he

was operating on prior data that I didn't know a damn thing about. He assumed it was *me* out there, but *I* didn't know *me,* so I couldn't act according to his script. . . . He's still the best. He saved both our lives in Hong Kong."

"Then you're saying what I'm saying, aren't you? We're in good hands."

"Alex's, yes. Not Mo's. That poor beautiful man is dead. They'll take him and break him!"

"He'd go to his grave before giving anyone information about us."

"He won't have a choice. They'll shoot him up to the moon with Amytals and his whole life will be on tape. Then they'll kill him and come after me . . . after us, which is why you and the kids are heading south, *way* south. The Caribbean."

"I'll send *them,* darling. Not me."

"Will you *stop* it! We agreed when Jamie was born. It's why we got the place down there, why we damn near bought your kid brother's *soul* to look after it for us. . . . Also, he's done pretty damn well. We now own half interest in a flourishing inn down a dirt road on an island nobody ever heard of until that Canadian hustler landed there in a seaplane."

"Johnny was always the aggressive type. Dad once said he could sell a broken-down heifer as a prime steer and no one would check the parts."

"The point is he loves you . . . and the kids. I'm also counting on that wild man's— Never mind, I trust Johnny."

"While you're trusting so much in my younger brother, don't trust your sense of direction. You just passed the turn to the cabin."

"Goddamn it!" cried Webb, braking the car and swerving around. *"Tomorrow!* You and Jamie and Alison are heading out of Logan Airport. To the island!"

"We'll discuss it, David."

"There's nothing to discuss." Webb breathed deeply, steadily, imposing a strange control. "I've been here before," he said quietly.

Marie looked at her husband, his suddenly passive face outlined in the dim wash of the dashboard lights. What she saw frightened her far more than the specter of the Jackal. She was not looking at David Webb the soft-spoken scholar. She was staring at a man they both thought had disappeared from their lives forever.

2

Alexander Conklin gripped his cane as he limped into the conference room at the Central Intelligence Agency in Langley, Virginia. He stood facing a long impressive table, large enough to seat thirty people, but instead there were only three, the man at the head the gray-haired DCI, director of Central Intelligence. Neither he nor his two highest-ranking deputy directors appeared pleased to see Conklin. The greetings were perfunctory, and rather than taking his obviously assigned seat next to the CIA official on the DCI's left, Conklin pulled out the chair at the far end of the table, sat down, and with a sharp noise slapped his cane against the edge.

"Now that we've said hello, can we cut the crap, gentlemen?"

"That's hardly a courteous or an amiable way to begin, Mr. Conklin," observed the director.

"Neither courtesy nor amiability is on my mind just now, *sir.* I just want to know why airtight Four Zero regulations were ignored and maximum-classified information was released that endangers a number of lives, including mine!"

"That's *outrageous,* Alex!" interrupted one of the two associates.

"Totally inaccurate!" added the other. "It couldn't happen and you know it!"

"I don't know it and it did happen and I'll tell you what's outrageously *accurate,*" said Conklin angrily. "A man's out there with a wife and two children, a man this country and a large part of the world owe more to than anyone could ever repay, and he's running, hiding, frightened out of his mind that he and his family are targets. We gave that man our word, *all* of us, that no part of the official record would ever see the light of day until it was confirmed beyond *doubt* that Ilich Ramirez Sanchez, also known as Carlos the Jackal, was dead. . . . All right, I've heard the same rumors you have, probably from the same or much better sources, that the Jackal was killed here or executed there, but no one—repeat *no one*—has come forward with indisputable proof. . . . Yet a part of that file was leaked, a very vital part, and it concerns me deeply because my name is there. . . . Mine and Dr. Morris Panov, the chief psychiatrist of record. We were the only—repeat *only*—two individuals acknowledged to have been close associates of the unknown man who assumed the name of Jason Bourne, considered in more sectors than we can count to be the rival of Carlos in the killing game. . . . But that information is buried in the vaults here in Langley. How did it get out? According to the rules, if anyone wants any part of that record—from the White House to the State Department to the holy Joint Chiefs—he has to go through the offices of the director and his chief analysts right here at Langley. They have to be briefed on all the details of the request, and even if they're satisfied as to the legitimacy, there's a final step. *Me.* Before a release is signed, *I'm* to be contacted, and in the event I'm not around any longer, Dr. Panov is to be reached, either one of us legally empowered to turn the request down flat. . . . That's the way it is, gentlemen, and no one knows the rules better than I do because I'm the one who *wrote* them—again right here at Langley, because this was the place I knew best. After twenty-eight years in this corkscrew business, it was my final contribution—with the full authority of the president of the United States and the consent of Congress through the select committees on intelligence in the House and the Senate."

"That's heavy artillery, Mr. Conklin," commented the gray-haired director, sitting motionless, his voice flat, neutral.

"There were heavy reasons for pulling out the cannons."

"So I gather. One of the sixteen-inchers reached me."

"You're damned right he did. Now, there's the question of accountability. I want to know how that information surfaced and, most important, *who got* it."

Both deputy directors began talking at once, as angrily as Alex, but they were stopped by the DCI, who touched their arms, a pipe in one hand, a lighter in the other. "Slow down and back up, Mr. Conklin," said the director gently, lighting his pipe. "It's obvious that you know my two associates, but you and I never met, have we?"

"No. I resigned four and a half years ago, and you were appointed a year after that."

"Like many others—quite justifiably, I think— did you consider me a crony appointment?"

"You obviously were, but I had no trouble with that. You seemed qualified. As far as I could tell, you were an apolitical Annapolis admiral who ran naval intelligence and who just happened to work with an FMF marine colonel during the Vietnam war who became president. Others were passed over, but that happens. No sweat."

"Thank you. But do you have any 'sweat' with my two deputy directors?"

"It's history, but I can't say either one of them was considered the best friend an agent in the field ever had. They were analysts, not field men."

"Isn't that a natural aversion, a conventional hostility?"

"Of course it is. They analyzed situations from thousands of miles away with computers we didn't know who programmed and with data we hadn't passed on. You're damned right it's a natural aversion. We dealt with human quotients; they didn't. They dealt with little green letters on a computer screen and made decisions they frequently shouldn't have made."

"Because people like you had to be *controlled,*" interjected the deputy on the director's right. "How many times, even today, do men and women like you lack the full picture? The *total* strategy and not just *your* part of it?"

"Then we should be given a fuller picture going in, or at least an overview so we can try to figure out what makes sense and what doesn't."

"Where does an overview stop, Alex?" asked the deputy on the DCI's left. "At what point do we say, 'We can't reveal this . . . for everyone's benefit'?"

"I don't know, you're the analysts, I'm not. On a case-by-case basis, I suppose, but certainly with better communication than I ever got when I was in the field. . . . Wait a minute. *I'm* not the issue, *you* are." Alex stared at the director. "Very smooth, *sir,* but I'm not buying a change of subject. I'm here to find out who got what and how. If you'd rather, I'll take my credentials over to the White House or up to the Hill and watch a few heads roll. I want answers. I want to know what to *do*!"

"I wasn't trying to change the subject, Mr. Conklin, only to divert it momentarily to make a point. You obviously objected to the methods and the compromises employed in the past by my colleagues, but did either of these men ever mislead you, lie to you?"

Alex looked briefly at the two deputy directors. "Only when they had to lie to me, which had nothing to do with field operations."

"That's a strange comment."

"If they haven't told you, they should have. . . . Five years ago I was an alcoholic—I'm still an alcoholic but I don't drink anymore. I was riding out the time to my pension, so nobody told me anything and they damn well shouldn't have."

"For your enlightenment, all my colleagues said to me was that you had been ill, that you hadn't been functioning at the level of your past accomplishments until the end of your service."

Again Conklin studied both deputies, nodding to both as he spoke. "Thanks, Casset, and you, too, Valentino, but you didn't have to do that. I was a drunk and it shouldn't be a secret whether it's me or anybody else. That's the dumbest thing you can do around here."

"From what we heard about Hong Kong, you did a hell of a job, Alex," said the man named Casset softly. "We didn't want to detract from that."

"You've been a pain in the ass for longer than I care to remember," added Valentino. "But we couldn't let you hang out as an accident of booze."

"Forget it. Let's get back to Jason Bourne. That's why I'm here, why you damn well had to see me."

"That's also why I momentarily sidetracked us, Mr. Conklin. You have professional differences with my deputies, but I gather you don't question their integrity."

"Others, yes. Not Casset or Val. As far as I was concerned, they did their jobs and I did mine; it was the system that was fouled up—it was buried in fog. But *this* isn't, *today* isn't. The rules are clear-cut and absolute, and since I wasn't reached, they were broken and I *was* misled, in a very real sense, *lied* to. I repeat. How did it happen and *who* got the information?"

"That's all I wanted to hear," said the director, picking up the telephone on the table. "Please call Mr. DeSole down the hall and ask him to come to the conference room." The DCI hung up and turned to Conklin. "I assume you're aware of Steven DeSole."

"DeSole the mute mole." Alex nodded.

"I beg your pardon?"

"It's an old joke around here," explained Casset to the director. "Steve knows where the bodies are buried, but when the time comes he won't even tell God unless He shows him a Four Zero clearance."

"I assume that means the three of you, especially Mr. Conklin, consider Mr. DeSole a thorough professional."

"I'll answer that," Alex said. "He'll tell you anything you have to know but no more than that. Also, he won't lie. He'll keep his mouth shut, or tell you he can't tell you, but he won't lie to you."

"That's another thing I wanted to hear." There was a brief knock on the door, and the DCI called out for the visitor to enter. A medium-sized, slightly overweight man with wide eyes magnified behind steel-rimmed glasses walked into the room, closing the door behind him. His casual second glance at the table revealed Alexander Conklin to him; he was obviously startled by the sight of the retired intelligence officer. Instantly, he changed his reaction to one of pleasant surprise, crossing to Conklin's chair, his hand extended.

"Good to see you, old boy. It's been two or three years now, hasn't it?"

"More like four, Steve," replied Alex, shaking hands. "How's the analysts' analyst and keeper of the keys?"

"Not much to analyze or to lock up these days. The White House is a sieve and the Congress isn't much better. I should get half pay, but don't tell anyone."

"We still keep some things to ourselves, don't we?" interrupted the DCI, smiling. "At least from past operations. Perhaps you earned double your pay then."

"Oh, I suspect I did." DeSole nodded his head humorously as he released Conklin's hand. "However, the days of archive custodians and armed transfers to underground warehouses are over. Today it's all computerized photo scans entered by machines from on high. I don't get to go on those wonderful trips any longer with military escorts, pretending I'll be deliciously attacked by Mata Hari. I haven't had a briefcase chained to my wrist since I can't remember when."

"A lot safer that way," said Alex.

"But very little I can tell my grandchildren about, old boy. . . . 'What did you do as a big spy, Grandpa?' . . . 'Actually, in my last years, a great many crossword puzzles, young man.'"

"Be careful, Mr. DeSole," said the DCI, chuckling. "I shouldn't care to put in a recommendation to cut your pay. . . . On the other hand, I couldn't, because I don't believe you for an instant."

"Neither do I." Conklin spoke quietly, angrily. "This is a setup," he added, staring at the overweight analyst.

"That's quite a statement, Alex," countered DeSole. "Would you mind explaining it?"

"You know why I'm here, don't you?"

"I didn't know you *were* here."

"Oh, I see. It just happened to be convenient for you to be 'down the hall' and ready to come in here."

"My *office* is down the hall. Quite far down, I might add."

Conklin looked at the DCI. "Again, very smooth, *sir.* Bring in three people you figure I've had no major run-ins with outside of the system itself, three men you've determined I basically trust, so I'll believe whatever's said."

"That's fundamentally accurate, Mr. Conklin, because what you'll hear is the truth. Sit down, Mr. DeSole. . . . Perhaps at this end of the table so that our former colleague can study us as we explain to him. I understand it's a technique favored by field officers."

"I haven't a *damn* thing to explain," said the analyst as he headed for the chair next to Cas-

set. "But in light of our former colleague's somewhat gross remarks, I'd like to study *him.* . . . Are
you *well,* Alex?"

"He's well," answered the deputy director
named Valentino. "He's snarling at the wrong
shadows but he's well."

"That information couldn't have surfaced
without the consent and cooperation of the people in this room!"

"What information?" asked DeSole, looking
at the DCI, suddenly widening his large eyes
behind his glasses. "Oh, the max-classified
thing you asked me about this morning?"

The director nodded, then looked at Conklin.
"Let's go back to this morning. . . . Seven hours
ago, shortly after nine o'clock, I received a call
from Edward McAllister, formerly of the State
Department and currently chairman of the National Security Agency. I'm told Mr. McAllister
was with you in Hong Kong, Mr. Conklin, is that
correct?"

"Mr. McAllister was with us," agreed Alex
flatly. "He flew undercover with Jason Bourne to
Macao, where he was shot up so badly he damn
near died. He's an intellectual oddball and one
of the bravest men I've ever met."

"He said nothing about the circumstances,

only that he was there, and I was to shred my calendar, if need be, but to consider our meeting with you as Priority Red. . . . Heavy artillery, Mr. Conklin."

"To repeat. There are heavy reasons for the cannons."

"Apparently. . . . Mr. McAllister gave me the precise maximum-classified codes that would clarify the status of the file you're talking about—the record of the Hong Kong operation. I, in turn, gave the information to Mr. DeSole, so I'll let him tell you what he learned."

"It hasn't been touched, Alex," said DeSole quietly, his eyes leveled on Conklin. "As of nine-thirty this morning, it's been in a black hole for four years, five months, twenty-one days, eleven hours and forty-three minutes without penetration. And there's a very good reason why that status is pure, but I have no idea whether you're aware of it or not."

"Where that file is concerned I'm aware of *everything*!"

"Perhaps, perhaps not," said DeSole gently. "You were known to have a problem, and Dr. Panov is not that experienced where security matters are concerned."

"What the hell are you driving at?"

"A third name was added to the clearance procedures for that official record on Hong Kong. . . . Edward Newington McAllister, by his own insistence and with both presidential and congressional authority. He made sure of it."

"Oh, my *God,*" said Conklin softly, hesitantly. "When I called him last night from Baltimore he said it was *impossible.* Then he said I had to understand for myself, so he'd set up the conference. . . . Jesus, what *happened*?"

"I'd say we'd have to look elsewhere," said the DCI. "But before we do that, Mr. Conklin, you have to make a decision. You see, none of us at this table knows what's in that maximum-classified file. . . . We've talked, of course, and as Mr. Casset said, we understood that you did a hell of a job in Hong Kong, but we don't know what that job *was.* We heard the rumors out of our Far East stations which, frankly, most of us believed were exaggerated in the spreading, and paramount among them was your name and that of the assassin Jason Bourne. The scuttlebutt then was that you were responsible for the capture and execution of the killer we knew *as* Bourne, yet a few moments ago in your anger you used the phrase 'the unknown man who *assumed* the name of Jason Bourne,' stating that he was alive and in hiding. In terms of specifics, we're at a loss—at least *I* am, God knows."

"You didn't pull the record out?"

"No," answered DeSole. "That was my decision. As you may or may not know, every invasion of a maximum-classified file is automatically marked with the date and hour of penetration. . . . Since the director informed me that there was a large Security Agency flap over an illegal entry, I decided to leave well enough alone. Not penetrated in nearly five years, therefore not read or even known about and consequently not given to the evil people, whoever they are."

"You were covering your ass right down to the last square inch of flesh."

"Most assuredly, Alex. That data has a White House flag on it. Things are relatively stable around here now and it serves no one to ruffle feathers in the Oval Office. There's a new man at that desk, but the former president is still very much alive and opinionated. He'd be consulted, so why risk trouble?"

Conklin studied each face and spoke quietly. "Then you really *don't* know the story, do you?"

"It's the truth, Alex," said Deputy Director Casset.

"Nothing but, you pain," agreed Valentino, permitting himself a slight smile.

"My word on it," added Steven DeSole, his clear, wide eyes rigid on Conklin.

"And if you want our help, we should know something besides contradictory rumors," continued the director, leaning back in his chair. "I don't know if we *can* help, but I do know there's little we can do so completely in the dark."

Again Alex looked at each man, the lines in his pained face more pronounced than ever, as if the decision was momentarily too agonizing for him. "I won't tell you his name because I've given my word—maybe later, not now. And it can't be found in the record, it's not there either; it's a cover—I gave my word on that, too. The rest I'll tell you because I do want your help and I want that record to remain in its black hole. . . . Where do I begin?"

"With this meeting perhaps?" suggested the director. "What prompted it?"

"All right, that'll be quick." Conklin stared pensively at the surface of the table, absently gripping his cane, then raised his eyes. "A woman was killed last night at an amusement park outside Baltimore—"

"I read about it in the *Post* this morning," interrupted DeSole, nodding, his full cheeks jiggling. "Good *Lord,* were you—"

"So did I," broke in Casset, his steady brown eyes on Alex. "It happened in front of a shooting gallery. They closed the guns down."

"I saw the article and figured it was some kind of terrible accident." Valentino shook his head slowly. "I didn't actually read it."

"I was given my usual thick sheaf of scissored newspaper stories, which is enough journalism for anyone in the morning," said the director. "I don't remember any such article."

"Were you involved, old boy?"

"If I wasn't, it was a horrible waste of life. . . . I should say if we weren't involved."

"We?" Casset frowned in alarm.

"Morris Panov and I received identical telegrams from Jason Bourne asking us to be at the amusement park at nine-thirty last night. It was urgent, and we were to meet him in front of the shooting gallery, but we were not, under any condition, to call his house or anyone else. . . . We both independently assumed that he didn't want to alarm his wife, that he had something to tell us individually that he didn't want her to know. . . . We arrived at the same time, but I saw Panov first and figured it was a bad scene. From any point of view, especially Bourne's, we should have reached each other and talked before going up there; instead, we had been told not to. It smelled, so I did my best to get us out of there fast. The only way seemed to be a diversion."

"You stampeded then," said Casset, making a statement.

"It was the only thing I could think of, and one of the few things this goddamned cane is good for other than keeping me upright. I cracked every shin and kneecap I could see and lanced a few stomachs and tits. We got out of the circle, but that poor woman was killed."

"How did you figure it—*do* you figure it?" asked Valentino.

"I just don't know, Val. It was a trap, no question about that, but what kind of trap? If what I thought then and what I think now are correct, how could a hired marksman miss at that distance? The shot came from my upper left—not that I necessarily heard it—but the position of the woman and the blood all over her throat indicated that she had turned and caught the bullet in her body swing. It couldn't have come from the gallery; those guns are chained and the massive hemorrhage in her neck was caused by a far larger caliber than any of the toys there. If the killer wanted to take out either Mo Panov or me, his telescopic cross hairs wouldn't be that far off the mark. Not if my thinking is right."

" 'Right,' Mr. Conklin," interjected the DCI, "meaning the assassin, Carlos the Jackal."

"Carlos?" exclaimed DeSole. "What in heaven's name has the Jackal to do with a killing in *Baltimore*?"

"Jason Bourne," answered Casset.

"Yes, I gather that, but this is all terribly confusing! Bourne was a scum hit man out of Asia who moved to Europe to challenge Carlos and lost. As the director just said, he went back to the Far East and was killed four or five years ago, yet Alex talks as if he's still alive, that he and someone named Panov got telegrams from him. . . . What in God's name does a dead scumball and the world's most elusive assassin have to do with last night?"

"You weren't here a few minutes ago, Steve," again Casset answered quietly. "Apparently they had a lot to do with last night."

"I *beg* your pardon."

"I think you should start at the beginning, Mr. Conklin," said the director. "Who *is* Jason Bourne?"

"As the world knew him, a man who never existed," replied the former intelligence officer.

3

"The original Jason Bourne was garbage, a paranoid drifter from Tasmania who found his way into the Vietnam war as part of an operation no one wants to acknowledge even today. It was a collection of killers, misfits, smugglers and thieves, mostly escaped criminals, many under death sentences, but they knew every inch of Southeast Asia and operated behind enemy lines—funded by us."

"Medusa," whispered Steven DeSole. "It's all buried. They were animals, killing wantonly without reason or authorization and stealing millions. *Savages*."

"Most, not all," said Conklin. "But the original

Bourne fitted every rotten profile you could come up with, including the betrayal of his own men. The leader of a particularly hazardous mission—hazardous, *hell,* it was suicidal—found Bourne radioing their position to the North Vietnamese. He executed him on the spot, shoving the body into a swamp to rot in the jungles of Tam Quan. Jason Bourne disappeared from the face of the earth."

"He obviously reappeared, Mr. Conklin," observed the director, leaning forward on the table.

"In another body," agreed Alex, nodding. "For another purpose. The man who executed Bourne in Tam Quan took his name and agreed to be trained for an operation that we called Treadstone Seventy-one, after a building on New York's Seventy-first Street, where he went through a brutal indoctrination program. It was a brilliant strategy on paper, but ultimately failed because of something no one could predict, even consider. After nearly three years of living the role of the world's second most lethal assassin and moving into Europe—as Steve accurately described—to challenge the Jackal in his own territory, our man was wounded and lost his memory. He was found half dead in the Mediterranean and brought by a fisherman to the island of Port Noir. He had no idea who he was or what he was—only that he was a master of various martial arts, spoke a couple of Oriental languages, and was obviously an extremely well-educated man. With the help of a British doctor, an alcoholic banished to Port Noir, our man started to piece his life—his identity—back together from fragments both mental and physical. It was a hell of a journey. . . . and we who had mounted the operation, who invented the myth, were no help to him. Not knowing what had happened, we thought he had turned, had actually become the mythical assassin we'd created to trap Carlos. I, myself, tried to kill him in Paris, and when he might have blown my head off, he couldn't do it. He finally made his way back to us only through the extraordinary talents of a Canadian woman he met in Zurich and is now his wife. That lady had more guts and brains than any woman I've ever met. Now she and her husband and their two kids are back in the nightmare, running for their lives."

Aristocratic mouth agape, his pipe in midair in front of his chest, the director spoke. "Do you mean to sit there and tell us that the assassin we knew as Jason Bourne was an *invention*? That he *wasn't* the killer we all presumed he was?"

"He killed when he had to kill in order to survive, but he was no assassin. We created the myth as the ultimate challenge to Carlos, to draw the Jackal out."

"Good *Christ!*" exclaimed Casset. *"How?"*

"Massive disinformation throughout the Far East. Whenever a killing of consequence took place, whether in Tokyo or Hong Kong, Macao or Korea—wherever—Bourne was flown there and took the credit, planting evidence, taunting the authorities, until he became a legend. For three years our man lived in a world of filth— drugs, warlords, crime, tunneling his way in with only one objective: Get to Europe and bait Carlos, threaten his contracts, force the Jackal out into the open if only for a moment, just long enough to put a bullet in his head."

The silence around the table was electric. DeSole broke it, his voice barely above a whisper. "What kind of man would accept an assignment like that?"

Conklin looked at the analyst and answered in a monotone. "A man who felt there wasn't much left to live for, someone who had a death wish, perhaps . . . a decent human being who was driven into an outfit like Medusa out of hatred and frustration." The former intelligence officer stopped; his anguish was apparent.

"Come on, Alex," said Valentino softly. "You can't leave us with that."

"No, of course not." Conklin blinked several times, adjusting to the present. "I was thinking how horrible it must be for him now—the memories, what he can remember. There's a lousy parallel I hadn't considered. The wife, the kids."

"What's the parallel?" asked Casset, hunched forward, staring at Alex.

"Years ago, during Vietnam, our man was a young foreign service officer stationed in Phnom Penh, a scholar married to a Thai woman he'd met here in graduate school. They had two children and lived on the banks of a river. . . . One morning while the wife and kids were swimming, a stray jet from Hanoi strafed the area killing the three of them. Our man went crazy; he chucked everything and made his way to Saigon and into Medusa. All he wanted to do was kill. He became Delta One— no names were ever used in Medusa—and he was considered the most effective guerrilla leader in the war, as often as not fighting Command Saigon over orders as he did the enemy with death squads."

"Still, he obviously supported the war," observed Valentino.

"Outside of having no use for Saigon and the ARVN, I don't think he gave a damn one way or another. He had his own private war and it was way behind enemy lines, the nearer Hanoi the better. I think in his mind he kept looking for the pilot who had killed his family. . . . That's the parallel. Years ago there was a wife and two kids and they were butchered in front of his eyes. Now there's another wife and two children and the Jackal is closing in, hunting him down. That's got to be driving him close to the edge. *Goddamn* it!"

The four men at the opposite end of the table looked briefly at one another and let Conklin's sudden emotion pass. Again, the director spoke, again gently. "Considering the time span," he began, "the operation mounted to trap Carlos had to have taken place well over a decade ago, yet the events in Hong Kong were much more recent. Were they related? Without giving us a name or names at this juncture, what do you feel you can tell us about Hong Kong?"

Alex gripped his cane and held it firmly, his knuckles white as he replied. "Hong Kong was both the filthiest black operation ever conceived in this town and without question the most extraordinary I've ever heard of. And to my profound relief we here at Langley had nothing to do with the initial strategy, the plaudits can go to hell. I came in late and what I found turned my stomach. It sickened McAllister, too, for he *was* in at the beginning. It was why he was willing to risk his life, why he damn near ended up a corpse across the Chinese border in Macao. His intellectualized morality couldn't let a decent man be killed for the strategy."

"That's a hell of an indictment," offered Casset. "What happened?"

"Our own people arranged to have Bourne's wife kidnapped, the woman who had led that man without a memory back to us. They left a trail that forced him to go after her—to Hong Kong."

"Jesus, *why*?" cried Valentino.

"The strategy; it was perfect, and it was also abominable. . . . I told you the 'assassin' called Jason Bourne had become a legend in Asia. He disappeared in Europe, but he was no less a legend for that in the Far East. Then suddenly, out of nowhere, a new enterprising killer operating out of Macao revived that legend. He took the name of 'Jason Bourne' and the killings for hire started all over again. A week rarely went by, often only days, when another hit was made, the same evidence planted, the same taunting of the police. A false Bourne was back in business, and he had studied every trick of the original.''

"So who better to track him down than the one who invented those tricks—the original, *your* original,'' interjected the director. "And what better way to force the original Bourne into the hunt than by taking his wife from him. But *why*? Why was Washington so consumed? There were no longer any ties to *us*.''

"There was something much worse. Among the new Jason Bourne's clients was a madman in Beijing, a Kuomintang traitor in the government who was about to turn the Far East into a firestorm. He was determined to destroy the Sino-British Hong Kong Accords, shutting down the colony, leaving the whole territory in chaos.''

"*War,*'' said Casset quietly. "Beijing would march into Hong Kong and take over. We'd all have to choose sides. . . . *War.*''

"In the nuclear age,'' added the director. "How far had it all progressed, Mr. Conklin?''

"A vice premier of the People's Republic was killed in a private massacre in Kowloon. The impostor left his calling card. 'Jason Bourne.' "

"Good God, he *had* to be stopped!" exploded the DCI, gripping his pipe.

"He was," said Alex, releasing his cane. "By the only man who could hunt him down. Our Jason Bourne. . . . That's all I'll tell you for now, except to repeat that that man is back here with his wife and children, and Carlos is closing in. The Jackal won't rest until he knows the only person alive who can identify him is dead. So call in every debt that's owed to us in Paris, London, Rome, Madrid—especially *Paris.* Someone's got to know *something.* Where is Carlos *now*? Who are his points over *here*? He's got eyes here in Washington, and whoever they are, they found Panov and me!" The former field officer again absently gripped his cane, staring at the window. "Don't you see?" he added quietly, as if talking to himself. "We can't let it happen. Oh, my *God,* we can't let it *happen*!"

Once more the emotional moment passed in silence as the men of the Central Intelligence Agency exchanged glances. It was as though a consensus had been reached among them without a word being said; three pairs of eyes fell on Casset. He nodded, accepting his selection as the one closest to Conklin, and spoke.

"Alex, I agree that everything points to Carlos, but before we start spinning our wheels in Europe, we have to be sure. We can't afford a false alarm because we'd be handing the Jackal a grail he'd have to go after, showing him how vulnerable we were where Jason Bourne is concerned. From what you've told us, Carlos would pick up on a long-dormant operation known as Treadstone Seventy-one if only because none of our agents or subagents has been in his personal neighborhood for over a decade."

The retired Conklin studied Charles Casset's pensive sharp-featured face. "What you're saying is that if I'm wrong and it isn't the Jackal, we're ripping open a thirteen-year-old wound and presenting him with an irresistible kill."

"I guess that's what I'm saying."

"And I guess that's pretty good thinking, Charlie. . . . I'm operating on externals, aren't I? They're triggering instincts, but they're still externals."

"I'd trust those instincts of yours far more than I would any polygraph—"

"So would I," interrupted Valentino. "You saved our personnel in five or six sector crises when all the indicators said you were wrong. However, Charlie's got a legitimate query. Suppose it isn't Carlos? We not only send the wrong message to Europe, but, more important, we've wasted time."

"So stay out of Europe," mused Alex softly, again as if to himself. "At least for now. . . . Go after the bastards *here.* Draw *them* out. Pull them in and break them. I'm the target, so let them come after me."

"That would entail far looser protection than I envisage for you and Dr. Panov, Mr. Conklin," said the director firmly.

"Then disenvisage, sir." Alex looked back and forth at Casset and Valentino, suddenly raising his voice. "We can *do* it if you two will listen to me and let me mount it!"

"We're in a gray area," stated Casset. "This thing may be foreign-oriented, but it's domestic turf. The Bureau should be brought in—"

"No *way,*" exclaimed Conklin. *"Nobody's* brought in outside of this room!"

"Come on, Alex," said Valentino kindly, slowly shaking his head. "You're retired. You can't give orders here."

"Good, *fine!*" shouted Conklin, awkwardly getting out of the chair and supporting himself on his cane. *"Next* stop the White House, to a certain chairman of the NSA named McAllister!"

"Sit *down,*" said the DCI firmly.

"I'm retired! You can't give orders to me."

"I wouldn't dream of it, I'm simply concerned for your life. As I read the scenario, what you're suggesting is based on the questionable supposition that whoever fired at you last night intended to miss, not caring whom he hit, only determined to take you alive during the subsequent chaos."

"That's a couple of leaps—"

"Based on a couple of dozen operations I've been involved with both here and at the Department of the Navy *and* in places you couldn't pronounce or know anything about." The director's elbows were planted on the arms of his chair, his voice suddenly harsh, commanding. "For your information, *Conklin,* I didn't suddenly bloom as a gold-braided admiral running naval intelligence. I was in the SEALs for a few years and made runs off submarines into Kaesong and later into Haiphong harbor. I *knew* a number of those Medusa pricks, and I can't think of one that I didn't want to put a bullet in his head! Now *you* tell me there *was* one, and he became your 'Jason Bourne' and you'll break your balls or bust open your heart to see that he stays alive and well and out of the Jackal's gun sights.

. . . So let's cut the crap, *Alex.* Do you want to work with me or not?"

Conklin slowly sank back in his chair, a smile gradually emerging on his lips. "I told you I had no sweat with your appointment, *sir.* It was just intuition, but now I know why. You were a field man. . . . I'll work with you."

"Good, *fine,"* said the director. "We'll work up a controlled surveillance and hope to Christ your theory that they want you alive is correct because there's no way we can cover every window or every rooftop. You'd better understand the risk."

"I do. And since two chunks of bait are better than one in a tank of piranhas, I want to talk to Mo Panov."

"You can't ask him to be a part of this," countered Casset. "He's not one of us, Alex. Why should he?"

"Because he *is* one of us and I'd *better* ask him. If I didn't, he'd give me a flu shot filled with strychnine. You see, he was in Hong Kong, too—for reasons not much different from mine. Years ago I tried to kill my closest friend in Paris because I'd made a terrible mistake believing my friend had turned when the truth was that he had lost his memory. Only days later, Morris

Panov, one of the leading psychiatrists in the country, a doctor who can't stand the chicken-shit psychobabble so popular these days, was presented with a 'hypothetical' psychiatric profile that required his immediate reaction. It described a rogue deep-cover agent, a walking time bomb with a thousand secrets in his head, who had gone over the edge. . . . On the basis of Mo's on-the-spot evaluation of that hypothetical profile—which he hours later suspected was no more hypothetical than Campbell's soup—an innocent amnesiac was nearly blown away in a government ambush on New York's Seventy-first Street. When what was left of that man survived, Panov demanded to be assigned as his *only* head doctor. He's never forgiven himself. If any of you were he, what would you do if I didn't talk to you about what we're talking about right now?"

"Tell you it's a flu shot and pump you full of strychnine, old boy," concluded DeSole, nodding.

"Where is Panov now?" asked Casset.

"At the Brookshire Hotel in Baltimore under the name of Morris, Phillip Morris. He called off his appointments today—he has the flu."

"Then let's go to work," said the DCI, pulling a yellow legal pad in front of him. "Incidentally,

Alex, a competent field man doesn't concern himself with rank and won't trust a man who can't convincingly call him by his first name. As you well know, my name is Holland and my first name is Peter. From here on we're Alex and Peter, got it?"

"I've got it—Peter. You must have been one son of a bitch in the SEALs."

"Insofar as I'm here—geographically, not in this chair—it can be assumed I was competent."

"A field man," mumbled Conklin in approval.

"Also, since we've dropped the diplomatic drivel expected of someone in this job, you should understand that I was a hard-nosed son of a bitch. I want pro input here, Alex, not emotional output. Is that clear?"

"I don't operate any other way, Peter. A commitment may be based on emotions and there's nothing wrong with that, but the execution of a strategy is ice-cold. . . . I was never in the SEALs, you hard-nosed son of a bitch, but I'm also geographically here, limp and all, and that presumes I'm also competent."

Holland grinned; it was a smile of youth belied by streaked gray hair, the grin of a professional momentarily freed of executive concerns so as to return to the world he knew best. "We may even get along," said the DCI. And then, as if to drop the last vestige of his directorial image, he placed his pipe on the table, reached into his pocket for a pack of cigarettes, propped one up to his mouth and snapped his lighter as he began to write on the legal pad. "To hell with the Bureau," he continued. "We'll use only our men and we'll check every one out under a fast microscope."

Charles Casset, the lean, bright heir apparent of the CIA's directorship, sat back in his chair and sighed. "Why do I have the idea that I'm going to have to ride herd on both you gentlemen?"

"Because you're an analyst at heart, Charlie," answered Holland.

The object of controlled surveillance is to expose those who shadow others so as to establish their identities or take them into custody, whichever suits the strategy. The aim in the present case was to trap the agents of the Jackal who had lured Conklin and Panov to the amusement park in Baltimore. Working through the night and most of the following day, the men of the Central Intelligence Agency formed a detail of eight experienced field personnel, defined and redefined the specific routes that Conklin and Panov were to take both individually and together for the next twenty-four hours—these routes covered by the armed professionals in swift progressive relays—and finally to design an irresistible rendezvous, unique in terms of time and location. The early morning hours at the Smithsonian Institution. It was the *Dionaea muscipula,* the Venus flytrap.

Conklin stood in the narrow, dimly lit lobby of his apartment house and looked at his watch, squinting to read the dial. It was precisely 2:35 in the morning; he opened the heavy door and limped out into the dark street, which was devoid of any signs of life. According to their plan he turned left, maintaining the pace agreed upon; he was to arrive at the corner as close to 2:38 as possible. Suddenly, he was alarmed; in a shadowed doorway on his right was the figure of a man. Unobtrusively Alex reached under his jacket for his Beretta automatic. There was nothing in the strategy that called for someone to be in a doorway on this section of the street! Then, as suddenly as he had been alarmed, he relaxed, feeling equal parts of guilt and relief at what he understood. The figure in shadows was an indigent, an old man in worn-out clothes, one of the homeless in a land of so much plenty. Alex kept going; he reached the corner and heard the low, single click of two fingers snapped apart. He crossed the avenue and proceeded down the pavement, passing an alleyway. The *alleyway.* Another *figure* . . . another old man in disheveled clothing moving slowly out into the street and then back into the alley. Another derelict protecting his concrete cave. At any other time Conklin might have approached the unfortunate and given him a few dollars, but not now. He had a long way to go and a schedule to keep.

Morris Panov approached the intersection still bothered by the curious telephone conversation he had had ten minutes ago, still trying to recall each segment of the plan he was to follow, afraid to look at his watch to see if he had reached a specific place within a specific time span—he had been told *not* to look at his watch in the street . . . and why couldn't they say "at approximately such and such" rather than the somewhat unnerving term "time span," as if a military invasion of Washington were imminent. Regardless, he kept walking, crossing the streets he was told to cross, hoping some unseen clock kept him relatively in tune with the goddamned "time spans" that had been determined by his striding back and forth between two pegs on some lawn behind a garden apartment in Vienna, Virginia. . . . He would do anything for David Webb—good Christ, *anything*!—but this was insane. . . . Yet, of course, it wasn't. They would not ask him to do what he was doing if it were.

What was *that*? A face in shadows peering at him, just like the other *two*! This one hunched over on a curb, raising wine-soaked eyes up at him. Old men—weather-beaten, old, *old* men who could barely move—*staring* at him! Now he was allowing his imagination to run away with him—the cities were filled with the homeless, with perfectly harmless people whose psychoses or poverty drove them into the streets. As much as he would like to help them, there was nothing he could do but professionally badger an unresponsive Washington. . . . There was *another*! In an indented space between two storefronts barricaded by iron gates—he, too, was *watching* him. *Stop* it! You're being irrational. . . . Or was he? Of *course,* he was. Go *on,* keep to the schedule, that's what you're supposed to do. . . . Good *God*! There's *another.* Across the street. . . . Keep *going*!

The vast moonlit grounds of the Smithsonian dwarfed the two figures as they converged from intersecting paths, joining each other and proceeding to a bench. Conklin lowered himself with the aid of his cane while Mo Panov looked around nervously, listening, as if he expected the unexpected. It was 3:28 in the predawn morning, the only noises the subdued rattle of crickets and mild summer breezes through the trees. Guardedly Panov sat down.

"Anything happen on the way here?" asked Conklin.

"I'm not sure," replied the psychiatrist. "I'm as lost as I was in Hong Kong, except that over there we knew where we were going, whom we expected to meet. You people *are* crazy."

"You're contradicting yourself, Mo," said Alex, smiling. "You told me I was cured."

"Oh, that? That was merely obsessive manic-depression bordering on dementia praecox. This is *nuts*! It's nearly four o'clock in the morning. People who aren't nuts do not play games at four o'clock in the morning."

Alex watched Panov in the dim wash of a distant Smithsonian floodlight that illuminated the massive stone structure. "You said you weren't sure. What does that mean?"

"I'm almost embarrassed to say—I've told too many patients that they invent uncomfortable images to rationalize their panic, justify their fears."

"What the hell does *that* mean?"

"It's a form of transference—"

"Come on, Mo!" interrupted Conklin. "What bothered you? What did you see?"

"Figures . . . some bent over, walking slowly, awkwardly—not like you, Alex, incapacitated not by injuries but by age. Worn out and old and staying in the darkness of storefronts and side streets. It happened four or five times between my apartment house and here. Twice I almost stopped and called out for one of your men, and then I thought to myself, My God, *Doctor,* you're overreacting, mistaking a few pathetic homeless people for what they're not, seeing things that aren't there."

"Right on!" Conklin whispered emphatically. "You saw exactly what *was* there, Mo. Because

I saw the same, the same kind of old people *you* saw, and they *were* pathetic, mostly in beat-up clothes and who moved slower than I move. . . . What does it mean? What do *they* mean? Who are they?"

Footsteps. Slow, hesitant, and through the shadows of the deserted path walked two short men—old men. At first glance they, indeed, appeared to be part of the swelling army of indigent homeless, yet there was something different about them, a sense of purpose, perhaps. They stopped nearly twenty feet away from the bench, their faces in darkness. The old man on the left spoke, his voice thin, his accent strange. "It is an odd hour and an unusual place for two such well-dressed gentlemen to meet. Is it fair for you to occupy a place of rest that should be for others not so well off as you?"

"There are a number of unoccupied benches," said Alex pleasantly. "Is this one reserved?"

"There are no reserved seats here," replied the second old man, his English clear but not native to him. "But why are *you* here?"

"What's it to you?" asked Conklin. "This is a private meeting and none of your business."

"Business at this hour and in this place?" The first aged intruder spoke while looking around.

"I repeat," repeated Alex. "It's none of your business and I really think you should leave us alone."

"Business is business," intoned the second old man.

"What in God's name is he *talking* about?" whispered the bewildered Panov to Conklin.

"Ground zero," said Alex under his breath. "Be quiet." The retired field agent turned his head up to the two old men. "Okay, fellas, why don't you go on your way?"

"Business is business," again said the second tattered ancient, glancing at his colleague, both their faces still in shadows.

"You don't have any business with us—"

"You can't be sure of that," interrupted the first old man, shaking his head back and forth. "Suppose I were to tell you that we bring you a message from Macao?"

"What?" exclaimed Panov.

"Shut *up!*" whispered Conklin, addressing the psychiatrist but his eyes on the messenger. "What does Macao mean to us?" he asked flatly.

"A great taipan wishes to meet with you. The greatest taipan in Hong Kong."

"Why?"

"He will pay you great sums. For your services."

"I'll say it again. *Why?*"

"We are to tell you that a killer has returned. He wants you to find him."

"I've heard that story before; it doesn't wash. It's also repetitious."

"That is between the great taipan and yourselves, sir. Not with us. He is waiting for you."

"Where is he?"

"At a great hotel, sir."

"Which one?"

"We are again to tell you that it has a great-sized lobby with always many people, and its name refers to this country's past."

"There's only one like that. The Mayflower." Conklin directed his words toward his left lapel, into a microphone sewn into the buttonhole.

"As you wish."

"Under what name is he registered?"

"Registered?"

"Like in reserved benches, only rooms. Who do we ask for?"

"No one, sir. The taipan's secretary will approach you in the lobby."

"Did that same secretary approach you also?"

"Sir?"

"Who hired you to follow us?"

"We are not at liberty to discuss such matters and we will not do so."

"That's it!" shouted Alexander Conklin, yelling over his shoulder as floodlights suddenly lit up the Smithsonian grounds around the deserted path, revealing the two startled old men to be Orientals. Nine personnel from the Central Intelligence Agency walked rapidly into the glare of light from all directions, their hands under their jackets. Since there was no apparent need for them, their weapons remained hidden.

Suddenly the need was there, but the realization came too late. Two high-powered rifle shots exploded from the outer darkness, the bullets ripping open the throats of the two Oriental messengers. The CIA men lunged to the ground, rolling for cover as Conklin grabbed Panov, pulling him down to the path in front of the bench for protection. The unit from Langley lurched to their feet and, like the combat veterans they were, including the former commando Director Peter Holland, they started scrambling, zigzagging one after another toward the source of the gunfire, weapons extended, shadows sought. In moments, an angry cry split the silence.

"Goddamn it!" shouted Holland, the beam of

his flashlight angled down between tree trunks. "They made their break!"

"How can you tell?"

"The grass, son, the heel imprints. Those bastards were overqualified. They dug in for one shot apiece and got out—look at the slip marks on the lawn. Those shoes were running. Forget it! No use now. If they stopped for a second position, they'd blow us into the Smithsonian."

"A *field* man," said Alex, getting up with his cane, the frightened, bewildered Panov beside him. Then the doctor spun around, his eyes wide, rushing toward the two fallen Orientals.

"Oh, my God, they're *dead,*" he cried, kneeling beside the corpses, seeing their blown-apart throats. *"Jesus,* the amusement park! It's the *same*!"

"A message," agreed Conklin, nodding, wincing. "Put rock salt on the trail," he added enigmatically.

"What do you mean?" asked the psychiatrist, snapping his head around at the former intelligence officer.

"We weren't careful enough."

"Alex!" roared the gray-haired Holland, running to the bench. "I heard you, but this neuters the hotel," he said breathlessly. "You can't go there now. I won't let you."

"It neuters—*fucks* up—more than the hotel. This isn't the Jackal! It's *Hong Kong*! The externals were right, but my instincts were wrong. *Wrong!*"

"Which way do you want to go?" asked the director softly.

"I don't know," answered Conklin, a plaint in his voice. "I was *wrong*. . . . Reach our man, of course, as soon as possible."

"I spoke to David—I spoke to *him* about an hour ago," said Panov, instantly correcting himself.

"You *spoke* to him?" cried Alex. "It's late and you were at home. *How?*"

"You know my answering machine," said the doctor. "If I picked up every crazy call after midnight, I'd never get to the office in the morning. So I let it ring, and because I was getting ready to go out and meet you, I listened. All he said was 'Reach me,' and by the time I got to the phone, he'd hung up. So I called him back."

"You called him *back*? On *your* phone?"

"Well . . . yes," answered Panov hesitantly. "He was very quick, very guarded. He just wanted us to know what was happening, that 'M'—he called her 'M'—was leaving with the children first thing in the morning. That was it; he hung up right away."

"They've got your boy's name and address by now," said Holland. "Probably the message as well."

"A location, yes; the message, maybe," broke in Conklin, speaking quietly, rapidly. "Not an address, not a name."

"By morning they will have—"

"By morning he'll be on his way to Tierra del Fuego, if need be."

"Christ, what have I *done*?" exclaimed the psychiatrist.

"Nothing anybody else in your place wouldn't have done," replied Alex. "You get a message at two o'clock in the morning from someone you care about, someone in trouble, you call back as fast as you can. Now we have to reach him as fast as *we* can. So it's not Carlos, but somebody with a lot of firepower is still closing in, making breakthroughs we thought were impossible."

"Use the phone in my car," said Holland. "I'll put it on override. There'll be no record, no log."

"Let's go!" As quickly as possible, Conklin limped across the lawn toward the Agency vehicle.

"David, it's Alex."

"Your timing's pretty scary, friend, we're on

our way out the door. If Jamie hadn't had to hit the potty we'd be in the car by now."

"At this hour?"

"Didn't Mo tell you? There was no answer at your place, so I called him."

"Mo's a little shook up. Tell me yourself. What's happening?"

"Is this phone secure? I wasn't sure his was."

"None more so."

"I'm packing Marie and the kids off south— *way* south. She's screaming like hell, but I chartered a Rockwell jet out of Logan Airport, everything precleared thanks to the arrangements you made four years ago. The computers spun and everyone cooperated. They take off at six o'clock, before it's light—I want them *out*."

"And you, David? What about you?"

"Frankly, I thought I'd head to Washington and stay with you. If the Jackal's coming for me after all these years, I want to be in on what we're doing about it. I might even be able to help. . . . I'll arrive by noon."

"No, David. Not today and not here. Go with Marie and the children. Get out of the country. Stay with your family and Johnny St. Jacques on the island."

"I can't do that, Alex, and if you were me you couldn't, either. My *family*'s not going to be free—really *free*—until Carlos is out of our lives."

"It's not Carlos," said Conklin, interrupting.

"What? Yesterday you told me—"

"Forget what I told you, I was wrong. This is out of Hong Kong, out of Macao."

"That doesn't make sense, Alex! Hong Kong's finished, *Macao's* finished. They're dead and forgotten and there's no one alive with a reason to come after me."

"There is somewhere. A great taipan, 'the greatest taipan in Hong Kong,' according to the most recent and most recently dead source."

"They're *gone.* That whole house of Kuomintang cards collapsed. There's no one left!"

"I repeat, there is somewhere."

David Webb was briefly silent; then Jason Bourne spoke, his voice cold. "Tell me everything you've learned, every detail. Something happened tonight. What was it?"

"All right, every detail," said Conklin. The retired intelligence officer described the controlled surveillance engineered by the Central Intelligence Agency. He explained how he and Morris Panov spotted the old men who followed them, picking each up in sequence as they made their separate ways to the Smithsonian, none showing himself in the light until the confrontation on a deserted path on the Smithsonian grounds, where the messenger spoke of Macao and Hong Kong and a great taipan. Finally, Conklin described the shattering gunfire that silenced the two aged Orientals. "It's out of Hong Kong, David. The reference to Macao confirms it. It was your impostor's base camp."

Again there was silence on the line, only Jason Bourne's steady breathing audible. "You're wrong, Alex," he said at last, his voice pensive, floating. "It's the Jackal—by way of Hong Kong and Macao, but it's still the Jackal."

"David, now *you're* not making sense. Carlos hasn't anything to do with taipans or Hong Kong or messages from Macao. Those old men were *Chinese,* not French or Italian or German or whatever. This is out of Asia, *not* Europe."

"The old men, they're the only ones he trusts," continued David Webb, his voice still low and cold, the voice of Jason Bourne. " 'The old men of Paris,' that's what they were called. They were his network, his couriers throughout Europe. Who suspects decrepit old men, whether they're beggars or whether they're just holding on to the last remnants of mobility? Who would think of interrogating them, much less putting them on a rack. And even then they'd stay silent. Their deals were made—*are* made—and they move with impunity. For Carlos."

For a moment, hearing the strange, hollow voice of his friend, the frightened Conklin stared at the dashboard, unsure of what to say. "David, I don't understand you. I know you're upset—we're *all* upset—but please be clearer."

"What? . . . Oh, I'm sorry, Alex, I was going back. To put it simply, Carlos scoured Paris looking for old men who were either dying or knew they hadn't long to live because of their age, all with police records and with little or nothing to show for their lives, their crimes. Most of us forget that these old men have loved ones and children, legitimate or not, that they care for. The Jackal would find them and swear to provide for the people his about-to-die couriers left behind if they swore the rest of their lives to him. In their places, with nothing to leave those who survive us but suspicion and poverty, which of us would do otherwise?"

"They *believed* him?"

"They had good reason to—they still have. Scores of bank checks are delivered monthly from multiple unlisted Swiss accounts to inheritors from the Mediterranean to the Baltic.

There's no way to trace those payments, but the people receiving them know who makes them possible and why. . . . Forget your buried file, Alex. Carlos dug around Hong Kong, that's where his penetration was made, where he found you and Mo."

"Then we'll do some penetrating ourselves. We'll infiltrate every Oriental neighborhood, every Chinese bookie joint and restaurant, in every city within a fifty-mile radius of D.C."

"Don't do anything until I get there. You don't know what to look for, I do. . . . It's kind of remarkable, really. The Jackal doesn't know that there's still a great deal I can't remember, but he just assumed that I'd forgotten about the old men of Paris."

"Maybe he didn't, David. Maybe he's counting on the fact that you'd remember. Maybe this whole charade is a prelude to the real trap he's setting for you."

"Then he made another mistake."

"Oh?"

"I'm better than that. Jason Bourne's better than that."

4

David Webb walked through the National Airport terminal and out the automatic doors onto the crowded platform. He studied the signs and proceeded across the walkway leading to the Short-Term Parking area. According to plan, he was to go to the farthest aisle on the right, turn left, and continue down the row of parked cars until he saw a metallic gray 1986 Pontiac Le-Mans with an ornamental crucifix suspended from the rearview mirror. A man would be in the driver's seat wearing a white cap, the window lowered. Webb was to approach him and say, "The flight was very smooth." If the man removed his cap and started the engine, David was to climb in the backseat. Nothing more would be said.

Nothing more *was* said, not between Webb and the driver. However, the latter reached under the dashboard, removed a microphone and spoke quietly but clearly. "Our cargo's on board. Please commence rotating vehicle cover."

David thought that the exotic procedures bordered on the laughable, but since Alex Conklin had traced him to the Rockwell jet's departure area at Logan Airport, and, further, had reached him on Director Peter Holland's private override telephone, he assumed the two of them knew what they were doing. It crossed Webb's mind that it had something to do with Mo Panov's call to him nine hours ago. It was all but confirmed when Holland himself got on the phone insisting that he drive down to Hartford and take a commercial flight out of Bradley to Washington, adding enigmatically that he wanted no further telephone communication or private or government aircraft involved.

This particular government-oriented car, however, wasted no time getting out of National Airport. It seemed as if in only minutes they were rushing through the countryside and, only minimally less rapidly, through the suburbs of Virginia. They swung up to the private gate of an expensive garden apartment complex, the sign reading VIENNA VILLAS, after the township in which it was located. The guard obviously recognized the driver and waved him through as the heavy bar across the entrance was raised. It was only then that the driver spoke directly to Webb.

"This place has five separate sections over as many acres, sir. Four of them are legitimate condominiums with regular owners, but the fifth, the one farthest from the gate, is an Agency proprietary with its own road and security. You couldn't be healthier, sir."

"I didn't feel particularly sick."

"You won't be. You're DCI cargo and your health is very important to him."

"That's nice to know, but how do *you* know?"

"I'm part of the team, sir."

"In that case, what's your name?"

The driver was silent for a moment, and when he answered, David had the uneasy feeling that he was being propelled back in time, to a time he knew he was reentering. "We don't have names, sir. You don't and I don't."

Medusa.

"I understand," said Webb.

"Here we are." The driver swung the car around a circular drive and stopped in front of a two-story Colonial structure that looked as though the fluted white pillars might have been made of Carrara marble. "Excuse me, sir, I just noticed. You don't have any luggage."

"No, I don't," said David, opening the door.

"How do you like my temporary digs?" asked Alex, waving his hand around the tastefully appointed apartment.

"Too neat and too clean for a cantankerous old bachelor," replied David. "And since when did you go in for floral curtains with pink and yellow daisies?"

"Wait'll you see the wallpaper in my bedroom. It's got baby roses."

"I'm not sure I care to."

"Your room has hyacinths. . . . Of course, I wouldn't know a hyacinth if it jumped up and choked me, but that's what the maid said."

"The maid?"

"Late forties and black and built like a sumo wrestler. She also carries two popguns under her skirt and, rumor has it, several straight razors."

"Some maid."

"Some high-powered patrol. She doesn't let a bar of soap or a roll of toilet paper in here that doesn't come from Langley. You know, she's a pay-grade *ten* and some of these clowns leave her tips."

"Do they need any waiters?"

"That's good. Our scholar, Webb the waiter."

"Jason Bourne's been one."

Conklin paused, then spoke seriously. "Let's get to him," he said, limping to an armchair. "By the way, you've had a rough day and it's not even noon, so if you want a drink there's a full bar behind those puce shutters next to the window. . . . *Don't* look at me like that, our black Brunhilde *said* they were puce."

Webb laughed; it was a low, genuine laugh as he looked at his friend. "It doesn't bother you a bit, does it, Alex?"

"Hell, no, you know that. Have you ever hid any liquor from me when I visited you and Marie?"

"There was never any stress—"

"Stress is irrelevant," Conklin broke in. "I made a decision because there was only one other one to make. Have a drink, David. We have to talk and I want you calm. I look at your eyes and they tell me you're on fire."

"You once told me that it's always in the eyes," said Webb, opening the purplish shutters and reaching for a bottle. "You can still see it, can't you?"

"I told you it was *behind* the eyes. Never accept the first level. . . . How are Marie and the children? I assume they got off all right."

"I went over the flight plan ad nauseam with the pilot and knew they were all right when he finally told me to get off his case or fly the run myself." Webb poured a drink and walked back to the chair opposite the retired agent. "Where are we, Alex?" he asked, sitting down.

"Right where we were last night. Nothing's moved and nothing's changed, except that Mo refuses to leave his patients. He was picked up this morning at his apartment, which is now as secure as Fort Knox, and driven to his office under guard. He'll be brought here later this afternoon with four changes of vehicles, all made in underground parking lots."

"Then it's open protection, no one's hiding any longer?"

"That'd be pointless. We sprung a trap at the Smithsonian and our men were very obvious."

"It's why it might work, isn't it? The unexpected? Backups behind a protection unit told to make mistakes."

"The unexpected works, David, not the dumb." Conklin quickly shook his head. "I take that back. Bourne could turn the dumbs into smarts, but not an officially mounted surveillance detail. There are too many complications."

"I don't understand."

"As good as those men are, they're primarily concerned with guarding lives, maybe saving them; they also have to coordinate with each other and make reports. They're career people, not one-shot, prepaid lowlife with an assassin's knife at their throats if they screw up."

"That sounds so melodramatic," said Webb softly, leaning back in the chair and drinking. "I guess I did operate like that, didn't I?"

"It was more image than reality, but it was real to the people you used."

"Then I'll find those people again, use them again." David shot forward, gripping his glass in both hands. "He's forcing me *out,* Alex! The Jackal's calling my cards and I have to show."

"Oh, shut up," said Conklin irritably. "Now you're the one who's being melodramatic. You sound like a grade-Z Western. You show yourself, Marie's a widow and the kids have no father. *That's* reality, David."

"You're wrong." Webb shook his head, staring at his glass. "He's coming after me, so I have to go after him; he's trying to pull me out, so I have to pull him out first. It's the only way it can happen, the only way we'll get him out of our lives. In the final analysis it's Carlos against Bourne. We're back where we were thirteen years ago. 'Alpha, Bravo, Cain, Delta . . . Cain is for Carlos and Delta is for Cain.' "

"That was a crazy Paris code thirteen years ago!" interrupted Alex sharply. "Medusa's *Delta* and his mighty challenge to the Jackal. But this *isn't* Paris and it's thirteen years *later!*"

"And in five more years it'll be eighteen; five years after that, twenty-three. What the hell do you want me to do? Live with the specter of that son of a bitch over my family, frightened every time my wife or my children leave the house, living in fear for the rest of my life? . . . No, *you* shut up, field man! You know better than that. The analysts can come up with a dozen strategies and we'll use bits and pieces of maybe six and be grateful, but when it gets down to the mud, it's between the Jackal and me. . . . And I've got the advantage. I've got you on my side."

Conklin swallowed while blinking. "That's very flattering, David, maybe too flattering. I'm better in my own element, a couple of thousand miles away from Washington. It was always a little stifling for me here."

"It wasn't when you saw me off on that plane to Hong Kong five years ago. You'd put together half the equation by then."

"That was easier. It was a down-and-dirty D.C. operation that had the smell of rotten halibut, so rotten it offended my nostrils. This is different; this is Carlos."

"That's my point, Alex. It *is* Carlos, not a voice over the telephone neither of us knew. We're dealing with a known quantity, someone predictable—"

"Predictable?" broke in Conklin, frowning. "That's also crazy. In what way?"

"He's the hunter. He'll follow a scent."

"He'll examine it first with a very experienced nose, then check the spoors under a microscope."

"Then we'll have to be authentic, won't we?"

"I prefer foolproof. What did you have in mind?"

"In the gospel according to Saint Alex, it's written that in order to bait a trap one has to use a large part of the truth, even a dangerous amount."

"That chapter and verse referred to a target's microscope. I think I just mentioned it. What's the relevance here?"

"Medusa," said Webb quietly. "I want to use Medusa."

"Now you're *out* of your mind," responded Conklin, no louder than David. "That name is as off-limits as you are—let's be honest, a hell of a lot more so."

"There were rumors, Alex, stories all over Southeast Asia that floated up the China Sea to Kowloon and Hong Kong, where most of those bastards ran with their money. Medusa wasn't exactly the secret evil you seem to think it was."

"Rumors, yes, and stories, of course," interrupted the retired intelligence officer. "Which of those animals didn't put a gun or a knife to the heads of a dozen or two dozen or two *hundred* marks during their so-called 'tours'? Ninety percent were killers and thieves, the original death squads. Peter Holland said that when he was a SEAL in the northern operations he never met a member of that outfit he didn't want to waste."

"And without them, instead of fifty-eight thousand casualties, there could well have been sixty-plus. Give the animals their due, Alex. They knew every inch of the territories, every square foot of jungle in the triangle. They—*we*—sent back more functional intelligence than all the units sent out by Saigon put together."

"My *point,* David, is that there can never be any connection between Medusa and the United States government. Our involvement was never logged, much less acknowledged; the name itself was concealed as much as possible. There's no statute of limitations on war crimes, and Medusa was officially determined to be a private organization, a collection of violent misfits who wanted the corrupt Southeast Asia back the way they knew it and used it. If it was ever established that Washington was behind Medusa, the reputation of some very important people in the White House and the State Department would be ruined. They're global power brokers now, but twenty years ago they were hotheaded junior staffers in Command Saigon. . . . We can live with questionable tactics in time of war, but not with being accomplices in the slaughter of noncombatants and the diversion of funds totaling millions, both unknowingly paid for by the taxpayers. It's like those still-sealed archives that detail how so many of our fat-cat financiers bankrolled the Nazis. Some things we never want out of their black holes, and Medusa's one of them."

Webb again leaned back in the chair—now, however, taut, his eyes steady on his old friend, who was once briefly his deadly enemy. "If what memory I have left serves me, Bourne was identified as having come out of Medusa."

"It was an entirely believable explanation and a perfect cover," agreed Conklin, returning David's gaze. "We went back to Tam Quan and 'discovered' that Bourne was a paranoid Tasmanian adventurer who disappeared in the jungles of North Vietnam. Nowhere in that very creative dossier was there the slightest clue of a Washington connection."

"But that's all a lie, isn't it, Alex? There was and is a Washington connection, and the Jackal *knows* it now. He knew it when he found you and Mo Panov in Hong Kong—found your names in the ruins of that sterile house on Victoria Peak where Jason Bourne was supposedly blown away. He confirmed it last night when his messengers approached you at the Smithsonian and—your words—'our men were very obvious.' He knew finally that everything he's believed for thirteen years is true. The member of Medusa who was called Delta was Jason Bourne, and Jason Bourne was a creation of American intelligence—and he's still alive. Alive and in hiding and protected by his government."

Conklin slammed his fist on the arm of his chair. "How did he find us, find *me*? Everything, *everything,* was under a black drape. McAllister and I made sure of it!"

"I can think of several ways, but that's a question we can postpone, we haven't time for it now. We have to move now on what we know Carlos knows. . . . *Medusa*, Alex."

"What? Move *how*?"

"If Bourne was plucked from Medusa, it has to follow that our covert operations were working with it—with them. Otherwise, how could the Bourne switch be created? What the Jackal doesn't know or hasn't put together yet is how far this government—especially certain people in this government—will go to keep Medusa in its black hole. As you pointed out, some very important men in the White House and the State Department could get burned, a lot of nasty labels branded on the foreheads of global power brokers, I think you called them."

"And suddenly we've got a few Waldheims of our own." Conklin nodded, frowning and looking down, his thoughts obviously racing.

"Nuy Dap Ranh," said Webb, barely above a whisper. At the sound of the Oriental words, Alex's eyes snapped back up at David. "That's

the key, isn't it?" continued Webb. *"Nuy Dap Ranh—*Snake Lady."

"You remembered."

"Just this morning," replied Jason Bourne, his eyes cold. "When Marie and the kids were airborne, the plane disappeared into the mists over Boston harbor and suddenly I was there. In another plane, in another time, the words crackling out of a radio through the static. 'Snake Lady, Snake Lady, abort. . . . Snake Lady, do you read me? *Abort!'* I responded by turning the damn thing off and looked around at the men in the cabin, which seemed ready to break apart in the turbulence. I studied each man, wondering, I guess, whether this one or that one would come out alive, whether I'd come out alive, and if we didn't, how we would die. . . . Then I saw two of the men rolling up their sleeves, comparing those small ugly tattoos on their forearms, those lousy little emblems that obsessed them—"

"Nuy Dap Ranh," said Conklin flatly. "A woman's face with snakes for strands of hair. Snake Lady. You refused to have one done on you—"

"I never considered it a mark of distinction," interrupted Webb-Bourne, blinking. "Somewhat the reverse, in fact."

"Initially it was meant for identification, not a standard or a banner of any distinction one way or the other. An intricate tattoo on the underside of the forearm, the design and the colors produced by only one artist in Saigon. No one else could duplicate it."

"That old man made a lot of money during those years; he was special."

"Every officer in Command Headquarters who was connected to Medusa had one. They were like manic kids who'd found secret code rings in cereal boxes."

"They weren't kids, Alex. Manic, you can bet your ass on it, but not kids. They were infected with a rotten virus called unaccountability, and more than a few millionaires were made in the ubiquitous Command Saigon. The real kids were being maimed and killed in the jungles while a lot of pressed khaki in the South had personal couriers routed through Switzerland and the banks on Zurich's Bahnhofstrasse."

"Careful, David. You could be speaking of some very important people in our government."

"Who are they?" asked Webb quietly, his glass poised in front of him.

"The ones I knew who were up to their necks

in garbage I made damn sure faded after Saigon fell. But I was out of the field a couple of years before then, and nobody talks very much about those months and nothing at all about Snake Lady.''

''Still, you've got to have some ideas.''

''Sure, but nothing concrete, nothing even close to proof. Just possibilities based on life-styles, on real estate they shouldn't have or places they go they shouldn't be able to afford or the positions some hold or held in corporations justifying salaries and stock options when nothing in their backgrounds justified the jobs.''

''You're describing a network,'' said David, his voice now tight, the voice of Jason Bourne.

''If it is, it's very tight,'' agreed Conklin. ''Very exclusive.''

''Draw up a list, Alex.''

''It'd be filled with holes.''

''Then keep it at first to those important people in our government who were attached to Command Saigon. Maybe even further to the ones who have real estate they shouldn't have or who held high-paying jobs in the private sector they shouldn't have gotten.''

''I repeat, any such list could be worthless.''

''Not with your instincts.''

"David, what the *hell* has any of this to do with Carlos?"

"Part of the truth, Alex. A dangerous part, I grant you, but foolproof and irresistible to the Jackal."

Stunned, the former field officer stared at his friend. "In what way?"

"That's where your creative thinking comes in. Say you come up with fifteen or twenty names, you're bound to hit three or four targets we can confirm one way or another. Once we ascertain who they are, we apply pressure, squeezing them in different ways, delivering the same basic message: A former Medusan has gone over the edge, a man who's been in protective custody for years is about to blow the head off Snake Lady and he's got the ammunition—names, crimes, the locations of secret Swiss accounts, the whole Caesar salad. Then—and this'll test the talents of the old Saint Alex we all knew and revered—word is passed on that there's someone who wants this dangerous, disgruntled turncoat more than they do."

"Ilich Ramirez Sanchez," supplied Conklin softly. "Carlos the Jackal. And what follows is equally impossible: Somehow—only God knows how—word gets out calling for a meeting between the two interested parties. That is to say, interested in a joint assassination, the parties of the first part unable to participate actively, due to the sensitive nature of their high official positions, is that about it?"

"Just about, except that these same powerful men in Washington can gain access to the identity and the whereabouts of this much desired corpse-to-be."

"Naturally," agreed Alex, nodding in disbelief. "They simply wave a wand and all the restrictions applicable to maximum-classified files are lifted and they're given the information."

"Exactly," said David firmly. "Because whoever meets with Carlos's emissaries has to be so high up, so authentic, that the Jackal has no choice but to accept him or them. He can't have any doubts, all thoughts of a trap gone with their coming forward."

"Would you also like me to make baby roses bloom during a January blizzard in Montana?"

"Close to it. Everything's got to happen within the next day or two while Carlos is still stinging from what happened at the Smithsonian."

"*Impossible!* . . . Oh, hell, I'll try. I'll set up shop here and have Langley send me what I need. Four Zero security, of course. . . . I hate like hell to lose whoever it is at the Mayflower."

"We may not," said Webb. "Whoever it is

won't fold so fast. It's not like the Jackal to leave an obvious hole like that."

"The Jackal? You think it's Carlos himself?"

"Not him, of course, but someone on his payroll, someone so unlikely he could carry a sign around his neck with the Jackal's name on it and we wouldn't believe him."

"Chinese?"

"Maybe. He might play that out and then he might not. He's geometric; whatever he does is logical, even his logic seems illogical."

"I hear a man from the past, a man who never was."

"Oh, he *was*, Alex. He was indeed. And now he's back."

Conklin looked toward the door of the apartment, David's words suddenly provoking another thought. "Where's your suitcase?" he asked. "You brought some clothes, didn't you?"

"No clothes, and these will be dropped in a Washington sewer once I have others. But first I have to see another old friend of mine, another genius who lives in the wrong section of town."

"Let me guess," said the retired agent. "An elderly black man with the improbable name of Cactus, a genius where false papers such as passports and driver's licenses and credit cards are concerned."

"That's about it. Him."

"The Agency could do it all."

"Not as well and too bureaucratically. I want nothing traceable, even with Four Zero security. This is solo."

"Okay. Then what?"

"You get to work, field man. By tomorrow morning I want a lot of people in this town shaken up."

"Tomorrow *morning* . . . ? That is *impossible*!"

"Not for you. Not for Saint Alex, the prince of dark operations?"

"Say whatever the hell you like, I'm not even in training."

"It comes back quickly, like sex and riding a bicycle."

"What about you? What are *you* going to do?"

"After I consult with Cactus, I'll get a room at the Mayflower hotel," answered Jason Bourne.

Culver Parnell, hotel magnate from Atlanta whose twenty-year reign in the hostelry business had led to his appointment as chief of protocol for the White House, angrily hung up his office phone as he scribbled a sixth obscenity on a legal pad. With the election and now the turnover of White House personnel, he had replaced the previous administration's well-born female who knew nothing about the political ramifications of 1600's invitation list. Then, to his profound irritation, he found himself at war with his own first assistant, another middle-aged female, also from one of the ass-elegant Eastern colleges, and, to make it worse, a popular Washington socialite who contributed her salary to some la-di-da dance company whose members pranced around in their underwear when they wore any.

"Hog damn!" fumed Culver, running his hand through his fringed gray hair; he picked up the telephone and poked four digits on his console. "Gimme the Redhead, you sweet thing," he intoned, exaggerating his already pronounced Georgia accent.

"Yes, *sir,*" said the flattered secretary. "He's on another line but I'll interrupt. Just hold on a sec, Mr. Parnell."

"You're the loveliest of the peaches, lovely child."

"Oh, golly, *thank* you! Now just hold *on.*"

It never failed, mused Culver. A little soft oil from the magnolia worked a hell of a lot better than the bark of a gnarled oak. That bitch of a first assistant of his might take a lesson from her

Southern superiors; she talked like some Yankee dentist had bonded her fucking teeth together with permanent cement.

"That you, Cull?" came the voice of Redhead over the line, intruding on Parnell's thoughts as he wrote a seventh obscenity on the legal pad.

"You're momma-letchin' right, boy, and we got a *problem*! The fricassee bitch is doin' it again. I got our Wall Streeters inked in for a table at the reception on the twenty-fifth, the one for the new French ambassador and *she* says we gotta bump 'em for some core-dee-ballet fruit-cakes—she says she and the *First Lady* feel mighty strong about it. *Shee-it!* Those money boys gotta lot of French interests goin' for them, and this White House bash could put 'em on top. Every frog on the Bourse will think they got the ears of the whole town here!"

"Forget it, Cull," broke in the anxious Redhead. "We may have a bigger problem, and I don't know what it means."

"What's that?"

"When we were back in Saigon, did you ever hear of something or someone called Snake Lady?"

"I heard a hell of a lot about snake eyes," chuckled Parnell, "but no Snake Lady. Why?"

"The fellow I was just talking to—he's going to call back in five minutes—sounded as though he was threatening me. I mean actually *threatening* me, Cull! He mentioned Saigon and implied that something terrible happened back then and repeated the name Snake Lady several times as if I should have run for cover."

"You leave that son of a bitch to *me*!" roared Parnell, interrupting. "I know *exactly* what that bastard's talking about! This is that snotty bitch first assistant of mine—*that's* the fuckin' Snake Lady! You give that slug worm my number and tell him I know all about his horseshit!"

"Will you please tell *me*, Cull?"

"What the hell, you were there, Redhead. . . . So we had a few games going, even a few mini casinos, and some clowns lost a couple of shirts, but there was nothin' soldiers haven't done since they threw craps for Christ's *clothes*! . . . We just put it on a higher plane and maybe tossed in a few broads who'd have been walkin' the streets anyway. . . . No, Redhead, that elegant-ass, so-called assistant thinks she's got somethin' on me—that's why she's goin' through you, 'cause everybody knows we're buddies. . . . You tell that slime to call me and *I'll* settle his grits along with that bitch's twat! *Oh,* boy, she made a wrong move! My Wall Streeters are in and her pansies are *out!*"

"Okay, Cull, I'll simply refer him to you," said the Redhead, otherwise known as the vice president of the United States, as he hung up the phone.

It rang four minutes later and the words were spat out at Parnell. *"Snake Lady,* Culver, and we're all in trouble!"

"No, you listen to me, Divot Head, and I'll tell you who's in trouble! She's no lady, she's a *bitch*! One of her thirty or forty eunuch husbands may have thrown a few snake eyes in Saigon and lost some of her well-advertised come-and-take-me cash, but nobody gave a shit then and nobody gives a shit now. Especially a marine colonel who liked a sharp game of poker every once in a while, and that man is sitting in the Oval Office at this moment. And furthermore, you ball-less scrotum, when he learns that she's trying to further defame the brave boys who wanted only a little relaxation while fighting a thankless war—"

In Vienna, Virginia, Alexander Conklin replaced the phone. *Misfire One* and *Misfire Two* . . . and he had never heard of Culver Parnell.

The chairman of the Federal Trade Commission, Albert Armbruster, swore out loud as he turned off the shower at the sound of his wife's shrieking voice in the steam-filled bathroom. "What the hell is it, Mamie? I can't take a shower without you *yammering*?"

"It could be the White House, Al! You know how they talk, so low and quiet and always saying it's urgent."

"Shit!" yelled the chairman, opening the glass door and walking naked to the phone on the wall. "This is Armbruster. What is it?"

"There's a crisis that requires your immediate attention."

"Is this 1600?"

"No, and we hope it never goes up there."

"Then who the hell *are* you?"

"Someone as concerned as you're going to be. After all these years—oh, *Christ!*"

"Concerned about *what*? What are you talking about?"

"Snake Lady, Mr. Chairman."

"Oh, my *God!*" Armbruster's hushed voice was a sudden involuntary cry of panic. Instantly, he controlled himself but it was too late. *Mark*

One. "I have no idea what you're talking about. . . . What's a snake whatever-it-is? Never heard of it."

"Well, hear it now, Mr. *Medusa.* Somebody's got it all, everything. Dates, diversions of matériel, banks in Geneva and Zurich—even the names of a half-dozen couriers routed out of Saigon—and worse. . . . Jesus, *the* worst! Other names—MIAs established as never having been in combat . . . eight investigating personnel from the inspector general's office. *Everything.*"

"You're not making sense! You're talking gibberish!"

"And you're on the list, Mr. *Chairman.* That man must have spent fifteen years putting it together, and now he wants payment for all those years of work or he blows it open—everything, *everyone.*"

"Who? Who *is* he, for Christ's sake?"

"We're centering in. All we know is that he's been in the protection program for over a decade, and no one gets rich in those circumstances. He must have been cut out of the action in Saigon and now he's making up for lost time. Stay tight. We'll be back in touch." There was a click and the line went dead.

Despite the steam and the heat of the bathroom, the naked Albert Armbruster, chairman of the Federal Trade Commission, shivered as the sweat rolled down his face. He hung up the phone, his eyes straying to the small, ugly tattoo on the underside of his forearm.

Over in Vienna, Virginia, Alex Conklin looked at the telephone.

Mark One.

General Norman Swayne, chief of Pentagon procurements, stepped back from the tee satisfied with his long straight drive down the fairway. The ball would roll to an optimum position for a decent five-iron approach shot to the seventeenth green. "That ought to do it," he said, turning to address his golfing partner.

"Certainly ought to, Norm," replied the youngish senior vice president of Calco Technologies. "You're taking my butt for a ride this afternoon. I'm going to end up owing you close to three hundred clams. At twenty a hole, I've only gotten four so far."

"It's your hook, young fella. You ought to work on it."

"That's certainly the truth, Norm," agreed the Calco executive in charge of marketing as he approached the tee. Suddenly, there was the high grating sound of a golf cart's horn as a three-wheeled vehicle appeared over the incline from the sixteenth fairway going as fast as it could go. "That's your driver, General," said the armaments marketer, immediately wishing he had not used his partner's formal title.

"So it is. That's odd; he never interrupts my golf game." Swayne walked toward the rapidly approaching cart, meeting it thirty feet away from the tee. "What is it?" he asked a large, middle-aged beribboned master sergeant who had been his driver for over fifteen years.

"My guess is that it's rotten," answered the noncommissioned officer gruffly while he gripped the wheel.

"That's pretty blunt—"

"So was the son of a bitch who called. I had to take it inside, on a *pay* phone. I told him I wouldn't break into your game, and he said I goddamned well better if I knew what was good for me. Naturally, I asked him who he was and what rank and all the rest of the bullshit but he cut me off, more scared than anything else. 'Just tell the general I'm calling about Saigon and some reptiles crawling around the city damn near twenty years ago.' Those were his exact words—"

"Jesus *Christ!*" cried Swayne, interrupting. *"Snake . . . ?"*

"He said he'd call back in a half hour—that's eighteen minutes now. Get in, Norman. I'm part of this, remember?"

Bewildered and frightened, the general mumbled. "I . . . I have to make excuses. I can't just walk away, drive away."

"Make it quick. And, *Norman,* you've got on a short-sleeved shirt, you goddamned idiot! Bend your arm."

Swayne, his eyes wide, stared at the small tattoo on his flesh, instantly crooking his arm to his chest in British brigadier fashion as he walked unsteadily back to the tee, summoning a casualness he could not feel. "Damn, young fella, the army calls."

"Well, damn also, Norm, but I've got to pay you. I *insist!*"

The general, half in a daze, accepted the debt from his partner, not counting the bills, not realizing that it was several hundred dollars more than he was owed. Proffering confused thanks, Swayne walked swiftly back to the golf cart and climbed in beside his master sergeant.

"So much for my hook, soldier boy," said the armaments executive to himself, addressing the tee and swinging his club, sending the little pocked white ball straight down the fairway far beyond the general's and with a much better lie. "Four hundred million's worth, you brass-plated bastard."

Mark Two.

"What in heaven's name are you *talking* about?" asked the senator, laughing as he spoke into the phone. "Or should I say, what's Al Armbruster trying to pull? He doesn't need my support on the new bill and he wouldn't get it if he did. He was a jackass in Saigon and he's a jackass now, but he's got the majority vote."

"We're not talking about votes, Senator. We're talking about *Snake Lady*!"

"The only snakes I knew in Saigon were jerks like Alby who crawled around the city pretending to know all the answers when there weren't any. . . . Who the hell *are* you anyway?"

In Vienna, Virginia, Alex Conklin replaced the telephone.

Misfire Three.

Phillip Atkinson, ambassador to the Court of St. James's, picked up his phone in London, assuming that the unnamed caller, code "courier

D.C.," was bearing an exceptionally confidential instruction from the State Department and automatically, as was the order, Atkinson snapped the switch on his rarely used scrambler. It would create an eruption of static on British intelligence's intercepts and later he would smile benignly at good friends in the Connaught bar who asked him if there was anything new out of Washington, knowing that this one or that one had "relatives" in MI-Five.

"Yes, Courier District?"

"Mr. Ambassador, I assume we can't be picked up," said the low, strained voice from Washington.

"Your assumption's correct unless they've come up with a new type of Enigma, which is unlikely."

"Good. . . . I want to take you back to Saigon, to a certain operation no one talks about—"

"Who *is* this?" broke in Atkinson, bolting forward in his chair.

"The men in that outfit never used names, Mr. Ambassador, and we didn't exactly advertise our commitments, did we?"

"Goddamn you, who *are* you? I *know* you?"

"No way, Phil, although I'm surprised you don't recognize my voice."

Atkinson's eyes widened as they roamed rapidly about his office, seeing nothing, only trying to remember, trying desperately to put a voice with a face. "Is that you, Jack—*believe* me, we're on a scrambler!"

"Close, Phil—"

"The Sixth Fleet, Jack. A simple reverse Morse. Then bigger things, *much* bigger. It's *you*, isn't it?"

"Let's say it's a possible, but it's also irrelevant. The point is we're in heavy weather, *very* heavy—"

"It *is* you!"

"Shut up. Just listen. A bastard frigate got loose from its moorings and is crashing around, hitting too many shoals."

"Jack, I was ground, not sea. I can't understand you."

"Some swab-jockey must have been cut out of the action back in Saigon, and from what I've learned he was put in protection for something or other and now he's got it all put together. He's got it *all*, Phil. *Everything.*"

"Holy Christ!"

"He's ready to launch—"

"*Stop* him!"

"That's the problem. We're not sure who he

is. The whole thing's being kept very close over in Langley."

"Good God, man, in your position you can give them the order to back off! Say it's a DOD dead file that was never completed—that it was designed to spread *disinformation*! It's all *false*!"

"That could be walking into a salvo—"

"Have you called Jimmy T over in Brussels?" interrupted the ambassador. "He's tight with the top max at Langley."

"At the moment I don't want anything to go any further. Not until I do some missionary work."

"Whatever you say, Jack. You're running the show."

"Keep your halyards taut, Phil."

"If that means keep my mouth shut, don't you worry about it!" said Atkinson, crooking his elbow, wondering who in London could remove an ugly tattoo on his forearm.

Across the Atlantic in Vienna, Virginia, Alex Conklin hung up the telephone and leaned back in his chair a frightened man. He had been following his instincts as he had done in the field for over twenty years, words leading to other words, phrases to phrases, innuendos snatched out of the air to support suppositions, even con-

clusions. It was a chess game of instant invention and he knew he was a skilled professional—sometimes too skilled. There were
things that should remain in their black holes,
undetected cancers buried in history, and what
he had just learned might well fit that category.

Marks Three, Four and Five.

Phillip Atkinson, ambassador to Great Britain.
James Teagarten, supreme commander of
NATO. Jonathan "Jack" Burton, former admiral
of the Sixth Fleet, currently chairman of the
Joint Chiefs of Staff.

Snake Lady. Medusa.

A network.

5

It was as if nothing had changed, thought Jason Bourne, knowing that his other self, the self called David Webb, was receding. The taxi had brought him out to the once elegant, now run-down neighborhood in northeast Washington, and, as happened five years ago, the driver refused to wait. He walked up the overgrown flag-stone path to the old house, thinking as he did the first time that it was too old and too fragile and too much in need of repair; he rang the bell, wondering if Cactus was even alive. He was; the thin old black man with the gentle face and warm eyes stood in the doorframe exactly as he had stood five years before, squinting beneath a green eyeshade. Even Cactus's first words were a minor variation of those he had used five years ago.

"You got hubcaps on your car, Jason?"

"No car and no cab; it wouldn't stay."

"Musta heard all those scurrilous rumors circulated by the fascist press. Me, I got howitzers in the windows just to impress this neighborly turf of my friendly persuasion. Come on in, I think of you a lot. Why didn't you phone this old boy?"

"Your number's not listed, Cactus."

"Musta been an oversight." Bourne walked into the hallway as the old man closed the door. "You got a few streaks of gray in your hair, Br'er Rabbit," added Cactus, studying his friend. "Other than that you ain't changed much. Maybe a line or six in your face, but it adds character."

"I've also got a wife and two kids, Uncle Remus. A boy and a girl."

"I know that. Mo Panov keeps me up on things even though he can't tell me where you are—which I don't care to know, Jason."

Bourne blinked while slowly shaking his head. "I still forget things, Cactus. I'm sorry. I forgot you and Mo are friends."

"Oh, the good doctor calls me at least once a month and says, 'Cactus, you rascal, put on your Pierre Cardin suit and your Gucci shoes and let's have lunch.' So I say to him, 'Where's this old nigger gonna get such threads?' and he says to me, 'You probably own a shopping center in the best part of town.' . . . Now that's an exaggeration, s' help me. I do have bits and pieces of decent white real estate but I never go near them."

As both men laughed, Jason stared at the dark face and warm black eyes in front of him. "Something else I just remembered. Thirteen years ago in that hospital in Virginia . . . you came to see me. Outside of Marie and those government bastards you were the only one."

"Panov understood, Br'er Rabbit. When in my very unofficial status I worked on you for Europe, I told Morris that you don't study a man's face in a lens without learning things about that face, that man. I wanted you to talk about the things I found missing in that lens and Morris thought it might not be a bad idea. . . . And now that confessional hour is over, I gotta say that it's really *good* to see you, Jason, but to tell you the truth I'm not *happy* to see you, if you catch my meaning."

"I need your help, Cactus."

"That's the root of my unhappiness. You've been through enough and you wouldn't be here unless you were itching for more, and in my professional, lens-peering opinion, that ain't healthy for the face I'm lookin' at."

"You've got to help me."

"Then you'd better have a damn good reason that passes muster for the good doctor. 'Cause I ain't gonna' mess around with anything that could mess you up further. . . . I met your lovely lady with the dark red hair a few times in the hospital—she's somethin' special, Br'er, and your kids have got to be outstanding, so you see I can't mess around with anything that might hurt them. Forgive me, but you're all like kinfolk from a distance, from a time we don't talk about, but it's on my mind."

"They're why I need your help."

"Be clearer, Jason."

"The Jackal's closing in. He found us in Hong Kong and he's zeroing in on me and my family, on my wife and my children. Please, *help* me."

The old man's eyes grew wide under the green shade, a moral fury in his expanded pupils. "Does the good doctor know about this?"

"He's part of it. He may not approve of what I'm doing, but if he's honest with himself, he knows that the bottom line is the Jackal and me. *Help* me, Cactus."

The aged black studied his pleading client in the hallway, in the afternoon shadows. "You in good shape, Br'er Rabbit?" he asked. "You still got juices?"

"I run six miles every morning and I press weights at least twice a week in the university gym—"

"I didn't hear that. I don't want to know anything about colleges or universities."

"Then you didn't hear it."

"Course I didn't. You look in pretty fair condition, I'll say that."

"It's deliberate, Cactus," said Jason quietly. "Sometimes it's just a telephone suddenly ringing, or Marie's late or out with the kids and I can't reach her . . . or someone I don't know stops me in the street to ask directions, and it comes back—*he* comes back. The Jackal. As long as there's a possibility that he's alive, I have to be ready for him because he won't stop looking for me. The awful irony is that his hunt is based on a supposition that may not be true. He thinks I can identify him, but I'm not sure I could. Nothing's really in focus yet."

"Have you considered sending that message to him?"

"With his assets maybe I'll take an ad out in the *Wall Street Journal.* 'Dear Old Buddy Carlos: Boy, have I got news for *you.*' "

"Don't chortle, Jason, it's not inconceivable. Your friend Alex could find a way. His gimp doesn't affect that head of his. I believe the fancy word is serpentine."

"Which is why if he hasn't tried it there's a reason."

"I guess I can't argue with that. . . . So let's go to work, Br'er Rabbit. What did you have in mind?" Cactus led the way through a wide archway toward a door at the rear of a worn-out living room replete with ancient furniture and yellowed antimacassars. "My studio isn't as elegant as it was but all the equipment's there. You see, I'm sort of semiretired. My financial planners worked out a hell of a retirement program with great tax advantages, so the pressure's not so great."

"You're only incredible," said Bourne.

"I imagine some people might say that, the ones not doin' time. What *did* you have in mind?"

"Pretty much myself. Not Europe or Hong Kong, of course. Just papers, actually."

"So the Chameleon retreats to another disguise. Himself."

Jason stopped as they approached the door. "That was something else I forgot. They used to call me that, didn't they?"

"Chameleon? . . . They sure did and not without cause, as they say. Six people could come face-to-face with our boy Bourne and there'd be six different descriptions. Without a jar of makeup, incidentally."

"It's all coming back, Cactus."

"I wish to almighty God that it didn't have to, but if it does, you make damn *sure* it's all back. . . . Come on into the magic room."

Three hours and twenty minutes later the magic was completed. David Webb, Oriental scholar and for three years Jason Bourne, assassin, had two additional aliases with passports, driver's licenses and voter registration cards to confirm the identities. And since no cabs would travel out to Cactus's "turf," an unemployed neighbor wearing several heavy gold chains around his neck and wrists drove Cactus's client into the heart of Washington in his new Cadillac Allanté.

Jason found a pay phone in Garfinkel's department store and called Alex in Virginia, giving him both aliases and selecting one for the May-flower hotel. Conklin would officially secure a room through the management in the event that summer reservations were tight. Further, Langley would activate a Four Zero imperative and do its best to furnish Bourne with the material he needed, delivering it to his room as soon as possible. The estimate was a minimum of an additional three hours, no guarantees as to the time or authenticity. Regardless, thought Jason, as Alex reconfirmed the information on a second direct line to the CIA, he needed at least two of those three hours before going to the hotel. He had a small wardrobe to put together; the Chameleon was reverting to type.

"Steve DeSole tells me he'll start spinning the disks, cross-checking ours with the army data banks and naval intelligence," said Conklin, returning to the line. "Peter Holland can make it happen; he's the president's crony."

"Crony? That's an odd word coming from you."

"Like in crony appointment."

"Oh? . . . Thanks, Alex. How about you? Any progress?"

Conklin paused, and when he answered his quiet voice conveyed his fear; it was controlled

but the fear was there. "Let's put it this way.
. . . I'm not equipped for what I've learned. I've
been away too long. I'm afraid, Jason—sorry
. . . David."

"You're right the first time. Have you discussed—"

"Nothing by name," broke in the retired intelligence officer quickly, firmly.

"I see."

"You couldn't," contradicted Alex. *"I* couldn't.
I'll be in touch." With these cryptic words Conklin abruptly hung up.

Slowly Bourne did the same, frowning in concern. Alex was the one now sounding melodramatic, and it was not like him to think that
way or act that way. Control was his byword,
understatement his persona. Whatever he had
learned profoundly disturbed him . . . so much so
as to make it seem to Bourne that he no longer
trusted the procedures he himself had set up, or
even the people he was working with. Otherwise
he would have been clearer, more forthcoming;
instead, for reasons Jason could not fathom,
Alexander Conklin did not want to talk about
Medusa or whatever he had learned in peeling
away twenty years of deceit. . . . Was it *possible*?

No time! No use, not now, considered Bourne,

looking around the huge department store. Alex was not only as good as his word, he lived by it, as long as one was not an enemy. Ruefully, suppressing a short throated laugh, Jason remembered Paris thirteen years ago. He knew *that* side of Alex, too. But for the cover of gravestones in a cemetery on the outskirts of Rambouillet, his closest friend would have killed him. That was then, not now. Conklin said he'd "be in touch." He would. Until then the Chameleon had to build several covers. From the inside to the outside, from underwear to outerwear and everything in between. No chance of a laundry or a cleaning mark coming to light, no microscopic chemical evidence of a regionally distributed detergent or fluid—*nothing*. He had given too much. If he had to kill for David's family . . . oh, my *God*! For *my* family! . . . he refused to live with the consequences of that killing or those killings. Where he was going there were no rules; the innocent might well die in the cross fire. So be it. David Webb would violently object, but Jason Bourne didn't give a goddamn. He'd been there before; he knew the statistics, Webb knew nothing.

Marie, I'll *stop* him! I *promise* you I'll rip him out of your lives. I'll take the Jackal and leave a dead man. He'll never be able to touch you again—you'll be *free.*

Oh, *Christ,* who *am* I? Mo, help me! . . . No, Mo, *don't*! I am what I have to be. I am cold and I'm getting colder. Soon I'll be ice . . . clear, transparent ice, ice so cold and pure it can move anywhere without being seen. Can't you understand, Mo—you, too, Marie—I *have* to! David has to go. I can't have him around any longer.

Forgive me, Marie, and you forgive me, Doctor, but I'm thinking the truth. A truth that has to be faced right now. I'm not a fool, nor do I fool myself. You both want me to let Jason Bourne get out of my life, release him to some infinity, but the *reverse* is what I have to do now. David has to leave, at least for a while.

Don't bother me with such considerations! I have *work* to do.

Where the hell is the men's department? When he was finished making his purchases, all paid for in cash with as many different clerks as possible, he would find a men's room where he would replace every stitch of clothing on his body. After that he would walk the streets of Washington until he found a hidden sewer grate. The Chameleon, too, was back.

———

It was 7:35 in the evening when Bourne put down the single-edged razor blade. He had removed all the labels from the assortment of new clothes, hanging up each item in the closet when he had finished except for the shirts; these he steamed in the bathroom to remove the odor of newness. He crossed to the table, where room service had placed a bottle of Scotch whisky, club soda and a bucket of ice. As he passed the desk with the telephone he stopped; he wanted so terribly to call Marie on the island but knew he could not, not from the hotel room. That she and the children had arrived safely was all that mattered and they had; he had reached John St. Jacques from another pay phone in Garfinkel's.

"Hey, Davey, they're bushed! They had to hang around the big island for damn near four hours until the weather cleared. I'll wake Sis if you want me to, but after she fed Alison she just crashed."

"Never mind, I'll call later. Tell her I'm fine and take care of them, Johnny."

"Will do, fella. Now you tell *me*. Are you okay?"

"I said I'm fine."

"Sure, you can say it and she can say it, but Marie's not just my only sister, she's my favorite sister, and I know when that lady's shook up."

"That's why you're going to take care of her."

"I'm also going to have a talk with her."

"Go easy, Johnny."

For a few moments he had been David Webb again, mused Jason, pouring himself a drink. He did not like it; it felt wrong. An hour later, however, Jason Bourne was back. He had spoken to the clerk at the Mayflower about his reservation; the night manager had been summoned.

"Ah, yes, Mr. *Simon*," the man had greeted him enthusiastically. "We understand you're here to argue against those terrible tax restrictions on business travel and entertainment. Godspeed, as they say. These politicians will ruin us all! . . . There were no double rooms, so we took the liberty of providing you with a suite, no additional charge, of course."

All that had taken place over two hours ago, and since then he had removed the labels, steamed the shirts and scuffed the rubber-soled shoes on the hotel's window ledge. Drink in hand, Bourne sat in a chair staring blankly at the wall; there was nothing to do but wait and think.

A quiet tapping at the door ended the waiting in a matter of minutes. Jason walked rapidly across the room, opened the door and admitted the driver who had met him at the airport. The CIA man carried an attaché case; he handed it to Bourne.

"Everything's there, including a weapon and a box of shells."

"Thanks."

"Do you want to check it out?"

"I'll be doing that all night."

"It's almost eight o'clock," said the agent. "Your control will reach you around eleven. That'll give you time to get started."

"My control . . . ?"

"That's who he is, isn't he?"

"Yes, of course," replied Jason softly. "I'd forgotten. Thanks again."

The man left and Bourne hurried to the desk with the attaché case. He opened it, removing first the automatic and the box of ammunition, then picking up what had to be several hundred computer printouts secured in file folders. Somewhere in those myriad pages was a name that linked a man or a woman to Carlos the Jackal. For these were the informational print-outs of every guest currently at the hotel, including those who had checked out within the past twenty-four hours. Each printout was supplemented by whatever additional information was found in the data banks of the CIA, Army G-2 and naval intelligence. There could be a score of reasons why it might all be useless, but it was a place to start. The hunt had begun.

Five hundred miles north, in another hotel suite, this on the third floor of Boston's Ritz-Carlton, there was another tapping on another hotel door. Inside, an immensely tall man, whose well-tailored pin-striped suit made him appear even larger than his nearly six feet five inches of height, came rushing out of the bedroom. His bald head, fringed by perfectly groomed gray hair above his temples, was like the skull of an anointed éminence grise of some royal court where kings, princes and pretenders deferred to his wisdom, delivered no doubt with the eyes of an eagle and the soaring voice of a prophet. Although his rushing figure revealed a vulnerable anxiety, even that did not diminish his image of dominance. He was important and powerful and he knew it. All this was in contrast to the older man he admitted through the door. There was little that was distinguished about this short, gaunt, elderly visitor; instead, he conveyed the look of defeat.

"Come in. *Quickly!* Did you bring the information?"

"Oh, yes, yes, indeed," answered the gray-faced man whose rumpled suit and ill-fitting collar had both seen better days perhaps a decade ago. "How grand you look, Randolph," he continued in a thin voice while studying his host and glancing around at the opulent suite. "And how grand a place this is, so proper for such a distinguished professor."

"The information, please," insisted Dr. Randolph Gates of Harvard, expert in antitrust law and highly paid consultant to numerous industries.

"Oh, give me a moment, my old friend. It's been a long time since I've been near a hotel suite, much less stayed in one. . . . Oh, how things have changed for us over the years. I read about you frequently and I've watched you on television. You're so—erudite, Randolph, that's the word, but it's not enough. It's what I said before—'grand,' that's what you are, grand and erudite. So tall and imperious."

"You might have been in the same position, you know," broke in the impatient Gates. "Unfortunately, you looked for shortcuts where there weren't any."

"Oh, there were lots of them. I just chose the wrong ones."

"I gather things haven't gone well for you—"

"You don't 'gather,' Randy, you *know.* If your spies didn't inform you, certainly you can tell."

"I was simply trying to find you."

"Yes, that's what you said on the phone, what a number of people said to me in the street—people who had been asked a number of questions having nothing to do with my residence, such as it is."

"I had to know if you were capable. You can't fault me for that."

"Good heavens, no. Not considering what you had me do, what I *think* you had me do."

"Merely act as a confidential messenger, that's all. You certainly can't object to the money."

"Object?" said the visitor, with a high-pitched and tremulous laugh. "Let me tell you something, Randy. You can be disbarred at thirty or thirty-five and still get by, but when you're disbarred at fifty and your trial is given national press along with a jail sentence, you'd be shocked at how your options disappear—even for a learned man. You become an untouchable, and I was never much good at selling anything but my wits. I proved that, too, over the last twenty-odd years, incidentally. Alger Hiss did better with greeting cards."

"I haven't time to reminisce. The information, please."

"Oh, yes, of course. . . . Well, first the money was delivered to me on the corner of Commonwealth and Dartmouth, and naturally I wrote down the names and the specifics you gave me over the phone—"

"*Wrote down*?" asked Gates sharply.

"Burned as soon as I'd committed them to memory—I *did* learn a few things from my difficulties. I reached the engineer at the telephone company, who was overjoyed with your—excuse me—*my* largess, and took his information to that repulsive private detective, a sleaze if I ever saw one, Randy, and considering his methods, someone who could really use my talents."

"*Please,*" interrupted the renowned legal scholar. "The facts, not your appraisals."

"Appraisals often contain germane facts, Professor. Surely you understand that."

"If I want to build a case, I'll ask for opinions. Not now. What did the man find out?"

"Based on what you told me, a lone woman with children—how many being undetermined—

and on the data provided by an underpaid telephone company mechanic, namely, a narrowed-
down location based on the area code and the
first three digits of a number, the unethical
sleaze went to work at an outrageous hourly
rate. To my astonishment, he was productive.
As a matter of fact, with what's left of my legal
mind, we may form a quiet, unwritten partner-
ship."

"Damn you, what did he *learn*?"

"Well, as I say, his hourly rate was beyond
belief, I mean it really invaded the corpus of my
own well-deserved retainer, so I think we should
discuss an adjustment, don't you?"

"Who the hell do you think you *are*? I sent you
three thousand dollars! Five hundred for the telephone man and fifteen hundred for that miserable keyhole slime who calls himself a private
detective—"

"Only because he's no longer on the public
payroll of the police department, Randolph. Like
me, he fell from grace, but he obviously does
very good work. Do we negotiate or do I leave?"

In fury, the balding imperious professor of law
stared at the gray-faced old disbarred and dis-
honored attorney in front of him. "How *dare*
you?"

"Dear me, Randy, you really do believe your press, don't you? Very well, I'll tell why I dare, my arrogant old friend. I've read you, seen you, expounding on your esoteric interpretations of complex legal matters, assaulting every decent thing the courts of this country have decreed in the last thirty years, when you haven't the vaguest idea what it is to be poor, or hungry, or have an unwanted mass in your belly you neither anticipated nor can provide a life for. You're the darling of the royalists, my unprofound fellow, and you'd force the average citizen to live in a nation where privacy is obsolete, free thought suspended by censorship, the rich get richer, and for the poorest among us the beginnings of potential life itself may well have to be abandoned in order to survive. And you expound on these unoriginal, medieval concepts only to promote yourself as a brilliant maverick—of disaster. Do you want me to go on, *Doctor* Gates? Frankly, I think you chose the wrong loser to contact for your dirty work."

"How . . . *dare* you?" repeated the perplexed professor, sputtering as he regally strode to the window. "I don't have to listen to this!"

"No, you certainly don't, Randy. But when I was an associate at the law school and you were one of my kids—one of the best but not the brightest—you damn well had to listen. So I suggest you listen now."

"What the hell do you *want*?" roared Gates, turning away from the window.

"It's what *you* want, isn't it? The information you underpaid me for. It's that important to you, isn't it?"

"I must have it."

"You were always filled with anxiety before an exam—"

"*Stop* it! I *paid*. I demand the information."

"Then I must demand more money. Whoever's paying you can afford it."

"Not a dollar!"

"Then I'm leaving."

"*Stop!* . . . Five hundred more, that's it."

"Five thousand or I go."

"*Ridiculous!*"

"See you in another twenty years—"

"All right. . . . All *right*, five thousand."

"Oh, Randy, you're so obvious. It's why you're not really one of the brightest, just someone who can use language to make yourself appear bright, and I think we've seen and heard enough of that these days. . . . *Ten* thousand, Dr. Gates, or I go to the raucous bar of my choice."

"You can't *do* this."

"Certainly I can. I'm now a confidential legal consultant. *Ten* thousand dollars. How do you want to pay it? I can't imagine you have it with you, so how will you honor the debt—for the information?"

"My word—"

"*Forget* it, Randy."

"All right. I'll have it sent to the Boston Five in the morning. In your name. A bank check."

"That's very endearing of you. But in case it occurs to your superiors to stop me from collecting, please advise them that an unknown person, an old friend of mine in the streets, has a letter detailing everything that's gone on between us. It is to be mailed to the Massachusetts's Attorney General, Return Receipt Requested, in the event I have an accident."

"That's absurd. The information, *please*."

"Yes, well, you should know that you've involved yourself in what appears to be an extremely sensitive government operation, that's the bottom line. . . . On the assumption that anyone in an emergency leaving one place for another would do so with the fastest transportation possible, our rumbottom detective went to Logan Airport, under what guise I don't know.

Nevertheless, he succeeded in obtaining the manifests of every plane leaving Boston yesterday morning from the first flight at six-thirty to ten o'clock. As you recall, that corresponds with the parameters of your statement to me—'leaving first thing in the morning.' "

"And?"

"Patience, Randolph. You told me not to write anything down, so I must take this step by step. Where was I?"

"The manifests."

"Oh, yes. Well, according to Detective Sleaze, there were eleven unaccompanied children booked on various flights, and eight women, two of them nuns, who had reservations with minors. Of these eight, including the nuns who were taking nine orphans to California, the remaining six were identified as follows." The old man reached into his pocket and shakily took out a typewritten sheet of paper. "Obviously, I did not write this. I don't own a typewriter because I can't type; it comes from Führer Sleaze."

"Let me have it!" ordered Gates, rushing forward, his hand outstretched.

"Surely," said the seventy-year-old disbarred attorney, giving the page to his former student.

"It won't do you much good, however," he added. "Our Sleaze checked them out, more to inflate his hours than for anything else. Not only are they all squeaky clean, but he performed that unnecessary service after the *real* information was uncovered."

"What?" asked Gates, his attention diverted from the page. "What information?"

"Information that neither Sleaze nor I would write down anywhere. The first hint of it came from the morning setup clerk for Pan American Airlines. He mentioned to our lowbrow detective that among his problems yesterday was a hotshot politician, or someone equally offensive, who needed diapers several minutes after our clerk went on duty at five forty-five. Did you know that diapers come in sizes and are locked away in an airline's contingency supplies?"

"What are you trying to tell me?"

"All the stores in the airport were closed. They open at seven o'clock."

"So?"

"So someone in a hurry forgot something. A lone woman with a five-year-old child and an infant were leaving Boston on a private jet taking off on the runway nearest the Pan Am shuttle counters. The clerk responded to the request and was personally thanked by the mother. You see, he's a young father and understood about diaper sizes. He brought three different packages—''

"For God's sake, will you get to the *point*, Judge?"

"Judge?" The gray-faced old man's eyes widened. "Thank you, Randy. Except for my friends in various gin mills, I haven't been called that in years. It must be the aura I exude."

"It was a throwback to that same *boring* circumlocution you used both on the bench and in the classroom!"

"Impatience was always your weak suit. I ascribed it to your annoyance with other people's points of view that interfered with your conclusions. . . . Regardless, our Major Sleaze knew a rotten apple when the worm emerged and spat in his face, so he hied himself off to Logan's control tower, where he found a bribable off-duty traffic controller who checked yesterday morning's schedules. The jet in question had a computer readout of Four Zero, which to our Captain Sleaze's astonishment he was told meant it was government-cleared and maximum-classified. No manifest, no names of anyone on board, only a routing to evade commercial aircraft and a destination.''

"Which *was*?"

"Blackburne, Montserrat."

"What the hell is that?"

"The Blackburne Airport on the Caribbean island of Montserrat."

"That's where they went? That's *it*?"

"Not necessarily. According to Corporal Sleaze, who I must say does his follow-ups, there are small flight connections to a dozen or so minor offshore islands."

"*That's* it?"

"That's it, Professor. And considering the fact that the aircraft in question had a Four Zero government classification, which, incidentally, in my letter to the attorney general I so specified, I think I've earned my ten thousand dollars."

"You drunken *scum*—"

"Again you're wrong, Randy," interrupted the judge. "Alcoholic, certainly, drunk hardly ever. I stay on the edge of sobriety. It's my one reason for living. You see in my cognizance I'm always amused—by men like you, actually."

"Get out of here," said the professor ominously.

"You're not even going to offer me a drink to help support this dreadful habit of mine? . . . Good heavens, there must be half a dozen unopened bottles over there."

"Take one and leave."

"Thank you, I believe I will." The old judge walked to a cherry-wood table against the wall where two silver trays held various whiskies and a brandy. "Let's see," he continued, picking up several white cloth napkins and wrapping them around two bottles, then a third. "If I hold these tightly under my arm, they could be a pile of laundry I'm taking out for quick service."

"Will you *hurry*!"

"Will you please open the door for me? I'd hate like hell dropping one of these while manipulating the knob. If it smashed it wouldn't do much for your image, either. You've never been known to have a drink, I believe."

"Get *out*," insisted Gates, opening the door for the old man.

"Thank you, Randy," said the judge, walking out into the hallway and turning. "Don't forget the bank check at the Boston Five in the morning. Fifteen thousand."

"*Fifteen . . . ?*"

"My word, can you imagine what the attorney general would say just knowing that you'd even consorted with me? Good-bye, Counselor."

Randolph Gates slammed the door and ran into the bedroom, to the bedside telephone. The smaller enclosure was reassuring, as it removed him from the exposure to scrutiny inherent in larger areas—the room was more private, more personal, less open to invasion. The call he had to make so unnerved him he could not understand the pull-out flap of instructions for overseas connections. Instead, in his anxiety, he dialed the operator.

"I want to place a call to Paris," he said.

6

Bourne's eyes were tired, the strain painful as he studied the results of the computer printouts spread across the coffee table in front of the couch. Sitting forward, he had analyzed them for nearly four hours, forgetting time, forgetting that his "control" was to have reached him by then, concerned only with a link to the Jackal at the Mayflower hotel.

The first group, which he temporarily put aside, was the foreign nationals, a mix of British, Italian, Swedish, West German, Japanese and Taiwanese. Each of them had been extensively examined with respect to authentic credentials and fully substantiated business or personal reasons for entering the country. The State Department and the Central Intelligence Agency had done their homework. Each person was professionally and personally vouched for by a minimum of five reputable individuals or companies; all had long-standing communications with such people and firms in the Washington area; none had a false or questionable statement on record. If the Jackal's man was among them— and he might well be—it would take far more information than was to be found in the printouts before Jason could refine the list. It might be necessary to go back to this group, but for the moment he had to keep reading. There was so little time!

Of the remaining five hundred or so American guests at the hotel, two hundred and twelve had entries in one or more of the intelligence data banks, the majority because they had business with the government. However, seventy-eight had raw-file negative evaluations. Thirty-one were Internal Revenue Service matters, which meant they were suspected of destroying or falsifying financial records and/or had tax havens in Swiss or Cayman Island accounts. They were zero, nothing, merely rich and not very bright thieves, and, further, the sort of "messengers" Carlos would avoid like lepers.

That left forty-seven possibles. Men and

women—in eleven cases ostensibly husbands and wives—with extensive connections in Europe, in the main with technological firms and related nuclear and aerospace industries, all under intelligence microscopes for possibly selling classified information to brokers of the Eastern bloc and therefore to Moscow. Of these forty-seven possibles, including two of the eleven couples, an even dozen had made recent trips to the Soviet Union—scratch *all* of them. The Komitet Gosudarstvennoi Bezopasnosti, otherwise known as the KGB, had less use for the Jackal than the Pope. Ilich Ramirez Sanchez, later Carlos the assassin, had been trained in the American compound of Novgorod, where the streets were lined with American gas stations and grocery stores, boutiques and Burger Kings, and everyone spoke American English with diverse dialects—no Russian was allowed—and only those who passed the course were permitted to proceed to the next level of infiltrators. The Jackal had, indeed, passed, but when the Komitet discovered that the young Venezuelan revolutionary's solution for all things disagreeable was to eliminate them violently, it was too much for even the inheritors of the brutal OGPU. Sanchez was expelled and

Carlos the Jackal was born. Forget about the twelve people who had traveled to the Soviet Union. The assassin would not touch them, for there was a standing order in all branches of Russian intelligence that if Carlos was tracked he was to be shot. Novgorod was to be protected at all cost.

The possibles were thus narrowed to thirty-five, the hotel's register listing them as nine couples, four single women and thirteen single men. The raw-file printouts from the data banks described in detail the facts and speculations that resulted in the negative evaluation of each individual. In truth, the speculations far outnumbered the facts and were too often based on hostile appraisals given by enemies or competitors, but each had to be studied, many with distaste, for among the information might be a word or phrase, a location or an act, that was the link to Carlos.

The telephone rang, breaking Jason's concentration. He blinked at the harsh, intrusive sound as if trying to locate the source, then he sprang from the couch and rushed to the desk, reaching the phone on the third ring.

"Yes?"

"It's Alex. I'm calling from down the street."

"Are you coming up?"

"Not through that lobby, I'm not. I've made arrangements for the service entrance, with a temporary guard hired this afternoon."

"You're covering all the bases, aren't you?"

"Nowhere near as many as I'd like to," replied Conklin. "This isn't your normal ball game. See you in a few minutes. I'll knock once."

Bourne hung up the phone and returned to the couch and the printouts, separating three that had caught his attention, not that any of them contained anything that evoked the Jackal. Instead, it was seemingly offhand data that might conceivably link the three to each other when no apparent connection existed between them. According to their passports, these three Americans had flown in to Philadelphia's International Airport within six days of one another eight months ago. Two women and a man, the women from Marrakesh and Lisbon, the man from West Berlin. The first woman was an interior decorator on a collecting trip to the old Moroccan city, the second an executive for the Chase Bank, Foreign Department; the man was an aerospace engineer on loan to the Air Force from McDonnell-Douglas. Why would three such obviously different people, with such dissimilar professions, converge on the same city within a week of one another? Coincidence? Entirely possible, but considering the number of international airports in the country, including the most frequented—New York, Chicago, Los Angeles, Miami—the coincidence of Philadelphia seemed unlikely. Stranger still, and even more unlikely, was the fact that these same three people were staying at the same hotel at the same time in Washington eight months later. Jason wondered what Alex Conklin would say when he told him.

"I'm getting the book on each of them," said Alex, sinking into an armchair across from the couch and the printouts.

"You *knew*?"

"It wasn't hard to put together. Of course, it was a hell of a lot easier with a computer doing the scanning."

"You might have included a note! I've been poring over these things since eight o'clock."

"I didn't find it—them—until after nine and I didn't want to call you from Virginia."

"That's another story, isn't it?" said Bourne, sitting down on the couch, once again leaning forward anxiously.

"Yes, it is, and it's God-awful."

"Medusa?"

"It's worse than I thought, and worse than that, I didn't think it could be."

"That's a mouthful."

"It's a bowelful," countered the retired intelligence officer. "Where do I start? . . . Pentagon procurements? The Federal Trade Commission? Our ambassador in London, or would you like the supreme commander of NATO?"

"My *God* . . . !"

"Oh, I can go one better. For size, try on the chairman of the Joint Chiefs."

"Christ, what is it? Some kind of *cabal*?"

"That's so academic, Dr. Scholar. Now try collusion, down deep and elusive and after all these years still breathing, still alive. They're in contact with each other in high places. Why?"

"What's the purpose? The objective?"

"I just said that, asked that, really."

"There has to be a *reason*!"

"Try motive. I just said that, too, and it may be as simple as hiding past sins. Isn't that what we were looking for? A collection of former Medusans who'd run to the hills at the thought of the past coming to light?"

"Then that's it."

"No, it's not, and this is Saint Alex's instincts

searching for words. Their reactions were too immediate, too visceral, too loaded with today, not twenty years ago."

"You've lost me."

"I've lost myself. Something's different from what we expected, and I'm goddamned sick of making mistakes. . . . But this isn't a mistake. You said this morning that it could be a network, and I thought you were way the hell off base. I thought that maybe we'd find a few high profiles who didn't want to be publicly drawn and quartered for things they did twenty years ago, or who legitimately didn't want to embarrass the government, and we could use them, force them in their collective fear to do things and say things we told them to do. But this is different. It's *today*, and I can't figure it out. It's more than fear, it's panic; they're frightened out of their minds. . . . We've bumbled and stumbled onto something, Mr. Bourne, and in your rich friend Cactus's old-time minstrel-show language, 'In the focus, it could be bigger than bo'fus."

"In my considered opinion there's *nothing* bigger than the Jackal! Not for me. The rest can go to hell."

"I'm on *your* side and I'll go to the wall shouting it. I just wanted you to know my thoughts.

. . . Except for a brief and pretty rotten interlude, we never kept anything from each other, David."

"I prefer Jason these days."

"Yes, I know," interrupted Conklin. "I hate it but I understand."

"*Do* you?"

"Yes," said Alex softly, nodding as he closed his eyes. "I'd do anything to change it but I can't."

"Then *listen* to me. In that serpentine mind of yours—Cactus's description, incidentally—conjure up the worst scenario you can think of and shove those bastards against another wall, one they can't get away from unscathed unless they follow your instructions down to the letter. Those orders will be to stay quiet and wait for you to call and tell them who to reach and what to say."

Conklin looked over at his damaged friend with guilt and concern. "There may be a scenario in place that I can't match," said Alex quietly. "I won't make another mistake, not in that area. I need more than what I've got."

Bourne clasped his hands, flesh angrily grinding flesh in frustration. He stared at the scattered printouts in front of him, frowning, wincing, his jaw pulsating. In seconds a sudden passivity came over him; he sat back on the couch and spoke as quietly as Conklin. "All right, you'll get it. Quickly."

"How?"

"Me. I'll get it for you. I'll need names, residences, schedules and methods of security, favorite restaurants and bad habits, if any are known. Tell your boys to go to work. Tonight. All night, if necessary."

"What the hell do you think you're going to *do*?" shouted Conklin, his frail body lurching forward in the armchair. "Storm their houses? Stick needles in their asses between the appetizer and the entrée?"

"I hadn't thought of the last option," replied Jason, smiling grimly. "You've really got a terrific imagination."

"And you're a *madman*! . . . I'm sorry, I didn't mean that—"

"Why not?" broke in Bourne gently. "I'm not lecturing on the rise of the Manchu and the Ching dynasty. Considering the accepted state of my mind and memory, the allusion to mental health isn't inappropriate." Jason paused, then spoke as he leaned slowly forward. "But let me tell you something, Alex. The memories may not all be there, but the part of my mind that you and

Treadstone formed is *all* there. I proved it in Hong Kong, in Beijing and Macao, and I'll prove it again. I *have* to. There's nothing left for me if I don't. . . . Now, get me the information. You mentioned several people who have to be here in Washington. Pentagon supplies or provisions—"

"Procurements," corrected Conklin. "It's a lot more expansive and expensive; he's a general named Swayne. Then there's Armbruster, he's head of the Federal Trade Commission, and Burton over at—"

"Chairman of the Joint Chiefs," completed Bourne. "Admiral 'Joltin' Jack Burton, commander of the Sixth Fleet."

"One and the same. Formerly the scourge of the South China Sea, now the largest of the large brass."

"I repeat," said Jason. "Tell your boys to go to work. Peter Holland will get you all the help you need. Find me everything there is on each of them."

"I can't."

"What?"

"I can get us the books on our three Philadelphians because they're part of the immediate Mayflower project—that's the Jackal. I can't touch our five—so far, five—inheritors of Medusa."

"For Christ's sake, why *not*? You *have* to. We can't waste time!"

"Time wouldn't mean much if both of us were dead. It wouldn't help Marie or the children either."

"What the hell are you talking about?"

"Why I'm late. Why I didn't want to call you from Virginia. Why I reached Charlie Casset to pick me up at that real estate proprietary in Vienna, and why, until he got there, I wasn't sure I'd ever get here alive."

"Spell it out, field man."

"All right, I will. . . . I've said nothing to anyone about going after former Medusa personnel—that was between you and me, nobody else."

"I wondered. When I spoke to you this afternoon you were playing it close. Too close, I thought, considering where you were and the equipment you were using."

"The rooms and the equipment proved secure. Casset told me later that the Agency doesn't want any traceable records of anything that takes place over there, and that's the best guarantee you can ask for. No bugs, no phone intercepts, nothing. Believe me, I breathed a lot easier when I heard that."

"Then what's the problem? Why are you *stopping*?"

"Because I have to figure out another admiral before I move any further into Medusa territory. . . . Atkinson, our impeccable WASP ambassador to the Court of St. James's in London, was very clear. In his panic, he pulled the masks off Burton and Teagarten in Brussels."

"So?"

"He said Teagarten could handle the Agency if anything about the old Saigon surfaced—because he was very tight with the top max at Langley."

"And?"

" 'Top max' is the Washington euphemism for maximum-classified security, and where Langley is concerned that's the director of Central Intelligence. . . . That's also Peter Holland."

"You told me this morning he'd have no problem wasting any *member* of Medusa."

"Anyone can say anything. But would he?"

Across the Atlantic, in the old Paris suburb of Neuilly-sur-Seine, an old man in a dark threadbare suit trudged up the concrete path toward the entrance of the sixteenth-century cathedral known as the Church of the Blessed Sacrament. The bells in the tower above tolled the first Angelus and the man stopped in the morning sunlight, blessing himself and whispering to the sky.

"Angelus domini nuntiavit Mariae." With his right hand he blew a kiss to the bas-relief crucifix atop the stone archway and proceeded up the steps and through the huge doors of the cathedral, aware that two robed priests eyed him with distaste. *I apologize for defiling your rich parish, you tight-assed snobs,* he thought as he lit a candle and placed it in the prayer rack, *but Christ made it clear that he preferred me to you. 'The meek shall inherit the earth'—what you haven't stolen of it.*

The old man moved cautiously down the center aisle, his right hand gripping the backs of successive pews for balance, his left fingering the rim of his outsized collar and slipping down to his tie so as to make sure the knot had not somehow come apart. His woman was so weak now that she could barely fold the damn thing together, but, as in the old days, she insisted on putting the finishing touches on his appearance before he went to work. She was still a good woman; they had both laughed, remembering the time she swore at his cuff links over forty years ago because she had put too much starch in his shirt. That night, so long ago, she had wanted him to look the proper bureaucrat when he went to the whore-mongering Oberführer's headquarters on the rue St. Lazare carrying a briefcase—a briefcase that, left behind, had blown up half the block. And twenty years later, one winter afternoon she'd had trouble making his stolen expensive overcoat hang properly on his shoulders before he set off to rob the Grande Banque Louis IX on the Madeleine, run by an educated but unappreciative former member of the Résistance who refused him a loan. Those were the good times, followed by bad times and bad health, which led to worse times—in truth, destitute times. Until a man came along, a strange man with an odd calling and an even odder unwritten contract. After that, respect returned in the form of sufficient money for decent food and acceptable wine, for clothes that fit, making his woman look pretty again, and, most important, for the doctors who made his woman feel better. The suit and shirt he wore today had been dug out of a closet. In many ways he and his woman were like the actors in a provincial touring company. They had costumes for their various roles. It was their business. . . . Today was business. This morning, with the bells of the Angelus, was business.

The old man awkwardly, only partially, genuflected in front of the holy cross and knelt down in the first seat of the sixth row from the altar, his eyes on his watch. Two and a half minutes later he raised his head and, as unobtrusively as possible, glanced around. His weakened sight had adjusted to the dim light of the cathedral; he could see, not well but clearly enough. There were no more than twenty worshipers scattered about, most in prayer, the others staring in meditation at the enormous gold crucifix on the altar. Yet these were not what he was looking for; and then he saw what he was seeking and knew that everything was on schedule. A priest in a priestly black suit walked down the far left aisle and disappeared beyond the dark red drapes of the apse.

The old man again looked at his watch, for everything now was timing; that was the way of the monseigneur—that was the way of the Jackal. Again two minutes passed and the aged courier got unsteadily up from his pew, sidestepped into the aisle, genuflected as best his body would permit, and made his way, step by imperfect step, to the second confessional booth on the left. He pulled back the curtain and went inside.

"Angelus Domini," he whispered, kneeling and repeating the words he had spoken several hundred times over the past fifteen years.

"Angelus Domini, child of God," replied the unseen figure behind the black latticework. The blessing was accompanied by a low rattling cough. "Are your days comfortable?"

"Made more so by an unknown friend . . . my friend."

"What does the doctor say about your woman?"

"He says to me what he does not say to her, thanks be for the mercy of Christ. It appears that against the odds I will outlive her. The wasting sickness is spreading."

"My sympathies. How long does she have?"

"A month, no more than two. Soon she will be confined to her bed. . . . Soon the contract between us will be void."

"Why is that?"

"You will have no further obligations to me, and I accept that. You've been good to us and I've saved a little and my wants are few. Frankly, knowing what's facing me, I'm feeling terribly tired—"

"You insufferable *ingrate!*" whispered the voice behind the confessional screen. "After all I've done, all I've promised you!"

"I beg your pardon?"

"Would you *die* for me?"

"Of course, that's our contract."

"Then, conversely, you will *live* for me!"

"If that's what you want, naturally I will. I simply wanted you to know that soon I would no longer be a burden to you. I am easily replaced."

"Do not presume, *never* with me!" The anger erupted in a hollow cough, a cough that seemed to confirm the rumor that had spread through the dark streets of Paris. The Jackal himself was ill, perhaps deathly ill.

"You are our life, our respect. Why should I do that?"

"You just did. . . . Nevertheless, I have an assignment for you that will ease your woman's departure for both of you. You will have a holiday in a lovely part of the world, the two of you together. You will pick up the papers and the money at the usual place."

"Where are we going, if I may ask?"

"To the Caribbean island of Montserrat. Your

instructions will be delivered to you there at the Blackburne Airport. Follow them precisely."

"Of course. . . . Again, if I may ask, what is my objective?"

"To find and befriend a mother and two children."

"Then what?"

"Kill them."

Brendan Prefontaine, former federal judge of the first circuit court of Massachusetts, walked out of the Boston Five Bank on School Street with fifteen thousand dollars in his pocket. It was a heady experience for a man who had lived an impecunious existence for the past thirty years. Since his release from prison he rarely had more than fifty dollars on his person. This was a very special day.

Yet it was more than very special. It was also very disturbing because he had never thought for an instant that Randolph Gates would pay him a sum anywhere near the amount he had demanded. Gates had made an enormous error because by acceding to the demand he had revealed the gravity of his endeavors. He had crossed over from ruthless, albeit nonfatal, greed into something potentially quite lethal. Prefontaine had no idea who the woman and the children were or what their relationship was to Lord Randolph of Gates, but whoever they were and whatever it was, Dandy Randy meant them no good.

An irreproachable Zeus-like figure in the legal world did not pay a disbarred, discredited, deniable alcoholic "scum" like one Brendan Patrick Pierre Prefontaine an outrageous sum of money because his soul was with the archangels of heaven. Rather, that soul was with the disciples of Lucifer. And since this was obviously the case, it might be profitable for the scum to pursue a little knowledge, for as the bromide declared, a little knowledge is a dangerous thing—frequently more so in the eyes of the beholder than in the one possessing scant tidbits of information, so slanted as to appear many times more. Fifteen thousand today might well become fifty thousand tomorrow if—if a scum flew to the island of Montserrat and began asking questions.

Besides, thought the judge, the Irish in him chuckling, the French sector in minor rebellion, he had not had a vacation in years. Good *Christ*, it was enough keeping body and soul together;

who thought of an unenforced suspension of the hustle?

So Brendan Patrick Pierre Prefontaine hailed a taxi, which he had not done sober for at least ten years, and directed the skeptical driver to take him to Louis's men's store at Faneuil Hall.

"You got the scratch, old man?"

"More than enough to get you a haircut and cure the acne on your pubescent face, young fellow. Drive on, Ben Hur. I'm in a hurry."

The clothes were off the racks, but they were expensive racks, and after he had shown a roll of hundred-dollar bills, the purple-lipped clerk was extremely cooperative. A midsized suitcase of burnished leather soon held casual apparel, and Prefontaine discarded his worn-out suit, shirt and shoes for a new outfit. Within the hour he looked not unlike a man he had known years ago: the Honorable Brendan P. Prefontaine. (He had always dropped the second *P.,* for Pierre, for obvious reasons.)

Another taxi took him to his rooming house in Jamaica Plains, where he picked up a few essentials, including his passport, which he always kept active for rapid exits—preferable to prison walls—and then delivered him to Logan Airport, this driver having no concern regarding his ability to pay the fare. Clothes, of course, never made the man, thought Brendan, but they certainly helped to convince dubious underlings. At Logan's information desk he was told that three airlines out of Boston serviced the island of Montserrat. He asked which counter was the nearest and then bought a ticket for the next available flight. Brendan Patrick Pierre Prefontaine naturally flew first class.

The Air France steward rolled the wheelchair slowly, gently through the ramp and onto the 747 jet in Paris's Orly Airport. The frail woman in the chair was elderly and overly made-up with an imbalance of rouge; she wore an outsized feather hat made of Australian cockatoo. She might have been a caricature except for the large eyes beneath the bangs of gray hair imperfectly dyed red—eyes alive and knowing and filled with humor. It was as if she were saying to all who observed her, Forget it, *mes amis,* he likes me this way and that's all I care about. I don't give a pile of *merde* about you or your opinions. The *he* referred to the old man walking cautiously beside her, every now and then touching her shoulder, lovingly as well as perhaps for balance, but in the touch there was a volume of poetry that was theirs alone. Closer inspection revealed a sporadic welling of tears in his eyes that he promptly wiped away so she could not see them.

"Il est ici, mon capitaine," announced the steward to the senior pilot, who greeted his two preboarding passengers at the aircraft's entrance. The captain reached for the woman's left hand and touched his lips to it, then stood erect and solemnly saluted the balding gray-haired old man with the small Légion d'honneur medal in his lapel.

"It is an honor, monsieur," said the captain. "This aircraft is my command, but you are my commander." They shook hands and the pilot continued. "If there's anything the crew and I can do to make the flight most comfortable for you, don't hesitate to ask, monsieur."

"You're very kind."

"We are all beholden—all of us, all of France."

"It was nothing, really—"

"To be singled out by Le Grand Charles himself as a true hero of the Résistance is hardly nothing. Age cannot dull such glory." The captain snapped his fingers, addressing three stewardesses in the still-empty first-class cabin. "Quickly, mesdemoiselles! Make everything perfect for a brave warrior of France and his lady."

So the killer with many aliases was escorted to the wide bulkhead on the left, where his woman was gently transferred from the wheelchair to the seat on the aisle; his was next to the window. Their trays were set up and a chilled bottle of Cristal was brought in their honor and for their enjoyment. The captain raised the first glass and toasted the couple; he returned to the flight deck as the old woman winked at her man, the wink wicked and filled with laughter. In moments, the passengers began boarding the plane, a number of whom glancing appreciatively at the elderly "man and wife" in the front row. For the rumors had spread in the Air France lounge. *A great hero . . . Le Grand Charles himself . . . In the Alps he held off six hundred Boche—or was it a thousand?*

As the enormous jet raced down the runway and with a thump lumbered off the ground into the air, the old "hero of France"—whose only heroics he could recall from the Résistance were based on theft, survival, insults to his woman, and staying out of whatever army or labor force that might draft him—reached into his pocket for his papers. The passport had his picture duly inserted, but that was the only item he recognized. The rest—name, date and place of birth, occupation—all were unfamiliar, and the attached list of honors, well, they were *formidable.* Totally out of character, but in case anyone should ever refer to them, he had better restudy the "facts" so he could at least nod in self-effacing modesty. He had been assured that the individual originally possessing the name and the achievements had no living relatives and few friends, and had disappeared from his apartment in Marseilles supposedly on a world trip from which he presumably would not return.

The Jackal's courier looked at the name—he *must* remember it and respond whenever it was spoken. It should not be difficult, for it was such a common name. And so he repeated it silently to himself over and over again.

Jean Pierre Fontaine, Jean Pierre Fontaine, Jean Pierre . . .

A sound! Sharp, abrasive. It was wrong, not *normal*, not part of a hotel's routine noise of hollow drumming at night. Bourne grabbed the weapon by his pillow and rolled out of bed in his shorts, steadying himself by the wall. It came again! A single, loud knock on the bedroom door of the suite. He shook his head trying to remember. . . . Alex? *I'll knock once.* Jason lurched half in sleep to the door, his ear against the wood.

"*Yes?*"

"Open this damn thing before somebody sees me!" came Conklin's muffled voice from the corridor. Bourne did so and the retired field officer limped quickly into the room, treating his cane as if he loathed it. "Boy, are *you* out of training!" he exclaimed as he sat on the foot of the bed. "I've been standing there tapping for at least a couple of minutes."

"I didn't hear you."

"Delta would have; Jason Bourne would have. David Webb didn't."

"Give me another day and you won't find David Webb."

"*Talk.* I want you better than talk!"

"Then stop talking and tell me why you're here—at whatever time it is."

"When last I looked I met Casset on the road at three-twenty. I had to gimp through a bunch of woods and climb over a goddamned fence—"

"*What?*"

"You heard me. A fence. Try it with your foot in cement. . . . You know, I once won the fifty-yard dash when I was in high school."

"Cut the digression. What happened?"

"Oh, I hear Webb again."

"What *happened*? And while you're at it, who the hell is this Casset you keep talking about?"

"The only man I trust in Virginia. He and Valentino."

"Who?"

"They're analysts, but they're straight."

"What?"

"Never mind. *Jesus,* there are times when I wish I could get pissed—"

"Alex, why are you *here*?"

Conklin looked up from the bed as he angrily gripped his cane. "I've got the books on our Philadelphians."

"That's why? Who are they?"

"No, that's not why. I mean it's interesting, but it's not why I'm here."

"Then why?" asked Jason, crossing to a chair next to a window and sitting down, frowning, perplexed. "My erudite friend from Cambodia and beyond doesn't climb over fences with his foot in cement at three o'clock in the morning unless he thinks he has to."

"I had to."

"Which tells me nothing. Please tell."

"It's DeSole."

"What's the soul?"

"Not 'the,' *De*Sole."

"You've lost me."

"He's the keeper of the keys at Langley. Nothing happens that he doesn't know about and nothing gets done in the area of research that he doesn't pass on."

"I'm still lost."

"We're in deep shit."

"That doesn't help me at all."

"Webb again."

"Would you rather I took a nerve out of your neck?"

"All right, all right. Let me get my breath." Conklin dropped his cane on the rug. "I didn't even trust the freight elevator. I stopped two floors below and walked up."

"Because we're in deep shit?"

"Yes."

"Why? Because of this *De*Sole?"

"Correct, Mr. Bourne. Steven DeSole. The man who has his finger on every computer at Langley. The one person who can spin the disks and put your old virginal Aunt Grace in jail as a hooker if he wants her there."

"What's your point?"

"He's the connection to Brussels, to Tea-garten at NATO. Casset learned down in the cellars that he's the *only* connection—they even have an access code bypassing everyone else."

"What does it mean?"

"Casset doesn't know, but he's goddamned angry."

"How much did you tell him?"

"The minimum. That I was working on some possibles and Teagarten's name came up in an odd way—most likely a diversion or used by someone trying to impress someone else—but I wanted to know who he talked to at the Agency, frankly figuring it was Peter Holland. I asked Charlie to play it out in the dark."

"Which I assume means confidentially."

"Ten times that. Casset is the sharpest knife in Langley. I didn't have to say any more than I did; he got the message. Now he's also got a problem he didn't have yesterday."

"What's he going to do?"

"I asked him not to do anything for a couple of days and that's what he gave me. Forty-eight hours, to be precise, and then he's going to confront DeSole."

"He can't do that," said Bourne firmly. "Whatever these people are hiding we can use it to pull out the Jackal. Use *them* to pull him out as others like them used me thirteen years ago."

Conklin stared first down at the floor, then up at Jason Bourne. "It comes down to the almighty ego, doesn't it?" he said. "The bigger the ego the bigger the fear—"

"The bigger the bait, the bigger the fish," completed Jason, interrupting. "A long time back you told me that Carlos's 'spine' was as big as his head, which had to be swollen all out of proportion for him to be in the business he's in. That was true then and it's true now. If we can get any one of these high government profiles to send a message to him—namely, to come after me, kill *me*—he'll jump at it. Do you know why?"

"I just told you. Ego."

"Sure, that's part of it, but there's something else. It's the respect that's eluded Carlos for more than twenty years, starting with Moscow cutting him loose and telling him to get lost. He's made millions, but his clients have mainly been the crud of the earth. For all the fear he's engendered he still remains a punk psychopath. No legends have been built around him, only contempt, and at this stage it's got to be driving him close to the edge. The fact that he's coming after me to settle a thirteen-year-old score supports what I'm saying. . . . I'm vital to him—his killing me is vital—because I was the product of our covert operations. That's who he wants to show up, show that he's better than all of us put together."

"It could also be because he still thinks you can identify him."

"I thought that at first, too, but after thirteen years and nothing from me—well, I had to think again."

"So you moved into Mo Panov's territory and came up with a psychiatric profile."

"It's a free country."

"Compared with most, yes, but where's all this leading us?"

"Because I know I'm right."

"That's hardly an answer."

"*Nothing* can be false or faked," insisted Bourne, leaning forward in the armchair, his elbows on his bare knees, his hands clasped. "Carlos would find the contrivance; it's the first thing he'll look for. Our Medusans have to be genuine and genuinely panicked."

"They're both, I told you that."

"To the point where they'd actually *consider*

making contact with someone like the Jackal."

"That I don't know—"

"That we'll never know," broke in Jason, "until we learn what they're hiding."

"But if we start the disks spinning at Langley, DeSole will find out. *And,* if he's part of whatever the hell it is, he'll alert the others."

"Then there'll be no research at Langley. I've got enough to go on anyway, just get me addresses and private telephone numbers. You can do that, can't you?"

"Certainly, that's low-level. What are you going to do?"

Bourne smiled and spoke quietly, even gently. "How about storming their houses or sticking needles in their asses between the appetizers and the entrées?"

"Now I hear Jason Bourne."

"So be it."

7

Marie St. Jacques Webb greeted the Caribbean morning by stretching in bed and looking over at the crib several feet away. Alison was deep in sleep, which she had not been four or five hours ago. The little dear had been a basket case then, so much so that Marie's brother Johnny had knocked on the door, walked cowardly inside, and asked if he could do anything, which he profoundly trusted he could not.

"How are you at changing a nasty diaper?"

"I don't even want to think about it," said St. Jacques, fleeing.

Now, however, she heard his voice through the shutters outside. She also knew that she was meant to hear it; he was enticing her son,

Jamie, into a race in the pool and speaking so loudly he could be heard on the big island of Montserrat. Marie literally crawled out of bed, headed for the bathroom, and four minutes later, ablutions completed, her auburn hair brushed and, wearing a bathrobe, walked out through the shuttered door to the patio over-looking the pool.

"Well, hi there, Mare!" shouted her tanned, dark-haired, handsome younger brother beside her son in the water. "I hope we didn't wake you up. We just wanted to take a swim."

"So you decided to let the British coastal pa-trols in Plymouth know about it."

"Hey, come on, it's almost nine o'clock. That's late in the islands."

"Hello, Mommy. Uncle John's been showing me how to scare off sharks with a stick!"

"Your uncle is full of terribly important infor-mation that I hope to God you'll never use."

"There's a pot of coffee on the table, Mare. And Mrs. Cooper will make you whatever you like for breakfast."

"Coffee's fine, Johnny. The telephone rang last night—was it David?"

"Himself," replied the brother. "And you and I are going to talk. . . . Come on, Jamie, up we go. Grip the ladder."

"What about the sharks?"

"You got 'em all, buddy. Go get yourself a drink."

"Johnny!"

"Orange juice, there's a pitcher in the kitchen." John St. Jacques walked around the rim of the pool and up the steps to the bedroom patio as his nephew raced into the house.

Marie watched her brother approach, noting the similarities between him and her husband. Both were tall and muscular; both had in their strides an absence of compromise, but where David usually won, Johnny more often than not lost, and she did not know why. Or why David had such trust in his younger brother-in-law when the two older St. Jacques sons would appear to be more responsible. David—or was it Jason Bourne?—never discussed the question in depth; he simply laughed it off and said Johnny had a streak in him that appealed to David—or was it Bourne?

"Let's level," said the youngest St. Jacques sitting down, the water dripping off his body onto the patio. "What kind of trouble is David in? He couldn't talk on the phone and you were in no shape last night for an extended chat. What's happened?"

"The Jackal. . . . The Jackal's what's happened."

"Christ!" exploded the brother. "After all these *years*?"

"After all these years," repeated Marie, her voice drifting off.

"How far has that bastard gotten?"

"David's in Washington trying to find out. All we know for certain is that he dug up Alex Conklin and Mo Panov from the horrors of Hong Kong and Kowloon." She told him about the false telegrams and the trap at the amusement park in Baltimore.

"I presume Alex has them all under protection or whatever they call it."

"Around the clock, I'm sure. Outside of ourselves and McAllister, Alex and Mo are the only two people still alive who know that David was— oh, *Jesus,* I can't even say the *name*!" Marie slammed the coffee mug down on the patio table.

"Easy, Sis." St. Jacques reached for her hand, placing his on top of hers. "Conklin knows what he's doing. David told me that Alex was the best—'field man,' he called him—that ever worked for the Americans."

"You don't *understand*, Johnny!" cried Marie,

trying to control her voice and emotions, her wide eyes denying the attempt. "David never said that, David Webb never *knew* that! Jason Bourne said it, and he's back! . . . That ice-cold calculating monster they created is back in David's head. You don't know what it's like. With a look in those unfocused eyes that see things I can't see—or with a tone of voice, a quiet freezing voice I don't *know*—and I'm suddenly with a stranger."

St. Jacques held up his free hand telling her to stop. "Come on," he said softly.

"The children? Jamie . . . ?" She looked frantically around.

"No, you. What do you expect David to do? Crawl inside a Wing or Ming dynasty vase and pretend his wife and children aren't in danger— that only he is? Whether you ladies like it or not, we boys still think it's up to us to keep the big cats from the cave. We honestly believe we're more equipped. We revert to those strengths, the ugliest of them, of course, because we have to. That's what David's doing."

"When did little brother get so philosophical?" asked Marie, studying John St. Jacques's face.

"That ain't philosophy, girl, I just know it. Most men do—apologies to the feminist crowd."

"Don't apologize; most of us wouldn't have it any other way. Would you believe that your big scholarly sister who called a lot of economic shots in Ottawa still yells like hell when she sees a mouse in our country kitchen, and goes into panic if it's a rat?"

"Certain bright women are more honest than others."

"I'll accept what you say, Johnny, but you're missing my point. David's been doing so well these last five years, every month just a little bit better than the last. He'll never be totally cured, we all know that—he was damaged too severely—but the furies, his own personal furies, have almost disappeared. The solitary walks in the woods when he'd come back with hands bruised from attacking *tree* trunks; the quiet, stifled tears in his study late at night when he couldn't remember what he was or what he'd done, thinking the worst of himself—they were *gone*, Johnny! There was real sunlight, do you know what I mean?"

"Yes, I do," said the brother solemnly.

"What's happening now could bring them all back, that's what's frightening me so!"

"Then let's hope it's over quickly."

Marie stopped, once again studying her

brother. "Hold it, little bro, I know you too well. You're pulling back."

"Not a bit."

"Yes, you are. . . . You and David—I never understood. Our two older brothers, so solid, so on top of everything, perhaps not intellectually but certainly pragmatically. Yet he turned to you. Why, Johnny?"

"Let's not go into it," said St. Jacques curtly, removing his hand from his sister's.

"But I *have* to. This is my life, *he's* my life! There can't be any more secrets where he's concerned—I can't *stand* any more! . . . Why *you*?"

St. Jacques leaned back in the patio chair, his stretched fingers now covering his forehead. He raised his eyes, an unspoken plea in them. "All right, I know where you're coming from. Do you remember six or seven years ago I left our ranch saying I wanted to try things on my own?"

"Certainly. I think you broke both Mom's and Dad's hearts. Let's face it, you were always kind of the favorite—"

"I was always the *kid*!" interrupted the youngest St. Jacques. "Playing out some moronic *Bonanza* where my thirty-year-old brothers were

blindly taking orders from a pontificating, bigoted French Canadian father whose only smarts
came with his money and his land."

"There was more to him than that, but I won't
argue—from a 'kid's' viewpoint."

"You couldn't, Mare. You did the same thing,
and sometimes you didn't come home for over
a year."

"I was busy."

"So was I."

"What did you do?"

"I killed two men. Two animals who'd killed a
friend of mine—raped her and killed her."

"What?"

"Keep your voice down—"

"My God, what *happened*?"

"I didn't want to call home, so I reached your
husband . . . my friend, David, who didn't treat
me like a brain-damaged kid. At the time it
seemed like a logical thing to do and it was the
best decision I could have made. He was owed
favors by his government, and a quiet team of
bright people from Washington and Ottawa flew
up to James Bay and I was acquitted. Self-defense, and it *was* just that."

"He never said a *word* to me—"

"I begged him not to."

"So that's why. . . . But I still don't understand!"

"It's not difficult, Mare. A part of him knows I can kill, *will* kill, if I think it's necessary."

A telephone rang inside the house as Marie stared at her younger brother. Before she could get her voice back, an elderly black woman emerged from the door to the kitchen. "It's for you, Mr. John. It's that pilot over on the big island. He says it's real important, *mon*."

"Thanks, Mrs. Cooper," said St. Jacques, getting out of the chair and walking rapidly down to an extension phone by the pool. He spoke for several moments, looked up at Marie, slammed down the telephone and rushed back up to his sister. "Pack up. You're getting out of here!"

"*Why?* Was that the man who flew us—"

"He's back from Martinique and just learned that someone was asking questions at the airport last night. About a woman and two small children. None of the crews said anything, but that may not last. Quickly."

"My God, where will we go?"

"Over to the inn until we think of something else. There's only one road and my own Tonton Macoute patrols it. No one gets in or out. Mrs. Cooper will help you with Alison. *Hurry!*"

The telephone started ringing again as Marie dashed through the bedroom door. St. Jacques raced down the steps to the pool extension, reaching it as Mrs. Cooper once more stepped out of the kitchen. "It's Government House over in 'Serrat, Mr. John."

"What the hell do *they* want . . . ?"

"Shall I ask them?"

"Never mind, I'll get it. Help my sister with the kids and pack everything they brought with them into the Rover. They're leaving right away!"

"Oh, a bad time pity, *mon*. I was just getting to know the little babies."

" 'Bad time pity' is right," mumbled St. Jacques, picking up the telephone. "Yes?"

"Hello, John?" said the chief aide to the Crown governor, a man who had befriended the Canadian developer and helped him through the maze of the colony's Territorial Regulations.

"Can I call you back, Henry? I'm kind of harried at the moment."

"I'm afraid there's no time, chap. This is straight from the Foreign Office. They want our immediate cooperation, and it won't do you any harm, either."

"Oh?"

"It seems there's an old fellow and his wife

arriving on Air France's connecting flight from Antigua at ten-thirty and Whitehall wants the red-carpet treatment. Apparently the old boy had a splendid war, with a slew of decorations, and worked with a lot of our chaps across the Channel."

"Henry, I'm really in a hurry. What's any of this got to do with *me*?"

"Well, I rather assumed you might have more of an idea about that than we do. Probably one of your rich Canadian guests, perhaps a Frenchie from Montreal who came out of the Résistance and who thought of you—"

"Insults will only get you a bottle of superior French Canadian wine. What do you *want*?"

"Put up our hero and his lady in the finest accommodations you've got, with a room for the French-speaking nurse we've assigned to them."

"On an hour's *notice*?"

"Well, chap, our buns could be in a collective sling, if you know what I mean—and your so vital but erratic telephone service does depend on a degree of Crown intervention, if you also know what I mean."

"Henry, you're a terrific negotiator. You so politely kick a person so accurately where it hurts. What's our hero's name? *Quickly, please!*"

"Our names are Jean Pierre and Regine Fontaine, *Monsieur le Directeur,* and here are our passports," said the soft-spoken old man inside the immigration officer's glass-enclosed office, the chief aide of the Crown governor at his side. "My wife can be seen over there," he added, pointing through the window. "She is talking with the mademoiselle in the white uniform."

"Please, Monsieur Fontaine," protested the stocky black immigration official in a pronounced British accent. "This is merely an informal formality, a stamping procedure, if you like. Also to remove you from the inconvenience of so many admirers. Rumors have gone throughout the airport that a great man has arrived."

"Really?" Fontaine smiled; it was a pleasant smile.

"Oh, but not to be concerned, sir. The press has been barred. We know you want complete privacy, and you shall have it."

"Really?" The old man's smile faded. "I was to meet someone here, an associate, you might say, I must consult with confidentially. I hope your most considerate arrangements do not prevent him from reaching me."

"A small, select group with proper standing and credentials will greet you in Blackburne's honored-guest corridor, Monsieur Fontaine," said the Crown governor's chief aide. "May we proceed? The reception line will be swift, I assure you."

"Really? That swift?"

It was, less than five minutes actually, but five seconds would have been enough. The first person the Jackal's courier-killer met was the beribboned Crown governor himself. As the Queen's royal representative embraced the hero in Gallic style, he whispered into Jean Pierre Fontaine's ear. "We've learned where the woman and her children were taken. We are sending you there. The nurse has your instructions."

The rest was somewhat anticlimactic for the old man, especially the absence of the press. He had never had his picture in the newspapers except as a felon.

Morris Panov, M.D., was a very angry man, and he always tried to control his very angry moments because they never helped him or his patients. At the moment, however, sitting at his office desk, he was having difficulty curbing his emotions. He had not heard from David Webb. He *had* to hear from him, he had to *talk* to him. What was happening could negate thirteen years of therapy, couldn't they *understand* that? . . . No, of course they couldn't; it was not what interested them; they had other priorities and did not care to be burdened by problems beyond their purview. But *he* had to care. The damaged mind was so fragile, so given to setbacks, the horrors of the past were so capable of taking over the present. It could not happen with David! He was so close to being as normal as he would ever be (and who the hell was "normal" in this fucked-up world). He could function wonderfully as a teacher; he had near-total recall where his scholarly expertise was called upon, and he was remembering more and more as each year progressed. But it could all blow apart with a single act of violence, for violence was the way of life for Jason Bourne. *Damn!*

It was crippling enough that they even permitted David to stay around; he had tried to explain the potential damage to Alex, but Conklin had an irrefutable reply: *We can't stop him. At least this way we can watch him, protect him.* Perhaps so. "They" did not stint where protection was involved—the guards down the hall from his office and on the roof of the building, to say nothing of a temporary receptionist bearing arms as well as a strange computer, attested to their concern. Still it would be so much better for David if he was simply sedated and flown down to his island retreat, leaving the hunt for the Jackal to the professionals. . . . Panov suddenly caught himself as the realization swept over him: there was no one more professional than Jason Bourne.

The doctor's thoughts were interrupted by the telephone, the telephone he could not pick up until all the security procedures were activated. A trace was placed on the incoming call; a scanner determined whether there were intercepts on the line, and finally the identity of the caller was approved by Panov himself. His intercom buzzed; he flipped the switch on his console. "Yes?"

"All systems are cleared, sir," announced the temporary receptionist, who was the only one in the office who would know. "The man on the line said his name was Treadstone, Mr. D. Treadstone."

"I'll take it," said Mo Panov firmly. "And you

can remove whatever other 'systems' you've got on that machine out there. This is doctor-patient confidentiality."

"Yes, sir. Monitor is terminated."

"It's what? . . . Never mind." The psychiatrist picked up the phone and was barely able to keep from shouting. "Why didn't you call me *before* this, you son of a bitch!"

"I didn't want to give you cardiac arrest, is that sufficient?"

"Where are you and what are you doing?"

"At the moment?"

"That'll suffice."

"Let's see, I rented a car and right now I'm a half a block from a town house in Georgetown owned by the chairman of the Federal Trade Commission, talking to you on a pay phone."

"For Christ's sake, *why*?"

"Alex will fill you in, but what I want you to do is call Marie on the island. I've tried a couple of times since leaving the hotel but I can't get through. Tell her I'm fine, that I'm perfectly *fine*, and not to worry. Have you got that?"

"I've got it, but I don't buy it. You don't even sound like yourself."

"You can't tell her that, Doctor. If you're my friend, you can't tell her anything like that."

"*Stop* it, David. This Jekyll-and-Hyde crap doesn't *wash* anymore."

"Don't tell her that, not if you're my friend."

"You're *spiraling*, David. Don't let it happen. Come to me, *talk* to me."

"No time, Mo. The fat cat's limousine is parking in front of his house. I've got to go to work."

"*Jason!*"

The line went dead.

Brendan Patrick Pierre Prefontaine walked down the jet's metal steps into the hot Caribbean sun of Montserrat's Blackburne Airport. It was shortly past three o'clock in the afternoon, and were it not for the many thousands of dollars on his person he might have felt lost. It was remarkable how a supply of hundred-dollar bills in various pockets made one feel so secure. In truth, he had to keep reminding himself that his loose change—fifties, twenties and tens—were in his right front trousers pocket so as not to make a mistake and either appear ostentatious or be a mark for some unprincipled hustler. Above all, it was vital for him to keep a low profile to the point of insignificance. He had to insignificantly ask significant questions around the airport regarding a woman and two small children who had arrived on a private aircraft the previous afternoon.

Which was why to his astonishment and alarm he heard the absolutely adorable black female immigration clerk say to him after hanging up a telephone, "Would you be so kind, sir, as to come with me, please?"

Her lovely face, lilting voice and perfect smile did nothing to allay the former judge's fears. Far too many extremely guilty criminals had such assets. "Is there something wrong with my passport, young lady?"

"Not that I can see, sir."

"Then why the delay? Why not simply stamp it and allow me to proceed?"

"Oh, it is stamped and entry is permitted, sir. There is no problem."

"Then *why* . . . ?"

"Please come with me, sir."

They approached a large glass-enclosed cubicle with a sign on the left window, the gold letters announcing the occupant: DEPUTY DIRECTOR OF IMMIGRATION SERVICES. The attractive clerk opened the door and, again smiling, gestured for the elderly visitor to go inside. Prefontaine did so, suddenly terrified that he would be searched, the money found, and all manner of charges leveled against him. He did not know which islands were involved in narcotics, but if this was one of them the thousands of dollars in his pockets would be instantly suspect. Explanations raced through his mind as the clerk crossed to the desk handing his passport to the short, heavyset deputy of immigration. The woman gave Brendan a last bright smile and went out the door, closing it behind her.

"Mr. Brendan Patrick Pierre Prefontaine," intoned the immigration official reading the passport.

"Not that it matters," said Brendan kindly but with summoned authority. "However, the 'Mister' is usually replaced with 'Judge'—as I say, I don't believe it's relevant under the circumstances, or perhaps it is, I really don't know. Did one of my law clerks make an error? If so, I'll fly the whole group down to apologize."

"Oh, not at all, sir—*Judge*," replied the uniformed wide-girthed black man with a distinct British accent as he rose from the chair and extended his hand over the desk. "Actually, it is I who may have made the error."

"Come now, Colonel, we all do occasionally." Brendan gripped the official's hand. "Then perhaps I may be on my way? There's someone here I must meet."

"That's what *he* said!"

Brendan released the hand. "I beg your pardon?"

"I may have to beg yours. . . . The confidentiality, of course."

"The what? Could we get to the point, please?"

"I realize that privacy," continued the official, pronouncing the word as *privvissy*, "is of utmost importance—that's been explained to us—but whenever we can be of assistance, we try to oblige the Crown."

"Extremely commendable, Brigadier, but I'm afraid I don't understand."

The official needlessly lowered his voice. "A great man arrived here this morning, are you aware of that?"

"I'm sure many men of stature come to your beautiful island. It was highly recommended to me, in fact."

"Ah, yes, the privvissy!"

"Yes, of course, the privvissy," agreed the ex-convict judge, wondering if the official had both his oars in the water. "Could you be clearer?"

"Well, *he* said he was to meet someone, an

associate he had to consult with, but after the very private reception line—no press, of course—he was taken directly to the charter that flew him to the out island, and obviously never met the person he was to confidentially meet. *Now,* am I clearer?"

"Like Boston harbor in a squall, General."

"Very good. I understand. *Privvissy.* . . . So all our personnel are alerted to the fact that the great man's friend might be seeking him here at the airport—confidentially, of course."

"Of course." *Not even a paddle,* thought Brendan.

"Then I considered another possibility," said the official in minor triumph. "Suppose the great man's friend was also flying to our island for a *rendezvous* with the great man?"

"Brilliant."

"Not without logic. *Then* it struck me to obtain the passenger manifests of all the incoming flights, concentrating, of course, on those in first class, which would be proper for the great man's associate."

"Clairvoyance," mumbled the once and former judge. "And you selected me?"

"The *name*, my good man! Pierre Prefontaine!"

"My pious, departed mother would no doubt take offense at your omitting the 'Brendan Patrick.' Like the French, the Irish are quite sensitive in such matters."

"But it was the *family*. I understood that immediately!"

"You did?"

"Pierre *Prefontaine*! . . . Jean *Pierre Fontaine*. I am an expert on immigration procedures, having studied the methods in many countries. Your own name is a fascinating example, most honored Judge. Wave after wave of immigrants flocked to the United States, the melting pot of nations, races and languages. In the process names were altered, combined or simply misunderstood by armies of confused, overworked clerks. But roots frequently survived and thus it was for you. The family Fontaine became *Prefontaine* in America and the great man's associate was in reality an esteemed member of the American branch!"

"Positively awesome," muttered Brendan, eyeing the official as if he expected several male nurses to barge into the room with restraining equipment. "But isn't it possible that this is merely coincidence? Fontaine is a common name throughout France, but, as I understand it, the Prefontaines were distinctly centered around Alsace-Lorraine.''

"Yes, of course," said the deputy, again lowering his voice rather than conceivably winking. "Yet without any prior word whatsoever, the Quai d'Orsay in Paris calls, then the UK's Foreign Office follows with instructions—a great man is soon to drop out of the sky. Acknowledge him, honor him, spirit him off to a remote resort known for its confidentiality—for that, too, is paramount. The great one is to have total *privvissy*. ... Yet that same great warrior is anxious; he is to confidentially meet with an associate he does not find. Perhaps the great man has secrets—all great men *do*, you know.''

Suddenly, the thousands of dollars in Prefontaine's pockets felt very heavy. Washington's Four Zero clearance in Boston, the Quai d'Orsay in Paris, the Foreign Office in London—Randolph Gates needlessly parting with an extraordinary amount of money out of sheer panic. There was a pattern of strange convergence, the strangest being the inclusion of a frightened, unscrupulous attorney named Gates. Was he an inclusion or an aberration? What did it all mean? "You are an extraordinary man," said Brendan quickly, covering his thoughts with rapid words. "Your perceptions are nothing short of brilliant, but you do understand that confidentiality *is* paramount."

"I will hear no more, honored Judge!" exclaimed the deputy. "Except to add that your appraisal of my abilities might not be lost on my superiors."

"They will be made clear, I assure you. . . . Precisely where did my not too distant and distinguished cousin go?"

"A small out island where the seaplanes must land on the water. Its name is Tranquility Isle and the resort is called Tranquility Inn."

"You will be personally thanked by those above you, be assured of that."

"And I shall personally clear you through customs."

Brendan Patrick Pierre Prefontaine, carrying his suitcase of burnished leather, walked out into the terminal of Blackburne Airport a bewildered man. Bewildered, *hell,* he was stunned! He could not decide whether to take the next flight back to Boston or to . . . his feet were apparently deciding for him. He found himself walking toward a counter beneath a large sea-blue sign with white lettering: INTER-ISLAND AIRWAYS. It couldn't do any harm to inquire, he mused, *then* he would buy a ticket on the next plane to Boston.

On the wall beyond the counter a list of nearby "Out Isles" was next to a larger column of the well-known Leeward and Windward Islands from St. Kitts and Nevis south to the Grenadines. Tranquility was sandwiched between Canada Cay and Turtle Rock. Two clerks, both young, one black and one white, the former a young woman, the latter a blond-haired man in his early twenties, were talking quietly. The girl approached. "May I help you, sir?"

"I'm not really sure," replied Brendan hesitantly. "My schedule's so unsettled, but it seems I have a friend on Tranquility Isle."

"At the inn, sir?"

"Yes, apparently so. Does it take long to fly over there?"

"If the weather's clear, no more than fifteen minutes, but that would be an amphibious charter. I'm not sure one's available until tomorrow morning."

"Sure, there is, babe," interrupted the young man with small gold wings pinned crookedly on his white shirt. "I'm running over some supplies to Johnny St. Jay pretty soon," he added, stepping forward.

"*He's* not scheduled for today."

"As of an hour ago he is. Pronto."

At that instant and with those words, Prefontaine's eyes fell in astonishment on two stacks of cartons moving slowly down Inter-Island's luggage carousel toward the exterior loading area. Even if he had the time to debate with himself, he knew his decision was made.

"I'd like to purchase a ticket on that flight, if I may," he said, watching the boxes of Gerber's Assorted Baby Foods and Pampers Medium Diapers disappear into the hold.

He had found the unknown woman with the small male child and the infant.

8

Routine secondhand inquiries at the Federal Trade Commission confirmed the fact that its chairman, Albert Armbruster, did, indeed, have ulcers as well as high blood pressure and under doctor's orders left the office and returned home whenever discomfort struck him. Which was why Alex Conklin telephoned him after a generally overindulgent lunch—also established—with an "update" of the Snake Lady crisis. As with Alex's initial call, catching Armbruster in the shower, he anonymously told the shaken chairman that someone would be in touch with him later in the day—either at the office or at home. The contact would identify himself simply as Cobra. ("Use all the banal trigger words you can come up with" was the gospel according to St. Conklin.) In the meantime, Armbruster was instructed to talk to no one. *"Those are orders from the Sixth Fleet."*

"Oh, Christ!"

Thus Albert Armbruster called for his chariot and was driven home in discomfort. Further nausea was in store for the chairman, however, as Jason Bourne was waiting for him.

"Good afternoon, Mr. Armbruster," said the stranger pleasantly as the chairman struggled out of the limousine, the door held open by the chauffeur.

"Yes, *what*?" Armbruster's response was immediate, unsure.

"I merely said 'Good afternoon.' My name's Simon. We met at the White House reception for the Joint Chiefs several years ago—"

"I wasn't *there*," broke in the chairman emphatically.

"Oh?" The stranger arched his brows, his voice still pleasant but obviously questioning.

"Mr. Armbruster?" The chauffeur had closed the door and now turned courteously to the chairman. "Will you be needing—"

"No, *no*," said Armbruster, again interrupting.

"You're relieved—I won't need you anymore today . . . tonight."

"Same time tomorrow morning, sir?"

"Yes, tomorrow—unless you're told otherwise. I'm not a well man; check with the office."

"Yes, sir." The chauffeur tipped his visored cap and climbed back into the front seat.

"I'm sorry to hear that," said the stranger, holding his place as the limousine's engine was started and the automobile rolled away.

"*What?* . . . Oh, you. I was never at the White House for that damned reception!"

"Perhaps I was mistaken—"

"Yes, well, nice to see you again," said Armbruster anxiously, impatiently, hurrying to the steps that led up to his Georgetown house.

"Then again, I'm quite sure Admiral Burton introduced us—"

"*What?*" The chairman spun around. "What did you just say?"

"This is a waste of time," continued Jason Bourne, the pleasantness gone from his voice and his face. "I'm Cobra."

"Oh, *Jesus*! . . . I'm not a well man." Armbruster repeated the statement in a hoarse whisper, snapping his head up to look at the front of his house, to the windows and the door.

"You'll be far worse unless we talk," added Jason, following the chairman's eyes. "Shall it be up there? In your house?"

"*No!*" cried Armbruster. "She yaps all the time and wants to know everything about everybody, then blabs all over town exaggerating everything."

"I assume you're talking about your wife."

"All of 'em! They don't know when to keep their traps shut."

"It sounds like they're starved for conversation."

"What . . . ?"

"Never mind. I've got a car down the block. Are you up to a drive?"

"I damn well better be. We'll stop at the drugstore down the street. They've got my prescription on file. . . . Who the hell *are* you?"

"I told you," answered Bourne. "Cobra. It's a snake."

"Oh, *Jesus!*" whispered Albert Armbruster.

The pharmacist complied rapidly, and Jason quickly drove to a neighborhood bar he had chosen an hour before should one be necessary. It was dark and full of shadows, the booths deep, the banquettes high, isolating those meeting one another from curious glances. The ambience was important, for it was vital that he stare into the eyes of the chairman when he asked questions, his own eyes ice-cold, demanding . . . threatening. Delta was back, Cain had returned; Jason Bourne was in full command, David Webb forgotten.

"We have to cover ourselves," said the Cobra quietly after their drinks arrived. "In terms of damage control that means we have to know how much harm each of us could do under the Amytals."

"What the hell does *that* mean?" asked Armbruster, swallowing most of his gin and tonic while wincing and holding his stomach.

"Drugs, chemicals, truth serums."

"What?"

"This isn't your normal ball game," said Bourne, remembering Conklin's words. "We've got to cover all of the bases because there aren't any constitutional rights in this series."

"So who are *you*?" The chairman of the Federal Trade Commission belched and brought his glass briefly to his lips, his hand trembling. "Some kind of one-man *hit* team? John Doe knows something, so he's shot in an alley?"

"Don't be ridiculous. Anything like that would be totally counterproductive. It would only fuel those trying to find us, leave a trail—"

"Then what are you *talking* about?"

"Saving our lives, which includes our reputations and our life-styles."

"You're one cold prick. How do we do that?"

"Let's take your case, shall we? . . . You're not a well man by your own admission. You could resign under doctor's orders and we take care of you—*Medusa* takes care of you." Jason's imagination floated, making quick sharp forays into reality and fantasy, swiftly searching for the words that might be found in the gospel according to St. Alex. "You're known to be a wealthy man, so a villa might be purchased in your name, or perhaps a Caribbean island, where you'd be completely secure. No one can reach you; no one can talk to you unless you agree, which would mean predetermined interviews, harmless and even favorable results guaranteed. Such things are not impossible."

"Pretty sterile existence in my opinion," said Armbruster. "Me and the yapper all by ourselves? I'd kill her."

"Not at all," went on the Cobra. "There'd be constant distractions. Guests of your choosing could be flown to wherever you are. Other women also—either of your choice or selected by those who respect your tastes. Life goes on much as before, some inconveniences, some pleasant surprises. The point is that you'd be protected, inaccessible and therefore *we're* also protected, the rest of us. . . . But, as I say, that option is merely hypothetical at this juncture. In my case, frankly, it's a necessity because there's little I don't know. I leave in a matter of days. Until then I'm determining who goes and who stays. . . . How much *do* you know, Mr. Armbruster?"

"I'm not involved with the day-to-day operations, naturally. I deal with the big picture. Like the others, I get a monthly coded telex from the banks in Zurich listing the deposits and the companies we're gaining control of—that's about it."

"So far you don't get a villa."

"I'll be damned if I want one, and if I do I'll buy it myself. I've got close to a hundred million, American, in Zurich."

Bourne controlled his astonishment and simply stared at the chairman. "I wouldn't repeat that," he said.

"Who am I going to tell? The yapper?"

"How many of the others do you know personally?" asked the Cobra.

"Practically none of the staff, but then they don't know me, either. Hell, they don't know anybody. . . . And while we're on the subject, take you, for instance. I've never heard of you. I figure you work for the board and I was told to expect you, but I don't *know* you."

"I was hired on a very special basis. My background's deep-cover security."

"Like I said, I figured—"

"What about the Sixth Fleet?" interrupted Bourne, moving away from the subject of himself.

"I see him now and then but I don't think we've exchanged a dozen words. He's military; I'm civilian—very civilian."

"You weren't once. Where it all began."

"The hell I wasn't. No uniform ever made a soldier and it sure didn't with me."

"What about a couple of generals, one in Brussels, the other at the Pentagon?"

"They were career men; they stayed in. I wasn't and I didn't."

"We have to expect leaks, rumors," said Bourne almost aimlessly, his eyes now wandering. "But we can't permit the slightest hint of military orientation."

"You mean like in junta style?"

"Never," replied Bourne, once more staring at Armbruster. "That kind of thing creates whirlwinds—"

"*Forget* it!" whispered the chairman of the Federal Trade Commission, angrily interrupting. "The Sixth Fleet, as you call him, calls the shots only *here* and only because it's convenient. He's a blood-and-guts admiral with a whiz-bang record and a lot of clout where we want it, but that's in *Washington*, not anywhere else!"

"I know that and you know it," said Jason emphatically, the emphasis covering his bewilderment, "but someone who's been in a protection program for over fifteen years is putting together his own scenario and *that* comes out of Saigon—*Command* Saigon."

"It may have come out of Saigon but it sure as hell didn't stay there. The soldier boys couldn't run with it, we *all* know that. . . . But I see what you mean. You tie in Pentagon brass with anything like us, the freaks are in the streets and the bleeding-heart fairies in Congress have a field day. Suddenly a dozen subcommittees are in session."

"Which we can't tolerate," added Bourne.

"Agreed," said Armbruster. "Are we any closer to learning the name of the bastard who's putting this scenario together?"

"Closer, not close. He's been in contact with Langley but on what level we don't know."

"*Langley?* For Christ's sake, we've *got* someone over there. He can squelch it and find out who the son of a bitch is!''

"DeSole?" offered the Cobra simply.

"That's right." Armbruster leaned forward. "There *is* very little you don't know. That connection's very quiet. What does DeSole say?"

"Nothing, we can't touch him," replied Jason, suddenly, frantically reaching for a credible answer. He had been David Webb too long! Conklin was right; he wasn't thinking fast enough. Then the words came . . . part of the truth, a dangerous part, but credible, and he could *not* lose credibility. "He thinks he's being watched and we're to stay away from him, no contact whatsoever until he says otherwise."

"What *happened*?" The chairman gripped his glass, his eyes rigid, bulging.

"Someone in the cellars learned that Teagarten in Brussels has an access fax code directly to DeSole bypassing routine confidential traffic."

"Stupid goddamned *soldier boys*!" spat out Armbruster. "Give 'em gold braid and they prance around like debutantes and want every new toy in town! . . . *Faxes, access* codes! Jesus, he probably punched the wrong numbers and got the NAACP."

"DeSole says he's building a cover and can

handle it, but it's no time for him to go around asking questions, especially in this area. He'll check quietly on everything he can, and if he learns something he'll reach us, but we're not to reach him."

"Wouldn't you *know* it'd be a lousy soldier boy who puts us out on a limb? If it wasn't for that jackass with his *access* code, we wouldn't have a problem. Everything would be taken care of."

"But he does exist, and the problem—the crisis—won't go away," said Bourne flatly. "I repeat, we have to cover ourselves. Some of us will have to leave—disappear at least for a while. For the good of all of us."

The chairman of the Federal Trade Commission leaned back in the booth, his expression pensively disagreeable. "Yeah, well let me tell you something, Simon, or whatever your name is. You're checking out the wrong people. We're businessmen, some of us rich enough or egotistical enough or for other reasons willing to work for government pay, but first we're *businessmen* with investments all over the place. We're also appointed, not elected, and that means nobody expects full financial disclosures. Do you see what I'm driving at?"

"I'm not sure," said Jason, instantly concerned that he was losing control, losing the threat. *I've been away too long* . . . and Albert Armbruster was not a fool. He was given to first-level panic, but the second level was colder, far more analytical. "What are you driving at?"

"Get rid of our soldier boys. Buy *them* villas or a couple of Caribbean islands and put *them* out of reach. Give 'em their own little courts and let 'em play kings; that's what they're all about anyway."

"Operate without them?" asked Bourne, trying to conceal his astonishment.

"You said it and I agree. Any hint of big brass and we're in big trouble. It goes under the heading of 'military industrial complex,' which freely translated means military-industrial collusion." Again Armbruster leaned forward over the table. "We don't need them anymore! Get rid of them."

"There could be very loud objections—"

"No *way*. We've got 'em by their brass balls!"

"I'll have to think about it."

"There's nothing to think about. In six months we'll have the controls we need in Europe."

Jason Bourne stared at the chairman of the Federal Trade Commission. *What controls?* he thought to himself. *For what reason? Why?*

"I'll drive you home," he said.

"I talked to Marie," said Conklin from the Agency garden apartment in Virginia. "She's at the inn, not at your house."

"How *come*?" asked Jason at a gas-station pay phone on the outskirts of Manassas.

"She wasn't too clear. . . . I think it was lunchtime or nap time—one of those times when mothers are never clear. I could hear your kids in the background. They were loud, pal."

"What did she say, Alex?"

"It seems your brother-in-law wanted it that way. She didn't elaborate, and other than sounding like one harried mommy, she was the perfectly normal Marie I know and love— which means she only wanted to hear about you."

"Which means you told her I was perfectly fine, didn't you?"

"Hell, yes. I said you were holed up under guard going over a lot of computer printouts, sort of a variation on the truth."

"Johnny must have had his talk with her. She told him what's happened, so he moved them all to his exclusive bunker."

"His what?"

"You never saw Tranquility Inn, or did you?

Frankly, I can't remember whether you did or not."

"Panov and I saw only the plans and the site; that was four years ago. We haven't been back since, at least I haven't. Nobody's asked me."

"I'll let that pass because you've had a standing invitation since we got the place. . . . Anyway, you know it's on the beach and the only way to get there except by water is up a dirt road so filled with rocks no normal car could make it twice. Everything is flown in by plane or brought over by boat. Almost nothing from the town."

"And the beach is patrolled," interrupted Conklin. "Johnny isn't taking any chances."

"It's why I sent them down there. I'll call her later."

"What about now?" said Alex. "What about Armbruster?"

"Let's put it this way," replied Bourne, his eyes drifting up at the white plastic shell of the pay phone. "What does it mean when a man who has a hundred million dollars in Zurich tells me that Medusa—point of origin Command Saigon, emphasis on 'command,' which is hardly civilian—should get rid of the military because Snake Lady doesn't need them any longer?"

"I don't *believe* it," said the retired intelli-

gence officer in a quiet, doubting voice. "He
didn't."

"Oh, yes, he did. He even called them soldier
boys, and he wasn't memorializing them in
song. He verbally dismissed the admirals and
the generals as gold-braided debutantes who
wanted every new toy in town."

"Certain senators on the Armed Services
Committee would agree with that assessment,"
concurred Alex.

"There's more. When I reminded him that
Snake Lady came out of Saigon—*Command
Saigon*—he was very clear. He said it may have,
but it sure as hell didn't stay there because—
and this is a direct quote—'The soldier boys
couldn't run with it.' "

"That's a provocative statement. Did he tell
you why they couldn't run with it?"

"No, and I didn't ask. I was supposed to know
the answer."

"I wish you did. I like less and less the sound
of what I'm hearing; it's big and it's ugly. . . . How
did the hundred million come up?"

"I told him Medusa might get him a villa someplace out of the country where he couldn't be
reached if we thought it was necessary. He
wasn't too interested and said if he wanted one,

he'd buy it himself. He had a hundred million, American, in Zurich—a fact I think I was also expected to know."

"That was all? Just a simple little one hundred million?"

"Not entirely. He told me that like everybody else he gets a monthly telex—in code—from the banks in Zurich listing his deposits. Obviously, they've been growing."

"Big, ugly and growing," added Conklin. "Anything else? Not that I particularly want to hear it, I'm frightened enough."

"Two more items and you'd better have some fear in reserve. . . . Armbruster said that along with the deposit telexes he gets a listing of the companies they're gaining control of."

"*What* companies? What was he *talking* about? . . . Good *God*."

"If I had asked, my wife and children might have to attend a private memorial service, no casket in evidence because I wouldn't be there."

"You've got more to tell me. Tell me."

"Our illustrious chairman of the Federal Trade Commission said that the ubiquitous 'we' could get rid of the military because in six months 'we' would have all the controls we needed in

Europe. . . . Alex, what controls? What are we *dealing* with?"

There was silence on the unbroken line, and Jason Bourne did not interrupt. David Webb wanted to shout in defiance and confusion, but there was no point; he was a nonperson. Finally, Conklin spoke.

"I think we're dealing with something we can't handle," he said softly, his words barely audible over the phone. "This has to go upstairs, David. We can't keep it to ourselves."

"*Goddamn* you, you're not talking to David!" Bourne did not raise his voice in anger; he did not have to, its tone was enough. "This isn't going anywhere unless or until I say it does and I may not ever say it. Understand me, field man, I don't owe anyone anything, especially not the movers and the shakers in this city. They moved and shook my wife and me too much for any concessions where our lives or the lives of our children are concerned! I intend to use every-thing I can learn for one purpose and one pur-pose *only*. That's to draw out the Jackal and kill him so we can climb out of our personal hell and go on living. . . . I know now that this *is* the way to do it. Armbruster talked tough and he proba-bly is tough, but underneath he's frightened.

They're all frightened—panicked, as you put it—and you were right. Present them with the Jackal and he's a *solution* they can't refuse. Present Carlos with a client as rich and as powerful as our current Medusa and it's *irresistible* to him—he's got the respect of the international big boys, not just the crud of the world, the fanatics of the left and right. . . . Don't stand in my way, *don't,* for God's sake!"

"That's a threat, isn't it?"

"*Stop* it, Alex. I don't want to talk like that."

"But you just did. It's the reverse of Paris thirteen years ago, isn't it? Only now you'll kill *me* because I'm the one who hasn't a memory, the memory of what we did to you and Marie."

"That's my *family* out there!" cried David Webb, his voice tight, sweat forming on his hairline as his eyes filled with tears. "They're a thousand miles away from me and in *hiding*. It can't be any other way because I won't risk letting them be harmed! . . . *Killed*, Alex, because that's what the Jackal will do if he finds them. It's an island this week; where is it *next*? How many thousands of miles more? And after that, where will they go—where will *we* go? Knowing what we know now, we can't stop—he's after me; that goddamned filthy psychopath is *after* me, and everything we've learned about him tells us he wants a maximum kill. His ego demands it, and that kill includes my family! . . . No, field man, don't burden me with things I don't care about—not where they interfere with Marie and the kids—I'm owed that much.''

''I hear you,'' said Conklin. ''I don't know whether I'm hearing David or Jason Bourne, but I hear you. All right, no reverse Paris, but we have to move fast and I'm talking to Bourne now. What's next? Where are you?''

''I judge about six or seven miles from General Swayne's house,'' replied Jason, breathing deeply, the momentary anguish suppressed, the coldness returning. ''Did you make the call?''

''Two hours ago.''

''Am I still 'Cobra'?''

''Why not? It's a snake.''

''That's what I told Armbruster. He wasn't happy.''

''Swayne will be less so, but I sense something and I can't really explain it.''

''What do you mean?''

''I'm not sure, but I have an idea that he's answerable to someone.''

''In the Pentagon? Burton?''

''I suppose so, I just don't know. In his partial

paralysis he reacted almost as if he was an on-
looker, someone involved but not in the middle
of the game. He slipped a couple of times and
said things like 'We'll have to think about this,'
and 'We'll have to confer.' Confer with *whom*?
It was a one-on-one conversation with my usual
warning that he wasn't to talk to *anyone*. His
response was a lame editorial 'we,' meaning
that the illustrious general was conferring with
himself. I don't buy it."

"Neither do I," agreed Jason. "I'm going to
change clothes. They're in the car."

"What?"

Bourne turned partially in the plastic shell of
the pay phone and glanced around the gas station. He saw what he hoped for, a men's room
in the side of the building. "You said that
Swayne lives on a large farm west of Manassas—"

"Correction," interrupted Alex. "*He* calls it a
farm; his neighbors and the tax rolls call it a
twenty-eight-acre estate. Not bad for a career
soldier from a lower-middle-class family in Ne-
braska who married a hairdresser in Hawaii
thirty years ago, and supposedly bought his
manse ten years ago on the strength of a very
sizable inheritance from an untraceable bene-

factor, an obscure wealthy uncle I couldn't find. That's what made me curious. Swayne headed up the Quartermaster Corps in Saigon and supplied Medusa. . . . What's his place got to do with your changing clothes?''

''I want to look around. I'll get there while it's light to see what it's like from the road, then when it's dark I'll pay him a surprise visit.''

''That'll be effective, but why the looking around?''

''I like farms. They're so spread out and extended and I can't imagine why a professional soldier who knows that he can be transferred anywhere in the world at a moment's notice would saddle himself with such a large investment.''

''The same as my reasoning except I was concerned about the how, not the why. Your approach may be more interesting.''

''We'll see.''

''Be careful. He may have alarms and dogs, things like that.''

''I'm prepared,'' said Jason Bourne. ''I did some shopping after I left Georgetown.''

The summer sun was low in the western sky as he slowed down the rental car and lowered the visor to keep from being blinded by the yellow globe of fire. Soon it would drop behind the Shenandoah mountains, twilight descending, prelude to darkness. And it was the darkness that Jason Bourne craved; it was his friend and ally, the blackness in which he moved swiftly, with sure feet and alert hands and arms that served as sensors against all the impediments of nature. The jungles had welcomed him in the past, knowing that although he was an intruder he respected them and used them as a part of him. He did not fear the jungles, he embraced them, for they protected him and allowed him passage to accomplish whatever his objective was; he was at one with the jungles—as he would have to be with the dense woods that flanked the estate of General Norman Swayne.

The main house was set back no less than the distance of two football fields from the country road. A stockade fence separated the entrance on the right from the exit on the left, both with iron gates, fronting a deep drive that was basically an elongated U-turn. Immediately bordering each opening was a profusion of tall trees and shrubbery that was in itself a natural extension of the stockade fence both left and right. All that was missing were guardhouses at each point of entry and exit.

His mind floated back to China, to Beijing and the wild bird sanctuary where he had trapped a killer posing as Jason Bourne. There had been a guardhouse then and a series of armed patrols in the dense forest . . . and a madman, a butcher who controlled an army of killers, foremost among them the false Jason Bourne. He had penetrated that deadly sanctuary, crippled a small fleet of trucks and automobiles by plunging the blade of his knife into every tire, then proceeded to take out each patrol in the Jing Shan forest until he found the torch-lit clearing that held a swaggering maniac and his brigade of fanatics. Could he do it all today? wondered Bourne as he drove slowly past Swayne's property for the third time, his eyes absorbing everything he could see. Five years later, thirteen years after Paris? He tried to evaluate the reality. He was not the younger man that he had been in Paris, nor the more mature man in Hong Kong, Macao and Beijing; he was now fifty and he felt it, every year of it. He would not dwell on it. There was too much else to think about, and the twenty-eight acres of General Norman Swayne's property were not the forest primeval of the Jing Shan sanctuary.

However, as he had done on the primitive

outskirts of Beijing, he drove the car off the country road deep into a mass of tall grass and foliage. He climbed out and proceeded to cover the vehicle with bent and broken branches. The rapidly descending darkness would complete the camouflage, and with the darkness he would go to work. He had changed his clothes in the men's room at the gas station: black trousers below a black long-sleeved, skintight pullover; and black thick-soled sneakers with heavy tread. These were his working apparel. The items he spread on the ground were his equipment, the shopping he had done after leaving Georgetown. They included a long-bladed hunting knife whose scabbard he threaded into his belt; a dual-chambered CO_2 pistol, encased in a nylon shoulder holster, that silently shot immobilizing darts into attacking animals, such as pit bulls; two flares designed to assist stranded drivers in broken-down cars to attract or deter other motorists; a pair of small Zeisslkon 8 x 10 binoculars attached to his trousers by a Velcro strip; a penlight; raw-hide laces; and finally, pocket-sized wire cutters in case there was a metal fence. Along with the automatic supplied by the Central Intelligence Agency, the gear was either lashed to his belt or concealed in his clothing. The darkness came and Jason Bourne walked into the woods.

The white sheet of ocean spray burst up from the coral reef and appeared suspended, the dark blue waters of the Caribbean serving as a backdrop. It was that hour of early evening, a long sundown imminent, when Tranquility Isle was bathed in alternating hot tropical colors, pockets of shadows constantly changing with each imperceptible descent of the orange sun. The resort complex of Tranquility Inn had seemingly been cut out of three adjacent rock-strewn hills above an elongated beach sandwiched between huge natural jetties of coral. Two rows of balconied pink villas with bright red roofs of terra-cotta extended from each side of the resort's central hub, a large circular building of heavy stone and thick glass, all the structures overlooking the water, the villas connected by a white concrete path bordered by low-cut shrubbery and lined with ground lamps. Waiters in yellow guayabera jackets wheeled room-service tables along the path, delivering bottles and ice and canapés to Tranquility's guests, the majority of whom sat on their individual balconies savor-

ing the end of the Caribbean day. And as the
shadows became more prominent, other people
unobtrusively appeared along the beach and on
the long dock that extended out over the water.
These were neither guests nor service employ-
ees; they were armed guards, each dressed in
a dark brown tropical uniform and—again unobtrusively—with a MAC-10 machine pistol
strapped to his belted waist. On the opposite
side of each jacket and hooked to the cloth was
a pair of Zeiss Ikon 8 x 10 binoculars continuously used to scan the darkness. The owner of
Tranquility Inn was determined that it live up to
its name.

On the large circular balcony of the villa nearest the main building and the attached glass-
enclosed dining room, an elderly infirm woman
sat in a wheelchair sipping a glass of Château
Carbonnieux '78 while drinking in the splendors
of sundown. She absently touched the bangs of
her imperfectly dyed red hair as she listened.
She heard the voice of her man talking with the
nurse inside, then the sound of his less than
emphatic footsteps as he walked out to join her.

"My God," she said in French. "I'm going to
get pissed!"

"Why not?" asked the Jackal's courier. "This

is the place for it. I see everything through a haze of disbelief myself."

"You still will not tell me why the monseigneur sent you here—us here?"

"I told you, I'm merely a messenger."

"And I don't believe you."

"Believe. It's important for him but of no consequence for us. Enjoy, my lovely."

"You always call me that when you won't explain."

"Then you should learn from experience not to inquire, is it not so?"

"It is *not* so, my dear. I'm dying—"

"We'll hear no more of that!"

"It's true nevertheless; you cannot keep it from me. I don't worry for myself, the pain will end, you see, but I worry about you. *You,* forever better than your circumstances, Michel— No, *no,* you are *Jean Pierre,* I must not forget that. . . . Still, I must concern myself. This place, these extraordinary lodgings, this *attention.* I think you will pay a terrible price, my dear."

"Why do you say that?"

"It's all so grand. Too grand. Something's wrong."

"You concern yourself too deeply."

"No, you deceive yourself too easily. My

brother, Claude, has always said you take too much from the monseigneur. One day the bill will be presented to you."

"Your brother, Claude, is a sweet old man with feathers in his head. It's why the monseigneur gives him only the most insignificant assignments. You send him out for a paper in Montparnasse he ends up in Marseilles not knowing how he got there." The telephone inside the villa rang, interrupting the Jackal's man. He turned. "Our new friend will get it," he said.

"She's a strange one," added the old woman. "I don't trust her."

"She works for the monseigneur."

"Really?"

"I haven't had time to tell you. She will relay his instructions."

The uniformed nurse, her light brown hair pulled severely back into a bun, appeared in the doorway. "Monsieur, it is Paris," she said, her wide gray eyes conveying an urgency missing in her low, understated voice.

"Thank you." The Jackal's courier walked inside, following the nurse to the telephone. She picked it up and handed it to him. "This is Jean Pierre Fontaine."

"Blessings upon you, child of God," said the

voice several thousand miles away. "Is every-thing suitable?"

"Beyond description," answered the old man. "It is . . . so grand, so much more than we deserve."

"You will earn it."

"However I may serve you."

"You'll serve me by following the orders given to you by the woman. Follow them precisely with no deviation whatsoever, is that understood?"

"Certainly."

"Blessings upon you." There was a click and the voice was no more.

Fontaine turned to address the nurse, but she was not at his side. Instead, she was across the room, unlocking the drawer of a table. He walked over to her, his eyes drawn to the contents of the drawer. Side by side were a pair of surgical gloves, a pistol with a cylindrical silencer attached to the barrel, and a straight razor, the blade recessed.

"These are your tools," said the woman, handing him the key, her flat, expressionless gray eyes boring into his own, "and the targets are in the last villa on this row. You are to familiarize yourself with the area by taking extended walks on the path, as old men do for circulatory purposes, and you are to kill them. You are to do this wearing the gloves and firing the gun into each skull. It *must* be the head. Then each throat must be slit—"

"Mother of *God*, the *children*'s?"

"Those are the orders."

"They're barbaric!"

"Do you wish me to convey that judgment?"

Fontaine looked over at the balcony door, at his woman in the wheelchair. "No, no, of course not."

"I thought not. . . . There is a final instruction. With whosever blood is most convenient, you are to write on the wall the following: 'Jason Bourne, brother of the Jackal.' "

"Oh, my God. . . . I'll be caught, of course."

"That's up to you. Coordinate the executions with me and I'll swear a great warrior of France was in this villa at the time."

"Time? . . . What is the time? When is this to be done?"

"Within the next thirty-six hours."

"*Then* what?"

"You may stay here until your woman dies."

9

Brendan Patrick Pierre Prefontaine was again astonished. Though he had no reservation, the front desk of Tranquility Inn treated him like a visiting celebrity, then only moments after he had secured a villa told him that he already *had* a villa and asked How was the flight from Paris? Confusion descended for several minutes as the owner of Tranquility Inn could not be reached for consultation; he was not at his residence, and if he was on the premises he could not be found. Ultimately hands were thrown up in frustration and the former judge from Boston was taken to his lodgings, a lovely miniature house overlooking the Caribbean. By accident, hardly by design, he had reached into the wrong pocket and given the manager behind the desk a fifty-dollar American bill for his courtesy. Prefontaine instantly became a man to be reckoned with; fingers snapped and palms hit bells rapidly. Nothing was too splendid for the bewildering stranger who had suddenly flown in on the seaplane from Montserrat. . . . It was the *name* that had thrown everyone behind Tranquility's front desk into confusion. Could such a coincidence be possible? . . . Still the Crown governor— Err on the safe side. Get the man a villa.

Once settled, his casual clothes distributed in the closet and the bureau, the craziness continued. A chilled bottle of Château Carbonnieux '78 accompanied fresh-cut flowers, and a box of Belgian chocolates arrived, only to have a confused room-service waiter return to remove them, apologizing for the fact that they were for another villa down the line—or up the line—he thought, *mon*.

The judge changed into Bermuda shorts, wincing at the sight of his spindly legs, and put on a subdued paisley sport shirt. White loafers and a white cloth cap completed his tropical outfit; it would be dark soon and he wanted a stroll. For several reasons.

"I know who Jean Pierre Fontaine is," said John St. Jacques, reading the register behind the front desk, "he's the one the CG's office called me about, but who the hell is B. P. *Pre*fontaine?"

"An illustrious judge from the United States," declared the tall black assistant manager in a distinct British accent. "My uncle, the deputy director of immigration, phoned me from the airport roughly two hours ago. Unfortunately, I was upstairs when the confusion arose, but our people did the right thing."

"A judge?" asked the owner of Tranquility Inn as the assistant manager touched St. Jacques's elbow, gesturing for him to move away from the desk and the clerks. Both men did so. "What did your uncle say?"

"There must be total privvissy where our two distinguished guests are concerned."

"Why wouldn't there be? What does that mean?"

"My uncle was very discreet, but he did allow that he watched the honored judge go to the Inter-Island counter and purchase a ticket. He further permitted himself to say that he knew he had been right. The judge and the French war hero are related and wish to meet confidentially on matters of great import."

"If that was the case, why didn't the honored judge have a reservation?"

"There appear to be two possible explanations, sir. According to my uncle, they were originally to meet at the airport but the Crown governor's reception line precluded it."

"What's the second possibility?"

"An error may have been made in the judge's own offices in Boston, Massachusetts. According to my uncle, there was a brief discussion regarding the judge's law clerks, how they are prone to errors and if one had been made with his passport, he'd fly them all down to apologize."

"Then judges are paid a lot more in the States than they are in Canada. He's damned lucky we had space."

"It's the summer season, sir. We usually have available space during these months."

"Don't remind me. . . . All right, so we've got two illustrious relatives who want to meet privately but go about it in a very complicated way. Maybe you should call the judge and tell him what villa Fontaine is in. Or Prefontaine—whichever the hell it is."

"I suggested that courtesy to my uncle, sir, and he was most adamant. He said we should do and say absolutely nothing. According to my uncle, all great men have secrets and he would not care to have his own brilliant deduction revealed except by the parties themselves."

"Beg your pardon?"

"If such a call were made to the judge, he would know the information could only come from my uncle, the deputy director of Montserrat's immigration."

"Christ, do whatever you want, I've got other things on my mind. . . . Incidentally, I've doubled the patrols on the road and the beach."

"We'll be stretched thin, sir."

"I've shifted a number off the paths. I know who's *here*, but I don't know who may want to get *in* here."

"Do we expect trouble, sir?"

John St. Jacques looked at the assistant manager. "Not now," he said. "I've been out checking every inch of the grounds and the beach. By the way, I'll be staying with my sister and her children in Villa Twenty."

The hero of World War II's Résistance known as Jean Pierre Fontaine walked slowly up the concrete path toward the last villa overlooking the sea. It was similar to the others, with walls of pink stucco and a red tiled roof, but the surrounding lawn was larger, the bordering shrubbery taller and denser. It was a place for prime ministers and presidents, foreign secretaries and secretaries of state, men and women of international stature seeking the peace of pampered isolation.

Fontaine reached the end of the path where there was a four-foot-high white stuccoed wall and beyond it the impenetrable overgrown slope of the hill leading down to the shoreline. The wall itself extended in both directions, curving around the hill below the villas' balconies, at once demarcation and protection. The entrance to Villa Twenty was a pink wrought-iron gate bolted into the wall. Beyond the gate the old man could see a small child running about the lawn in a bathing suit. In moments a woman appeared in the frame of the open front door.

"Come on, Jamie!" she called out. "Time for dinner."

"Has Alison eaten, Mommy?"

"Fed and asleep, darling. She won't yell at her brother."

"I like our house better. Why can't we go back to our house, Mommy?"

"Because Uncle John wants us to stay here.
. . . The boats are here, Jamie. He can take you
fishing and sailing just like he did last April during the spring vacation."

"We stayed at our house then."

"Yes, well, Daddy was with us—"

"And we had lots of fun driving over in the
truck!"

"*Dinner*, Jamie. Come along now."

Mother and child went into the house and
Fontaine winced thinking about his orders from
the Jackal, the bloody executions he was sworn
to carry out. And then the child's words came
back to him. *Why can't we go back to our house,
Mommy? . . . We stayed at our house then.* And
the mother's answers: *Because Uncle John
wants us to stay here. . . . Yes, well, Daddy was
with us then.*

There might be any number of explanations
for the brief exchange he had overheard, but
Fontaine could sense warnings quicker than
most men, for his life had been filled with them.
He sensed one now, and for that reason an old
man would take a number of walks late at night
for "circulatory purposes."

He turned from the wall and started down the
concrete path so absorbed in thought that he

nearly collided with a guest at least his own age wearing a foolish-looking little white cap and white shoes.

"Excuse me," said the stranger, sidestepping out of Fontaine's way.

"Pardon, monsieur!" exclaimed the embarrassed hero of France, unconsciously slipping into his native tongue. *"Je regrette*—that is to say, it is I who must be excused."

"Oh?" At his words the stranger's eyes briefly widened, almost as if there had been recognition that was quickly hidden. "Not at all."

"Pardon, we have met, monsieur?"

"I don't believe so," replied the old man in the silly white cap. "But we've all heard the rumors. A great French hero is among the guests."

"Foolishness. The accidents of war when we were all much younger. My name is Fontaine. Jean Pierre Fontaine."

"Mine's . . . Patrick. Brendan Patrick—"

"A pleasure to make your acquaintance, monsieur." Both men shook hands. "This is a lovely place, is it not?"

"Simply beautiful." Again the stranger seemed to be studying him, thought Fontaine, yet, oddly enough, avoiding any prolonged eye contact. "Well, I must be on my way," added the elderly guest in the brand-new white shoes. "Doctor's orders."

"Moi aussi," said Jean Pierre, purposely speaking French, which evidently had an effect on the stranger. *"Toujours le médecin à notre âge, n'est-ce pas?"*

"All too true," replied the old man with the bony legs, nodding and making the gesture of a wave as he turned and walked rapidly up the path.

Fontaine stood motionless watching the receding figure, waiting, knowing it would happen. And then it did. The old man stopped and slowly turned around. From a distance their eyes locked; it was enough. Jean Pierre smiled, then proceeded down the concrete path toward his villa.

It was another warning, he mused, and a far more deadly one. For three things were apparent: first, the elderly guest in the foolish white cap spoke French; second, he knew that "Jean Pierre Fontaine" was in reality someone else—sent to Montserrat by someone else; third . . . he had the mark of the Jackal in his eyes. *Mon Dieu,* how like the monseigneur! Engineer the kill, make sure it is done, then remove all physical traces that could lead back to his methods of operation, in particular his private army of old men. No wonder the nurse had said that after his orders were carried out they could remain here in this paradise until his woman died, a date that was imprecise at best. The Jackal's generosity was not so grand as it appeared; his woman's death, as well as his own, had been scheduled.

John St. Jacques picked up the phone in his office. "Yes?"

"They have *met*, sir!" said the excited assistant manager at the front desk.

"Who have met?"

"The great man and his illustrious relative from Boston, Massachusetts. I would have called you at once, but there was a mix-up concerning a box of Belgian chocolates—"

"What *are* you talking about?"

"Several minutes ago, sir, I saw them through the windows. They were conferring on the path. My esteemed uncle, the deputy director, was right in all things!"

"That's nice."

"The Crown governor's office will be most pleased, and I'm certain we shall be commended, as will, of course, my brilliant uncle."

"Good for all of us," said St. Jacques wearily.

"Now we don't have to concern ourselves about them any longer, do we?"

"Offhand I would say not, sir. . . . Except that as we speak the honored judge is walking down the path in haste. I believe he's coming inside."

"I don't think he'll bite you; he probably wants to thank you. Do whatever he says. There's a storm coming up from Basse-Terre and we'll need the CG's input if the phones go out."

"I myself shall perform whatever service he requires, sir!"

"Well, there are limits. Don't brush his teeth."

Brendan Prefontaine hurried through the door of the circular glass-walled lobby. He had waited until the old Frenchman had turned into the first villa before reversing direction and heading straight for the main complex. As he had done so many times over the past thirty years, he was forced to think quickly on his feet—usually running feet—building plausible explanations that would support a number of obvious possibilities as well as others not so obvious. He had just committed an unavoidable yet stupid error, unavoidable because he was not prepared to give Tranquility Inn's desk a false name in case identification was required, and stupid because he *had* given a false name to the hero of France. . . . Well, not stupid; the similarity of their surnames might have led to unwanted complications where the purpose of his trip to Montserrat was concerned, which was quite simply extortion—to learn what so frightened Randolph Gates that he would part with fifteen thousand dollars, and having learned it perhaps collect a great deal more. No, the stupidity was in not taking the precautionary step he was about to take. He approached the front desk and the tall, slender clerk behind it.

"Good evening, *sir,*" fairly yelled the inn's employee, causing the judge to look around, grateful that there were very few guests in the lobby. "However I may assist you, be assured of my perfection!"

"I'd rather be assured of your keeping your voice down, young man."

"I shall *whisper,*" said the clerk inaudibly.

"What did you say?"

"How may I help you?" intoned the man, now sotto voce.

"Let's just talk quietly, all right?"

"Certainly. I am so very privileged."

"You are?"

"Of course."

"Very well," said Prefontaine. "I have a favor to ask of you—"

"Anything!"

"Shhh!"

"Naturally."

"Like many men of advanced age I frequently forget things, you can understand that, can't you?"

"A man of your wisdom I doubt forgets anything."

"What? . . . Never mind. I'm traveling incognito, you *do* know what I mean."

"Most assuredly, sir."

"I registered under my name, Prefontaine—"

"You certainly did," interrupted the clerk. "I *know*."

"It was a mistake. My office and those I've told to reach me expect to ask for a 'Mr. Patrick,' my middle name. It's harmless subterfuge to allow me some much needed rest."

"I *understand*," said the clerk confidentially, leaning over the counter.

"You do?"

"Of course. If such an eminent person as yourself were known to be a guest here, you might find little rest. As *another*, you must have complete privvissy! Be assured, I understand."

" 'Privvissy'? Oh, good Lord. . . ."

"I shall myself alter the directory, Judge."

"Judge . . . ? I said nothing about being a judge."

Consternation was apparent on the man's embarrassed face. "A slip born of wishing to serve you, sir."

"And of something else—some*one* else."

"On my word, no one here other than the owner of Tranquility Inn is aware of the confidential nature of your visit, sir," whispered the clerk, again leaning over the counter. "All is total privvissy!"

"Holy Mary, that asshole at the airport—"

"My astute uncle," continued the clerk, overriding and not hearing Prefontaine's soft monotone, "made it completely clear that we were privileged to be dealing with illustrious men who required total confidentiality. You see, he called me in that spirit—"

"All right, all right, young man, I understand now and appreciate everything you're doing. Just make sure that the name is changed to Patrick, and should anyone here inquire about me, he or she is to be given that name. Do we understand each other?"

"With clairvoyance, honored Judge!"

"I hope not."

Four minutes later the harried assistant manager picked up the ringing telephone. "Front desk," he intoned, as if giving a benediction.

"This is Monsieur Fontaine in Villa Number Eleven."

"Yes, sir. The honor is mine . . . ours . . . everyone's!"

"*Merci.* I wondered if you might help me. I met a charming American on the path perhaps a quarter of an hour ago, a man about my own age wearing a white walking cap. I thought I might ask him for an apéritif one day, but I'm not sure I heard his name correctly."

He was being tested, thought the assistant manager. *Great men not only had secrets but concerned themselves with those guarding them.* "I would have to say from your description, sir, that you met the very charming Mr. Patrick."

"Ah, yes, I believe that was the name. An Irish name, indeed, but he's American, is he not?"

"A very *learned* American, sir, from Boston, Massachusetts. He's in Villa Fourteen, the third west of yours. Simply dial seven-one-four."

"Yes, well, thank you so much. If you see Monsieur Patrick, I'd prefer you say nothing. As you know, my wife is not well and I must extend the invitation when it is comfortable for her."

"I would never say *anything*, great sir, unless told to do so. Where you and the learned Mr. Patrick are concerned, we follow the Crown governor's confidential instructions to the letter."

"You do? That's most commendable. . . . *Adieu.*"

He had done it! thought the assistant manager, hanging up the phone. Great men understood subtleties, and he had been subtle in ways his brilliant uncle would appreciate. Not only with the instant offering of the Patrick name, but, more important, by using the word "learned" which conveyed that of a scholar—or a *judge.* And, finally, by stating that he would not say anything without the Crown governor's instructions. By the use of subtlety he had insinuated himself into the confidentiality of great men. It was a breathtaking experience, and he must call his uncle and share their combined triumph.

Fontaine sat on the edge of the bed, the telephone in its cradle yet still in his hand, staring at his woman out on the balcony. She sat in her wheelchair, her profile to him, the glass of wine on the small table beside the chair, her head bent down in pain. . . . *Pain!* The whole terrible world was filled with pain! And he had done his share inflicting it; he understood that and expected no quarter, but not for his woman. That was never part of the contract. *His* life, yes, of course, but not hers, not while she had breath in her frail body. *Non, monseigneur. Je refuse! Ce n'est pas dans le contrat!*

So the Jackal's army of very old men now extended to America—it was to be expected. And an old Irish American in a foolish white cap, a *learned* man who for one reason or another had embraced the cult of the terrorist, was to be their executioner. A man who had studied him and pretended to speak no French, who had the sign of the Jackal in his eyes. *Where you and the learned Mr. Patrick are concerned, we follow the instructions of the Crown governor.* The Crown governor who took his instructions from a master of death in Paris.

A decade ago, after five productive years with the monseigneur, he had been given a telephone number in Argenteuil, six miles north of Paris, that he was never to use except in the most extreme emergency. He had used it only once before, but he would use it now. He studied the international codes, picked up the phone and dialed. After the better part of two minutes, a voice answered.

"Le Coeur du Soldat," said a flat male voice, martial music in the background.

"I must reach a blackbird," said Fontaine in French. "My identity is Paris Five."

"If such a request is possible, where can such a bird reach you?"

"In the Caribbean." Fontaine gave the area code, the telephone number and the extension to Villa Eleven. He hung up the phone and sat despondent on the edge of the bed. In his soul he knew that this might be his and his woman's last few hours on earth. If so, he and his woman could face their God and speak the truth. He had killed, no question about that, but he had never harmed or taken the life of a person who had not committed greater crimes against others—with a few minor exceptions that might be called innocent bystanders caught in the heat of fire or in an explosion. All life was pain, did not the Scriptures tell us that? . . . On the other hand, what kind of God allowed such brutalities? *Merde!* Do not think about such things! They are beyond your understanding.

The telephone rang and Fontaine grabbed it,

pulling it to his ear. "This is Paris Five," he said.

"Child of God, what can be so extreme that you would use a number you have called only once before in our relationship?"

"Your generosity has been absolute, monseigneur, but I feel we must redefine our contract."

"In what way?"

"My life is yours to do with as you will, as mercifully as you will, but it does not include my woman."

"What?"

"A man is here, a learned man from the city of Boston who studies me with curious eyes, eyes that tell me he has other purposes in mind."

"That arrogant fool flew down to Montserrat *himself*? He knows *nothing*!"

"Obviously he does, and I beg you, I shall do as you order me to do, but let us go back to Paris ... I *beg* of you. Let her die in peace. I will ask no more of you."

"You ask of *me*? I've given you my *word*!"

"Then why is this learned man from America here following me with a blank face and inquisitive eyes, monseigneur?"

The deep, hollow roll of a throated cough

filled the silence, and then the Jackal spoke. "The great professor of law has transgressed, inserted himself where he should not be. He's a dead man."

Edith Gates, wife of the celebrated attorney and professor of law, silently opened the door of the private study in their elegant town house on Louisburg Square. Her husband sat motionless in his heavy leather armchair staring at the crackling fire, a fire he insisted upon despite the warm Boston night outside and the central air conditioning inside.

As she watched him, Mrs. Gates was once again struck by the painful realization that there were ... *things* ... about her husband she would never understand. Gaps in his life she could never fill, leaps in his thinking she could not comprehend. She only knew that there were times when he felt a terrible pain and would not share it, when by sharing it he would lessen the burden on himself. Thirty-three years ago a passably attractive young woman of average wealth had married an extremely tall, gangling, brilliant but impoverished law school graduate whose anxiety and eagerness to please had turned off the major firms in those days of the cool, restrained late fifties. The veneer of so-phistication and the pursuit of security were valued over a smoldering, wandering first-rate mind of unsure direction, especially a mind in-side a head of unkempt hair and a body dressed in clothes that were cheap imitations of J. Press and Brooks Brothers, which appeared even worse because his bank account precluded any additional expenses for alterations and few dis-count stores carried his size.

The new Mrs. Gates, however, had several ideas that would improve the prospects of their life together. Among them was to lay aside an immediate law career—better none than with an inferior firm, or, God forbid, a private practice with the sort of clients he was bound to attract, namely, those who could not afford established attorneys. Better to use his natural endow-ments, which were his impressive height and a quick, spongelike intelligence that, combined with his drive, disposed of heavy academic workloads with ease. Using her modest trust fund, Edith shaped the externals of her man, buying the correct clothes and hiring a theatrical voice coach who instructed his student in the ways of dramatic delivery and effective stage presence. The gangling graduate soon took on a Lincolnesque quality with subtle flashes of John Brown. Too, he was on his way to becoming a legal expert, remaining in the milieu of the university, piling one degree upon another while teaching at the graduate level until the sheer depth of his expertise in specific areas was incontestable. And he found himself sought after by the prominent firms that had rejected him earlier.

The strategy took nearly ten years before concrete results appeared, and while the early returns were not earthshaking, still they represented progress. Law reviews, first minor and then major, began publishing his semicontroversial articles as much for their style as for their content, for the young associate professor had a seductive way with the written word, at once riveting and arcane, by turns flowery and incisive. But it was his opinions, latently emerging, that made segments of the financial community take notice. The mood of the nation was changing, the crust of the benevolent Great Society beginning to crack, the lesions initiated with code words coined by the Nixon boys, such as the Silent Majority and Bums-on-Welfare and the pejorative *them*. A meanness was rising out of the ground and spreading, and it was more than the perceptive, decent Ford could stop, weakened as he was by the wounds of Watergate; and too much as well for the brilliant Carter, too consumed by minutiae to exercise compassionate leadership. The phrase ". . . what you can do for your country" was out of fashion, replaced by "what I can do for *me*."

Dr. Randolph Gates found a relentless wave on which to ride, a mellifluous voice with which to speak, and a growing acerbic vocabulary to match the dawning new era. In his now refined scholarly opinion—legally, economically and so-cially—*bigger* was better, and *more* far preferable to less. The laws that supported competition in the marketplace he attacked as stifling to the larger agenda of industrial growth from which would flow all manner of benefits for everyone—well, practically everyone. It was, after all, a Darwinian world and, like it or not, the fittest would always survive. The drums went bang and the cymbals clanged and the financial manipulators found a champion, a legal *scholar* who lent re-spectability to their righteous dreams of merger and consolidation; buy out, take over and sell off, all for the good of the many, of course.

Randolph Gates was summoned, and he ran

into their arms with alacrity, stunning one courtroom after another with his elocutionary gym-
nastics. He had made it, but Edith Gates was not
sure what it all meant. She had envisioned a
comfortable living, naturally, but not millions, not
the private jets flying all over the world, from
Palm Springs to the South of France. Nor was
she comfortable when her husband's articles
and lectures were used to support causes that
struck her as unrelated or patently unfair; he
waved her arguments aside, stating that the
cases in point were legitimate intellectual paral-
lels. Above everything, she had not shared a
bed or a bedroom with her husband in over six
years.

She walked into the study, abruptly stopping
as he gasped, swerving his head around, his
eyes glazed and filled with alarm.

"I'm sorry, I didn't mean to startle you."

"You always knock. Why didn't you knock?
You know how it is when I'm concentrating."

"I said I'm sorry. Something's on my mind and
I wasn't thinking."

"That's a contradiction."

"Thinking about knocking, I mean."

"What's on your *mind*," asked the celebrated
attorney as if he doubted his wife had one.

"Please don't be clever with me."

"What *is* it, Edith?"

"Where were you last night?"

Gates arched his brows in mock surprise. "My God, are you suspicious? I told you where I was. At the Ritz. In conference with someone I knew years ago, someone I did not care to have at my house. If, at your age, you want confirmation, call the Ritz."

Edith Gates was silent for a moment; she simply looked at her husband. "My dear," she said, "I don't give a damn if you had an assignation with the most voluptuous whore in the Combat Zone. Somebody would probably have to give her a few drinks to restore her confidence."

"Not bad, bitch."

"In that department you're not exactly a stud, bastard."

"Is there a point to this colloquy?"

"I think so. About an hour ago, just before you came home from your office, a man was at the door. Denise was doing the silver, so I answered it. I must say he looked impressive; his clothes were terribly expensive and his car was a black Porsche—"

"*And?*" broke in Gates, lurching forward in the chair, his eyes suddenly wide, rigid.

"He said to tell you that *le grand professeur* owed him twenty thousand dollars and 'he' wasn't where he was supposed to be last night, which I assumed was the Ritz."

"It wasn't. Something came up. . . . Oh, Christ, he doesn't *understand.* What did you say?"

"I didn't like his language or his attitude. I told him I hadn't the vaguest idea where you were. He knew I was lying, but there wasn't anything he could do."

"Good. Lying's something he knows about."

"I can't imagine that twenty thousand is such a problem for you—"

"It's not the money, it's the method of payment."

"For what?"

"Nothing."

"I believe that's what you call a contradiction, Randy."

"Shut up!"

The telephone rang. Gates lunged up from the chair and stared at it. He made no move to go to the desk; instead, he spoke in a guttural voice to his wife. "Whoever it is, you tell him I'm not here. . . . I'm away, out of town—you don't know when I'll be back."

Edith walked over to the phone. "It's your very

private line," she said as she picked it up on the third ring. "The Gates residence," began Edith, a ploy she had used for years; her friends knew who it was, others did not matter to her any longer. "Yes. . . . Yes? I'm sorry, he's away and we don't know when he'll return." Gates's wife looked briefly at the phone, then hung up. She turned to her husband. "That was the operator in Paris. . . . It's strange. Someone was calling you, but when I said you weren't here, she didn't even ask where you could be reached. She simply got off the line—very abruptly."

"Oh, my *God*!" cried Gates, visibly shaken. "Something happened . . . something's gone wrong, someone *lied*!" With those enigmatic words the attorney whipped around and raced across the room, fumbling in his trousers pocket. He reached a section of the floor-to-ceiling bookshelves where the center of the chest-high shelf had been converted into a safe-like cupboard, a carved wooden door superimposed on the brown steel. In panic, as an afterthought stunned him further, he spun around and screamed at his wife. "Get *out* of here! Get out, get out, get *out*!"

Edith Gates walked slowly to the study door, where she turned to her husband and spoke quietly. "It all goes back to Paris, doesn't it, Randy? Seven years ago in Paris. *That's* where something happened, isn't it? You came back a frightened man, a man with a pain you won't share."

"Get *out of here*!" shrieked the vaunted professor of law, his eyes wild.

Edith went out the door, closing it behind her but not releasing the knob, her hand twisted so the latch would not close. Moments later she opened it barely a few inches and watched her husband.

The shock was beyond anything she could imagine. The man she had lived with for thirty-three years, the legal giant who neither smoked nor drank a drop of alcohol, was plunging a hypodermic needle into his forearm.

10

Darkness had descended on Manassas, the countryside alive with nocturnal undercurrents, as Bourne crept through the woods bordering the "farm" of General Norman Swayne. Startled birds fluttered out of their black recesses; crows awoke in the trees and cawed their alarms, then, as if calmed by a foraging co-conspirator, kept silent.

He reached it, wondering, if indeed *it* would be there. A fence—high, with thick crisscrossing links embedded in green plastic, a coiled-barbed-wire addition above slanting outward. Entry prohibited. *Beijing. The Jing Shan Sanctuary.* There had been things to conceal within that Oriental wildlife preserve, so it was protected by an all but impassable government barrier. But why would a desk-bound general on military pay erect such a barricade around a "farm" in Manassas, Virginia, an obstruction costing thousands of dollars? It was not designed to fence in livestock; it was, instead, built to keep out human life.

As with the sanctuary in China, there would be no electric alarms threaded through the links, for the animals and the birds of the forest would set them off repeatedly. Nor would there be the unseen beams of trip lights for the same reason; instead, they would be on the flat ground nearer the house, and waist-high, if they existed. Bourne pulled the small wire cutters out of his rear pocket and started with the links at earth level.

With each scissoring cut, he again understood the obvious, the inevitable, confirmed by his heavy breathing and the sweat that had formed on his hairline. No matter how hard he tried—not fanatically but at least assiduously—to keep himself in reasonably good shape, he was now fifty and his body knew it. Again, it was something to think about, not dwell upon, and with every inch of progress not think about at all.

There were Marie and the children, his *family*; there was nothing he could not do as long as he willed it. David Webb was gone from his psyche, only the predator Jason Bourne remained.

He was through! The parallel vertical links were cut, the ground wires as well. He gripped the fence and pulled the opening toward him, making each half foot of space an ordeal. He crawled inside this strangely fortified acreage and stood up, listening, his eyes darting in every direction, scanning the darkness—which was not complete darkness. He saw—filtered through the thick branches of the tall overlapping pines bordering the tamed grounds—flickerings of light coming from the large house. Slowly, he made his way toward what he knew was the circular drive. He reached the outer border of the asphalt and lay prone beneath a spreading pine, gathering his thoughts and his breath as he studied the scene in front of him. Suddenly there was a flash of light on his far right, deep inside the grounds at the end of a straight graveled road that branched off from the circular drive.

A door had been opened; it belonged to what appeared to be a small house or a large cabin and it remained open. Two men and a woman came out and were talking . . . no, they were not just talking, they were arguing heatedly. Bourne ripped the short powerful binoculars out of their Velcro recess and put them up to his eyes. Quickly he focused on the trio, whose voices grew in volume, the words indistinguishable but the anger apparent. As the blurred image sharpened, he studied the three people, knowing instantly that the medium-sized, medium-built, ramrod-straight protesting man on the left was the Pentagon's General Swayne, and the large-breasted woman with streaked dark hair his wife, but what struck him—and fascinated him— was the hulking overweight figure nearest the open door. He *knew* him! Jason could not remember from where or when, which was certainly not unusual, but his visceral reaction to the sight of the man was *not* usual. It was one of instant loathing and he did not know why, since no connection with anything in the past came to him. Only feelings of disgust and revulsion. Where were the images, the brief flashes of time or circumstance that so often illuminated his inner screen? They did not come; he only knew that the man he focused on in the binoculars was his enemy.

Then that huge man did an extraordinary

thing. He reached for Swayne's wife, throwing his large left arm protectively around her shoulders, his right hand accusingly jabbing the space between him and the general. Whatever he said—or yelled—caused Swayne to react with what seemed to be stoic resolve mixed with feigned indifference. He turned around, and in military fashion strode back across the lawn toward a rear entrance to the house. Bourne lost him in the darkness and swung back to the couple in the light of the door. The large obese man released the general's wife and spoke to her. She nodded, brushed her lips against his, and ran after her husband. The obvious consort walked back into the small house and slammed the door shut, removing the light.

Jason reattached the binoculars to his trousers and tried to understand what he had observed. It had been like watching a silent movie minus the subtitles, the gestures far more real and without exaggerated theatricality. That there was in the confines of this fenced acreage a *ménage à trois* was obvious, but this could hardly explain the fence. There was another reason, a reason he had to learn.

Further, instinct told him that whatever it was, was linked to the huge overweight man who had walked angrily back into the small house. He had to reach that house; he had to reach that man who had been a part of his forgotten past. He slowly got to his feet, and ducking from one pine to the next, he made his way to the end of the circular drive, and then continued down the tree-lined border of the narrow graveled road.

He stopped, lurching to the ground at a sudden sound that was no part of the murmuring woods. Somewhere wheels were spinning, crushing stone and displacing it; he rolled over and over into the dark recesses of the low-hanging, wide-spreading branches of a pine tree, swinging his body around to locate the disturbance.

Within seconds he saw something racing out of the shadows of the circular drive, rushing over the gravel of the extended road. It was a small odd-shaped vehicle, half three-wheeled motorbike, half miniature golf cart, the tires large and deeply treaded, capable of both high speed and balance. It was also, in its way, ominous, for, in addition to a high flexible antenna, thick curved Plexiglas shields shot up from all sides, bulletproof windows that protected the driver from gunfire while alerting by radio anyone inside the residences of an assault. General Norman

Swayne's "farm" took on an even stranger ambience. . . . Then, abruptly, it was macabre.

A second three-wheeled cart swung out from the shadows behind the cabin—and it *was* a cabin with split logs on the exterior—and came to a stop only feet from the first vehicle on the graveled road. Both drivers' heads swung militarily toward the small house as if they were robots in a public gallery, and then the words shot out from an unseen speaker.

"Secure the gates," said the amplified voice, a voice in command. "Release the dogs and resume your rounds."

As if choreographed, the vehicles swung in unison, each in the opposite direction, the drivers gunning their engines as one, the strange-looking carts racing forward into the shadows. At the mention of dogs Bourne had automatically reached into his back pocket and removed the CO_2 gun; he then crawled laterally, rapidly, through the underbrush to within feet of the extended fence. If the dogs were in a pack, he would have no choice but to scramble up the links and spring over the coiled barbed wire to the other side. His dual-chambered dart pistol could eliminate two animals, not more; there would be no time to reload. He crouched, waiting, ready to leap up on the fence, the sightlines beneath the lower branches relatively clear.

Suddenly a black Doberman raced by on the graveled road, no hesitation in his pace, no scent picked up, the animal's only objective apparently to reach a given place. Then another dog appeared, this a long-haired shepherd. It slowed down, awkwardly yet instinctively, as if programmed to halt at a specific area; it stopped, an obscure moving silhouette up the road. Standing motionless, Bourne understood. These were trained male attack dogs, each with its own territory, which was constantly urinated upon, forever its own turf. It was a behavioral discipline favored by Oriental peasants and small landowners who knew too well the price of feeding the animals who guarded their minuscule fiefdoms of survival. Train a few, as few as possible, to protect their separated areas from thieves, and if alarms were raised the others would converge. Oriental. Vietnam. . . . Medusa. It was coming back to him! Vague, obscure outlines—*images*. A young, powerful man in uniform, driving a Jeep, stepping out, and—through the mists of Jason's inner screen—yelling at what was left of an assault team that had returned from interdicting an ordnance route paralleling the Ho Chi Minh Trail. That *same man*, older, larger, had been in his binoculars only moments ago! And years ago that same man had promised *supplies*. Ammunition, mortars, grenades, *radios*. He had brought *nothing*! Only complaints from Command Saigon that "you fucking illegals fed us crap!" But they hadn't. Saigon had acted too late, *reacted* too late, and twenty-six men had been killed or captured for nothing.

As if it were an hour ago, a minute ago, Bourne remembered. He had yanked his .45 out of his holster and, without warning, jabbed the barrel into the approaching noncom's forehead.

"One more word and you're dead, Sergeant." The man had been a sergeant! "You bring us our requisitions by O-five-hundred tomorrow morning or I'll get to Saigon and personally blow you into the wall of whatever whorehouse you're frequenting. Do I make myself clear or do you care to save me a trip to publicity city? Frankly, in light of our losses, I'd rather waste you now."

"You'll get what you need."

"Très bien!" had yelled the oldest French member of Medusa, who years later would save his life in a wildlife sanctuary in Beijing. *"Tu es formidable, mon fils!"* How right he was. And

how dead he was. D'Anjou, a man legends were written about.

Jason's thoughts were abruptly shattered. The long-haired attack dog was suddenly circling in the road, its snarls growing louder, his nostrils picking up the human scent. Within seconds, as the animal found its directional bearings, a frenzy developed. The dog lunged through the foliage, its teeth bared, the snarls now the throated growls of a kill. Bourne sprang back into the fence, pulling the CO_2 pistol out of its nylon shoulder holster with his right hand; his left arm crooked, extended, prepared for a vital counterassault that if not executed properly would cost him the night. The crazed animal leaped, a hurling mass of rage. Jason fired, first one cartridge and then the second, and as the darts were embedded, he whipped his left arm around the attack dog's head, yanking the skull counterclockwise, slamming his right knee up into the animal's body to ward off the lashing sharp-nailed paws. It was over in moments— moments of raging, panicked, finally disintegrating fury—without the howling sounds that might have carried across the lawn of the general's estate. The long-haired dog, its narcotized eyes wide, fell limp in Bourne's arms. He lowered it to the ground and once again waited, afraid to move until he knew that no converging inhuman alarms had been sent to the other animals.

There were none; there was only the constant murmuring of the forest beyond the prohibiting fence. Jason replaced the CO_2 pistol in his holster and crept forward, back to the graveled road, beads of sweat rolling down his face and into his eyes. He *had* been away too long. Years ago such a feat as silencing an attack dog would have rolled off him—*un exercice ordinaire*, as the legend d'Anjou would have said—but it was no longer ordinary. What permeated his being was fear. Pure, unadulterated *fear*. Where was the man that was? Still, Marie and the children were out there; that man had to be summoned. *Summon* him!

Bourne stripped out the binoculars and raised them to his eyes again. The moonlight was sporadic, low-flying clouds intercepting the rays, but the yellow wash was sufficient. He focused on the shrubbery that fronted the stockade fence that bordered the road outside. Pacing back and forth on a bisecting dirt path like an angry, impatient panther was the black Doberman, stopping now and then to urinate and poke its long snout into the bushes. As he had been programmed to do, the animal roamed between the opposing closed iron gates of the enormous circular drive. At each halting checkpoint it snarled, spinning around several times as if both expecting and loathing the sharp electrical shock it would receive through its collar if it transgressed without cause. Again, the method of training went back to Vietnam; soldiers disciplined the attack dogs around ammunition and matériel depots with such remote-signaling devices. Jason focused the binoculars on the far side of the expansive front lawn. He zeroed in on a third animal, this a huge Weimaraner, gentle in appearance but lethal in attack. The hyperactive dog raced back and forth, aroused perhaps by squirrels or rabbits in the brush, but not by human scent; it did not raise a throated growl, the signal of assault.

Jason tried to analyze what he observed, for that analysis would determine his moves. He had to assume that there was a fourth or a fifth, or even a sixth animal patrolling the perimeters of Swayne's grounds. But why this way? Why not a pack roaming at will and in unison, a far more frightening and inhibiting sight? The expense that concerned the Oriental farmer was no object. . . . Then the explanation struck him; it was so basic it was obvious. He shifted the binoculars back and forth between the Weimaraner and the Doberman, the picture of the long-haired German shepherd still all too clear in his mind. Beyond the fact that these were trained attack dogs, they were also something else. They were the top of their breeds, groomed to a fare-thee-well—vicious animals posing as champion show dogs by day, violent predators at night. Of *course*. General Norman Swayne's "farm" was not unrecorded property, not concealed real estate, but very much out in the open and undoubtedly, jealously perhaps, visited by friends, neighbors and colleagues. During the daylight hours, guests could admire these docile champions in their well-appointed kennels without realizing what they really were. Norman Swayne, Pentagon Procurements and alumnus of Medusa, was merely a dog aficionado, attested to by the quality of his animals' bloodlines. He might very well charge stud fees, but there was nothing in the canon of military ethics that precluded the practice.

A sham. If one such aspect of the general's "farm" was a sham, it had to follow that the estate itself was a sham, as false as the "inheritance" that made its purchase possible. Medusa.

One of the two strange three-wheeled carts appeared far across the lawn, out of the shadows of the house and down the exit road of the circular drive. Bourne focused on it, not surprised to see the Weimaraner romp over and playfully race beside the vehicle, yapping and seeking approval from the driver. The *driver*. The drivers were the handlers! The familiar scent of their bodies was calming to the dogs, reassuring them. The observation formed the analysis and the analysis determined his next tactic. He had to move, at least more freely than he was moving now, about the general's grounds. To do so he had to be in the company of a handler. He had to take one of the roving patrols; he raced back in the cover of the pine trees to his point of penetration.

The mechanized, bulletproof vehicle stopped on the narrow path at midpoint between the two front gates nearly obscured by the shrubbery; Jason adjusted his binoculars. The black Doberman was apparently a favored dog; the driver opened the right panel as the animal sprang up, placing his huge paws on the seat. The man chucked biscuits or pieces of meat into the wide, anticipating jaws, then reached over and massaged the dog's throat.

Bourne knew instantly that he had only moments to put his uncertain strategy together. He had to stop the cart and force the driver outside but without alarming the man, without giving him any reason whatsoever to use his radio and call for help. The *dog*? Lying in the road? No, the driver might assume it had been shot from the other side of the fence and alert the house. What could he *do*? He looked around in the near-total darkness feeling the panic of indecision, his anxiety growing as his eyes swept the area. Then, again, the obvious struck him.

The large expanse of close-cropped manicured lawn, the precisely cut shrubbery, the swept circular drive—neatness was the order of the general's turf. Jason could almost hear Swayne commanding his groundskeepers to "police the area!"

Bourne glanced over at the cart by the Doberman; the driver was playfully pushing the dog away, about to close the shielded panel. Only seconds now! What? *How?*

He saw the outlines of a tree limb on the ground; a rotted branch had fallen from the pine above him. He crossed quickly to it and crouched, yanking it out of the dirt and debris and dragged it toward the paved asphalt. To lay it across the drive might appear too obvious a trap, but *partially* on the road—an intrusion on the pervasive neatness—would be offensive to the eye, the task of removing it better done now than later in the event the general drove out and saw it upon his return. The men in Swayne's compound were either soldiers or ex-soldiers still under military authority; they would try to avoid reprimands, especially over the inconse-quential. The odds were on Jason's side. He gripped the base of the limb, swung it around and pushed it roughly five feet into the drive. He heard the panel of the cart slam shut; the vehi-cle rolled forward, gathering speed as Bourne raced back into the darkness of the pine tree.

The driver steered the vehicle around the dirt curve into the drive. As rapidly as he had accel-erated, he slowed down, his single headlight beam picking up the new obstruction protruding on the road. He approached it cautiously, at min-imum speed, as if he were unsure of what it was; then he realized what it was and rushed forward. Without hesitation, he opened his side door, the tall Plexiglas shield swinging forward as he stepped out on the drive and walked around the front of the cart.

"Big Rex, you're one bad dog, buddy," said

the driver in a halfloud, very Southern voice. "What'd you drag out of there, you dumb bastard? The brass-plated asshole would shave your coat for messing up his *ee*state! . . . Rex? *Rex,* you come here, you fuckin' hound!" The man grabbed the limb and pulled it off the road under the pine tree into the shadows. "*Rex*, you hear me! You humpin' knotholes, you horny stud?"

"Stay completely still and put your arms out in front of you," said Jason Bourne, walking into view.

"Holy shit! Who are *you*?"

"Someone who doesn't give a damn whether you live or die," replied the intruder calmly.

"You got a gun! I can see it!"

"So do you. Yours is in your holster. Mine's in my hand and it's pointed at your head."

"The dog! Where the hell's the *dawg*?"

"Indisposed."

"What?"

"He looks like a good dog. He could be anything a trainer wanted him to be. You don't blame the animal, you blame the human who taught it."

"What are you talkin' about?"

"I guess the bottom line is that I'd rather kill

the man than the animal, do I make myself clear?"

"Nothin's clear! I jest know *this* man don't want to get killed."

"Then let's talk, shall we?"

"I got words, but only one life, mister."

"Lower your right arm and take out your gun—by the fingers, *mister*." The guard did so, holding the weapon by his thumb and forefinger. "Lob it toward me, please." The man obeyed. Bourne picked it up.

"What the hell's this all *about*?" cried the guard, pleading.

"I want information. I was sent here to get it."

"I'll give you what I got if you let me get out of here. I don't want nothin' more to do with this place! I figured it was comin' someday, I told Barbie Jo, you ask her! I told her someday people'd be comin' around asking questions. But not this way, not *your* way! Not with guns aimed at our heads."

"I assume Barbie Jo is your wife."

"Sort of."

"Then let's start with why 'people' would come out here asking questions. My superiors want to know. Don't worry, you won't be in-

volved, nobody's interested in you. You're just a
security guard."

"That's all I *am*, mister!" interrupted the frightened man.

"Then why did you tell Barbie Jo what you
did? That people would someday come out here
asking questions."

"Hell, I'm not sure. . . . . Jest so many crazy
things, y'know?"

"No, I don't know. Like what?"

"Well, like the brass-plated screamer, the
general. He's a big wheel, right? He's got Pentagon cars and drivers and even helicopters
whenever he wants 'em, right? He owns this
place, right?"

"So?"

"So that big mick of a sergeant—a lousy master *sergeant*—orders him around like he wasn't
toilet-trained, y'know what I mean? And that big-
titty wife of his—she's got a thing goin' with the
hulk and she don't give a damn who knows it.
It's all crazy, y'see what I mean?"

"I see a domestic mess, but I'm not sure it's
anybody's business. Why would people come
out here and ask questions?"

"Why are *you* out here, man? You figured
there was a meetin' tonight, didn't you?"

"A meeting?"

"Them fancy limousines with the chauffeurs and the big shots, right? Well, you picked the wrong night. The dogs are out and they're never let out when there's a meetin'."

Bourne paused, then spoke as he approached the guard. "We'll continue this in the cart," he said with authority. "I'll crouch down and you'll do exactly what I tell you to do."

"You promised me I could get out of here!"

"You can, you will. Both you and the other fellow making the rounds. The gates over there, are they on an alarm?"

"Not when the dogs are loose. If those hounds see something out on the road and get excited, they'd jump up and set it off."

"Where's the alarm panel?"

"There are two of 'em. One's in the sergeant's place, the other's in the front hall of the house. As long as the gates are closed, you can turn it on."

"Come on, let's go."

"Where are we goin'?"

"I want to see every dog on the premises."

Twenty-one minutes later, the remaining five attack dogs drugged and carried to their kennels, Bourne unlatched the entrance gate and let the two guards outside. He had given each three hundred dollars. "This will make up for any pay you lose," he said.

"Hey, what about my car?" asked the second guard. "It ain't much but it gets me around. Me and Willie come out here in it."

"Do you have the keys?"

"Yeah, in my pocket. It's parked in the back by the kennels."

"Get it tomorrow."

"Why don't I get it now?"

"You'd make too much noise driving out, and my superiors will be arriving any moment. It's best that they don't see you. Take my word for it."

"Holy shit! What'd I tell you, Jim-Bob? Jest like I tole Barbie Jo. This place is weird, man!"

"Three hundred bucks ain't weird, Willie. C'mon, we'll hitch. T'ain't late and some of the boys'll be on the road. . . . Hey, mister, who's gonna take care of the hounds when they wake up? They got to be walked and fed before the morning shift, and they'll tear apart any stranger who gets near 'em."

"What about Swayne's master sergeant? He can handle them, can't he?"

"They don't like him much," offered the guard

named Willie, "but they obey him. They're better with the general's wife, the horny bastards."

"What about the general?" asked Bourne.

"He pisses bright yeller at the sight of 'em," replied Jim-Bob.

"Thanks for the information. Go on now, get down the road a piece before you start hitchhiking. My superiors are coming from the other direction."

"You know," said the second guard, squinting in the moonlight at Jason, "this is the craziest fuckin' night I ever expect to see. You get in here dressed like some gawddamn terrorist, but you talk and act like a shit-kickin' army officer. You keep mentioning these 'soopeeriors' of yours; you drug the pups and pay us three hundred bucks to get out. I don't understand nothin'!"

"You're not supposed to. On the other hand, if I was really a terrorist, you'd probably be dead, wouldn't you?"

"He's right, Jim-Bob. Let's get *outta* here!"

"What the hell are we supposed to *say*?"

"Tell anyone who asks you the truth. Describe what happened tonight. Also, you can add that the code name is Cobra."

"My *Gawd*!" yelled Willie as both men fled into the road.

Bourne secured the gate and walked back to the patrol cart certain in the knowledge that whatever happened during the next hours, an appendage of Medusa had been thrown into a state of further anxiety. Questions would be asked feverishly—questions for which there were no answers. Nothing. Enigma.

He climbed into the cart, shifted gears and started for the cabin at the end of the graveled road that branched off from the immaculate circular drive.

He stood by the window peering inside, his face at the edge of the glass. The huge, overweight master sergeant was sitting in a large leather armchair, his feet on an ottoman, watching television. From the sounds penetrating the window, specifically the rapid, high-pitched speech of an announcer, the general's aide was engrossed in a baseball game. Jason scanned the room as best he could; it was typically rustic, a profusion of browns and reds, from dark furniture to checkered curtains, comfortable and masculine, a man's cabin in the country. However, there were no weapons in sight, not even the accepted antique rifle over the fireplace, and

no general-issue .45 automatic either on the
sergeant's person or on the table beside the
chair. The aide had no concerns for his immediate safety and why should he? The estate of
General Norman Swayne was totally secure—
fence, gates, patrols and disciplined roving attack dogs at all points of entry. Bourne stared
through the glass at the strong jowled face of
the master sergeant. What secrets did that large
head hold? He would find out. Medusa's Delta
One would find out if he had to carve that skull
apart. Jason pushed himself away from the window and walked around the cabin to the front
door. He knocked twice with the knuckles of his
left hand; in his right was the untraceable automatic supplied by Alexander Conklin, the crown
prince of dark operations.

"It's *open*, Rachel!" yelled the rasping voice
from within.

Bourne twisted the knob and shoved the door
back; it swung slowly on its hinges and made
contact with the wall. He walked inside.

"Jesus *Christ*!" roared the master sergeant,
his heavy legs plunging off the ottoman as he
wriggled his massive body out of the chair.
"*You*! . . . You're a goddamned *ghost*! You're
dead!"

"Try again," said Delta of Medusa. "The name's Flannagan, isn't it? That's what comes to mind."

"You're *dead*!" repeated the general's aide, screaming, his eyes bulging in panic. "You bought it in Hong Kong! You were killed in Hong Kong . . . four, five *years* ago!"

"You kept tabs—"

"We know . . . *I* know!"

"You've got connections in the right places, then."

"You're Bourne!"

"Obviously born again, you might say."

"I don't *believe* this!"

"Believe, Flannagan. It's the 'we' we're going to talk about. Snake Lady, to be precise."

"*You're* the one—the one Swayne called 'Cobra'!"

"It's a snake."

"I don't *get* it—"

"It's confusing."

"You're *one* of us!"

"I was. I was also cut out. I snaked back in, as it were."

The sergeant frantically looked at the door, then the windows. "How'd you get in here? Where are the guards, the *dogs*? *Jesus!* Where *are* they?"

"The dogs are asleep in the kennels, so I gave the guards the night off."

"You gave . . . ? The dogs are on the grounds!"

"Not any longer. They were persuaded to rest."

"The guards—the goddamned *guards*!"

"They were persuaded to leave. What they think is happening here tonight is even more confusing."

"What've you done—what are you *doing*?"

"I thought I just mentioned it. We're going to talk, Sergeant Flannagan. I want to get caught up with some old comrades."

The frightened man backed awkwardly away from the chair. "You're the maniac they called Delta before you turned and went in business for yourself!" he cried in a guttural whisper. "There was a picture, a photograph—you were laid out on a slab, bloodstains all over the sheet from the bullet wounds; your face was uncovered, your eyes wide open, holes still bleeding on your forehead and your throat. . . . They asked me who you were and I said, 'He's Delta. Delta One from the illegals,' and they said, 'No, he's not, he's Jason Bourne, the killer, the assassin,' so I said, 'Then they're one and the same because that man is *Delta*—I *knew* him.' They thanked me and told me to go back and join the others."

"Who were 'they'?"

"Some people over at Langley. The one who did all the talking had a limp; he carried a cane."

"And 'the others'—they told you to go back and join?"

"About twenty-five or thirty of the old Saigon crowd."

"Command Saigon?"

"Yeah."

"Men who worked with *our* crowd, the 'illegals'?"

"Mostly, yeah."

"When was this?"

"For Christ's sake, I *told* you!" roared the panicked aide. "Four or five *years* ago! I saw the photograph—you were *dead*!"

"Only a single photograph," interrupted Bourne quietly, staring at the master sergeant. "You have a very good memory."

"You held a gun to my head. Thirty-three years, two wars and twelve combat tours, nobody ever did that to me—nobody but you. . . . Yeah, I gotta good memory."

"I think I understand."

"I *don't*! I don't understand a goddamned thing! You were dead!"

"You've said that. But I'm not, am I? Or maybe I am. Maybe this is the nightmare that's been visited upon you after twenty years of deceit."

"What kind of crap is that? What the *hell*—"

"Don't move!"

"I'm *not*!"

Suddenly, in the distance, there was a loud report. *A gunshot!* Jason spun around . . . then instinct commanded him to keep turning! *All* around! The massive general's aide was lunging at him, his huge hands like battering rams grazing off Bourne's shoulders as Delta One viciously lashed up his right foot, catching the sergeant's kidney, embedding his shoe deep into the flesh while crashing the barrel of his automatic into the base of the man's neck. Flannagan lurched downward, splayed on the floor; Jason hammered his left foot into the sergeant's head, stunning him into silence.

A silence that was broken by the continuous hysterical screams of a woman racing outside toward the open door of the cabin. Within seconds, General Norman Swayne's wife burst into the room, recoiling at the sight in front of her, gripping the back of the nearest chair, unable to contain her panic.

"He's *dead*!" she shrieked, collapsing, swerving the chair to her side as she fell to the floor reaching for her lover. "He *shot* himself, Eddie! Oh, my *God*, he *killed* himself!"

Jason Bourne rose from his crouched position and walked to the door of the strange cabin that held so many secrets. Calmly, watching his two prisoners, he closed it. The woman wept, gasping, trembling, but they were tears not of sorrow but of fear. The sergeant blinked his eyes and raised his huge head. If any emotion could be defined in his expression, it was an admixture of fury and bewilderment.

11

"Don't *touch* anything," ordered Bourne as Flannagan and Rachel Swayne haltingly preceded him into the general's photograph-lined study. At the sight of the old soldier's corpse arched back in the chair behind the desk, the ugly gun still in his outstretched hand, and the horror beyond left by the blowing away of the back of his skull, the wife convulsed, falling to her knees as if she might vomit. The master sergeant grabbed her arm, holding her off the floor, his eyes dazed, fixed on the mutilated remains of General Norman Swayne.

"Crazy son of a bitch," whispered Flannagan, his voice strained and barely audible. Then

standing motionless, the muscles of his jaw pulsating, he roared. "You insane fuckin' son of a
bitch! What did you do it for—*why*? What do we
do *now*?"

"You call the police, Sergeant," answered
Jason.

"What?" yelled the aide, spinning around.

"No!" screamed Mrs. Swayne, lurching to her
feet. "We can't do that!"

"I don't think you've got a choice. You didn't
kill him. You may have driven him to kill himself
but you didn't kill him."

"What the hell are you talking about?" asked
Flannagan gruffly.

"Better a simple if messy domestic tragedy
than a far wider investigation, wouldn't you say?
I gather it's no secret that you two have an arrangement that's—well, no secret."

"He didn't give a shit about our 'arrangement,' and that was no secret, either."

"He encouraged us at every opportunity,"
added Rachel Swayne, hesitantly smoothing
her skirt, oddly, swiftly regaining her composure.
She spoke to Bourne but her eyes strayed to her
lover. "He consistently threw us together, often
for days at a time. . . . Do we *have* to stay in
here? My *God*, I was married to that man for

twenty-six years! I'm sure you can understand
. . . this is *horrible* for me!"

"We have things to discuss," said Bourne.

"Not in *here*, if you please. The living room;
it's across the hall. We'll talk there." Mrs.
Swayne, suddenly under control, walked out of
the study; the general's aide glanced over at the
blood-drenched corpse, grimaced, and followed
her.

Jason watched them. "Stay in the hallway
where I can see you and don't move!" he
shouted, crossing to the desk, his eyes darting
from one object to another, taking in the last
items Norman Swayne saw before placing the
automatic in his mouth. Something was wrong.
On the right side of the wide green blotter was
a Pentagon memorandum pad, Swayne's rank
and name printed below the insignia of the
United States Army. Next to the pad, to the left
of the blotter's leather border, was a gold ballpoint pen, its sharp silver point protruding, as if
recently used, the writer forgetting to twist it
back into its recess. Bourne leaned over the
desk within inches of the dead body, the acrid
smell of the exploded shell and burnt flesh still
pungent, and studied the memo pad. It was
blank, but Jason carefully tore off the top pages,

folded them, and put them into his trousers pocket. He stepped back still bothered. . . . What was it? He looked around the room, and as his eyes roamed over the furniture Master Sergeant Flannagan appeared in the doorway.

"What are you doing?" Flannagan asked suspiciously. "We're waiting for you."

"Your friend may find it too difficult to stay in here, but I don't. I can't afford to, there's too much to learn."

"I thought you said we shouldn't touch anything."

"Looking isn't touching, Sergeant. Unless you remove something, then no one knows it's been touched because it isn't here." Bourne suddenly walked over to an ornate brass-topped coffee table, the sort so common in the bazaars of India and the Middle East. It was between two armchairs in front of the study's small fireplace; off center was a fluted glass ashtray partially filled with the remains of half-smoked cigarettes. Jason reached down and picked it up; he held it in his hand and turned to Flannagan. "For instance, Sergeant, this ashtray. I've touched it, my fingerprints are on it, but no one will know that because I'm taking it away."

"What for?"

"Because I smelled something—I mean I really smelled it, with my nose, nothing to do with instincts."

"What the hell are you talking about?"

"Cigarette smoke, that's what I'm talking about. It hangs around a lot longer than you might think. Ask someone who's given them up more times than he can remember."

"So what?"

"So let's have a talk with the general's wife. Let's all have a talk. Come on, Flannagan, we'll play show and tell."

"That weapon in your pocket makes you pretty fuckin' brave, doesn't it?"

"*Move,* Sergeant!"

Rachel Swayne swung her head to her left, throwing back her long, dark streaked hair over her shoulder as she stiffened her posture in the chair. "That's offensive in the extreme," she pronounced with wide accusatory eyes, staring at Bourne.

"It certainly is," agreed Jason, nodding. "It also happens to be true. There are five cigarette butts in this ashtray and each has lipstick on it." Bourne sat down across from her, putting the ashtray on the small table next to the chair. "You were there when he did it, when he put his gun into his mouth and pulled the trigger. Perhaps you didn't think he'd go through with it; maybe you thought it was just another one of his hysterical threats—whatever, you didn't raise a word to stop him. Why should you have? For you and *Eddie* it was a logical and reasonable solution."

"Preposterous!"

"You know, Mrs. Swayne, to put it bluntly, that's not a word you should use. You can't carry it off, any more than you're convincing when you say something's 'offensive in the extreme.' . . . Neither expression is you, Rachel. You're imitating other people—probably rich, vacuous customers a young hairdresser heard repeating such phrases years ago in Honolulu."

"How *dare* you . . . ?"

"Oh, come on, that's ridiculous, Rachel. Don't even try the 'How dare you' bit, it doesn't work at all. Are you, in your nasal twang, going to have my head chopped off by royal decree?"

"Lay *off* her!" shouted Flannagan, standing beside Mrs. Swayne. "You got the iron but you don't have to do this! . . . She's a good woman, a *damn* good woman, and she was shit on by all the crap artists in this town."

"How could she be? She was the *general's* wife, the mistress of the manor, wasn't she? *Isn't* she?"

"She was *used*—"

"I was laughed at, always laughed at, Mr. Delta!" cried Rachel Swayne, gripping the arms of her chair. "When they weren't leering or drooling. How'd *you* like to be the special piece of meat passed out like a special dessert to *very* special people when the dinner and the drinks are over?"

"I don't think I'd like it at all. I might even refuse."

"I *couldn't*! He made me *do* it!"

"Nobody can make anybody do anything like that."

"Sure, they can, Mr. Delta," said the general's wife, leaning forward, her large breasts pressing the sheer fabric of her blouse, her long hair partially obscuring her aging but still sensual soft-featured face. "Try an uneducated grammar school dropout from the coal basins in West Virginia when the companies shut down the mines and nobody had no food—excuse me, *any* food. You take what you got and you run with it and that's what I did. I got laid from Aliquippa to Hawaii, but I got there and I learned a trade. That's where I met the Big Boy and I married him, but I didn't have no illusions from day *one*. 'Specially when he got back from 'Nam, y'know what I mean?''

"I'm not sure I do, Rachel."

"You don't have to explain *nothin'*, kiddo!" roared Flannagan.

"No, I wanna, Eddie! I'm sick of the whole shit, *okay*?''

"You watch your tongue!"

"The point is, I don't *know* nothin', Mr. Delta. But I can figure things, y'know what I mean?''

"*Stop* it, Rachel!" cried the dead general's aide.

"Fuck off, Eddie! You're not too bright either. This Mr. Delta could be our way out. . . . Back to the islands, *right*?''

"Absolutely right, Mrs. Swayne."

"You know what this place is—?''

"Shut *up*!" yelled Flannagan, awkwardly plodding forward, stopped by the sudden ear-shattering explosion of Bourne's gun, the bullet searing into the floor between the sergeant's legs.

The woman screamed. When she stopped, Jason continued: "What is this place, Mrs. Swayne?''

"*Hold* it," the master sergeant again interrupted, but his objection was not shouted now; instead, it was a plea, a strong man's plea. He looked at the general's wife and then back at Jason. "Listen, Bourne or Delta or whoever you are, Rachel's right. You could be our way out—there's nothing left for us over here—so what have you got to offer?"

"For what?"

"Say we tell you what we know about this place . . . and *I* tell you where you can start looking for a lot more. How can you help us? How can we get out of here and back to the Pac Islands without being hassled, our names and faces all over the papers?"

"That's a tall order, Sergeant."

"Goddamn it, she didn't *kill* him—*we* didn't kill him, you said so yourself!"

"Agreed, and I couldn't care less whether you did or not, whether you were responsible or not. I've got other priorities."

"Like getting 'caught up with some old comrades' or whatever the hell it was?"

"That's right, I'm owed."

"I still can't figure you—"

"You don't have to."

"You were dead!" broke in the perplexed Flannagan, the words rushing out. "Delta One from the illegals was *Bourne*, and Bourne was *dead* and Langley proved it to us! But you're *not* dead—"

"I was *taken*, Sergeant! That's all you have to know—that and the fact that I'm working alone. I've got a few debts I can call in, but I'm strictly solo. I need information and I need it quickly!"

Flannagan shook his head in bewilderment. "Well . . . maybe I can help you there," he said quietly, tentatively, "better than anyone else would. I was given a special assignment, so I had to learn things, things someone like me wouldn't normally be told."

"That sounds like the opening notes of a con song, Sergeant. What was your special assignment?"

"Nursemaid. Two years ago Norman began to fall apart. I controlled him, and if I couldn't I was given a number to call in New York."

"Said number being part of the help you can give me."

"That and a few license-plate ID's I wrote down just in case—"

"In case," completed Bourne, "someone decided your nursemaid's services were no longer required."

"Something like that. Those pricks never liked us—Norman didn't see it but I did."

"Us? You and Rachel and Swayne?"

"The *uniform*. They look down their rich civilian noses at us like we're necessary garbage, and they're right about the necessary. They needed Norman. With their eyes they spat on him, but they needed him."

The soldier boys couldn't run with it. Albert Armbruster, chairman of the Federal Trade Commission. Medusa—the civilian inheritors.

"When you say you wrote down the license-plate numbers, I assume that means you weren't part of the meetings that took place— *take* place—here on a fairly regular basis. That is, you didn't mingle with the guests; you weren't one of them."

"Are you *crazy*?" screeched Rachel Swayne, in her own succinct way answering Jason's question. "Whenever there was a real meeting and not a lousy drunken dinner party, Norm told me to stay upstairs, or if I wanted to, go over to Eddie's and watch television. Eddie couldn't leave the cabin. We weren't *good* enough for his big fancy asshole friends! It's been that way for years. . . . Like I said, he threw us together."

"I'm beginning to understand—at least, I think I am. But you got the license numbers, Sergeant. How did you do that? I gather you were confined to quarters."

"I didn't get 'em, my guards did. I called it a confidential security procedure. No one argued."

"I see. You said Swayne began to fall apart a couple of years ago. How? In what way?"

"Like tonight. Whenever something out of the ordinary happened, he'd freeze; he didn't want to make decisions. If it even smacked of Snake Lady, he wanted to bury his head in the sand until it went away."

"What *about* tonight? I saw you two arguing . . . it seemed to me the sergeant was giving the general his marching orders."

"You're damn right I was. Norman was in a panic—over you, over the man they called Cobra who was bringing out this heavy business about Saigon twenty years ago. He wanted me to be with him when you got here, and I told him no way. I said I wasn't nuts and I'd have to be nuts to do that."

"Why? Why would it be nuts for an aide to be with his superior officer?"

"For the same reason noncoms aren't called into situation rooms where the stars and the stripers are figuring out strategy. We're on different levels; it isn't done."

"Which is another way of saying there are limits to what you should know."

"You got it."

"But you were part of that Saigon twenty years ago, part of Snake Lady—hell, Sergeant, you were *Medusa,* you *are* Medusa."

"Nickels and dimes' worth, Delta. I sweep up and they take care of me, but I'm only a sweeper in a uniform. When my time comes to turn in that uniform, I go quietly into a nice distant retirement with my mouth shut, or I go out in a body bag. It's all very clear. I'm expendable."

Bourne watched the master sergeant closely as he spoke, noting Flannagan's brief glances at the general's wife, as if he expected to be applauded or, conversely, to be told with a look to shut up. Either the huge military aide was telling the truth or he was a very convincing actor. "Then it strikes me," said Jason finally, "that this is a logical time to move up your retirement. I can do that, Sergeant. You can fade quietly with your mouth shut and with whatever rewards you're given for sweeping up. A devoted general's aide with over thirty years' service opts for retirement when his friend and superior tragically takes his own life. No one will question you. . . . That's my offer."

Flannagan again looked at Rachel Swayne; she nodded sharply once, then stared at Bourne. "What's the guarantee that we can pack up our stuff and get out?" asked the woman.

"Isn't there a little matter of Sergeant Flannagan's discharge and his army pension?"

"I made Norman sign those papers eighteen months ago," broke in the aide. "I was posted permanently to his office at the Pentagon and billeted to his residence. I just have to fill in the date, sign my own name, and list a general delivery address, which Rachel and I already figured out."

"That's all?"

"What's left is maybe three or four phone calls. Norman's lawyer, who'll wrap up everything here; the kennels for the dogs; the Pentagon assigned-vehicle dispatcher—and a last call to New York. Then it's Dulles Airport."

"You must have thought about this for a long time, for years—"

"Nothing but, Mr. Delta," confirmed the general's wife, interrupting. "Like they say, we paid our dues."

"But before I can sign those papers or make those calls," added Flannagan, "I have to know we can break clean—now."

"Meaning no police, no newspapers, no involvement with tonight—you simply weren't here."

"You said it's a tall order. How tall are the debts you can call in?"

"You simply weren't here," repeated Bourne softly, slowly, looking at the fluted glass ashtray with the lipstick-stained cigarette butts on the table beside him. He pulled his eyes back to the general's aide. "You didn't touch anything in there; there's nothing to physically tie you in with his suicide. . . . Are you really prepared to leave—say, in a couple of hours?"

"Try thirty minutes, Mr. Delta," replied Rachel.

"My God, you had a *life* here, both of you—"

"We don't want anything from this life outside of what we've got," said Flannagan firmly.

"The estate here is yours, Mrs. Swayne—"

"Like hell it is. It's being turned over to some foundation, ask the lawyer. Whatever I get, *if* I get, he'll send on to me. I just want out—we want out."

Jason looked back and forth at the strange and strangely drawn-together couple. "Then there's nothing to stop you."

"How do we *know* that?" pressed Flannagan, stepping forward.

"It'll take a measure of trust on your part, but, believe me, I can do it. On the other hand, look at the alternative. Say you stay here. No matter

what you do with *him*, he won't show up in Arlington tomorrow or the next day or the day after
that. Sooner or later someone's going to come
looking for him. There'll be questions, searches,
an investigation, and as sure as God made little
Bobby Woodwards, the media will descend with
its bellyful of speculations. In short order your
'arrangement' will be picked up—hell, even the
guards talked about it—and the newspapers,
the magazines and television will have a collective field day. . . . Do you want that? Or would it
all lead to that body bag you mentioned?"

The master sergeant and his lady stared at
each other. "He's right, Eddie," said the latter.
"With him we got a chance, the other way we
don't."

"It sounds too easy," said Flannagan, his
breath coming shorter as he glanced toward the
door. "How are you going to handle everything?"

"That's my business," answered Bourne.
"Give me the telephone numbers, all of them,
and then the only call you'll have to make is the
one to New York, and if I were you, I'd make it
from whatever Pac island you're on."

"You're *nuts*! The minute the news breaks,
I'm on Medusa's rug—so's Rachel! They're
going to want to know what happened."

"Tell them the truth, at least a variation of it, and I think you may even get a bonus."

"You're a goddamned flake!"

"I wasn't a flake in 'Nam, Sergeant. Nor was I in Hong Kong, and I'm certainly not now. . . . You and Rachel came home, saw what had happened, packed up and left—because you didn't want any questions and the dead can't talk and trap themselves. Predate your papers by a day, mail them, and leave the rest to me."

"I dunno—"

"You don't have a *choice*, Sergeant!" shot back Jason, rising from the chair. "And I don't care to waste any more time! You want me to go, I'll *go*—figure it all out for yourselves." Bourne angrily started for the door.

"No, Eddie, *stop* him! We gotta do it his way, we gotta take the chance! The other way we're dead and you know it."

"All *right*, all right! . . . Cool it, Delta. We'll do what you say."

Jason stopped and turned. "*Everything* I say, Sergeant, down to the letter."

"You got it."

"First, you and I will go over to your place while Rachel goes upstairs and packs. You'll give me everything you've got—telephone and license numbers, every name you can remember, anything you can give me that I ask for. Agreed?"

"Yeah."

"Let's go. And Mrs. Swayne, I know that there are probably a lot of little things you'd like to take along, but—"

"*Forget* it, Mr. Delta. Mementos I don't have. Whatever I really wanted was long since shipped out of this hell hole. It's all in storage ten thousand miles away."

"My, you really were prepared, weren't you?"

"Tell me something I don't know. You see, the time had to come, one way or the other, y'know what I mean?" Rachel walked rapidly past the two men and into the hall; she stopped and came back to Master Sergeant Flannagan, a smile on her lips, a glow in her eyes, as she placed her hand on his face. "Hey, Eddie," she said quietly. "It's really gonna happen. We're gonna *live*, Eddie. Y'know what I mean?"

"Yeah, babe. I know."

As they walked out into the darkness toward the cabin, Bourne spoke. "I meant what I said about not wasting time, Sergeant. Start talking. What were you going to tell me about Swayne's place here?"

"Are you ready?"

"What does that mean? Of course I'm ready." But he wasn't. He stopped suddenly on the grass at Flannagan's words.

"For openers, it's a cemetery."

Alex Conklin sat back in the desk chair, the phone in his hand, stunned, frowning, unable to summon a rational response to Jason's astonishing information. All he could say was "I don't *believe* it!"

"Which part?"

"I don't know. Everything, I guess . . . the cemetery on down. But I have to believe it, don't I?"

"You didn't want to believe London or Brussels, either, or a commander of the Sixth Fleet or the keeper of the covert keys in Langley. I'm just adding to the list. . . . The point is, once you find out who they all are, we can *move*."

"You'll have to start from the beginning again; my head's shredded. The telephone number in New York, the license plates—"

"The *body*, Alex! Flannagan and the general's *wife*! They're on their way; that was the deal and you've got to cover it."

"Just like that? Swayne kills himself and the two people on the premises who can answer questions, we say *Ciao* to them and let them get away? That's only slightly more lunatic than what you've told me!"

"We don't have time for negotiating games— and besides, he can't answer any more questions. They were on different levels."

"Oh, boy, that's really clear."

"Do it. Let them go. We may need them both later."

Conklin sighed, his indecision apparent. "Are you sure? It's very complicated."

"*Do* it! For Christ's sake, Alex, I don't give a goddamn about complications or violations or all the manipulations you can dream up! I want *Carlos*! We're building a net and we can pull him *in*—*I* can pull him in!"

"All right, all right. There's a doctor in Falls Church that we've used before in special operations. I'll get hold of him, he'll know what to do."

"Good," said Bourne, his mind racing. "Now put me on tape. I'll give you everything Flannagan gave me. Hurry up, I've got a lot to do."

"You're on tape, Delta One."

Reading from the list he had written down in Flannagan's cabin, Jason spoke rapidly, enunciating clearly so that there would be no confusion on the tape. There were the names of seven frequent and acknowledged guests at the general's dinner parties, none guaranteed as to accuracy or spelling but with broad-brush descriptions; then came the license plates, all from the far more serious twice-monthly meetings. Next to last were the telephone numbers of Swayne's lawyer, all of the estate's guards, the dog kennels and the Pentagon extension for assigned vehicles; finally there was the unlisted telephone in New York, no name here, only a machine that took messages. "That's got to be a priority one, Alex."

"We'll break it," said Conklin, inserting himself on the tape. "I'll call the kennels and talk Pentagonese—the general's being flown to a hush-factor post and we pay double for getting the animals out first thing in the morning. Open the gates, incidentally. . . . The licenses are no problem and I'll have Casset run the names through the computers behind DeSole's back."

"What about Swayne? We've got to keep the suicide quiet for a while."

"How long?"

"How the hell do I know?" replied Jason, exasperated. "Until we find out who they all are

and I can reach them—or you can reach them—
and together we can start the wave of panic
rolling. That's when we plant the Carlos solution."

"Words," said Conklin, his tone not flattering.
"You could be talking about days, maybe a
week or even longer."

"Then that's what I'm *talking* about."

"Then we'd better damn well bring in Peter
Holland—"

"No, not yet. We don't know what he'd do and
I'm not giving him the chance to get in my way."

"You've got to trust someone besides me,
Jason. I can fool the doctor perhaps for twenty-
four or forty-eight hours—*perhaps*—but I doubt
much longer than that. He'll want higher authorization. And don't forget, I've got Casset breathing down my neck over DeSole—"

"Give me two days, *get* me two days!"

"While tracking down all this information and
stalling Charlie, and lying through my teeth to
Peter, telling them that we're making progress
running down the Jackal's possible couriers at
the Mayflower hotel—we *think* . . . Of course,
we're doing nothing of the sort because we're
up to our credentials in some off-the-wall,
twenty-year-old Saigon conspiracy involving

who knows *what*, damned if we know, except that the *who* is terribly impressive. Without going into statuses—or is it *statae*—we're now told they have their own private cemetery on the grounds of the general officer in charge of Pentagon procurements, who just happened to blow his head off, a minor incident we're sitting on. . . . *Jesus,* Delta, back up! The missiles are colliding!''

Though he was standing in front of Swayne's desk, the general's corpse in the chair beside him, Bourne managed a tentative, slow smile. "That's what we're counting on, isn't it? It's a scenario that could have been written by our beloved Saint Alex himself.''

"I'm only along for the ride, I'm not steering—''

"What about the doctor?'' interrupted Jason. "You've been out of operation for almost five years. How do you know he's still in business?''

"I run into him now and then; we're both museum mavens. A couple of months ago at the Corcoran Gallery he complained that he wasn't given much to do these days.''

"Change that tonight.''

"I'll try. What are you going to do?''

"Delicately pull apart everything in this room.''

"Gloves?"

"Surgical, of course."

"Don't touch the body."

"Only the pockets—very delicately. . . . Swayne's wife is coming down the stairs. I'll call you back when they're gone. Get hold of that *doctor*!"

Ivan Jax, M.D. by way of Yale Medical School, surgical training and residency at Massachusetts General, College of Surgeons by appointment, Jamaican by birth, and erstwhile "consultant" to the Central Intelligence Agency courtesy of a fellow black man with the improbable name of Cactus, drove through the gates of General Swayne's estate in Manassas, Virginia. There were times, thought Ivan, when he wished he had never met old Cactus and this was one of them, but tonight notwithstanding, he never regretted that Cactus had come into his life. Thanks to the old man's "magic papers," Jax had gotten his brother and sister out of Jamaica during the repressive Manley years when established professionals were all but prohibited from emigrating and certainly not with personal funds.

Cactus, however, using complex mock-ups of government permits had sprung both young adults out of the country along with bank transfers honored in Lisbon. All the aged forger requested were stolen blank copies of various official documents, including import/export bills of lading, the two people's passports, separate photographs and copies of several signatures belonging to certain men in positions of authority—easily obtainable through the hundreds of bureaucratic edicts published in the government-controlled press. Ivan's brother was currently a wealthy barrister in London and his sister a research fellow at Cambridge.

Yes, he owed Cactus, thought Dr. Jax as he swung his station wagon around the curve to the front of the house, and when the old man had asked him to "consult" with a few "friends over in Langley" seven years ago, he had obliged. Some consultation! Still, there were further perks forthcoming in Ivan's silent association with the intelligence agency. When his island home threw out Manley, and Seaga came to power, among the first of the "appropriated" properties to be returned to their rightful owners were the Jax family's holdings in Montego Bay and Port Antonio. That had been Alex Conklin's doing, but without Cactus there would have been no Conklin, not in Ivan's circle of friends. . . . But why did Alex have to call *tonight?* Tonight was his twelfth wedding anniversary, and he had sent the kids on an overnight with the neighbors' children so that he and his wife could be alone, alone with grilled Jamaic' ribs on the patio—prepared by the only one who knew how, namely, Chef Ivan—a lot of good dark Overton rum, and some highly erotic skinny-dipping in the pool. *Damn* Alex! Double damn the son-of-a-bitch bachelor who could only respond to the event of a wedding anniversary by saying, "What the hell? You made the year, so what's a day count? Get your jollies tomorrow, I need you tonight."

So he had lied to his wife, the former head nurse at Mass. General. He told her that a patient's life was in the balance—it was, but it had already tipped the wrong way. She had replied that perhaps her next husband would be more considerate of *her* life, but her sad smile and her understanding eyes denied her words. She knew death. *Hurry, my darling!*

Jax turned off the engine, grabbed his medical bag and got out of the car. He walked around the hood as the front door opened and a tall man in what appeared to be dark skin-tight clothing stood silhouetted in the frame. "I'm your doctor," said Ivan, walking up the steps. "Our mutual friend didn't give me your name, but I guess I'm not supposed to have it."

"I guess not," agreed Bourne, extending a hand in a surgical glove as Jax approached.

"And I guess we're both right," said Jax, shaking hands with the stranger. "The mitt you're wearing is pretty familiar to me."

"Our mutual friend didn't tell me you were black."

"Is that a problem for you?"

"Good Christ, no. I like our friend even more. It probably never occurred to him to say anything."

"I think we'll get along. Let's go, no-name."

Bourne stood ten feet to the right of the desk as Jax swiftly, expertly tended to the corpse, mercifully wrapping the head in gauze. Without explaining, he had cut away sections of the general's clothing, examining those parts of the body beneath the fabric. Finally, he carefully rolled the hooded body off the chair and onto the floor. "Are you finished in here?" he asked, looking over at Jason.

"I've swept it clean, Doctor, if that's what you mean."

"It usually is. . . . I want this room sealed. No one's to enter it after we leave until our mutual friend gives the word."

"I certainly can't guarantee that," said Bourne.

"Then he'll have to."

"Why?"

"Your general didn't commit suicide, no-name. He was murdered."

12

"The woman," said Alex Conklin over the line. "From everything you told me it had to be Swayne's wife. *Jesus!*"

"It doesn't change anything, but it looks that way," agreed Bourne halfheartedly. "She had reason enough to do it, God knows—still, if she did, she didn't tell Flannagan, and *that* doesn't make sense."

"No, it doesn't. . . ." Conklin paused, then spoke quickly. "Let me talk to Ivan."

"Ivan? Your doctor? His name is Ivan?"

"So?"

"Nothing. He's outside . . . 'packing the merchandise' was the way he put it."

"In his wagon?"

"That's right. We carried the body—"

"What makes him so sure it *wasn't* suicide?" broke in Alex.

"Swayne was drugged. He said he'd call you later and explain. He wants to get out of here and no one's to come into this room after we leave—after I leave—until you give the word for the police. He'll tell you that, too."

"Christ, it must be a mess in there."

"It's not pretty. What do you want me to do?"

"Pull the curtains, if there are any; check the windows and, if possible, lock the door. If there's no way to lock it, look around for—"

"I found a set of keys in Swayne's pocket," interrupted Jason. "I checked; one of them fits."

"Good. When you leave, wipe the door down clean. Find some furniture polish or a dusting spray."

"That's not going to keep out anyone who wants to get in."

"No, but if someone does, we might pick up a print."

"You're reaching—"

"I certainly am," concurred the former intelligence officer. "I've also got to figure out a way to seal up the whole place without using anybody from Langley, *and,* not incidentally, keep the Pentagon at bay just in case someone among those twenty-odd thousand people want to reach Swayne, and that includes his office and probably a couple of hundred buyers and sellers *a day* in procurements. . . . Christ, it's *impossible*!"

"It's perfect," contradicted Bourne as Dr. Ivan Jax suddenly appeared in the doorway. "Our little game of destabilization will start right here on the 'farm.' Do you have Cactus's number?"

"Not with me. I think it's probably in a shoe-box at home."

"Call Mo Panov, he's got it. Then reach Cactus and tell him to get to a pay phone and call me here."

"What the hell have you got in mind? I hear that old man's name, I get nervous."

"You told me I had to find someone else to trust besides you. I just did. Reach him, Alex." Jason hung up the telephone. "I'm sorry, Doctor . . . or maybe under the circumstances I can use your name. Hello, Ivan."

"Hello, *no*-name, which is the way I'd like to keep it on my end. Especially when I just heard you say another name."

"Alex? . . . No, of course it wasn't Alex, not our

mutual friend." Bourne laughed quietly, knowingly, as he walked away from the desk. "It was
Cactus, wasn't it?"

"I just came in to ask you if you wanted me to
close the gates," said Jax, bypassing the question.

"Would you be offended if I told you that I
didn't think of him until I saw you just now?"

"Certain associations are fairly obvious. The
gates, please?"

"Do you owe Cactus as much as I do, Doctor?" Jason held his place, looking at the Jamaican.

"I owe him so much that I could never think
of compromising him in a situation like tonight.
For God's sake, he's an old man, and no matter
what deviant conclusions Langley wants to
come up with, tonight was *murder*, a particularly
brutal killing. No, I wouldn't involve him."

"You're not me. You see, I have to. He'd
never forgive me if I didn't."

"You don't think much of yourself, do you?"

"Please close the gates, Doctor. There's an
alarm panel in the hallway I can activate when
they're shut."

Jax hesitated, as if unsure of what he wanted
to say. "Listen," he began haltingly, "most sane

people have reasons for saying things—doing things. My guess is you're sane. Call Alex if you need me—if old Cactus needs me." The doctor left, rushing out the door.

Bourne turned and glanced around the room. Since Flannagan and Rachel Swayne had left nearly three hours ago, he had searched every foot of the general's study, as well as the dead soldier's separate bedroom on the second floor. He had placed the items he intended to take on the brass coffee table; he studied them now. There were three brown leather-bound covers, each equal in size, each holding inserted spiral-bound pages; they were a desk set. The first was an appointments calendar; the second, a personal telephone book in which the names and numbers were entered in ink; the last was an expense diary, barely touched. Along with these were eleven office messages of the tele-phone notepad variety, which Jason found in Swayne's pockets, a golf-club scorecard and several memoranda written at the Pentagon. Fi-nally, there was the general's wallet containing a profusion of impressive credentials and very little money. Bourne would turn everything over to Alex and hope further leads would be found, but as far as he could determine, he had turned up nothing startling, nothing dramatically relevant to the modern Medusa. And that bothered him; there had to be *something*. This was the old soldier's home, his sanctum sanctorum inside that home—something! He knew it, he felt it, but he could not find it. So he started again, not foot by foot now; instead, inch by inch.

Fourteen minutes later, as he was removing and turning over the photographs on the wall behind the desk, the wall to the right of the cushioned bay window that overlooked the lawn outside, he recalled Conklin's words about checking the windows and the curtains so that no one could enter or observe the scene inside.

Christ, it must be a mess in there.

It's not very pleasant.

It wasn't. The panes of the central bay window frame were splattered with blood and membrane. And the . . . the small brass *latch*? Not only was it free from its catch, the window itself was open—barely open, but nevertheless it *was open*. Bourne knelt on the cushioned seat and looked closely at the shiny brass fixture and the surrounding panes of glass. There were smudges among the rivulets of dried blood and tissue, coarse pressings on the stains that appeared to widen and thin them out into irregular shapes. Then below the sill he saw what kept the window from closing. The end of the left drape had been drawn out, a small piece of its tasseled fabric wedged beneath the lower window frame. Jason stepped back bewildered but not really surprised. This was what he had been looking for, the missing piece in the complex puzzle that was the death of Norman Swayne.

Someone had climbed out that window *after* the shot that blew the general's skull apart. Someone who could not risk being seen going through the front hall or out the front door. Someone who knew the house and the grounds . . . and the dogs. A brutal killer from Medusa. *Goddamn* it!

Who? Who had been here? Flannagan . . . Swayne's wife! They would know, they *had* to know! Bourne lurched for the telephone on the desk; it began ringing before his hand touched it.

"Alex?"

"No, Br'er Rabbit, it's just an old friend, and I didn't realize we were so free with names."

"We're not, we shouldn't be," said Jason rapidly, imposing a control on himself he could barely exercise. "Something happened a moment ago—I found something."

"Calm down, boy. What can I do for you?"

"I need you—out here where I am. Are you free?"

"Well, let's see." Cactus chuckled as he spoke. "There are several board meetings I should rightfully attend, and the White House wants me for a power breakfast. . . . When and where, Br'er Rabbit?"

"Not alone, old friend. I want three or four others with you. Is that possible?"

"I don't know. What did you have in mind?"

"That fellow who drove me into town after I saw you. Are there any other like-minded citizens in the neighborhood?"

"Most are doin' time, frankly, but I suppose I could dig around the refuse and pull up a few. What for?"

"Guard duty. It's pretty simple really. You'll be on the phone and they'll be behind locked gates telling people that it's private property, that visitors aren't welcome. Especially a few honkies probably in limousines."

"Now, that might appeal to the brothers."

"Call me back and I'll give you directions." Bourne disconnected the line and immediately released the bar for a dial tone. He touched the numbers for Conklin's phone in Vienna.

"Yes?" answered Alex.

"The doctor was right and I let our Snake Lady executioner get away!"

"Swayne's wife, you mean?"

"No, but she and her fast-talking sergeant know who it was—they had to know who was *here*! Pick them up and hold them. They lied to me, so the deal's off. Whoever staged this gruesome 'suicide' had orders from high up in Medusa. I want him. He's our shortcut."

"He's also beyond our reach."

"What the hell are you talking about?"

"Because the sergeant and his paramour are beyond our reach. They've disappeared."

"That's crazy? If I know Saint Alex, and I *do*, you've had them covered since they left here."

"Electronically, not physically. Remember, you insisted we keep Langley and Peter Holland away from Medusa."

"What did you do?"

"I sent out a full-toned alert to the central reservations computers of all international airline carriers. As of eight-twenty this evening our subjects had seats on Pan Am's ten o'clock flight to London—"

"London?" broke in Jason. "They were heading the other way, to the Pacific. To Hawaii!"

"That's probably where they're going because they never showed up at Pan Am. Who
knows?"

"Damn it, *you* should!"

"How? Two United States citizens flying to
Hawaii don't have to present passports to enter
our fiftieth state. A driver's license or a voter's
registration card will do. You told me that they've
been considering this move for quite a while.
How difficult would it be for a master sergeant
with over thirty years' service to get a couple of
driver's licenses using different names?"

"But *why*?"

"To throw off people looking for them—like
us, or maybe a few Medusans, very high up."

"Shit!"

"Would you care to talk less in the vulgate,
Professor? It was the 'vulgate,' wasn't it?"

"Shut up, I've got to think."

"Then think about the fact that we're up to our
asses in the Arctic without a heater. It's time for
Peter Holland. We need him. We need Langley."

"No, not *yet*! You're forgetting something.
Holland took an oath, and everything we know
about him says he took it seriously. He may
bend a rule now and then, but if he's faced with

a Medusa, with hundreds of millions out of Geneva buying up whatever they're buying up in Europe, he may say, 'Halt, that's enough!' "

"That's a risk we have to take. We *need* him, David."

"*Not* David, *goddamn* you! I'm Bourne, Jason Bourne, *your* creation, and I'm owed! My family is owed! I won't have it any other way!"

"And you'll kill me if I go against you."

Silence. Neither spoke until Delta One of Saigon's Medusa broke the pause. "Yes, Alex, I'll kill you. Not because you tried to kill me in Paris, but for the same blind assumptions you made back then that led to your decision to come after me. Can you understand that?"

"Yes," replied Conklin, his voice so low it was barely audible. "The arrogance of ignorance, it's your favorite Washington theme; you always make it sound so Oriental. But somewhere along the line you're going to have to be a little less arrogant yourself. There's only so much we can do alone."

"On the other hand, there's so much that can be loused up if we're *not* alone. Look at the progress we've made. From zero to double digits in how long—forty-eight, seventy-two hours? Give me the two days, Alex, *please*.

We're closing in on what this whole thing's about, what *Medusa's* all about. One breakthrough, and we present them with the perfect solution to get rid of me. The Jackal."

"I'll do the best I can. Did Cactus reach you?"

"Yes. He'll call me back and then come out here. I'll explain later."

"I should tell you. He and our doctor are friends."

"I know. Ivan told me. . . . Alex, I want to get some things over to you—Swayne's telephone book, his wallet, appointments schedule, stuff like that. I'll wrap it all up and have one of Cactus's boys deliver the package to your place, to the security gate. Put everything into your high tech and see what you can find."

"Cactus's boys? What are you doing?"

"Taking an item off your agenda. I'm sealing this place up. Nobody'll be able to get in, but we'll see who tries."

"That could be interesting. The kennel people are coming for the dogs around seven in the morning, incidentally, so don't make the seals too tight."

"Which reminds me," interrupted Jason. "Be official again and call the guards on the other shifts. Their services are no longer required, but each will receive a month's pay by mail in lieu of notice."

"Who the hell's going to pay it? There's no Langley, remember? No Peter Holland and I'm not independently wealthy."

"I am. I'll phone my bank in Maine and have them Fed Ex you a cashier's check. Ask your friend Casset to pick it up at your apartment in the morning."

"It's funny, isn't it?" said Conklin slowly, pensively. "I forgot about your money. I never think about it, actually. I guess I've blocked it out of my mind."

"That's possible," added Bourne, a trace of lightness in his voice. "The official part of you may have visions of some bureaucrat coming up to Marie and saying, 'By the way, Mrs. Webb or Bourne or whoever you are, while you were in the employ of the Canadian government you made off with over five million dollars belonging to mine.' "

"She was only brilliant, David—Jason. You were owed every dollar."

"Don't press the point, Alex. *She* claimed at least twice the amount."

"She was right. It's why everyone shut up. . . . What are you going to do now?"

"Wait for Cactus's call, then make one of my own."

"Oh?"

"To my wife."

Marie sat on the balcony of her villa at Tranquility Inn staring out at the moonlit Caribbean, trying with every controlling instinct in her not to go mad with fear. Strangely, perhaps stupidly or even dangerously, it was not the fear of physical harm that consumed her. She had lived in both Europe and the Far East with the killing machine that was Jason Bourne; she knew what that stranger was capable of and it was brutally efficient. No, it wasn't Bourne, it was David—what Jason Bourne was doing to David Webb. She had to *stop* it! . . . They could go away, far away, to some remote safe haven and start a new life with new names, create a world for themselves that Carlos could never penetrate. They had all the money they would ever need, they could *do* it! It was done all the time—hundreds, thousands of men and women and children whose lives were threatened were shielded by their governments; and if ever a government anywhere had reason to protect a man, that man was David Webb! . . . Thoughts conceived in frenzy, reflected Marie, getting up from her chair and walking to the balcony's railing. It would never happen because David could never accept the solution. Where the Jackal was concerned, David Webb was ruled by Jason Bourne and Bourne was capable of destroying his host body. Oh, *God,* what's *happening* to us?

The telephone rang. Marie stiffened, then rushed into the bedroom and picked it up. "Yes?"

"Hello, Sis, it's Johnny."

"Oh . . ."

"Which means you haven't heard from David."

"No, and I'm going a little crazy, Bro."

"He'll call when he can, you know that."

"But you're not calling to tell me that."

"No, I'm just checking in. I'm stuck over here on the big island and it looks like I'll be here for a while. I'm at Government House with Henry, waiting for the CG to personally thank me for accommodating the Foreign Office."

"I don't understand a word you're saying—"

"Oh, sorry. Henry Sykes is the Crown governor's aide who asked me to take care of that old French war hero down the path from you. When the CG wants to thank you, you wait until you're thanked—when the phones go out, cowboys like me need Government House."

"You've totally lost me, Johnny."

"A storm out of Basse-Terre will hit in a few hours."

"Out of *whom*?"

"It's a what, but I should be back before then. Have the maid make up the couch for me."

"John, it's not necessary for you to stay here. Good heavens, there are men with guns outside the hedge and down on the beach and God knows where else."

"That's where they're going to stay. See you later, and hug the kids for me."

"They're asleep," said Marie as her younger brother hung up. She looked at the phone as she replaced it, unconsciously saying out loud, "How little I know about you, little Bro . . . our favorite, incorrigible Bro. And how much more does my husband know. Damn the *both* of you!"

The telephone instantly rang again, stunning her. She grabbed it. "Hello?"

"It's me."

"Thank *God*!"

"*He's* out of town, but everything's fine. I'm fine, and we're making headway."

"You don't have to *do* this! *We* don't have to!"

"Yes, we do," said Jason Bourne—no evidence of David Webb. "Just know I love you, *he* loves you—"

"*Stop* it! It's *happening—*"

"I'm sorry, I apologize—*forgive* me."

"You're *David!*"

"Of course I'm David. I was just joking—"

"No, you *weren't!*"

"I was talking to Alex, that's all. We argued, that's *all!*"

"No, it *isn't!* I want you back, I want you *here!*"

"Then I can't talk any longer. I love you." The line went dead and Marie St. Jacques Webb fell on the bed, her cries of futility muffled by the blankets.

Alexander Conklin, his eyes red with strain, kept touching the letters and the numbers of his computer, his head turned to the open pages of the ledgers sent over by Bourne from General Norman Swayne's estate. Two shrill beeps suddenly intruded on the silence of the room. It was the inanimate machine's robotic signal that another dual reference had been calculated. He checked the entry. *R.G.* What did it mean? He back-taped and found nothing. He pressed forward, typing like a mindless automaton. *Three beeps.* He kept punching the irritatingly beige buttons, faster and faster. *Four beeps . . . five . . . six.* Back space—stop—forward. *R.G. R.G. R.G. R.G.* What the hell was *R.G.?*

He cross-checked the data with the entries from the three different leather-bound notebooks. A common numeral sprang out in green letters on the screen. *617-202-0011.* A telephone number. Conklin picked up the Langley phone, dialed the night watch, and told the CIA operator to trace it.

"It's unlisted, sir. It's one of three numbers for the same residence in Boston, Massachusetts."

"The name, please."

"Gates, Randolph. The residence is—"

"Never mind, Operator," interrupted Alex, knowing that he had been given the essential information. Randolph Gates, scholar, attorney for the privileged, advocate of the bigger the better, the biggest the best. How right that Gates should be involved with amassing hundreds of millions in Europe controlled by American interests. . . . No, wait a moment. It wasn't right at all, it was *wrong*! It was completely illogical for the scholarly attorney to have any con-

nection whatsoever to a highly questionable, indeed illegal, operation like Medusa. It did not
make sense! One did not have to admire the
celebrated legal giant to grant him just about the
cleanest record for propriety in the Bar Association. He was a notorious stickler for the most
minute points of law, often using those minutiae
of his craft to obtain favorable decisions, but no
one ever dared question his integrity. So un-
popular were his legal and philosophical opinions to the brightest lawyers in the liberal
establishment that he would have been gleefully
discredited years ago at the slightest hint of im-
propriety.

Yet here was his name appearing six times in
the appointments calendar of a Medusan responsible for untold millions in the nation's defense expenditures. An unstable Medusan
whose apparent suicide was in fact murder.

Conklin looked at the screen, at the date of
Swayne's last entry referring to R.G. It was on
August second, barely a week ago. He picked
up the leather-bound diary and turned to the
day. He had been concentrating on names, not
comments, unless the information struck him as
relevant—to what he was not sure, but he was
trusting to instinct. If he had known up front who

R.G. was, the abbreviated handwritten notation beside the last entry would have caught his eye.

RG will nt cnsider app't fr Maj. Crft. Need Crft on hs stff. Unlock. Paris—7 yrs ago. Two file out and bur'd.

The *Paris* should have alerted him, thought Alex, but Swayne's notes throughout were filled with foreign or exotic names and places as if the general had been trying to impress whoever might read his personal observations. Also, Conklin regretfully considered, he was terribly tired; were it not for his computer he probably would not have centered in on Dr. Randolph Gates, legal Olympian.

Paris—7 yrs ago. Two file out and bur'd.

The first part was obvious, the second obscure but hardly concealed. The "Two" referred to the army's intelligence arm, G-2, and the "file" was just that, an event or a revelation uncovered by intelligence personnel in *Paris—7 yrs ago* and removed from the data banks. It was an amateur's attempt to use intelligence gibberish by misusing it. "Unlock" meant "key"—*Jesus,* Swayne was an idiot! Using his notepad, Alex wrote out the notation as he knew it to be:

"Randolph Gates will not consider the appointment for a Major Craft or Croft or even Christopher, for the *f* could be an *s*. (But) we need Crft on his staff. The key is to use the information in our G-2 file about Gates in Paris seven years ago, said file removed and in our possession.''

If that was not the exact translation of Swayne's insertion, it was certainly close enough in substance to act upon, mused Conklin, turning his wrist and glancing at his watch. It was twenty past three in the morning, a time when even the most disciplined person would be shaken by the shrill bell of a telephone. Why not? David—*Jason*—was right. Every hour counted now. Alex picked up the phone and touched the numbers for Boston, Massachusetts.

The telephone kept ringing and the *bitch* would not pick it up in her room! Then Gates looked at the lighted square and the blood drained from his head. It was his unlisted number, a number that was restricted to a very few. He thrashed wildly in the bed, his eyes wide; the strange call from Paris unnerved him the more he thought about it. It concerned Montserrat, he *knew* it!

The information he had relayed was *wrong*.
. . . Prefontaine had *lied* to him and now Paris
wanted an accounting! My *God*, they'd come
after him, *expose* him! . . . No, there was a way,
a perfectly acceptable explanation, the *truth*. He
would deliver the liars to Paris, to Paris's man
here in Boston. He would trap the drunken Prefontaine and the sleazeball detective and force
them to tell their lies to the one person who
could absolve him. . . . The phone! He had to
answer it. He could not appear as if he had
anything to hide! He reached out and grabbed
the incessantly ringing instrument, pulling it to
his ear. "Yes?"

"Seven years ago, Counselor," began the
quiet voice on the line. "Do I have to remind you
that we've got the entire file. The Deuxième Bureau was extremely cooperative, far more than
you have been."

"For God's sake, I was *lied* to!" cried Gates,
swinging his legs onto the floor in panic, his
voice hoarse. "You can't *believe* I'd forward er-
roneous information. I'd have to be insane!"

"We know you can be obstinate. We made a
simple request—"

"I *complied*, I swear I did! Good Christ, I paid
fifteen thousand dollars to make certain every-

thing was silent, absolutely untraceable—not that the money matters, of course—''

"You *paid* . . . ?" interrupted the quiet voice.

"I can show you the bank withdrawals!"

"For what?"

"The information, naturally. I hired a former judge who has contacts—''

"For information about Craft?"

"What?"

"Croft. . . . Christopher."

"Who?"

"Our major, Counselor. *The* major."

"If that's her code name, then yes, yes I did!"

"A code name?"

"The woman. The two children. They flew to the island of Montserrat. I swear that's what I was *told*!"

There was a sudden click and the line went dead.

13

His hand still on the telephone, Conklin broke out in a sweat. He released the phone and got up from his chair, limping away from the computer, looking back at it, down at it, as if it were some monstrous thing that had taken him into a forbidden land where nothing was as it appeared to be or *should* be. What had *happened*? How did Randolph Gates know anything about Montserrat, about Marie and the children? *Why?*

Alex lowered himself into the armchair, his pulse racing, his thoughts clashing, no judgments emerging, only chaos. He gripped his right wrist with his left hand, his nails digging into his flesh. He had to get hold of himself, he had to *think*—he had to act! For David's wife and children.

Associations. What were the conceivable *associations*? It was difficult enough to consider Gates as even unwittingly a part of Medusa, but impossible to think he was also connected to Carlos the Jackal. *Impossible!* . . . Yet both appeared to *be*; the connections existed. Was Carlos himself part of Swayne's Medusa? Everything they knew about the Jackal would deny it emphatically. The assassin's strength was in his total *disassociation* with any structured entity, Jason Bourne had proved that thirteen years ago in Paris. No group of people could ever reach *him*; they could only send out a message and he would reach *them*. The single organization the international killer for hire permitted was his army of old men, from the Mediterranean to the Baltic, lost misfits, criminals whose impoverished last days were made better by the assassin's largess, fealty unto death demanded and received. Where did—*could*—a man like Randolph Gates fit in?

He didn't, concluded Alex as the outer limits of his imagination explored an old territory—Be skeptical of the apparent. The celebrated attorney was no more part of Carlos than he was of

Medusa. He was the aberration, the flaw in the lens, an otherwise honorable man with a single weakness that had been uncovered by two disparate parties both with extraordinary resources. It was common knowledge that the Jackal could reach into the Sûreté and Interpol, and it took no clairvoyance to assume that Medusa could penetrate the army's G-2. It was the only *possible* explanation, for Gates had been too controversial, too powerful for too long to function as spectacularly as he did in the courts if his vulnerability was easily uncovered. No, it would take predators like the Jackal and the men of Medusa to bore deep enough to dredge up a secret so devastating as to turn Randolph Gates into a valuable pawn. Clearly, Carlos had gotten to him first.

Conklin reflected on a truth that was forever reconfirmed: the world of global corrupters was in reality a small multilayered neighborhood, geometric in design, the irregular avenues of corruption leading into one another. How could it be otherwise? The residents of those lethal streets had services to offer, their clients were a specific breed—the desperate dregs of humanity. Extort, compromise, kill. The Jackal and the men of Medusa belonged to the same fraternal order. The Brotherhood of I Must Have Mine.

Breakthrough. But it was a breakthrough Jason Bourne could handle—not David Webb—and Webb was still too much a part of Bourne. Especially since both parts of the same man were over a thousand miles away from Montserrat, the coordinates of death determined by Carlos. *Montserrat?* . . . Johnny St. Jacques! The "little brother" who had proved himself in a backwater town in the northern regions of Canada, proved himself beyond the knowledge and the understanding of his family, especially his beloved sister. A man who could kill in anger—who had killed in fury—and who would kill again if the sister he adored and her children were under the Jackal's gun. David believed in him—Jason Bourne believed in him, which was far more to the point.

Alex looked over at the telephone console, then quickly got out of the chair. He rushed to the desk, sat down, and touched the buttons that rewound the current tape, adjusting it to the spot where he wanted to pick it up. He went forward and back until he heard Gates's panicked voice.

"*. . . Good Christ, I paid fifteen thousand—*"

No, not there, thought Conklin. Later.

"*. . . I can show you the bank withdrawals—*"

Later!

". . . I hired a former judge who has contacts—"

That's it. A judge.

". . . They flew to the island of Montserrat—"

Alex opened the drawer where he kept a sheet of paper with each number he had called during the past two days on the assumption that he might need specific ones quickly. He saw the number in the Caribbean for Tranquility Inn, picked up the phone and dialed. After more rings than seemed necessary, a voice thick with sleep answered.

"Tranquility—"

"This is an emergency," broke in Conklin. "It's urgent that I speak with John St. Jacques. Quickly, please."

"I'm sorry, sir, Mr. St. Jacques isn't here."

"I've got to find him. I repeat, it's urgent. Where is he?"

"On the big island—"

"Montserrat?"

"Yes—"

"*Where?* . . . My name's Conklin. He wants to talk to me—he *has* to talk to me. *Please!*"

"A big wind came up from Basse-Terre and all flights are canceled until morning."

"A what?"

"A tropical depression—"

"Oh, a storm."

"We prefer a TD, sir. Mr. St. Jacques left a telephone number in Plymouth."

"What's your name?" interrupted Alex suddenly. The clerk replied Pritchard and Conklin continued: "I'm going to ask you a very delicate question, Mr. Pritchard. It's important that you have the right answer, but if it's the wrong one you must do as I tell you. Mr. St. Jacques will confirm everything I say when I reach him; however, I can't waste time now. Do you understand me?"

"What is your question?" asked the clerk with dignity. "I'm not a child, *mon*."

"I'm sorry, I didn't mean to—"

"The question, Mr. Conklin. You're in a hurry."

"Yes, of course. . . . Mr. St. Jacques's sister and her children, are they in a safe place? Did Mr. St. Jacques take certain precautions?"

"Such as armed guards about the villa and our usual men down on the beach?" said the clerk. "The answer is yes."

"It's the right answer." Alex took a deep breath, his breathing still erratic. "Now, what's the number where I can reach Mr. St. Jacques?"

The clerk gave it to Conklin, then added,

"Many phones are out, sir. It might be well if you left a number here. The wind is still strong, but Mr. Saint Jay will no doubt come over with the first light if he can."

"Certainly." Alex rattled off the number of the sterile telephone in the Vienna apartment and had the man in Montserrat repeat it. "That's it," said Conklin. "I'll try Plymouth now."

"The spelling of your name, please. It is C-o-n-c-h—"

"C-o-n-*k*," broke in Alex, snapping off the line and instantly dialing the number in the town of Plymouth, the capital of Montserrat. Once again a startled, drowsy voice answered; it was a barely coherent greeting. "Who's this?" asked Conklin impatiently.

"Who the hell is *this*—are *you*?" replied an angry Englishman.

"I'm trying to reach John St. Jacques. It's an emergency, and I was given this number by the desk at Tranquility Inn."

"Good Lord, their phones are intact . . . ?"

"Obviously. *Please,* is John there?"

"Yes, yes, of course. He's across the hall, I'll fetch him. Who shall I say—"

" 'Alex' is good enough."

"Just 'Alex'?"

"Hurry, please!" Twenty seconds later the voice of John St. Jacques filled the line.

"*Conklin?* Is that *you*?"

"Listen to me. They know Marie and the children flew into Montserrat."

"We heard that someone was asking questions over at the airport about a woman and two kids—"

"Then that's why you moved them from the house to the inn."

"That's right."

"Who was asking questions?"

"We don't know. It was done by telephone. . . . I didn't want to leave them, even for a few hours, but I had a command appearance at Government House, and by the time that son-of-a-bitch Crown governor showed up, the storm hit."

"I know. I talked to the desk and got this number."

"That's one consolation; the phones are still working. In weather like this they usually don't, which is why we suck up to the Crown."

"I understand you've got guards—"

"You're goddamned right!" cried St. Jacques. "The trouble is I don't know what to look for except strangers in boats or on the beach, and

if they don't stop and identify themselves satis-
factorily, my orders are to shoot!"

"I may be able to help—"

"Go ahead!"

"We got a break—don't ask how; it's from
outer space but that doesn't matter, it's real.
The man who traced Marie to Montserrat used
a judge who had contacts, presumably in the
islands."

"A *judge*?" exploded the owner of Tranquility
Inn. "My God, he's there! Christ, he's *there*! I'll
kill that *scum* bastard—"

"*Stop* it, Johnny! Get hold of yourself—*who's*
there?"

"A judge, and he insisted on using a different *name*! I didn't think anything about it—a
couple of whack-a-doo old men with similar
names—"

"*Old men?* . . . Slow down, Johnny, this is
important. What two old men?"

"The one you're talking about is from Boston—"

"*Yes!*" confirmed Alex emphatically.

"The other flew in from Paris—"

"*Paris?* Jesus *Christ*! The old men of Paris!"
"What . . . ?"

"The Jackal! Carlos has his *old men* in place!"

"Now, *you* slow down, Alex," said St. Jacques, his breathing audible. "Now *you* be clearer."

"There's no time, Johnny. Carlos has an army—*his* army—of old men who'll die for him, *kill* for him. There won't be any strangers on the beach, they're already *there*! Can you get back to the island?"

"Somehow, yes! I'll call my people over there. Both those pieces of garbage will be thrown into the cisterns!"

"*Hurry,* John!"

St. Jacques pressed down the small bar of the old telephone, released it, and heard the forever-pulsating dial tone. He spun the numbers for the inn on Tranquility Isle.

"*We are sorry,*" said the recorded voice. "*Due to weather conditions the lines are down to the area you are calling. Government is working very hard to restore communications. Please try your call later. Have a good day.*"

John St. Jacques slammed the phone down with such force that he broke it in two. "A *boat!*" he screamed. "Get me a *drug* boat!"

"You're crazy," objected the aide to the

Crown governor across the room. "In these swells?"

"A sea streak, Henry!" said the devoted brother, reaching into his belt and slowly pulling out an automatic. "Or I'll be forced to do something I don't even want to think about, but I'll get a boat."

"I simply can't believe this, chap."

"Neither can I, Henry. . . . I mean it, though."

Jean Pierre Fontaine's nurse sat at her dressing table in front of the mirror and adjusted her tightly knotted blond hair under the black rain hat. She looked at her watch, recalling every word of the most unusual telephone call she had received several hours ago from Argenteuil in France, from the great man who made all things possible.

"There is an American attorney who calls himself a judge staying near you."

"I know of no such person, monseigneur."

"He is there, nevertheless. Our hero rightfully complains of his presence, and a call to his home in the city of Boston confirms that it is he."

"His presence here is not desirable, then?"

"His presence there is abominable to me. He

pretends to be in my debt—an enormous debt, an event that could destroy him—yet his actions tell me that he's ungrateful, that he intends to cancel his debt by betraying me, and by betraying me he betrays you."

"He's dead."

"Exactly. In the past he's been valuable to me, but the past is over. Find him, kill him. Make his death appear to be a tragic accident. . . . Finally, since we will not speak until you are back on Martinique, are preparations complete for your last act on my behalf?"

"They are, monseigneur. The two syringes were prepared by the surgeon at the hospital in Fort-de-France. He sends you his devotion."

"He should. He's alive, as opposed to several dozen of his patients."

"They know nothing of his other life in Martinique."

"I'm aware of that. . . . Administer the doses in forty-eight hours, when the chaos has begun to subside. Knowing that the hero was my invention—which I'll make sure they know—will put a chameleon to shame."

"All will be done. You'll be here soon?"

"In time for the shock waves. I'm leaving within the hour and will reach Antigua before it's noon in Montserrat tomorrow. All things being on schedule, I'll arrive in time to observe the exquisite anguish of Jason Bourne before I leave my signature, a bullet in his throat. The Americans will then know who has won. *Adieu.*"

The nurse, like an ecstatic suppliant, arched her neck in front of the mirror remembering the mystical words of her omniscient lord. It was nearly time, she thought, opening the dresser drawer and picking out a diamond-clustered wire garrote from among her necklaces, a gift from her mentor. It would be so simple. She had easily learned who the judge was and where he was staying—the old, painfully thin man three villas away. Everything now was precision, the "tragic accident" merely a prelude to the horror that would take place at Villa Twenty in less than an hour. For all of Tranquility's villas had kerosene lamps in the event of electricity loss and generator malfunction. A panicked old man with loose bowels, or in plain fear, living through such a storm as they were experiencing, might well attempt to light a lamp for additional comfort. How tragic that his upper body would fall into the flowing spilled kerosene, his neck scorched into black tissue, the neck that had been garroted. *Do it,* insisted the echoing voices of her imagination. *You must obey. Without Carlos you would have been a headless corpse in Algeria.*

She would do it—she would do it now.

The harsh downpour of the rain on the roof and the windows, and the whistling, roaring wind outside were interrupted by a blinding streak of lightning followed by a deafening crack of thunder.

"Jean Pierre Fontaine" wept silently as he knelt beside the bed, his face inches from his woman's, his tears falling on the cold flesh of her arm. She was dead, and the note by her white rigid hand said it all: *Maintenant nous deux sommes libres, mon amour.*

They were both free. She from the terrible pain, he from the price demanded by the monseigneur, a price he had not described to her, but one she knew was too horrible to pay. He had known for months that his woman had ready access to pills that would end her life quickly if her living became unendurable; he had frequently, at times frantically, searched for them but he had never found them. Now he knew why as he stared at the small tin of her favorite pastilles, the harmless droplets of licorice she had popped laughingly into her mouth for years.

"Be thankful, *mon cher*, they might be caviar or those expensive drugs the rich indulge in!" They were not caviar but they were drugs, lethal drugs.

Footsteps. The nurse! She had come out of her room, but she could not see his woman! Fontaine pushed himself up from the bed, wiped his eyes as best he could, and hurried to the door. He opened it, stunned by the sight of the woman; she stood directly in front of him, her arm raised, the knuckles of her hand arcing forward to knock.

"*Monsieur!* . . . You startled me."

"I believe we startled each other." Jean Pierre slipped out, rapidly closing the door behind him. "Regine is finally asleep," he whispered, bringing his forefinger to his lips. "This terrible storm has kept her up most of the night."

"But it is sent from heaven for us—for you—isn't it? There are times when I think the monseigneur can order such things."

"Then I doubt they come from heaven. It's not the source of his influence."

"To business," interrupted the nurse, not amused and walking away from the door. "Are you prepared?"

"I will be in a matter of minutes," replied Fontaine, heading for the table where his killing equipment lay in the locked drawer. He reached into his pocket and took out the key. "Do you want to go over the procedure?" he asked, turning. "For my benefit, of course. At this age, details are often blurred."

"Yes, I do, because there is a slight change."

"Oh?" The old Frenchman arched his brows. "Also at my age sudden changes are not welcome."

"It's only a question of timing, no more than a quarter of an hour, perhaps much less."

"An eternity in this business," said Fontaine as yet another streak of lightning, separated only milliseconds from its crash of thunder, interrupted the pounding rain on the windows and the roof. "It's dangerous enough to be outside; that bolt was too near for safety."

"If you believe that, think how the guards feel."

"The 'slight change,' please? Also an explanation."

"I'll give you no explanation except to say that it is an order from Argenteuil and you were responsible."

"The *judge*?"

"Draw your own conclusions."

"Then he was *not* sent to—"

"I'll say no more. The change is as follows. Rather than running up the path from here to the guards at Villa Twenty and demanding emergency assistance for your ill wife, I will say I was returning from the front desk where I was complaining about the telephone and saw a fire in Villa Fourteen, three away from ours. There'll no doubt be a great deal of confusion, what with the storm and everyone yelling and calling for help. That will be your signal. Use the confusion; get through and take out whoever remains at the woman's villa—make sure your silencer is secure. Then go inside and do the work you have sworn to do."

"So I wait for the fire, for the guards and for you to return to Number Eleven."

"Exactly. Stay on the porch with the door closed, of course."

"Of course."

"It may take me five minutes or perhaps even twenty, but *stay* there."

"Naturally. . . . May I ask, madame—or perhaps mademoiselle, although I see no evidence—"

"What *is* it?"

"It will take you five or twenty minutes to do what?"

"You're a fool, old man. What must be done."

"Of course."

The nurse pulled her raincoat around her, looped the belt and walked to the front door of the villa. "Get your equipment together and be out here in three minutes," she commanded.

"Of course." The door swung back with the wind as the woman opened it; she went outside into the torrential rain, pulling it shut behind her. Astonished and confused, the old Frenchman stood motionless, trying to make sense out of the inexplicable. Things were happening too fast for him, blurred in the agony of his woman's death. There was no time to mourn, no time to feel. . . . Only think and think quickly. Revelation came hard upon revelation, leaving unanswered questions that *had* to be answered so the whole could be understood—so that Montserrat itself made sense!

The nurse was more than a conduit for instructions from Argenteuil; the angel of mercy was herself an angel of death, a killer in her own right. So why was *he* sent thousands of miles to do the work another could do just as well and without the elaborate charade of his auspicious arrival? An old hero of France, indeed . . . it was all so unnecessary. And speaking of age, there was another—another old man who was no

killer at all. Perhaps, thought the false Jean
Pierre Fontaine, he had made a terrible mistake.
Perhaps, instead of coming to kill him, the other
"old man" had come to *warn* him!

"Mon Dieu," whispered the Frenchman. "The
old men of Paris, the Jackal's army! Too many
questions!" Fontaine walked rapidly to the
nurse's bedroom door and opened it. With the
swiftness developed over a lifetime of practice,
impaired only slightly by his years, he began
methodically to tear apart the woman's room—
suitcase, closet, clothes, pillows, mattress, bureau, dressing table, writing desk . . . the desk.
A locked drawer in the desk—a locked drawer
in the outer room. The "equipment." Nothing
mattered now! His woman was gone and there
were too many questions!

A heavy lamp on the desk with a thick brass
base—he picked it up, pulling out the cord, and
smashed it into the drawer. Again and again and
again until the wood splintered, shattering the
recess that held the tiny vertical latch. He
yanked the drawer open and stared in equal
parts of horror and comprehension at what he
saw.

Next to each other in a cushioned plastic case
were two hypodermic needles, their vials filled

with an identical yellowish serum. He did not have to know the chemical compounds; there were too many beyond his knowledge that would be effective. Liquid death in the veins.

Nor did he have to be told for whom they were intended. *Côte à côte dans le lit.* Two bodies beside each other in bed. He and his woman in a pact of final deliverance. How thoroughly had the monseigneur thought everything out! Himself dead! One dead old man from the Jackal's army of old men had outwitted all the security procedures, killing and mutilating those dearest to Carlos's ultimate enemy, Jason Bourne. And, naturally, behind that brilliant manipulation was the Jackal himself!

Ce n'est pas le contrat! Myself, *yes,* but not my woman! You promised me!

The *nurse.* The angel not of mercy but of death! The man known on Tranquility Isle as Jean Pierre Fontaine walked as fast as he could into the other room. To his equipment.

The huge silver racing craft with its two enormous engines crashed through the swells as often above the waves as in them. On the short low bridge, John St. Jacques maneuvered the drug boat through the dangerous reefs he knew by summoned memory, aided by the powerful searchlight that lit up the turbulent waters, now twenty, now two hundred feet in front of the bow. He kept screaming into his radio, the microphone weaving in front of his drenched face, hoping against all logic to raise someone on Tranquility.

He was within three miles of the island, a shrubbed volcanic intrusion on the water his landmark. Tranquility Isle was in kilometers much nearer Plymouth than to Blackburne Airport, and if one knew the shoals, not much longer to reach in a drug boat than in a seaplane, which had to bank east out of Blackburne to catch the prevailing west winds in order to land on the sea. Johnny was not sure why these calculations kept interfering with his concentration except that somehow they made him feel better, that he was doing the best he could— *Damn it!* Why was it always the best he could do rather than simply the *best*? He couldn't louse up anymore, not now, not *tonight*! Christ, he owed everything to Mare and David! Maybe even more to the crazy bastard who was his brother-in-law than to his own sister. David, wild-nuts *David*, a man he sometimes wondered if Marie ever knew existed!

"You back off, little Bro, I'll take care of this."

"You can't, David, I did it. I killed them!"

"I said 'Back off.' "

"I asked for your help, not for you to be me!"

"But you see I am you. I would have done the same thing and that makes me you in my eyes."

"That's crazy!"

"It's part of it. Someday I may teach you how to kill cleanly, in the dark. In the meantime, listen to the lawyers."

"Suppose they lose?"

"I'll get you out. I'll get you away."

"How?"

"I'll kill again."

"I can't believe you! A teacher, a scholar—I don't believe you, I don't want to believe you—you're my sister's husband."

"Then don't believe me, Johnny. And forget everything I've said, and never tell your sister I said it."

"It's that other person inside of you, isn't it?"

"You're very dear to Marie."

"That's no answer! Here, now, you're Bourne, aren't you? Jason Bourne!"

"We'll never, ever, discuss this conversation, Johnny. Do you understand me?"

No, he had never understood, thought St. Jacques, as the swirling winds and the cracks of lightning seemed to envelop the boat. Even when Marie and David appealed to his rapidly disintegrating ego by suggesting he could build a new life for himself in the islands. Seed money, they had said; build us a house and then see where you want to go from there. Within limits, we'll back you. Why would they do that? Why did they?

It was not "they," it was he. Jason Bourne.

Johnny St. Jacques understood the other morning when he picked up the phone by the pool and was told by an island pilot that someone had been asking questions at the airport about a woman and two children.

Someday I may teach you how to kill cleanly, in the dark. Jason Bourne.

Lights! He saw the beach lights of Tranquility. He was less than a mile from the shore!

The rain pounded down against the old Frenchman, the blasts of wind throwing him off balance as he made his way up the path toward Villa Fourteen. He angled his head against the elements, squinting, wiping his face with his left hand, his right gripping the weapon, a gun lengthened by the extension of the pocked cylinder that was its silencer. He held the pistol behind him as he had done years ago racing along railroad tracks, sticks of dynamite in one hand, a German Luger in the other, prepared to drop both at the appearance of Nazi patrols.

Whoever they were on the path above, they were no less than the Boche in his mind. All were Boche! He had been subservient to others long enough! His woman was gone; he would be his own man now, for there was nothing left but his own decisions, his own *feelings*, his own very private sense of what was right and what was wrong. . . . And the Jackal was wrong! The apostle of Carlos could accept the killing of the woman; it was a debt he could rationalize, but not the children, and certainly not the mutilations. Those acts were against God, and he and his woman were about to face Him; there had to be certain ameliorating circumstances.

Stop the angel of death! What could she be *doing*? What did the fire she talked about *mean*? . . . Then he saw it—a huge burst of flame through the hedges of Villa Fourteen. In a window! The same window that had to be the bedroom of the luxurious pink cottage.

Fontaine reached the flagstone walk that led to the front door as a bolt of lightning shook the ground under him. He fell to the earth, then struggled to his knees, crawling to the pink porch, its fluttering overhead light outlining the door. No amount of twisting or pulling or shoving could release the latch, so he angled his pistol up, squeezed the trigger twice and blew the lock apart. He pushed himself to his feet and went inside.

Inside. The screams came from beyond the door of the master bedroom. The old Frenchman lurched toward it, his legs unsteady, his weapon wavering in his right hand. With what strength he had left, he kicked the door open and observed a scene that he knew had to come from hell.

The nurse, with the old man's head in a metal leash, was forcing her victim down into a raging kerosene fire on the floor.

"Arrêtez!" screamed the man called Jean Pierre Fontaine. *"Assez! Maintenant!"*

Through the rising, spreading flames, shots rang out and bodies fell.

The lights of Tranquility's beach drew nearer as John St. Jacques kept yelling into the microphone: "It's *me*! It's Saint Jay coming in! Don't *shoot*!"

But the sleek silver drug boat was greeted by the staccato gunfire of automatic weapons. St. Jacques dived to the deck and kept shouting. "I'm coming in—I'm *beaching*! Hold your god-damned fire!"

"Is that *you, mon*?" came a panicked voice over the radio.

"You want to get *paid* next week?"

"Oh, yes, Mr. Saint Jay!" The loudspeakers on the beach erratically interrupted the winds and the thunder out of Basse-Terre. "Everyone down on the beach, stop shooting your guns! The *bo-att* is okay, *mon*! It is our *boss mon*, Mr. Saint Jay!"

The drug boat shot out of the water and onto the dark sand, its engines screaming, the blades instantly embedded, the pointed hull cracking under the impact. St. Jacques leaped up from his defensive fetal position and vaulted over the gunwale. *"Villa Twenty!"* he roared, racing through the downpour across the beach to the stone steps that led to the path. "All you men, *get* there!"

As he ran up the hard, rain-splattered staircase he suddenly gasped, his personal galaxy exploding into a thousand blinding stars of fire. *Gunshots!* One after another. On the east wing of the path! His legs cycled faster and faster, leaping over two and three steps at a time; he reached the path and like a man possessed raced up the path toward Villa Twenty, snapping his head to the right in furious confusion that only added to his panic. *People*—men and woman from his *staff*—were clustered around the doorway of Villa Fourteen! . . . Who was there? . . . My *God*, the *judge*!

His lungs bursting, every muscle and tendon in his legs stretched to the breaking point, St. Jacques reached his sister's house. He crashed through the gate, and ran to the door, hurling his body against it and bursting through to the room inside. Eyes bulging first in horror, then in unmeasurable pain, he fell to his knees, screaming. On the white wall with terrible clarity were the words scrawled in dark red:

Jason Bourne, brother of the Jackal.

14

"*Johnny!* Johnny, *stop* it!" His sister's voice crashed into his ear as she cradled his head in one arm, the other extended above him, her free hand gripping his hair, nearly pulling it out of his skull. "Can you *hear* me? We're *all right*, Bro! The children are in another villa—we're *fine!*"

The faces above him and around him came slowly into focus. Among them were the two old men, one from Boston, the other from Paris. "There they *are!*" screamed St. Jacques, lurching up but stopped by Marie, who fell across him. "I'll kill the bastards!"

"No!" roared his sister, holding him, helped by a guard whose strong black hands gripped her

brother's shoulders. "At this moment they're two of the best friends we have."

"You don't know who they *are*!" cried St. Jacques, trying to free himself.

"Yes, we do," broke in Marie, lowering her voice, her lips next to his ear. "Enough to know they can lead us to the Jackal—"

"They *work* for the Jackal!"

"One did," said the sister. "The other never heard of Carlos."

"You don't understand!" whispered St. Jacques. "They're old men—'the old men of Paris,' the Jackal's *army*! Conklin reached me in Plymouth and explained . . . they're killers!"

"Again, one was but he's not anymore; he has nothing to kill for now. The other . . . well, the other's a mistake, a stupid, outrageous mistake, but that's all he is, and thank God for it—for him."

"It's all crazy . . . !"

"It's crazy," agreed Marie, nodding to the guard to help her brother up. "Come on, Johnny, we have things to talk about."

The storm had blown away like a violent, un-wanted intruder racing off into the night leaving

behind the carnage of its rage. The early morning light broke over the eastern horizon, slowly
revealing through the mists the blue-green out
islands of Montserrat. The first boats cautiously, dolefully lumbered out to the favored
fishing grounds, for the catch of the day meant
one more day's survival. Marie, her brother and
the two old men were around a table on the
balcony of an unoccupied villa. Over coffee,
they had been talking for the better part of an
hour, treating each point of horror coldly, dissecting facts without feeling. The aged false
hero of France had been assured that all
proper arrangements would be made for his
woman once phone service had been restored
to the big island. If it was possible, he wanted
her to be buried in the islands; she would understand. There was nothing left for her in
France but the ignominy of a tawdry grave. If it
was possible—

"It's possible," said St. Jacques. "Because of
you my sister's alive."

"Because of me, young man, she might have
died."

"Would you have killed me?" asked Marie,
studying the old Frenchman.

"Certainly not after I saw what Carlos had

planned for me and my woman. *He* had broken the contract, not I.''

''Before then.''

''When I had not yet seen the needles, understood what was all too obvious?''

''Yes.''

''That's difficult to answer; a contract's a contract. Still, my woman was dead, and a part of her dying was because she sensed that a terrible thing had been demanded of me. To go through with that demand would deny that aspect of her death, don't you see? Yet again, even in her death, the monseigneur could not be totally denied—he had made possible years of relative happiness that would have been impossible without him. . . . I simply don't know. I might have reasoned that I owed him your life—your death—but certainly not the children's . . . and most certainly not the rest of it.''

''Rest of what?'' asked St. Jacques.

''It's best not to inquire.''

''I think you would have killed me,'' said Marie.

''I tell you, I simply don't know. There was nothing personal. You were not a person to me, you were simply an event that was part of a business arrangement. . . . Still, as I say, my woman was gone, and I'm an old man with limited time before me. Perhaps a look in your eyes or a plea for your children—who knows, I might have turned the pistol on myself. Then again, I might not have."

"Jesus, you are a killer," said the brother quietly.

"I am many things, monsieur. I don't ask forgiveness in this world; the other's another question. There were always circumstances—"

"Gallic logic," remarked Brendan Patrick Pierre Prefontaine, former judge of the first circuit court in Boston, as he absently touched the raw tender skin of his neck below his singed white hair. "Thank heavens I never had to argue before *les tribunaux*; neither side is ever actually wrong." The disbarred attorney chuckled. "You see before you a felon, justly tried and justly convicted. The only exculpatory aspect of my crimes is that I was caught and so many others were not and are not."

"Perhaps we are related, after all, *Monsieur le Juge.*"

"By comparison, sir, my life is far closer to that of St. Thomas Aquinas—"

"Blackmail," interrupted Marie.

"No, actually the charge was malfeasance. Accepting remunerations for favorable decisions, that sort of thing. . . . My God, we're hound's-tooth Boston! In New York City it's standard procedure: Leave your money with the bailiff, enough for everyone."

"I'm not referring to Boston, I'm talking about why you're here. It's blackmail."

"That's an oversimplification but essentially correct. As I told you, the man who paid me to find out where you'd gone also paid me an additional large sum of money to keep the information to myself. Under the circumstances, and because I have no pressing schedule of appointments, I thought it logical to pursue the inquiry. After all, if the little I knew brought so much, how much more might come to me if I learned a little more?"

"You talk of Gallic logic, monsieur?" inserted the Frenchman.

"It's simple interrogatory progression," replied the former judge, briefly glancing at Jean Pierre before turning back to Marie. "However, my dear, I may have glossed over an item that was extremely helpful in negotiations with my client. To put it plainly, your identity was being withheld and protected by the government. It was a strong point that frightened a very strong and influential man."

"I want his name," said Marie.

"Then I must have protection, too," rejoined Prefontaine.

"You'll have it—"

"And perhaps something more," continued the old disbarred attorney. "My client has no idea I came here, no knowledge of what's happened, all of which might fuel the fires of his largess if I described what I've experienced and observed. He'd be frightened out of his mind even to be associated with such events. Also, considering the fact that I was nearly killed by that Teutonic Amazon, I really deserve more."

"Am I then to be rewarded for saving your life, monsieur?"

"If I had anything of value—other than my legal expertise, which is yours—I'd happily share it. If I'm given anything, that still holds, Cousin."

"Merci bien, Cousin."

"D'accord, mon ami, but never let the Irish nuns hear us."

"You don't look like a poor man, Judge," said John St. Jacques.

"Then appearances are as deceiving as a long-forgotten title you so generously use. . . . I should add that my wants are not extravagant, for there's no one but myself, and my creature comforts do not require luxury."

"You've lost your woman, too, then?"

"Not that it's any of your damn business, but my wife left me twenty-nine years ago, and my thirty-eight-year-old son, now a successful attorney on Wall Street, uses her name and when questioned by curious people tells them he never knew me. I haven't seen him since he was ten; it was not in his interest, you understand."

"Quelle tristesse."

"Quel bullshit, Cousin. That boy got his brains from me, not from the airhead who bore him. . . . However, we stray. My French pureblood here has his own reasons—obviously based on betrayal—for cooperating with you. I have equally strong reasons for wanting to help you, too, but I must also consider myself. My aged new friend can go back and live what's left of his life in Paris, whereas I have no place to go but Boston and the few opportunities I've developed over the years to eke out a living. Therefore my deep-seated motives for wanting to help must themselves take a backseat. With what I know now I wouldn't last five minutes in the streets of Boston."

"Breakthrough," said John St. Jacques, staring at Prefontaine. "I'm sorry, Judge, we don't need you."

"What?" Marie sat forward in her chair. "Please, Bro, we need all the help we can get!"

"Not in this case. We know who hired him."

"We *do*?"

"Conklin knows; he called it a 'breakthrough.' He told me that the man who traced you and the children here used a judge to find you." The brother nodded across the table at the Bostonian. "Him. It's why I smashed up a hundred-thousand-dollar boat to get back over here. Conklin knows who his client is."

Prefontaine again glanced at the old Frenchman. "Now is the time for *'Quelle tristesse,'* Sir Hero. I'm left with nothing. My persistence brought me only a sore throat and a burned scalp."

"Not necessarily," interrupted Marie. "You're the attorney, so I shouldn't have to tell you. Corroboration is cooperation. We may want you to tell everything you know to certain people in Washington."

"Corroboration can be obtained with a subpoena, my dear. Under oath in a courtroom, take my personal as well as my professional word for it."

"We won't be going to court. Ever."

"Oh? . . . I see."

"You couldn't possibly, Judge, not at this juncture. However, if you agree to help us you'll be well paid. . . . A moment ago you said that you had strong reasons for wanting to help, reasons that had to be secondary to your own well-being—"

"Are you by any chance a lawyer, my dear?"

"No, an economist."

"Holy Mary, that's worse. . . . About my reasons?"

"Do they concern your client, the man who hired you to trace us?"

"They do. His august persona—as in Caesar Augustus—should be trashed. Slippery intellectuality aside, he's a whore. He had promise once, more than I let him know, but he let it all go by the boards in a flamboyant quest for his own personal grail."

"What the hell's he talking about, Mare?"

"A man with a great deal of influence or power, neither of which he should have, I think. Our convicted felon here has come to grips with personal morality."

"Is that an economist speaking?" asked Prefontaine, once more absently touching the blistered flesh of his neck. "An economist reflecting on her last inaccurate projection that caused inappropriate buying or selling on the stock exchanges, resulting in losses many could afford and many more could not?"

"My voice was never that important, but I'll grant you it's the reflection of a great many others whose projections were, because they never risked, they only theorized. It's a safe position. . . . Yours isn't, Judge. You may need the protection we can provide. What's your answer?"

"Jesus, Mary and Joseph, you're a cold one—"

"I have to be," said Marie, her eyes leveled on the man from Boston. "I want you with us, but I won't beg, I'll simply leave you with nothing and you can go back to the streets in Boston."

"Are you *sure* you're not a lawyer—or perhaps a lord high executioner?"

"Take your choice. Just give me your answer."

"Will somebody tell me what the hell is going on here!" yelled John St. Jacques.

"Your sister," answered Prefontaine, his gentle gaze on Marie, "has enlisted a recruit. She's made the options clear, which every attorney understands, and the inevitability of her logic, in addition to her lovely face, crowned by that dark red hair, makes my decision also inevitable."

"What . . . ?"

"He's opted for our side, Johnny. Forget it."

"What do we need him for?"

"Without a courtroom a dozen different reasons, young man," answered the judge. "In certain situations, volunteerism is not the best road to take unless one is thoroughly protected beyond the courts."

"Is that right, Sis?"

"It's not wrong, Bro, but it's up to Jason— *damn it*—David!"

"No, Mare," said John St. Jacques, his eyes boring into his sister's. "It's up to Jason."

"Are these names I should be aware of?" asked Prefontaine. "The name 'Jason Bourne' was sprayed on the wall of your villa."

"My instructions, Cousin," said the false yet not so false hero of France. "It was necessary."

"I don't understand . . . any more than I understood the other name, the 'Jackal,' or 'Carlos,' which you both rather brutally questioned me about when I wasn't sure whether I was dead or alive. I thought the 'Jackal' was fiction."

The old man called Jean Pierre Fontaine

looked at Marie; she nodded. "Carlos the Jackal is a legend, but he is not fiction. He's a professional killer now in his sixties, rumored to be ill, but still possessed with a terrible hatred. He's a man of many faces, many sides, some loved by those who have reasons to love him, others detested by those who consider him the essence of evil—and depending on the view, all have their reasons for being correct. I am an example of one who has experienced both viewpoints, but then my world is hardly yours, as you rightly suggested, St. Thomas of Aquinas."

"*Merci bien.*"

"But the hatred that obsesses Carlos grows like a cancer in his aging brain. One man drew him out; one man tricked him, usurped his kills, taking credit for the Jackal's work, kill after kill, driving Carlos mad when he was trying to correct the record, trying to maintain his supremacy as the ultimate assassin. That same man was responsible for the death of his lover—but one far more than a lover, the woman who was his keel, his beloved since childhood in Venezuela, his colleague in all things. That single man, one of hundreds, perhaps thousands sent out by governments everywhere, was the only one who ever saw his face—*as* the Jackal. The man who did all this was a product of American intelligence, a strange man who lived a deadly lie every day of his life for three years. And Carlos will not rest until that man is punished . . . and killed. The man is Jason Bourne."

Squinting, stunned by the Frenchman's story, Prefontaine leaned forward over the table. "Who *is* Jason Bourne?" he asked.

"My husband, David Webb," replied Marie.

"Oh, my *God*," whispered the judge. "May I have a drink, please?"

John St. Jacques called out. "Ronald!"

"Yes, boss-*mon*!" cried from within the guard whose strong hands had held his employer's shoulders an hour ago in Villa Twenty.

"Bring us some whisky and brandy, please. The bar should be stocked."

"Comin', sir."

The orange sun in the east suddenly took fire, its rays penetrating what was left of the sea mists of dawn. The silence around the table was broken by the soft, heavily accented words of the old Frenchman. "I am not used to such service," he said, looking aimlessly beyond the railing of the balcony at the progressively bright waters of the Caribbean. "When something is asked for, I always think the task should be mine."

"Not anymore," said Marie quietly, then after a beat, adding, ". . . Jean Pierre."

"I suppose one could live with that name. . . ."

"Why not here?"

"Qu'est-ce que vous dites, madame?"

"Think about it. Paris might not be any less dangerous for you than the streets of Boston for our judge."

The judge in question was lost in his own aimless reverie as several bottles, glasses and a bucket of ice were brought to the table. With no hesitation, Prefontaine reached out and poured himself an extravagant drink from the bottle nearest him. "I *must* ask a question or two," he said emphatically. "Is that proper?"

"Go ahead," replied Marie. "I'm not sure I can or will answer you, but try me."

"The gunshots, the spray paint on the wall— my 'cousin' here says the red paint and the words were by his instructions—"

"They were, *mon ami*. The loud firing of the guns as well."

"Why?"

"Everything must be as it is expected to be. The gunshots were an additional element to draw attention to the event that was to take place."

"Why?"

"A lesson we learned in the Résistance—not that I was ever a 'Jean Pierre Fontaine,' but I did my small part. It was called an *accentuation*, a positive statement making clear that the underground was responsible for the action. Everyone in the vicinity knew it."

"Why *here*?"

"The Jackal's nurse is dead. There is no one to tell him that his instructions have been carried out."

"Gallic logic. Incomprehensible."

"French common sense. Incontestable."

"Why?"

"Carlos will be here by noon tomorrow."

"Oh, dear *God*!"

The telephone rang inside the villa. John St. Jacques lurched out of his chair only to be blocked by his sister, who threw her arm in front of his face and then raced through the doors into the living room. She picked up the phone.

"David?"

"It's Alex," said the breathless voice on the line. "Christ, I've had this goddamned thing on redial for three hours! Are you all right?"

"We're alive but we weren't supposed to be."

"The old men! The old men of Paris! Did Johnny—"

"Johnny *did*, but they're on our side!"

"Who?"

"The old men—"

"You're not making one damn bit of sense!"

"Yes, I am! We're in control here. What about *David*?"

"I don't know! The telephone lines were cut. Everything's a mess! I've got the police heading out there—"

"*Screw* the police, Alex!" screamed Marie. "Get the army, the marines, the lousy CIA! We're *owed*!"

"Jason won't allow that. I can't turn on him now."

"Well, try this for size. The Jackal will be here *tomorrow*!"

"Oh, Jesus! I have to get him a jet somewhere."

"You have to do *something*!"

"You don't understand, Marie. The old Medusa surfaced—"

"You tell that husband of mine that Medusa's *history*! The Jackal *isn't*, and he's flying in here tomorrow!"

"David'll be there, you know that."

"Yes, I do. . . . Because he's Jason Bourne now."

"Br'er Rabbit, this ain't thirteen years ago, and you just happen to be thirteen years older. You're not only gonna be useless, you're gonna be a positive liability unless you get some rest, preferably sleep. Turn off the lights and grab some sack time in that big fancy couch in the living room. I'll man the phones, which ain't gonna ring 'cause nobody's callin' at four o'-clock in the morning."

Cactus's voice had faded as Jason wandered into the dark living room, his legs heavy, his lids falling over his eyes like lead weights. He dropped to the couch, swinging his legs slowly, with effort, one at a time, up on the cushions; he stared at the ceiling. *Rest is a weapon, battles won and lost . . .* Philippe d'Anjou. Medusa. His inner screen went black and sleep came.

A screaming, pulsating siren erupted, deafening, incessant, echoing throughout the cavern-ous house like a sonic tornado. Bourne spastically whipped his body around and sprang off the couch, at first disoriented, unsure of where he was and for a terrible moment . . . of who he was.

"*Cactus!*" he roared, racing out of the ornate living room into the hallway. "*Cactus!*" he shouted again, hearing his voice lost in the rapid, rhythmic crescendos of the siren-alarm. "Where *are* you?"

Nothing. He ran to the door of the study, gripping the knob. It was locked! He stepped back and crashed his shoulder against it, once, twice, a third time with all the speed and strength he could summon. The door splintered, then gave way and Jason hammered his foot against the central panel until it collapsed; he went inside and what he found caused the killing machine that was the product of Medusa and beyond to stare in ice-cold fury. Cactus was sprawled over the desk, under the light of the single lamp, in the same chair that had held the murdered general, his blood forming a pool of red on the blotter—a corpse. . . . No, *not* a corpse! The right hand moved, Cactus was alive!

Bourne ran to the desk and gently raised the old man's head, the shrill, deafening, all-encompassing alarm making communication—if communication were possible—impossible. Cactus opened his dark eyes, his trembling right hand moving down the blotter, his forefinger curved and tapping the top of the desk.

"What *is* it?" yelled Jason. The hand kept moving back toward the edge of the blotter, the tapping more rapid. "Below? Underneath?" With minuscule—nearly imperceptible—motions of his head, Cactus nodded in the affirmative. "*Under* the desk!" shouted Bourne, beginning to understand. He knelt down to the right of Cactus and felt under the thin top drawer, then to the side— He found it! A button. Again gently, he moved the heavy rolling chair inches to the left and centered his eyes on the button. Beneath it, in tiny white letters on a black plastic strip, was the answer.

Aux. Alarm

Jason pressed the button; instantly the shrieking pandemonium was cut off. The ensuing silence was nearly as deafening, the adjustment to it nearly as terrifying.

"How were you hit?" asked Bourne. "How long ago? . . . If you can talk, just whisper, no energy at all, do you understand?"

"Oh, Br'er, you're too much," whispered Cactus, in pain. "I was a black cabdriver in Washington, man. I've been here before. It ain't fatal, boy, I gotta slug in the upper chest."

"I'll get a doctor right away—our friend Ivan, incidentally—but if you can, tell me what happened while I move you to the floor and look at the damage." Jason slowly, carefully lowered the old man off the chair and onto the throw rug beneath the bay window. He tore off Cactus's shirt; the bullet had gone through the flesh of the left shoulder. With short, swift movements Bourne ripped the shirt into strips and tightly wrapped a primitive bandage around his friend's chest and between the underarm and the shoulder. "It's not much," said Jason, "but it'll hold you for a while. Go on."

"He's *out* there, Br'er!" Cactus coughed weakly, lying back on the floor. "He's got a big mother 'fifty-seven magnum with a silencer; he pinned me through the window, then smashed it and climbed inside. . . . He—he . . . "

"Easy! Don't talk, never mind—"

"I gotta. The brothers out there, they ain't got no hardware. He'll pick 'em off! . . . I played deep dead and he was in a hurry—oh, was *he* in a hurry! Look over there, will ya?" Jason swung his head in the direction of Cactus's gesture. A dozen or so books had been yanked out of a shelf on the side wall and strewn on the floor. The old man continued, his voice growing weaker. "He went over to the bookcase like in

a panic, until he found what he wanted . . . then
to the door, that 'fifty-seven ready for bear, if you
follow me. . . . I figured it was you he was after,
that he'd seen you through the window go out to
the other room, and I tell ya, I was workin' my
right knee like a runnin' muskrat 'cause I found
that alarm button an hour ago and knew I had
to stop him—''

"Easy!"

"I gotta tell you . . . I couldn't move my hands
'cause he'd see me, but my knee hit that sucker
and the siren damn near blew me out of the
chair. . . . The honky bastard fell apart. He
slammed the door, locked it, and beat his way
out of here back through the window." Cactus's
neck arched back, the pain and the exhaustion
overtaking him. "He's out there, Br'er Rabbit—''

"That's enough!" ordered Bourne as he cautiously reached up, snapping off the desk lamp,
leaving the dim light from the hallway through
the shattered door as the only illumination. "I'm
calling Alex; he can send the doctor—''

Suddenly, from somewhere outside, there
was a high-pitched scream, a roar of shock and
anguish Jason knew only too well. So did Cactus, who whispered, his eyes shut tight: "He got
one. That fucker got one of the brothers!"

"I'm reaching Conklin," said Jason, pulling the phone off of the desk. "Then I'll go out and get *him*. . . . Oh, Christ! The line's out—it's been *cut*!"

"That honky knows his way around here."

"So do I, Cactus. Stay as quiet as you can. I'll be back for you—"

There was another scream, this lower, more abrupt, an expulsion of breath more than a roar.

"May sweet Jesus forgive me," muttered the old black man painfully, meaning the words. "There's only one brother left—"

"If anyone should ask forgiveness, it's *me*," cried Bourne, his voice guttural, half choking. "*Goddamn* it! I swear to you, Cactus, I never thought, never even considered, that anything like this would happen."

"Course you didn't. I know you from back to the old days, Br'er, and I never heard of you asking anyone to risk anything for you. . . . It's always been the other way around."

"I'm going to pull you over," interrupted Jason, tugging on the rug, maneuvering Cactus to the right side of the desk, the old man's left hand close enough to reach the auxiliary alarm. "If you hear anything or see anything or *feel* anything, turn on the siren."

"Where are you going? I mean how?"

"Another room. Another window."

Bourne crept across the floor to the mutilated door, lurched through it and ran into the living room. At the far end was a pair of French doors that led to an outside patio; he recalled seeing white wrought-iron lawn furniture on the south end of the house when he was with the guards. He twisted the knob and slipped outside, pulling the automatic from his belt, shutting the right door, and crouching, making his way to the shrubbery at the edge of the grass. He had to move *quickly*. Not only was there a third life in the balance, a third unrelated, unwarranted death, but a killer who could be his shortcut to the crimes of the new Medusa, and those crimes were his bait for the Jackal! A diversion, a magnet, a trap . . . the *flares*—part of the equipment he had brought with him to Manassas. The two emergency "candles" were in his left rear pocket, each six inches long and bright enough to be seen for miles; ignited together yet spaced apart they would light up Swayne's property like two searchlights. One in the south drive, the other by the kennels, possibly waking the drugged dogs, bewildering them, infuriating them— Do it! *Hurry.*

Jason scrambled across the lawn, his eyes darting everywhere, wondering where the stalking killer was and how the innocent quarry that Cactus had enlisted was evading him. One was experienced, the other not, and Bourne could not permit the latter's life to be wasted.

It *happened*! He had been spotted! Two cracks on either side of him, bullets from a silenced pistol slicing the air. He reached the south leg of the paved drive and, racing across it, dived into the foliage. Ripping a flare from his pocket, he put down the weapon, snapped up the flame of his lighter, ignited the fuse and threw the sizzling candle to his right. It landed on the road; in seconds it would spew out the blinding fire. He ran to his left beneath the pine trees toward the rear of the estate, his lighter and the second flare in one hand, the automatic in the other. He was parallel to the kennels; the flare in the road exploded into bluish-white flames. He ignited the second and threw it end over end, arcing it forty yards away to the front of the kennels. He waited.

The second flare burst into sputtering fire, two balls of blinding white light eerily illuminating the house and grounds of the estate's south side. Three of the dogs began to wail, then made feeble attempts to howl; soon their confused anger would be heard. A *shadow*. Against the west wall of the white house—it *moved*, caught in the light between the flare by the kennels and the house. The figure darted for the protection of the shrubbery; it crouched, an immobile but intrusive part of the silhouetted foliage. Was it the killer or the killer's target, the last "brother" recruited by Cactus? . . . There was one way to find out, and if it was the former and he was a decent marksman, it was not the best tactic, but still it was the quickest.

Bourne leaped up from the underbrush, yelling in full view as he lunged to his right, at the last half second plunging his foot into the soft dirt and pivoting, lowering his body and diving to his left. "Head for the *cabin*!" he roared. And he got his answer. Two more spits, two more cracks in the air, the bullets digging up the earth to his right. The killer was good; perhaps not an expert but good enough. A .357 held six shells; five had been fired, but there had been sufficient time to reload the emptied cylinder. Another strategy—*quickly*!

Suddenly another figure appeared, a man running up the road toward the rear of Flannagan's cabin. He was in the open—he could be killed!

"Over here, you *bastard*!" screamed Jason, jumping up and firing his automatic blindly into the shrubbery by the house. And then he got another answer, a welcome one. There was a single spit, a single crack in the air and then no more. The killer had *not* reloaded! Perhaps he had no more shells—*whatever*, the primary target was now on the high ground. Bourne raced out of the bushes and across the lawn through the opposing light of the flares; the dogs were now really aroused, the yelps and throated growls of attack becoming louder. The killer ran out of the shrubbery and into the road, racing through shadows toward the front gates. Jason had the bastard, he *knew* it. The gates were closed, the Medusan was cornered. Bourne roared: "There's no way out, Snake Lady! Make it easy on yourself—"

A spit, a *crack*. The man had reloaded while running! Jason fired; the man fell in the road. And as he did so, the intermittent silence of the night was ripped open by the sound of a powerful, racing engine, the vehicle in question speeding up the outside road, its flashing red and blue lights signifying the police. The *police*! The alarm must have been wired into the Manassas headquarters, a fact that had never occurred to

Bourne; he had assumed that such a measure was impossible where Medusa was concerned. It wasn't logical; the security was *internal*; no external force could be permitted for Snake Lady. There was too much to learn, too much that had to be kept secret—a *cemetery*!

The killer writhed in the road, rolling over and over toward the bordering pine trees. There was something clutched in his hand. Jason approached him as two police officers got out of the patrol car beyond the gate. He lashed his foot out, kicking the man's body, releasing whatever it was in his grip and reaching down to pick it up. It was a leather-bound book, one of a set, like a volume of Dickens or Thackeray, the embossed letters in gold, more for display than for reading. It was *crazy*! Then he flipped open a page and understood it was not crazy at all. There was no print inside, only the scrawl of handwritten notes on blank pages. It was a diary, a *ledger*!

There could be no *police*! Especially not now. He could not allow them to be aware of his and Conklin's penetration into Medusa. The leather-bound book in his hand could not see the official light of day! The Jackal was *everything*. He had to get *rid* of them!

"We got a call, mister," intoned a middle-aged patrolman walking toward the grilled gate, a younger associate joining him. "HQ said he was uptight as hell. We're responding, but like I told dispatch, there've been some pretty wild parties out here, no criticism intended, sir. We all like a good time now and then, right?"

"Absolutely right, Officer," replied Jason, trying his utmost to control the painful heaving in his chest, his eyes straying to the wounded killer—he had *disappeared*! "There was a momentary shortage in electricity that somehow interfered with the telephone lines."

"Happens a lot," confirmed the younger patrolman. "Sudden showers and summer heat lightnin'. Someday they'll put all them cables underground. My folks got a place—"

"The point *is*," interrupted Bourne, "everything's getting back to normal. As you can see, some of the lights in the house are back on."

"I can't see nothin' through them flares," said the young police officer.

"The general always takes the ultimate precautions," explained Jason. "I guess he feels he has to," added Bourne, somewhat lamely. "Regardless, everything's—as I said—getting back to normal. Okay?"

"Okay by me," answered the older patrolman, "but I got a message for someone named Webb. He in there?"

"I'm Webb," said Jason Bourne, alarmed.

"That makes things easier. You're supposed to call a 'Mister Conk' right away. It's urgent."

"Urgent?"

"An emergency, we were told. It was just radioed to us."

Jason could hear the rattling of the fence on the perimeter of Swayne's property. The killer was getting away! "Well, Officer, the phones are still out here. . . . Do you have one in your car?"

"Not for personal use, sir. Sorry."

"But you just said it was an emergency."

"Well, I suppose since you're a guest of the general's I could permit it. If it's long distance, though, you'd better have a credit card number."

"Oh, my *God*." Bourne unlocked the gate and rushed to the patrol car as the siren-alarm was activated back at the house—activated and then instantly shut off. The remaining brother had apparently found Cactus.

"What the hell was *that*?" yelled the young policeman.

"*Forget* it!" screamed Jason, jumping into the car and yanking an all too familiar patrol phone out of its cradle. He gave Alex's number in Virginia to the police switchboard and kept repeating the phrase: *"It's an emergency, it's an emergency!"*

"Yes?" answered Conklin, acknowledging the police operator.

"It's me!"

"What *happened*?"

"Too involved to go into. What's the emergency?"

"I've got you a private jet out of the Reston airport."

"Reston? That's north of here—"

"The field in Manassas doesn't have the equipment. I'm sending a car for you."

"Why?"

"Tranquility. Marie and the kids are okay; they're *okay*! She's in charge."

"What the hell does *that* mean?"

"Get to Reston and I'll tell you."

"I want *more*!"

"The Jackal's flying in today."

"Jesus *Christ*!"

"Wrap things up there and wait for the car."

"I'll take this one!"

"No! Not unless you want to blow everything. We've got time. Wrap it up out there."

"Cactus . . . he's hurt—shot."

"I'll call Ivan. He'll get back in a hurry."

"There's one brother left—only *one*, Alex. I killed the other two—I was responsible."

"Cut that out. *Stop* it. Do what you have to do."

"Goddamn you, I *can't*. Someone's got to be here and I *won't* be!"

"You're right. There's too much to keep under wraps out there and you've got to be in Montserrat. I'll drive out with the car and take your place."

"Alex, tell me what happened on *Tranquility*!"

"The old men . . . your 'old men of Paris,' that's what happened."

"They're dead," said Jason Bourne quietly, simply.

"Don't be hasty. They've turned—at least I gather the real one turned and the other's a God-given mistake. They're on our side now."

"They're never on anyone's side but the Jackal's, you don't know them."

"Neither do you. Listen to your wife. But now you go back to the house and write out everything I should know. . . . And Jason, I must tell you something. I hope to Christ you can find your solution—*our* solution—on Tranquility. Because all things considered, including my life, I can't keep this Medusa on our level much longer. I think you know that."

"You *promised*!"

"Thirty-six hours, Delta."

In the woods beyond the fence a wounded man crouched, his frightened face against the green links. In the bright wash of the headlights, he observed the tall man who had gone into the patrol car and now came out, awkwardly, nervously thanking the policemen. He did not, however, permit them inside.

Webb. The killer had heard the name "Webb."

It was all they had to know. All Snake Lady had to know.

15

"God, I love you!" said David Webb, leaning into the pay phone in the preboarding room at the private airfield in Reston, Virginia. "The waiting was the worst part, waiting to talk to you, to hear from *you* that you were all all right."

"How do you think I felt, darling? Alex said the telephone lines had been cut and he was sending the police when I wanted him to send the whole damned army."

"We can't even allow the police, nothing official anywhere at the moment. Conklin's promised me at least another thirty-six hours. . . . We may not need that now. Not with the Jackal in Montserrat."

"David, what happened? Alex mentioned Medusa—"

"It's a mess and he's right, he has to go higher up with it. *Him,* not us. We stay out. Far away out."

"What *happened*?" repeated Marie. "What's the old Medusa got to do with anything?"

"There's a new Medusa—an extension of the old one, actually—and it's big and ugly and it kills, they kill. I saw that tonight; one of their guns tried to kill me after thinking he'd killed Cactus and murdering two innocent men."

"Good *God*! Alex told me about Cactus when he called me back, but nothing else. How is your Uncle Remus?"

"He'll make it. The Agency doctor came out and took him and the last brother away."

" 'Brother'?"

"I'll tell you when I see you. . . . Conklin's out there now. He'll take care of everything and have the telephone fixed. I'll call him from Tranquility."

"You're exhausted—"

"I'm tired, but I'm not sure why. Cactus insisted I get some sleep and I must have had all of twelve minutes."

"My poor darling."

"I like the tone of your voice," said David. "The words even better, except I'm not poor. You took care of that in Paris thirteen years ago." Suddenly his wife was silent and Webb was alarmed. "What is it? Are you all right?"

"I'm not sure," answered Marie softly, but with a strength that was the result of thought, not feeling. "You say this new Medusa is big and ugly and it tried to kill you—they tried to kill you."

"They didn't."

"Yet they, or it, wanted you dead. Why?"

"Because I was there."

"You don't kill a man because he was at someone's *house*—"

"A lot happened at that house tonight. Alex and I penetrated its circle of secrets and I was seen. The idea was to bait the Jackal with a few rich and all too famous bandits from the old Saigon who would hire him to come after me. It was a hell of a strategy but it spiraled out of control."

"My God, David, don't you understand? You're marked! They'll come after you *themselves*!"

"How can they? The hit man from Medusa who was there never saw my face except while I was running in shadows, and *they* have no idea who I am. I'm a nonperson who'll simply disappear. . . . No, Marie, if Carlos shows up and if I can do what I *know* I can do in Montserrat, we'll be free. To borrow a phrase, 'free at last.' "

"Your voice changes, doesn't it?"

"My what does which?"

"It really does. I can tell."

"I don't know what you're talking about," said Jason Bourne. "I'm being signaled. The plane's here. Tell Johnny to keep those two old men under guard!"

The whispers spread through Montserrat like rolling pockets of mist. Something terrible had happened on the out island of Tranquility. . . . "Bad times, *mon*." . . . "The evil *obeah* come across the Antilles from Jamaic' and there was death and madness." . . . "And blood on the walls of death, *mon,* a curse put on the family of an animal." . . . "*Sshh!* There was a cat mother and two cat children . . . !"

And there were other voices. . . . "Dear God, keep it *quiet*! It could ruin what tourism we've built!" . . . "Never anything like this before—an isolated incident, obviously drug-related, brought over from another island!" . . . "All too true, *mon*! I hear it was a madman, his body filled with dope." . . . "I'm told a fast boat running like the wind of a hurricane took him out to sea. He's gone!" . . . "Keep it quiet, I say! Remember the Virgins? The Fountainhead massacre? It took them years to recover. *Quiet!*"

And a single voice. "It's a trap, sir, and if successful, as we believe it will be, we'll be the talk of the West Indies, the heroes of the Caribbean. It'll be positively *mahvelous* for our image. Law and order and all that."

"Thank heavens! Was anyone actually killed?"

"One person, and she was in the act of taking another's life."

"*She?* Good God, I don't want to hear another word until it's all over."

"It's better that you not be available for comment."

"Damned good idea. I'll go out on the boat; the fish are running well after the storm."

"Excellent, sir. And I'll stay in radio contact with developments."

"Perhaps you shouldn't. Anything can be picked up out there."

"I only meant so as to advise you when to return—at the appropriate moment to make a most advantageous appearance. I'll fill you in, of course."

"Yes, of course. You're a good man, Henry."

"Thank you, Crown Governor."

It was ten o'clock in the morning and they held each other fiercely, but there was no time for talk, only the brief comfort of being together, safe together, secure in the knowledge that they knew things the Jackal did not know and that knowledge gave them an enormous advantage. Still, it was only an advantage, not a guarantee, not where Carlos was concerned. And both Jason and John St. Jacques were adamant: Marie and the children were being flown south to Guadeloupe's Basse-Terre island. They would stay there with the Webbs' regal maid, Mrs. Cooper, all under guard until they were called back to Montserrat. Marie objected, but her objections were met with silence; her husband's orders were delivered abruptly, icily.

"You're leaving because I have work to do. We won't discuss it any further."

"It's Switzerland again . . . Zurich again, isn't it, *Jason*?"

"It's whatever you like," replied Bourne, now

preoccupied as the three of them stood at the base of the dock, two seaplanes bobbing in the water only yards apart at the far end. One had brought Jason directly to Tranquility from Antigua; the other was fueled for the flight to Guadeloupe with Mrs. Cooper and the children already inside. "Hurry up, Marie," added Bourne. "I want to go over things with Johnny and then grill those two old scumballs."

"They're not scumballs, David. Because of them we're alive."

"Why? Because they blew it and had to turn to save their asses?"

"That's not fair."

"It's fair until I say otherwise, and they're scum until they convince me they're not. You don't know the Jackal's old men, I do. They'll say anything, do anything, lie and snivel to hell and back, and if you turn the other way, they'll shove a knife in your spine. He *owns* them—body, mind and what's left of their souls. . . . Now get to the plane, it's waiting."

"Don't you want to see the children, tell Jamie that—"

"*No,* there isn't time! Take her out there, Johnny. I want to check the beach."

"There's nothing I haven't checked, David,"

said St. Jacques, his voice on the edge of defiance.

"*I'll* tell you whether you have or not," shot
back Bourne, his eyes angry as he started
across the sand, adding in a loud voice without
looking around, "I'm going to have a dozen
questions for you, and I hope to Christ you can
answer them!"

St. Jacques tensed, taking a step forward but
stopped by his sister. "Leave it alone, Bro," said
Marie, her hand on his arm. "He's frightened."

"He's *what*? He's one nasty son of a bitch is
what he is!"

"Yes, I know."

The brother looked at his sister. "That stranger you were talking about yesterday at the
house?"

"Yes, only now it's worse. That's why he's
frightened."

"I don't understand."

"He's older, Johnny. He's fifty now and he
wonders if he can still do the things he did
before, years ago—in the war, in Paris, in Hong
Kong. It's all gnawing at him, eating into him,
because he knows he's got to be better than he
ever was."

"I think he can be."

"I know he will be, for he has an extraordinary reason going for him. A wife and two children were taken from him once before. He barely remembers them, but they're at the core of his torment; Mo Panov believes that and I do, too. . . . Now, years later, another wife and two children are threatened. Every nerve in him has to be on fire."

Suddenly, from three hundred feet away on the beach, Bourne's voice erupted, splitting through the breezes from the sea. "Goddamn it, I told you to *hurry*! . . . And you, Mr. *Expert*, there's a reef out here with the color of a sandbar beyond it! Have you *considered* that?"

"Don't answer, Johnny. We'll go out to the plane."

"A sandbar? What the hell's he talking about? . . . Oh, my God, I *do* see!"

"I don't," said Marie as they walked rapidly up the pier.

"There are reefs around eighty percent of the island, ninety-five percent where this beach is concerned. They brake the waves, it's why it's called Tranquility; there's no surf at all."

"So what?"

"So someone using a tank under water wouldn't risk crashing into a reef, but he would into a sandbar in *front* of a reef. He could watch the beach and the guards and crawl up when his landing was clear, lying in the water only feet from shore until he could take the guard. I never thought about that."

"*He* did, Bro."

Bourne sat on the corner of the desk, the two old men on a couch in front of him, his brother-in-law standing by a window fronting the beach in the unoccupied villa.

"Why would I—why would *we*—lie to you, monsieur?" asked the hero of France.

"Because it all sounds like a classic French farce. Similar but different names; one door opening as another closes, look-alikes disappearing and entering on cue. It smells, gentlemen."

"Perhaps you are a student of Molière or Racine . . . ?"

"I'm a *student* of uncanny coincidence, especially where the Jackal is concerned."

"I don't think there's the slightest similarity in our appearances," offered the judge from Boston. "Except, perhaps, our ages."

The telephone rang. Jason quickly reached down and picked it up. "Yes?"

"Everything checks out in Boston," said Conklin. "His name's Prefontaine, Brendan Prefontaine. He was a federal judge of the first circuit caught in a government scam and convicted of felonious misconduct on the bench—read that as being very large in the bribery business. He was sentenced to twenty-one years and did ten, which was enough to blow him away in every department. He's what they call a functioning alcoholic, something of a character in Bean Town's shadier districts, but harmless—actually kind of liked in a warped sort of way. He's also considered very bright when he's clearheaded, and I'm told a lot of crumbs wouldn't have gone court-free and others would be doing longer jail terms if he hadn't given shrewd advice to their attorneys of record. You might say he's a behind-the-scenes storefront lawyer, the 'stores' in his case being saloons, pool halls and probably warehouses. . . . Since I've been where he's at in the booze terrain, he sounds straight arrow to me. He's handling it better than I ever did."

"You quit."

"If I could have managed better in that twilight zone, I might not have. There's something to be said for the grape on many occasions."

"What about his client?"

"Awesome, and our once and former judge was an adjunct professor at Harvard Law, where

Gates was a student in two of his classes. No question about it, Prefontaine knows the man. . . . Trust him, Jason. There's no reason for him to lie. He was simply after a score."

"You're following up on the client?"

"With all the quiet ammunition I can pull out of my personal woodwork. He's our link to Carlos. . . . The Medusa connection was a false lead, a stupid attempt by a stupid general in the Pentagon to put someone inside Gates's inner legal circle."

"You're sure of that?"

"I am now. Gates is a highly paid consultant to a law firm representing a megadefense contractor under antitrust scrutiny. He wouldn't even return Swayne's calls, which, if he did, would make him more stupid than Swayne, which he isn't."

"That's your problem, friend, not mine. If everything goes the way I intend it to go here, I don't even want to hear about Snake Lady. In fact, I can't remember *ever* having heard of it."

"Thanks for dumping it in my lap—and in a way I guess I mean that. Incidentally, the grammar-school notebook you grabbed from the gunslinger in Manassas has some interesting things in it."

"Oh?"

"Do you remember those three frequent fliers from the Mayflower's registry who flew into Philadelphia eight months ago and just happened to be at the hotel at the same time eight months later?"

"Certainly."

"Their names are in Swayne's Mickey Mouse loose-leaf. They had nothing to do with Carlos; they're part of Medusa. It's a mother lode of disconnected information."

"I'm not interested. Use it in good health."

"We will, and very quietly. That notebook'll be on the most wanted list in a matter of days."

"I'm happy for you, but I've got work to do."

"And you refuse any help?"

"Absolutely. This is what I've been waiting thirteen years for. It's what I said at the beginning, it's one on one."

"*High Noon*, you goddamn fool?"

"No, the logical extension of a very intellectual chess game, the player with the better trap wins, and I've got that trap because I'm using *his*. He'd smell out any deviation."

"We trained you too well, scholar."

"Thank you for that."

"Good hunting, Delta."

"Good-bye." Bourne hung up the phone and looked over at the two pathetically curious old

men on the couch. "You passed a sleaze-fac-
tored muster, Judge," he said to Prefontaine.
"And you, 'Jean Pierre,' what can I say? My own
wife, who admits to me that you might very well
have killed her without the slightest compunc-
tion, tells me that I have to trust you. Nothing
makes a hell of a lot of sense, does it?"

"I am what I am, and I did what I did," said the
disgraced attorney with dignity. "But my client
has gone too far. His magisterial persona must
come to an end in ashes."

"My words are not so well phrased as those
of my learned, newfound relative," added the
aged hero of France. "But I know the killing
must stop; it's what my woman tried to tell me.
I am a hypocrite, of course, for I am no stranger
to killing, so I shall only say that *this* kind of
killing must stop. There is no business arrangement here, no profit in the kill, only a sick madman's vengeance that demands the
unnecessary death of a mother and her children. Where is the profit there? . . . No, the
Jackal has gone too far. He, too, must now be
stopped."

"That's the most cold-blooded fucking reasoning I've ever *heard*!" cried John St. Jacques
by the window.

"I thought your words were very well chosen,"

said the former judge to the felon from Paris.
"Très bien."

"D'accord."

"And I think I'm out of my mind to have anything to do with either of you," broke in Jason
Bourne. "But right now I don't have a choice.
. . . It's eleven-thirty-five, gentlemen. The clock
is running."

"The what?" asked Prefontaine.

"Whatever's going to happen will happen during the next two, five, ten or twenty-four hours.
I'm flying back to Blackburne Airport, where I'll
create a scene, the bereaved husband and father who's gone crazy over the killing of his wife
and children. It won't be difficult for me, I assure
you; I'll make a hell of a ruckus. . . . I'll demand
an immediate flight to Tranquility, and when I get
here there'll be three pine coffins on the pier,
supposedly containing my wife and children."

"Everything as it should be," interrupted the
Frenchman. *"Bien."*

"Very *bien*," agreed Bourne. "I'll insist that
one be opened, and then I'll scream or collapse
or both, whatever comes to mind, so that whoever's watching won't forget what they've seen.
St. Jacques here will have to control me—be
rough, Johnny, be convincing—and finally I'll be

taken up to another villa, the one nearest the steps to the beach on the east path. . . . Then the waiting begins."

"For this Jackal?" asked the Bostonian. "He'll know where you are?"

"Of course he will. A lot of people, including the staff, will have seen where I was taken. He'll find out, that's child's play for him."

"So you wait for him, monsieur? You think the monseigneur will walk into such a trap? *Ridicule!*"

"Not at all, monsieur," replied Jason calmly. "To begin with, I won't be there, and by the time he finds that out, I'll have found him."

"For Christ's sake, *how*?" half shouted St. Jacques.

"Because I'm better than he is," answered Jason Bourne. "I always was."

The scenario went as planned, the personnel at Montserrat's Blackburne Airport still smoldering from the abuse hurled at them by the tall hysterical American who accused them all of murder, of allowing his wife and children to be killed by terrorists—of being willing *nigger* accomplices of filthy killers! Not only were the people of the island quietly furious, but they were also hurt. Quiet because they understood his anguish, hurt because they could not understand how he could blame *them* and use such vicious words, words he had never used before. Was this good *mon*, this wealthy brother of the gregarious Johnny Saint Jay, this rich-rich friend who had put so much money into Tranquility Isle not a friend at all but, instead, white garbage who blamed them for terrible things they had nothing to do with because their skins were dark? It was an evil puzzle, *mon*. It was part of the madness, the *obeah* that had crossed the waters from the mountains of Jamaic' and put a curse on their islands. *Watch him,* brothers. *Watch his every move.* Perhaps he is another sort of storm, one not born in the south or the east, but whose winds are more destructive. *Watch him, mon.* His anger is dangerous.

So he was watched. By many—the uninformed, civilians and authorities alike—as a nervous Henry Sykes at Government House kept his word. The official investigation was solely under his command. It was quiet, thorough—and nonexistent.

Bourne behaved far worse on the pier of Tranquility Inn, striking his own brother, the amiable

Saint Jay, until the younger man subdued him and had him carried up the steps to the nearest villa. Servants came and went bringing trays of food and drink to the porch. Selected visitors were permitted to pay their condolences, including the chief aide to the Crown governor who wore his full military regalia, a symbol of the Crown's concern. And an old man who knew death from the brutalities of war and who insisted on seeing the bereaved husband and father—he was accompanied by a woman in a nurse's uniform, properly topped by a hat and a dark mourning veil. And two Canadian guests of the hotel, close friends of the owner, both of whom had met the disconsolate man when Tranquility Inn opened with great fireworks several years ago—they asked to pay their respects and offer whatever support or comfort they could. John St. Jacques agreed, suggesting that their visit be brief and to understand that his brother-in-law remained in a corner of the darkened living room, the drapes having been drawn.

"It's all so horrible, so meaningless!" said the visitor from Toronto softly to the shadowed figure in a chair across the room. "I hope you're a religious man, David. I am. Faith helps in such times as these. Your loved ones are in the arms of Christ now."

"Thank you." A momentary breeze off the water rustled the drapes, permitting a narrow shaft of sunlight to flash across the room. It was enough.

"Wait a minute," said the second Canadian. "You're not—good Lord, *you're* not Dave Webb? Dave has—"

"Be quiet," ordered St. Jacques, standing at the door behind the two visitors.

"Johnny, I spent seven hours in a fishing boat with Dave and I damn well know him when I see him!"

"Shut up," said the owner of Tranquility Inn.

"Oh, dear *God*!" cried the aide to the Crown governor of Montserrat in a clipped British accent.

"Listen to me, both of you," said St. Jacques, rushing forward between the two Canadians and turning to stand in front of the armchair. "I wish I'd never let you in here, but there's nothing we can do about that now. . . . I thought you'd add weight, two more observers, if anyone asked you questions, which they will, and that's *exactly* what you're going to do. You've been talking to David Webb, consoling *David Webb*. Do you understand that?"

"I don't understand a damn thing," objected the bewildered visitor who had spoken of the comfort of faith. "Who the hell is he?"

"He's the senior aide to the Crown governor," answered St. Jacques. "I'm telling you this so you *will* understand—"

"You mean the army brass who showed up in full uniform with a squad of black soldiers?" asked the guest who had fished with David Webb.

"Among his duties is chief military aide-de-camp. He's a brigadier—"

"We saw the bastard leave," protested the fisherman. "From the dining room, we all saw him *leave*! He was with the old Frenchman and the nurse—"

"You saw someone else leave. Wearing sunglasses."

"Webb . . . ?"

"Gentlemen!" The governor's aide rose from the chair, wearing the ill-fitting jacket worn by Jason Bourne when he had flown back to Tranquility from Blackburne Airport. "You are welcome guests on our island but, as guests, you will abide by the Crown's decisions in emergencies. You will either abide by them, or, as we would do in extreme weather, we will be forced to place you in custody."

"Hey, come on, Henry. They're friends. . . ."

"Friends do not call brigadiers 'bastards'—"

"You might if you were once a busted corporal, General," inserted the man of faith. "My companion here didn't mean anything. Long before the whole damned Canadian army needed his company's engineers, he was a screwed-up infantry grunt. *His* company, incidentally. He wasn't too bright in Korea."

"Let's cut the crap," said Webb's fishing companion. "So we've been in here talking to Dave, right?"

"Right. And that's all I can tell you."

"It's enough, Johnny. Dave's in trouble, so what can we do?"

"Nothing—absolutely nothing but what's on the inn's agenda. You all got a copy delivered to your villas an hour ago."

"You'd better explain," said the religious Canadian. "I never read those goddamn happy-hour schedules."

"The inn's having a special buffet, everything on the house, and a meteorologist from the Leeward Islands Weather Control will speak for a few minutes on what happened last night."

"The storm?" asked the fisherman, the former busted corporal and current owner of Canada's largest industrial engineering company. "A storm's a storm in these islands. What's to explain?"

"Oh, things like why they happen and why they're over so quickly; how to behave—the elimination of fear, basically."

"You want us all up there, is that what you mean?"

"Yes, I do."

"That'll help Dave?"

"Yes, it will."

"Then the whole place'll be up there. I guarantee it."

"I appreciate that, but how can you?"

"I'll circulate another happy-hour notice that Angus MacPherson McLeod, chairman of All Canada Engineering, will award ten thousand dollars to whoever asks the most intelligent question. How about that, Johnny? The rich always want more for nothing, that's our profound weakness."

"I'll take your word for it," mumbled St. Jacques.

"C'mon," said McLeod to his religious friend from Toronto. "We'll circulate with tears in our eyes and spread the word. Then, you idiot colonel—that's what you were, y' bastard—in an hour or so we'll shift gears and only talk of ten thousand dollars and a free-for-all dinner. With the beach and the sun, people's attention spans are roughly two and a half minutes; in cold weather, no more than four. Believe me, I've had it calculated by computer research. . . . You'll have a full party tonight, Johnny." McLeod turned and walked toward the door.

"Scotty," cried the man of faith following the fisherman. "You're going off half-cocked again! Attention spans, two minutes, four minutes, computer research—I don't believe a *word* of it!"

"Really?" said Angus, his hand on the knob. "You believe in ten thousand dollars, don't you?"

"I certainly do."

"You watch, that's my market research. . . . That's also why I own the company. And now I intend to summon those tears to my eyes; it's another reason I own the company."

In a dark storage room on the third floor of Tranquility Inn's main complex, Bourne, who had shed the military tunic, and the old Frenchman sat on two stools in front of a window overlooking the east and west paths of the shoreline resort. The villas below extended out on both sides of the stone steps leading down to the beach and the dock. Each man held a pair of powerful binoculars to his eyes, scanning the people walking back and forth on the paths and up and down the rock staircase. A hand-held radio with the hotel's private frequency was on the sill in front of Jason.

"He's near us," said Fontaine softly.

"What?" shot out Bourne, yanking the glasses from his face and turning to the old man. "Where? Tell me *where!*"

"He's not in our vision, monsieur, but he is near us."

"What do you mean?"

"I can feel it. Like an animal that senses the approach of distant thunder. It's inside of you; it's the fear."

"That's not very clear."

"It is to me. Perhaps you wouldn't understand. The Jackal's challenger, the man of many appearances, the Chameleon—the killer known as Jason Bourne—was not given to fear, we are told, only a great bravado that came from his strength."

Jason smiled grimly, in contradiction. "Then

you were told a lie," he said softly. "A part of that man lives with a kind of raw fear few people have ever experienced."

"I find that hard to believe, monsieur—"

"Believe. I'm he."

"Are you, Mr. Webb? It's not difficult to piece things together. Do you force yourself to assume your other self because of this fear?"

David Webb stared at the old man. "For God's sake, what choice do I have?"

"You could disappear for a time, you and your family. You could live peacefully, in complete security, your government would see to it."

"He'd come after me—after us—wherever we were."

"For how long? A year? Eighteen months? Certainly less than two years. He's a sick man; all Paris—my Paris—knows it. Considering the enormous expense and complexity of the current situation—these events designed to trap you—I would suggest that it's Carlos's last attempt. Leave, monsieur. Join your wife in Basse-Terre and then fly thousands of miles away while you can. Let him go back to Paris and die in frustration. Is it not enough?"

"*No.* He'd come after me, after us! It's got to be settled here, *now.*"

"I will soon join my woman, if such is to be, so I can disagree with certain people, men like you, for instance, *Monsieur le Caméléon,* whom I would have automatically agreed with before. I do so now. I think you *can* go far away. I think you know that you *can* put the Jackal in a side pocket and get on with your life, altered only slightly for a while, but you won't do it. Something inside stops you; you cannot permit yourself a strategic retreat, no less honorable for its avoidance of violence. Your family is safe but others may die, but even that doesn't stop you. You have to *win*—"

"I think that's enough psychobabble," interrupted Bourne, bringing the binoculars again to his eyes, concentrating on the scene below beyond the windows.

"That's it, isn't it?" said the Frenchman, studying Le Caméléon, his binoculars still at his side. "They trained you too well, instilled in you too completely the person you had to become. Jason Bourne against Carlos the Jackal and Bourne must win, it's imperative that he *win*. . . . Two aging lions, each pitted against the other years ago, both with a burning hatred created by far-off strategists who had no idea what the consequences would be. How many have lost their lives because they crossed your converging paths? How many unknowing men and women have been killed—"

"Shut *up*!" cried Jason as flashing images of Paris, even peripherally of Hong Kong, Macao and Beijing—and most recently last night in Manassas, Virginia—assaulted his fragmented inner screen. So much death!

Suddenly, abruptly, the door of the dark storage room opened and Judge Brendan Prefontaine walked rapidly, breathlessly inside. "He's here," said the Bostonian. "One of St. Jacques's patrols, a three-man unit a mile down the east shoreline, couldn't be reached by radio. St. Jacques sent a guard to find them and he just returned—then ran away himself. All three were killed, each man with a bullet in his throat."

"The Jackal!" exclaimed the Frenchman. "It is his *carte de visite*—his calling card. He announces his arrival."

16

The midafternoon sun was suspended, immobile, burning the sky and the land, a ringed globe of fire intent only on scorching everything beneath it. And the alleged "computerized research" offered by the Canadian industrialist Angus McLeod appeared to be confirmed. Although a number of seaplanes flew in to take frightened couples away, the collective attention span of average people after a disturbing event, if certainly longer than two and a half to four minutes, was certainly not more than a few hours. A horrible thing had happened during the predawn storm, an act of terrible vengeance, as they understood it. It involved a single man with a vendetta against old enemies, a killer who had long since fled from the island. With the removal of the ugly coffins, as well as the beached, damaged speedboat, and the soothing words over the government radio along with the intermittent, unobtrusive appearances of the armed guards, a sense of normalcy returned—not total, of course, for there was a mourning figure among them, but he was out of sight and, they were told, would soon leave. And despite the depth of the horrors, as the rumors had them— naturally exaggerated out of all proportion by the hypersuperstitious island natives—the horrors were not *theirs*. It was an act of violence completely unrelated to them, and, after all, life had to go on. Seven couples remained at the inn.

"Christ, we're paying six hundred dollars a day—"

"No one's after *us*—"

"Shit, man, next week it's back to the commodities grind, so we're going to enjoy—"

"No sweat, Shirley, they're not giving out names, they *promised* me—"

With the burning, immobile afternoon sun, a small soiled plot of the vast Caribbean playground came back to its own particular ambience, death receding with each application of

Bain de Soleil and another rum punch. Nothing was quite as it had been, but the blue-green waters lapped on the beach, enticing the few bathers to walk into them, immersing their bodies in the cool liquid rhythm of wet constancy. A progressively less tentative peace returned to Tranquility Isle.

"There!" cried the hero of France.

"Where?" shouted Bourne.

"The four priests. Walking down the path in a line."

"They're black."

"Color means nothing."

"He was a priest when I saw him in Paris, at Neuilly-sur-Seine."

Fontaine lowered the binoculars and looked at Jason. "The Church of the Blessed Sacrament?" he asked quietly.

"I can't remember. . . . Which one *is* he?"

"You saw him in his priest's habit?"

"And that son of a bitch saw *me*. He knew I *knew* it was him! Which *one*?"

"He's not there, monsieur," said Jean Pierre, slowly bringing the binoculars back to his eyes. "It is another *carte de visite*. Carlos anticipates; he is a master of geometry. There is no straight line for him, only many sides, many levels."

"That sounds damned Oriental."

"Then you understand. It has crossed his mind that you may not be in that villa, and if you are not, he wants you to know that he knows it."

"Neuilly-sur-Seine—"

"No, not actually. He can't be sure at the moment. He *was* sure at the Church of the Blessed Sacrament."

"How should I play it?"

"How does the Chameleon think he should play it?"

"The obvious would be to do nothing," answered Bourne, his eyes on the scene below. "And he wouldn't accept that because his uncertainty is too strong. He'd say to himself, He's better than that. I could blow him away with a rocket, so he's somewhere else."

"I think you're correct."

Jason reached down and picked up the handheld radio from the sill. He pressed the button and spoke. "Johnny?"

"Yes?"

"Those four black priests on the path, do you see them?"

"Yes."

"Have a guard stop them and bring them into the lobby. Tell him to say the owner wants to see them."

"Hey, they're not going into the villa, they're just passing by offering prayers to the bereaved inside. The vicar from town called and I gave him permission. They're okay, David."

"The hell they are," said Jason Bourne. "Do as I say." The Chameleon spun around on the stool, looking at the objects in the storage room. He slid off his perch and walked to a bureau with a mirror attached to its top. He yanked the automatic from his belt, smashed the glass, picked up a fragment and brought it to Fontaine. "Five minutes after I leave, flash this every now and then in the window."

"I shall do so from the *side* of the window, monsieur."

"Good thinking." Jason relented to the point of a brief slight smile. "It struck me that I didn't really have to suggest that."

"And what will you do?"

"What he's doing now. Become a tourist in Montserrat, a roving 'guest' at Tranquility Inn." Bourne again reached down for the radio; he picked it up, pressed the button and gave his orders. "Go to the men's shop in the lobby and get me three different guayabera jackets, a pair of sandals, two or three wide-brimmed straw hats and gray or tan walking shorts. Then send someone to the tackle shop and bring me a reel of line, hundred-pound test, a scaling knife— and two distress flares. I'll meet you on the steps up here. *Hurry.*"

"You will not heed my words, then," said Fontaine, lowering the binoculars and looking at Jason. "Monsieur le Caméléon goes to work."

"He goes to work," replied Bourne, replacing the radio on the sill.

"If you or the Jackal or both of you are killed, others may die, innocent people slaughtered—"

"Not because of me."

"Does it matter? Does it matter to the victims or their families who is responsible?"

"I didn't choose the circumstances, old man, they were chosen for me."

"You can change them, alter them."

"So can he."

"He has no conscience—"

"You're one hell of an authority on *that* score."

"I accept the rebuke, but I have lost something of great value to me. Perhaps it's why I discern a conscience in you—a part of you."

"Beware the sanctimonious reformer." Jason started for the door and the beribboned military tunic that hung on an old coatrack alongside the visored officer's hat. "Among other things he's a bore."

"Shouldn't you be watching the path below while the priests are detained? It will take some time for St. Jacques to get the items you asked for."

Bourne stopped and turned, his eyes cold on the verbose old Frenchman. He wanted to *leave*, to get away from this old, *old* man who talked too much—said too much! But Fontaine was right. It would be stupid not to watch what happened below. An awkward, unusual reaction on the part of someone, an abrupt, startled glance by someone in an unexpected direction—it was the little things, the sudden involuntary, precisely imprecise small motions that so often pointed to the concealed string that was the fuse leading to the explosive trap. In silence, Jason walked back to the window, picked up the binoculars and put them to his face.

A police officer in the tan-and-scarlet uniform of Montserrat approached the procession of four priests on the path; he was obviously as bewildered as he was deferential, nodding courteously as the four gathered together to listen, gesturing politely toward the glass doors of the lobby. Bourne's eyes shifted within the frame of vision, studying the black features of each cleric, one after another in rapid succession. He spoke quietly to the Frenchman. "Do you see what I see?"

"The fourth one, the priest who was last," replied Fontaine. "He's alarmed, but the others are not. He's afraid."

"He was bought."

"Thirty pieces of silver," agreed the Frenchman. "You'll go down and take him, of course."

"Of course not," corrected Jason. "He's right where I want him to be." Bourne grabbed the radio off the sill. "Johnny?"

"Yes? . . . I'm in the shop. I'll be up in a few minutes—"

"Those priests, do you know them?"

"Only the one who calls himself the 'vicar'; he comes around for contributions. And they're not really priests, David, they're more like 'ministers' in a religious order. Very religious and very local."

"Is the vicar there?"

"Yes. He's always first in line."

"Good. . . . Slight change of plans. Bring the clothes to your office, then go and see the priests. Tell them an official of the government wants to meet them and make a contribution in return for their prayers."

"What?"

"I'll explain later. Now hurry up. I'll see you in the lobby."

"You mean my office, don't you? I've got the clothes, remember?"

"They'll come later—roughly a minute later, after I get out of this uniform. Do you have a camera in your office?"

"Three or four of them. Guests are always leaving them behind—"

"Put all of them with the clothes," interrupted Jason. "Get going!" Bourne shoved the radio into his belt, then changed his mind. He pulled it out and handed it to Fontaine. "Here, you take this. I'll get another and stay in contact. . . . What's happening down there?"

"Our alarmed priest looks around as they go to the lobby doors. He's truly frightened now."

"Where's he looking?" asked Bourne, grabbing the binoculars.

"That's of no help. In every direction."

"Damn!"

"They're at the doors now."

"I'll get ready—"

"I'll help you." The old Frenchman got off the stool and went to the coatrack. He removed the tunic and the hat. "If you are about to do what

I think you intend doing, try to stay by a wall and don't turn around. The governor's aide is somewhat stouter than you and we must bunch the jacket in the back."

"You're pretty good at this, aren't you?" said Jason, holding out his arms so as to be helped into the tunic.

"The German soldiers were always much fatter than we were, especially the corporals and the sergeants—all that sausage, you know. We had our tricks." Suddenly, as if he had been shot or seized by a convulsion, Fontaine gasped, then lurched in front of Bourne. "*Mon Dieu! . . . C'est terrible!* The governor—"

"What?"

"The *Crown governor*!"

"What about him?"

"At the airport, it was so quick, so rapid!" cried the old Frenchman. "And everything that has happened, my woman, the killing— Still, it is *unforgivable* of me!"

"What are you talking about?"

"That man in the villa, the military officer whose uniform you wear. He's his *aide*!"

"We know that."

"What you do not know, monsieur, is that my very first instructions came from the Crown governor."

"Instructions?"

"From the Jackal! He is the contact."

"Oh, my *God*," whispered Bourne, rushing to the stool where Fontaine had put the radio. He took a deep breath as he picked it up, his thoughts racing, control imperative. "Johnny?"

"For Christ's sake, my arms are full and I'm on my way to the office and those goddamned monks are in the lobby waiting for me! What the hell do you want *now*?"

"Take it easy and listen very carefully. How well do you know Henry?"

"Sykes? The CG's man?"

"Yes. I've met him a few times but I don't know him, Johnny."

"I know him very well. You wouldn't have a house and I wouldn't have Tranquility Inn if it wasn't for him."

"Is he in touch with the governor? I mean right *now*, is he keeping the CG posted about what's going on here. *Think,* Johnny. It's important. There's a phone in that villa; he could be in contact with Government House. *Is* he?"

"You mean with the CG himself?"

"With *anyone* over there."

"Believe me, he's not. Everything's so quiet not even the police know what's going on. And as far as the CG is concerned, he's only been given the vaguest scenario, no names, nothing, only a trap. He's also out on his boat and doesn't want to know a damn thing until it's all over. . . . Those were his orders."

"I'll bet they were."

"Why do you ask?"

"I'll explain later. Hurry *up*!"

"Will you stop *saying* that?"

Jason put down the radio and turned to Fontaine. "We're clear. The governor isn't one of the Jackal's army of old men. He's a different kind of recruit, probably like that lawyer Gates in Boston—just bought or frightened, no soul involved."

"You're certain? Your brother-in-law is certain?"

"The man's out on his boat. He was given a bare-bones outline but that's all, and his orders were that he's not to be told anything else until it's all over."

The Frenchman sighed. "It's a pity my mind is so old and so filled with salt. If I had remembered, we could have used him. Come, the jacket."

"How could we have used him?" asked Bourne, again holding out his arms.

"He removed himself to the *gradins*—how is it said?"

"The bleachers. He's out of the game, only an observer."

"I've known many like him. They want Carlos to lose; *he* wants Carlos to lose. It's his only way out, but he's too terrified to raise a hand against the Jackal."

"Then how could we turn him?" Jason buttoned the tunic as Fontaine manipulated the belt and the cloth behind him.

"*Le Caméléon* asks such a question?"

"I've been out of practice."

"Ah, yes," said the Frenchman, yanking the belt firmly. "That man I've appealed to."

"Just shut up. . . . How?"

"*Très simple, monsieur.* We tell him the Jackal already knows he's turned—*I* tell him. Who better than the monseigneur's emissary?"

"You *are* good." Bourne held in his stomach as Fontaine turned him around, pressing the lapels and the ribbons of the jacket.

"I'm a survivor, neither better nor worse than others—except with my woman. Then I was better than most."

"You loved her very much, didn't you?"

"Love? Oh, I imagine that's taken for granted although rarely expressed. Perhaps it's the comfort of being familiar, although, again, hardly with grand passion. One does not have to finish a sentence to be understood, and a look in the eyes will bring on laughter without a word being said. It comes with the years, I suppose.''

Jason stood motionless for a moment, staring strangely at the Frenchman. "I want the years you had, old man, I want them very, very much. The years I've had with my . . . woman . . . are filled with scars that won't heal, can't heal, until something inside is changed or cleansed or goes away. That's the way it is.''

"Then you are too strong, or too stubborn or too *stupid*! . . . Don't look at me that way. I told you, I'm not afraid of you, I'm not afraid of any- one any longer. But if what you say is true, that this is the way things really are with you, then I suggest you leave aside all thoughts of love and concentrate on hatred. Since I cannot reason with David Webb, I must prod Jason Bourne. A Jackal filled with hate must die, and only Bourne can kill him. . . . Here are your hat and sun- glasses. Stay against a wall or you'll look like a military peacock, your khaki tail raised for the purpose of passing *merde*.''

Without speaking, Bourne adjusted the vi- sored hat and sunglasses, walked to the door and let himself out. He crossed to the solid wood staircase and started rapidly down, nearly colliding with a white-jacketed black steward carrying a tray out of the second-floor exit. He nodded to the young man, who backed away, allowing him to proceed, when a quiet, ziplike noise along with a sudden movement caught in the corner of his eyes caused him to turn. The waiter was pulling an electronic beeper out of his pocket! Jason spun around, lurching up the steps, his hands lunging into the youngster's body, ripping the device out of his grip as the tray crashed to the floor of the landing. Straddling the youth, with one hand on the beeper and the other grasping the steward's throat, he spoke breathlessly, quietly. "Who had you do this? *Tell* me!"

"Hey, *mon,* I *fight* you!" cried the youngster, writhing, freeing his right hand and smashing a fist into Bourne's left cheek. "We don't want no bad *mon* here! Our boss-*mon* the best! You don't scare *me!*" The steward crashed his knee into Jason's groin.

"You young son of a *bitch!*" cried Le Caméléon, slapping the youngster's face back and forth while grabbing his aching testicles with his left hand. "I'm his friend, his *brother!* Will you cut it *out?* . . . Johnny Saint Jay's my brother! In-law, if it makes any goddamned difference!"

"Oh?" said the large, youthful, obviously athletic steward, a touch of resentment in his wide, embarrassed brown eyes. "You are the *mon* with Boss Saint Jay's sister?"

"I'm her husband. Who the fuck are you?"

"I am first head steward of the second floor, *sir*! Soon I will be on the first floor because I am very good. I am also a very fine fighter—my father taught me, although he is old now, like you. Do you wish to fight more? I think I can beat you! You have gray in your hair—"

"Shut up! . . . What's the beeper all about?" asked Jason, holding up the small brown plastic instrument as he crawled off the young waiter.

"I don't know, *mon*—sir! Bad things have happened. We are told that if we see men running on the staircases we should press the buttons."

"Why?"

"The lifts, sir. Our very fast elevators. Why would guests use the stairs?"

"What's your name?" asked Bourne, replacing his hat and sunglasses.

"Ishmael, sir."

"Like in *Moby Dick*?"

"I do not know such a person, sir."

"Maybe you will."

"Why?"

"I'm not sure. You're a very good fighter."

"I see no connection, *mon*—sir."

"Neither do I." Jason got to his feet. "I want you to help me, Ishmael. Will you?"

"Only if your brother permits it."

"He will. He *is* my brother."

"I must hear it from him, sir."

"Very good. You doubt me."

"Yes, I do, sir," said Ishmael, getting to his knees and reassembling the tray, separating the broken dishes from the whole ones. "Would you take the word of a strong man with gray in his hair who runs down the stairs and attacks you and says things anyone could say? . . . If you wish to fight, the loser must speak the truth. Do you wish to fight?"

"No, I do not wish to fight and don't you press it. I'm not that old and you're not that good, young man. Leave the tray and come with me. I'll explain to Mr. St. Jacques, who, I remind you, is my brother—my wife's brother. To hell with it, come *on*!"

"What do you want me to do, sir?" asked the steward, getting to his feet and following Jason.

"Listen to me," said Bourne, stopping and turning on the steps above the first-floor landing. "Go ahead of me into the lobby and walk to the front door. Empty ashtrays or something and look busy, but keep glancing around. I'll come out in a few moments and you'll see me go over and talk to Saint Jay and four priests, who'll be with him—"

"Priests?" interrupted the astonished Ishmael. "Men of the cloth, sir? *Four* of them? What they doing here, *mon*? More bad things happen? The *obeah*?"

"They came here to pray so the bad things will stop—no more *obeah*. But what's important to me is that I must speak to one of them alone. When they leave the lobby, this priest I have to see may break away from the others to be by himself . . . or possibly to meet someone else. Do you think you could follow him without his seeing you?"

"Would Mr. Saint Jay tell me to do that?"

"Suppose I have him look over at you and nod his head."

"Then I can do it. I am faster than the mongoose and, like the mongoose, I know every foot trail on Tranquility. He goes one way, I know where he's going and will be there first. . . . But how will I know which priest? More than one may go off by himself."

"I'll talk to all four separately. He'll be the last one."

"Then I will know."

"That's pretty fast thinking," said Bourne. "You're right; they could separate."

"I think good, *mon*. I am fifth in my class at 'Serrat's Technical Academy. The four ahead of me are all girls, so they don't have to work."

"That's an interesting observation—"

"In five or six years I'll have the money to attend the university in Barbados!"

"Maybe sooner. Go on now. Walk into the lobby and head for the door. Later, after the priests leave, I'll come out looking for you, but I won't be in this uniform, from any distance you won't know me. If I don't find you, meet me in an hour— Where? Where's a quiet place?"

"Tranquility Chapel, sir. The path in the woods above the east beach. No one ever goes there, even on the Sabbath."

"I remember it. Good idea."

"There is a remaining subject, sir—"

"Fifty dollars, American."

"*Thank* you, sir!"

Jason waited by the door for ninety seconds, then opened it barely an inch. Ishmael was in place by the entrance, and he could see John St. Jacques talking with the four priests several feet to the right of the front desk. Bourne tugged at his jacket, squared his shoulders in military fashion, and walked out into the lobby toward the priests and the owner of Tranquility Inn.

"It's an honor and a privilege, Fathers," he said to the four black clerics as a surprised and curious St. Jacques watched him. "I'm new here in the islands and I must say I'm very impressed. The government is particularly pleased that you saw fit to help calm our troubled waters," continued Jason, his hands clasped firmly behind his back. "For your efforts, the Crown governor has authorized Mr. St. Jacques here to issue you a check in the amount of one hundred pounds for your church—to be reimbursed by the treasury, of course."

"It is such a magnificent gesture, I hardly know what to say," intoned the vicar, his high lilting voice sincere.

"You could tell me whose idea it was," said the Chameleon. "Most touching, most touching, indeed."

"Oh, I cannot take the credit, sir," replied the vicar, looking, as the two others did, at the fourth man. "It was Samuel's. Such a good and decent leader of our flock."

"Good show, Samuel." Bourne stared briefly, his eyes penetrating, at the fourth man. "But I should like to thank each of you personally. And know your names." Jason went down the line shaking the three hands and quietly exchanging pleasantries. He came to the last priest, whose eyes kept straying away from his. "Of course I know your name, Samuel," he said, his voice even lower, barely audible. "And I should like to know whose idea it was before you took the credit."

"I don't understand you," whispered Samuel.

"Certainly you do—such a good and decent man—you must have received another very generous contribution."

"You mistake me for someone else, sir," mumbled the fourth priest, his dark eyes for an instant betraying deep fear.

"I don't make mistakes, your friend knows that. I'll find you, Samuel. Maybe not today, but surely tomorrow or the day after that." Bourne raised his voice as he released the cleric's hand. "Again, the government's profound thanks, Fathers. The Crown is most grateful. And now I must be on my way; a dozen telephone calls should be answered. . . . Your office, St. Jacques?"

"Yes, of course, *General.*"

Inside the office, Jason took out his automatic and tore off the uniform as he separated the pile of clothing Marie's brother had brought for him. He slipped on a pair of knee-length gray Bermuda walking shorts, chose a red-and-white-striped guayabera jacket, and the widest-brimmed straw hat. He removed his socks and shoes, put on the sandals, stood up and swore. "*Goddamn* it!" He kicked off the sandals and shoved his bare feet back into his heavy rubber-soled shoes. He studied the various cameras and their accessories, choosing the lightest but most complicated, and crossed the straps over his chest. John St. Jacques walked into the room carrying a small hand-held radio.

"Where the hell did you come from? Miami Beach?"

"Actually, a little north—say, Pompano. I'm not that gaudy. I won't stand out."

"Actually, you're right. I've got people out there who'd swear you were old-time Key West conservative. Here's the radio."

"Thanks." Jason put the compact instrument into his breast pocket.

"Where to now?"

"After Ishmael, the kid I had you nod at."

"*Ishmael?* I didn't nod at Ishmael, you simply said I should nod my head at the entrance."

"Same thing." Bourne squeezed the automatic under his belt beneath the guayabera and looked at the equipment brought from the tackle shop. He picked up the reel of one-hundred-test line and the scaling knife, placing both in his pockets, then opened an empty camera case and put the two distress flares inside. It was not everything he wanted, but it was enough. He was not who he was thirteen years ago and he was not so young even then. His mind had to work better and faster than his body, a fact he reluctantly accepted. *Damn!*

"That Ishmael's a good boy," said Marie's brother. "He's pretty smart and strong as a prize Saskatchewan steer. I'm thinking of making him a guard in a year or so. The pay's better."

"Try Harvard or Princeton if he does his job this afternoon."

"Wow, *that's* a wrinkle. Did you know his father was the champion wrestler of the islands? Of course, he's sort of getting on now—"

"Get the hell out of my way," ordered Jason, heading for the door. "You're not exactly *eighteen*, either!" he added, turning briefly before he let himself out.

"Never said I was. What's your problem?"

"Maybe it's the sandbar you never saw, Mr.

Security." Bourne slammed the door as he ran out into the hallway.

"Touchy, touchy." St. Jacques slowly shook his head as he unclenched his thirty-four-year-old fist.

Nearly two hours had passed and Ishmael was nowhere to be found! His leg locked in place as if crippled, Jason limped convincingly from one end of Tranquility Inn's property to the other, his eye focused through the mirrored lens of the camera, seeing everything, but no sign of young Ishmael. Twice he had gone up the path into the woods to the isolated square structure of logs, thatched roof and stained glass that was the multidenominational chapel of the resort, a sanctuary for meditation built more for its quaint appearance than for utility. As the young black steward had observed, it was rarely visited but had its place in vacation brochures.

The Caribbean sun was growing more orange, inching its way down toward the water's horizon. Soon the shadows of sundown would crawl across Montserrat and the out islands. Soon thereafter darkness would come, and the Jackal approved of darkness. But then, so did the Chameleon.

"Storage room, anything?" said Bourne into his radio.

"*Rien, monsieur.*"

"Johnny?"

"I'm up on the roof with six scouts at all points. Nothing."

"What about the dinner, the party tonight?"

"Our meteorologist arrived ten minutes ago by boat from Plymouth. He's afraid to fly. . . . And Angus tacked a check for ten thousand on the bulletin board, signature and payee to be entered. Scotty was right, all seven couples will be there. We're a society of who-gives-a-shit after an appropriate few minutes of silence."

"Tell me something I don't know, Bro. . . . Out. I'm heading back to the chapel."

"Glad to hear somebody goes there. A travel bastard in New York said it'd be a nice touch, but I haven't heard from him since. Stay in touch, David."

"I will, Johnny," replied Jason Bourne.

The path to the chapel was growing dark, the tall palms and dense foliage above the beach hastening nature's process by blocking the rays of the setting sun. Jason was about to turn around and head for the tackle shop and a flashlight when suddenly, as if on photoelectric cue, blue and red floods came alive, shooting their wide circles of light up from the ground into the palms above. For a moment Bourne felt that he had abruptly, too abruptly, entered a lush Technicolor tunnel cut out of tropical forest. It was disorienting, then disturbing. He was a moving, illuminated target in a garishly colored gallery.

He quickly walked into the underbrush beyond the border of floodlights, the nettles of the wild shrubbery stinging his bare legs. He went deeper into the enveloping foliage and continued in the now semidarkness toward the chapel, his pace slow, difficult, the moist branches and vines tangling about his hands and feet. Instinct. Stay out of the light, the gaudy bombastic lights that belonged more properly to an island *carnivale.*

A blunt sound! A thud that was no part of the shoreline woods. Then the start of a moan growing into a convulsion—stopped, thwarted . . . suppressed? Jason crouched and foot by foot broke through the inhibiting, succeeding walls of bush until he could see the thick cathedral door of the chapel. It was partially open, the soft, pulsating glow of the electric candles penetrating the wash of the red and blue floods on the outside path.

Think. Memory. *Remember!* He had been to

the chapel only once before, humorously berating his brother-in-law for spending good money
on a useless addition to Tranquility Inn.

At least it's quaint, St. Jacques had said.

It ain't, Bro, Marie had replied. *It doesn't belong. This isn't a retreat.*

*Suppose someone gets bad news. You know,
really bad—*

Get him a drink, David Webb had said.

*Come on inside. I've got symbols of five differ-
ent religions in stained glass, including Shinto.*

Don't show your sister the bills on this one,
Webb had whispered.

Inside. Was there a door inside? Another exit?
. . . No, there was not. Only five or six rows of
pews, then a railing of some sort in front of a
raised lectern, beneath primitive stained-glass
windows done by native artisans.

Inside. Someone was inside. Ishmael? A distraught guest of Tranquility? A honeymooner
who had sudden, deep reservations embarrass-
ingly too late? He again reached into his breast
pocket for the miniaturized radio. He brought it
to his lips and spoke softly.

"Johnny?"

"Right here on the roof."

"I'm at the chapel. I'm going inside."

"Is Ishmael there?"

"I don't know. Someone is."

"What's wrong, Dave? You sound—"

"Nothing's wrong," interrupted Bourne. "I'm just checking in. . . . What's behind the building? East of it."

"More woods."

"Any paths?"

"There was one several years ago; it's overgrown by now. The construction crews used it to go down to the water. . . . I'm sending over a couple of guards—"

"*No!* If I need you, I'll call. Out." Jason replaced the radio and, still crouching, stared at the chapel door.

Silence now. No sound at all from inside, no human movement, nothing but the flickering "candlelight." Bourne crept to the border of the path, removed the camera equipment and the straw hat and opened the case holding the flares. He removed one, inserted it under his belt, and took out the automatic beside it. He reached into the left pocket of his guayabera jacket for his lighter, gripping it in his hand as he got to his feet, and walked quietly, rapidly, to the corner of the small building—this unlikely sanctuary in the tropical woods above a tropical beach. Flares and the means to light them went back long before Manassas, Virginia, he considered, as he inched his way around the corner toward the chapel's entrance. They went back to Paris—thirteen years ago to Paris, and a cemetery in Rambouillet. And Carlos. . . . He reached the frame of the partially opened door and slowly, cautiously moved his face to the edge and looked inside.

He gasped, his breath suspended, the horror filling him as disbelief and fury spread within him. On the raised platform in front of the rows of glistening wood was the young Ishmael, his body bent forward over the lectern, his arms hanging down, his dark face bruised and lacerated, blood trickling out of his mouth onto the floor. The guilt overwhelmed Jason; it was sudden and complete and devastating, the words of the old Frenchman screaming in his ears: *Others may die, innocent people slaughtered.*

Slaughtered! A child had been *slaughtered*! Promises were implied, but death had been delivered. Oh, *Christ,* what have I *done*? . . . What can I *do*?

Sweat pouring down his face, his eyes barely focusing, Bourne ripped the distress flare out of his pocket, snapped the lighter and, trembling, held it to the red tip. Ignition was instant; the white fire spewed out in white heat, hissing like a hundred angry snakes. Jason threw it into the chapel toward the far end, leaped through the frame, pivoted, and slammed the heavy door shut behind him. He lunged to the floor below the last row, pulled the radio from his pocket and pushed the *Send* button.

"Johnny, the chapel. *Surround* it!" He did not wait for St. Jacques's reply; that there was a voice was enough. The automatic in his hand, the hissing flare continuously erupting as shafts of color shot down from the stained-glass windows, Bourne crept to the far aisle, his eyes moving constantly, seeking out everything he no longer remembered about Tranquility Inn's chapel. The one place where he could not look again was the lectern that held the body of the child he had killed. . . . On both sides of the raised platform were narrow draped archways, like scenic doors on a stage leading to minimum wing space, entrances both left and right. Despite the anguish he felt, there welled up in Jason Bourne a deep sense of satisfaction, even of morbid elation. The lethal game was his for the winning. Carlos had mounted an elaborate trap and the Chameleon had reversed it, Medusa's Delta had turned it around! Behind

one of those two draped archways was the assassin from Paris.

Bourne got to his feet, his back pressed
against the right wall, and raised his gun. He
fired twice into the left archway, the drapes fluttering with each shot, as he sprang behind the
last row, scrambling to the far side, getting to his
knees and firing twice more into the archway on
the right.

A figure lunged in panic through the drapes,
clutching the cloth as it fell forward, the dark red
fabric ripped from the hooks, bunched around
the target's shoulders as he fell to the floor.
Bourne rushed forward, screaming Carlos's
name, firing again and again until the automatic's magazine was empty. Suddenly, from
above there was an explosion, blowing out a
whole section of stained glass high on the left
wall. As the colored fragments shot through the
air and down into the floor, a man on a ledge
outside moved into the center of the open space
above the hissing, blinding flare.

"You're out of bullets," said Carlos to the
stunned Jason Bourne below. "Thirteen years,
Delta, thirteen loathsome years. But now they'll
know who won."

The Jackal raised his gun and fired.

17

The searing ice-cold heat ripped through his neck as Bourne lunged over the pews, crashing down between the second and third rows, smashing his head and his hips on the glistening brown wood as he clawed at the floor. His vision spun out of control as a cloud of darkness enveloped him. In the distance, far, far away, he heard the sound of voices shouting hysterically. Then the darkness was complete.

"David." There was no shouting now; the single voice was low and urgent and used a name he did not care to acknowledge. "David, can you hear me?"

Bourne opened his eyes, instantly aware of two facts. There was a wide bandage around his throat and he was lying fully clothed on a bed. To his right, the anxious face of John St. Jacques came into focus; on his left was a man he did not know, a middle-aged man with a level, steady gaze. "Carlos," Jason managed to say, finding his voice. "It was the *Jackal*!"

"Then he's still on the island—this island." St. Jacques was emphatic. "It's been barely an hour and Henry's got Tranquility ringed. Patrols are hovering offshore, roving back and forth, all in visual and radio contact. He's calling it a 'drug exercise,' very quiet and very official. A few boats come in, but none go out and none will go out."

"Who's *he*?" asked Bourne, looking at the man on his left.

"A doctor," answered Marie's brother. "He's staying at the inn and he's a friend of mine. I was a patient of his in—"

"I think we should be circumspect here," interrupted the Canadian doctor firmly. "You asked for my help and my confidence, John, and I give both gladly, but considering the nature of the events and the fact that your brother-in-law won't be under my professional care, let's dispense with my name."

"I couldn't agree with you more, Doctor," added Jason, wincing, then suddenly snapping his head up, his eyes wide in an admixture of pleading and panic. "*Ishmael!* He's dead—I *killed* him!"

"He isn't and you didn't," said St. Jacques calmly. "He's a goddamned mess but he's not dead. He's one tough kid, like his father, and he'll make it. We're flying him to the hospital in Martinique."

"*Christ,* he was a corpse!"

"He was savagely beaten," explained the doctor. "Both arms were broken, along with multiple lacerations, contusions, I suspect internal injuries and a severe concussion. However, as John accurately described the young man, he's one tough kid."

"I want the best for him."

"Those were my orders."

"Good." Bourne moved his eyes to the doctor. "How damaged am I?"

"Without X rays or seeing how you move—symptomatically, as it were—I can only give you a cursory judgment."

"Do that."

"Outside of the wound, I'd say primarily traumatic shock."

"Forget it. That's not allowed."

"Who says?" said the doctor, smiling kindly.

"I do and I'm not trying to be funny. The body, not the head. I'll be the judge of the head."

"Is he a native?" asked the doctor, looking at the owner of Tranquility Inn. "A white but older Ishmael? I'll tell you he's not a physician."

"Answer him, please."

"All right. The bullet passed through the left side of your neck, missing by millimeters several vital spots that would certainly have rendered you voiceless and probably dead. I've bathed the wound and sutured it. You'll have difficulty moving your head for a while, but that's only a superficial opinion of the damage."

"In short words, I've got a very stiff neck, but if I can walk . . . well, I can walk."

"In shorter words, that's about it."

"It was the flare that did it, after all," said Jason softly, carefully moving his neck back over the pillow. "It blinded him just enough."

"What?" St. Jacques leaned over the bed.

"Never mind. . . . Let's see how well I walk— symptomatically, that is." Bourne slid off the bed, swinging his legs cautiously to the floor, shaking his head at his brother-in-law, who started to help him. "No thanks, Bro. This has got to be me on me." He stood up, the inhibiting bandage around his throat progressively becoming more uncomfortable. He stepped forward, pained by the bruises on his thighs, but they *were* bruises—they were minor. A hot bath would reduce the pain, and medication, extrastrength aspirin and liniment, would permit more normal mobility. It was the goddamned dressing around his neck; it not only choked him but forced him to move his shoulders in order to look in any direction. . . . Still, he considered, he was far less incapacitated than he might have been—for a man of his age. *Damn.* "Can we loosen this necklace, Doctor? It's strangling me."

"A bit, not much. You don't want to risk rupturing those sutures."

"What about an Ace bandage? It gives."

"Too much for a neck wound. You'd forget about it."

"I promise not to."

"You're very amusing."

"I don't feel remotely amusing."

"It's your neck."

"It certainly is. Can you get one, Johnny?"

"Doctor?" St. Jacques looked at the physician.

"I don't think we can stop him."

"I'll send someone to the pro shop."

"Excuse me, Doctor," said Bourne as Marie's brother went to the telephone. "I want to ask Johnny a few questions and I'm not sure you want to hear them."

"I've heard more than I care to already. I'll wait in the other room." The doctor crossed to the door and let himself out.

While St. Jacques talked on the phone, Jason moved about the room raising and lowering his arms and shaking his hands to check the functioning of his motor controls. He crouched, then rose to his feet four times in succession, each movement faster than the previous one. He had to be ready—he *had* to be!

"It'll only be a few minutes," said the brother-in-law, hanging up the phone. "Pritchard will have to go down and open the shop. He'll bring different sizes of tape."

"Thanks." Bourne stopped moving and stood in place. "Who was the man I shot, Johnny? He fell through the curtains in that archway, but I couldn't see his face."

"No one I know, and I thought I knew every white man in these islands who could afford an expensive suit. He must have been a tourist—a tourist on assignment . . . for the Jackal. Naturally, there wasn't any identification. Henry's shipped him off to 'Serrat."

"How many here know what's going on?"

"Outside of the staff, there are only fourteen guests, and no one's got a clue. I've sealed off the chapel—the word is storm damage. And even those who have to know something—like the doctor and the two guys from Toronto—they don't know the whole story, just pieces, and they're friends. I trust them. The others are heavy into island rum."

"What about the gunshots at the chapel?"

"What about the loudest and lousiest steel band in the islands? Also, you were a thousand feet away in the woods. . . . Look, David, most everyone's left but some diehards who wouldn't stay here if they weren't old Canadian buddies showing me loyalty, and a few casuals who'd probably take a vacation in Teheran. What can I tell you except that the bar is doing a hell of a business."

"It's like a mystifying charade," murmured Bourne, again carefully arching his neck and staring at the ceiling. "Figures in silhouette playing out disconnected, violent events behind white screens, nothing really making sense, everything's whatever you want it to be."

"That's a little much for me, Professor. What's your point?"

"Terrorists aren't born, Johnny, they're made, schooled in a curriculum you won't find in any academic catalog. Leaving aside the reasons why they are what they are—which can range from a justifiable cause to the psychopathic megalomania of a Jackal—you keep the charades going because *they're* playing out their own."

"So?" St. Jacques frowned in bewilderment.

"So you control your players, telling them what to act out but not why."

"That's what we're doing here and that's what Henry's doing out on the water all around Tranquility."

"Is he? Are we?"

"Hell, yes."

"I thought I was too, but I was wrong. I overestimated a big clever kid doing a simple, harmless job and underestimated a humble, frightened priest who took thirty pieces of silver."

"What *are* you talking about?"

"Ishmael and Brother Samuel. Samuel must have witnessed the torture of a child through the eyes of Torquemada."

"Turkey who?"

"The point is we don't really know the players.

The guards, for instance, the ones you brought to the chapel—"

"I'm not a fool, David," protested St. Jacques, interrupting. "When you called for us to surround the place, I took a small liberty and chose two men, the only two I would choose, figuring a pair of Uzis made up for the absence of one man and the four points of the compass. They're my head boys and former Royal Commandos; they're in charge of all the security here and, like Henry, I trust them."

"Henry? He's a good man, isn't he?"

"He's a pain in the ass sometimes, but he's the best in the islands."

"And the Crown governor?"

"He's just an ass."

"Does Henry know that?"

"Sure, he does. He didn't get to be a brigadier on his looks, potbelly and all. He's not only a good soldier, he's a good administrator. He covers for a lot around here."

"And you're certain he hasn't been in touch with the CG."

"He told me he'd let me know before he reached the pompous idiot and I believe him."

"I sincerely hope you're right—because that pompous idiot is the Jackal's contact in Montserrat."

"*What?* I don't *believe* it!"

"Believe. It's confirmed."

"It's incredible!"

"No, it's not. It's the way of the Jackal. He finds vulnerability and he recruits it, buys it. There are very few in the gray areas beyond his ability to purchase them."

Stunned, St. Jacques wandered aimlessly to the balcony doors coming to terms with the un- believable. "I suppose it answers a question a lot of us have asked ourselves. The governor's old-line landed gentry with a brother high up in the Foreign Office who's close to the prime min- ister. Why at his age was he sent out here, or, maybe more to the point, why did he accept it? You'd think he'd settle for nothing less than Ber- muda or the British Virgins. Plymouth can be a stepping-stone, not a final post."

"He was banished, Johnny. Carlos probably found out why a long time ago and has him on a list. He's been doing it for years. Most people read newspapers and books and magazines for diversion; the Jackal pores over volumes of in- depth intelligence reports from every conceiv- able source he can unearth, and he's unearthed more than the CIA, the KGB, MIFive and Six, Interpol and a dozen other services even want to think about. . . . Those seaplanes flew in four

or five times after I got back here from Blackburne. Who was on them?"

"Pilots," answered St. Jacques, turning
around. "They were taking people out, not
bringing anyone in, I told you that."

"Yes, you told me. Were you watching?"

"Watching who?"

"Each plane when it came in."

"Hey, come on! You had me doing a dozen
different things."

"What about the two black commandos? The
ones you trust so much."

"They were checking and positioning the
other guards, for Christ's sake."

"Then we don't really know who may have
come in on those planes, do we? Maybe slipping
into the water over the pontoons as they taxied
through the reefs—perhaps before the sandbar."

"For God's sake, David, I've known those
charter jocks for years. They wouldn't let anything like that happen. No way!"

"You mean it's kind of unbelievable."

"You bet your ass."

"Like the Jackal's contact in Montserrat. The
Crown governor."

The owner of Tranquility Inn stared at his

brother-in-law. "What kind of world do you live in?"

"One I'm sorry you ever became a part of. But you are now and you'll play by its rules, my rules." A fleck, a *flash*, an infinitesimal streak of deep red light from the darkness outside! *Infrared!* Arms extended, Bourne lunged at St. Jacques, propelling him off his feet, away from the balcony doors. "Get *out* of there!" Jason roared in midair as both crashed to the floor, three successive snaps crackling the space above them as bullets thumped with finality into the walls of the villa.

"What the *hell*—"

"He's out there and he wants me to *know* it!" said Bourne, shoving his brother-in-law into the lower molding, crawling beside him, and reaching into the pocket of his guayabera. "He knows who you are, so you're the first corpse, the one he realizes will drive me to the edge because you're Marie's brother—you're *family* and that's what he's holding over my head. My *family*!"

"Jesus *Christ*! What do we *do*?"

"*I* do!" replied Jason, pulling the second flare out of his pocket. "I send him a message. The message that tells him why I'm alive and why I *will* be when he's dead. *Stay* where you are!"

Bourne pulled his lighter out of his right pocket and ignited the flare. Scrambling, he raced across the balcony doors hurling the hissing, blinding missile out into the darkness. Two snaps followed, the bullets ricocheting off the tiled ceiling and shattering the mirror of a dressing table. "He's got a MAC-ten with a silencer," said Medusa's Delta, rolling into the wall, grabbing his inflamed neck as he did so. "I have to get *out* of here!"

"David, you're *hurt*!"

"That's nice." Jason Bourne got to his feet and raced to the door; slamming it back, he rushed into the villa's living room, only to face a frowning Canadian physician.

"I heard some noise in there," said the doctor. "Is everything all right?"

"I have to leave. Get to the *floor*."

"Now, see here! There's blood on your bandage, the sutures—"

"Get your ass on the *floor*!"

"You're not twenty-one, Mr. Webb—"

"Get out of my *life*!" shouted Bourne, running to the entrance, letting himself outside, and rushing up the lighted path toward the main complex, suddenly aware of the deafening steel band, its sound amplified throughout the grounds by a score of speakers nailed to the trees.

The undulating cacophony was overwhelming, and that was not to his disadvantage, thought Jason. Angus McLeod had been true to his word. The huge glass-enclosed circular dining room held the few remaining guests and the fewer staff, and that meant the Chameleon had to change colors. He knew the mind of the Jackal as well as he knew his own, and that meant that the assassin would do exactly what he himself would do under the circumstances. The hungry, salivating wolf went into the cave of its confused, rabid quarry and pulled out the prized piece of meat. So would he, shedding the skin of the mythical chameleon, revealing a much larger beast of prey—say, a Bengal tiger—which could rip a jackal apart in his jaws. . . . Why were the images important? *Why?* He knew why, and it filled him with a feeling of emptiness, a longing for something that had passed—he was no longer Delta, the feared guerrilla of Medusa; nor was he the Jason Bourne of Paris and the Far East. The older, much older, David Webb kept intruding, invading, trying to find reason within insanity and violence.

No! Get *away* from me! You are nothing and I am everything! . . . Go away, David, for Christ's sake, go *away*.

Bourne spun off the path and ran across the harsh, sharp tropical grass toward the side entrance of the inn. Instantly, breathlessly, he cut his pace to a walk at the sight of a figure coming through the door; then upon recognizing the man, he resumed running. It was one of the few members of Tranquility's staff he remembered and one of the few he wished he could forget. The insufferable snob of an assistant manager named Pritchard, a loquacious bore, albeit hard-working, who never let anyone forget his family's importance in Montserrat—especially an uncle who was deputy director of immigration, a not so incidental plus for Tranquility Inn, David Webb suspected.

"Pritchard!" shouted Bourne, approaching the man. "Have you got the bandages?"

"Why, *sir*!" cried the assistant manager, genuinely flustered. "You're *here*. We were told you left this afternoon—"

"Oh, shit!"

"Sir? . . . Such condolences of sorrow so pain my lips—"

"Just keep them shut, Pritchard. Do you understand me?"

"Of course, I was not here this morning to greet you or this afternoon to bid you farewell and express my deepest feelings, for Mr. Saint Jay asked me to work this evening, through the night, actually—"

"Pritchard, I'm in a hurry. Give me the bandages and don't tell anyone—*anyone*—that you saw me. I want that very clear."

"Oh, it is clear, sir," said Pritchard, handing over the three different rolls of elasticized tape. "Such privileged information is safe with me, as safe as the knowledge that your wife and children were staying here—oh, God *forgive* me! *Forgive* me, sir!"

"I will and He will if you keep your mouth shut."

"Sealed. It is sealed. I am so privileged!"

"You'll be shot if you abuse the privilege. Is *that* clear?"

"*Sir?*"

"Don't faint, Pritchard. Go down to the villa and tell Mr. Saint Jay that I'll be in touch with him and he's to stay there. Have you got that? He's to *stay* there. . . . You, too, for that matter."

"Perhaps I could—"

"Forget it. Get *out* of here!"

The talkative assistant manager ran across the lawn toward the path to the east villas as

Bourne raced to the door and went inside. Jason climbed the steps two at a time—only years before, it would have been three at a time—and again, out of breath, reached St. Jacques's office. He entered, closed the door, and quickly went to the closet where he knew his brother-in-law kept several changes of clothing. Both men were approximately the same size—outsized, as Marie claimed—and Johnny had frequently borrowed jackets and shirts from David Webb when visiting. Jason selected the most subdued combination in the closet. Lightweight gray slacks and an all-cotton dark blue blazer; the only shirt in evidence, again tropical cotton, was thankfully short-sleeved and brown. Nothing would pick up or reflect light.

He started to undress when he felt a sharp, hot jolt on the left side of his neck. He looked in the closet mirror, alarmed, then furious at what he saw. The constricting bandage around his throat was deep red with spreading blood. He tore open the box of the widest tape; it was too late to change the dressing, he could only reinforce it and hope to stem the bleeding. He unraveled the elasticized tape around his neck, tearing it after several revolutions, and applied the tiny clamps to hold it in place. It was more inhibiting than ever; it was also an impediment he would put out of his mind.

He changed clothes, pulling the collar of the brown shirt high over his throat and putting the automatic in his belt, the reel of fishing line in the blazer's pocket. . . . *Footsteps!* The door opened as he pressed his back against the wall, his hand on the weapon. Old Fontaine walked in; he stood for a moment, looking at Bourne, then closed the door.

"I've been trying to find you, frankly not knowing if you were still alive," said the Frenchman.

"We're not using the radios unless we have to." Jason walked away from the wall. "I thought you got the message."

"I did and it was right. Carlos may have his own radio by now. He's not alone, you know. It's why I've been wandering around looking for you. Then it occurred to me that you and your brother-in-law might be up here in his office, a headquarters, as it were."

"It's not very smart for you to be walking around out in the open."

"I'm not an idiot, monsieur. I would have perished long before now if I were. Wherever I walked I did so with great caution. . . . In truth, it's why I made up my mind to find you, assuming you were not dead.''

''I'm not and you found me. What is it? You and the judge are supposed to be in an empty villa somewhere, not wandering around.''

''We are; we were. You see, I have a plan, a *stratagème*, I believe would interest you. I discussed it with Brendan—''

''Brendan?''

''His name, monsieur. He thinks my plan has merit and he's a brilliant man, very *sagace*—''

''Shrewd? Yes, I'm sure he is, but he's not in our business.''

''He's a survivor. In that sense we are all in the same business. He thinks there is a degree of risk, but what plan under these circumstances is without risk?''

''What's your plan?''

''It is a means to trap the Jackal with minimum danger to the other people here.''

''That really worries you, doesn't it?''

''I told you why, so there's no reason to repeat it. There are men and women together out there—''

''Go on,'' broke in Bourne, irritated. ''What's this strategy of yours, and you'd better understand that I intend to take out the Jackal if I have to hold this whole goddamned island hostage. I'm not in a giving mood. I've given too much."

"So you and Carlos stalk each other in the night? Two crazed middle-aged hunters obsessed with killing each other, not caring who else is killed or wounded or maimed for life in the bargain?"

"You want compassion, go to a church and appeal to that God of yours who pisses on this planet! He's either got one hell of a warped sense of humor or he's a sadist. Now either talk sense or I'm getting out of here."

"I've thought this out—"

"Talk!"

"I know the monseigneur, know the way he thinks. He planned the death of my woman and me but not to coincide with yours, not in a way that would detract from the high drama of his immediate victory over you. It would come later. The revelation that I, the so-called hero of France, was in reality the Jackal's instrument, his creation, would be the final proof of his triumph. Don't you see?"

Briefly silent, Jason studied the old man. "Yes, I do," he replied quietly. "Not that I ever figured on someone like you, but that approach is the basis of everything I believe. He's a megalomaniac. In his head he's the king of hell and wants the world to recognize him and his throne. By his lights, his genius has been overlooked, relegated to the level of punk killers and Mafia hit men. He wants trumpets and drums, when all he hears are tired sirens and weary questions in police lineups."

"*C'est vrai.* He once complained to me that almost no one in America knew who he was."

"They don't. They think he's a character out of novels or films, if they think about him at all. He tried to make up for that thirteen years ago, when he flew over from Paris to New York to kill me."

"Correction, monsieur. You forced him to go after you."

"It's history. What's all this got to do with now, tonight . . . your plan?"

"It provides us with a way to force the Jackal to come out after *me*, to meet with *me*. Now. Tonight."

"How?"

"By my wandering around the grounds very much in the open where he or one of his scouts will see me and hear me."

"Why would that force him to come out after you?"

"Because I will not be with the nurse he had assigned to me. I will be with someone else, unknown to him, someone who would have no reason at all to kill me."

Again Bourne looked at the old Frenchman in silence. "Bait," he said finally.

"A lure so provocative it will drive him into a frenzy until he has it in his possession—has me in his grip so he can question me. . . . You see, I'm vital to him—more specifically, my death is vital—and everything is timing to him. Precision is his . . . his *diction*, how is it said?"

"His byword, his method of operation, I suppose."

"It is how he has survived, how he has made the most of each kill, each over the years adding to his reputation as the *assassin suprême*. Until a man named Jason Bourne came out of the Far East . . . he has never been the same since. But you know all that—"

"I don't care about all that," interrupted Jason. "The 'timing.' Go on."

"After I'm gone he can reveal who Jean Pierre Fontaine, the hero of France, really was. An impostor, *his* impostor, *his* creation, the instrument of death who was the snare for Jason Bourne. What a triumph for him! . . . But he cannot do that until I'm dead. Quite simply, it would be too inconvenient. I know too much, too many of my colleagues in the gutters of Paris. No, I must be dead before he has his triumph."

"Then he'll kill you when he sees you."

"Not until he has his answers, monsieur. Where is his killer nurse? What has happened to her? Did Le Caméléon find her, turn her, do away with her? Have the British authorities got her? Is she on her way to London and MI-Six with all their chemicals, to be turned over at last to Interpol? So many questions. . . . No, he will not kill me until he learns what he must learn. It may take only minutes to satisfy him, but long before then I trust that you will be at my side insuring my survival, if not his."

"The nurse? Whoever it is, she'll be shot."

"No, not at all. I'll order her away in anger, out of my sight at the first sign of contact. As I walk with her I shall lament the absence of my new dear friend, the angel of mercy who takes such good care of my wife, wondering out loud, What has happened to her? Where has she gone? Why haven't I seen her all *day*? Naturally, I will conceal on my person the radio, activated, of course. Wherever I am taken—for surely one of Carlos's men will make contact first—I will ask an enfeebled old man's questions. Why am I going here? Why are we there? . . . You will follow—in full force, I sincerely hope. If you do so, you'll have the Jackal."

Holding his head straight, his neck rigid, Bourne walked to St. Jacques's desk and sat on the edge. "Your friend, Judge Brendan what's-his-name, is right—"

"*Pre*fontaine. Although Fontaine is not my true name, we've decided it's all the same family. When the earliest members left Alsace-Lorraine for America in the eighteenth century with Lafayette, they added the *Pre* to distinguish them from the Fontaines who spread out all over France."

"He told you that?"

"He's a brilliant man, once an honored judge."

"Lafayette came from Alsace-Lorraine?"

"I don't know, monsieur. I've never been there."

"He's a brilliant man. . . . More to the point, he's right. Your plan has a lot of merit, but there's also considerable risk. And I'll be honest with you, Fontaine, I don't give a damn about the risk you're taking or about the nurse, whoever it is. I want the Jackal, and if it costs your life or the life of a woman I don't know, it doesn't matter to me. I want you to understand that."

The old Frenchman stared at Jason with amused rheumy eyes and laughed softly. "You are such a transparent contradiction. Jason Bourne would never have said what you just did. He would have remained silent, accepting my proposition without comment but knowing the advantage. Mrs. Webb's husband, however, must have a voice. *He* objects and must be heard." Fontaine suddenly spoke sharply. "Get *rid* of him, Monsieur Bourne. *He* is not my protection, not the death of the Jackal. Send him away."

"He's gone. I promise you, he's *gone*." The Chameleon sprang up from the desk, his neck frozen in pain. "Let's get started."

The steel band continued its deafening assault, but now restricted to the confines of the glass-enclosed lobby and adjacent dining room. The speakers on the grounds were switched off on St. Jacques's orders, the owner of Tranquility Inn having been escorted up from the unoccupied villa by the two Uzi-bearing former commandos along with the Canadian doctor and the incessantly chattering Mr. Pritchard. The assistant manager was instructed to return to the front desk and say nothing to anyone about the things he had witnessed during the past hour.

"Absolutely nothing, sir. If I am asked, I was on the telephone with the authorities over in 'Serrat."

"About *what*?" objected St. Jacques.

"Well, I thought—"

"Don't think. You were checking the maid service on the west path, that's all."

"Yes, sir." The deflated Pritchard headed for the office door, which had been opened moments before by the nameless Canadian doctor.

"I doubt it would make much difference what he said," offered the physician as the assistant manager left. "That's a small zoo down there. The combination of last night's events, too much sun today and excessive amounts of alcohol this evening, will augur a great deal of guilt in the morning. My wife doesn't think your meteorologist will have much to say, John."

"Oh?"

"He's having a few himself, and even if he's halfway lucid, there aren't five sober enough to listen to him."

"I'd better get down there. We may as well turn it into a minor *carnivale*. It'll save Scotty ten thousand dollars, and the more distraction we have, the better. I'll speak to the band and the bar and be right back."

"We may not be here," said Bourne as his brother-in-law left and a strapping young black woman in a complete nurse's uniform walked out of St. Jacques's private bathroom into the office. At the sight of her, old Fontaine approached.

"Very good, my child, you look splendid," said the Frenchman. "Remember now, I'll be holding your arm as we walk and talk, but when I squeeze you and raise my voice, telling you to leave me alone, you'll do as I say, correct?"

"Yes, sir. I am to hurry away quite angry with you for being so unnice."

"That's it. There's nothing to be afraid of, it's just a game. We want to talk with someone who's very shy."

"How's the neck?" asked the doctor, looking at Jason, unable to see the bandage beneath the brown shirt.

"It's all right," answered Bourne.

"Let's take a look at it," said the Canadian, stepping forward.

"Thanks but not now, Doctor. I suggest you go downstairs and rejoin your wife."

"Yes. I thought you'd say that, but may I say something very quickly?"

"*Very* quickly."

"I'm a doctor and I've had to do a great many things I didn't like doing and I'm sure this is in that category. But when I think of that young man and what was done to him—"

"Please," broke in Jason.

"Yes, yes, I understand. Nevertheless, I'm here if you need me, I just wanted you to know that. . . . I'm not terribly proud of my previous statements. I saw what I saw and I do have a name and I'm perfectly willing to testify in a court of law. In other words, I withdraw my reluctance."

"There'll be no courts, Doctor, no testimony."

"Really? But these are serious *crimes*!"

"We *know* what they are," interrupted Bourne. "Your help is greatly appreciated, but nothing else concerns you."

"I see," said the doctor, staring curiously at Jason. "I'll go, then." The Canadian went to the door and turned. "You'd better let me check that neck later. If you've got a neck." The doctor left and Bourne turned to Fontaine.

"Are we ready?"

"We're ready," replied the Frenchman, smiling pleasantly at the large, imposing, thoroughly mystified young black woman. "What are you going to do with all the money you're earning tonight, my dear?"

The girl giggled shyly, her broad smile alive with bright white teeth. "I have a good boyfriend. I'm going to buy him a fine present."

"That's lovely. What's your boyfriend's name?"

"Ishmael, sir."

"Let's go," said Jason firmly.

The plan was simple to mount and, like most good strategies, however complex, simple to execute. Old Fontaine's walk through the grounds of Tranquility Inn had been precisely mapped out. The trek began with Fontaine and the young woman returning to his villa presumably to look in on his ill wife before his established, medically required evening stroll. They stayed on the lighted main path, straying now and then across the floodlit lawns but always visible, a crotchety old man supposedly walking wherever his whims led him, to the annoyance of his companion. It was a familiar sight the world over, an enfeebled, irascible septuagenarian taunting his keeper.

The two former Royal Commandos, one rather short, the other fairly tall, had selected a series of stations between the points where the Frenchman and his "nurse" would turn and head in different directions. As the old man and the girl proceeded into the next planned leg, the second commando bypassed his colleague in darkness to the next location, using unseen routes only they knew or could negotiate, such as that beyond the coastline wall above the tangled tropical brush that led to the beach below the villas. The black guards climbed like two enormous spiders in a jungle, crawling swiftly, effortlessly from branch and rock to limb and vine, keeping pace with their two charges. Bourne followed the second man, his radio on Receive, the angry words of Fontaine pulsating through the static.

Where is that other nurse? That lovely girl who takes care of my woman? Where is she? I haven't seen her all day! The emphatic phrases were repeated over and over again with growing hostility.

Jason slipped. He was caught! He was behind

the coastal wall, his left foot entangled in thick vines. He could not pull his leg loose—the strength was not there! He moved his head—his shoulders—and the hot flashes of pain broke out on his neck. It is *nothing*. Pull, yank, *rip*! . . . His lungs bursting, the blood now drenching his shirt, he worked his way free and crawled on.

Suddenly there were lights, *colored* lights spilling over the wall. They had reached the path to the chapel, the red and blue floodlights that lit up the entrance to Tranquility Inn's sealed-off sanctuary. It was the last destination before the return route back to Fontaine's villa, and one they all agreed was designed more to permit the old Frenchman time to catch his breath than for any other purpose. St. Jacques had stationed a guard there to prevent entrance into the demolished chapel. There would be no contact here. Then Bourne heard the words over the radio— the words that would send the false nurse racing away from her false charge.

"Get *away* from me!" yelled Fontaine. "I don't like you. Where is our regular nurse? What have you *done* with her?"

Up ahead, the two commandos were side by side, crouching below the wall. They turned and looked at Jason, their expressions in the eerie wash of colored lights telling him what he knew only too well. From that moment on, all decisions were his; they had led him, escorted him, to his enemy. The rest was up to him.

The unexpected rarely disturbed Bourne; it did now. Had Fontaine made a mistake? Had the old man forgotten about the inn's guard and erroneously presumed he was the Jackal's contact? In his aged eyes had an understandably surprised reaction on the guard's part been misinterpreted as an approach? Anything was possible, but considering the Frenchman's background—the life of a survivor—and the state of his alert mind, such a mistake was not realistic.

Then the possibility of another reality came into focus and it was sickening. Had the guard been killed or bribed, replaced by another? Carlos was a master of the turn-around. It was said he had fulfilled a contract on the assassination of Anwar Sadat without firing a weapon, by merely replacing the Egyptian president's security detail with inexperienced recruits—money dispersed in Cairo returned a hundredfold by the anti-Israel brotherhoods in the Middle East. If it were true, the exercise on Tranquility Isle was child's play.

Jason rose to his feet, gripped the top of the coastal wall, and slowly, painfully, his neck causing agony, pulled himself up over the ledge, again slowly, inch by inch, sending one arm after the other across the surface to grab the opposing edge for support. What he saw stunned him!

Fontaine was immobile, his mouth gaped in shock, his wide eyes disbelieving, as another old man in a tan gabardine suit approached him and threw his arms around the aged hero of France. Fontaine pushed the man away in panic and bewilderment. The words erupted out of the radio in Bourne's pocket. *"Claude! Quelle secousse! Vous êtes ici!"*

The ancient friend replied in a tremulous voice, speaking French. "It is a privilege our monseigneur permitted me. To see for a final time my sister, and to give comfort to my friend, her husband. I am here and I am with you!"

"With *me*? He brought you *here*? But, of course, he did!"

"I am to take you to him. The great man wishes to speak with you."

"Do you know what you're doing—what you've *done*?"

"I am with you, with her. What else matters?"

"She's *dead*! She took her own life last night! *He* intended to kill us both."

Shut off your radio! screamed Bourne in the silence of his thoughts. *Kill the radio!* It was too late. The left door of the chapel opened and the silhouetted figure of a man walked out into the floodlit corridor of colored lights. He was young, muscular and blond, with blunt features and rigid posture. Was the Jackal training someone else to take his place?

"Come with me, please," said the blond man, his French gentle but icily commanding. "You," he added, addressing the old man in the tan gabardine suit. "Stay where you are. At the slightest sound, fire your gun. . . . Take it out. Hold it in your hand."

"Oui, monsieur."

Jason watched helplessly as Fontaine was escorted through the door of the chapel. From the pocket of his jacket there was an eruption of static followed by a snap; the Frenchman's radio had been found and destroyed. Yet something was wrong, off-center, out of balance—or perhaps too symmetrical. It made no sense for Carlos to use the location of a failed trap a second time, no sense at all! The appearance of the brother of Fontaine's wife was an exceptional move, worthy of the Jackal, a truly unexpected move within the swirling winds of confusion, but not this, not again Tranquility Inn's superfluous chapel. It was too orderly, too repetitive, too obvious. *Wrong.*

And therefore right? considered Bourne. Was it the illogical logic of the assassin who had eluded a hundred special branches of the international intelligence community for nearly thirty years? "He wouldn't do *that*—it's crazy!" ". . . Oh, yes, he might because he knows we think it's crazy." Was the Jackal in the chapel or wasn't he? If not, where *was* he? Where had he set his trap?

The lethal chess game was not only supremely intricate, it was sublimely intimate. Others might die, but only one of *them* would live. It was the only way it could end. Death to the seller of death or death to the challenger, one seeking the preservation of a legend, the other seeking the preservation of his family and himself. Carlos had the advantage; ultimately he would risk everything, for, as Fontaine revealed, he was a dying man and he did not care. Bourne had everything to live for, a middle-aged hunter whose life was indelibly marked, split in two by the death of a vaguely remembered wife and children long ago in far-off Cambodia. It could not, *would* not, happen again!

Jason slid down off the coastal wall to the

slanting precipice at its base. He crawled forward to the two former commandos and whispered, "They've taken Fontaine inside."

"Where is the *guard*?" asked the man nearest Bourne, confusion and anger in his whisper. "I myself placed him here with specific instructions. *No* one was permitted inside. He was to be on the radio the instant he saw *anyone*!"

"Then I'm afraid he didn't see him."

"Who?"

"A blond man who speaks French."

Both commandos whipped their heads toward each other, exchanging glances as the second guard instantly looked at Jason and spoke quietly. "Describe him, please," he said.

"Medium height, large chest and shoulders—"

"Enough," interrupted the first guard. "Our man saw him, sir. He is third provost of the government police, an officer who speaks several languages and is chief of drug investigations."

"But why is he here, *mon*?" the second commando asked his colleague. "Mr. Saint Jay said the Crown police are not told everything, they are not part of us."

"Sir Henry, *mon*. He has Crown boats, six or seven, running back and forth with orders to stop anyone leaving Tranquility. They are drug boats, *mon*. Sir Henry calls it a patrol exercise, so naturally the chief of investigations must be—" The lilting whisper of the West Indian trailed off in midsentence as he looked at his companion. ". . . Then why isn't he out on the water, *mon*? On the lead boat, *mon*?"

"Do you like him?" asked Bourne instinctively, surprising himself by his own question. "I mean, do you respect him? I could be wrong but I seem to sense something—"

"You are not wrong, sir," answered the first guard, interrupting. "The provost is a cruel man and he doesn't like the 'Punjabis,' as he calls us. He's very quick to accuse us, and many have lost work because of his rash accusations."

"Why don't you complain, get rid of him? The British will listen to you."

"The Crown governor will not, sir," explained the second guard. "He's very partial to his strict chief of narcotics. They are good friends and often go out after the big fish together."

"I see." Jason did see and was suddenly alarmed, *very* alarmed. "Saint Jay told me there used to be a path behind the chapel. He said it might be overgrown, but he thought it was still there."

"It is," confirmed the first commando. "The

help still use it to go down to the water on their off times."

"How long is it?"

"Thirty-five, forty meters. It leads to an incline where steps have been cut out of the rocks that take one down to the beach."

"Which of you is faster?" asked Bourne, reaching into his pocket and taking out the reel of fishing line.

"I am."

"*I* am!"

"I choose you," said Jason, nodding his head at the shorter first guard, handing him the reel. "Go down on the border of that path and wherever you can, string this line across it, tying it to limbs or trunks or the strongest branches you can find. You mustn't be seen, so be alert, see in the dark."

"Is no pro*blem, mon*!"

"Have you got a knife?"

"Do I have eyes?"

"Good. Give me your Uzi. *Hurry!*"

The guard scrambled away along the vine-tangled precipice and disappeared into the dense foliage beyond. The second Royal Commando spoke. "In truth, sir, I am much faster, for my legs are much longer."

"Which is why I chose him and I suspect you

know it. Long legs are no advantage here, only an impediment, which / happen to know. Also, he's much shorter and less likely to be spotted."

"The smaller ones always get the better assignments. They parade *us* up front and put *us* in boxing rings with rules we don't understand, but the small soldiers get the plumbies."

" 'Plumbies'? The better jobs?"

"Yes, sir."

"The most dangerous jobs?"

"Yes, *mon*!"

"Live with it, big fella."

"What do we do now, sir?"

Bourne looked above at the wall and the soft wash of colored lights. "It's called the waiting game—no love songs implied, only the hatred that comes from wanting to live when others want to kill you. There's nothing quite like it because you can't *do* anything. All you can do is think about what the enemy may or may not be doing, and whether he's thought of something you haven't considered. As somebody once said, I'd rather be in Philadelphia."

"Where, *mon*?"

"Nothing. It isn't true."

Suddenly, filling the air above in chilling horror, came a prolonged excruciating scream, followed by words shrieked in pain. *"Non, non! Vous êtes monstrueux! . . . Arrêtez, arrêtez, je vous en supplie!"*

"Now!" cried Jason, slinging the strap of his Uzi over his shoulder as he leaped onto the wall, gripping the edge, pulling himself up as the blood poured out of his neck. He could not *get* up! He could not get *over*! Then strong hands pulled him and he fell over the top of the wall. "The *lights*!" he shouted. "Shoot them out!"

The tall commando's Uzi blazing, the lines of floodlights exploded in the ground on both sides of the chapel's path. Again, strong black hands pulled him to his feet in the new darkness. And then a single shaft of yellow appeared, roving swiftly in all directions; it was a powerful halogen flashlight in the commando's left hand. The figure of a blood-drenched old man in a tan gabardine suit lay curled up in the path, his throat slit.

"Stop! In the name of almighty *God*, stop where you *are*!" came Fontaine's voice from inside the chapel, the open half door revealing the flickering light of the electric candles. They approached the entrance, automatic weapons leveled, prepared for continuous fire . . . but not prepared for what they saw. Bourne closed his eyes, the sight was too painful. Old Fontaine,

like young Ishmael, was sprawled over the lectern on the raised platform beneath the blown-out, stained-glass windows of the left wall, his face running with blood where he had been slashed, and attached to his body were thin cables that led to various black boxes on both sides of the chapel.

"Go *back*!" screamed Fontaine. "*Run,* you fools! I'm wired—"

"Oh, *Christ*!"

"Mourn not for me, Monsieur le Caméléon. I gladly join my woman! This world is too ugly even for me. It is no longer amusing. *Run!* The charge will go off—they are watching!"

"You, *mon*! *Now*!" roared the second commando, grabbing Jason's jacket and racing him to the wall, holding Bourne in his arms as they plummeted over the stone surface into the thick foliage.

The explosion was massive, blinding and deafening. It was as if this small corner of the small island had been taken out by a heat-seeking nuclear missile. Flames erupted into the night sky, but the burning mass was quickly diffused in the still wind to fiery rubble.

"The *path*!" shouted Jason, in a hoarse whisper, as he crawled to his feet in the sloping brush. "Get to the path!"

"You're in bad condition, *mon*—"

"I'll take care of *me*, you take care of *you*!"

"I believe I've taken care of both of us."

"So you've got a fucking medal and I'll add a lot of money to it. Now, get us up to the *path*!"

Pulling, pushing, and finally with Bourne's feet grinding like a machine out of control, the two men reached the border of the path thirty feet behind the smoldering ruins of the chapel. They crept into the weeds and within seconds the first commando found them. "They're in the south palms," he said breathlessly. "They wait until the smoke has cleared to see if anyone is alive, but they cannot stay long."

"You were *there*?" asked Jason. "*With* them?"

"No problem, *mon,* I told you, sir."

"What's happening? How many are there?"

"There were four, sir. I killed the man whose place I assumed. He was black, so it made no matter in appearance with the darkness. It was quick and silent. The throat."

"Who's left?"

" 'Serrat's chief of narcotics, of course, and two others—"

"*Describe* them!"

"I could not see clearly, but one I think was another black man, tall and without much hair.

The third I could not see at all, for he—or she—was wearing strange clothes, with cloth over the head like a woman's sun hat or insect veil.''

"A *woman*?"

"It is possible, sir."

"A woman . . . ? They've got to get *out* of there—*he's* got to get out of there!"

"Very soon they will run to this path and race down to the beach, where they will hide in the woods of the cove until a boat comes for them. They have no choice. They cannot go back to the inn, for strangers are seen instantly, and even though we are far away and the steel band is loud, the explosion was certainly heard by the guards posted outside. They will report it."

"Listen to me," said Bourne, his voice hoarse, tense. "One of those three people is the man I want, and I want him for *myself*! So hold your fire because I'll know him when I see him. I don't give a *damn* about the others; they can be flushed out of that cove later."

There was a sudden burst of gunfire from the tropical forest accompanied by screams from the once floodlit corridor beyond the ruins of the chapel. Then one after another the figures raced out of the tangled brush into the path. The first to be caught was the blond-haired police officer from Montserrat, the waist-high invisible fishing line tripping him as he fell into the dirt, breaking the thin, taut string. The second man, slender, tall, dark-featured, with only a fringe of hair on his bald head, was hard upon the first, pulling him to his feet, sight or instinct making the second killer wield his automatic weapon in slashing arcs, cutting the impeding lines across the path to the ledge that led down to the beach. The third figure appeared. It was *not* a woman. It was a man, in the robes of a monk. A priest. It was *he*. The *Jackal*!

Bourne rose to his feet and stumbled out of the brush into the path, the Uzi in his hands; the victory was his, his *freedom* his, his *family* his! As the robed figure reached the top of the primitive rock-hewn staircase, Jason pressed his trigger finger, holding it in place, the fusillade of bullets exploding out of the automatic weapon.

The monk arched in silhouette, then fell, his body tumbling, rolling, sprawling down the steps carved out of volcanic rock, finally lurching over the edge and plummeting to the sand below. Bourne raced down the awkward, irregular stone staircase, the two commandos behind him. He reached the beach, raced over to the corpse, and pulled the drenched hood away from the face. In horror, he looked at the black features of Samuel, the brother priest of Tranquility Isle, the Judas who had sold his soul to the Jackal for thirty pieces of silver.

Suddenly, in the distance, there was the roar of powerful dual engines as a huge speedboat lurched out of a shadowed section of the cove and sped for a break in the reefs. The beam of a searchlight shot out, firing the barriers of rock protruding above the choppy black water, its wash illuminating the fluttering ensign of the government's drug fleet. *Carlos!* . . . The Jackal was no chameleon, but he had changed! He had aged, grown thinner and bald—he was not the sharp, broad, full-headed muscular image of Jason's memory. Only the indistinct dark Latin features remained, the face and the unfamiliar expanse of bare skin above burned by the sun. He was *gone!*

The boat's motors screamed in unison as the craft breached a precarious opening in the reef and burst out into open water. Then the words in heavily accented English, metallically spewing from the distant loudspeaker, echoed within the tropical cove.

"*Paris,* Jason Bourne! Paris, if you *dare!* Or

shall it be a certain minor university in Maine, *Dr. Webb*?''

Bourne, his neck wound ripped open, collapsed in the lapping waves, his blood trickling into the sea.

18

Steven DeSole, keeper of the deepest secrets for the Central Intelligence Agency, forced his overweight frame out of the driver's seat. He stood in the deserted parking lot of the small shopping center in Annapolis, Maryland, where the only source of light was the storefront neons of a closed gas station, with a large German shepherd sleeping in the window. DeSole adjusted his steel-rimmed glasses and squinted at his watch, barely able to see the radium hands. As near as he could determine, it was between 3:15 and 3:20 in the morning, which meant he was early and that was good. He had to adjust his thoughts; he was unable to do so while driving, as his severe night blindness necessitated complete concentration on the road, and hiring a taxi or a driver was out of the question.

The information was at first . . . well, merely a name . . . a rather common name. *His name is Webb,* the caller had said. *Thank you,* he had replied. A sketchy description was given, one fitting several million men, so he had thanked the informer again and hung up the phone. But then, in the recesses of his analyst's mind, by profession and training a warehouse for both essential and incidental data, an alarm went off. Webb, Webb . . . *amnesia?* A clinic in Virginia years ago. A man more dead than alive had been flown down from a hospital in New York, the medical file so maximum classified it could not even be shown to the Oval Office. Yet interrogation specialists talk in dark corners, as often to relieve frustration as to impress a listener, and he had heard about a recalcitrant, unmanageable patient, an amnesiac they called "Davey" and sometimes just a short, sharp, hostile "Webb," formerly a member of Saigon's infamous Medusa, and a man they suspected of feigning his loss of memory. . . . Loss of memory? Alex Conklin had told them that the Medusan they had trained to go out in deep cover for

Carlos the Jackal, an agent provocateur they called Jason Bourne, had lost his *memory*. Lost his memory and nearly lost his life because his controls disbelieved the story of *amnesia*! That was the man they called "Davey" . . . David. David Webb was Conklin's Jason Bourne! How could it be otherwise?

David Webb! And he had been at Norman Swayne's house the night the Agency was told that poor cuckolded Swayne had taken his own life, a suicide that had not been reported in the papers for reasons DeSole could not possibly understand! David Webb. The old Medusa. Jason Bourne. Conklin. *Why?*

The headlights of an approaching limousine shot through the darkness at the far end of the parking lot, swerving in a semicircle toward the CIA analyst, causing him to shut his eyes— the refracted light through his thick lenses was painful. He had to make the sequence of his revelations clear to these men. They were his means to a life he and his wife had dreamed of—*money*. Not bureaucratic less-than-money, but *real* money. Education at the best universities for their grandchildren, not the state colleges and the begged-for scholarships that came with the government salary of a bureaucrat—a bureaucrat so much better than those around him it was pitiful. *DeSole the Mute Mole,* they called him, but would not pay him for his expertise, the very expertise that prohibited him from going into the private sector, surrounding him with so many legal restrictions that it was pointless to apply. Someday Washington would learn; that day would not come in his lifetime, so six grandchildren had made the decision for him. The empathetic new Medusa had beckoned with generosity, and in his bitterness he had come running.

He rationalized that it was no more an unethical decision on his part than those made every year by scores of Pentagon personnel who walked out of Arlington and into the corporate arms of their old friends the defense contractors. As an army colonel once said to him, "It's work now and get paid later," and God knew that one Steven DeSole worked like hell for his country, but his country hardly reciprocated in kind. He hated the name Medusa, though, and rarely if ever used it because it was a symbol from another time, ominous and misleading. The great oil companies and railroads sprang from the chicanery and the venality of the robber barons, but they were not now what they were then. Medusa may have been born in the corruption of a war-ravaged Saigon, its early funding may have been a result of it, but that Medusa no longer existed; it had been replaced by a dozen different names and companies.

"We're not pure, Mr. DeSole, no American-controlled international conglomerate is," said his recruiter, "and it's true that we seek what some might call unfair economic advantage based on privileged information. Secrets, if you like. You see, we have to because our competitors throughout Europe and the Far East consistently have it. The difference between them and us is that *their* governments support their efforts—ours doesn't. . . . Trade, Mr. DeSole, trade and profits. They're the healthiest pursuits on earth. Chrysler may not like Toyota, but the astute Mr. Iacocca does not call for an air strike against Tokyo. At least not yet. He finds ways to join forces with the Japanese."

Yes, mused DeSole as the limousine came to a stop ten feet away from him. What he did for the "corporation," which he preferred to call it, as opposed to what he did for the Company, might even be considered benevolent. Profits, after all, were more desirable than bombs . . . and his grandchildren would go to the finest schools and universities in the country. Two men got out of the limousine and approached him.

"What's this Webb look like?" asked Albert Armbruster, chairman of the Federal Trade Commission, as they walked along the edge of the parking lot.

"I only have a description from the gardener, who was hiding behind a fence thirty feet away."

"What did he tell you?" The unidentified associate of the chairman, a short stocky man with penetrating dark eyes and dark eyebrows beneath dark hair, looked at DeSole. "Be precise," he added.

"Now, just a minute," protested the analyst defensively but firmly. "I'm precise in everything I say, and, frankly, whoever you are, I don't like the tone of your voice one bit."

"He's upset," said Armbruster, as if his associate was dismissible. "He's a spaghetti head from New York and doesn't trust anybody."

"Who's to trust in New *Yawk*?" asked the short, dark man, laughing and poking his elbow into the wide girth of Albert Armbruster. "You WASPs are the worst, you got the banks, *amico*!"

"Let's keep it that way and out of the courts.

. . . The description, please?'' The chairman looked at DeSole.

"It's incomplete, but there *is* a long-ago tie-in with Medusa that I'll describe—*precisely.*"

"Go ahead, pal,'' said the man from New York.

"He's rather large—tall, that is—and in his late forties or early fifties and—''

"Has he got some gray around his temples?'' asked Armbruster, interrupting.

"Well, yes, I think the gardener said something to that effect—graying, or gray in his hair, or something like that. It's obviously why he judged him to be in his forties or fifties.''

"It's Simon,'' said Armbruster, looking at the New Yorker.

"Who?" DeSole stopped, as the other two stopped and looked at him.

"He called himself Simon, and he knew all about you, Mr. CIA,'' said the chairman. "About you and Brussels and our whole thing.''

"What are you *talking* about?''

"For starters, your goddamn fax machine exclusively between you and that fruitcake in Brussels.''

"It's a buried, dedicated line! It's locked up!''

"Someone found the key, Mr. Precision,'' said the New Yorker, not smiling.

"Oh, my God, that's *terrible*! What should I *do*?"

"Make up a story between you and Teagarten, but do it from public phones," continued the mafioso. "One of you will come up with something."

"*You* know about . . . Brussels?"

"There's very little I don't know."

"That son of a bitch conned me into thinking he was one of us and he had me by the balls!" said Armbruster angrily, continuing to walk along the edge of the parking lot, the other two joining him, DeSole hesitantly, apprehensively. "He seemed to know everything, but when I think back, he only brought up bits and pieces—damned *big* bits and pieces like Burton and you and Brussels—and I, like a fucking idiot, filled in a hell of a lot more. *Shit!*"

"Now, just *wait* a minute!" cried the CIA analyst, once again forcing the others to stop. "I don't understand—I'm a strategist, and I don't *understand*. What was David Webb—Jason Bourne, if he *is* Jason Bourne—doing at Swayne's place the other night?"

"Who the hell is *Jason Bourne*?" roared the chairman of the Federal Trade Commission.

"He's the tie-in with Saigon's Medusa that I just mentioned. Thirteen years ago the Agency

gave him the name Jason Bourne, the original
Bourne a dead man by then, and sent him out
in deep cover on a Four Zero assignment—a
termination with extreme prejudice, if you
like—"

"A hit, if you want to speak English, *paisan*."

"Yes, yes, that's what it was. . . . But things
went wrong; he had a loss of memory and the
operation collapsed. It collapsed, but he survived."

"Holy Christ, what a bunch of zucchinis!"

"What can you tell us about this Webb . . . or
Bourne—this Simon or the 'Cobra'? Jesus, he's
a walking vaudeville act!"

"Apparently that's what he did before. He assumed different names, different appearances,
different personalities. He was trained to do that
when he was sent out to challenge the assassin
called the Jackal—to draw him out and kill him."

"The *Jackal*?" asked the astonished capo supremo of the Cosa Nostra. "Like in the movie?"

"No, not the movie *or* the book, you idiot—"

"Hey, easy, *amico*."

"Oh, shut up. . . . Ilich Ramirez Sanchez, otherwise known as Carlos the Jackal, is a living
person, a professional killer the international authorities have been hunting for over a quarter of

a century. Outside of scores of confirmed hits, many think he was the puff of smoke on the grassy knoll in Dallas, the true killer of John Kennedy."

"You're shittin' me."

"I can assure you, I am not shitting you. The word we got at the Agency at the highest secure levels was that after all these years Carlos had tracked down the only man alive who could identify him, Jason Bourne—or, as I'm firmly convinced, David Webb."

"That *word* had to come from somebody!" exploded Albert Armbruster. "Who *was* it?"

"Oh, yes. Everything's so sudden, so bewildering. . . . He's a retired field agent with a crippled leg, a man named Conklin, Alexander Conklin. He and a psychiatrist—Panov, Morris Panov—are close friends of Webb . . . or Jason Bourne."

"Where are they?" asked the capo supremo grimly.

"Oh, you couldn't reach either one, talk to either of them. They're both under maximum security."

"I didn't ask for the rules of engagement, *paisan,* I asked where they were."

"Well, Conklin's at a condominium in Vienna,

a proprietary of ours no one could penetrate, and Panov's apartment and office are both under round-the-clock surveillance.''

"You'll give me the addresses, won't you?''

"Certainly, but I guarantee they won't talk to you.''

"Oh, that would be a pity. We're just looking for a guy with a dozen names, asking questions, offering assistance.''

"They won't buy it.''

"Maybe I can sell it.''

"Goddamn it, *why*?'' spouted Armbruster, then immediately lowered his voice. "Why was this Webb or Bourne or whoever the hell he is at *Swayne's*?''

"It's a gap I can't fill,'' said DeSole.

"A *what*?''

"That's an Agency term for no answer.''

"No wonder the country's up shit's creek.''

"That's not true—''

"Now *you* shut up!'' ordered the man from New York, reaching into his pocket and pulling out a small notepad and a ballpoint pen. "Write out the addresses of this retired spook and the yid shrink. *Now!*''

"It's difficult to see,'' said DeSole, writing, angling the small pad of paper toward the neon lights of the closed gas station. "There. The apartment number may be wrong but it's close, and Panov's name will be on the mailbox. But I tell you again, he won't talk to you."

"Then we'll just have to apologize for interrupting him."

"Yes, you probably will. I gather he's very dedicated where his patients are concerned."

"Oh? Like that telephone line into your fax machine."

"No, no, that's a technical term. Number Three wire, to be precise."

"And you're always precise, aren't you, *paisan*?"

"And you're very irritating—"

"We've got to go," broke in Armbruster, watching the New Yorker take back the pad and the ballpoint pen. "Stay calm, Steven," he added, obviously suppressing his anger and heading back to the limousine. "Remember, there's nothing we can't handle. When you talk to Jimmy T in Brussels, see if you two can come up with a reasonable explanation, okay? If not, don't worry, we'll figure it out upstairs."

"Of course, Mr. Armbruster. But if I may ask? Is my account in Bern ready for immediate release—in case . . . well, you understand . . . in case—"

"Of course it is, Steven. All you have to do is

fly over and write out the numbers of your account in your own handwriting. That's your signature, the one on file, remember?''

"Yes, yes, I do."

"It must be over two million by now."

"Thank you. *Thank* you . . . sir."

"You've earned it, Steven. Good night."

The two men settled back in the rear seat of the limousine, but there was no lack of tension. Armbruster glanced at the mafioso as the chauffeur, beyond the glass partition, turned on the ignition. "Where's the other car?"

The Italian switched on the reading light and looked at his watch. "By now he's parked less than a mile down the road from the gas station. He'll pick up DeSole on his way back and stay with him until the circumstances are right."

"Your man knows exactly what to do?"

"Come on, a virgin he's not. He's got a searchlight mounted on that car so powerful it can be seen in Miami. He comes alongside, switches it on high, and wiggles the handle. Your two-million-dollar flunky is blinded and out of business, and we're only charging a quarter of that amount for the job. It's your day, Alby."

The chairman of the Federal Trade Commission sat back in the shadows of the left rear seat and stared out the window at the dark, rushing images beyond the smoked glass. "You know," he said quietly, "if anyone had ever told me twenty years ago that I'd be sitting in this car with someone like you, saying what I'm saying, I would've told him it was impossible."

"Oh, that's what we like about you class-act characters. You look down your noses and drip your snot on us until you need us. Then all of a sudden we're 'associates.' Live and be well, Alby, we're eliminating another problem for you. Go back to your big federal commission and decide which companies are clean and which aren't—decisions not necessarily based on soap, right?"

"Shut up!" roared Armbruster, pounding his hand on the armrest. "This Simon—this *Webb*! Where's he coming from? What's he on our case for? What's he *want*?"

"Something to do with that Jackal character maybe."

"That doesn't make sense. We don't have anything to do with the Jackal."

"Why should you?" asked the mafioso, grinning. "You got us, right?"

"It's a very loose association and don't you forget it. . . . Webb—*Simon,* god*damn* it, whoever he is, we've got to find him! With what he already knew, plus what I told him, he's a fucking *menace*!"

"He's a real major item, isn't he?"

"A major item," agreed the chairman, again staring out the window, his right fist clenched, the fingers of his left hand drumming furiously on the armrest.

"You want to negotiate?"

*"What?"*snappedArmbruster,turningandlooking at the calm Sicilian face of his companion.

"You heard me, only I used the wrong word and I apologize for that. I'll give you a *non*negotiable figure and you can either accept it or reject it."

"A . . . contract? On Simon—*Webb*?"

"No," replied the mafioso, slowly shaking his head. "On a character named Jason Bourne. It's cleaner to kill someone who's already dead, isn't it? . . . Since we just saved you one and a half mill, the price of the contract is five."

"Five *million*?"

"The cost of eliminating problems in the category of major items is high. Menaces are even higher. Five million, Alby, half on acceptance within the usual twenty-four hours."

"That's outrageous!"

"Then turn me down. You come back, it's seven fifty; and if you come back again, it's double that. Fifteen million."

"What guarantee do we have that you can even *find* him? You heard DeSole. He's Four Zero, which means he's out of reach, buried."

"Oh, we'll dig him up just so we can replant him."

"How? Two and a half million is a lot to pay on your word. *How?*"

Again smiling, the Mafia supremo reached into his pocket and pulled out the small notebook Steven DeSole had returned to him. "Close friends are the best sources, Alby. Ask the sleazes who write all those gossip books. I got two addresses."

"You won't get near them."

"Hey, come on. You think you're dealing with old Chicago and the animals? With Mad Dog Capone and Nitti, the nervous finger. We got sophisticated people on the payroll these days. *Geniuses.* Scientists, electronics whiz kids— doctors. By the time we get finished with the spook and the yid, they won't know what happened. But we'll have Jason Bourne, the character who doesn't exist because he's already dead."

Albert Armbruster nodded once and turned to the window in silence.

"I'll close up for six months, change the name, then start a promotional campaign in the magazines before reopening," said John St. Jacques, standing by the window as the doctor worked on his brother-in-law.

"There's no one left?" asked Bourne, wincing as he sat in a chair dressed in a bathrobe, the last suture on his neck being pincered.

"Sure, there is. Seven crazy Canadian couples, including my old buddy, who's needlepointing your throat at the moment. Would you believe they wanted to start up a brigade, Renfrews of the Mounties, after the evil people."

"That was Scotty's idea," interrupted the doctor softly, concentrating on the wound. "Count me out. I'm too old."

"So's he but he doesn't know it. Then he wanted to advertise a reward to the tune of a hundred thousand for information leading to the *et cetera*! I finally convinced him that the less said the better."

"Nothing said is the best," added Jason. "That's the way it's got to be."

"That's a little tough, David," said St.

Jacques, misunderstanding the sharp glance *Bourne* leveled at him. "I'm sorry, but it is. We're deflecting most of the local inquiries with an ersatz story about a massive propane-gas leak, but not too many people are buying it. Of course, to the world outside, an earthquake down here wouldn't rate six lines buried in the last pages of the want ads, but rumors are flying around the Leewards."

"You said local inquiries . . . what about that world outside? Has there been anything from it?"

"There will be but not about here, not about Tranquility. Montserrat, yes, and the news will get a column in the London *Times* and maybe an inch in the New York and Washington papers, but I don't think it'll touch us."

"Stop being so cryptic."

"We'll talk later."

"Say whatever you like, John," broke in the doctor. "I'm just about finished, so I'm not paying much attention, and even if I heard you, I'm entitled to."

"I'll make it brief," said St. Jacques, walking to the right of the chair. "The Crown governor," he continued. "You were right, at least I have to assume you were right."

"Why?"

"The news came in while you were getting cleaned up. The CG's boat was found smashed on one of the nastier reefs off Antigua, halfway to Barbuda. There was no sign of survivors. Plymouth assumes it was one of those whipsaw squalls that can come out of south Nevis, but it's hard to swallow. Not a squall necessarily, but the circumstances."

"Which were?"

"His usual two crewmen weren't with him. He dismissed them at the yacht club, saying he wanted to take the boat out by himself, yet he told Henry he was going out for the running big fish—"

"Which means he would've had to have a crew," interrupted the Canadian physician. "Oh, sorry."

"Yes, he would've," agreed the owner of Tranquility Inn. "You can't fish the big fellas and skipper a boat at the same time—at least the CG couldn't. He was afraid to take his eyes off the charts."

"But he could read them, couldn't he?" asked Jason. "The charts?"

"As a navigator, he was no Captain Bligh sailing by the Pacific stars, but he was good enough to stay out of trouble."

"He was told to go out alone," said Bourne. "Ordered to rendezvous with a boat in waters that called for him to *really* keep his eyes on the charts." Jason suddenly realized that the doctor's nimble fingers were no longer touching his neck; instead, there was the constricting bandage and the physician was standing beside him looking down. "How are we doing?" asked Bourne, looking up, an appreciative smile creasing his lips.

"We're done," said the Canadian.

"Well . . . then I think we'd better meet later, for a drink, all right?"

"Good heavens, you're just getting to the good part."

"It's not good, Doctor, it's not good at all, and I'd be a very ungrateful patient—which I'm not— if I even unwittingly let you hear things I don't think you should hear."

The elderly Canadian locked his eyes with Jason's. "You mean that, don't you? In spite of everything that's happened, you really don't want to involve me any further. And you're not playing melodramatic games, secrecy for secrecy's sake—an old dodge for inferior doctors, incidentally—but you're really concerned, aren't you?"

"I guess I am."

"Considering what's happened to you, and I don't just mean these past few hours, which I've been a part of, but what the scars on your body tell me you've been through before, it's rather remarkable that you can be concerned for anyone but yourself. You're a strange man, Mr. Webb. At times you even sound like two different people."

"I'm not strange, Doctor," said Jason Bourne, momentarily closing his eyes, his lids briefly tight. "I don't want to be strange or different or anything exotic at all. I want to be as normal and ordinary as the next fellow, no *games* at all. I'm just a teacher, and that's all I want to be. But in the present circumstances, I have to do things my way."

"Which means I leave for my own benefit?"

"Yes, it does."

"And if I ever learn all the facts, I'll realize that your instructions were very educational."

"I hope so."

"I'll bet you're one hell of a teacher, Mr. Webb."

"*Doctor* Webb," interjected John St. Jacques spontaneously, as if the clarification were mandatory. "My brother-in-law's a doctor, too. Like my sister, he's got a Ph.D.; he speaks a couple of Oriental languages and is a full professor. Places like Harvard, McGill and Yale have been after him for years, but he won't budge—"

"Will you please be *quiet*," said Bourne, close to laughing, albeit kindly, at his wife's brother. "My entrepreneurial young friend is impressed with any alphabet after a name despite the fact that left to my own resources I couldn't afford one of these villas for more than a couple of days."

"That's a crock."

"I said my *own* resources."

"You've got a point."

"I've got a rich wife. . . . Forgive us, Doctor, it's an old family argument."

"Not only a good teacher," the physician repeated, "but under the grim exterior I suspect a very engaging one." The Canadian walked to the door; he turned and added, "I'll take you up on that drink later, I'd really like that."

"Thanks," said Jason. "Thanks for everything." The doctor nodded and left, closing the door firmly behind him. Bourne turned to his brother-in-law. "He's a good friend, Johnny."

"Actually, he's a cold fish but a hell of a doctor. That's the most human I've ever seen him.

. . . So you figure the Jackal had the Crown governor meet him somewhere off the Antigua coast, got the CG's information, killed him, and fed him to the sharks."

"Conveniently foundering the boat in reef waters," completed Jason. "Perhaps opening the throttle and setting a short high-speed course into the shoals. A tragedy at sea and a link to Carlos vanishes—that's vital to him."

"That's also something I have trouble with," said St. Jacques. "I didn't go into it, but the section of reef north of Falmouth where he bought it is called Devil's Mouth, and it's not the kind of place that's advertised. Charters just stay away from it, and no one boasts about the number of lives and boats it's claimed."

"So?"

"So assuming the Jackal told the CG where to rendezvous, someplace obviously close to Devil's Mouth, how the hell did the Jackal know about it?"

"Your two commandos didn't tell you?"

"Tell me what? I sent them right over to Henry to give *him* a full report while we took care of you. There wasn't time to sit down and talk and I figured every moment counted."

"Then Henry knows by now; he's probably in

shock. He's lost two drug boats in two days, and only one is likely to be paid for, and he still doesn't know about his boss, the so honorable Crown governor, lackey of the Jackal who made fools of the Foreign Office by passing off a small-time Paris hit man as a venerable hero of France. The wires will be burning all night between Government House and Whitehall."

"Another *drug* boat? What are you trying to tell me? What does Henry know *now*—what could my guards tell him?"

"Your question a minute ago was how did the Jackal know about the reef off the coast of Antigua called Devil's Mouth."

"Take my word for it, *Doctor* Webb, I remember the question. How could he?"

"Because he had a third man here, that's what your Royal Commandos have told Henry by now. A blond-haired son of a bitch who heads up Montserrat's drug patrols."

"*Him?* Rickman? The one-man British Ku Klux Klan? By-the-Rules-Rickman, scourge of anybody who's afraid to yell back at him? Holy *Christ*, Henry won't *believe* it!"

"Why not? You just described a likely disciple of Carlos."

"I suppose I did, but it seems so *un*likely. He's

the original sanctimonious deacon. Prayer
meetings before work in the morning, calling on
God to aid him in his battle against Satan, no
alcohol, no women—"

"Savonarola?"

"I'd say that fits—from what I remember reading for history courses."

"Then I'd say he's prime meat for the Jackal.
And Henry *will* believe it when his lead boat
doesn't come back to Plymouth and the bodies
of the crew float up on shore or simply don't
show up for the prayer meetings."

"That's how Carlos got away?"

"Yes." Bourne nodded and gestured at the
couch several feet in front of him, the space
between taken up by a glass-topped coffee
table. "Sit down, Johnny. We have to talk."

"What have we been doing?"

"Not about what *has* happened, Bro, but
about what's going to happen."

"What's going to happen?" asked St.
Jacques, lowering himself on the couch.

"I'm leaving."

"No!" cried the younger man, shooting to his
feet as if propelled by a bolt of electricity. "You
can't!"

"I have to. He knows our names, where we
live. Everything."

"Where are you *going*?"

"Paris."

"Goddamn it, *no*! You can't *do* that to Marie! Or to the kids, for Christ's sake. I won't *let* you!"

"You can't stop me."

"For God's sake, David, listen to me! If Washington's too cheap or doesn't give a shit, believe me, Ottawa's cut from better stock. My sister *worked* for the government and *our* government doesn't kiss people off because it's inconvenient or too expensive. I know people—like Scotty, the Doc and others. A few words from them and you'll be put in a fortress in Calgary. No one could touch you!"

"You think my government wouldn't do the same? Let me tell you something, Bro, there are people in Washington who've put their lives on the line to keep Marie and the children and me alive. Selflessly, without any reward for themselves *or* the government. If I wanted a safe house where no one could touch us, I'd probably get an estate in Virginia, with horses and servants and a full platoon of armed soldiers protecting us around the clock."

"Then that's the answer. *Take* it!"

"To what end, Johnny? To live in our own personal prison? The kids not allowed to go over to friends' houses, guards with them *if* they

go to school and not tutored by themselves, no
overnights, no pillow fights—no neighbors?
Marie and I staring at each other, glancing over
at the searchlights outside the windows, hearing
the footsteps of the guards, the occasional
cough or sneeze, or, heaven forbid, the crack of
a rifle bolt because a rabbit disturbed a garden?
That's not living, that's imprisonment. Your sister and I couldn't handle it."

"Neither could I, not the way you describe it.
But what can Paris solve?"

"I can find him. I can take him."

"He's got the manpower over there."

"I've got Jason Bourne," said David Webb.

"I don't buy that crap!"

"Neither do I, but it seems to work. . . . I'm
calling in your debt to me, Johnny. Cover for me.
Tell Marie I'm fine, not hurt at all, and that I've
got a lead on the Jackal that only old Fontaine
could have provided—which is the truth, actually. A café in Argenteuil called Le Coeur du
Soldat. Tell her I'm bringing in Alex Conklin and
all the help Washington can provide."

"But you're not, are you?"

"No. The Jackal would hear about it; he's got
ears up and down the Quai d'Orsay. Solo's the
only way."

"Don't you think she'll know that?"

"She'll suspect it, but she can't be certain. I'll have Alex call her, confirming that he's in touch with all the heavy covert firepower in Paris. But first it comes from you."

"Why the lie?"

"You shouldn't have to ask that, Bro. I've put her through enough."

"All right, I'll tell her, but she won't believe me. She'll see right through me, she always has. Since I was a kid, those big brown eyes would look into mine, most of the time pissed off, but not like our brothers', not—oh, I don't know— not with that disgust in their faces because the 'kid' was a screwup. Can you understand that?"

"It's called caring. She's always cared for you—even when you were a screwup."

"Yeah, Mare's okay."

"Somewhat more than that, I think. Call her in a couple of hours and bring them back here. It's the safest place they can be."

"What about you? How are you going to get to Paris? The connections out of Antigua and Martinique are lousy, sometimes booked days in advance."

"I can't use those airlines anyway. I've got to get in secretly under a shroud. Somehow, a man in Washington will have to figure it out. Somehow. He's *got* to."

Alexander Conklin limped out of the small kitchen in the CIA's Vienna apartment, his face and hair soaking wet. In the old days, before the old days fell into a distillery vat, he would calmly leave the office—wherever it was—when things got too heavy too fast and indulge himself in an unwavering ritual. He would seek out the best steak house—again, wherever he was—have two dry martinis and a thick rare slab of meat with the greasiest potatoes on the menu. The combination of the solitude, the limited intake of alcohol, the blood-rare hunk of beef and, in particular, the grease-laden potatoes, had such a calming effect on him that all the rushing, conflicting complexities of the hectic day sorted themselves out and reason prevailed. He would return to his office—whether a smart flat in London's Belgravia Square or the back rooms of a whorehouse in Katmandu—with multiple solutions. It was how he got the sobriquet of Saint Alex of Conklin. He had once mentioned this gastronomical phenomenon to Mo Panov, who had a succinct reply: "If your crazy head doesn't kill you, your stomach will."

These days, however, with postalcoholic vacuum and various other impediments, such as high cholesterol and dumb little triglycerides, whatever the hell *they* were, he had to come up with a different solution. It came about by accident. One morning during the Iran-contra hearings, which he found to be the finest hours of comedy on television, his set blew out. He was furious, so he turned on his portable radio, an instrument he had not used in months or perhaps years, as the television set had a built-in radio component—also inoperable at the time—but the portable radio's batteries had long since melted into white slime. His artificial foot in pain, he walked to his kitchen telephone, knowing that a call to his television repairman, for whom he had done several favors, would bring the man running to his emergency. Unfortunately, the call only brought forth a hostile diatribe from the repairman's wife, who screamed that her husband, the "customerfucker," had run off with a "horny rich black bitch from Embassy Row!" (Zaire, as it later turned out in the Puerta Vallarta papers.) Conklin, in progressive apoplexy, had rushed to the kitchen sink, where his stress and blood pressure pills stood on the windowsill above the sink, and turned on the cold water. The faucet exploded, surging out of its recess into the ceiling as a powerful gush of water inundated his entire head. *Caramba!* The shock calmed him down, and he remembered that the Cable Network was scheduled to rebroadcast the hearings in full that evening. A happy man, he called the plumber and went out and bought a new television set.

So, since that morning, whenever his own furies or the state of the world disturbed him—the world he knew—he lowered his head in a kitchen sink and let the cold water pour over his head. He had done so this morning. This goddamned, fucked-up morning!

DeSole! *Killed* in an accident on a deserted country road in Maryland at 4:30 that morning. What the hell was Steven DeSole, a man whose driver's license clearly stated that he was afflicted with night blindness, doing on a back-country road outside Annapolis at 4:30 in the morning? And then Charlie Casset, a very angry Casset, calling him at six o'clock, yelling his usually cool head off, telling Alex he was going to put the commander of NATO on the goddamned spit and demand an explanation for the buried fax connection between the general and the dead chief of clandestine reports, who was not a victim of an accident but of murder! Furthermore, one retired field officer named Conklin had better damned well come clean with everything he knew about DeSole and Brussels and related matters, or all bets were off where said retired field agent and his elusive friend Jason Bourne were concerned. Noon at the latest! And *then*, Ivan Jax! The brilliant black doctor from Jamaica phoned, telling him he wanted to put Norman Swayne's body back where he had found it because he did not want to be loused up by another Agency fiasco. But it was *not* Agency, cried Conklin to himself, unable to explain to Ivan Jax the real reason he had asked for his help. *Medusa.* And Jax could *not* simply drive the corpse back to Manassas because the police, on federal orders—the orders of one retired field agent using appropriated codes he was not entitled to use—had sealed off General Norman Swayne's estate without explanation.

"What do I do with the *body*?" Jax had yelled.

"Keep it cold for a while, Cactus would want it that way."

"*Cactus?* I've been with him at the hospital all night. He's going to be okay, but he doesn't know what the hell is going on any more than *I* do!"

"We in the clandestine services can't always

explain things,'' Alex said, wincing as he spoke the ridiculous words. ''I'll call you back.''

So he had gone into the kitchen and put his head under a spray of cold water. What else could go wrong? And naturally the telephone rang.

''Dunkin' Donuts,'' said Conklin, the phone to his ear.

''Get me *out* of here,'' said Jason Bourne, not a trace of David Webb in his voice. ''To *Paris*!''

''What happened?''

''He got away, that's what happened, and I have to get to Paris under a cover, no immigration, no customs. He's got them all wired and I can't give him the chance to track me. . . . Alex, are you *listening* to me?''

''DeSole was killed last night, killed in an accident that was no accident at four o'clock in the morning. Medusa's closing in.''

''I don't give a *damn* about Medusa! For me it's history; we made a wrong turn. I want the Jackal and I've got a place to start. I can find him, *take* him!''

''Leaving me with Medusa . . .''

''You said you wanted to go higher—you said you'd only give me forty-eight hours until you did. Shove the clock ahead. The forty-eight hours are over, so *go* higher, just get me out of here and over to Paris."

"They'll want to talk to you."

"Who?"

"Peter Holland, Casset, whoever else they bring in . . . the attorney general, Christ, the President himself."

"About *what*?"

"You spoke at length with Armbruster, with Swayne's wife and that sergeant, Flannagan. I didn't. I just used a few code words that triggered responses from Armbruster and Ambassador Atkinson in London, nothing substantive. You've got the fuller picture firsthand. I'm too deniable. They'll have to talk to you."

"And put the Jackal on a back *burner*?"

"Just for a day, two at the most."

"Goddamn it, *no*. Because it doesn't work that way and you know it! Once I'm back there I'm their only material witness, shunted from one closed interrogation to another; and if I refuse to cooperate, I'm in custody. No *way*, Alex. I've got only one priority and he's in Paris!"

"Listen to me," said Conklin. "There are some things I can control, others I can't. We needed Charlie Casset and he helped us, but he's not someone you can con, nor would I want to. He knows DeSole's death was no accident—a man with night blindness doesn't take a five-hour drive at four o'clock in the morning—and he also knows that *we* know a lot more about DeSole and Brussels than we're telling him. If we want the Agency's help, and we need it for things like getting you on a military or a diplomatic flight into France, and God knows what else when you're there, I can't ignore Casset. He'll step on us and by his lights, he should.''

Bourne was silent; only his breathing was heard. ''All right,'' he said. ''I see where we're at. You tell Casset that if he gives us whatever we ask for now, we'll give him—no, *I'll* give him; keep yourself cleaner than me—enough information for the Department of Justice to go after some of the biggest fish in the government, assuming Justice isn't part of Snake Lady. . . . You might add that'll include the location of a cemetery that might prove enlightening.''

It was Conklin's turn to be silent for a moment. ''He may want more than that, considering your current pursuits.''

''Oh . . . ? Oh, I see. In case I lose. Okay, add that when I get to Paris I'll hire a stenographer and dictate everything I know, everything I've learned, and send it to *you*. I'll trust Saint Alex to carry it from there. Maybe a page or two at a time to keep them cooperative."

"I'll handle that part. . . . Now Paris, or close by. From what I recall, Montserrat's near Dominica and Martinique, isn't it?"

"Less than an hour to each, and Johnny knows every pilot on the big island."

"Martinique's French, we'll go with that. I know people in the Deuxième Bureau. Get down there and call me from the airport terminal. I'll have made the arrangements by then."

"Will do. . . . There's a last item, Alex. Marie. She and the children will be back here this afternoon. Call her and tell her I'm covered with all the firepower in Paris."

"You lying son of a bitch—"

"*Do* it!"

"Of course I will. On that score and not lying, if I live through the day, I'm having dinner with Mo Panov at his place tonight. He's a terrible cook, but he thinks he's the Jewish Julia Child. I'd like to bring him up to date; he'll go crazy if I don't."

"Sure. Without him we'd both be in padded cells chewing rawhide."

"Talk to you later. Good luck."

The next day at 10:25 in the morning, Washington time, Dr. Morris Panov, accompanied by his guard, walked out of Walter Reed Hospital after a psychiatric session with a retired army lieutenant suffering from the aftereffects of a training exercise in Georgia that took the lives of twenty-odd recruits under his command eight weeks before. There was not much Mo could do; the man was guilty of competitive overachievement, military style, and had to live with his guilt. The fact that he was a financially privileged black and a graduate of West Point did not help. Most of the twenty dead recruits were also black and they had been underprivileged.

Panov, muddling over the available options with his patient, looked at his guard, suddenly startled. "You're a new man, aren't you? I mean, I thought I knew all of you."

"Yes, sir. We're often reassigned on short notice, keeps all of us on our toes."

"Habit-oriented anticipation—it can lull anybody." The psychiatrist continued across the pavement to where his armor-plated car was usually waiting for him. It was a different vehicle. "This isn't my car," he said, bewildered.

"Get in," ordered his guard, politely opening the door.

"What?" A pair of hands from inside the car grabbed him and a uniformed man pulled him into the backseat as the guard followed, sandwiching Panov between them. The two men held the psychiatrist as the one who had been inside yanked Mo's seersucker jacket off his shoulder and shoved up the short sleeve of his summer shirt. He plunged a hypodermic needle into Panov's arm.

"Good night, Doctor," said the soldier with the insignia of the Medical Corps on the lapels of his uniform. "Call New York," he added.

19

The Air France 747 from Martinique circled Orly Airport in the early evening haze over Paris; it was five hours and twenty-two minutes behind schedule because of the severe weather patterns in the Caribbean. As the pilot entered his final approach the flight officer acknowledged their clearance to the tower, then switched to his prescribed sterile frequency and sent a last message in French to an off-limits communications room.

"Deuxième, special cargo. Please instruct your interested party to go to his designated holding area. Thank you. Out."

"Instructions received and relayed" was the terse reply. "Out."

The special cargo in question sat in the left rear bulkhead seat in the first-class section of the aircraft; the seat beside him was unoccupied, on orders of the Deuxième Bureau in cooperation with Washington. Impatient, annoyed and unable to sleep because of the constricting bandage around his neck, Bourne, close to exhaustion, reflected on the events of the past nineteen hours. To put it mildly, they had not gone as smoothly as Conklin had anticipated. The Deuxième had balked for over six hours as phone calls went back and forth feverishly between Washington, Paris and, finally, Vienna, Virginia. The stumbling block, and it was more of a hard rock, was the CIA's inability to spell out the covert operation in terms of one Jason Bourne, for only Alexander Conklin could release the name and he refused to do so, knowing that the Jackal's penetrations in Paris extended to just about everywhere but the kitchens of the Tour d'Argent. Finally, in desperation and realizing it was lunchtime in Paris, Alex placed ordinary, unsafe overseas telephone calls to several cafés on the Rive Gauche, finding an old Deuxième acquaintance at one on the rue de Vaugirard.

"Do you remember the tinamou and an American somewhat younger than he is now who made things a little simpler for you?"

"Ah, the tinamou, the bird with hidden wings and ferocious legs! They were such better days, younger days. And if the somewhat older American was at the time given the status of a saint, I shall never forget him."

"Don't now, I need you."

"It *is* you, Alexander?"

"It is and I've got a problem with D. Bureau."

"It is solved."

And it was, but the weather was insoluble. The storm that had battered the central Leeward Islands two nights before was only a prelude to the torrential rain and winds that swept up from the Grenadines, with another storm behind it. The islands were entering the hurricane season, so the weather was not astonishing, it was merely a delaying factor. Finally, when clearance for takeoff was around the chronological corner, it was discovered that there was a malfunction in the far starboard engine; no one argued while the problem was traced, found and repaired. The elapsed time, however, was an additional three hours.

Except for the churning of his mind, the flight itself was uneventful for Jason; only his guilt interfered with his thoughts of what was before him—Paris, Argenteuil, a café with the provocative name of Le Coeur du Soldat, The Soldier's Heart. The guilt was most painful on the short flight from Montserrat to Martinique when they passed over Guadeloupe and the island of Basse-Terre. He knew that only a few thousand feet below were Marie and his children, preparing to fly back to Tranquility Isle, to the husband and father who would not be there. His infant daughter, Alison, would, of course, know nothing, but Jamie would; his wide eyes would grow larger and cloud over as words tumbled out about fishing and swimming . . . and Marie—*Christ,* I can't think about her! It hurts too much!

She'd think he had betrayed her, run away to seek a violent confrontation with an enemy from long ago in another far-off life that was no longer *their* life. She would think like old Fontaine, who had tried to persuade him to take his family thousands of miles away from where the Jackal prowled, but neither of them understood. The aging Carlos might die, but on his deathbed he would leave a legacy, a bequest that would hinge on the mandatory death of Jason Bourne—David Webb and his family. *I'm right, Marie! Try to understand me. I have to find him,*

I have to kill him! We can't live in our personal prison for the rest of our lives!

"Monsieur Simon?" said the stoutish well-tailored Frenchman, an older man with a close-cropped white chin beard, pronouncing the name *Seemohn*.

"That's right," replied Bourne, shaking the hand extended to him in a narrow deserted hallway somewhere in Orly Airport.

"I am Bernardine, François Bernardine, an old colleague of our mutual friend, Alexander the Saint."

"Alex mentioned you," said Jason, smiling tentatively. "Not by name, of course, but he told me you might bring up his sainthood. It was how I'd know you were—his colleague."

"How is he? We hear stories, of course." Bernardine shrugged. "Banal gossip, by and large. Wounded in the futile Vietnam, alcohol, dismissed, disgraced, brought back a hero of the Agency, so many contradictory things."

"Most of them true; he's not afraid to admit that. He's a cripple now, and he doesn't drink, and he *was* a hero. I know."

"I see. Again stories, rumors, who can believe

what? Flights of fancy out of Beijing, Hong Kong—some concerning a man named Jason Bourne."

"I've heard them."

"Yes, of course. . . . But now Paris. Our saint said you would need lodgings, clothes purchased *en scène*, as it were, French to the core."

"A small but varied closet," agreed Jason. "I know where to go, what to buy, and I have sufficient money."

"Then we are concerned with lodgings. A hotel of your choice? La Trémoille? George Cinq? Plaza-Athénée?"

"Smaller, much smaller and far less expensive."

"Money *is* a problem, then?"

"Not at all. Only appearances. I'll tell you what, I know Montmartre. I'll find a place myself. What I will need is a car—registered under another name, preferably a name that's a dead end."

"Which means a dead man. It's been arranged; it is in the underground garage on the Capucines, near the Place Vendôme." Bernardine reached into his pocket, pulled out a set of keys, and handed them to Jason. "An older

Peugeot in Section E. There are thousands like them in Paris and the license number is on the tab."

"Alex told you I'm traveling deep?"

"He didn't really have to. I believe our saint scoured the cemeteries for useful names when he worked here."

"I probably learned it from him."

"We all learned things from that extraordinary mind, the finest in our profession, yet so self-effacing, so . . . *je ne sais quoi* . . . so 'why not try it,' yes?"

"Yes, why not try it."

"I must tell you, though," said Bernardine, laughing. "He once chose a name, admittedly from a tombstone, that drove the Sûreté *folle*— crazy! It was the alias of an ax murderer the authorities had been hunting for months!"

"That *is* funny," agreed Bourne, chuckling.

"Yes, very. He told me later that he found it in Rambouillet—in a cemetery on the outskirts of Rambouillet."

Rambouillet! The cemetery where Alex had tried to kill him thirteen years ago. All traces of a smile left Jason's lips as he stared at Alex's friend from the Deuxième Bureau. "You know who I am, don't you?" he asked softly.

"Yes," answered Bernardine. "It was not so difficult to piece together, not with the rumors and the gossip out of the Far East. After all, it was here in Paris where you made your mark on Europe, Mr. Bourne."

"Does anyone else know?"

"*Mon Dieu, non!* Nor will they. I must explain, I owe my life to Alexander Conklin, our modest saint of *les opérations noires*—the black assignments in your language."

"That's not necessary, I speak French fluently . . . or didn't Alex tell you that?"

"Oh, my God, you doubt me," said the Deuxième man, his gray eyebrows arched. "Take into account, young man—younger man—that I am in my seventieth year, and if I have lapses of language and try to correct them, it is because I mean to be kind, not *subreptice*."

"*D'accord. Je regrette.* I mean that."

"*Bien.* Alex is several years younger than I am, but I wonder how he's handling it. The age, that is."

"Same as you. Badly."

"There was an English poet—a Welsh poet, to be exact—who wrote, 'Do not go gently into that good night.' Do you remember it?"

"Yes. His name was Dylan Thomas and he

died in his mid-thirties. He was saying fight like a son of a bitch. Don't give in."

"I mean to do that." Bernardine again reached into a pocket and pulled out a card. "Here is my office—merely consultant status, you understand—and on the back I've written down my home phone; it is a special telephone, actually unique. Call me; whatever you need will be provided. Remember, I am the only friend you have in Paris. No one else knows you are here."

"May I ask you a question?"

"*Mais certainement.*"

"How can you do the things you're doing for me when for all intents and purposes you've been put out to pasture?"

"*Ah,*" exclaimed the consultant to the Deuxième Bureau. "The younger man grows older! Like Alex, I carry my credentials in my head. I know the *secrets.* How it is otherwise?"

"You could be taken out, neutralized—have an accident."

"*Stupide,* young man! What is in both our heads we say is written down, locked away, to be revealed should such unnatural acts occur. . . . Of course, it's all nonsense, for what do we really know that could not be denied, labeled as the ramblings of old men, but *they* do not know that. *Fear,* monsieur. It is the most potent weapon in our profession. Second, of course, is embarrassment, but that is usually reserved for the Soviet KGB and your Federal Bureau of Investigation, both of which fear embarrassment more than their nations' enemies."

"You and Conklin come from the same street, don't you?"

"But of course. To the best of my knowledge, neither of us has a wife or a family, only sporadic lovers to fill our beds, and loud, annoying nephews and nieces to fill our flats on certain holidays; no really close friends except now and then an enemy we respect, who, for all we know and in spite of our truce, might shoot us or poison us with a drink. We *must* live alone, you see, for we are the professionals—we have nothing to do with the normal world; we merely use it as a *couverture*—as we slink around in dark alleys, paying or compromising people for secrets that mean nothing where summit conferences are concerned."

"Then why do you do it? Why not walk away if it's so useless?"

"It's in the blood rushing through our veins. We've been trained. Beat the enemy in the deadly game—he takes you or you take him, and it is better that you take him."

"That's dumb."

"But of course. It's all dumb. So why does Jason Bourne go after the Jackal here in Paris? Why doesn't he walk away and say *Enough*. Complete protection is yours for the asking."

"So's prison. Can you get me out of here and into the city? I'll find a hotel and be in touch with you."

"Before you are in touch with me, reach Alex."

"What?"

"Alex wants you to call him. Something happened."

"Where's a phone?"

"Not now. Two o'clock, Washington time; you have well over an hour. He won't be back before then."

"Did he say what it was?"

"I think he's trying to find out. He was very upset."

The room at the Pont-Royal on the rue Montalembert was small and in a secluded corner of the hotel, reached by taking the slow, noisy brass elevator to the top floor and walking down two narrow intersecting hallways, all of which was satisfactory to Bourne. It reminded him of a mountain cave, remote and secure.

To chew up the minutes before calling Alex, he walked along the nearby boulevard Saint-Germain, making necessary purchases. Various toiletries joined several articles of clothing; casual denims called for summer shirts and a lightweight safari jacket; dark socks required tennis shoes, to be scuffed and soiled. Whatever he could supply himself now would save time later. Fortunately, there was no need to press old Bernardine for a weapon. During the drive into Paris from Orly, the Frenchman had opened the glove compartment of his car in silence, withdrawn a taped brown box and handed it to Jason. Inside was an automatic with two boxes of shells. Underneath, neatly layered, were thirty thousand francs, in varying denominations, roughly five thousand dollars, American.

"Tomorrow I will arrange a method for you to obtain funds whenever necessary. Within limits, of course."

"No limits," Bourne had contradicted. "I'll have Conklin wire you a hundred thousand, and then another hundred after that, if it's necessary. You just tell him where."

"Of *contingency* funds?"

"No. Mine. Thanks for the gun."

With both his hands holding the looped strings of shopping bags, he headed back to Montalembert and the hotel. In a few minutes it would be two in the afternoon in Washington, eight at night in Paris. As he walked rapidly down the street he tried not to think about Alex's news—an impossible demand on himself. If anything had happened to Marie and the children, he'd go out of his mind! Yet what could have happened? They were back on Tranquility by now, and there was no safer place for them. There was *not*! He was sure of that. As he entered the old elevator and lowered the bags in his right hand so as to push the number of his floor and remove the hotel key from his pocket, there was a stinging sensation in his neck; he gasped—he had moved too fast, stretched the gut of a suture perhaps. He felt no warm trickle of blood; it was merely a warning this time. He rushed down the two narrow corridors to his room, unlocked the door, threw the shopping bags on the bed, and rapidly took the three necessary steps to the desk and the telephone. Conklin was true to his word; the phone in Vienna, Virginia, was picked up on the first ring.

"Alex, it's me. What happened? *Marie* . . . ?"

"No," interrupted Conklin curtly. "I spoke to her around noon. She and the kids are back at the inn and she's ready to kill me. She doesn't believe a word I told her and I'm going to erase the tape. I haven't heard that kind of language since the Mekong Delta."

"She's upset—"

"So am I," broke in Alex, not bothering to make light of Bourne's understatement. "Mo's disappeared."

"What?"

"You heard me. Panov's gone, vanished."

"My God, *how*? He was guarded every minute!"

"We're trying to piece it together; that's where I was, over at the hospital."

"Hospital?"

"Walter Reed. He was in a psych session with a military this morning, and when it was over he never came out to his detail. They waited twenty minutes or so, then went in to find him and his escort because he was on a tight schedule. They were told he left."

"That's crazy!"

"It gets crazier and scarier. The head floor nurse said an army doctor, a surgeon, came to the desk, showed his ID, and instructed her to tell Dr. Panov that there was a change of routing for him, that he was to use the east-wing exit because of an expected protest march at the main entrance. The east wing has a different hallway to the psych area than the one to the main lobby, yet the army surgeon used the main doors.''

"Come again?''

"He walked right past our escort in the hall-way.''

"And obviously out the same way and around to the east-wing hall. Nothing on-scene unusual. A doctor with clearance in a restricted area, in and out, and while he's in, he delivers false in-structions. . . . But, Christ, Alex, *who*? Carlos was on his way back here, to Paris! Whatever he wanted in Washington he got. He found me, he found *us*. He didn't *need* any more!''

"DeSole,'' said Conklin quietly. "DeSole knew about me and Mo Panov. I threatened the Agency with both of us, and DeSole was there in the conference room.''

"I'm not with you. What are you telling me?''

"DeSole, Brussels . . . Medusa.''

"All right, I'm slow.''

"It's not *he,* David, it's *they.* DeSole was taken out, our connection removed. It's Medusa.''

"To *hell* with them! They're on *my* back burner!"

"You're not on theirs. You cracked their shell. They want you."

"I couldn't care *less.* I told you yesterday, I've only got one priority and he's in Paris, *square* one in Argenteuil."

"Then I haven't been clear," said Alex, his voice faint, the tone defeated. "Last night I had dinner with Mo. I told him everything. Tranquility, your flying to Paris, Bernardine . . . *everything*!"

A former judge of the first circuit court, residing in Boston, Massachusetts, United States of America, stood among the small gathering of mourners on the flat surface of the highest hill on Tranquility Isle. The cemetery was the final resting place—*in voce verbatim via amicus curiae,* as he legally explained to the authorities on Montserrat. Brendan Patrick Pierre Prefontaine watched as the two splendid coffins provided by the generous owner of Tranquility Inn were lowered into the ground along with the absolutely incomprehensible blessings of the native priest, who no doubt usually had the neck of a dead chicken in his mouth while intoning his benediction in voodoo language.

"Jean Pierre Fontaine" and his wife were at peace.

Nevertheless, barbarism notwithstanding, Brendan, the quasi-alcoholic street lawyer of Harvard Square, had found a cause. A cause beyond his own survival, and that in itself was remarkable. Randolph Gates, Lord Randolph of Gates, Dandy Randy of the Courts of the Elite, was in reality a scumball, a conduit of death in the Caribbean. And the outlines of a scheme were forming in Prefontaine's progressively clearer mind, clearer because, among other inhumane deprivations, he had suddenly decided to do without his four shots of vodka upon waking up in the morning. Gates had provided the essential information that led the would-be killers of the Webb family to Tranquility Isle. *Why?* . . . That was basically, even legally, irrelevant; the fact that he had supplied their whereabouts to known killers, with prior knowledge that they *were* killers, was not. That was accomplice to murder, *multiple* murder. Dandy Randy's testicles were in a vise, and as the plates closed, he would—he *had* to—reveal information that would assist the Webbs, especially the glorious auburn-headed woman he wished to almighty God he had met fifty years ago.

Prefontaine was flying back to Boston in the morning, but he had asked John St. Jacques if he might return one day. Perhaps not with a prepaid reservation.

"Judge, my house is your house" was the reply.

"I might even earn that courtesy."

Albert Armbruster, chairman of the Federal Trade Commission, got out of his limousine and stood on the pavement before the steep steps of his town house in Georgetown. "Check with the office in the morning," he said to the chauffeur, holding the rear door. "As you know, I'm not a well man."

"Yes, sir." The driver closed the door. "Would you like assistance, sir?"

"*Hell,* no. Get out of here."

"Yes, sir." The government chauffeur climbed into the front seat; the sudden roar of his engine was not meant as a courteous exit as he sped down the street.

Armbruster climbed the stone staircase, his stomach and chest heaving with each step, cursing under his breath at the sight of his wife's silhouette beyond the glass door of their Victorian entrance. "Shit-kicking *yapper*," he said to himself as he neared the top, gripping the railing before facing his adversary of thirty years.

A spit exploded out of the darkness from somewhere within the grounds of the property next door. Armbruster's arms flew up, his wrists bent as if trying to locate the bodily chaos; it was too late. The chairman of the Federal Trade Commission tumbled back down the stone staircase, his thumping dead weight landing grotesquely on the pavement below.

Bourne changed into the French denim trousers, slipped on a dark short-sleeved shirt and the cotton safari jacket, put his money, his weapon and all his IDs—authentic and false—into his pockets and left the Pont-Royal. Before doing so, however, he stuffed the bed with pillows, and hung his traveling clothes in clear view over the chair. He walked casually past the ornate front desk, and once outside on Montalembert ran to the nearest telephone kiosk. He inserted a coin and dialed Bernardine's home.

"It's Simon," he said.

"I thought so," replied the Frenchman. "I was

hoping so. I've just heard from Alex and told him *not* to tell me where you were; one cannot reveal what one does not know. Still, if I were you, I'd go to another place, at least for the night. You may have been spotted at the airport."

"What about you?"

"I intend to be a *canard*."

"A duck?"

"The sitting variety. The Deuxième has my flat under watch. Perhaps I'll have a visitor; it would be convenient, *n'est-ce pas*?"

"You didn't tell your office about—"

"About *you*?" interrupted Bernardine. "How could I, monsieur, when I don't *know* you? My protective Bureau believes I had a threatening call from an old adversary known to be a psychopath. Actually I removed him in the Maritimes years ago but I never closed the file—"

"Should you be telling me this on your telephone?"

"I thought I mentioned that it was a unique instrument."

"You did."

"Suffice it to say it cannot be tapped and still function. . . . You need rest, monsieur. You are no good to anyone, least of all yourself, without it. Find a bed, I cannot help you there."

" 'Rest is a weapon,' " said Jason, repeating a phrase he had come to believe was a vital truth, vital for survival in a world he loathed.

"I beg your pardon?"

"Nothing. I'll find a bed and call you in the morning."

"Tomorrow then. *Bonne chance, mon ami.* For both of us."

He found a room at the Avenir, an inexpensive hotel on the rue Gay-Lussac. Registering under a false name, promptly forgotten, he climbed the stairs to his room, removed his clothes, and fell into the bed. "Rest is a weapon," he said to himself, staring at the ceiling, at the flickering lights of the Paris streets as they traveled across the plaster. Whether rest came in a mountain cave or a rice paddy in the Mekong Delta, it did not matter; it was a weapon frequently more powerful than firepower. That was the lesson drummed into his head by d'Anjou, the man who had given his life in a Beijing forest so that Jason Bourne might live. Rest *is* a weapon, he considered, touching the bandage around his neck yet not really feeling it, its constricting presence fading as sleep came.

He woke up slowly, cautiously, the noise of the traffic in the streets below pounding up to his window, the metallic horns like the erratic cawing of angry crows amid the irregular bursts of angry engines, full bore one moment, abrupt quiet the next. It was a normal morning in the narrow streets of Paris. Holding his neck rigid, Jason swung his legs to the floor from the inadequate bed and looked at his watch, startled at what he saw, wondering for an instant whether he had adjusted the watch for Paris time. Of course he had. It was 10:07 in the morning— Paris time. He had slept nearly eleven hours, a fact confirmed by the rumbling in his stomach. Exhaustion was now replaced by acute hunger.

Food, however, would have to wait; there were things to take care of, and first on the list was to reach Bernardine, and then to learn the security status of the Pont-Royal hotel. He got to his feet, stiffly, unsteadily, numbness momentarily invading his legs and arms. He needed a hot shower, which was not to be had at the Avenir, then mild exercise to limber up his body, therapies unnecessary only a few years ago. He removed his wallet from his trousers, pulled out Bernardine's card and returned to the bed to use the telephone beside it; he dialed.

"*Le canard* had no visitors, I'm afraid," said the Deuxième veteran. "Not even the hint of a hunter, which I presume is favorable news."

"It's not until we find Panov—*if* we find him. The *bastards*!"

"Yes, that must be faced. It's the ugliest part of our work."

"Goddamn it, I can't dismiss a man like Mo with 'That must be *faced*'!"

"I'm not asking you to. I'm only remarking upon the reality. Your feelings are meaningful to you, but they don't change reality. I did not mean to offend you."

"And I didn't mean to mouth off. Sorry. It's just that he's a very special person."

"I understand. . . . What are your plans? What do you need?"

"I don't know yet," answered Bourne. "I'll pick up the car in the Capucines and an hour or so later I'll know more. Will you be home or at the Deuxième Bureau?"

"Until I hear from you I will stay in my flat and near my very unique telephone. Under the circumstances I prefer that you do not call me at the office."

"That's an astonishing statement."

"I don't know everyone these days at the

Deuxième, and at my age, caution is not merely the better part of valor, it's frequently a substitute. Besides, to call off my protection so swiftly might generate rumors of senility. . . . Speak to you later, *mon ami.*"

Jason replaced the phone, tempted to pick it up again and reach the Pont-Royal, but this was Paris, the city of discretion, where hotel clerks were loath to give information over the telephone, and would refuse to do so with guests they did not know. He dressed quickly, went down to pay his bill, and walked out onto the rue Gay-Lussac. There was a taxi stand at the corner; eight minutes later he walked into the lobby of the Pont-Royal and up to the concierge. *"Je m'appelle Monsieur Simon,"* he said to the man, giving his room number. "I ran into a friend last night," he continued in flawless French, "and I stayed at her place. Would you know if anyone came around looking for me, perhaps asking for me." Bourne removed several large franc notes, his eyes telling the man he would pay generously for confidentiality. "Or even describing someone like me," he added softly.

"Merci bien, monsieur. . . . I understand. I will check further with the night concierge, but I'm sure he would have left a note for my personal

attention if someone had come here seeking you."

"Why are you so sure?"

"Because he *did* leave such a note for me to speak with you. I've been calling your room since seven o'clock this morning when I came on duty."

"What did the note say?" asked Jason, his breathing on hold.

"It's what I'm to say to you. 'Reach his friend across the Atlantic. The man has been phoning all night.' I can attest to the accuracy of that, monsieur. The switchboard tells me that last call was less than thirty minutes ago."

"Thirty minutes ago?" said Jason, looking hard at the concierge and then at his watch. "It's five A.M. over there . . . all *night*?"

The hotel man nodded as Bourne started for the elevator.

"Alex, for Christ's sake, what *is* it? They told me you've been calling all—"

"Are you at the hotel?" interrupted Conklin quickly.

"Yes, I am."

"Get to a public phone in the street and call me back. Hurry."

Again the slow, cumbersome elevator; the faded ornate lobby now half filled with Parisians talking manically, many heading for the bar and their prenoon apéritifs; and again the hot bright summer street outside and the maddening congested traffic. Where was a telephone? He walked rapidly down the pavement toward the Seine—where was a *phone*? There! Across the converging rue du Bac, a red-domed booth with posters covering the sides.

Dodging the onslaught of automobiles and small trucks, all with furious drivers, he raced to the other side of the street and down to the booth. He sped inside, deposited a coin, and after an agonizing few moments during which he explained that he was *not* calling Austria, the international operator accepted his AT&T credit number and put the call through to Vienna, Virginia.

"Why the hell couldn't I talk from the hotel?" asked Bourne angrily. "I called you last night from there!"

"That was last night, not today."

"Any news about Mo?"

"Nothing yet, but they may have made a mistake. We may have a line on the army doctor."

"Break him!"

"With pleasure. I'll take off my foot and smash

his face with it until he begs to cooperate—if the line on him is rumb."

"That's not why you've been calling me all night, though, is it?"

"No. I was with Peter Holland for five hours yesterday. I went over to see him after we talked, and his reaction was exactly what I thought it would be, with a few generous broadsides in the bargain."

"Medusa?"

"Yes. He insists you fly back immediately; you're the only one with direct knowledge. It's an order."

"Bullshit! He can't insist I do anything, much less give me an order!"

"He can cut you off, and I can't do anything about it. If you need something in a hurry, he won't deliver."

"Bernardine's offered to help. 'Whatever you need,' those were his words."

"Bernardine's limited. Like me, he can call in debts, but without access to the machine he's too restricted."

"Did you tell Holland I'm writing down everything I know, every statement that was made to me, every answer to every question I asked?"

"Are you?"

"I will."

"He doesn't buy it. He wants to question you; he says he can't question pages of paper."

"I'm too close to the Jackal! I won't *do* it. He's an unreasonable son of a bitch!"

"I think he wanted to be reasonable," said Conklin. "He knows what you're going through, what you've been through, but after seven o'-clock last night he closed the doors."

"Why?"

"Armbruster was shot to death outside his house. They're calling it a Georgetown robbery, which, of course, it isn't and wasn't."

"Oh, *Jesus*!"

"There are a couple of other things you ought to know. To begin with, we're releasing Swayne's 'suicide.' "

"For God's sake, why?"

"To let whoever killed him think he's off the hook, and, more important, to see who shows up during the next week or so."

"At the funeral?"

"No, that's a 'closed family affair,' no guests, no formal ceremony."

"Then who's going to show up where?

"At the estate, in one form or another. We checked with Swayne's attorney, very officially, of course, and he confirmed what Swayne's wife told you about his leaving the whole place to a foundation."

"Which one?" asked Bourne.

"One you've never heard of, funded privately a few years ago by wealthy close friends of the august 'wealthy' general. It's as touching as can be. It goes under the title of the Soldiers, Sailors and Marines Retreat; the board of directors is already in place."

"Medusans."

"Or their surrogates. We'll see."

"Alex, what about the names I gave you, the six or seven names Flannagan gave *me*? And that slew of license plate numbers from their meetings?"

"Cute, real cute," said Conklin enigmatically.

"What's cute?"

"Take the names—they're the dregs of the wing-ding social set, no relation to the George-town upper crust. They're out of the *National Enquirer,* not *The Washington Post.*"

"But the *licenses,* the meetings! That's got to be the ball of wax."

"Even cuter," observed Alex. "A ball of sheep dip. . . . Every one of those licenses is registered to a limousine company, read that companies. I don't have to tell you how authentic the names would be even if we had the dates to trace them."

"There's a cemetery out there!"

"Where is it? How big, how small? There are twenty-eight acres—"

"Start looking!"

"And advertise what we know?"

"You're right; you're playing it right. . . . Alex, tell Holland you couldn't reach me."

"You're joking."

"No, I mean it. I've got the concierge, I can cover. Give Holland the hotel and the name and tell him to call himself, or send over whoever he likes from the embassy to verify. The concierge will swear I checked in yesterday and he hasn't seen me since. Even the switchboard will confirm it. Buy me a few days, *please*."

"Holland could still pull all the plugs and probably will."

"He won't if he thinks I'll come back when you find me. I just want him to keep looking for Mo and keep my name out of Paris. Good *or* bad, no Webb, no Simon, no Bourne!"

"I'll try."

"Was there anything else? I've got a lot to do."

"Yes. Casset is flying over to Brussels in the morning. He's going to nail Teagarten—*him* we can't allow and it won't touch you."

"Agreed."

On a side street in Anderlecht, three miles south of Brussels, a military sedan bearing the flags of a four-star general officer pulled up to the curb in front of a sidewalk café. General James Teagarten, commander of NATO, his tunic emblazoned with five rows of ribbons, stepped gingerly out of the car into the bright early afternoon sunlight. He turned and offered his hand to a stunning WAC major, who smiled her thanks as she climbed out after him. Gallantly, with military authority, Teagarten released the woman's hand and took her elbow; he escorted her across the wide pavement toward a cluster of umbrella-topped tables behind a row of flowering planter boxes that was the alfresco section of the café. They reached the entrance, a latticework archway profusely covered with baby roses, and walked inside. All the tables were occupied save one at the far end of the enclosed pavement; the hum of luncheon conversation was punctuated by the tinkling of wine bottles gently touching wineglasses and the delicate clatter of utensils lowered on china plates. The decibel level of the conversation was suddenly reduced, and the general, aware that his presence inevitably brought stares, amiable waves and not infrequently mild applause, smiled benignly at no one in particular and yet at everyone as he guided his lady to the deserted table where a small folded card read *Réservé.*

The owner, with two waiters trailing behind him like anxious egrets, practically flew between the tables to greet his distinguished guest. When the commander was seated, a chilled bottle of Corton-Charlemagne was presented and the menu discussed. A young Belgian child, a boy of five or six, walked shyly up to the table and brought his hand to his forehead; he smiled and saluted the general. Teagarten rose to his feet, standing erect, and saluted the child back.

"Vous êtes un soldat distingué, mon camarade," said the general, his commanding voice ringing through the sidewalk café, his bright smile winning the crowd, who responded with appreciative applause. The child retreated and the meal continued.

A leisurely hour later, Teagarten and his lady

were interrupted by the general's chauffeur, a middle-aged army sergeant whose expression conveyed his anxiety. The commander of NATO had received an urgent message over his vehicle's secure phone, and the chauffeur had had the presence of mind to write it down and repeat it for accuracy. He handed Teagarten the note.

The general stood up, his tanned face turning pale as he glanced around the now-half-empty sidewalk café, his eyes narrowed, angry, afraid. He reached into his pocket and pulled out a folded wad of Belgian franc notes, peeled off several large ones and dropped them on the table. "Come on," he said to the woman major. "Let's go. . . . You"—he turned to his driver— "get the car started!"

"What is it?" asked his luncheon companion.

"London. Over the wire. Armbruster and DeSole are dead."

"Oh, my God! *How?*"

"It doesn't matter. Whatever they say is a lie."

"What's happening?"

"I don't know. I just know we're getting out of here. Come *on!*"

The general and his lady rushed through the

latticework archway, across the wide pavement and into the military vehicle. On either side of the hood, something was missing. The middle-aged sergeant had removed the two red-and-gold flags denoting the impressive rank of his superior, the commander of NATO. The car shot forward, traveling less than fifty yards when it happened.

A massive explosion blew the military vehicle into the sky, shards of glass and metal, pieces of flesh and streaks of blood filling the narrow street in Anderlecht.

"Monsieur!" cried the petrified waiter as crews of police, firemen and sanitation workers went about their grisly business in the road.

"What is it?" replied the distraught owner of the sidewalk café, still shaking from the harsh interrogation he had gone through by the police and the descending hordes of journalists. "I am ruined. We will be known as the Café de la Mort, the restaurant of death."

"Monsieur, *look!*" The waiter pointed at the table where the general and his lady had sat.

"The police have gone over it," said the disconsolate owner.

"No, monsieur. *Now!*"

Across the glass top of the table, the capital letters scrawled in glistening red lipstick, was a name.

JASON BOURNE

20

Stunned, Marie stared at the television set, at the satellite news program beamed from Miami. Then she screamed as a camera moved in on a glass table in a town called Anderlecht in Belgium and the name printed in red across the top. *"Johnny!"*

St. Jacques burst through the bedroom door of the suite he had built for himself on the second floor of Tranquility Inn. *"Christ,* what *is* it?"

Tears streaming down her face, Marie pointed in horror at the set. The announcer on the overseas "feed" was speaking in the monotonic drone peculiar to such satellite transmissions.

". . . as if a bloodstained savage from the past

had returned to terrorize civilized society. The infamous killer, Jason Bourne, second only to Carlos the Jackal in the assassin-for-hire market, has claimed responsibility for the explosion that took the lives of General James Teagarten and his companions. Conflicting reports have come from Washington and London intelligence circles and police authorities. Sources in Washington claim that the assassin known as Jason Bourne was hunted down and killed in Hong Kong five years ago in a joint British-American operation. However, spokesmen for both the Foreign Office and British intelligence deny any knowledge of such an operation and say that a joint effort as was described is highly unlikely. Still other sources, these from Interpol's headquarters in Paris, have stated that their branch in Hong Kong knew of the supposed death of Jason Bourne, but as the widely circulated reports and photographs were so sketchy and unidentifiable, they did not give much credence to the story. They assumed, as was also reported, that Bourne disappeared into the People's Republic of China for a last contract fatal to himself. All that's clear today is that in the quaint city of Anderlecht in Belgium, General James Teagarten, commander of NATO, was assassinated and someone calling himself Jason Bourne has taken credit for killing this great and popular soldier. . . . We now show you an old composite photograph from Interpol's files produced by a consensus of those who purportedly had seen Bourne at close range. Remember, this is a composite, the features put together separately from scores of other photographs and, considering the killer's reputation for changing his appearance, probably not of great value."

The screen was suddenly filled with the face of a man, somewhat irregular and lacking definition.

"It's not David!" said John St. Jacques.

"It could be, Bro," said his sister.

"And now to other news. The drought that has plagued large areas of Ethiopia—"

"Turn that goddamned thing off!" shouted Marie, lurching out of the chair and heading for the telephone as her brother switched off the set. "Where's Conklin's number? I wrote it down here on your desk somewhere. . . . Here it is, on the blotter. *Saint Alex* has a hell of a lot to explain, that son of a *bitch*!" She dialed angrily but accurately, sitting in St. Jacques's chair, tapping her clenched fist as the tears continued to roll down her cheeks. Tears of sorrow and fury. "It's me, you *bastard*! . . . You've killed him! You let him go—*helped* him to go—and you've *killed* him!"

"I can't talk to you now, Marie," said a cold, controlled Alexander Conklin. "I've got Paris on the other line."

"Screw Paris! Where is he? Get him *out*!"

"Believe me, we're trying to find him. All fucking hell has broken out here. The British want Peter Holland's ass for even hinting at a Far East connection, and the French are in an uproar over something they can't figure out but suspect, like special Deuxième cargo on a plane from Martinique, which was originally rejected. I'll call you back, I *swear* it!"

The line was disconnected, and Marie slammed down the phone. "I'm flying to Paris, Johnny," she said, breathing deeply and wiping the tears from her face.

"You're *what*?"

"You heard me. Bring Mrs. Cooper over here. Jamie loves her and she's better with Alison than I could ever be—and why not? She's had seven children, all grown up who still come back to her every Sunday."

"You're *crazy*! I won't let you!"

"Somehow," said Marie, giving her brother a withering look, "I have an idea you probably said

something like that to David when he told you
he was going to Paris.''

"Yes, I did!''

"And you couldn't stop him any more than
you can stop me.''

"But *why*?''

"Because I know every place he knows in
Paris, every street, every café, every alley, from
one end to the other. He has to *use* them, and
I'll find him long before the Deuxième or the
Sûreté.'' The telephone rang; Marie picked it up.

"I told you I'd call you right back,'' said the
voice of Alex Conklin. "Bernardine has an idea
that might work.''

"Who's Bernardine?''

"An old Deuxième colleague and a good
friend who's helping David.''

"What's his idea?''

"He got Jason—*David*—a rental car. He
knows the license-plate number and is having it
radioed to all the Paris police patrols to report it
if seen, but not to stop the car or harass the
driver. Simply keep it in sight and report directly
to him.''

"And you think David—*Jason*—won't spot
something like that? You've got a terrible memory, worse than my husband's.''

"It's only one possibility, there are others.''

"Such as?"

"Well . . . well, he's bound to call *me.* When he hears the news about Teagarten, he's *got* to call me."

"Why?"

"Like you say, to get him out!"

"With Carlos in the offing? Fat chance, fathead. I've got a better idea. I'm flying to Paris."

"You *can't!*"

"I don't want to hear that anymore, I *won't* hear that anymore. Are you going to help me or do I do it by myself?"

"I couldn't get a postage stamp from a dispensing machine in France, and Holland couldn't get the address of the Eiffel Tower."

"Then I'm on my own, which, frankly, under the circumstances, makes me feel a lot safer."

"What can you *do,* Marie?"

"I won't give you a litany, but I can go to all those places he and I went to, *used* when we were running. He'll use them again, somehow, some way. He has to because in your crazy jargon they were 'secure,' and in his crazy frame of mind he'll return to them because he knows they're secure."

"God bless, favorite lady."

"*He* abandoned us, Alex. God doesn't exist."

Prefontaine walked through the terminal at Boston's Logan Airport to the crowded platform and raised his hand to hail a cab. But after looking around, he lowered his hand and stood in line; things had changed in thirty years. Everything, including airports, had become cafeterias; one stood in line for a plate of third-rate mulligan stew, as well as for a taxi.

"The Ritz-Carlton," said the judge to the driver.

"You h'ain'd got no luggage?" asked the man. "Nudding but d'liddle bag?"

"No, I do not," replied Prefontaine and, unable to resist a follow-up added, "I keep wardrobes wherever I go."

"Tutti-fruitee," said the driver, removing an outsized, wide-toothed comb from his hair as he swung out into the traffic.

"You have a reservation, sir?" asked the tuxedoed clerk behind the counter at the Ritz.

"I trust one of my law clerks made it for me. The name's Scofield, Justice William Scofield of the Supreme Court. I'd hate to think that the Ritz had lost a reservation, especially these days

when everyone's screaming for consumer protection."

"*Justice* Scofield . . . ? I'm sure it's here somewhere, sir."

"I specifically requested Suite Three-C, I'm
sure it's in your computer."

"Three-C . . . it's booked—"

"*What?*"

"No, no, I'm wrong, Mr. Justice. They haven't
arrived . . . I mean it's an error . . . they're in
another suite." The clerk pounded his bell with
ferocity. "Bellboy, *bellboy*!"

"No need for that, young fella, I travel light.
Just give me the key and point me in the right
direction."

"Yes, *sir*!"

"I trust you've got a few bottles of decent
whisky up there, as usual?"

"If they're not, they will be, Mr. Justice. Any
particular brands?"

"Good rye, good bourbon and good brandy.
The white stuff is for sissies, right?"

"*Right,* sir. Right away, sir!"

Twenty minutes later, his face washed and a
drink in his hand, Prefontaine picked up the
phone and dialed Dr. Randolph Gates.

"The Gates residence," said the woman on
the line.

"Oh, come on, Edie, I'd know your voice under water and it's been almost thirty years."

"I know yours, too, but I simply can't place it."

"Try a rough adjunct professor at the law school who kept beating the hell out of your husband, which made no impression upon him and he was probably right because I ended up in jail. The first of the local judges to be put away, and rightfully so."

"Brendan? Dear God, it's you! I never believed all those things they said about you."

"Believe, my sweet, they were true. But right now I have to speak to the lord of the Gates. Is he there?"

"I suppose he is, I don't really know. He doesn't speak to me very much anymore."

"Things are not well, my dear?"

"I'd love to talk to you, Brendan. He's got a problem, a problem I never knew about."

"I suspect he has, Edie, and of course we'll talk. But at the moment I have to speak with *him.* Right now."

"I'll call him on the intercom."

"Don't tell him it's me, Edith. Tell him it's a man named Blackburne from the island of Montserrat in the Caribbean."

"What?"

"Do as I say, dear Edie. It's for his sake as

well as yours—perhaps more for you, if truth were told."

"He's *sick,* Brendan."

"Yes, he is. Let's try to make him well. Get him on the line for me."

"I'll put you on hold."

The silence was interminable, the two minutes more like two hours until the graveled voice of Randolph Gates exploded on the line. "Who *are* you?" whispered the celebrated attorney.

"Relax, Randy, it's Brendan. Edith didn't recognize my voice, but I sure remembered hers. You're one lucky fellow."

"What do you *want*? What's this about Montserrat?"

"Well, I just came back from there—"

"You *what*?"

"I decided I needed a vacation."

"You *didn't* . . . !" Gates's whisper was now essentially a cry of panic.

"Oh, but I did, and because I did your whole life is going to change. You see, I ran into the woman and her two children that you were so interested in, remember them? It's quite a story and I want to tell it to you in all its fascinating detail. . . . You set them up to be killed, Dandy Randy, and that's a no-no. A dreadful no-no."

"I don't know what you're *talking* about! I've never heard of Montserrat or any woman with two children. You're a desperate sniveling drunk and I'll deny your insane allegations as the alcoholic fantasies of a convicted felon!"

"Well done, Counselor. But denying any allegations made by me isn't the core of your dilemma. No, that's in Paris."

"Paris . . . ?"

"A certain man in Paris, someone I didn't realize was a living person, but I learned otherwise. It's somewhat murky how it came about, but a strange thing happened in Montserrat. I was mistaken for *you.*"

"You were . . . what?" Gates was barely audible, his thin voice tremulous.

"Yes. Odd, isn't it? I imagine that when this man in Paris tried to reach you here in Boston, someone told him your imperial presence was out or away and that's how the mix-up began. Two brilliant legal minds, both with an elusive connection to a woman and her two children, and Paris thought I was you."

"What *happened*?"

"Calm down, Randy. At the moment he probably thinks you're dead."

"What?"

"He tried to have me killed—you killed. For transgression."

"Oh, my God!"

"And when he finds out you're very much alive and eating well in Boston, he won't permit a second attempt to fail."

"Jesus *Christ* . . . !"

"There may be a way out, Dandy Boy, which is why you must come and see me. Incidentally, I'm in the same suite at the Ritz that you were in when I came to see *you*. Three-C; just take the elevator. Be here in thirty minutes, and remember, I have little patience with clients who abuse schedules, for I'm a very busy man. By the way, my fee is twenty thousand dollars an hour or any part thereof, so bring money, Randy. Lots of it. In cash."

He was ready, thought Bourne, studying himself in the mirror, satisfied with what he saw. He had spent the last three hours getting ready for his drive to Argenteuil, to a restaurant named Le Coeur du Soldat, the message center for a "blackbird," for Carlos the Jackal. The Chameleon had dressed for the environment he was about to enter; the clothes were simple, the body and the face less so. The first required a trip to the secondhand stores and pawn shops in Montmartre, where he found faded trousers and a surplus French army shirt, and an equally faded small combat ribbon that denoted a wounded veteran. The second, somewhat more complex, demanded hair coloring, a day's growth of beard, and another constricting bandage, this bound around his right knee so tight he could not forget the limp he had quickly perfected. His hair and eyebrows were now a dull red—dirty, unkempt red, which fit his new surroundings, a cheap hotel in Montparnasse whose front desk wanted as little contact as possible with its clientele.

His neck was more an irritant now than an impediment; either he was adjusting to the stiff, restricted movement or the healing process was doing its mysterious work. And that restricted movement was not a liability where his current appearance was concerned; in truth, it was an asset. An embittered wounded veteran, a discarded son of France, would be hard pressed to forget his dual immobility. Jason shoved Bernardine's automatic into his trousers pocket, checked his money, his car keys, and his scabbarded hunting knife, the latter purchased at a sporting goods store and strapped inside his shirt, and limped to the door of the small, filthy, depressing room. Next stop, the Capucines and a nondescript Peugeot in an underground garage. He *was* ready.

Out on the street, he knew he had to walk a number of blocks before he found a taxi station; cabs were not the fashion in this section of Montparnasse. . . . Neither was the commotion around a newspaper kiosk at the second corner. People were shouting, many waving their arms, clutching papers in their fists, anger and consternation in their voices. Instinctively, he quickened his pace, reached the stand, threw down his coins and grabbed a newspaper.

The breath went out of him as he tried to suppress the shock waves that swept through him. *Teagarten killed!* The assassin, Jason Bourne! *Jason Bourne!* Madness, *insanity*! What had *happened*? Was it a resurrection of *Hong Kong* and *Macao*? Was he losing what was left of his *mind*? Was he in some nightmare so real he had entered its dimensions, the horror of demented sleep, the fantasy of conjured, improvised terror turned into *reality*? He broke away from the crowd, reeled across the pavement, and leaned against the stone wall of a building,

gasping for air, his neck now in pain, trying desperately to find a reasonable train of thought.
Alex! *A telephone!*

"What *happened*?" he screamed into the
mouthpiece to Vienna, Virginia.

"Come down and stay cold," said Conklin in
a low monotone. "Listen to me. I want to know
exactly where you are. Bernardine will pick you
up and get you out. He'll make the arrangements and put you on the Concorde to New
York."

"Wait a minute—*wait* a minute! . . . The Jackal
did this, didn't he?"

"From what we're told, it was a contract from
a crazy jihad faction out of Beirut. They're claiming it was their kill. The actual executioner is
unimportant. That may be true and it may not. At
first I didn't buy it, not after DeSole and Armbruster, but the numbers add up. Teagarten was
forever sounding off about sending NATO
forces into Lebanon and leveling every suspected Palestinian enclave. He's been threatened before; it's just that the Medusa
connection is too *damned* coincidental for me.
But to answer your question, of course it was the
Jackal."

"So he laid it on me, *Carlos* laid it on *me!*"

"He's an ingenious fucker, I'll say that for him. You come after him and he uses a contract that freezes you in Paris."

"Then we turn it *around*!"

"What the hell are you talking about? You get out!"

"No way. While he thinks I'm running, hiding, evading—I'm walking right into his nest."

"You're nuts! You get out while we can still *get* you out!"

"No, I stay in. Number one, he figures I have to in order to reach him, but, as you say, he's locked me in ice. He thinks that after all these years I'll panic in my fashion and make stupid moves—God knows I made enough on Tranquility—but so stupid here that his army of old men will find me by looking in the right places and knowing what to look for. *Christ,* he's good! Shake the bastard up so he'll make a mistake. I *know* him, Alex. I know the way he thinks and I'll outthink *him.* I'll stay on course, no prolonged safe cave for me."

"Cave? *What* cave?"

"A figure of speech, forget it. I was in place *before* the news of Teagarten. I'm okay."

"You're not okay, you're a fruitcake! Get *out*!"

"Sorry, Saint Alex, this is exactly where I want to be. I'm going after the Jackal."

"Well, maybe I can move you off that place you're clinging to. I spoke to Marie a couple of hours ago. Guess what, you aging Neanderthal? She's flying to Paris. To find you."

"She *can't*!"

"That's what *I* said, but she wasn't in a listening mode. She said she knew all the places you and she used when you were running from us thirteen years ago. That you'd use them again."

"I have. Several. But she *mustn't*!"

"Tell *her,* not me."

"What's the Tranquility number? I've been afraid to call her—to be honest, I've tried like *hell* to put her and the kids out of my mind."

"That's the most reasonable statement you've made. Here it is." Conklin recited the 809 area code number, and the instant he had done so, Bourne slammed down the phone.

Frantically, Jason went through the agonizing process of relaying destination and credit card numbers, accompanied by the beeps and stutters of an overseas call to the Caribbean, and, finally, after subduing some idiot at the front desk of Tranquility Inn, got through to his brother-in-law.

"Get Marie for me!" he ordered.

"David?"

"Yes . . . David. Get Marie."

"I can't. She's gone. She left an hour ago."

"Where to?"

"She wouldn't tell me. She chartered a plane out of Blackburne, but she wouldn't tell me what international island she was going to. There's only Antigua or Martinique around here, but she could have flown to Sint Maarten or Puerto Rico. She's on her way to Paris."

"Couldn't you have *stopped* her?"

"Christ, I tried, David. Goddamn it, I *tried*!"

"Did you ever think about locking her up?"

"Marie?"

"I see what you mean. . . . She can't get here until tomorrow morning at the earliest."

"Have you heard the news?" cried St. Jacques. "General *Teagarten* was killed and they say it was Jason—"

"Oh, shut up," said Bourne, replacing the phone and leaving the booth, walking down the street to collect what thoughts he could generate.

Peter Holland, director of the Central Intelligence Agency, rose to his feet behind his desk and roared at the crippled man seated in front of him. "Do *nothing*? Have you lost your fucking *senses*?"

"Did you lose yours when you issued that statement about a joint British-American operation in Hong Kong?"

"It was the goddamned truth!"

"There are truths, and then again there are other truths, such as denying the truth when it doesn't serve the service."

"Shit! Fairy politicians!"

"I'd hardly say that, Genghis Khan. I've heard of such men going to the wall, accepting execution rather than betraying the current truth they had to live by. . . . You're off base, Peter."

Exasperated, Holland sank back into his chair. "Maybe I really don't belong here."

"Maybe you don't, but give yourself a little more time. Maybe you'll become as dirty as the rest of us; it could happen, you know."

The director leaned back, arching his head over the chair; he spoke in a broken cadence. "I was dirtier than any of you in the field, Alex. I still wake up at night seeing the faces of young men staring at me as I ripped a knife up their chests, taking their lives away, somehow knowing that they had no idea why they were there."

"It was either you or them. They would have put a bullet in your head if they could have."

"Yes, I suppose so." The DCI shot forward,

his eyes locked with Conklin's. "But that's not what we're talking about, is it?"

"You might say it's a variation on the theme."

"Cut the horseshit."

"It's a musician's term. I like music."

"Then get to the main symphonic line, Alex. I like music, too."

"All right. Bourne's disappeared. He told me that he thinks he's found a cave—his word, not mine—where he's convinced he can track the Jackal. He didn't say where it is, and God knows when he'll call me again."

"I sent our man at the embassy over to the Pont-Royal, asking for Simon. What they told you is true. Simon checked in, went out, and never came back. Where *is* he?"

"Staying out of sight. Bernardine had an idea, but it blew up in his face. He thought he could quietly close in on Bourne by circulating the license number of the rental car, but it wasn't picked up at the garage and we both agree it won't be. He doesn't trust anybody now, not even me, and considering his history, he has every right not to."

Holland's eyes were cold and angry. "You're not lying to me, are you, Conklin?"

"Why would I lie at a time like this, about a friend like this?"

"That's not an answer, it's a question."

"Then no, I'm not lying. I don't know where he is." And, in truth, Alex did not.

"So your idea is to do nothing."

"There's nothing we can do. Sooner or later he'll call me."

"Have you any idea what a Senate investigating committee will say a couple of weeks or months down the road when all this explodes, and it *will* explode? We covertly send a man known to be 'Jason Bourne' over to Paris, which is as close to Brussels as New York is to Chicago—"

"Closer, I think."

"Thanks, I need that. . . . The illustrious commander of NATO is assassinated with said 'Jason Bourne' taking credit for the kill, and we don't say a goddamned thing to anybody! *Jesus,* I'll be cleaning latrines on a tugboat!"

"But he didn't kill him."

"You know that and *I* know that, but speaking of his history, there's a little matter of mental illness that'll come out the minute our clinical records are subpoenaed."

"It's called amnesia; it has nothing to do with violence."

"Hell, no, it's worse. He can't remember what he did."

Conklin gripped his cane, his wandering eyes intense. "I don't give a goddamn what everything appears to be, there's a gap. Every instinct I have tells me Teagarten's assassination is tied to *Medusa.* Somehow, somewhere, the wires crossed; a message was intercepted and a hell of a diversion was put in a game plan."

"I believe I speak and understand English as well as you do," said Holland, "but right now I can't follow you."

"There's nothing to follow, no arithmetic, no line of progression. I simply don't know. . . . But Medusa's there."

"With your testimony, I can pull in Burton on the Joint Chiefs, and certainly Atkinson in London."

"No, leave them alone. Watch them, but don't sink their dinghies, Admiral. Like Swayne's 're-treat,' the bees will flock to the honey sooner or later."

"Then what are you suggesting?"

"What I said when I came in here. Do nothing; it's the waiting game." Alex suddenly slammed his cane against the table. "Son of a bitch, it's *Medusa.* It *has* to be!"

The hairless old man with a wrinkled face struggled to his feet in a pew of the Church of the Blessed Sacrament in Neuilly-sur-Seine on the outskirts of Paris. Step by difficult step he made his painful way to the second confessional booth on the left. He pulled back the black curtain and knelt in front of the black latticework covered with black cloth, his legs in agony.

"*Angelus domini,* child of God," said the voice from behind the screen. "Are you well?"

"Far better for your generosity, monseigneur."

"That pleases me, but I must be pleased more than that, as you know. . . . What *happened* in Anderlecht? What does my beloved and well-endowed army *tell* me? Who has *presumed*?"

"We have dispersed and worked for the past eight hours, monseigneur. As near as we can determine, two men flew over from the United States—it is assumed so, for they spoke only American English—and took a room in a *pension de famille* across the street from the restaurant. They left the premises within minutes after the assault."

"A frequency-detonated explosive!"

"Apparently, monseigneur. We have learned nothing else."

"But why? *Why?*"

"We cannot see into men's minds, monseigneur."

Across the Atlantic Ocean, in an opulent apartment in Brooklyn Heights with the lights of the East River and the Brooklyn Bridge seductively pulsating beyond the windows, a capo supremo lounged in an overstuffed couch, a glass of Perrier in his hand. He spoke to his friend sitting across from him in an armchair, drinking a gin and tonic. The young man was slender, dark-haired and striking.

"You know, Frankie, I'm not just bright, I'm brilliant, you know what I mean? I pick up on nuances—that's hints of what could be important and what couldn't—and I got a hell of sense. I hear a spook *paisan* talk about things and I put four and four together and instead of eight, I get twelve. *Bingo!* It's the answer. There's this cat who calls himself 'Bourne,' a creep who makes like he's a major hit man but who isn't—he's a lousy *esca,* bait to pull in someone else, but *he's* the hot cannoli *we* want, see? Then the Jew shrink, being very under the weather, spits out everything I need. This cannoli's got only half a head, a *testa balzana;* a lot of the time he don't know who he is, or maybe what he does, right?"

"That's right, Lou."

"And there this Bourne is in Paris, France, a couple of blocks away from a real big impediment, a fancy general the quiet boys across the river want taken out, like the two fatsoes already planted. *Capisce?"*

"I *capisco,* Lou," said the clean-cut young man from the chair. "You're real intelligent."

"You don't know what the fuck I'm talking about, you *zabaglione.* I could be talking to myself, so why not? . . . So I get my twelve and I figure let's slam the loaded dice right into the felt, *see*?"

"I see, Lou."

"We got to eliminate this asshole general because he's the impediment to the fancy crowd who needs us, right?"

"Right on, Lou. An imped—an im*ped*—"

"Don't bother, *zabaglione.* So I say to myself, let's blow him away and say the hot cannoli did it, *got* it?"

"Oh, yeah, Lou. You're *real* intelligent."

"So we get rid of the impediment and put the cannoli, this Jason Bourne, who's not all there, in everybody's gun sights, right? If we don't get him, and this Jackal don't get him, the federals will, *right*?"

"Hey, that's terrific, Lou. I gotta say it, I really respect you."

"Forget respect, *bello ragazzo.* The rules are different in this house. Come on over and make good love to me."

The young man got up from the chair and walked over to the couch.

Marie sat in the back of the plane drinking coffee from a plastic cup, trying desperately to recall every place—every hiding and resting place—she and David had used thirteen years ago. There were the rock-bottom cafés in Montparnasse, the cheap hotels as well; and a motel—where was it?—ten miles outside of Paris, and an inn with a balcony in Argenteuil where David—*Jason*—first told her he loved her but could not stay with her *because* he loved her—the goddamned ass! And there was the Sacré-Coeur, far up on the steps where Jason—*David*—met the man in a dark alley who gave them the information they needed—what *was* it, who *was* he?

"Mesdames et messieurs," came the voice over the flight deck's loudspeaker. *"Je suis votre capitaine. Bienvenu."* The pilot continued first in French, then he and his crew repeated the information in English, German, Italian and, finally with a female interpreter, in Japanese. "We anticipate a very smooth flight to Marseilles. Our estimated flight time is seven hours and fourteen minutes, landing on or before schedule at six o'clock in the morning, Paris time. Enjoy."

The moonlight outside bathed the ocean below as Marie St. Jacques Webb looked out the window. She had flown to San Juan, Puerto Rico, and taken the night flight to Marseilles, where French immigration was at best a mass of confusion and at worst intentionally lax. At least that was the way it was thirteen years ago, a time she was reentering. She would then take a domestic flight to Paris and she would find him. As she had done thirteen years ago, she *would find* him. She had to! As it had been thirteen years ago, if she did not, the man she loved was a dead man.

21

Morris Panov sat listlessly in a chair by a window looking out over the pasture of a farm somewhere, he assumed, in Maryland. He was in a small second-floor bedroom dressed in a hospital nightshirt, his bare right arm confirming the story he knew only too well. He had been drugged repeatedly, taken up to the moon, in the parlance of those who usually administered such narcotics. He had been mentally raped, his mind penetrated, violated, his innermost thoughts and secrets brought chemically to the surface and exposed.

The damage he had done was incalculable, he understood that; what he did not understand was why he was still alive. Even more perplexing was why he was being treated so deferentially. Why was his guard with the foolish black mask so courteous, the food plentiful and decent? It was as if the present imperative of his captivity was to restore his strength—profoundly sapped by the drugs—and make him as comfortable as possible under the extraordinarily difficult circumstances. *Why?*

The door opened and his masked guard walked in, a short heavyset man with a rasping voice Panov placed somewhere in the northeastern United States or possibly Chicago. In another situation he might have appeared comic, his large head too massive for the asinine Lone Ranger eye-covering, which would certainly not impede instant identification. However, in the current state of affairs, he was not comic at all; his obsequiousness was in itself menacing. Over his left arm were the psychiatrist's clothes.

"Okay, Doc, you gotta get dressed. I made sure everything was cleaned and pressed, even the undershorts. How about that?"

"You mean you have your own laundry and dry cleaners out here?"

"Fuck no, we take 'em over to— *Oh,* no, you

don't get me *that* way, Doc!" The guard grinned with slightly yellowed teeth. "Pretty smart, huh? You figure I'll tell you where we are, huh?"

"I was simply curious."

"Yeah, sure. Like I got a nephew, my sister's kid, who's always 'simply curious,' askin' me questions I don't wanna answer. Like, 'Hey, Unc, how'd you put me through medical school, huh?' *Yeah!* He's a *doctor,* like *you,* what do you think of *that*?"

"I'd say his mother's brother is a very generous person."

"Yeah, well, wadda you gonna do, huh? . . . Come on, put on the threads, Doc, we're going on a little trip." The guard handed Mo his clothes.

"I suppose it would be foolish to ask where," said Panov, getting out of the chair, removing his hospital nightshirt and putting on his shorts.

"Very foolish."

"I hope not as foolish as your nephew not telling you about a symptom you have that I'd find somewhat alarming if I were you." Mo casually pulled up his trousers.

"Wadda you talkin'?"

"Perhaps nothing," replied Panov, putting on his shirt and sitting down to pull up his socks. "When did you last see your nephew?"

"A couple of weeks ago. I put in some bread to cover his insurance. Shit, those mothers are *bleeders*! . . . Wadda you mean when did I last see the prick?"

"I just wondered if he said anything to you."

"About *what*?"

"About your mouth." Mo laced his shoes and gestured with his head. "There's a mirror over the bureau, go take a look."

"At what?" The capo subordinato walked quickly to the mirror.

"Smile."

"At *what*?"

"Yourself. . . . See the yellow on your teeth, the fading red of your gums and how the gums recede the higher they go?"

"So? They always been like that—"

"It might be nothing, but he should have spotted it."

"Spotted *what,* for Christ's sake?"

"Oral ameloblastoma. Possibly."

"What the hell is *that*? I don't brush too good and I don't like dentists. They're butchers!"

"You mean you haven't seen a dentist or an oral surgeon in quite a while?"

"So?" The capo bared his teeth again in front of the mirror.

"That could explain why your nephew didn't say anything."

"Why?"

"He probably figures you have regular dental checkups, so let those people explain it to you." Shoes tied, Panov stood up.

"I don't getcha."

"Well, he's grateful for everything you've done for him, appreciative of your generosity. I can understand why he'd hesitate telling you."

"Telling me *what*?" The guard spun away from the mirror.

"I could be wrong but you really ought to see a periodontist." Mo put on his jacket. "I'm ready," he said. "What do we do now?"

The capo subordinato, his eyes squinting, his forehead creased in ignorance and suspicion, reached into his pocket and pulled out a large black kerchief. "Sorry, Doc, but I gotta blindfold you."

"Is that so you can put a bullet in my head when, mercifully, I don't know it's going to happen?"

"No, Doctor. No bam-bam for you. You're too valuable."

———

"Valuable?" asked the capo supremo rhetorically in his opulent living room in Brooklyn Heights. "Like a gold mine just popped out of the ground and landed in your minestrone. This Jew has worked on the heads of some of the biggest lasagnas in Washington. His files have got to be worth the price of Detroit."

"You'll never get them, Louis," said the attractive middle-aged man dressed in an expensive tropical worsted suit sitting across from his host. "They'll be sealed and carted off out of your reach."

"Well, we're working on that, Mr. Park Avenue, Manhattan. Say—just for laughs—say we got 'em. What are they worth to you?"

The guest permitted himself a thin aristocratic smile. "Detroit?" he replied.

"Va bene! I like you, you got a sense of humor." As abruptly as he had grinned, the mafioso became serious, even ugly. "The five mill still holds for this Bourne-Webb character, right?"

"With a proviso."

"I don't like provisos, Mr. Lawyer, I don't like them at *all.*"

"We can go elsewhere. You're not the only game in town."

"Let me explain something to you, Signor Avvocato. In a lot of ways, we—all of *we*—are the only game in town. We don't mess with other families' hits, you know what I mean? Our councils have decided hits are too personal; it makes for bad blood."

"Will you listen to the proviso? I don't think you'll be offended."

"Shoot."

"I wish you'd use another word—"

"Go ahead."

"There'll be a two-million-dollar bonus because we insist you include Webb's wife and his government friend Conklin."

"Done, Mr. Park Avenue, Manhattan."

"Good. Now to the rest of our business."

"I want to talk about the Jew."

"We'll get to him—"

"Now."

"Please don't give orders to me," said the attorney from one of Wall Street's most prestigious firms. "You're really not in a position to do that, *wop.*"

"Hey, *farabutto!* You don't talk to me like that!"

"I'll talk to you any way I like. . . . On the outside, and to your credit in negotiations, you're a very masculine, very macho fellow."

The lawyer calmly uncrossed and crossed his legs. "But the inside's quite different, isn't it? You've got a soft heart, or should I say hard loins, for pretty young men."

"*Silenzio!*" The Italian shot forward on the couch.

"I have no wish to exploit the information. On the other hand, I don't believe Gay Rights are very high on the Cosa Nostra's agenda, do you?"

"You son of a *bitch*!"

"You know, when I was a young army lawyer in Saigon, I defended a career lieutenant who was caught *in flagrante delicto* with a Vietnamese boy, a male prostitute obviously. Through legal maneuvers, using ambiguous phrases in the military code regarding civilians, I saved him from a dishonorable discharge, but it was obvious that he had to resign from the service. Unfortunately, he never went on to a productive life; he shot himself two hours after the verdict. You see, he'd become a pariah, a disgrace before his peers and he couldn't handle the burden."

"Get on with your business," said the capo supremo named Louis, his voice low and flat and filled with hatred.

"Thank you. . . . First, I left an envelope on

your foyer table. It contains payment for Armbruster's tragic confrontation in Georgetown
and Teagarten's equally tragic assassination in
Brussels."

"According to the yid head doctor," interrupted the mafioso, "you got two more they
know about. An ambassador in London and that
admiral on the Joint Chiefs. You wanna add another bonus?"

"Possibly later, not now. They both know very
little and nothing about the financial operations.
Burton thinks that we're essentially an ultracon-
servative veterans' lobbying effort that grew out
of the Vietnam disgrace—legally borderline for
him, but then he has strong patriotic feelings.
Atkinson's a rich dilettante; he does what he's
told, but he doesn't know why or by whom. He'd
do anything to hold on to the Court of Saint
James's and has; his only connection was with
Teagarten. . . . Conklin hit pay dirt with Swayne
and Armbruster, Teagarten and, of course,
DeSole, but the other two are window dressing,
quite respectable window dressing. I wonder
how it happened."

"When I find out, and I *will* find out, I'll let you
know, gratis."

"Oh?" The attorney raised his eyebrows.
"How?"

"We'll get to it. What's your other business?"

"Two items, both vital, and the first I'll give *you*—gratis. Get rid of your current boyfriend. He goes to places he shouldn't and throws money around like a cheap hoodlum. We're told he boasts about his connections in high places. We don't know what else he talks about or what he knows or what he's pieced together, but he concerns us. I'd think he'd concern you, too."

"Il prostituto!" roared Louis, slamming his clenched fist down on the arm of the couch. *"Il pinguino!* He's dead."

"I accept your thanks. The other item is far more important, certainly to us. Swayne's house in Manassas. A book was removed, an office diary, which Swayne's lawyer in Manassas—our lawyer in Manassas—could not find. It was on a bookshelf, its binding identical with all the other books in that row, the entire row on the shelf. A person would have to know *exactly* which one to take."

"So what do you want from me?"

"The gardener was your man. He was put in place to do his job, and he was given the only number we knew was totally secure, namely, DeSole's."

"So?"

"To do his job, to mount the suicide authentically, he had to study Swayne's every move. You yourself explained that to me ad nauseam when you demanded your outrageous fee. It's not hard to picture your man peering through the window at Swayne in his study, the place where Swayne supposedly would take his life. Gradually your man realizes that the general keeps taking a specific book from off his shelf, writes in it, and returns it to the same spot. That has to intrigue him; that particular book has to be valuable. Why wouldn't he take it? I would, *you* would. So where is it?"

The mafioso got slowly, menacingly to his feet. "Listen to me, *avvocato,* you gotta lot of fancy words that make for conclusions, but we ain't got no book like that and I'll tell you how I can *prove* it! If there was anything anywhere written down that could burn your ass, I'd be shoving it in your face right now, *capisce*?"

"That's not illogical," said the well-dressed attorney, once again uncrossing and crossing his legs as the resentful capo sullenly returned to the couch. "Flannagan," added the Wall Street lawyer. "Naturally . . . of course, *Flannagan.* He and his hairdresser bitch had to have their insurance policy, no doubt with minor extortion in the bargain. Actually, I'm relieved. They could never use it without exposing themselves. Accept my apologies, Louis."

"Your business finished?"

"I believe so."

"Now, the Jew shrink."

"What about him?"

"Like I said, he's a gold mine."

"Without his patients' files, less than twenty-four carat, I think."

"Then you think wrong," countered Louis. "Like I told Armbruster before he became another big impediment for you, we got doctors, too. Specialists in all kinds of medical things, including what they call motor responses and, get this, 'triggered mental recall under states of external control'—I remembered that one especially. It's a whole different kind of gun at your head, only no blood."

"I assume there's a point to this."

"You can bet your country club on it. We're moving the Jew to a place in Pennsylvania, a kind of nursing home where only the richest people go to get dried out or straightened out, if ya know what I mean."

"I believe I do. Advanced medical equipment, superior staff—well-patrolled grounds."

"Yeah, sure you do. A lot of your crowd passes through—"

"Go on," interrupted the attorney, looking at his gold Rolex watch. "I haven't much time."

"Make time for this. According to my specialists—and I purposely used the word 'my,' if you follow me—on a prearranged schedule, say every fourth or fifth day, the new patient is 'shot up to the moon'—that's the phrase they use, it's not mine, Christ knows. Between times he's been treated real good. He's been fed the right neutermints or whatever they are, given the proper exercise, a lot of sleep and all the rest of that shit. . . . We should all be so careful of our bodies, right, *avvocato*?"

"Some of us play squash every other day."

"Well, you'll forgive me, Mr. Park Avenue, Manhattan, but squash to me is zucchini and I eat it."

"Linguistic and cultural differences do crop up, don't they?"

"Yeah, I can't fault you there, Consigliere."

"Hardly. And my title is attorney."

"Give me time. It could be Consigliere."

"There's not enough years in our lifetimes, Louis. Do you go on or do I leave?"

"I go on, Mr. *Attorney.* . . . So each time the

Jew shrink is shot up to that moon my specialist talks about, he's in pretty good shape, right?"

"I see the periodic remissions to normalcy, but then I'm not a doctor."

"I don't know what the fuck you're talking about, but then I'm not a doctor, either, so I'll take my specialist's word for it. You see, every time he's shot up, his mind is pretty clear inside, and then he's fed name after name after name. A lot, maybe most, won't mean a thing, but every now and then one will, and then another, and another. With each, they start what they call a probe, finding out bits and pieces of information, just enough to get a sketch of the patient he's talking about—just enough to scare the shit out of that lasagna when he's reached. Remember, these are stressful times and this Hebe doctor treats some of the fattest cats in Washington, in and outside the government. How does that grab you, Mr. Attorney?"

"It's certainly unique," replied the guest slowly, studying the capo supremo. "His files, of course, would be infinitely preferable."

"Yeah, well, like I say, we're working on that, but it'll take time. This is now, *immediato.* He'll be in Pennsylvania in a couple of hours. You want to deal? You and me?"

"Over what? Something you don't have and may never get?"

"Hey, come on, what do you think I am?"

"I'm sure you don't want to hear that—"

"Cut the crap. Say in a day or so, maybe a week, we meet, and I give you a list of names I think you might be interested in, all of which we got information on—let's say information not readily available. You pick one or two or maybe none, what can you lose? We're talkin' spitballs anyway, 'cause the deal's between you and me only. No one else is involved except my specialist and his assistant who don't know you and you don't know them."

"A side arrangement, as it were?"

"Not as it were, like it is. Depending on the information, I'll figure out the charge. It may only be a thou or two, or it may go to twenty, or it may be gratis, who knows? I'd be fair because I want your business, *capisce*?"

"It's very interesting."

"You know what my specialist says? He says we could start our own cottage industry, he called it. Snatch a dozen shrinks, all with heavy government connections, like in the Senate or even the White House—"

"I understand fully," interrupted the attorney,

getting to his feet, "but my time's up. . . . Bring me a list, Louis." The guest walked toward the short marble foyer.

"No fancy attaché case, Signor Avvocato?" said the capo, rising from the couch.

"And upset the not so delicate mechanisms in your doorway?"

"Hey, it's a violent world out there."

"I wouldn't know about that."

The Wall Street attorney left, and at the sound of the closing door, Louis rushed across the room to the inlaid Queen Anne desk and virtually pounced on the ivory French telephone—as usual, tipping over the tall thin instrument twice before securing the stem with one hand while dialing with the other. "Fucking swish horn!" he mumbled. "Goddamned fairy decorator! . . . *Mario?*"

"Hello, Lou," said the pleasant voice in New Rochelle. "I'll bet you called to wish Anthony a happy birthday, huh?"

"Who?"

"My kid, Anthony. He's fifteen today, did you forget? The whole family's out in the garden and we miss you, Cousin. And hey, Lou, what a garden this year. I'm a real artist."

"You also may be something else."

"What?"

"Buy Anthony a present and send me the bill. At fifteen, maybe a broad. He's ready for manhood."

"Lou, you're too much. There are other things—"

"There's only *one* thing now, Mario, and I want the truth from your lips or I'll carve them out of your face!"

There was a brief pause from New Rochelle before the pleasant sounding executioner spoke. "I don't deserve to be talked to that way, *cugino.*"

"Maybe, maybe not. There was a book taken from that general's place in Manassas, a very valuable book."

"They found out it was missing, huh?"

"Holy *shit*! You got it?"

"I *had* it, Lou. It was going to be a present to you, but I lost it."

"You *lost* it? What the fuck did you do, leave it in a *taxi*?"

"No, I was running for my life, that maniac with the flares, what's his name, Webb, unloading at me in the driveway. He grazed me and I fell and the lousy book flew out of my hand—just as the police car arrived. He picked it up and I ran like hell for the fence."

"Webb's got it?"

"I guess so."

"Christ on a trampoline . . . !"

"Anything else, Lou? We're about to light the candles on the cake."

"Yeah, Mario, I may need you in Washington—a big cannoli without a foot but with a book."

"Hey, wait a minute, *cugino,* you know my rules. Always a month between business trips. What did Manassas take? Six weeks? And last May in Key West, three, almost four weeks? I can't call, I can't write a postcard—no, Lou, always a month. I got responsibilities to Angie and the children. I'm not going to be an absentee parent; they've got to have a role model, you know what I mean?"

"I got Ozzie Nelson for a fuckin' cousin!" Louis slammed down the phone, and instantly grabbed it as it crashed over on the desk, its delicate ivory stem displaying a crack. "The best hit man in the business and he's a freak," mumbled the capo supremo as he dialed frantically. When the line was picked up, the anxiety and the anger disappeared from his voice; it was not apparent but it had not gone away. "Hello, Frankie baby, how's my closest friend?"

"Oh, hi, Lou," came the floating, but hesitant,

languorous tones from an expensive apartment in Greenwich Village. "Can I call you back in two minutes? I'm just putting my mother into a cab to take her back to Jersey. Okay?"

"Sure, kid. Two minutes." *Mother?* The whore! *Il pinguino!* Louis walked to his mirrored marble bar with the pink angels flying over the Lalique inset above the whisky bottles. He poured himself a drink and took several calming swallows. The bar phone rang. "Yeah?" he said, carefully picking up the fragile crystal instrument.

"It's me, Lou. Frankie. I said good-bye to Mama."

"That's a good boy, Frankie. Never forget your mama."

"Oh, I never do, Lou. You taught me that. You told me you gave your mama the biggest funeral they ever saw in East Hartford."

"Yeah, I bought the fuckin' church, man."

"Real nice, real nice."

"Now let's get to something else real nice, okay? It's been one of those days, Frankie, lots of turmoil, you know what I mean?"

"Sure, Lou."

"So I got an itch. I gotta get some relief. Come on over here, Frankie."

"As fast as a cab can take me, Lou."

Prostituto! It would be Frankie the Big Mouth's last service for him.

Out on the street the well-dressed attorney walked two blocks south and a block east to his waiting limousine parked beneath the canopy of another impressive residence in Brooklyn Heights. His stocky chauffeur of middle years was talking pleasantly with the uniformed door-man, whom he had generously tipped by now. Spotting his employer, the driver walked rapidly to the limousine's rear door and opened it. Several minutes later they were in traffic heading for the bridge.

In the quiet of the backseat, the lawyer undid his alligator belt, pressed the upper and lower rims of the buckle, and a small cartridge fell out between his legs. He picked it up and refastened the belt.

Holding the cartridge up to the filtered light from the window, he studied the miniaturized voice-activated recording device. It was an ex-traordinary machine, tiny enough and with an acrylic mechanism that permitted it to fly through the most sophisticated detectors. The attorney leaned forward in his seat and spoke to the driver. "William?"

"Yes, sir." The chauffeur glanced up at his rearview mirror and saw his employer's out-stretched hand; he reached back.

"Take this over to the house and put it on a cassette, will you, please?"

"Right, Major."

The Manhattan lawyer reclined in the seat, smiling to himself. Louis would give him anything he wanted from now on. A capo did not make side arrangements where the family was con-cerned, to say nothing of acknowledging certain sexual preferences.

Morris Panov sat blindfolded in the front seat of the sedan with his guard, his hands loosely, al-most courteously bound, as if the capo subor-dinato felt he was following unnecessary orders. They had been driving for about thirty minutes in silence when the guard spoke.

"What's a perry-oh-dentist?" he asked.

"An oral surgeon, a doctor trained to operate inside patients' mouths on problems relating to teeth and gum tissue."

Silence. Then seven minutes later: "What kind of problems?"

"Any number of them, from infections to scraping the roots to more complicated surgery usually in tandem with an oncologist."

Silence. Four minutes later: "What was that last—the tandy-uncle stuff?"

"Oral cancer. If it's caught in time, it can be arrested with minor bone removal. . . . If not, the entire jaw might have to go." Panov could feel the car briefly swerve as the driver momentarily lost control.

Silence. A minute and a half later: "The whole fuckin' jaw? Half the face?"

"It's either that or the whole of the patient's life."

Thirty seconds later: "You think I could *have* something like that?"

"I'm a doctor, not an alarmist. I merely noted a symptom, I did not make a diagnosis."

"So *bullshit*! So make a dagassnossis!"

"I'm not qualified."

"Bullshit! You're a doctor, ain't you? I mean a real doctor, not a *fasullo* who says he is but ain't got no shingle that's legit."

"If you mean medical school, yes, I'm that kind of doctor."

"So look at me!"

"I can't. I'm blindfolded." Panov suddenly felt the guard's thick strong hand clawing at his head, yanking the kerchief off him. The dark interior of the automobile answered a question for Mo: How could anyone travel in a car with a blindfolded passenger? In that car it was no problem; except for the windshield, the windows were not merely tinted, they were damn near opaque, which meant from the outside they *were* opaque. No one could see inside.

"Go on, *look*!" The capo subordinato, his eyes on the road, tilted his large head grotesquely toward Panov; his thick lips were parted and his teeth bared like those of a child playing monster in the mirror, he shouted again. "So tell me what you see!"

"It's too dark in here," replied Mo, seeing essentially what he wanted to see in the front window; they were on a country road, so narrow and so country the next step lower was dirt. Wherever he was being taken, he was being driven there by an extremely circuitous route.

"Open the fuckin' *window*!" yelled the guard, his head still twisted, his eyes still on the road, his gaping mouth approaching a caricature of Orca, the about-to-vomit whale. "Don't hold nothin' back. I'll break every goddamn finger in that prick's hands! He can do his fuckin' surgery with his elbows! . . . I told that stupid sister of mine he was no fuckin' good, that fairy. Always readin' books, no action on the street, y'know what I mean?''

"If you'll stop shouting for a few seconds, I can get a closer look," said Panov, having lowered the window at his side, seeing nothing but trees and the coarse underbrush of a distinctly backcountry road, one he doubted was on too many maps. "There we are," continued Mo, raising his loosely bound hands to the capo's mouth, his eyes, however, not on that mouth but on the road ahead. "Oh, my God!" cried Panov.

"What?" screamed the guard.

"Pus. Pockets of pus everywhere. In the upper and lower mandibles. The worst sign."

"Oh, *Christ!"* The car swerved wildly, but it did not swerve enough.

A huge *tree.* Up ahead. On the left-hand side of the deserted road! Morris Panov surged his bound hands over to the wheel, lifting his body off the seat as he propelled the steering wheel to the left. Then at the last second before the car hit the tree, he hurled himself to the right, curling into a fetal position for protection.

The crash was enormous. Shattered glass and crushed metal accompanied the rising mists of steam from burst cylinders, and the growing fires of viscous fluids underneath that would soon reach a gas tank. The guard was moaning, semiconscious, his face bleeding; Panov pulled him out of the wreck and into the grass as far as he could until exhaustion overtook him, just before the car exploded.

In the moist overgrowth, his breath somewhat restored but his fear still at the forefront, Mo released his loosely bound hands and picked the fragments of glass out of his guard's face. He then checked for broken bones—the right arm and the left leg were candidates—and with stolen stationery from a hotel he had never heard of from the capo's pocket, he used the guard's pen to write out his diagnosis. Among the items he removed was a gun—what kind, he had no idea—but it was heavy and too large for his pocket and sagged in his belt.

Enough. Hippocrates had his limits.

Panov searched the guard's clothing, astonished at the money that was there—some six thousand dollars—and the various driver's licenses—five different identities from five different states. He took the money and the licenses to turn them over to Alex Conklin, but he left the capo's wallet otherwise intact. There were photographs of his family, his children, grand-

children and assorted relatives—and somewhere among them a young surgeon he had put
through medical school. *Ciao, amico,* thought
Mo as he crawled over to the road, stood up and
smoothed his clothes, trying to look as respectable as possible.

Standing on the hard coarse surface, common sense dictated that he continue north, in
the direction the car was heading; to return
south was not only pointless but conceivably
dangerous. Suddenly, it struck him.

Good God! Did I just do what I just did?

He began to tremble, the trained psychiatri-
cally oriented part of him telling him it was posttraumatic stress.

Bullshit, you asshole. It wasn't you!

He started walking, and then kept walking and
walking and walking. He was not on a backcountry road, he was on *Tobacco* Road. There were
no signs of civilization, not a car in either direction, not a house—not even the ruins of an old
farmhouse—or a primitive stone wall that would
at least have proved that humans had visited
the environs. Mile after mile passed and Mo
fought off the effects of the drug-induced exhaustion. How long had it been? They had taken
his watch, his watch with the day and date in

impossible small print, so he had no idea of either the present time or the time that had elapsed since he had been taken from Walter Reed Hospital. He had to find a telephone. He had to reach Alex Conklin! Something had to happen soon!

It did.

He heard the growing roar of an engine and spun around. A red car was speeding up the road from the south—no, not speeding, but racing, with its accelerator flat on the floor. He waved his arms wildly—gestures of helplessness and appeal. To no avail; the vehicle rushed past him in a blur . . . then to his delighted surprise the air was filled with dust and screeching brakes. The car *stopped*! He ran ahead as the automobile actually backed up, the tires still screaming. He remembered the words his mother incessantly repeated when he was a youngster in the Bronx: *Always tell the truth, Morris. It's the shield God gave us to keep us righteous.*

Panov did not precisely subscribe to the admonition, but there were times when he felt it had socially interactive validity. This might be one of them. So, somewhat out of breath he approached the opened passenger window of the red automobile. He looked inside at the woman driver, a platinum blonde in her mid-thirties with an overly made-up face and large breasts encased in décolletage more fitting to an X-rated film than a backcountry road in Maryland. Nevertheless, his mother's words echoed in his ears, so he spoke the truth.

"I realize that I look rather shabby, madam, but I assure you it's purely an exterior impression. I'm a doctor and I've been in an accident—"

"Get in, for Christ's sake!"

"Thank you so very much." No sooner had Mo closed the door than the woman slammed the car into gear, gunned the engine to its maximum, and seemingly launched off the rough pavement and down the road. "You're obviously in a hurry," offered Panov.

"So would you be, pal, if you were me. I gotta husband back there who's puttin' his truck together to come after my ass!"

"Oh, really?"

"Stupid fuckin' jerk! He rolls across the country three weeks outta the month layin' every broad on the highways, then blows his keister when he finds out I had a little fun of my own."

"Oh, I'm terribly sorry."

"You'll be a hell of a lot sorrier if he catches up with us."

"I beg your pardon?"

"You really a doctor?"

"Yes, I am."

"Maybe we can do business."

"I *beg* your pardon?"

"Can you handle an abortion?"

Morris Panov closed his eyes.

22

Bourne walked for nearly an hour through the streets of Paris trying to clear his head, ending up at the Seine, on the Pont de Solferino, the bridge that led to the Quai des Tuileries and the gardens. As he leaned against the railing absently watching the boats lazily plowing the waters below, the question kept assaulting him: Why, why, *why*? What did Marie think she was *doing*? Flying over to Paris! It wasn't just foolish, it was stupid—yet his wife was neither a fool nor an idiot. She was a very bright lady with reserves of control and a quick, analytical mind. That was what made her decision so untenable; what could she possibly hope to accomplish?

She had to know he was far safer working alone rather than worrying about her while tracking the Jackal. Even if she found him, the risk was doubled for both of them, and *that* she had to understand completely. Figures and projections were her profession. So *why*?

There was only one conceivable answer, and it infuriated him. She thought he might slip back over the edge as he had done in Hong Kong, where she alone had brought him to his senses, to the reality that was uniquely his own, a reality of frightening half truths and only partial remembrances, episodic moments she lived with every day of their lives together. *God,* how he adored her; he loved her so! And the fact that she had made this foolish, stupid, *untenable* decision only fueled that love because it was so—so giving, so outrageously unselfish. There were moments in the Far East when he had craved his own death, if only to expunge the guilt he felt at putting her in such dangerous—untenable?—positions. The guilt was still there, *always* there, but the aging man in him recognized another reality. Their children. The cancer of the Jackal had to be ripped out of *all* their lives. Couldn't she realize that and leave him *alone*?

No. For she was not flying to Paris to save his

life—she had too much confidence in Jason Bourne for that. She was coming to Paris to save his mind. *I'll handle it, Marie. I can and will handle it!*

Bernardine. He could do it. The Deuxième could find her at Orly or De Gaulle. Find her and take her, put her under guard at a hotel and claim no one knew where he was. Jason ran from the Pont de Solferino to the Quai des Tuileries and to the first telephone he could find.

"Can you *do* it?" asked Bourne. "She's only got one updated passport and it's American, not Canadian."

"I can try on my own," answered Bernardine, "but not with any help from the Deuxième. I don't know how much Saint Alex told you, but at the moment my consultant status has been canceled and I think my desk has been thrown out the window."

"Shit!"

"Merde to the triple, *mon ami.* The Quai d'Orsay wants my underwear burned with me in it, and were it not for certain information I possess regarding several members of the Assembly, they would no doubt revive the guillotine."

"Can you pass around some money at immigration?"

"It would be better if I acted in my former official capacity on the assumption that the Deuxième does not so swiftly advertise its embarrassments. Her full name, please."

"Marie Elise St. Jacques Webb—"

"Ah, yes, I recall now, at least the St. Jacques," broke in Bernardine. "The celebrated Canadian economist. The newspapers were filled with her photograph. *La belle mademoiselle.*"

"It was exposure she could have done without."

"I'm certain it was."

"Did Alex say anything about Mo Panov?"

"Your doctor friend?"

"Yes."

"I'm afraid not."

"Goddamn it!"

"If I may suggest, you must think of yourself now."

"I understand."

"Will you pick up the car?"

"Should I?"

"Frankly, I wouldn't if I were you. It's unlikely, but the invoice might be traced back to me. There's risk, however minor."

"That's what I thought. I bought a *métro* map. I'll use the trains. . . . When can I call you?"

"Give me four, perhaps five hours to get back here from the airports. As our saint explained, your wife could be leaving from several different points of embarkation. To get all those passenger manifests will take time."

"Concentrate on the flights arriving early tomorrow morning. She can't fake a passport, she wouldn't know how to do it."

"According to Alex, one does not underestimate Marie Elise St. Jacques. He even spoke French. He said she was *formidable.*"

"She can come at you from the outer limits, I'll tell you that."

"Qu'est-ce que c'est?"

"She's an original, let's leave it there."

"And you?"

"I'm taking the subway. It's getting dark. I'll call you after midnight."

"Bonne chance."

"Merci."

Bourne left the booth knowing his next move as he limped down the Quai, the bandage around his knee forcing him to assume a damaged leg. There was a *métro* station by the Tuileries where he would catch a train to Havre-Caumartin and switch to the Regional Express north line past St.-Denis–Basilique to Argenteuil. Argenteuil, a town of the Dark Ages founded by Charlemagne in honor of a nunnery fourteen centuries ago, now fifteen hundred years later a city that housed the message center of a killer as brutal as any man who roamed the bloody fields with a broadsword in Charlemagne's barbaric days, then as now celebrating and sanctifying brutality in the shadows of religiosity.

Le Coeur du Soldat was not on a street or a boulevard or an avenue. Instead, it was in a dead-end alleyway around the corner and across from a long-since-closed factory whose faded signs indicated a once flourishing metallurgical refining plant in what had to be the ugliest part of the city. Nor was the Soldat listed in the telephone directory; it was found by innocently asking strangers where it was, as the inquirer was to meet *une grosse secousse* at this undiscoverable *pissoir.* The more dilapidated the buildings and the filthier the streets, the more cogent were the directions.

Bourne stood in the dark narrow alley leaning against the aged rough brick of the opposing structure across from the bistro's entrance. Above the thick massive door in square block letters, several missing, was a dull red sign: L C eur d Soldat. As the door was sporadically

opened for entering or departing clientele, metallic martial music blared forth into the alley;
and the clientele were not candidates for an
haute couture cotillion. His appearance was in
keeping, thought Jason, as he struck a wooden
match against the brick, lighting a thin black
cigar as he limped toward the door.

Except for the language and the deafening
music, it might have been a waterfront bar in
Sicily's Palermo, reflected Bourne as he made
his way to the crowded bar, his squinting eyes
roaming, absorbing everything he could observe—briefly confused, wondering when he
had been in Palermo, Sicily.

A heavyset man in a tank shirt got off a stool;
Jason slid on top of it. The clawlike hand gripped
his shoulder; Bourne slapped his right hand up,
grabbing the wrist and twisting it clockwise,
pushing the barstool away and rising to his full
height. "What's your problem?" he asked
calmly in French but loud enough to be heard.

"That's my seat, *pig*! I'm just taking a piss!"

"So maybe when you're finished, I'll take
one," said Jason, his gaze boring into the man's
eyes, the strength of his grip unmistakable—
emphasized by pressing a nerve with his thumb,
which had nothing to do with strength.

"Ah, you're a fucking *cripple . . .* !'' cried the man, trying not to wince. "I don't pick on invalids."

"I'll tell you what," said Bourne, releasing his thumb. "You come back, we'll take turns, and I'll buy you a drink each time you let me get off this bum leg of mine, okay?"

Looking up at Jason, the heavyset man slowly grinned. "Hey, you're all right."

"I'm not all right, but I'm certainly not looking for a fight, either. Shit, you'd hammer me to the floor." Bourne released the muscular Tank Shirt's arm.

"I'm not so sure of *that,"* said the man, now laughing and holding his wrist. "Sit, *sit!* I'll take a piss and come back and buy *you* a drink. You don't look like you're loaded with francs."

"Well, like they say, appearances are deceiving," replied Jason, sitting down. "I've got different, better clothes and an old friend told me to meet him here but not to wear them. . . . I just got back from good money in Africa. You know, training the savages—"

Cymbals crashed in the metallic, deafening martial music as Tank Shirt's eyes widened. *"Africa?"* interrupted the stranger. "I knew it! That grip—*LPN."*

What remained of the Chameleon's memory data banks expanded into the code. LPN—*Legion Patria Nostra.* France's Foreign Legion, the mercenaries of the world. It was not what he had in mind, but it would certainly do. "Christ, you too?" he asked, again coarsely but innocently.

"La Légion etrangère! 'The Legion is our Fatherland'!"

"This is crazy!"

"We don't announce ourselves, of course. There's great jealousy, naturally, because we were the best and we were paid for it, but still these are our people. *Soldiers!*"

"When did you leave the Legion?" asked Bourne, sensing a cloud that could be troublesome.

"*Ah,* nine years ago! They threw me out before my second conscription for overweight. They were right and they probably saved my life. I'm from Belgique, a corporal."

"I was discharged a month ago, before my first term was over. Wounds during our incursion into Angola and the fact that they figured I was older than my papers said. They don't pay for extended recoveries." How easily the words came.

"Angola? We did *that*? What was the Quai d'Orsay *thinking* about."

"I don't know. I'm a soldier, I follow orders and don't question those I can't understand."

"*Sit!* My kidneys are bursting. I'll be right back. Maybe we know friends. . . . I never heard of any Angola operation."

Jason leaned forward over the bulging bar and ordered *une bière,* grateful that the bartender was too busy and the music too loud for the man to have overheard the conversation. However, he was infinitely more grateful to Saint Alex of Conklin, whose primary advice to a field agent was to "get in bad with a mark first before you get in good," the theory being that the reversal from hostility to amiability was far stronger for the change. Bourne swallowed the beer in relief. He had made a friend at Le Coeur du Soldat. It was an inroad, minor but vital, and perhaps not so minor.

Tank Shirt returned, his thick arm around the shoulders of a younger man in his early twenties, of medium height and with the physique of a large safe; he was wearing an American field jacket. Jason started to get off the barstool. "Sit, *sit!*" cried his new friend, leaning forward to be heard through the crowds and the music. "I brought us a virgin."

"*What?*"

"You forgot so quickly? He's on his way to becoming a Legion recruit."

"Oh, that," laughed Bourne, covering his gaffe. "I wondered in a place like this—"

"In a place like this," broke in Tank Shirt, "half will take it or give it either way as long as it's rough. But that's neither here nor there. I thought he should talk to you. He's American and his French is *grotesque,* but if you speak slow, he'll catch on."

"No need to," said Jason in faintly accented English. "I grew up in Neufchâtel, but I spent several years in the States."

"That's nice to heah." The American's speech was distinctly Deep South, his smile genuine, his eyes wary but unafraid.

"Then let us start again," said the Belgian in heavily accented English. "My name is . . . Maurice, it's as good a name as any. My young friend here is Ralph, at least he says it is. What's yours, my wounded hero?"

"François," replied Jason, thinking of Bernardine and wondering briefly how he was doing at the airports. "And I'm no hero; they died too quickly. . . . Order your drinks, I'm paying." They did and Bourne did, his mind racing, trying to recall the little he knew about the French Foreign Legion. "A lot has changed in nine years, Maurice." *How very easily the words came,* thought the Chameleon. "Why are you enlisting, Ralph?"

"Ah figure it's the wisest thing I can do—kinda disappear for a few years, and I understand five is the minimum."

"If you last the first, *mon ami,*" interjected the Belgian.

"Maurice is right. Listen to him. The officers are tough and difficult—"

"All *French*!" added the Belgian. "Ninety percent, at least. Only one foreigner in perhaps three hundred reach the officer corps. Have no illusions."

"But Ah'm a college man. An engineer."

"So you'll build fine latrines for the camps and design perfect shit holes in the field," laughed Maurice. "Tell him, François. Explain how the *savants* are treated."

"The educated ones must first know how to fight," said Jason, hoping he was right.

"Always first!" exclaimed the Belgian. "For their schooling is suspicious. Will they doubt? Will they think when they are paid only to follow orders? . . . Oh, no, *mon ami,* I would not emphasize your *érudition.*"

"Let it come out gradually," added Bourne.

"When they need it, not when you want to offer it."

"Bien!" cried Maurice. "He knows what he's talking about. A true *légionnaire*!"

"Can you fight?" asked Jason. "Could you go after someone to kill him?"

"Ah killed mah *feeancee* and her two brothers and a cousin, all with a knife and my bare hands. She was fuckin' a big banker in Nashville and they were coverin' for her because he was payin' all of 'em a lot of money. . . . Yeah, I can kill, Mr. François."

Manhunt for Crazed Killer in Nashville

Young engineer with promising future escapes dragnet. . . .

Bourne remembered the newspaper headlines of only weeks ago, as he stared at the face of the young American. "Go for the Legion," he said.

"If push comes to shove, Mr. François, could I use you as a reference?"

"It wouldn't help you, young man, it might only hurt. If you're pressed, just tell the truth. It's your credentials."

"Très bien! He knows the Legion. They will not take maniacs if they can help it, but they— how do you say it, François?"

"Look the other way, I think."

"Oui. They look the other way when there are—*encore,* François?"

"When there are extenuating circumstances."

"See? My friend François also has brains. I wonder how he survived."

"By not showing them, Maurice."

A waiter wearing about the filthiest apron Jason had ever seen clapped the Belgian on the neck. *"Votre table, René."*

"So?" shrugged Tank Shirt. "Just another name. *Quelle différence?* We eat and with good fortune we will not be poisoned."

Two hours later, with four bottles of rough *vin ordinaire* consumed by Maurice and Ralph, along with suspicious fish, Le Coeur du Soldat settled in for its nightly endurance ritual. Fights occurred episodically, broken up by muscular waiters. The blaring music marshaled memories of battles won and lost, engendering arguments between old soldiers who had basically been the assault troops, cannon fodder, at once resentful and filled with the pride of survival because they *had* survived the blood and horror their gold-braided superiors knew nothing about. It was the collective roar of the underprivileged foot soldiers heard from the time of the Pharaoh's legions to the grunts of Korea and

Vietnam. The properly uniformed officers decreed from far behind the lines, and the foot
soldiers died to preserve their superiors' wisdom. Bourne remembered Saigon and could not
fault the existence of Le Coeur du Soldat.

The head bartender, a massive bald man with
steel-rimmed glasses, picked up a telephone
concealed below the far end of the bar and
brought it to his ear. Jason watched him between the roving figures. The man's eyes spun
around the crowded room—what he heard appeared to be important; what he saw, dismissible. He spoke briefly, plunged his hand below
the bar and kept it there for several moments;
he had dialed. Again, he spoke quickly, then
calmly replaced the phone out of sight. It was
the kind of sequence described by old Fontaine
on Tranquility Isle. Message received, message
relayed. And at the end of that receiving line was
the Jackal.

It was all he wanted to see that evening; there
were things to consider, perhaps men to hire, as
he had hired men in the past. Expendable men
who meant nothing to him, people who could be
paid or bribed, blackmailed or threatened into
doing what he wanted them to do without explanation.

"I just spotted the man I was to meet here,"

he said to the barely conscious Maurice and Ralph. "He wants me to go outside."

"You're *leaving* us?" whined the Belgian.

"Hey, man, you shouldn't do *thay-at,*" added the young American from the South.

"Only for tonight." Bourne leaned over the table. "I'm working with another *légionnaire,* someone who's on to something that involves a lot of money. I don't know you, but you seem like decent men." Bourne pulled out his roll of bills and peeled off a thousand francs, five hundred for each of his companions. "Take this, both of you—shove it in your pockets, *quickly!*"

"Holy *shee-itt!*"

"Merde!"

"It's no guarantee, but maybe we can use you. Keep your mouths shut and get out of here ten or fifteen minutes after I leave. Also, no more wine. I want you sober tomorrow. . . . When does this place open, Maurice?"

"I'm not sure it closes. I myself have been here at eight o'clock in the morning. Naturally, it is not so crowded—"

"Be here around noon. But with clear heads, all right?"

"I shall be *le caporal extraordinaire* of La Légion. The man that I once was! Should I wear my uniform?'' Maurice belched.

"Hell, no."

"Ah'll wear a suit and a tie. I got a suit and a tie, honest!" The American hiccupped.

"No. Both of you be like you are now, but with your heads straight. Do you understand me?''

"You sound *très américain, mon ami.*"

"He sure do."

"I'm not, but then the truth's not a commodity here, is it?''

"Ah know what he means. I learned it real well. You kinda fib with a tie on.''

"No tie, Ralph. See you tomorrow." Bourne slid out of the booth, and suddenly a thought struck him. Instead of heading for the door, he cautiously made his way to the far end of the bar and the huge bald bartender. No seats were available, so, again cautiously, politely, he squeezed sideways between two customers, ordered a Pernod and asked for a napkin on which to write a message, ostensibly personal, to no one who might concern the establishment. On the back of the napkin's crude coat of arms, he wrote the following with his ballpoint pen in French:

The nest of a blackbird is worth a million

francs. Object: confidential business advice. If interested, be at the old factory around the corner in thirty minutes. Where is the harm? An additional 5000 F for being there alone.

Bourne palmed the napkin along with a hundred-franc note and signaled the bartender, who adjusted his steel-rimmed glasses as if the unknown patron's gesture were an impertinence. Slowly he moved his large body forward, and leaned his thick tattooed arms on the bar. "What is it?" he asked gruffly.

"I have written out a message for you," replied the Chameleon, his eyes steady, focused on the bartender's glasses. "I am by myself and hope you will consider the request. I am a man who carries wounds but I am not a poor man." Bourne quickly but gently—very gently—reached for the bartender's hand, passing the napkin and the franc note. With a final imploring look at the astonished man, Jason turned and headed for the door, his limp pronounced.

Outside, Bourne hurried up the cracked pavement toward the alley's entrance. He judged that his interlude at the bar had taken between eight and twelve minutes. Knowing the bartender was watching him, he had purposely not tried to see if his two companions were still at the table, but he assumed they were. Tank Shirt and Field Jacket were not at their sharpest, and in their condition minutes did not count; he could only hope five hundred francs apiece might bring about a degree of responsibility and that they would leave soon as instructed. Oddly enough, he had more faith in Maurice-René than in the young American who called himself Ralph. A former corporal in the Foreign Legion was imbued with an automatic reflex where orders were concerned; he followed them blind drunk or blind sober. Jason hoped so; it was not mandatory, but he could use their assistance— if, *if,* the bartender at Le Coeur du Soldat had been sufficiently intrigued by the excessive sums of money, as well as by a solitary conversation with a cripple he could obviously kill with one tattooed arm.

Bourne waited in the street, the wash of the streetlights diminishing in the alley, fewer and fewer people going in or coming out, those arriving in better shape than those departing, all passing Jason without a glance at the derelict weaving against the brick.

Instinct prevailed. Tank Shirt pulled the much younger Field Jacket through the heavy door, and at one point after the door had swung shut, slapped the American across the face, telling him in unclear words to follow orders, for they were rich and could become much richer.

"It is better than being shot in Angola!" cried the former *légionnaire,* loud enough for Bourne to hear. "Why did they *do* that?"

Jason stopped them at the entrance to the alley, pulling both men around the edge of the brick building. "It's *me*," he said, his voice commanding.

"Sacrebleu . . . !"

"What the Gawdamn hell . . . !"

"Be *quiet*! You can make another five hundred francs tonight, if you want to. If not, there are twenty other men who will."

"We are comrades!" protested Maurice-René.

"And Ah could bust your ass for scarin' us like *thay*-at. . . . But mah buddy's right, we're comrades—that ain't Commie stuff, is it, Maurice?"

"Taisez-vous!"

"That means shut up," explained Bourne.

"Ah know *thay*-at. I hear it a lot—"

"Listen to me. Within the next few minutes the bartender in there may come out looking for me. He *may*, he also may not, I simply don't know. He's the large bald man wearing glasses. Do either of you know him?"

The American shrugged, but the Belgian nodded his floating head, his lips flat until he spoke. "His name is Santos and he is *espagnol*."

"Spanish?"

"Or *latino-américain*. No one knows."

Ilich Ramirez Sanchez, thought Jason. *Carlos the Jackal,* Venezuelan by birth, rejected terrorist, whom even the Soviets could not handle. Of course he would return to his own. "How well do you know him?"

It was the Belgian's turn to shrug. "He is the complete authority where Le Coeur du Soldat is concerned. He has been known to crush men's heads if they behave too badly. He always takes off his glasses first, and that is the first sign that something will happen that even proven soldiers do not care to witness. . . . If he is coming out here to see you, I would advise you to leave."

"He may come because he *wants* to see me, not because he wants to harm me."

"That is not Santos—"

"You don't have to know the particulars, they don't concern you. But if he does come out that door, I want you to engage him in conversation, can you do that?"

"*Mais certainement.* On several occasions I have slept on his couch upstairs, personally carried there by Santos himself when the cleaning women came in."

"Upstairs?"

"He lives above the café on the second floor. It is said that he never leaves, never goes into the streets, even to the markets. Other people purchase all the supplies, or they are simply delivered."

"I see." Jason pulled out his money and distributed another five hundred francs to each weaving man. "Go back into the alley, and if Santos comes out, stop him and behave like you've had too much to drink. Ask him for money, a bottle, whatever."

Like children, Maurice-René and Ralph clutched the franc notes, glancing at each other both as conspirators and as victors. François, the crazy *légionnaire*, was passing out money as if he printed it himself! Their collective enthusiasm grew.

"How long do you want us to hassle this turkey?" asked the American from the Deep South.

"I will talk the ears off his bald head!" added the Belgian.

"No, just long enough for me to see that he's alone," said Bourne, "that no one else is with him or comes out after him."

"Piece a' cake, man."

"We shall earn not only your francs but your respect. You have the word of a Légion corporal!"

"I'm touched. Now, get back in there." The two inebriated men lurched down the alley, Field Jacket slapping Tank Shirt triumphantly across the shoulders. Jason pressed his back against the street-side brick inches from the edge of the building and waited. Six minutes passed, and then he heard the words he so desperately wanted to hear.

"*Santos!* My great and good friend Santos!"

"What are you doing here, René?"

"My young American friend was sick to his stomach but it has gone—he vomited."

"American . . . ?"

"Let me introduce you, Santos. He's about to become a great soldier."

"There is a Children's Crusade somewhere?" Bourne peered around the corner as the bald bartender looked at Ralph. "Good luck, baby face. Go find your war in a playground."

"You talk French awful fast, mistuh, but I caught some of that. You're a big mother, but *I* can be a mean son of a bitch!"

The bartender laughed and switched effortlessly to English. "Then you'd better be mean someplace else, baby face. We only permit peaceable gentlemen in Le Coeur du Soldat. . . . Now I must go.''

"Santos!" cried Maurice-René. "Lend me ten francs. I left my billfold back at my flat.''

"If you ever had a billfold, you left it back in North Africa. You know my policy. Not a sou for any of you.''

"What money I had went for your lousy fish! It made my friend vomit!''

"For your next meal, go down to Paris and dine at the Ritz. . . . Ah, *yes*! You did have a meal—but you did not pay for it.'' Jason pulled quickly back as the bartender snapped his head around and looked up the alley. "Good night, René. You too, baby warrior. I have business.''

Bourne ran down the pavement toward the gates of the old factory. Santos was coming to meet him. *Alone.* Crossing the street into the shadows of the shut-down refinery, he stood still, moving only his hand so as to feel the hard steel and the security of his automatic. With every step Santos took the Jackal was closer! Moments later, the immense figure emerged from the alley, crossed the dimly lit street and approached the rusted gates.

"I am here, monsieur,'' said Santos.

"And I am grateful."

"I'd rather you'd keep your word first. I believe you mentioned five thousand francs in your note."

"It's here." Jason reached into his pocket, removed the money, and held it out for the manager of Le Coeur du Soldat.

"Thank you," said Santos, walking forward and accepting the bills. "*Take* him!" he added.

Suddenly, from behind Bourne, the old gates of the factory burst open. Two men rushed out, and before Jason could reach his weapon, a heavy blunt instrument crashed down on his skull.

23

"We're alone," said the voice across the dark room as Bourne opened his eyes. Santos's huge frame minimized the size of his large armchair, and the low wattage of the single floor lamp heightened the whiteness of his immense bald head. Jason arched his neck and felt the angry swelling on top of his skull; he was angled into the corner of a sofa. "There's no break, no blood, only what I imagine is a very painful lump," commented the Jackal's man.

"Your diagnosis is accurate, especially the last part."

"The instrument was hard rubber and cushioned. The results are predictable except where concussions are concerned. At your side, on a tray, is an ice bag. It might be well to use it.''

Bourne reached down in the dim light, grabbed the bulky cold bag and brought it to his head. "You're very considerate," he said flatly.

"Why not? We have several things to discuss . . . perhaps a million, if broken down into francs."

"It's yours under the conditions stated."

"Who *are* you?" asked Santos sharply.

"That's not one of the conditions."

"You're not a young man."

"Not that it matters, but neither are you."

"You carried a gun and a knife. The latter is for younger men."

"Who said so?"

"Our reflexes. . . . What do you know about a blackbird?"

"You might as well ask me how I knew about Le Coeur du Soldat."

"How did you?"

"Someone told me."

"Who?"

"Sorry, not one of the conditions. I'm a broker and that's the way I work. My clients expect it."

"Do they also expect you to bind your knee so as to feign an injury? As your eyes opened I pressed the area; there was no sign of pain, no sprain, no break. Also, you carry no identification but considerable amounts of money?"

"I don't explain my methods, I only clarify my restrictions as I understand them to be. I got my message through to you, didn't I? Since I had no telephone number, I doubt I could have done so very successfully had I arrived at your establishment in a business suit carrying an attaché case."

Santos laughed. "You never would have gotten inside. You would have been rudely stopped in the alley and stripped."

"The thought occurred to me. . . . Do we do business, say a million francs' worth?"

The Jackal's man shrugged. "It would seem to me that if a buyer mentions such an amount in his first offer, he will go higher. Say a million and a half. Perhaps even two."

"But I'm not the buyer, I'm the broker. I was authorized to pay one million, which is far too much in my opinion, but time is of the essence. Take it or leave it, I have other options."

"Do you really?"

"Certainly."

"Not if you're a corpse found floating in the Seine without any identification."

"I see." Jason looked around the darkened flat; it bore little relationship to the shabby café below. The furniture was large, as required by the oversized owner, but tastefully selected, not elegant but certainly not cheap. What was mildly astonishing were the bookshelves covering the wall between the two front windows. The academic in Bourne wished he could read the titles; they might give him a clearer picture of this strange, huge man whose speech might have been formed at the Sorbonne—a committed brute on the outside, perhaps someone else inside. His eyes returned to Santos. "Then my leaving here freely under my own power is not a given, is it?"

"No," answered the Jackal's conduit. "It might have been had you answered my simple questions, but you tell me that your conditions, or should I say your restrictions, forbid you to do so. . . . Well, I, too, have conditions and you will live or die by them."

"That's succinct."

"There's no reason not to be."

"Of course, you're forfeiting any chance of collecting a million francs—or, as you suggested, perhaps a great deal more."

"Then may I also suggest," said Santos,

crossing his thick arms in front of him and absently glancing at the large tattoos on his skin, "that a man with such funds available will not only part with them in exchange for his life, but will happily deliver the information requested so as to avoid unnecessary and excruciating pain." The Jackal's man suddenly slammed his clenched right fist down on the armrest and shouted, "What do you know about a *blackbird*? Who told you about Le Coeur du Soldat? Where do you come from and who *are* you and who is your *client*?"

Bourne froze, his body rigid but his mind spinning, whirling, racing. He had to get *out*! He had to reach Bernardine—how many hours was his call overdue? Where was *Marie*? Yet what he wanted to do, *had* to do, could not be done by opposing the giant across the room. Santos was neither a liar nor a fool. He would and could kill his prisoner handily and without hesitation . . . and he would not be duped by outright false or convoluted information. The Jackal's man was protecting two turfs—his own and his mentor's. The Chameleon had only one option open: to expose a part of the truth so dangerous as to be credible, the ring of authenticity so plausible that the risk of rejecting it was unacceptable. Jason put the ice bag on the tray and spoke slowly from the shadows of the large couch.

"Obviously I don't care to die for a client or be tortured to protect his information, so I'll tell you what I know, which isn't as much as I'd like under the present circumstances. I'll take your points in order if I'm not too damned frightened to forget the sequence. To begin with, the funds are not available to me personally. I meet with a man in London to whom I deliver the information, and he releases an account in Bern, Switzerland, to a name and a number—any name, any number—that I give him. . . . We'll skip over my life and the 'excruciating pain'—I've answered both. Let's see, what do I know about a blackbird? The Coeur du Soldat is part of that question, incidentally. . . . I was told that an old man—name and nationality unknown, at least to me, but I suspect French—approached a well-known public figure and told him he was the target of an assassination. Who believes a drunken old man, especially one with a long police record looking for a reward? Unfortunately the assassination took place, but fortunately an aide to the deceased was by his side when the old man warned him. Even more fortunate, the aide was and is extremely close to my client and the assassination was a welcome event to both. The aide secretly passed on the old man's information. A blackbird is sent a message through a café known as Le Coeur du Soldat in Argenteuil. This blackbird must be an extraordinary man, and now my client wants to reach him. . . . As for myself, my offices are hotel rooms in various cities. I'm currently registered under the name of Simon at the Pont-Royal, where I keep my passport and other papers." Bourne paused, his palms outstretched. "I've just told you the entire truth as I know it."

"*Not* the entire truth," corrected Santos, his voice low and guttural. "Who is your client?"

"I'll be killed if I tell you."

"I'll kill you right now if you don't," said the Jackal's conduit, removing Jason's hunting knife from his wide leather belt, the blade glistening in the light of the floor lamp.

"Why not give me the information my client wants along with a name and a number—any name, any number—and I'll guarantee you two million francs. All my client asks is for me to be the *only* intermediary. Where's the harm? The blackbird can turn me down and tell me to go to hell. . . . *Three* million!"

Santos's eyes wavered as if the temptation

were almost too much for his imagination. "Perhaps we'll do business later—"

"Now."

"No!" Carlos's man pushed his immense body out of the chair and walked toward the couch, the knife held threateningly in front of him. "Your client."

"Plural," replied Bourne. "A group of powerful men in the United States."

"Who?"

"They guard their names like nuclear secrets, but I know of one and he should be enough for you."

"Who?"

"Find out for yourself—at least learn the enormity of what I'm trying to tell you. *Protect* your blackbird by all means! Ascertain that I'm telling you the truth and in the process make yourself so rich you can do anything you want to do for the rest of your life. You could travel, disappear, perhaps have time for those books of yours rather than being concerned with all that garbage downstairs. As you pointed out, neither of us is young. I make a generous brokering fee and you're a wealthy man, free of care, of unpleasant drudgery. . . . Again, where's the harm? I can be turned down, my clients turned down.

There's no trap. My clients don't ever want to see him. They want to *hire* him."

"How could this be done? How could I be satisfied?"

"Invent some high position for yourself and reach the American ambassador in London— the name is Atkinson. Tell him you've received confidential instructions from Snake Lady. Ask him if you should carry them out."

"Snake Lady? What's that?"

"Medusa. They call themselves Medusa."

Mo Panov excused himself and slid out of the booth. He made his way through the crowded highway diner toward the men's room, frantically scanning the wall at the far end for a pay phone. There was none! The only goddamned phone was ten feet from the booth and in clear sight of the wild-eyed platinum blonde whose paranoia was as deeply embedded as the dark roots of her hair. He had casually mentioned that he thought he should call his office and tell his staff about the accident and where he was, and was instantly met with invective.

"And have a swarm of cops coming out to pick you *up*! Not on your fuckin' life, Medicine

Man. Your office calls the fuzz, they call my devoted Chief Fork-in-Mouth, and my ass is bouncing into every barbed-wire fence in the county. He's in with every cop on the roads. I think he tells 'em where to get laid.''

"There'd be no reason for me to mention you and I certainly wouldn't. If you recall, you said he might resent me.''

"Resent don't count. He'd just cut your cute little nose off. I'm not takin' any chances—you don't look like you're too with-it. You'd blurt out about your accident—next thing the cops.''

"You know, you're not really making sense.''

"All right, I'll make sense. I'll yell 'Rape!' and tell these not-so-pansy truckers I picked you up on the road two days ago and I've been a sex slave ever since. How does that grab you?''

"Very firmly. May I at least go to the men's room? It's urgent that I do.''

"Be my guest. They don't put phones in the can in these places.''

"Really? . . . No, honestly, I'm not chagrined, not disappointed—just curious. Why don't they? Truckers make good money; they're not interested in stealing dimes or quarters.''

"Boy, you're from La La Land, Doc. Things happen on the highways; things get switched or snitched, you dig? If people make phone calls, other people want to know who makes them."

"Really . . . ?"

"Oh, *Jesus*. Hurry up. We only got time for a couple of greasies, so I'll order. He'll head up Seventy, not Ninety-seven. He wouldn't figure."

"Figure what? What are Seventy and Ninety-seven?"

"Routes, for Christ's sake! There are routes and there are *routes*. You are one dumb medicine man. Hit the head, then maybe later we'll stop at a motel where we can continue our business discussion while you get an advance bonus."

"I beg your pardon?"

"I'm pro-choice. Is that against your religion?"

"Good Lord, no. I'm a firm advocate."

"Good. Hurry *up*!"

So Panov headed for the men's room, and indeed the woman was right. There was no phone, and the window to the outside was too small for anyone but a small cat or a large rat to crawl through. . . . But he had money, a great deal of money, along with five driver's licenses from five different states. In Jason Bourne's lexicon these were weapons, especially the money. Mo went to the urinal—long overdue—and then to the door; he pulled it back several inches to observe the blonde. Suddenly, the door swung violently back several feet and Panov crashed into the wall.

"Hey, *sorry,* pal!" cried a short heavyset man, who grabbed the psychiatrist by the shoulders as Mo grabbed his face. "You okay, buddy?"

"Oh, certainly. Yes, of course."

"The hell you are, you got a nosebleed! C'mon over here by the towels," ordered the T-shirted trucker, one sleeve rolled up to hold a pack of cigarettes. "C'mon, put your head back while I get some cold water on your schnoz. . . . Loosen up and lean against the wall. There, that's better; we'll stop this sucker in a moment or two." The short man reached up and gently pressed the wet paper towels across Panov's face while holding the back of his neck, and every few seconds checking the flow of blood from Mo's nostrils. "There y'are, buddy, it's damned near stopped. Just breathe through your mouth, deep breaths, you got me? Head tilted, okay?"

"Thank you," said Panov, holding the towels and amazed that a nosebleed could be stopped so quickly. "Thank you very much."

"Don't thank me, I bashed you one by mistake," answered the trucker, relieving himself. "Feel better now?" he asked, zipping up his trousers.

"Yes, I do." And against the advice of his dear deceased mother, Mo decided to take advantage of the moment and forgo righteousness. "But I should explain that it was my mistake, not yours."

"Waddaya mean?" asked the trucker, washing his hands.

"Frankly, I was hiding behind the door looking at a woman I'm trying to get away from—if that makes sense to you."

Panov's personal medic laughed as he dried his hands. "Whose sense wouldn't it make? It's the story of mankind, pal! They getcha in their clutches and *whammo*, they whine and you don't know what to do, they scream and you're at their feet. Now me, I got it different. I married a real Eur'pean, you know? She don't speak so good English, but she's grateful. . . . Great with the kids, great with me, and I still get excited when I see her. Not like these fuckin' princesses over here."

"That's an extremely interesting, even visceral, statement," said the psychiatrist.

"It's who?"

"Nothing. I still want to get out of here without her seeing me leave. I have some money—"

"Hold the money, who is she?"

Both men went to the door and Panov pulled it back a few inches. "She's the one over there, the blonde who keeps looking in this direction and at the front door. She's getting very agitated—"

"Holy shit," interrupted the short trucker. "That's the Bronk's wife! She's way off course."

"Off course? The *Bronk*?"

"He trucks the eastern routes, not these. What the *hell* is she doing here?"

"I think she's trying to avoid him."

"Yeah," agreed Mo's companion. "I heard she's been messing around and don't charge no money."

"Do you know her?"

"Hell, yeah. I been to a couple of their barbecues. He makes a hell of a sauce."

"I have to get *out* of here. As I told you, I have some money—"

"So you told me and we'll discuss it later."

"Where?"

"In my truck. It's a red semi with white stripes, like the flag. It's parked out front, on the right. Get around the cab and stay out of sight."

"She'll see me leave."

"No she won't. I'm goin' over and give her a big surprise. I'll tell her all the CBs are hummin' and the Bronk is headin' south to the Carolinas—at least that's what I heard."

"How can I ever repay you?"

"Probably with some of that money you keep talkin' about. Not too much, though. The Bronk's an animal and I'm a born-again Christian." The short trucker swung back the door, nearly shoving Panov back into the wall again. Mo watched as his conspiratorial colleague approached the booth, his conspiratorial arms extended as the trucker embraced an old friend and started talking rapidly; the woman's eyes were attentive—she was mesmerized. Panov rushed out of the men's room, through the diner's entrance and toward the huge red-and-white-striped truck. He crouched breathlessly behind the cab, his chest pounding, and waited.

Suddenly, the Bronk's wife came racing out of the diner, her platinum hair rising grotesquely in the air behind her as she ran to her bright red automobile. She climbed inside and in seconds the engine roared; she continued north as Mo watched, astonished.

"How are y'doing, buddy—wherever the hell

you are?'' shouted the short man with no name who had not only amazingly stopped a nosebleed but had rescued him from a manic wife whose paranoid mood swings were rooted in equal parts of vengeance and guilt.

Stop it, asshole, cried Panov to himself as he raised his voice. ''Over here . . . buddy!''

Thirty-five minutes later they reached the outskirts of an unidentified town and the trucker stopped in front of a cluster of stores that bordered the highway. ''You'll find a phone there, buddy. Good luck.''

''Are you sure?'' asked Mo. ''About the money, I mean.''

''Sure I'm sure,'' replied the short man behind the wheel. ''Two hundred dollars is fine—maybe even what I earned—but more than that corrupts, don't it? I been offered fifty times that to haul stuff I won't haul, and you know what I tell 'em?''

''What do you tell them?''

''I tell 'em to go piss into the wind with their poison. It's gonna flash back and blind 'em.''

''You're a good person,'' said Panov, climbing out onto the pavement.

''I got a few things to make up for.'' The door of the cab slammed shut and the huge truck shot forward as Mo turned away, looking for a telephone.

"Where the hell *are* you?" shouted Alexander Conklin in Virginia.

"I don't *know*!" answered Panov. "If I were a patient, I'd ponderously explain that it was an extension of some Freudian dream sequence because it never *happens* but it happened to *me*. They shot me *up*, Alex!"

"Stay cold. We assumed that. We have to know where you are. Let's face it, others are looking for you, too."

"All right, all right. . . . Wait a minute! There's a drugstore across the street. The sign says 'Battle Ford's Best,' will that help?"

The sigh on the line from Virginia was the reply. "Yes, it does. If you were a socially productive Civil War buff rather than an insignificant shrink, you'd know it, too."

"What the hell does that mean?"

"Head for the old battleground at Ford's Bluff. It's a national landmark; there are signs everywhere. A helicopter will be there in thirty minutes, and don't say a goddamned thing to *anybody*!"

"Do you know how extreme you sound? Yet *I* was the object of hostility—"

"*Out,* coach!"

Bourne walked into the Pont-Royal and immediately approached the night concierge, peeling off a five-hundred-franc note and placing it quietly in the man's hand. "The name is Simon," he said, smiling. "I've been away. Any messages?"

"No messages, Monsieur Simon," was the quiet reply, "but two men are outside, one on Montalembert, the other across on the rue du Bac."

Jason removed a thousand-franc note and palmed it to the man. "I pay for such eyes and I pay well. Keep it up."

"Of course, monsieur."

Bourne crossed to the brass elevator. Reaching his floor, he walked rapidly down the intersecting corridors to his room. Nothing was disturbed; everything was as he had left it, except that the bed had been made up. The bed. Oh, God, he needed to rest, to sleep. He couldn't *do* it any longer. Something was happening inside him—less energy, less breath. Yet he had to have both, now more than ever. Oh, Christ, he wanted to lie down. . . . *No.* There was Marie. There was Bernardine. He went to the telephone and dialed the number he had committed to memory.

"I'm sorry I'm late," he said.

"Four hours late, *mon ami*. What happened?"

"No time. What about Marie?"

"There is nothing. Absolutely nothing. She is not on any international flight currently in the air or scheduled for departure. I even checked the transfers from London, Lisbon, Stockholm and Amsterdam—nothing. There is no Marie Elise St. Jacques Webb en route to Paris."

"There *has* to be. She wouldn't change her mind, it's not like her. And she wouldn't know how to bypass immigration."

"I repeat. She's not listed on any flight from any country coming into Paris."

"Damn!"

"I will keep trying, my friend. The words of Saint Alex keep ringing in my ears. Do not underestimate *la belle mademoiselle*."

"She's not a goddamned mademoiselle, she's my wife. . . . She's not one of us, Bernardine; she's not an agent in the field who can cross and double-cross and triple-cross. That's not *her*. But she's on her way to Paris. I know it!"

"The airlines do not, what more can I say?"

"Just what you said," said Jason, his lungs seemingly incapable of absorbing the air he needed, his eyelids heavy. "Keep trying."

"What happened tonight? *Tell* me."

"Tomorrow," replied David Webb, barely audible. "Tomorrow. . . . I'm so tired and I have to be somebody else."

"What are you talking about? You don't even sound like yourself."

"Nothing. Tomorrow. I have to think. . . . Or maybe I shouldn't think."

Marie stood in Marseilles's immigration line, mercifully short because of the early hour, and assumed an air of boredom, the last thing she felt. It was her turn to go to the passport counter.

"Américaine," said the half-awake official. "Are you heer on bizziness or playseeoor, madame?"

"Je parle français, monsieur. Je suis canadienne d'origine—Quebec. Séparatiste."

"Ah, bien!" The sleepy clerk's eyes opened somewhat wider as he proceeded in French. "You are in business?"

"No, I'm not. This is a journey of memories. My parents came from Marseilles and both died recently. I want to see where they came from, where they lived—perhaps what I missed."

"How extraordinarily touching, lovely lady,"

said the immigration official, appraising the most appealing traveler. "Perhaps also you might need a guide? There is no part of this city that is not indelibly printed on my mind."

"You're most kind. I'll be at the Sofitel Vieux Port. What's your name? You have mine."

"Lafontaine, madame. At your service!"

"*Lafontaine?* You don't say?"

"I do indeed!"

"How interesting."

"I am *very* interesting," said the official, his eyelids half closed but not with sleepiness, as his rubber stamps flew recklessly down to process the tourist. "I am at your every service, madame!"

It must run in that very peculiar clan, thought Marie as she headed for the luggage area. From there she would board a domestic flight to Paris under any name she chose.

François Bernardine awoke with a start, shooting up on his elbows, frowning, disturbed. *She's on her way to Paris, I know it!* The words of the husband who knew her best. *She's not listed on any flight from any other country coming into Paris.* His own words. Paris. The operative word was *Paris*!

But suppose it was *not* Paris?

The Deuxième veteran crawled rapidly out of bed in the early morning light shining through the tall narrow windows of his flat. In fewer minutes than his face appreciated, he shaved, then completed his ablutions, dressed, and walked down into the street to his Peugeot, where there was the inevitable ticket on the windshield; alas, it was no longer officially dismissible with a quiet phone call. He sighed, picked it off the glass, and climbed in behind the wheel.

Fifty-eight minutes later he swung the car into the parking lot of a small brick building in the huge cargo complex of Orly Airport. The building was nondescript; the work inside was not. It was a branch of the Department of Immigration, an all-important arm known simply as the Bureau of Air Entries, where sophisticated computers kept up-to-the-minute records of every traveler flying into France at all the international airports. It was vital to immigration but not often consulted by the Deuxième, for there were far too many other points of entry used by the people in which the Deuxième was interested. Nevertheless, over the years, Bernardine, operating on the theory of the obvious being unnoticed, had sought information from the Bureau of Air Entries. Every now and then he had been rewarded. He wondered if that would be the case this morning.

Nineteen minutes later he had his answer. It was the case, but the reward was considerably diminished in value, for the information came too late. There was a pay phone in the bureau's lobby; Bernardine inserted a coin and dialed the Pont-Royal.

"Yes?" coughed the voice of Jason Bourne.

"I apologize for waking you."

"François?"

"Yes."

"I was just getting up. There are two men down in the street far more tired than I am, unless they're replacements."

"Relative to last night? All night?"

"Yes. I'll tell you about it when I see you. Is that why you called?"

"No. I'm out at Orly and I'm afraid I have bad news, information that proves me an *idiot*. I should have considered it. . . . Your wife flew into Marseilles slightly over two hours ago. Not Paris. Marseilles."

"Why is that *bad* news?" cried Jason. "We know where she *is*! We can— Oh, Christ, I see what you mean." Subdued, Bourne's words trailed off. "She can take a train, hire a car. . . ."

"She can even fly up to Paris under any name she cares to," added Bernardine. "Still, I have an idea. It's probably as worthless as my brain but I suggest it anyway. . . . Do you and she have special—how do you say it?—nicknames for each other? *Sobriquets* of endearment perhaps?"

"We're not much for the cute stuff, frankly. . . . Wait a minute. A couple of years ago, Jamie, that's our son, had trouble with 'Mommy.' He turned it around and called her 'Meemom.' We kidded about it and I called her that for a few months off and on until he got it right."

"I know she speaks French fluently. Does she read the papers?"

"Religiously, at least the financial pages. I'm not sure she goes seriously much beyond them; it's her morning ritual."

"Even in a crisis?"

"Especially in a crisis. She claims it calms her."

"Let's send her a message—on the financial pages."

Ambassador Phillip Atkinson settled in for a morning of dreary paperwork at the American embassy in London. The dreariness was compounded by a dull throbbing at his temples and a sickening taste in his mouth. It was hardly a typical hangover because he rarely drank whisky and for over twenty-five years had never been drunk. He had learned a long time ago, roughly thirty months after Saigon fell, the limits of his talents, his opportunities and, above all, his resources. When he returned from the war with reasonable, if not exceptional, commendations at twenty-nine, his family had purchased him an available seat on the New York Stock Exchange, where in thirty additional months he had lost something over three million dollars.

"Didn't you ever learn a goddamned *thing* at Andover and Yale?" his father had roared. "At least make a few connections on the *Street*?"

"Dad, they were all jealous of me, you know that. My looks, the girls—I look like you, Dad—they all conspired against me. Sometimes I think they were really getting at you through *me*! You know how they talk. Senior and Junior, dashing socialites and all that crap. . . . Remember the column in the *Daily News* when they compared us to the Fairbankses?"

"I've known Doug for forty years!" yelled the father. "He's got it upstairs, one of the best."

"He didn't go to Andover and Yale, Dad."

"He didn't *have* to, for Christ's sake! . . . Hold it. Foreign Service . . . ? What the hell was that degree you got at Yale?"

"Bachelor of Arts."

"Screw that! There was something else. The courses or something."

"I majored in English literature and minored in political science."

"*That's* it! Shove the fairy stuff on the back burner. You were outstanding in the other one— the political science bullshit."

"Dad, it wasn't my strongest course."

"You passed?"

"Yes. . . . Barely."

"*Not* barely, with *honors*! That's *it!*"

And so Phillip Atkinson III began his career in the Foreign Service by way of a valuable political contributor who was his father, and never looked back. And although that illustrious man had died eight years ago, he never forgot the old war horse's last admonition: "Don't fuck this up, son. You want to drink or you want to whore around, you do it inside your own house or in a goddamned desert somewhere, understand? And you treat that wife of yours, whatever the hell her name is, with real affection wherever anybody can see you, *got* it?"

"Yes, Dad."

Which was why Phillip Atkinson felt so *blah* on this particular morning. He had spent the previous evening at a dinner party with unimportant royals who drank until the drink flowed out of their nostrils, and with his wife who excused their behavior because they *were* royals, all of which he could tolerate only with seven glasses of Chablis. There were times when he longed for the freewheeling, free-drinking days of the old Saigon.

The telephone rang, causing Atkinson to blur his signature on a document that made no sense to him. "Yes?"

"The high commissioner from the Hungarian Central Committee is on the line, sir."

"*Oh?* Who's that—who *are* they? Do we recognize them—it—*him*?"

"I don't know, Mr. Ambassador. I really can't pronounce his name."

"Very well, put him through."

"Mr. Ambassador?" said the deep accented voice on the phone. "Mr. Atkinson?"

"Yes, this is Atkinson. Forgive me, but I don't recollect either your name or the Hungarian affiliation you speak for."

"It does not matter. I speak on behalf of Snake Lady—"

"Stop!" cried the ambassador to the Court of St. James's. "Stay on the line and we'll resume talking in twenty seconds." Atkinson reached down, snapped on his scrambler, and waited until the spiraling sounds of the pre-interceptor subsided. "All right, continue."

"I have received instructions from Snake Lady and was told to confirm the origin from you."

"Confirmed!"

"And therefore I am to carry out these instructions?"

"Good Lord, *yes*! Whatever they say. My God, look what happened to Teagarten in Brussels, Armbruster in Washington! Protect me! Do whatever they *say*!"

"Thank you, Mr. Ambassador."

Bourne first sat in the hottest tub he could endure, then took the coldest shower he could tolerate. He then changed the dressing around his neck, walked back into the small hotel room and fell on the bed. . . . So Marie had found a simple, ingenious way to reach Paris. Goddamn it! How could he find her, *protect* her? Had she any idea what she was *doing*? David would go out of his mind. He'd panic and make a thousand mistakes. . . . Oh, my God, I *am* David!

Stop it. Control. Pull back.

The telephone rang; he grabbed it off the bed-side table. "Yes?"

"Santos wants to see you. With peace in his heart."

24

The Emergency Medical Service helicopter was lowered into its threshold; the rotors were cut and the blades thumped to a stop. Following EMS procedure when disembarking ambulatory patients, only then did the exit door open and the metal steps slap down to the ground. A uniformed paramedic preceded Panov, turning and assisting the doctor to the tarmac, where a second man in civilian clothes escorted him to a waiting limousine. Inside were Peter Holland, director of the CIA, and Alex Conklin, the latter in the right jump seat, obviously for conversational purposes. The psychiatrist climbed in beside Holland; he took several deep breaths, sighed audibly and fell back into the seat.

"I am a maniac," he stated, emphasizing each word. "Certifiably insane and I'll sign the papers of commitment myself."

"You're safe, that's all that matters, Doctor," said Holland.

"Good to see you, Crazy Mo," added Conklin.

"Have you any idea what I *did*? . . . I purposely crashed a car into a tree with me *in* it! Then after walking at least half the distance to the Bronx, I was picked up by the only person I know who may have more loose bananas in her head than *I* do. Her libido is unhinged and she's running away from her trucker husband—hot on her French heels—who I subsequently learned has the cuddly name of the Bronk. My hooker chauffeur proceeds to hold me hostage with such wiles as threatening to yell 'Rape!' in a diner filled with a collection of the NFL's most carnivorous linebackers—except for one who got me out." Panov abruptly stopped and reached into his pocket. "Here," he continued, thrusting the five driver's licenses and the roughly six thousand dollars into Conklin's hands.

"What's this?" asked the bewildered Alex.

"I robbed a bank and decided to become a professional driver! . . . What do you think it is? I took it from the man who was guarding me. I described as best I could to the chopper's crew where the crash took place. They're flying back to find him. They will; he's not walking any-where."

Peter Holland reached for the limousine's telephone, pushing three buttons. In less than two seconds, he spoke. "Get word to EMS-Arlington, Equipment Fifty-seven. The man they're picking up is to be brought directly to Langley. To the infirmary. And keep me informed as to their progress. . . . Sorry, Doctor. Go on."

"Go on? What's to go on to? I was kidnapped and held in some farmhouse and injected with enough sodium pentothal, if I'm not mistaken, to make me a resident of—of La La Land, which I was recently accused of being by Madame Scylla Charybdis."

"What the hell are you talking about?" said Holland flatly.

"Nothing, Admiral, or Mr. Director or—"

"Peter's fine, Mo," completed Holland. "I simply didn't understand you."

"There's nothing to understand but the facts. My allusions are compulsive attempts at false erudition. It's called posttraumatic stress."

"Of course, now you're perfectly clear."

Panov turned to the DCI with a nervous smile.

"It's my turn to be sorry, Peter. I'm still wound up. This last day or so hasn't exactly been representative of my normal life-style."

"I don't think it's anybody's," concurred Holland. "I've seen my share of rotten stuff, but nothing like this, nothing that tampers with the mind. I missed all that."

"There's no hurry, Mo," added Conklin. "Don't press yourself; you've taken a lot of punishment. If you like, we can postpone the briefing for a few hours so you can rest, calm down."

"Don't be a damn fool, Alex!" protested the psychiatrist sharply. "For the *second* time I've put David's life in jeopardy. The knowledge of *that* is far worse punishment. There's not a minute to lose. . . . Forget Langley, Peter. Take me to one of your clinics. Free-floating, I want to get out everything I can recall, consciously or unconsciously. *Hurry*. I'll tell the doctors what to do."

"You've got to be joking," said Holland, staring at Panov.

"I'm not joking for an instant. You both have to know what I know—whether I realize I know it or not. Can't you *understand* that?"

The director again reached for the telephone and pressed a single button. In the front seat, beyond the glass partition, the driver picked up the phone recessed in the seat beside him. "There's been a change of plans," said Holland. "Head for Sterile Five."

The limousine slowed down, and at the next intersection turned right toward the rolling hills and verdant fields of the Virginia hunt country. Morris Panov closed his eyes, as if in a trance or as a man might do facing some appalling ordeal—his own execution perhaps. Alex looked at Peter Holland; they both glanced at Mo, then back at each other. Whatever Panov was doing, there was a reason for it. Until they reached the gates of the estate that was Sterile House Five thirty minutes later, no one spoke.

"DCI and company," announced the driver to the guard wearing the uniform of a private security firm, in reality a CIA proprietary. The limousine proceeded down the long tree-lined entrance.

"Thanks," said Mo, opening his eyes and blinking. "As I'm sure you gathered, I'm trying to clear my head and with any luck bring down my blood pressure."

"You don't have to do this," insisted Holland.

"Yes, I do," said Panov. "Maybe with time I could piece things together with a degree of clarity, but I can't now and we don't *have* the time." Mo turned to Conklin. "How much can you tell me?"

"Peter knows everything. For the sake of that blood pressure of yours, I won't fill you in on all the details, but the bottom line is that David's all right. At least we haven't heard otherwise."

"Marie? The children?"

"On the island," replied Alex, avoiding Holland's eyes.

"What about this Sterile Five?" asked Panov, now looking at Holland. "I assume there's a specialist, or specialists, the kind I need."

"In relays and around the clock. You probably know a few of them."

"I'd rather not." The long dark vehicle swung around the circular drive and stopped in front of the stone steps of the pillared Georgian mansion that was the focal point of the estate. "Let's go," said Mo quietly, stepping outside.

The sculptured white doors, the rose-colored marble floors and the elegant winding staircase in the great hall all combined to furnish a superb cover for the work done at Sterile Five. Defectors, double and triple agents, and field officers returned from complex assignments for rest and debriefing were continuously processed through its various agendas. The staff, each with a Four Zero clearance, consisted of two doctors and three nurses in relay units, cooks and domestic attendants recruited from the foreign service—in the main, overseas embassies—and guards, all with Ranger training or its equivalent. They moved about the house and grounds unobtrusively, eyes constantly alert, each with either a concealed or an unconcealed weapon, except for the medical personnel. Visitors without exception were given small lapel pins by the well-spoken, dark-suited house steward, who admitted them and directed them to the locations of their scheduled appointments. The man was a retired gray-haired interpreter for the Central Intelligence Agency, but he suited his position so well in appearance he might have come from Central Casting.

Naturally, at the sight of Peter Holland, the steward was astonished. He prided himself on committing to memory every schedule at Sterile Five. "A surprise visit, sir?"

"Good to see you, Frank." The DCI shook hands with the former interpreter. "You may remember Alex Conklin—"

"Good Lord, is that you, Alex? It's been years!" Again hands were shaken. "When was the last time? . . . That crazy woman from Warsaw, wasn't it?"

"The KGB's been chuckling ever since," laughed Conklin. "The only secret she had was the recipe for the worst *golumpki* I've ever tasted. . . . Still keeping your hand in, Frank?"

"Every now and then," replied the steward, grimacing in mock disapproval. "These young translators don't know a quiche from a *kluski.*"

"Since I don't either," said Holland, "may I have a word with you, Frank?" The two older men walked off to the side speaking quietly as Alex and Mo Panov held their places, the latter frowning and sporadically breathing deeply. The director returned, handing lapel pins to his colleagues. "I know where to go now," he said. "Frank will call ahead."

The three of them walked up the curving ornate staircase, Conklin limping, and down a lushly carpeted hallway on the left to the rear of the enormous house. On the right wall was a door unlike any of the doors they had passed; it was made of thick varnished oak with four small windows in the upper recessed panels and two black buttons set in an outlet casing beside the knob. Holland inserted a key, twisted it and pressed the lower button; instantly a red light appeared in the small stationary camera mounted on the ceiling. Twenty seconds later there was the familiar muffled metallic clanking of an elevator coming to a stop. "Inside, gentlemen," ordered the DCI. The door closed and the elevator began its descent.

"We walked up to go *down*?" asked Conklin.

"Security," answered the director. "It's the only way to get where we're going. There's no elevator on the first floor."

"Why not, may the man with one foot missing ask?" said Alex.

"I'd think you'd be able to answer that better than me," retorted the DCI. "Apparently all accesses to the cellars are sealed off except for two elevators that bypass the first floor and for which you need a key. This one and another on the other side; this takes us to where we want to go, the other leads to the furnaces, air-conditioning units and all the rest of the normal basement equipment. Frank gave me the key, incidentally. If it doesn't return to its slot within a given period of time, another alarm goes off."

"It all strikes me as unnecessarily complicated," said Panov curtly, nervously. "Expensive games."

"Not necessarily, Mo," interrupted Conklin

gently. "Explosives can be concealed pretty easily in heating pipes and ducts. And did you know that during the last days of Hitler's bunker a few of his saner aides tried to insert poison gas into the air-filtering machinery? These are just precautions."

The elevator stopped and the door opened. "To your left, Doctor," Holland said. The hallway was a glistening pristine white, antiseptic in its way, which was altogether proper, as this underground complex was a highly sophisticated medical center. It was devoted not only to the healing of men and women, but also to the process of breaking them down, crippling their resistance so that information might be revealed, truths learned that could prevent the penetration of high-risk operations, frequently saving lives as a result.

They entered a room that was in stark contrast to the antiseptic quality of the fluorescent-lit hallway. There were heavy armchairs and soft indirect lighting, a coffee urn on a table with cups and saucers; newspapers and magazines were folded neatly on other tables, all the comforts of a lounge designed for those waiting for someone or something. From an inner door a man in a white medical jacket appeared; he was frowning, looking uncertain.

"Director Holland?" he said, approaching Peter, extending his hand. "I'm Dr. Walsh, second shift. Needless to say, we didn't expect you."

"I'm afraid it's an emergency and hardly one of my choosing. May I introduce you to Dr. Morris Panov—unless you know him?"

"*Of* him, of course." Walsh again extended his hand. "A pleasure, Doctor, also a privilege."

"You may take both back before we're finished, Doctor. May we talk privately?"

"Certainly. My office is inside." The two men disappeared through the inner door.

"Shouldn't you go with them?" asked Conklin, looking at Peter.

"Why not you?"

"Goddamn it, you're the *director*. You should insist!"

"You're his closest friend. So should you."

"I don't have any clout here."

"Mine disappeared when Mo dismissed us. Come on, let's have some coffee. This place gives me the proverbial creeps." Holland went to the table with the coffee urn and poured two cups. "How do you like it?"

"With more milk and sugar than I'm supposed to have. I'll do it."

"I still take it black," said the director, moving

away from the table and removing a pack of cigarettes from his shirt pocket. "My wife says the acid will kill me one day."

"Other people say tobacco will."

"What?"

"Look." Alex pointed at the sign on the opposite wall. It read: THANK YOU FOR NOT SMOKING.

"That I've got enough clout for," announced Holland quietly as he snapped his lighter and lit a cigarette.

Nearly twenty minutes passed. Every now and then one or the other of them picked up a magazine or a newspaper only to put it down moments later and look up at the inner door. Finally, twenty-eight minutes after he had disappeared with Panov, the doctor named Walsh reappeared.

"He tells me you know what he's requesting and that you have no objections, Director Holland."

"I've got plenty of objections, but it seems he's overruled them. . . . Oh, excuse me, Doctor, this is Alex Conklin. He's one of us and a close friend of Panov."

"How do *you* feel, Mr. Conklin?" asked Walsh, nodding at Alex as he returned the greeting.

"I hate what he's doing—what he wants to do—but he says it makes sense. If it does, it's right for him and I understand why he insists on doing it. If it doesn't make sense, I'll pull him out of there myself, one foot and all. *Does* it make sense, Doctor? And what's the risk of damage?"

"There's always a risk where drugs are concerned, especially in terms of chemical balance, and he knows that. It's why he's designed an intravenous flow that prolongs his own psychological pain but somewhat reduces the potential damage."

"Somewhat?" cried Alex.

"I'm being honest. So is he."

"Bottom line, Doctor," said Holland.

"If things go wrong, two or three months of therapy, not permanent."

"And the sense?" insisted Conklin. "Does it make *sense*?"

"Yes," replied Walsh. "What happened to him is not only recent, it's consumed him. It's obsessed his conscious, which can only mean that it's inflamed his subconscious. He's right. His unreachable recall is on the cutting edge. . . . I came in here as a courtesy. He's insisted we proceed, and from what he's told me, I'd do the same thing. Each of us would."

"What's the security?" asked Alex.

"The nurse will be dismissed and stay outside the door. There'll be only a single battery-operated tape recorder and me . . . and one or both of you." The doctor turned to the door, then glanced back. "I'll send for you at the proper time," he added, again disappearing inside.

Conklin and Peter Holland looked at each other. The second period of waiting began.

To their astonishment, it ended barely ten minutes later. A nurse came out into the lounge and asked them to follow her. They walked through what appeared to be a maze of antiseptic white walls broken up only by recessed white panels with glass knobs that denoted doors. Only once on their brief journey did they see another human being; it was a man in a white smock, wearing a white surgical mask, who walked out of yet another white door, his sharp, intense eyes above the white cloth somehow accusing, determining them to be aliens from some different world that had not been cleared for Sterile House Five.

The nurse opened a door; there was a blinking red light above its top frame. She put her index finger to her lips, indicating silence. Holland and Conklin walked quietly inside a dark

room and confronted a drawn white curtain concealing a bed or an examining table beyond, a
small circle of intense light shining through the
cloth. They heard the softly spoken words of Dr.
Walsh.

"You are going back, Doctor, not far back, just
a day or so, just when you began to feel the dull,
constant pain in your arm . . . your *arm,* Doctor.
Why are they inflicting pain on your *arm*? You
were in a farmhouse, a small farmhouse with
fields outside your window, and then they put a
blindfold on you and began hurting your arm.
Your *arm*, Doctor."

Suddenly, there was a muted flashing of
green light reflected on the ceiling. The curtain
parted electronically several feet, revealing the
bed, the patient and the doctor. Walsh took his
finger off a bedside button and looked at them,
gesturing slowly with his hands as if to say,
There's no one else here. Confirmed?

Both witnesses nodded, at first mesmerized,
then repelled at the sight of Panov's grimacing
pale face and the tears that began to flow from
his wide-open eyes. Then, as one, they saw the
white straps that emerged from under the white
sheet, holding Mo in place; the order had to be
his.

"The *arm*, Doctor. We have to begin with the *physically* invasive procedure, don't we? Because you know what it does, Doctor, don't you? It leads to another invasive procedure that you cannot permit. You must stop its progression."

The ear-shattering scream was a prolonged shriek of defiance and horror. "No, *no*! *I won't tell you*! I *killed* him once, I won't kill him *again*! Get away from *meeeee* . . . !"

Alex slumped, falling to the floor. Peter Holland grabbed him and gently the strong, broad-shouldered admiral, a veteran of the darkest operations in the Far East, led Conklin silently through the door to the nurse. "Get him away from here, please."

"Yes, sir."

"Peter," coughed Alex, trying to stand, collapsing on his false foot. "I'm sorry, Christ, I'm *sorry*!"

"What for?" whispered Holland.

"I should watch but I *can't* watch!"

"I understand. It's all too close. If I were you, I probably couldn't either."

"No, you *don't* understand! Mo said he killed David, but of course he didn't. But *I* meant to, I really *wanted* to kill him! I was wrong, but I tried with all the expertise in my bones to *kill* him! And

now I've done it again. I sent him to Paris.
. . . It's not Mo, it's *me*!"

"Put him against the wall, miss. Let him sink
to the floor and leave us alone."

"Yes, *sir*!" The nurse did as she was ordered
and fled, leaving Holland and Alex alone in the
antiseptic maze.

"Now, you listen to me, Field Man," whispered the gray-haired director of the Central Intelligence Agency, kneeling in front of Conklin.
"This fucking merry-go-round of guilt had better
stop—has *got* to stop—or nobody's going to be
any good to *anybody*. I don't give a good goddamn what you or Panov did thirteen years ago,
or five years ago, or *now*! We're all reasonably
bright people, and we did what each of us did
because we thought they were the right moves
at the time. . . . Guess what, *Saint* Alex? Yes, I've
heard the term. We make *mistakes*. Fucking inconvenient, isn't it? Maybe we're not so *brilliant*
after all. Maybe Panov isn't the greatest behavioral whatever-the-hell-it-is; maybe you're not
the shrewdest son of a bitch in the field, the one
who got canonized, and maybe *I'm* not the
superjock behind-the-lines strategist they've
made me out to be. So *what*? We take our baggage and go where we have to go."

"Oh, for *Christ's* sake, *shut* up!" yelled Conklin, struggling against the wall.

"Shhh!"

"Oh, shit! The last thing I need is a sermon from you! If I had a foot, I'd take you."

"Now we're physical?"

"I was Black Belt. First class, Admiral."

"Golly, gee. I don't even know how to wrestle."

Their eyes met and Alex was the first to laugh quietly. "You're too much, Peter. I got your message. Help me up, will you? I'll go back to the lounge and wait for you. Come on, give me a hand."

"The hell I will," said Holland, getting to his feet and standing over Conklin. "Help yourself. Someone told me that the Saint made it back through a hundred and forty miles in enemy territory, through rivers and streams and jungle, and arrived at the Foxtrot base camp asking if anybody had a bottle of bourbon."

"Yeah, well, that was different. I was a hell of a lot younger and I had another foot."

"Pretend you got one now, Saint Alex." Holland winked. "I'm going back inside. One of us has to be there."

"Bastard!"

For an hour and forty-seven minutes Conklin sat in the lounge. His attachable footless foot never throbbed, but it was throbbing now. He did not know what the impossible feeling meant, but he could not dismiss the beat that surged through his leg. If nothing else, it was something to think about, and he thought wistfully of the younger days, when he had both feet, and before. Oh, how he had wanted to change the world! And how he had felt so *right* in a destiny that forced him to become the youngest valedictorian in his high school's history, the youngest freshman ever accepted at Georgetown, a bright, *bright* light that shimmered at the end of the tunnels of academe. His decline started when someone, somewhere, found out that his name at birth was not Alexander Conklin but Aleksei Nikolae Konsolikov. That now faceless man had casually asked him a question, the answer to which had changed Conklin's life.

"Do you by any chance speak Russian?"

"Of course," he had replied, amused that his visitor would even think he might not. "As you obviously know, my parents were immigrants. I grew up not only in a Russian home but in a Russian neighborhood—at least in the early years. You couldn't buy a loaf of bread at the *ovoshchnoi otdel* if you didn't. And at church school the older priests and nuns, like the Poles, held ferociously on to the language. . . . I'm sure it contributed to my leaving the faith."

"Those were the early years, however, as I believe you mentioned."

"Yes."

"What changed?"

"I'm sure it's in your government report somewhere and will hardly satisfy your iniquitous Senator McCarthy."

The face came back to Alex with the memory of those words. It was a middle-aged face and it had suddenly become expressionless, the eyes clouded but with suppressed anger in them. "I assure you, Mr. Conklin, I am in no way associated with the senator. You call him iniquitous, I have other terms, but they're not pertinent here. . . . What changed?"

"Quite late in his life my father became what he had been in Russia, a highly successful merchant, a capitalist. At last count he owned seven supermarkets in upscale malls. They're called Conklin's Corners. He's over eighty now, and although I love him dearly, I regret to say he's an ardent supporter of the senator. I simply consider his years, his struggles, his hatred of the Soviets, and avoid the subject."

"You're very bright and very diplomatic."

"Bright and diplomatic," Alex had agreed.

"I've shopped at a couple of Conklin's Corners. Kind of expensive."

"Oh, yes."

"Where did the 'Conklin' come from?"

"My father. My mother says he saw it on a billboard advertising motor oil, she thinks, about four or five years after they got here. And, of course, the Konsolikov had to go. As my considerably bigoted father once said, 'Only the Jews with Russian names can make money over here.' Again, I avoid the subject."

"*Very* diplomatic."

"It's not difficult. He has his share of good points as well."

"Even if he didn't, I'm sure you could be convincing in your diplomacy, in the concealment of your feelings."

"Why do I think that's a leading statement?"

"Because it is, Mr. Conklin. I represent a government agency that's extremely interested in you, and one in which your future would be as unlimited as that of any potential recruit I've spoken to in a decade. . . ."

That conversation had taken place nearly thirty years ago, mused Alex, his eyes drifting up once again to the inner door of Sterile Five's waiting lounge in its own private medical center. And how crazy the intervening years had been. In a stress-defying bid for unrealistic expansion, his father had overextended himself, committing enormous sums of money that existed only in his imagination and in the minds of avaricious bankers. He lost six of his seven supermarkets, the smallest and last supporting a life-style that he found unacceptable, so he conveniently had a massive stroke and died as Alex's own adult life was about to begin.

Berlin—East and West. Moscow, Leningrad, Tashkent and Kamchatka. Vienna, Paris, Lisbon and Istanbul. Then back across the world to stations in Tokyo, Hong Kong, Seoul, Cambodia, Laos, and finally Saigon and the tragedy that was Vietnam. Over the years, with his facile mastery of languages and the expertise that came with survival, he had become the Agency's point man in clandestine operations, its primary scout and often the on-scene strategist for covert activities. Then one morning with the mists hanging over the Mekong Delta, a land mine shattered his life as well as his foot. There was little left for a field man who depended on mobility in his chosen work; the rest was downhill and out of the field. His excessive drinking he accepted, and excused as genetic. The Russian's winter of depression carried over into spring, summer and autumn. The skeletal, trembling wreck of a man who was about to go under was given a reprieve. David Webb—Jason Bourne—came back into his life.

The door opened, mercifully cutting short his reverie, and Peter Holland walked slowly into the lounge. His face was pale and drawn, his eyes glazed, and in his left hand were two small plastic containers, each presumably holding a cassette tape.

"As long as I live," said Peter, his voice low and hollow, barely above a whisper, "I hope to Christ I never go through anything like this again, never witness anything like this again."

"How's Mo?"

"I didn't think he'd live. . . . I thought he'd kill himself. Every now and then Walsh would stop. Let me tell you, he was one frightened doctor."

"Why didn't he call it *off*, for God's sake?"

"I asked him that. He said Panov's instructions were not only explicit but that he'd written them out and signed them and expected them to be followed to the letter. Maybe there's some kind of unwritten code of ethics between doctors, I don't know, but I do know Walsh hooked him up to an EKG, which he rarely took his eyes off. Neither did I; it was easier than looking at Mo. Jesus, let's get *out* of here!"

"Wait a minute. What about Panov?"

"He's not ready for a welcome-home party. He'll stay here for a couple of days under observation. Walsh will call me in the morning."

"I'd like to see him. I want to see him."

"There's nothing to see but a human dishrag. Believe me, you don't and he wouldn't want you to. Let's go."

"Where?"

"Your place in Vienna—our place in Vienna. I assume you've got a cassette machine."

"I've got everything but a moon rocket, most of which I can't operate."

"I want to stop and get a bottle of whisky."

"There's whatever you want at the apartment."

"It doesn't bother you?" asked Holland, studying Alex.

"Would it matter if it did?"

"Not a bit. . . . If I remember, there's an extra bedroom, isn't there?"

"Yes."

"Good. We may be up most of the night listening to these." The director held up the cassettes. "The first couple of times won't mean anything. All we'll hear is the pain, not the information."

It was shortly past five o'clock in the afternoon when they left the estate known within the Agency as Sterile House Five. The days were growing shorter, September on the cusp, the descending sun announcing the forthcoming change with an intensity of color that was the death of one season and the birth of another.

"The light's always brightest before we die," said Conklin, leaning back in the seat beside Holland in the limousine, staring out the window.

"I find that not only inappropriate but quite possibly sophomoric," declared Peter wearily. "I won't commit to the latter until I know who said it. Who was it?"

"Jesus, I think."

"The Scriptures were never edited. Too many campfires, no on-scene confirmation."

Alex laughed softly, reflectively. "Did you ever actually read them? The Scriptures, I mean."

"Most of it—most of them."

"Because you had to?"

"Hell, no. My father and mother were as agnostic as any two people could be without being branded godless pariahs. They shut up about it and sent me and my two sisters to a Protestant service one week, a Catholic mass on another, and a synagogue after that. Never with any regularity, but I guess they figured we should catch the whole scene. *That's* what makes kids want to read. Natural curiosity wrapped in mysticism."

"Irresistible," agreed Conklin. "I lost my faith, and now after years of proclaiming my spiritual independence, I wonder if I'm missing something."

"Like what?"

"Comfort, Peter. I have no comfort."

"For what?"

"I don't know. Things I can't control, maybe."

"You mean you don't have the comfort of an excuse, a metaphysical excuse. Sorry, Alex, we part company. We're accountable for what we do, and no confessional absolution can change that."

Conklin turned his head, his eyes wide open, and looked at Holland. "Thank you," he said.

"For what?"

"For sounding like me, even using a variation of the words I've used. . . . I came back from Hong Kong five years ago with the banner of Accountability on my lance."

"You've lost me."

"Forget it. I'm back on track. . . . 'Beware the pitfalls of ecclesiastical presumption and self-absorbed thought.' "

"Who the hell said that?"

"Either Savonarola or Salvador Dalí, I can't remember who."

"Oh, for Christ's sake, cut the crap!" laughed Holland.

"Why should I? It's the first chuckle we've had. And what about your two sisters? What happened to them?"

"It's a better joke," replied Peter, his head angled down into his chin, a mischievous smile on his lips. "One's a nun in New Delhi, and the other's president of her own public relations firm in New York and uses better Yiddish than most of her colleagues in the profession. A couple of years ago she told me they stopped calling her *shiksa*. She loves her life; so does my other sister in India."

"Yet you chose the military."

"Not *'yet,'* Alex. . . . *And* I chose it. I was an angry young man who really believed this country was being dumped on. I came from a privileged family—money, influence, an expensive prep school—that guaranteed me—*me,* not the black kid on the streets of Philadelphia or Harlem—automatic admittance to Annapolis. I simply figured I had to somehow earn that privilege. I had to show that people like me didn't just use our advantages to avoid, but instead to extend, our responsibilities."

"Aristocracy reborn," said Conklin. "Noblesse oblige—nobility imposes obligations."

"That's not fair," protested Holland.

"Yes, it is, in a very real sense. In Greek, *aristo* means the 'best,' and *kratia* is the word for 'rule.' In ancient Athens such young men led armies, their swords up front, not behind, if only to prove to the troops that they would sacrifice with the lowliest of them, for the lowliest were under their commands, the commands of the finest."

Peter Holland's head arched back into the top of the velvet seat, his eyes half closed. "Maybe that was part of it, I'm not sure—I'm not sure at all. We were asking so much . . . for what? Pork Chop Hill? Unidentifiable, useless terrain in the Mekong? Why? For Christ's sake, *why*? Men shot, their stomachs and chests blown away by an enemy two feet in front of them, by a 'Cong who knew jungles they didn't know? What kind of war was that? . . . If guys like me didn't go up with the kids and say, 'Look, here I am, I'm with you,' how the hell do you think we could have lasted as long as we did? There might have been mass revolts and maybe there should have been. Those kids were what some people call niggers, and spics and the foul-ups who couldn't read or write beyond a third-grade level. The privileged had deferments—deferments from getting soiled—or service that damn near guaranteed no combat. The others didn't. And if my being with them—this privileged son of a bitch—meant anything, it was the best gig I ever did in my life.'' Holland suddenly stopped talking and shut his eyes.

"I'm sorry, Peter. I didn't mean to rough up past roads, I really didn't. Actually, I started with my guilt, not yours. . . . It's crazy how it all dovetails and feeds upon itself, isn't it? What did you call it? The merry-go-round of guilt. Where does it stop?''

"Now," said Holland, sitting up in the seat, straightening his back and shoulders. He picked up the limousine telephone, punched two numbers and spoke. "Drop us off in Vienna, please. And when you've done that, go find a Chinese restaurant and bring us back the best they've got. . . . Frankly, I'm partial to spare ribs and lemon chicken.''

Holland proved to be half right. The first hearing of Panov's session under the serum was agonizing to listen to, the voice devastating, the emotional content blurring the information, especially for anyone who knew the psychiatrist. The second hearing, however, produced instantaneous concentration, engendered without question by the very pain they heard. There was no time to indulge in personal feelings; the information was suddenly everything. Both men began taking copious notes on legal pads, frequently stopping and replaying numerous sections for clarity and understanding. The third hearing refined the salient points further; by the end of the fourth, both Alex and Peter Holland had thirty to forty pages of notes apiece. They spent an additional hour in silence, each going over his own analysis.

"Are you ready?" asked the CIA's director from the couch, a pencil in his hand.

"Sure," said Conklin, seated at the desk with his various electronic equipment, the tape machine at his elbow.

"Any opening remarks?"

"Yes," replied Alex. "Ninety-nine point forty-four percent of what we listened to gives us nothing, except to tell us what a terrific prober this Walsh is. He hopscotched around picking up cues faster than I could find them, and I wasn't exactly an amateur when it came to interrogations."

"Agreed," said Holland. "I wasn't so bad either, especially with a blunt instrument. Walsh is good."

"Better than that, but that doesn't concern us. What he pulled out of Mo does—again with a 'but.' It's not in Panov's recapturing what he revealed because we have to assume he revealed almost everything I told him. Instead, it's in what he repeated having *heard.*" Conklin separated several pages. "Here's an example. 'The family will be pleased . . . our supreme will give us his blessing.' He's repeating someone else's words, not his own. Now, Mo isn't familiar with criminal jargon, certainly not to the point where he would automatically make a connection, but the connection's there. Take the word 'supreme' and change it by removing one vowel and inserting another. 'Supremo'—capo supremo, hardly a heavenly supreme being. Suddenly, 'the family' is light years away from Norman Rockwell, and 'blessing' is interchangeable with a reward or a bonus."

"Mafia," said Peter, his eyes steady and clear

despite a number of drinks that had obviously been burned out of his system. "I hadn't thought that one through, but I marked it instinctively. . . . Okay, here's something else along the same lines, the same lines because I also picked up on the unlike-Panov phrases." Holland flipped through his legal pad and stopped at a specific page. "Here. 'New York wants it all.' " Peter continued slapping over the pages. "Again here. 'That Wall Street is something.' " Once more the DCI progressed through his legal pad. "And this one. 'Blondie fruits'—the rest is garbled."

"I missed that. I heard it, but it didn't make any sense to me."

"Why should it, Mr. Aleksei Konsolikov?" Holland smiled. "Underneath that Anglo-Saxon exterior, education and all, beats the heart of a Russian. You're not sensitive to what some of us have to endure."

"Huh?"

"I'm a WASP, and 'blondie fruits' is but one more pejorative description given us by, I must admit, other trampled-upon minorities. Think about it. Armbruster, Swayne, Atkinson, Burton, Teagarten—'blondies' all. And Wall Street, certain firms in that originally WASP financial bastion, at any rate."

"Medusa," said Alex, nodding. "Medusa and the Mafia. . . . Holy Christ."

"We've got a *telephone* number!" Peter leaned forward on the couch. "It was in the ledger Bourne brought out of Swayne's house."

"I've tried it, remember? It's an answering machine, that's all it is."

"And that's enough. We can get a location."

"To what end? Whoever picks up the messages does it by remote, and if he or she has half a brain, it's done from a public phone. The relay is not only untraceable but capable of erasing all other messages, so we can't tap in."

"You're not very into high tech, are you, Field Man?"

"Let's put it this way," replied Conklin. "I bought one of those VCRs so I could watch old movies, and I can't figure out how to turn off the goddamn blinking clock. I called the dealer and he said, 'Read the instructions on the interior panel.' I can't find the interior panel."

"Then let me explain what we can do to an answering machine. . . . We can jam it externally."

"Gee willikers, Sandy, what's next for Orphan Annie? What the hell is that going to do? Other than kill the source."

"You're forgetting. We have the location from the numbers."

"Oh?"

"Someone has to come and repair the machine."

"Oh."

"We take him and find out who sent him there."

"You know, Peter, you've got possibilities. For a neophyte, you understand, your current outrageously undeserved position notwithstanding."

"Sorry I can't offer you a drink."

Bryce Ogilvie, of the law firm Ogilvie, Spofford, Crawford and Cohen, was dictating a highly complex reply to the Justice Department's anti-trust division when his very private telephone line rang; it rang only at his desk. He picked up the phone, pressed the green button and spoke rapidly. "Hold on," he ordered, looking up at his secretary. "Would you excuse me, please?"

"Certainly, sir." The secretary got out of her chair, walked across the large impressive office and disappeared beyond the door.

"Yes, what is it?" asked Ogilvie, returning to the phone.

"The machine isn't working," said the voice on the sacrosanct line.

"What happened?"

"I don't know. All I get is a busy signal."

"That's the best equipment available. Perhaps someone was calling in when *you* called."

"I've been trying for the past two hours. There's a glitch. Even the best machines break down."

"All right, send someone up to check it out. Use one of the niggers."

"Naturally. No white man would go up there."

25

It was shortly past midnight when Bourne got off the *métro* in Argenteuil. He had divided the day into segments, splitting the hours between the arrangements he had to make and looking for Marie, going from one arrondissement to an-other, scouting every café, every shop, every large and small hotel he could recall having been a part of their fugitive nightmare thirteen years ago. More than once he had gasped, see-ing a woman in the distance or across a café—the back of a head, a quick profile, and twice a crown of dark red hair, any of which from a dis-tance or in a café's dim light might have be-longed to his wife. None of these had turned out to be Marie, but he began to understand his own anxiety and, by understanding it, was better able to control it. These were the most impossible parts of the day; the rest was merely filled with difficulty and frustration.

Alex! Where the hell was *Conklin*? He could not reach him in Virginia! Because of the time difference, he had counted on Alex to take care of the details, swiftly expediting the transfer of funds, primarily. The business day on the eastern seaboard of the United States began at four o'clock, Paris time, and the business day in Paris stopped at five o'clock *or* before, *Paris* time. That left barely an hour to release and transfer over a million American dollars to one Mr. Simon at his chosen bank in Paris, and *that* meant said Mr. Simon had to make himself known to the aforementioned, as yet unchosen, Paris bank. Bernardine had been helpful. Helpful, *hell*! He had made it possible.

"There's a bank on the rue de Grenelle that the Deuxième frequently uses. They can be accommodating in terms of hours and the absence of an authentic signature or two, but they give nothing for nothing, and they trust no one, especially anyone associated with our benevolent socialist government."

"You mean regardless of the teletypes, if the money's not there you don't get it."

"Not a sou. The president, himself, could call and he would be told to pick it up in Moscow, where they firmly believe he belongs."

"Since I can't reach Alex, I've bypassed the bank in Boston and called our man in the Cayman Islands, where Marie put the bulk of the money. He's Canadian and so's the bank. He's waiting for instructions."

"I'll make a phone call. Are you at the Pont-Royal?"

"No. I'll call you back."

"Where are you?"

"I suppose you could say I'm an anxious and confused butterfly going from one vaguely remembered place to another."

"You are looking for her."

"Yes. But then that wasn't a question, was it?"

"Forgive me, but in some ways I hope you do not find her."

"Thanks. I'll call you back in twenty minutes."

He had gone to yet another point of recall, the Trocadéro, and the Palais de Chaillot. He had been shot at in the past on one of the terraces; there had been gunfire and men running down the endless stone steps, intermittently obscured by the huge gilded statues and the great sprays of the fountains, disappearing into the formal gardens, finally out of sight, out of range. What had happened? Why did he remember the Trocadéro? . . . But Marie had been there— *somewhere.* Where had she been in that enormous complex? Where? . . . A terrace! She had been on a *terrace.* Near a statue—*what* statue? . . . Descartes? Racine? Talleyrand? The statue of Descartes came to his mind first. He would find it.

He had found it and there was no Marie. He had looked at his watch; it had been nearly forty-five minutes since he had talked to Bernardine. Like the men in his inner screen, he had raced down the steps. To a telephone.

"Go to the Banque Normandie and ask for Monsieur Tabouri. He understands that a Monsieur Simon intends to transfer over seven million francs from the Caymans by way of voice authorization through his private banker in the islands. He is most happy to let you use his phone, but believe me, he'll charge you for the call."

"Thanks, François."

"Where are you now?"

"The Trocadéro. It's crazy. I have the damnedest feelings, like vibrations, but she's not there. It's probably the things I can't remember. Hell, I may have taken a bullet here, I simply don't know."

"Go to the bank."

He had done so, and within thirty-five minutes after his call to the Caymans, the olive-skinned, perpetually smiling Monsieur Tabouri confirmed that his funds were in place. He requested 750,-000 francs in the largest notes possible. They were delivered to him, and the grinning obsequious banker took him confidentially aside, away from the desk—which was rather foolish, as there was no one else in the office—and spoke quietly by a window.

"There are some marvelous real estate opportunities in Beirut, believe me, I *know*. I am the expert on the Middle East and these stupid conflagrations cannot last much longer. *Mon Dieu,* no one will be left alive! It will once again rise as the Paris of the Mediterranean. Estates for a fraction of their value, hotels for a ridiculous price!"

"It sounds interesting. I'll be in touch."

He had fled the Banque Normandie as if its confines held the germs of a lethal disease. He had returned to the Pont-Royal, and again tried to reach Alex Conklin in the United States. It was then close to one o'clock in the afternoon in Vienna, Virginia, and still all he had heard was an answering machine with Alex's disembodied voice instructing the caller to leave a message. For any number of reasons, Jason had chosen not to do so.

And now he was in Argenteuil, walking up the steps of the *métro* to the pavement, where he would slowly, cautiously make his way into the uglier streets and the vicinity of Le Coeur du Soldat. His instructions were clear. He was not to be the man he was last night, no limp, no ragged cast-off army clothing, no image that anyone might recognize. He was to be a simple laborer and reach the gates of the old closed-down refinery and smoke cigarettes while leaning against the wall. This was to take place between 12:30 and one o'clock in the morning. No sooner and no later.

When he had asked Santos's messengers—after giving them several hundred francs for their inconvenience—the reason these late-night precautions, the less inhibited man had replied, "Santos never leaves Le Coeur du Soldat."

"He left last evening."

"For minutes only," rejoined the more voluble messenger.

"I understand." Bourne nodded, but he had not understood, he could only speculate. Was Santos in some way the Jackal's prisoner, confined to the sleazy café night and day? It was a fascinating query in light of the manager's size and sheer raw power, both combined with a far-above-average intellect.

It was 12:37 when Jason, in blue jeans, cap and a dark, tattered V-necked sweater, reached the gates of the old factory. He took out a pack of Gauloise cigarettes and leaned against the wall, lighting one with a match, holding the flame longer than necessary before he blew it out. His thoughts returned to the enigmatic Santos, the premier conduit in Carlos's army, the most trusted satellite in the Jackal's orbit, a man whose French might have been formed at the Sorbonne, yet Santos was a Latin American. A Venezuelan, if Bourne's instincts had merit. *Fascinating.* And Santos wanted to see him 'with peace in his heart.' Bravo, *amigo,* thought Jason. Santos had reached a terrified ambassador in London with a question so loaded it made a political party's private poll look like the essence of nonpartisan neutrality. Atkinson had no choice but to state emphatically, if not in panic, that whatever instructions Snake Lady issued were to be carried out. The power of Snake Lady was the ambassador's only protection, his ultimate refuge.

So Santos could bend; that decision was rooted in intellect, not loyalty, not obligation. The conduit wanted to crawl out of his sewer, and with three million francs in the offing, combined with a multitude of faraway places across the globe to choose from, the conduit's mind told him to listen, to consider. There were alternatives in life if opportunities were presented. One had been presented to Santos, vassal to Carlos, whose fealty to his lord had perhaps run its suffocating course. It was this instinctive projection that made Bourne include in his plea—calmly but firmly, the emphasis in understatement—such phrases as *You could travel, disappear . . . a wealthy man, free of care and unpleasant drudgery.* The key words were "free" and "disappear," and Santos's eyes had responded. He was ready to take the three-million-franc bait, and Bourne was perfectly happy to let him break the line and swim with it.

Jason looked at his watch; fifteen minutes

had passed. No doubt Santos's minions were checking the streets, a final inspection before the high priest of conduits appeared. Bourne thought briefly of Marie, of the sensations he felt at the Trocadéro, remembering old Fontaine's words when the two of them watched the paths of Tranquility Inn from the high storage room, waiting for Carlos. *He's near, I feel it. Like the approach of distant thunder.* In a different—far different—way Jason had like feelings at the Trocadéro. *Enough!* Santos! The Jackal!

His watch read one o'clock, and the two messengers from the Pont-Royal walked out of the alley and across the street to the gates of the old refinery.

"Santos will see you now," said the voluble one.

"I don't see him."

"You are to come with us. He does not leave Le Coeur du Soldat."

"Why do I find that not to my liking?"

"There's no reason for such feelings. He has peace in his heart."

"What about his knife?"

"He has no knife, no weapon. He never carries either."

"That's nice to hear. Let's go."

"He has no need for such weapons," added the messenger, disquietingly.

He was escorted down the alley, past the neon-lit entrance, to a barely negotiable break in the buildings. One by one, Jason between the two men, they made their way to the rear of the café, where there was just about the last thing Bourne expected to see in this run-down section of the city. It was . . . well, an English garden. A plot of ground perhaps thirty feet in length, twenty in depth, and trellises supporting a variety of flowering vines, a barrage of color in the French moonlight.

"That's quite a sight," commented Jason. "It didn't come about through neglect."

"Ah, it is a passion with Santos! No one understands it, but no one touches a single flower, either."

Fascinating.

Bourne was led to a small outside elevator whose steel frame was attached to the stone wall of the building. There was no other access in sight. The conveyance barely held the three of them, and once the iron gate was closed, the silent messenger pressed a button in the darkness and spoke. "We are here, Santos. *Camellia.* Bring us up."

"Camellia?" asked Jason.

"He knows everything is all right. If not, my friend might have said 'lily' or 'rose.' "

"What would happen then?"

"You don't want to think about it. *I* don't care to think about it."

"Naturally. Of course."

The outside elevator stopped with a disturbing double jerk, and the quiet messenger opened a thick steel door that required his full weight to open. Bourne was led into the familiar room with the tasteful, expensive furniture, the bookcases and the single floor lamp that illuminated Santos in his outsized armchair.

"You may leave, my friends," said the large man, addressing the messengers. "Pick up your money from the faggot, and for God's sake, tell him to give René and the American who calls himself Ralph fifty francs apiece and get them out of here. They're pissing in the corners. . . . Say the money's from their friend from last night who forgot about them."

"Oh, *shit!*" exploded Jason.

"You did forget, didn't you?" Santos grinned.

"I've had other things on my mind."

"Yes, sir! Yes, Santos!" The two messengers, instead of heading for the back of the room and the elevator, opened a door in the left wall and disappeared. Bourne looked after them, bewildered.

"There is a staircase leading to our kitchen, such as it is," said Santos, answering Jason's unspoken question. "The door can be opened from this side, not from the steps below except by me. . . . Sit down, Monsieur Simon. You are my guest. How is your head?"

"The swelling's gone down, thank you." Bourne sat on the large couch, sinking into the pillows; it was not an authoritative position, nor was it not meant to be. "I understand you have peace in your heart."

"And a desire for three million francs in the avaricious section of that heart."

"Then you were satisfied with your call to London?"

"No one could have programmed that man into reacting the way he did. There *is* a Snake Lady and she instills extraordinary devotion and fear in high places—which means that female serpent is not without power."

"That's what I tried to tell you."

"Your word is accepted. Now, let me recapitulate your request, your demand, as it were—"

"My restrictions," interrupted Jason.

"Very well, your restrictions," agreed Santos. "You and you *alone* must reach the blackbird, correct?"

"It's an absolute."

"Again, I must ask why?"

"Speaking frankly, you already know too much, more than my clients realize, but then none of them was about to lose his own life on the second floor of a café in Argenteuil. They want nothing to do with you, they want no traces, and in that area you're vulnerable."

"How?" Santos crashed his fist against the arm of the chair.

"An old man in Paris with a police record who tried to warn a member of the Assembly that he was to be assassinated. *He* was the one who mentioned the blackbird; *he* was the one who spoke of Le Coeur du Soldat. Fortunately, *our* man heard him and silently passed the word to my clients, but that's not good enough. How many other old men in Paris in their senile delusions may mention Le Coeur du Soldat—and *you*? . . . No, you can have nothing to do with my clients."

"Even through *you*?"

"I disappear, you don't. Although, in all honesty, I believe you should think about doing so. . . . Here, I brought you something." Bourne sat forward on the couch and reached into his back pocket. He pulled out a roll of tightly wound franc notes held together by a thick elastic band. He threw it over to Santos, who caught it effortlessly in midair. "Two hundred thousand francs on account—I was authorized to give this to you. On a best-efforts basis. You give me the information I need, I deliver it to London, and whether or not the blackbird accepts my clients' offer, you still receive the balance of the three million."

"But you could disappear before then, couldn't you?"

"Have me watched as you've been doing, have me followed to London and back. I'll even call you with the names of the airlines and the flight numbers. What could be fairer?"

"One thing more could be fairer, Monsieur Simon," replied Santos, pushing his immense frame out of the chair and baronially striding to a card table against the lacquered brick wall of his flat. "If you will, please come over here."

Jason rose from the couch and walked over to the card table, instantly astonished. "You're thorough, aren't you?"

"I try to be. . . . Oh, don't blame the concierges, they belong to you. I'm much further below scale. Chambermaids and stewards are more to my liking. They're not so spoiled and nobody really misses them if they don't show up one day."

Spread across the table were Bourne's three passports, courtesy of Cactus in Washington, as well as the gun and the knife taken from him last night. "You're very convincing, but it doesn't solve anything, does it?"

"We'll see," answered Santos. "I'll accept your money now—for my best efforts—but instead of your flying to London, have London fly to Paris. Tomorrow morning. When he arrives at the Pont-Royal, you'll call me—I'll give you my private number, of course—and we'll play the Soviets' game. Exchange for exchange, like walking across a bridge with our respective prisoners in tow. The money for the information."

"You're crazy, Santos. My clients don't expose themselves that way. You just lost the rest of the three million."

"Why not try them? They could always hire a blind, couldn't they? An innocent tourist with a false bottom in his or her Louis Vuitton carryon? No alarms are set off with paper. *Try* it! It is the only way you'll get what you want, monsieur."

"I'll do what I can," said Bourne.

"Here is my telephone." Santos picked up a prearranged card from the table with numbers scrawled across it. "Call me when London arrives. In the meantime, I assure you, you *will* be watched."

"You're a real swell guy."

"I'll escort you to the elevator."

Marie sat up in bed, sipping hot tea in the dark room, listening to the sounds of Paris outside the windows. Not only was sleep impossible, but it was intolerable, a waste of time when every hour counted. She had taken the earliest flight from Marseilles to Paris and had gone directly to the Meurice on the rue de Rivoli, the same hotel where she had waited thirteen years ago, waited for a man to listen to reason or lose his life, and in doing so, losing a large part of hers. She had ordered a pot of tea then, and he had come back to her; she ordered tea now from the night floor steward, absently perhaps, as if the repeated ritual might bring about a repetition of his appearance so long ago.

Oh, God, she had *seen* him! It was no illusion, no mistake, it was *David*! She had left the hotel at midmorning and begun wandering, going down the list she had made on the plane, heading from one location to another without any logical sequence in mind, simply following the succession of places as they had come to her— that was her sequence. It was a lesson she had learned from Jason Bourne thirteen years ago: *When running or hunting, analyze your options but remember your first. It's usually the cleanest and the best. Most of the time you'll take it.*

So she had followed the list, from the pier of the Bateau Mouche at the base of the avenue George V to the bank on the Madeleine . . . to the Trocadéro. She had wandered aimlessly along the terraces of the last, as if in a trance, looking for a statue she could not remember, jostled by the intermittent groups of tourists led by loud, officious guides. The huge statues all began to look alike; she had felt light-headed. The late August sun was blinding. She was about to sit down on a marble bench, remembering yet another dictate from Jason Bourne: *Rest is a weapon.* Suddenly, up ahead, she saw a man wearing a cap and a dark V-necked sweater; he had turned and raced toward the palatial stone steps that led to the avenue Gustave V. She knew that run, that stride; she knew it better than *anyone*! How often had she watched him—frequently from behind bleachers, sight unseen—as he had pounded around the university track, ridding himself of the furies that had gripped him. It was *David*! She had leaped up from the bench and raced after him.

"*David!* David, it's me! . . . *Jason!*"

She had collided with a tour guide leading a group of Japanese. The man was incensed; she was furious, so she furiously pummeled her way through the astonished Orientals, the majority shorter than she was, but her superior sight lines were no help. Her husband had disappeared. Where had he *gone*? Into the gardens? Into the street with the crowds and the traffic from the Pont d'Iéna? For Christ's sake, *where*?

"*Jason!*" she had screamed at the top of her voice. "Jason, come *back*!"

People had looked at her, some with the empathetic glances of lovers burned, most simply disapproving. She had run down the never-ending steps to the street, spending—how long a time she could not recall—searching for him. Finally, in exhaustion, she had taken a taxi back to the Meurice. In a daze, she reached her room and fell on the bed, refusing to let the tears come. It was no time for tears. It was a time for a brief rest and food; energy to be restored, the lessons of Jason Bourne. Then back into the streets, the hunt to continue. And as she lay there, staring at the wall, she felt a swelling in her chest, in her lungs perhaps, and it was accompanied by a sense of passive elation. As she was looking for David, *he* was looking for *her*. Her husband had not run away, even Jason Bourne had not run away. Neither part of the same man could have seen her. There had been another unknown reason for the sudden, hurried exit from the Trocadéro, but there was only one reason for his being *at* the Trocadéro. He, too, was searching what memories he had of Paris thirteen years ago. He, too, understood that somewhere, someplace in those memories he would *find* her.

She had rested, ordered room service and two hours later gone out again into the streets.

Now, at the moment, as she drank her tea, she could not wait for the light to come. The day ahead was meant for searching.

"Bernardine!"

"*Mon Dieu,* it is four o'clock in the morning, so I can assume you have something vital to tell this seventy-year-old man."

"I've got a problem."

"I think you have many problems, but I suppose it's a minor distinction. What is it?"

"I'm as close as I can be but I need an end man."

"Please speak clearer English, or if you will, far clearer French. It must be an American term, this 'end man.' But then you have so many esoteric phrases. I'm sure someone sits in Langley and thinks them up."

"Come on, I haven't time for your *bon mots*."

"You come on, my friend. I'm not trying to be clever, I'm trying to wake up. . . . *There,* my feet are on the floor and a cigarette's in my mouth. *Now,* what is it?"

"My access to the Jackal expects an Englishman to fly over from London this morning with two million eight hundred thousand francs—"

"Far less than you have at your disposal, I assume," interrupted Bernardine. "The Banque Normandie was accommodating, was it not?"

"Very. The money's there, and that Tabouri of yours is a beaut. He tried to sell me real estate in Beirut."

"That Tabouri is a thief—but Beirut is interesting."

"Please."

"Sorry. Go ahead."

"I'm being watched, so I can't go to the bank, and I don't have any Englishman to bring what I can't get to the Pont-Royal."

"That's your problem?"

"Yes."

"Are you willing to part with, say, fifty thousand francs?"

"What for?"

"Tabouri."

"I suppose so."

"You signed papers, of course."

"Of course."

"Sign another paper, handwritten by you and also signed, releasing the money to— Wait a moment, I must go to my desk." There was silence on the line as Bernardine obviously went to another room in his flat; his voice returned. *"Allo?"*

"I'm here."

"Oh, this is lovely," intoned the former Deuxième specialist. "I sank him in his sailboat off the shoals of the Costa Brava. The sharks had a feeding frenzy; he was so fat and delectable. The name is Antonio Scarzi, a Sardinian who traded drugs for information, but you know nothing about that, of course."

"Of course." Bourne repeated the last name, spelling it out.

"Correct. Seal the envelope, rub a pencil or a pen over your thumb and press your prints along the seal. Then give it to the concierge for Mr. Scarzi."

"Understood. What about the Englishman? This morning? It's only a few hours away."

"The Englishman is not a problem. The morning is—the few hours are. It's a simple matter to transfer funds from one bank to another—buttons are pressed, computers instantly cross-check the data, and, poof, figures are entered on paper. It's quite another thing to collect nearly three million francs in cash, and your access certainly won't accept pounds or dollars for fear of being caught exchanging them or depositing them. Add to this the problem of collecting notes large enough to be part of a bundle small enough to be concealed from customs inspectors. . . . Your access, *mon ami,* has to be aware of these difficulties."

Jason looked aimlessly at the wall, his thoughts on Bernardine's words. "You think he's testing me?"

"He has to."

"The money could be gotten together from

the foreign departments of different banks. A small private plane could hop across the channel and land in a pasture where a car's waiting to bring the man to Paris."

"*Bien.* Of course. However, these logistics take time even for the most influential people. Don't make it all appear too simple, that would be suspect. Keep your access informed as to the progress being made, emphasizing the secrecy, how there can be no risk of exposure, explain the delays. If there were none, he might think it's a trap."

"I see what you mean. It comes down to what you just said—don't make it seem so easy because that's not credible."

"There's something else, *mon ami.* A chameleon may be many things in daylight; still, he is safer in darkness."

"You forgot something," said Bourne. "What about the Englishman?"

"Tallyho, old *chap,*" said Bernardine.

The operation went as smoothly as any Jason had ever engineered or been witness to, perhaps thanks to the flair of a resentful talented man who had been sent to the pastures too soon. While throughout the day Bourne made progress calls to Santos, Bernardine had some-

one other than himself pick up the sealed instructions from the concierge and bring them to
him, at which point he made his appointment
with Monsieur Tabouri. Shortly after four-thirty in
the afternoon, the Deuxième veteran walked
into the Pont-Royal dressed in a dark pin-striped
suit so obviously British that it screamed Savile
Row. He went to the elevator and eventually,
after two wrong turns, reached Bourne's room.

"Here's the money," he said, dropping the
attaché case on the floor and going straight to
Jason's hotel wet bar; he removed two miniature bottles of Tanqueray gin, snapped them
open and poured the liquor into a questionably
clean glass. *"A votre santé,"* he added, swallowing half his drink before breathing heavily
through his mouth and then rapidly swallowing
the rest. "I haven't done anything like that in
years."

"You haven't?"

"Frankly, no. I had others do such things. It's
far too dangerous. . . . Nevertheless, Tabouri is
forever in your debt, and, frankly, he's convinced me I should look into Beirut."

"What?"

"Of course, I haven't your resources, but a
percentage of forty years of *les fonds de contin-*

gence have found their way to Geneva on my behalf. I'm not a poor man."

"You may be a dead man if they pick you up leaving here."

"Oh, but I shan't go," said Bernardine, once again searching the small refrigerator. "I shall stay in this room until you have concluded your business." François ripped open two additional bottles and poured them into his glass. "Now, perhaps, my old heart will beat slower," he added as he walked to the inadequate desk, placed his drink on the blotter, and proceeded to take out two automatics and three grenades from his pockets, placing them all in a row in front of his glass. "Yes, I will relax now."

"What the hell is *that*—are *they*?" cried Jason.

"I think you Americans call it deterrence," replied Bernardine. "Although I frankly believe both you and the Soviets are playing with yourselves as you both put so much money into weaponry that doesn't work. Now, I come from a different era. When you go out to do your business, you will leave the door open. If someone comes down that narrow corridor, he will see a grenade in my hand. That is not nuclear abstraction, *that* is deterrence."

"I'll buy it," said Bourne, going to the door. "I want to get this over with."

Out on Montalembert, Jason walked to the corner, and as he had done at the old factory in Argenteuil, leaned against the wall and lit a cigarette. He waited, his posture casual, his mind in high gear.

A man walked across from the bisecting rue du Bac toward him. It was the talkative messenger from last night; he approached, his hand in his jacket pocket.

"Where's the money?" said the man in French.

"Where's the information?" answered Bourne.

"The money first."

"That's not the arrangement." Without warning, Jason grabbed the minion from Argenteuil by his lapel, yanking him forward off his feet. Bourne whipped up his free hand and gripped the messenger's throat, his fingers digging into the man's flesh. "You go back and tell Santos he's got a one-way ticket to hell. I don't *deal* this way."

"*Enough!*" said the low voice, its owner rounding the corner on Jason's right. The huge figure of Santos approached. "Let him go,

Simon. He is nothing. It is now only you and me."

"I thought you never left Le Coeur du Soldat?"

"You've changed that, haven't you?"

"Apparently." Bourne released the messenger, who looked at Santos. With a gesture of his large head, the man raced away.

"Your Englishman arrived," said Santos when they were alone. "He carried a valise, I saw for myself."

"He arrived carrying a valise," agreed Jason.

"So London capitulates, no? London is very anxious."

"The stakes are very high and that's all I'll say about it. The information, please."

"Let us first again define the procedure, shall we?"

"We've defined it several times. . . . You give me the information, my client tells me to act upon it; and if satisfactory contact is made, I bring you the remainder of the three million francs."

"You say 'satisfactory contact.' What will satisfy you? How will you know the contact is firm? How do *I* know that you will not claim it is unsatisfactory and steal my money when, indeed, you have made the connection your clients have paid for?"

"You're a suspicious fellow, aren't you?"

"Oh, *very* suspicious. Our world, Mr. Simon, is not peopled with saints, is it?"

"Perhaps more than you realize."

"That would astonish me. Please answer my questions."

"All right, I'll try. . . . How will I know the contact's firm? That's easy. I'll simply *know* because it's my business to know. It's what I'm paid for, and a man in my position does not make mistakes at this level and live to apologize. I've refined the process, done my research, and I'll ask two or three questions myself. Then I'll know—one way or another."

"That's an elusive reply."

"In our world, Mr. Santos, being elusive is hardly a negative, is it? . . . As to your concern that I would lie to you and take your money, let me assure you I don't cultivate enemies like you and the network your blackbird obviously controls any more than I would make enemies of my clients. That way is madness and a much shorter life."

"I admire your perspicacity as well as your caution," said the Jackal's intermediary.

"The bookcases didn't lie. You're a learned man."

"That's neither here nor there, but I have certain credentials. Appearances can be a liability as well as an asset. . . . What I am about to tell you, Mr. Simon, is known by only four men on the face of the earth, all of whom speak French fluently. How you wish to use that information is up to you. However, if you even hint at Argenteuil, I'll know it instantly and you will never leave the Pont-Royal alive."

"The contact can be made so quickly?"

"With a telephone number. But you will not place the call for at least an hour from the moment we part. If you do, again I will know it, and again I tell you you're a dead man."

"An hour. Agreed. . . . Only three other people have this number? Why not pick one you're not particularly fond of so I might peripherally allude to him—if it's necessary."

Santos permitted himself a small, flat smile. "Moscow," he said softly. "High up in Dzerzhinsky Square."

"The *KGB*?"

"The blackbird is building a cadre in Moscow, always Moscow, it's an obsession with him."

Ilich Ramirez Sanchez, thought Bourne.

Trained at Novgorod. Dismissed by the Komitet as a maniac. The Jackal!

"I'll bear it in mind—if it's called for. The number, please?"

Santos recited it twice along with the words Bourne was to say. He spoke slowly, obviously impressed that Bourne wrote nothing down. "Is it all clear?"

"Indelibly, no pencil or paper required. . . . If everything goes as I trust it will, how do you want me to get you the money?"

"Phone me; you've got my number. I will leave Argenteuil and come to you. And never return to Argenteuil."

"Good luck, Santos. Something tells me you deserve it."

"No one more so. I have drunk the hemlock far too many times."

"Socrates," said Jason.

"Not directly. Plato's dialogues, to be precise. *Au revoir.*"

Santos walked away, and Bourne, his chest pounding, headed back to the Pont-Royal, desperately suppressing his desire to run. *A running man is an object of curiosity, a target.* A lesson from the cantos of Jason Bourne.

"Bernardine!" he yelled, racing down the nar-

row, deserted hallway to his room, all too aware of the open door and the old man seated at the desk, a grenade in one hand, a gun in the other. "Put the hardware away, we've hit pay dirt!"

"Who's paying?" asked the Deuxième veteran as Jason closed the door.

"I am," answered Bourne. "If this works out the way I think it will, you can add to your account in Geneva."

"I do not do what I'm doing for that, my friend. It has never been a consideration."

"I know, but as long as we're passing out francs like we're printing them in the garage, why shouldn't you get a fair share?"

"I can't argue with that, either."

"An *hour,*" announced Jason. "Forty-three minutes now, to be exact."

"For what?"

"To find out if it's real, actually *real.*" Bourne fell on the bed, his arms behind his head on the pillow, his eyes alive. "Write this down, François." Jason recited the telephone number given him by Santos. "Buy, bribe, or threaten every high-level contact you've ever had in the Paris telephone service, but get me the location of that number."

"It's not such an expensive request—"

"Yes, it *is,*" countered Bourne. "He's got it guarded, inviolate; he wouldn't do it any other way. Only four people in his entire network have it."

"Then, perhaps, we do not go high-level, but, instead, far lower to the ground, underground actually. Into the tunnels of the telephone service beneath the streets."

Jason snapped his head over at Bernardine. "I hadn't thought of that."

"Why should you? You are not Deuxième. The technicians are the source, not the bureaucrats behind the desks. . . . I know several. I will find one and give him a quiet call at home later tonight—"

"Tonight?" broke in Bourne, raising himself off the bed.

"It will cost a thousand francs or so, but you'll get the location of the telephone."

"I can't wait until later tonight."

"Then you add a risk by trying to reach such a man at work. These men are monitored; no one trusts anyone in the telephone service. It's the Socialists' paradox: Give its laboring forces responsibility but no individual authority."

"*Hold* it!" said Jason from the bed. "You have the home phone numbers, right?"

"They're in the book, yes. These people don't keep private listings."

"Have someone's wife call. An emergency. Someone's got to get home."

Bernardine nodded his head. "Not bad, my friend. Not bad at all."

The minutes turned into quarter hours as the retired Deuxième officer went to work, unctuously, with promises of reward for the wives of telephone technicians, if they would do what he asked them to do. Two hung up on him, three turned him down with epithets born of the suspicious Paris curbsides; but the sixth, amid obscenities, declared, "Why not?" As long as the rodent she had married understood that the money was hers.

The hour was over, and Jason left the hotel, walking slowly, deliberately, down the pavement, crossing four streets until he saw a public phone on the Quai Voltaire by the Seine. A blanket of darkness was slowly floating down over Paris, the boats on the river and the bridges dotted with lights. As he approached the red kiosk he breathed steadily, inhaling deeply, exercising a control over himself that he never thought possible. He was about to place the most important phone call of his life, but he could not let the Jackal know that, if, indeed, it was the Jackal. He went inside, inserted the coin and dialed.

"Yes?" It was a woman's voice, the French *oui* sharp and harsh. A Parisienne.

"Blackbirds circle in the sky," said Bourne, repeating Santos's words in French. "They make a great deal of noise, all but one. He is silent."

"Where do you call from?"

"Here in Paris, but I am not from Paris."

"From where, then?"

"Where the winters are far colder," answered Jason, feeling the moisture on his hairline. Control. *Control!* "It is urgent that I reach a blackbird."

The line was suddenly filled with silence, a sonic void, and Bourne stopped breathing. Then came the voice, low, steady, and as hollow as the previous silence. "We speak to a Muscovite?"

The *Jackal!* It *was* the Jackal! The smooth, swift French could not hide the Latino trace. "I did not say that," answered Bourne; his own French dialect was one he employed frequently, with the guttural tinge of Gascony. "I merely said the winters were colder than Paris."

"Who is this?"

"Someone who is considered by someone who knows you sufficiently impressive to be given this number along with the proper words to go with it. I can offer you the contract of your career, of your *life.* The fee is immaterial—name your own—but those who pay are among the most powerful men in the United States. They control much of American industry, as well as that country's financial institutions, and have direct access to the nerve centers of the government."

"This is also a very strange call. Very unorthodox."

"If you're not interested, I'll forget this number and go elsewhere. I'm merely the broker. A simple yes or no will suffice."

"I do not commit to things I know nothing about, to people I never heard of."

"You'd recognize their positions, if I were at liberty to reveal them, believe that. However, I'm not seeking a commitment, only your interest at this point. If the answer is yes, I can reveal more. If it's no, well, I tried, but am forced to go elsewhere. The newspapers say he was in Brussels only yesterday. I'll find him." There was a short, sharp intake of breath at the mention of Brussels and the unspoken Jason Bourne. "Yes or no, blackbird?"

Silence. Finally the Jackal spoke. "Call me back in two hours," he ordered, hanging up the phone.

It was *done*! Jason leaned against the pay phone, the sweat pouring down his face and breaking out on his neck. The Pont-Royal. He had to get back to Bernardine!

"It was Carlos!" he announced, closing the door and crossing directly to the bedside phone while taking Santos's card out of his pocket. He dialed; in seconds, he spoke. "The bird's confirmed," he said. "Give me a name, any name." The pause was brief. "I've got it. The merchandise will be left with the concierge. It'll be locked and taped; count it and send my passports back to me. Have your best boy pick everything up and call off the dogs. They could lead a blackbird to you." Jason hung up and turned to Bernardine.

"The telephone number is in the fifteenth arrondissement," said the Deuxième veteran. "Our man knew that, or at least assumed it when I gave it to him."

"What's he going to do?"

"Go back into the tunnels and refine things further."

"Will he call us here?"

"Fortunately, he drives a motorbike. He said he would be back at work in ten minutes or so and reach us by this room number within the hour."

"Perfect!"

"Not entirely. He wants five thousand francs."

"He could have asked ten times that. . . . What's 'within the hour'? How long before he calls?"

"You were gone perhaps thirty, thirty-five minutes, and he reached me shortly after you left. I'd say within the next half hour."

The telephone rang. Twenty seconds later they had an address on the boulevard Lefebvre.

"I'm leaving," said Jason Bourne, taking Bernardine's automatic off the desk and putting two grenades in his pocket. "Do you mind?"

"Be my guest," replied the Deuxième, reaching under his jacket and removing a second weapon from his belt. "Pickpockets so abound in Paris one should always carry a backup. . . . But what for?"

"I've got at least a couple of hours and I want to look around."

"Alone?"

"How else? If we call for support, I risk being

gunned down or spending the rest of my life in jail for an assassination in Belgium I had nothing to do with."

Former judge of the first circuit court in Boston, the once Honorable Brendan Patrick Prefontaine, watched the weeping, disconsolate Randolph Gates as he sat forward on the couch at the Ritz-Carlton hotel, his face in his widespread hands.

"Oh, good Christ, how the mighty fall with such a thud of finality," observed Brendan, pouring himself a short bourbon on the rocks. "So you got snookered, Randy. French style. Your facile brain and your imperial presence didn't help you very much when you saw *Paree,* huh? You should have stayed 'down on the farm,' soldier boy."

"My *God,* Prefontaine, you don't know what it was *like*! I was setting up a cartel—Paris, Bonn, London and New York with the Far East labor markets—an enterprise worth billions when I was taken from the Plaza-Athénée and put in a car and *blindfolded.* Then I was thrown into a plane and flown to Marseilles, where the most horrible things happened to me. I was kept in a room, and every few hours I was injected—for over six weeks! Women were brought in, films taken—I wasn't *myself*!"

"Maybe you were the self you never recognized, Dandy Boy. The same self that learned to anticipate instant gratification, if I use the phrase correctly. Make your clients extraordinary profits on paper, which they trade on the exchanges while thousands of jobs are lost in buy-outs. Oh, yes, my dear royalist, that's instant gratification."

"You're *wrong*, Judge—"

"So lovely to hear that term again. Thank you, Randy."

"The unions became too strong. Industry was being crippled. Many companies had to go overseas to survive!"

"And not talk? Oddly enough, you may have a point, but you never considered an alternative. . . . Regardless, we stray. You emerged from your confinement in Marseilles an addict—and, of course, there were the films of the eminent attorney in compromising situations."

"What could I *do*?" screamed Gates. "I was ruined!"

"We know what you did. You became this Jackal's confidence man in the world of high

finance, a world where competition is undesir-
able baggage better lost along the way."

"It's how he found me to begin with. The cartel we were forming was opposed by Japanese
and Taiwanese interests. They hired him. . . .
Oh, my God, he'll *kill* me!"

"Again?" asked the judge.

"What?"

"You forget. He thinks you're already dead—
thanks to me."

"I have cases coming up, a congressional
hearing next week. He'll know I'm alive!"

"Not if you don't show up."

"I *have* to! My clients expect—"

"Then I agree," interrupted Prefontaine.
"He'll kill you. Sorry about that, Randy."

"What am I going to *do*?"

"There's a way, Dandy Boy, not only out of
your current dilemma but for years to come. Of
course, it will require some sacrifice on your
part. For starters, a long convalescence at a
private rehabilitation center, but even before
that, your complete cooperation right now. The
first ensures your imminent disappearance, the
second—the capture and elimination of Carlos
the Jackal. You'll be free, Randy."

"Anything!"

"How do you reach him?"

"I have a telephone number!" Gates fumbled for his wallet, yanking it out of his pocket and with trembling fingers digging into a recess. "Only four people alive have it!"

Prefontaine accepted his first $20,000-an-hour fee, instructed Randy to go home, beg Edith's forgiveness, and be prepared to leave Boston tomorrow. Brendan had heard of a private treatment center in Minneapolis, he thought, where the rich sought help incognito; he would refine the details in the morning and call him, naturally expecting a second payment for his services. The instant a shaken Gates left the room, Prefontaine went to the phone and called John St. Jacques at Tranquility Inn.

"John, it's the judge. Don't ask me questions, but I have urgent information that could be invaluable to your sister's husband. I realize I can't reach him, but I know he's dealing with someone in Washington—"

"His name is Alex Conklin," interrupted St. Jacques. "Wait a minute, Judge, Marie wrote the number down on the desk blotter. Let me get over there." The sound of one phone being placed on a hard surface preceded the clicks of another being picked up. "Here it is." Marie's brother recited the number.

"I'll explain everything later. Thank you, John."

"An awful lot of people keep telling me that, goddamn it!" said St. Jacques.

Prefontaine dialed the number with a Virginia area code. It was answered with a short, brusque "Yes?"

"Mr. Conklin, my name is Prefontaine and I was given this number by John St. Jacques. What I have to tell you is in the nature of an emergency."

"You're the judge," broke in Alex.

"Past tense, I'm afraid. Very past."

"What is it?"

"I know how to reach the man you call the Jackal."

"What?"

"Listen to me."

Bernardine stared at the ringing telephone, briefly debating with himself whether or not to pick it up. There was no question; he had to. "Yes?"

"Jason? It's you, isn't it? . . . Perhaps I have the wrong room."

"*Alex?* This is you?"

"François? What are *you* doing there? Where's Jason?"

"Things have happened so fast. I know he's been trying to reach you."

"It's been a rough day. We've got Panov back."

"That's good news."

"I've got other news. A telephone number where the Jackal can be reached."

"We've *got* it! And a location. Our man left an hour ago."

"For Christ's sake, how did you *get* it?"

"A convoluted process I sincerely believe only your man could have negotiated. He's brilliantly imaginative, a true *caméléon.*"

"Let's compare," said Conklin. "What's yours?"

Bernardine complied, reciting the number he had written down on Bourne's instructions.

The silence on the phone was a silent scream. "They're different," said Alex finally, his voice choked. "They're *different!*"

"A trap," said the Deuxième veteran. "God in heaven, it's a *trap!*"

26

Twice Bourne had passed the dark, quiet row of old stone houses on the boulevard Lefebvre in the concrete backwater of the fifteenth arrondissement. He then doubled back to the rue d'Alésia and found a sidewalk café. The outdoor tables, their candles flickering under glass, were peopled mostly by gesturing, argumentative students from the nearby Sorbonne and Montparnasse. It was nearing ten o'clock and the aproned waiters were growing irritable; the majority of customers were not full of largess, either in their hearts or in their pockets. Jason wanted only a strong espresso, but the perpetual scowl on the face of the approaching *garçon* convinced him he would get mud if he ordered only the coffee, so he added the most expensive brandy he could recall by name.

As the waiter returned to the service bar, Jason pulled out his small notebook and ball-point pen, shutting his eyes for a moment, then opening them and sketching out everything he could envision from the row of houses on his inner screen. There were three structures of two attached houses each, separated by two narrow alleyways. Each double complex was three stories high, each front entrance reached by climbing a steep flight of brick steps, and at either end of the row were vacant lots covered with rubble, the remains of demolished adjacent buildings. The address of the Jackal's buried telephone number—the address was available in the underground tunnels solely for repair purposes—was the final structure on the right, and it took no imagination to know he occupied the entire building, if not the entire row.

Carlos was the consummate self-protector, so one had to assume that his Paris command post would be a fortress, employing every human and electronic security device that loyalty and high technology could provide. And the seemingly isolated, all but deserted, section of the outlying fifteenth arrondissement served his purposes far better than any crowded section of the city. For that reason, Bourne had first paid a drunken tramp to walk with him during his initial foray past the houses, he himself limping unsteadily in the shadows beside his companion; and for his second appraisal, he had hired a middle-aged whore as his cover, with no limp or stagger in his gait. He knew the terrain now, for all the good it did him, but it was the beginning of the end. He *swore* himself to that!

The waiter arrived with his espresso and the cognac, and only when Jason placed a hundred-franc note on the table, accompanied by a wave of his hand, did the man's hostile countenance move to neutral ground. *"Merci,"* he mumbled.

"Is there a pay phone nearby?" asked Bourne, removing an additional ten-franc note.

"Down the street, fifty, sixty meters," replied the waiter, his eyes on the new money.

"Nothing closer?" Jason peeled off another note, twenty francs. "I'm calling right here within a few blocks."

"Come with me," said the aproned *garçon,* gingerly picking up the franc notes and leading Bourne through the open doors of the café to a cashier seated on high at the far end of the restaurant. The gaunt, sallow-faced woman looked annoyed; obviously she assumed that Bourne was a discontented customer.

"Let him use your telephone," said the waiter.

"Why?" spat out the harridan. "So he can call *China*?"

"He calls up the street. He will pay."

Jason proffered a ten-franc note, his innocent eyes looking blankly at the highly suspicious woman. *"Augh,* take it," she said, removing a phone from under her cash-register stand and grasping the money. "It has an extension so you can move to the wall, as they all do. *Men!* Business and the bed, it's all you think about!"

He dialed the Pont-Royal and asked for his room, expecting Bernardine to pick up on the first or second ring. By the fourth, he was concerned; by the eighth, he was profoundly disturbed. Bernardine was not there! Had *Santos* . . . ? No, the Deuxième veteran was armed and knew how to use his "deterrence"—there would have been at the least loud gunfire, at the last a room blown apart by a grenade. Bernardine had left under his own control. *Why?*

There could be any one of several reasons, thought Bourne, handing back the telephone and returning to his table outside. The first and most wished for was news of Marie; the old intelligence officer would not raise false hopes by detailing the nets he had spread throughout the city, but they were there, Jason was sure of it. . . . Bourne could not think of another reason, so it was best not to think about Bernardine. He had other pressing considerations, the most intensely pressing of his life. He returned to the strong coffee and his notebook; every detail had to be exact.

An hour later he finished his espresso, taking a sip of the cognac and spilling the rest on the pavement under the usual soiled red tablecloth. He left the café and the rue d'Alésia, turning right and walking slowly, as a far older man might walk, toward the boulevard Lefebvre. The closer he came to the last corner, the more he became aware of the undulating, erratic sounds from apparently different directions. *Sirens!* The two-note sirens of the Paris police! What had happened? What was *happening*? Jason abandoned his elderly gait and ran to the edge of the building fronting the Lefebvre and the row of old stone houses. Instantly, he was in shock, fury and astonishment joining together in panic. What were they *doing*?

Five patrol cars converged on the row of stone houses, each successively screeching to a halt in front of the structure on the right. Then a large black police van appeared, swinging directly around to face the two entrances of the building, its searchlight shooting out as a squad of black-uniformed men with automatic weapons leaped into the street and took up crouching attack positions only partially concealed by the patrol cars—an assault was in the making!

Fools. Goddamned *fools!* To give Carlos a warning was to lose the Jackal! Killing was his profession; escape, his *obsession.* Thirteen years ago Bourne had been told that Carlos's huge retreat in the village hills of Vitry-sur-Seine outside Paris had more false walls and concealed staircases than a nobleman's Loire château in the time of Louis XIV. The fact that no one had ever determined which estate it was, or whom it was assigned to, did not vitiate the all too acceptable rumors. And with three supposedly separated structures on the boulevard Lefebvre, it was also all too acceptable to presuppose hidden underground tunnels linking each to the others.

For Christ's sake, who had *done* this? Had a terrible error been made? Had he and Bernardine been so obtuse as to think the Deuxième *or* Peter Holland's Paris station of the CIA had overlooked tapping into his Pont-Royal telephone or bribed or enlisted the various relays of operators on the hotel's switchboard? If so, that obtuseness was rooted in an absolute: it was next to impossible to tap a phone on short notice in a relatively small hotel without being detected. Technology required a stranger on the premises, and bribe money spread around was countered with larger bribes by the subject under surveillance. *Santos?* Bugs placed in the room by a chambermaid or a bellman? Not likely. The huge conduit to the Jackal, especially if he had reneged on their contract, would not *expose* the Jackal. *Who? How?* The questions burned into Jason's imagination as he watched in horror and dismay the scene taking place on the boulevard Lefebvre.

"On police authority, all residents will evacuate the building." The orders over the loudspeaker metallically echoed throughout the street. *"You have one minute before we take aggressive procedures."*

What aggressive *procedures*? screamed Bourne into the silent void of his mind. You've *lost* him. *I've* lost him. Insanity! *Who? Why?*

The door at the top of the brick steps on the left side of the building opened first. A petrified man, short, obese, in an undershirt, his trousers held up by suspenders, cautiously walked out into the flood of the searchlight, spreading his hands in front of his face and turning his head away from the blinding beam. "What is it, messieurs?" he cried, his voice tremulous. "I am merely a baker—a *good* baker—but I know nothing about this street except that the rent is cheap! Is that a crime to the *police*?"

"Our concerns are not with you, monsieur," continued the amplified voice.

"Not with *me*, you say? You arrive here like an army, frightening my wife and children into thinking it is their last minutes on earth, and yet you say we don't *concern* you? What kind of reasoning is that? We live among *fascists*?"

Hurry up! thought Jason. *For God's sake, hurry! Every second is a minute in escape time, an hour for the Jackal!*

The door above the flight of brick steps on the right now opened, and a nun in the full flowing black robe of a religious habit appeared. She stood defiantly in the frame, no fear whatsoever in her almost operatic voice. "How *dare* you?" she roared. "These are the hours of vespers and you intrude. Better you should be asking forgiveness for your sins than interrupting those who plead with *God* for theirs!''

''Nicely said, Sister,'' intoned the unimpressed police officer over the loudspeaker. ''But we have other information and we respectfully insist on searching your house. If you refuse, we shall disrespectfully carry out our orders.''

''We are the Magdalen Sisters of Charity!'' exclaimed the nun. ''These are the sacrosanct quarters of women devoted to Christ!''

''We respect your position, Sister, but we are still coming inside. If what you say is so, I'm sure the authorities will make a generous contribution to your cause.''

You're wasting time! screamed Bourne to himself. *He's getting away!*

''Then may your souls be damned for transgression, but come ahead and invade this holy ground!''

''*Really,* Sister?'' asked another official over the loudspeaker. ''I don't believe there's anything in the canons that gives you the right to condemn souls to hell on such a flimsy excuse. . . . Go ahead, Monsieur Inspector. Under the habit, you may find lingerie more suited to the Faubourg.''

He knew that voice! It was Bernardine! What

had happened? Was Bernardine no friend after all? Was it all an act, the smooth talk of a traitor? If so, there would be another death that night!

The black-uniformed squad of antiterrorists, their automatic weapons bolted into firing modes, raced to the base of the brick steps as the gendarmes blocked off the boulevard Lefebvre, north and south, while the red and blue lights of the patrol cars incessantly blinked their bright warnings to all beyond the area: *Stay away.*

"May I go *inside*?" screamed the baker. No one replied, so the obese man ran through his door clutching his trousers.

An official in civilian clothes, the obvious leader of the assault, joined his invading unit on the pavement below the steps. With a nod of his head, he and his men raced up the brick staircase through the door held open by the defiant nun.

Jason held his place at the edge of the building, his body pressed against the stone, the sweat pouring from his hairline and his neck, his eyes on the incomprehensible scene being played out on the Lefebvre. He knew the *who* now, but *why*? Was it true? Was the man most trusted by Alex Conklin and himself in reality another pair of eyes and ears for the Jackal? *Christ,* he did not want to *believe* it!

Twelve minutes passed, and with the reemergence of Paris's version of a SWAT team and its leader, several members bowing and kissing the hand of the real or would-be abbess, Bourne understood that his and Conklin's instincts had been on true course.

"Bernardine!" screamed the official approaching the first patrol car. "You are finished! *Out!* Never are you to talk to the lowest recruit in the Deuxième, even the man who cleans the *toilets*! You are *ostracized*! . . . If I had my way, you'd be *shot*! . . . International murder in the boulevard Lefebvre! A friend of the *Bureau*! An agent we must *protect*! . . . A fucking *nunnery,* you miserable son of a bitch! *Shit! A nunnery!* . . . Get out of my *car,* you smelly pig. Get *out* before a weapon goes off by mistake and your stomach's on the street, where it belongs!"

Bernardine lurched out of the patrol car, his old unsteady legs barely able to maintain balance, twice falling into the street. Jason waited, wanting to rush to his friend, but knowing he had to wait. The patrol cars and the van raced away; *still* Bourne had to wait, his eyes alternately watching Bernardine and the front entrance of the Jackal's house. And it *was* the Jackal's house, the nun proved it. Carlos could never let go of his lost faith; he consistently used it as a viable cover, but it was much more than that. Much more.

Bernardine staggered into the shadows of a long-abandoned storefront across from the house on the boulevard Lefebvre. Jason breached the corner and ran down the pavement, racing into the recess and grabbing the Deuxième veteran as he leaned against a long glass window, breathing heavily.

"For God's sake, what *happened*?" cried Bourne, supporting Bernardine by both shoulders.

"Easy, *mon ami*," choked Bernardine. "The pig I sat next to—a politician, no doubt, looking for an issue—punched me in the chest before he threw me out of the car. . . . I told you, I don't know all the new people who attach themselves to the Bureau these days. You have the same problems in America, so, please, do not give me a lecture."

"It's the last thing I'm about to do. . . . This is the *house,* Bernardine. Right *here,* right in front of us!"

"This is also a trap."

"What?"

"Alex and I confirmed it. The telephone numbers were different. I gather you did not make
your call to Carlos, as he instructed you to."

"No. I had the address and I wanted him
stretched. What's the difference? This is the
house!"

"Oh, this is where your Mr. *Simon* was to go,
and if he was truly *Mr. Simon,* he would be taken
to another rendezvous. But if he was *not* Monsieur Simon but someone else, then he would
be shot—proof—another corpse in search of
the Jackal."

"You're *wrong*!" insisted Jason, shaking his
head and speaking quietly, rapidly. "This may be
a detour, but Carlos is still on the switch. He's
not going to allow anyone to waste me but himself. That's his commandment."

"As yours is regarding him?"

"Yes. I have a family; he has a borderline
legend. Mine is complete for me, but his is a
vacuum—without any real meaning for him any
longer. He's gone as far as he can go. The only
way he can go further is to move into my territory—David Webb's territory—and eliminate
Jason Bourne."

"*Webb?* David *Webb*? Who in the name of
almighty God is *that*?"

"Me," replied Bourne, smiling forlornly and

leaning beside Bernardine against the window. "It's nuts, isn't it?"

"Nuts!" cried the former Deuxième. "It is *fou! Insane,* not to be *believed!"*

"Believe it."

"You are a family man with children and you *do* this work?"

"Alex never told you?"

"If he did so, I passed it off as a cover—one goes along with anything." Shaking his head, the older man looked up at his taller companion. "You *really* have a family whom you do not wish to escape from?"

"On the contrary, I want to get back to them as soon as I can. They're the only people on earth I really care about."

"But you are *Jason Bourne,* the killer Chameleon! The deepest recesses of the criminal world tremble at your name!"

"Oh, come on, that's a bit much, even from you."

"Not for an instant! You are *Bourne,* second only to the Jackal—"

"No!" shouted the suddenly forgotten David Webb. "He's no *match* for me! I'll *take* him! I'll *kill* him!"

"Very well, very well, *mon ami,"* said Bernardine calmly, reassuringly, staring at the man he could not understand. "What do you want me to do?"

Jason Bourne turned and breathed heavily against the glass window for several moments—and then through the mists of indecision the Chameleon's strategy became clear. He swung around and looked across the dark street at the stone building on the right. "The police are gone," he said quietly.

"Of course, I realize that."

"Did you also realize that no one from the other two buildings came outside? Yet there are lights on in a number of the windows."

"I was preoccupied, what can I say? I did not notice." Bernardine raised his eyebrows in sudden recollection. "But there were faces at the windows, several faces, I saw them."

"Yet no one came outside."

"Very understandable. The police . . . men with weapons racing around. Best to barricade oneself, no?"

"Even after the police and the weapons and the patrol cars have left? They all just go back to their television sets as if nothing had happened? No one comes out to check with the neighbors? That's not natural, François; it's not

even unnaturally natural. It's been orches-
trated."

"What do you mean? How?"

"One man walks out on the porch and shouts
into a searchlight. Attention is drawn to him and
precious seconds of a minute's warning evapo-
rate. Then a nun emerges on the other side
draping herself in holy indignation—more seconds lost, more hours for Carlos. The assault's
mounted and the Deuxième comes up with zero.
. . . And when it's all over, everything's back to
normal—an abnormal normalcy. A job was done
according to a predesigned plan, so there's no
call for really normal curiosity—no gathering in
the street, no excitement, not even a collective
postcrisis indignation. Simply people inside undoubtedly checking with one another. Doesn't it
all tell you something?"

Bernardine nodded. "A prearranged strategy
carried out by professionals," said the veteran
field officer.

"That's what I think, too."

"It's what you saw and I did not," countered
Bernardine. "Stop being kind, Jason. I've been
too long away from the cold. Too soft, too old,
too unimaginative."

"So have I," said Bourne. "It's just that the

stakes are so high for me that I have to force myself into thinking like a man I wanted to forget."

"This is Monsieur Webb speaking?"

"I guess it is."

"So where does that leave us?"

"With an irate baker and an angry nun, and if they prove to be ciphers, several faces in various windows. At this juncture the pickings are ours but that won't last long, I doubt through the morning."

"I beg your pardon?"

"Carlos will close up shop here and he'll do it quickly. He hasn't got a choice now. Someone in his Praetorian guard gave someone else the location of his Paris headquarters, and you can bet your pension—if you've still got one—that he's climbing the walls trying to figure out who betrayed him—"

"Get *back*!" cried Bernardine, interrupting and grabbing Jason by the cloth of his black jacket, yanking him into the farthest recess of the dark storefront. "Get out of sight! Flat on the pavement!"

Both men threw themselves down, lying prone on the broken concrete, Bourne's face against the short wall below the glass, his head angled to see the street. A second dark van appeared from the right, but it was not police equipment. Instead, it was shinier and smaller, somehow thicker, lower to the ground and more powerful. The one glaring, blinding similarity it had to the police van was the searchlight. . . . No, not one, but *two* searchlights, one on either side of the windshield, both beams swinging back and forth scanning the vehicle's flanks. Jason reached for the weapon in his belt—the gun he had borrowed from Bernardine—knowing that his companion already had his backup automatic out of his pocket. The beam of the left searchlight shot over their bodies as Bourne whispered; "Good work, but how did you spot it?"

"The moving reflections of the lamps on the side windows," replied old François. "I thought for a moment it was my former colleague returning to finish the job he had contemplated. Namely, my stomach in the street. . . . My God, *look!*"

The van swept past the first two buildings, then suddenly swerved into the curb and stopped in front of the last structure, nearly two hundred feet from the storefront, the building farthest from the Jackal's telephone. The instant the vehicle came to a halt the rear door opened and four men jumped out, automatic weapons in their hands, two running to the street side, one racing down the pavement to the front, the last guard standing menacingly by the open doors, his MAC-10 ready to fire. A dull wash of yellow light appeared at the top of the brick steps; the door had been opened and a man in a black raincoat came outside. He stood for a moment looking up and down the boulevard Lefebvre.

"Is that *him*?" whispered François.

"No, not unless he's wearing high heels and a wig," answered Jason, reaching into his jacket pocket. "I'll know him when I see him—because I *see* him every day of my life!" Bourne took out one of the grenades he had also borrowed from Bernardine. He checked the release, laying down his gun and gripping the pockmarked steel oval, tugging at the pin to make certain it was free of corrosion.

"What the hell do you think you're *doing*?" asked the old Deuxième veteran.

"That man up there is a decoy," replied Jason, his soft voice suspended in a cold monotone. "In moments another will take his place, run down the steps and get into the van, either

in the front seat or through the rear doors—I
hope the latter, but it won't make much difference."

"You're *mad*! You'll be killed! What good is a
corpse to that family of yours?"

"You're not thinking, François. The guards
will run back and climb up through the rear
doors because there's no room in front. There's
a lot of difference between climbing into a truck
and jumping out of it. For starters, it's a slower
sequence. . . . By the time the last man gets in
and reaches out to close those wide doors, I'll
have a primed grenade inside that van. . . . And
I have no intention of becoming a corpse. Stay
here!"

Before Bernardine could object further,
Medusa's Delta crawled out into the dark boulevard, dark but for the harsh stationary beams of
the searchlights, which were now angled on the
flanks, thus actually enhancing Bourne's concealment. The hot white light around the vehicle
obscured the darkness beyond; his only extreme risk was the guard posted by the open
doors. Hugging the shadows of the successive
storefronts as though he were threading his way
through the high grass of the Mekong Delta toward a floodlit prisoner compound, Jason crept

slowly forward with each wayward glance of the rear guard, his eyes darting continuously up to the man by the door above the brick steps.

Suddenly another figure emerged; it was a woman carrying a small suitcase in one hand, a large purse in the other. She spoke to the man in the black raincoat as the guard's attention was drawn to both of them. Bourne scrambled, his elbows and knees silently pounding the hard pavement, until he reached that point nearest the van where he could observe the scene on the staircase with minimum risk of being spotted. He was relieved to see that the two guards in the street continuously winced and blinked under the beam of the searchlight. His status was as clean as it could be under the tenuous circumstances. Everything now was timing, precision, and all the expertise he could summon from times too often unremembered or too vague or too long ago. He had to remember now; instinct had to propel him through his personal mists. *Now.* The end of the nightmare was at hand.

It was happening! Suddenly there was furious activity at the door as a third figure came rushing out, joining the other two. The man was shorter than his male colleague, wearing a beret and carrying a briefcase. He obviously issued orders that included the rear guard, who ran up to the pavement as the new arrival hurled his briefcase down over the brick steps. The guard instantly clutched his weapon under his left arm and effortlessly caught the leather missile in midair.

"*Allez-vous-en. Nous partons! Vite!*" shouted the second man, gesturing for the other two on the brick steps to precede him down to the van. They did so, the man in the raincoat joining the guard at the rear doors, the woman accompanying the one who gave the orders. . . . The *Jackal*? Was it *Carlos*? *Was* it?

Bourne desperately wanted to believe that it was—therefore, it *was*! The sound of the vehicle's curbside door slamming shut was followed rapidly by the gunning of the vehicle's powerful engine; both were a signal. The three other guards raced from their posts to the rear doors of the van. One by one they climbed up inside after the man in the black raincoat, their legs stretched, arms bracing shoulders, curved hands gripping the two metal frames that with instant muscular strain propelled them inside as their weapons were thrown in front of them. Then a pair of hands reached out for the interior door handles—

Now! Bourne pulled the pin of the grenade and lurched to his feet, running as he had never run in his life toward the swinging rear doors of the van. He dived, twisting his body in flight, landing on his back as he gripped the left panel and threw the grenade inside, the bomb's release in his hand. *Six seconds* and it would detonate. Jason got to his knees, arms extended, and crashed the doors shut. A fusillade of gunfire erupted. But it was an unintended *miracle*— as the Jackal's van was bulletproof, it was also impervious to bullets shot from within! There were no penetrations of the steel, only thuds and the screaming whistles of ricochets . . . and the screams of the wounded inside.

The glistening vehicle shot forward on the boulevard Lefebvre as Bourne sprang to a crouch and raced toward the deserted storefronts on the east side of the street. He was nearly across the wide avenue when the impossible happened. The *impossible*!

The Jackal's van blew up, the explosion firing the dark Paris sky, and the moment it happened a brown limousine screeched around the nearest corner, the windows open, men in the black spaces, weapons in their grips, spraying the entire area with thunderous, indiscriminate fire.

Jason lunged into the nearest recess, curling up into a fetal position in the shadows, accepting the fact—not in fear but in fury—that it might well be his last moments of life. He had failed. Failed Marie and his children! . . . But not *this* way. He spun off the concrete, the weapon in his hand. He would kill, *kill*! That was the way of Jason Bourne.

Then the incredible happened. The *incredible.* A siren? The *police*? The brown limousine shot forward, skirting the flaming wreck of the Jackal's van and disappeared into the dark streets as a patrol car raced out of the opposing darkness, its siren screaming, the tires screeching as it skidded to a stop only yards from the flames of the demolished vehicle. Nothing made sense! thought Jason. Where before there had been five patrol cars, only one had returned. *Why?* And even that question was superfluous. Carlos had mounted a strategy employing not one but seven, conceivably eight, decoys, all *expendable,* all led to their terrible death by the consummate self-protector. The Jackal had sprung himself from the trap that had been reversed by his hated quarry, Delta, the product of Medusa, a creation of American intelligence. Once again, the assassin had outthought him, but he had not killed him. There would be another day, another night.

"Bernardine!" screamed the Deuxième official who less than thirty minutes ago had officially disowned his colleague. Leaping out of the patrol car, the man shouted again. "Bernardine! Where are you? . . . My God, where *are* you? I came back, old friend, for I could not *leave* you! My God, you were *right,* I see that now for myself! Oh, *Christ,* tell me you're alive! *Answer me!"*

"Another is dead," came the reply from Bernardine as his gaunt figure walked slowly, with difficulty, out of the storefront two hundred feet north of Bourne. "I tried to tell you but you would not listen—"

"I was perhaps too *hasty*!" roared the official, running to the old man and embracing him as the others in the patrol car, their arms crossed in front of their faces, surrounded the burning van but at a considerable distance. "I've radioed for our people to return!" added the official. "You must believe me, old friend, I came back because I couldn't leave you in anger, not my old comrade. . . . I had no idea that pig from the newspaper actually assaulted you, *struck* you. He told me and I threw him out! . . . I came back for you, you see that, don't you? But, my *God,* I never expected anything like this!"

"It's horrible," said the Deuxième veteran, while cautiously, his eyes straying rapidly up and down the boulevard, he surveyed the area. He specifically noted the many frightened, intense faces in the windows of the three stone buildings. The scenario had blown apart with the van's explosion and the disappearance of the brown limousine. The minions were without their leader and filled with anxiety. "It's not entirely your error alone—my old comrade," he continued, a note of apology in his voice. "I had the wrong building."

"Ah *ha,*" cried the Deuxième associate, relishing a minor triumph of self-vindication. "The wrong building? That is indeed a mistake of consequence, *eh,* François?"

"The consequences might have been far less tragic had you not abandoned me so hastily, as you so aptly phrased it. Instead of listening to a man with my vast experience, you ordered me out of your car only to have me witness the horror moments after you fled."

"We followed your orders! We searched the building—the *wrong* building!"

"Had you remained, if only for a brief conference, this might have been avoided and a friend
might be alive. I shall have to include that judgment in my report—"

"*Please,* old friend," broke in the associate.
"Let us reason together for the good of the Bureau—" The interruption now came with the
shrill appearance of a fire truck. Bernardine held
up his hand and led his protesting former comrade across the boulevard, ostensibly to get out
of the way of the firemen, more purposefully to
be within earshot of Jason Bourne. "When our
people arrive," went on the associate of the
Deuxième, his voice rising with authority, "we
shall empty the buildings and detain every resident for thorough interrogation!"

"My *God,*" exclaimed Bernardine, "don't add
asininity to incompetence!"

"What?"

"The limousine, the brown limousine—surely
you saw it."

"Yes, of course. The driver said it raced
away."

"That's all he told you?"

"Well, the truck was in flames and there was
so much confusion radioing for personnel—"

"Look at the shattered glass!" commanded
François, pointing at the storefronts away from

the recess where Bourne was hiding. "Look at the pits on the pavement and in the street. Gunfire, my old comrade. Those involved escaped believing they had killed me! . . . Say *nothing, do* nothing. Leave these people alone."

"You are incomprehensible—"

"And you are a fool. If for any reason whatsoever there is the slightest possibility that even one of those killers is ordered to return here, there can be no impediments."

"Now you are inscrutable."

"Not at all," protested Bernardine as the firemen hosed down the flames of the van, their efforts augmented by giant extinguishers. "Send your people into each building, inquiring if everything is all right, explaining that the authorities have determined the terrible events on the boulevard were criminally oriented. The crisis has passed; there is no further alarm."

"But is that true?"

"It's what we want them to believe." An ambulance stormed into the street followed by two additional patrol cars, all the sirens at maximum volume. From the rue d'Alésia, apartment dwellers had gathered at both corners, many in hastily pulled-on street attire—trousers and undershirts—while others were in night

clothes—frayed bathrobes and worn slippers.
Noting that the Jackal's van was now a smoldering mass of twisted steel and shattered glass,
Bernardine continued: "Give the crowds time to
satisfy their morbid viewing, then send men to
disperse them. In an hour or so, when the rubble
is under control and the bodies carted away,
proclaim loudly to your police detachment that
the emergency is over, ordering all but one man
back to the precinct. That man is to remain here
on duty until the debris is cleared from the boulevard. He is also to be instructed not to interfere with anyone leaving the buildings, is that
clear?"

"Not for a moment. You said that someone
might be hiding—"

"I know what I said," pressed the former
Deuxième consultant. "It changes nothing."

"You will stay here, then?"

"Yes. I will move slowly, inconspicuously,
around the area."

"I see. . . . What about the police report? And
my report?"

"Use some of the truth, not all of it, of course.
Word was passed to you—informer's name
withheld—that an act of violence related to the
Bureau's narcotics division was to take place on

the boulevard Lefebvre at precisely this hour. You commandeered a police contingent and found nothing, but shortly thereafter your highly professional instincts sent you back beyond the time span, unfortunately too late to stop the carnage.''

"I might even be commended,'' said the associate, suddenly frowning, wary. "And *your* report?'' he asked quietly.

"We'll see if one is necessary, won't we?'' replied the newly reinstated Deuxième consultant.

The medical team wrapped the bodies of the victims and placed them in the ambulance as a wrecker hoisted what was left of the destroyed vehicle into the huge attached dumpster. The crew swept the street, several remarking that they should not sweep too thoroughly or no one would recognize the Lefebvre. A quarter of an hour later the job was finished; the wrecker departed, the lone patrolman joining the crew to be dropped off at the nearest police phone several blocks away. It was well past four o'clock in the morning, and soon the dawn would light up the sky over Paris, preceding the boisterous human carnival below. Now, however, the only signs of life on the boulevard Lefebvre were five lighted windows in the row of stone buildings controlled by Carlos the Jackal. Inside those rooms were men and women for whom sleep was not permitted. They had work to do for their monseigneur.

Bourne sat on the pavement, his legs outstretched, his back against the inside wall of a storefront across from the building where the frightened yet argumentative baker and the indignant nun had confronted the police. Bernardine was in a similar recess several hundred feet away, opposite the first building where the Jackal's van had stopped for its condemned cargo. Their agreement was firm: Jason would follow and take by force whoever left first from any building; the old Deuxième veteran would follow whoever left second, ascertain his or her destination, but make no contact. Bourne's judgment was that either the baker or the nun would be the assassin's messenger, so he had selected the north end of the row of stone houses.

He was partially right, but he had not anticipated an embarrassment of personnel and conveyances. At 5:17, two bicycles ridden by nuns in full habits and white hats wheeled up from the south side of the boulevard, ringing the muted bells on their handlebars as they stopped in front of the house that was supposedly the quarters of the Magdalen Sisters of Charity. The door opened and three additional nuns, each carrying a bicycle, walked out and down the brick steps to join their charitable sisters. They discreetly mounted their saddles and the procession started up the street; the one consoling fact for Jason was that Carlos's indignant nun took up the single rear position. Not knowing how it would happen, knowing only that it *would* happen, Bourne lurched out of the storefront and ran across the dark boulevard. As he reached the shadows of the deserted lot adjacent to the Jackal's house, another door opened. He crouched, watching the overweight irate baker waddle rapidly down his brick steps and head south. Bernardine had his work cut out for him, too, thought Jason as he got to his feet and ran after his procession of cycling nuns.

Paris traffic is an endless enigma regardless of the hour of day or night. It also provides palpable excuses for anyone wishing to be early or late, or having arrived at the right destination or

the wrong one. In a phrase, Parisians behind a
steering wheel embody the last civilized vestiges of lethal abandon—possibly outdone by
their counterparts in Rome or Athens. And so it
was for the Magdalen Sisters of Charity, especially for the officious superior hen on the single
rear point. At an intersection of the rue Lecourbe in Montparnasse, a congestion of produce trucks prevented her from keeping up with
her religious colleagues. Benignly she waved
them on and abruptly turned into a narrow side
street, suddenly pedaling faster than before.
Bourne, his wound from Tranquility Isle now pulsating throughout his neck, did not increase his
pace; he did not have to. The white-lettered blue
sign on the building fronting the street read IM-
PASSE, a dead end; there was no other way out.

He found the bicycle chained to an extinguished street lamp and waited in the darkness
of a doorway no more than fifteen feet away. He
raised his hand and touched the warm moist-
ness of the bandage around his neck; the bleeding was slight. With luck, no more than one
suture had burst. . . . Oh, *Christ,* his legs were
tired—no, "tired" was inadequate. They ached
with the pain that came with unused and abused
muscles; the rhythmic strides of jogging, even
running, were no preparation for lurching or

weaving, or for violently sudden stops and starts. He leaned against the stone, breathing heavily, his eyes on the bicycle, trying to suppress a thought that kept recurring with infuriating regularity: only a few short years ago, he would never have noticed the discomfort in his legs. There would have been none.

The sound of an unlatched bolt broke the stillness of the predawn narrow street, followed rapidly by the grating noise of a heavy door being opened. It was the entrance to the flat in front of the chained bicycle. His back against the wall, Jason removed the gun from his belt and watched the woman in the nun's habit rush to the lamppost. She fumbled with a key in the dim light, awkwardly trying to insert it into the base of the lock. Bourne stepped out on the pavement and walked swiftly, silently forward.

"You'll be late for early Mass," he said.

The woman spun around, the key flying into the street, her black cloth snapping in the turn as she plunged her right hand between the folds of her habit. Jason lurched, gripping her arm with his left hand and tearing off the large white hat with his right. At the sight of the exposed face in front of him, he gasped.

"My *God,*" he whispered. "It's *you!*"

27

"I *know* you!" cried Bourne. "Paris . . . years ago . . . your name is Lavier . . . Jacqueline *Lavier.* You had one of those dress shops . . . Les Classiques—St.-Honoré—Carlos's drop in the Faubourg! I found you in a confessional booth in Neuilly-sur-Seine. I thought you were *dead."* The woman's sharp, creased, middle-aged face was contorted in frenzy. She tried to twist out of his grip, but Jason stepped sideways as she pivoted, yanking her away in a sweeping circular motion, crashing her against the wall, pinning her, his left forearm across her throat. "But you *weren't* dead. You were part of the trap that ended at the Louvre, blew apart at the Louvre!

. . . By Christ, you're coming with me. Men died in that trap—*Frenchmen* died—and I couldn't stay around and tell them how it happened or who was responsible. . . . In my country, you kill a cop, it doesn't go off the books. It's no different over here; and when it's *cops,* they don't stop looking. Oh, they'll remember the Louvre, they'll remember their men!"

"You're wrong!" choked the woman, her wide green eyes bulging. "I'm not who you think I am—"

"You're Lavier! Queen of the Faubourg, sole contact to the Jackal's woman, the general's wife. Don't tell me I'm wrong . . . I followed the two of you out to Neuilly—to that church with the bells ringing and priests everywhere—one of them *Carlos*! Moments later his whore came back out, but you didn't. She left in a hurry, so I ran inside and described you to an old priest— if he was a priest—and he told me you were in the second confessional from the left. I walked over and pulled the curtain and there you were. *Dead.* I thought you'd just been *killed* and everything was happening so fast. Carlos had to *be* there! He was within my reach, my gun—or maybe I was within his. I raced around like a maniac and finally I saw him! Out in the street in his priestly black clothes—I *saw* him, I *knew* it was him because he saw me and started to run through the traffic. And then I lost him, I *lost* him! . . . But I had a card to play. *You.* I passed the word—Lavier's dead. . . . It was just what I was supposed to do, wasn't it? *Wasn't* it?"

"I tell you again, you are *wrong*!" The woman no longer struggled; it was pointless. Instead, she remained rigid against the wall, no part of her body moving, as if by doing so she might be permitted to speak. "Will you listen to me?" she asked with difficulty, Jason's forearm still pressed against her throat.

"Forget it, lady," answered Bourne. "You're going out of here limp—a Sister of Charity being helped, not assaulted, by a stranger. You're about to have a fainting spell. At your age it's a fairly common occurrence, isn't it?"

"Wait."

"Too late."

"We must talk!"

"We will." Releasing his arm, Jason instantly crashed both his hands simultaneously into the woman's shoulder blades where the tendons weave into the neck muscles. She collapsed; he caught her in the fall and carried her out of the narrow street as an adoring supplicant might a religious social worker. The dawn light was beginning to fill the sky, and several early risers, one a young jogger in shorts, converged on the man carrying the nun. "She's been with my wife and sick children for nearly two days without sleep!" pleaded the Chameleon in street French. "Will someone please find me a taxi so I can take her back to her convent in the ninth arrondissement?"

"*I shall!*" roared the young runner. "There's an all-night stand on the rue de Sèvres, and I'm very fast!"

"You are a gift, monsieur," said Jason, appreciating but instantly disliking the all too confident, all too young jogger.

Six minutes later the taxi arrived, the youth inside. "I told the driver you have money," he said, climbing out. "I trust it's so."

"Of course. And thanks."

"Tell the sister what I did," added the young man in running shorts, helping Bourne gently insert the unconscious woman into the back of the taxi. "I'll need all the help I can get when my time comes."

"I trust that's not imminent," said Jason, trying to return the youth's grin.

"Not likely! I represent my firm in the marathon." The overgrown child began running in place.

"Thanks again. I hope you win the next one."

"Tell the sister to pray for me!" cried the athlete, racing away.

"The Bois de Boulogne," said Bourne, closing the door and addressing the driver.

"The *Bois*? That ventilating nut told me it was an emergency! You had to get the nun to a hospital."

"She drank too much wine, what can I tell you?"

"The Bois de Boulogne," said the driver, nodding his head. "Let her walk it off. I have a second cousin in the Lyons convent. She gets out for a week she's soused to the temples. Who can blame her?"

The bench on the graveled path of the Bois progressively received the warm rays of the early sun as the middle-aged woman in the religious habit began shaking her head. "How are you doing, *Sister*?" asked Jason, sitting beside his prisoner.

"I believe I was struck by an army tank," replied the woman, blinking and opening her mouth to swallow air. "At least a tank."

"Which I suspect you know more about than

a welfare wagon from the Magdalen Sisters of Charity."

"Quite so," agreed the woman.

"Don't bother to look for your gun," said Bourne. "I removed it from the very expensive belt under your habit."

"I'm glad you recognized the value. It's part of what we must talk about. . . . Since I am not in a police station, I assume you've granted me my request to talk."

"Only if what you say suits my purpose, I assume you understand that."

"But it must, you see. Suit your purpose, as you say. I've failed. I've been taken. I'm not where I should be, and whatever the time is, the light tells me I'm too late for excuses. Also, my bicycle has either disappeared or is still chained to the lamppost."

"I didn't take it."

"Then I'm a dead woman. And if it's gone I'm just as dead, don't you see?"

"Because you've disappeared? Not where you're supposed to be?"

"Of course."

"You're *Lavier*!"

"That's true. I'm Lavier. But I'm not the woman you knew. You knew my sister Jacqueline—I am Dominique Lavier. We were close in age and since we were children strongly resembled each other. But you are not wrong about Neuilly-sur-Seine or what you saw there. My sister was killed because she broke a cardinal rule, committed a mortal sin, if you like. She panicked and led *you* to Carlos's woman, his most cherished and useful secret."

"Me? . . . You know who I am?"

"All Paris—the Jackal's Paris—knows who you are, Monsieur Bourne. Not by sight, I grant you, but they know you are here and they know you're tracking Carlos."

"And you're part of that Paris?"

"I am."

"Good Christ, lady, he killed your *sister*!"

"I'm aware of that."

"Still you work for him?"

"There are times when a person's choices are considerably reduced. Say, to live or to die. Until six years ago when Les Classiques changed ownership, it was vital to the monseigneur. I took Jacqui's place—"

"Just like that?"

"It wasn't difficult. I was younger, and more to the point I looked younger." The lines in the middle-aged Lavier's face cracked with a brief pensive smile. "My sister always said it came with living on the Mediterranean. . . . At any rate, cosmetic surgery is commonplace in the world of haute couture. Jacqui supposedly went to Switzerland for a face-lift . . . and I returned to Paris after eight weeks of preparation."

"How could you? Knowing what you knew, how the hell *could* you?"

"I did not know earlier what I learned later, by which time it was irrelevant. By then I had the choice I just mentioned. To live or to die."

"It never occurred to you to go to the police or the Sûreté?"

"Regarding Carlos?" The woman looked at Bourne as if rebuking a foolish child. "As the British say in Cap Ferrat, surely you jest."

"So you blithely went into the killing game?"

"Not consciously. I was gradually led into it, my education slow, piecemeal. . . . In the beginning I was told Jacqueline had died in a boating accident with her lover of the month and that I would be enormously well paid to carry on in her place. Les Classiques was far more than a grand salon—"

"*Far* more," agreed Jason, interrupting. "It was the drop for France's most highly classified military and intelligence secrets funneled to the

Jackal by his woman, a celebrated general's wife."

"I was not aware of that until long after the general killed her. Villiers was his name, I believe."

"It was." Jason looked across the path at the still dark waters of a pond, white lilies floating in clusters. Images came back to him. "I'm the one who found him, found them. Villiers was in a high-backed chair, a gun in his hand, his wife lying on the bed, naked, bleeding, dead. He was going to kill himself. It was a proper execution for a traitor, he said, for his devotion to his wife had blinded his judgment and in that blindness he had betrayed his beloved France. . . . I convinced him there was another way; it almost worked—thirteen years ago. In a strange house on Seventy-first Street in New York."

"I don't know what happened in New York, but General Villiers left instructions that after his death what happened in *Paris* was to be made part of the public record. When he died and the truth was known, it was said that Carlos went mad with fury, killing several high-ranking military commanders simply because they were generals."

"It's all an old story," interrupted Bourne

sharply. "This is now, thirteen years later. What happens *now*?"

"I don't know, monsieur. My choices are zero, aren't they? One or the other of you will kill me, I suppose."

"Maybe not. Help me take him and you're free of both of us. You can go back to the Mediterranean and live in peace. You won't even have to disappear—you merely return to wherever it is after a number of profitable years in Paris."

"Disappear?" asked Lavier, studying the haggard face of her captor. "As in the word 'vanish'?"

"No need for that. Carlos can't reach you because he'll be dead."

"Yes, I understand that part. It's the disappearance that interests me along with the 'profitable' years. Does this profit come from you?"

"Yes."

"I see. . . . Is that what you offered Santos? A profitable disappearance?"

It was as if the words were hard flesh and had slapped him across the face. Jason looked at his prisoner. "So it was Santos, after all," he said softly. "The Lefebvre *was* a trap. Christ, he's good."

"He's dead, Le Coeur du Soldat cleaned out and closed down."

"What?" Stunned, Bourne again stared at the Lavier woman. "That was his reward for cornering me?"

"No, for betraying Carlos."

"I don't understand."

"The monseigneur has eyes everywhere, I'm sure that's no surprise to you. Santos, the total recluse, was observed sending several heavy boxes out with his main food supplier, and yesterday morning he did not clip and water his precious garden, a summer ritual as predictable as the sun. A man was sent to the supplier's warehouse and opened the boxes—"

"Books," broke in Jason quietly.

"Placed in storage until further instructions," completed Dominique Lavier. "Santos's departure was to be swift and secret."

"And Carlos knew there was no one in Moscow giving out a telephone number."

"I beg your pardon?"

"Nothing. . . . What kind of man was Santos?"

"I never knew him, never even saw him. I've only heard the downstairs rumors, which weren't many."

"I haven't time for many. What were they?"

"Apparently he was a very large man—"

"I know that," interrupted Jason impatiently. "And from the books we both know that he was well read, probably well educated, if his speech was indicative. Where did he come from and why did he work for the Jackal?"

"They say he was Cuban and fought in Fidel's revolution, that he was a deep thinker, as well as a law student with Castro, and once a great athlete. Then, of course, as in all revolutions, the internal strife sours the victories—at least that's what my old friends from the May Day barricades tell me."

"Translation, please?"

"Fidel was jealous of the leaders of certain cadres, especially Che Guevara and the man you knew as Santos. Where Castro was larger than life, those two were larger than he was, and Fidel could not tolerate the competition. Che was sent on a mission that ended his life, and trumped up counterrevolutionary charges were brought against Santos. He was within an hour of being executed when Carlos and his men broke into the prison and spirited him away."

"Spirited? Dressed as priests, no doubt."

"I have no doubts. The Church with all its medieval lunacies once held sway over Cuba."

"You sound bitter."

"I'm a woman, the Pontiff is not; he's merely medieval."

"Judgment decreed. . . . So Santos joined

forces with Carlos, two disillusioned Marxists in search of their personal cause—or maybe their own personal Hollywood."

"That's beyond me, monsieur, but if I vaguely understand you, the fantasy belongs to the brilliant Carlos; the bitter disillusion was Santos's fate. He owed his life to the Jackal, so why not give it? What was left for him? . . . Until you came along."

"That's all I need. Thanks. I just wanted a few gaps filled in."

"Gaps?"

"Things I didn't know."

"What do we do now, Monsieur Bourne? Wasn't that your original question?"

"What do you *want* to do, Madame Lavier?"

"I know I don't want to die. And I am not Madame Lavier in the marital sense. The restrictions never appealed to me and the benefits seemed unnecessary. For years I was a high-priced call girl in Monte Carlo, Nice and Cap Ferrat until my looks and my body deserted me. Still, I once had friends from the old days, intermittent lovers who took care of me for old times' sake. Most are dead now, a pity, really."

"I thought you said you were enormously well paid for assuming your sister's identity."

"Oh, I was and to a degree I still am, for I'm

still valuable. I move among the elite of Paris, where gossip abounds, and that's often helpful. I have a beautiful flat on the avenue Montaigne. Antiques, fine paintings, servants, charge accounts—everything a woman once in high fashion should be expected to have for the circles she still travels in. And money. Every month my bank receives eighty thousand francs from Geneva—somewhat more than enough for me to pay the bills. For, you see, *I* have to pay them, no one else can do so."

"So then you've got money."

"No, monsieur. I have a *life-style,* not money. That's the way of the Jackal. Except for the old men, he pays only for what he gets in terms of immediate service. If the money from Geneva does not arrive at my bank on the tenth of every month, I'd be thrown out in thirty days. But then if Carlos decided to get rid of me, there would be no need for Geneva. I'd be finished—as I am no doubt finished now. If I returned to my flat in the Montaigne this morning, I'd never come out . . . as my sister never came out of that church in Neuilly-sur-Seine. At least not alive."

"You're convinced of that?"

"Of course. The stop where I chained the bicycle was made to receive instructions from one of the old men. The orders were precise and to be precisely followed. A woman I know would meet me in twenty minutes at a bakery in Saint-Germain where we were to exchange clothes. She was to proceed to the Magdalen mission and I was to meet a courier from Athens in a room at the Hôtel Trémoille."

"The Magdalen mission . . . ? You mean those women on the bicycles were actually nuns?"

"Complete with vows of chastity and poverty, monsieur. I am a frequent visiting superior from the convent at Saint-Malo."

"And the woman at the bakery. Is she—?"

"She falls from grace now and then, but she's a perfectly splendid administrator."

"Jesus," mumbled Bourne.

"He's frequently on their lips. . . . Do you see now the hopelessness of my position?"

"I'm not sure I do."

"Then I am forced to wonder if you really are the Chameleon. I was *not* at the bakery. The meeting with the Greek courier never took place. Where was I?"

"You were delayed. The bicycle chain broke; you got grazed by one of those trucks on the rue Lecourbe. Hell, you got mugged. What's the difference? You were delayed."

"How long has it been since you rendered me unconscious?"

Jason looked at his watch, now easily seen in the bright morning sunlight. "Something over an hour-plus, I think; perhaps an hour and a half. Considering how you were dressed, the taxi driver cruised around trying to find a place to park where we could help you to a bench on the path with as little scrutiny as possible. He was well paid for his assistance."

"An hour and a half?" asked Lavier pointedly. "So?"

"So why didn't I call the bakery or the Hôtel Trémoille?"

"Complications? . . . No, too easily verified," added Bourne, shaking his head.

"Or?" Lavier locked her large green eyes with his. "*Or,* monsieur?"

"The boulevard Lefebvre," replied Jason slowly, softly. "The trap. As I reversed his on me, he reversed mine for him three hours later. Then I broke the strategy and took *you.*"

"Exactly." The once and former whore of Monte Carlo nodded. "And he cannot know what transpired between us . . . therefore, I'm marked for execution. A pawn is removed, for she is merely a pawn. She can tell the authorities nothing of substance; she's never seen the Jackal; she can only repeat the gossip of lowly subordinates."

"You've never *seen* him?"

"I may have, but not to my knowledge. Again, the rumors fly around Paris. This one with swarthy Latin skin, or that one with black eyes and a dark mustache; 'He is really Carlos, you know'—how often have I heard the phrases! But no, no man has ever come up to me and said, 'I am he and I make your life pleasant, you aging elegant prostitute.' I simply report to old men who every now and then convey information that I must have—such as this evening on the boulevard Lefebvre."

"I see." Bourne got to his feet, stretching his body and looking down at his prisoner on the bench. "I can get you out," he said quietly. "Out of Paris, out of Europe. Beyond Carlos's reach. Do you want that?"

"As eagerly as Santos did," answered Lavier, her eyes imploring. "I willingly trade my allegiance from him to you."

"Why?"

"Because he is old and gray-faced and is no match for you. You offer me life; he offers death."

"That's a reasonable decision, then," said Jason, a tentative but warm smile on his lips. "Do you have any money? With you, I mean?"

"Nuns are sworn to poverty, monsieur," replied Dominique Lavier, returning his smile. "Actually, I have several hundred francs. Why?"

"It's not enough," continued Bourne, reaching into his pocket and taking out his impressive roll of franc notes. "Here's three thousand," he said, handing her the money. "Buy some clothes somewhere—I'm sure you know how— and take a room at the . . . the Meurice on the rue de Rivoli."

"What name should I use?"

"What suits you?"

"How about Brielle? A lovely seaside town."

"Why not? . . . Give me ten minutes to get out of here and then leave. I'll see you at the Meurice at noon."

"With all my *heart,* Jason Bourne!"

"Let's forget that name."

The Chameleon walked out of the Bois de Boulogne to the nearest taxi station. Within minutes an ecstatic cabdriver accepted a hundred francs to remain in place at the end of the three-vehicle line, his passenger slumped in the rear seat waiting to hear the words.

"The nun comes out, monsieur!" cried the driver. "She enters the first taxi!"

"Follow it," said Jason, sitting up.

On the avenue Victor Hugo, Lavier's taxi slowed down and pulled up in front of one of Paris's few exceptions to tradition—an open plastic-domed public telephone. "Stop *here,*" ordered Bourne, who climbed out the instant the driver swung into the curb. Limping, the Chameleon walked swiftly, silently, to the telephone directly behind and unseen by the frantic nun under the plastic dome. He was not seen, but he could hear clearly as he stood several feet behind her.

"The *Meurice*!" she shouted into the phone. "The name is *Brielle.* He'll be there at noon. . . . Yes, yes, I'll stop at my flat, change clothes, and be there in an hour." Lavier hung up and turned, gasping at the sight of Jason. *"No!"* she screamed.

"Yes, I'm afraid," said Bourne. "Shall we take my taxi or yours? . . . 'He's old and gray-faced'— those were your words, Dominique. Pretty god-damned descriptive for someone who never met Carlos."

A furious Bernardine walked out of the Pont-Royal with the doorman, who had summoned him. "This is *preposterous*!" he shouted as he approached the taxi. "No, it's not," he amended, looking inside. "It's merely insane."

"Get in," said Jason on the far side of the woman dressed in the habit of a nun. François did so, staring at the black clothes, the white pointed hat and the pale face of the religious female between them. "Meet one of the Jackal's more talented performers," added Bourne. "She could make a fortune in your *cinéma-vérité,* take my word for it."

"I'm not a particularly religious man, but I trust you have not made a mistake. . . . I did—or should I say *we* did—with that pig of a baker."

"Why?"

"He's a *baker,* that's all he is! I damn near put a grenade in his ovens, but no one but a French *baker* could plead the way *he* did!"

"It fits," said Jason. "The illogical logic of Carlos—I can't remember who said that, probably me." The taxi made a U-turn and entered the rue du Bac. "We're going to the Meurice," added Bourne.

"I'm sure there's a reason," stated Bernardine, still looking at the enigmatically passive face of Dominique Lavier. "I mean, this sweet old lady says nothing."

"I'm not *old!*" cried the woman vehemently.

"Of course not, my dear," agreed the Deuxième veteran. "Only more desirable in your mature years."

"Boy, did *you* hit it!"

"Why the Meurice?" asked Bernardine.

"It's the Jackal's final trap for me," answered Bourne. "Courtesy of our persuasive Magdalen Sister of Charity here. He expects me to be there and I'll be there."

"I'll call in the Deuxième. Thanks to a frightened bureaucrat, they'll do anything I ask. Don't endanger yourself, my friend."

"I don't mean to insult you, François, but you yourself told me you didn't know all of the people in the Bureau these days. I can't take the chance of a leak. One man could send out an alarm."

"Let me help." The low soft-spoken voice of Dominique Lavier broke the hum of the outside traffic like the initial burr of a chain saw. "I *can* help."

"I listened to your help before, lady, and it was leading me to my own execution. No thanks."

"That was before, not now. As must be obvious to you, my position now is truly hopeless."

"Didn't I hear those words recently?"

"No, you did not. I just added the word 'now.' . . . For God's sake, put yourself in my place. I can't pretend to understand, but this ancient boulevardier beside me casually mentions that he'll call in the Deuxième—the *Deuxième*, Monsieur Bourne! For some that is no less than France's Gestapo! Even if I survived, I'm marked by that infamous branch of the government. I'd no doubt be sent to some horrible penal colony halfway across the world—oh, I've heard the stories of the Deuxième!"

"Really?" said Bernardine. "I haven't. Sounds positively marvelous. How *wonderful*."

"Besides," continued Lavier, looking hard at Jason as she yanked the pointed white hat off her head, a gesture that caused the driver, seeing it in the rearview mirror, to raise his eyebrows. "*Without* me, without my presence in decidedly different clothing at the Meurice, Carlos won't come near the rue de Rivoli." Bernardine tapped the woman's shoulder, bringing his index finger to his lips and nodding toward the front seat. Dominique quickly added, "The man you wish to *confer* with will not be there."

"She's got a point," said Bourne, leaning forward and looking past Lavier at the Deuxième veteran. "She's also got an apartment on the Montaigne, where she's supposed to change clothes, and neither of us can go in with her."

"That poses a dilemma, doesn't it?" responded Bernardine. "There's no way we can monitor the telephone from outside in the street, is there?"

"You *fools*! . . . I have no *choice* but to cooperate with you, and if you can't see that you should be led around by trained dogs! This old, *old* man here will have my name in the Deuxième files the first chance he gets, and as the notorious Jason Bourne knows if he has even a nodding acquaintance with the Deuxieme, several profound questions are raised—once raised by my sister, Jacqueline, incidentally. Who is this Bourne? Is he real or unreal? Is he the assassin of Asia or is he a fraud, a *plant*? She phoned me herself one night in Nice after too many brandies—a night perhaps you recall, Monsieur le Caméléon—a terribly expensive restaurant outside Paris. You threatened her . . . in the name of powerful, *unnamed* people you *threatened* her! You demanded that she reveal what she knew about a certain acquaintance of hers— who it was at the time I had no idea—but you frightened her. She said you appeared deranged, that your eyes became glazed and you uttered words in a language she could not understand."

"I remember," interrupted Bourne icily. "We had dinner and I threatened her and she was frightened. She went to the ladies' room, paid someone to make a phone call, and I had to get out of there."

"And now the *Deuxième* is allied with those powerful unnamed people?" Dominique Lavier shook her head repeatedly and lowered her voice. "No, messieurs, I am a survivor and I do not fight against such odds. One knows when to pass the shoe in baccarat."

After a short period of silence, Bernardine spoke. "What's your address on the avenue Montaigne? I'll give it to the driver, but before I do, understand me, madame. If your words prove false, all the true horrors of the Deuxième will be visited upon you."

Marie sat at the room-service table in her small suite at the Meurice reading the newspapers. Her attention constantly strayed; concentration was out of the question. Her anxiety had kept her awake after she returned to the hotel shortly past midnight, having made the rounds of five cafés she and David had frequented so many years ago in Paris. Finally by four-something in the morning, exhaustion had short-circuited her tossing and turning; she fell asleep with the bedside lamp switched on, and was awakened by the same light nearly six hours later. It was the longest she had slept since that first night on Tranquility Isle, itself a distant memory now except for the very real pain of not seeing and hearing the children. *Don't think about them, it hurts too much. Think about David. . . . No, think about Jason Bourne! Where? Concentrate!*

She put down the Paris *Tribune* and poured herself a third cup of black coffee, glancing over at the French doors that led to a small balcony overlooking the rue de Rivoli. It disturbed her that the once bright morning had turned into a dismal gray day. Soon the rain would come, making her search in the streets even more difficult. Resigned, she sipped her coffee and replaced the elegant cup in the elegant saucer, annoyed that it was not one of the simple pottery mugs favored by David and her in their rustic country kitchen in Maine. Oh, *God,* would they ever be back there again? *Don't think about such things! Concentrate!* Out of the question.

She picked up the *Tribune*, aimlessly scanning the pages, seeing only isolated words, no sentences or paragraphs, no continuity of thought or meaning, merely words. Then one stood out at the bottom of a meaningless column, a single meaningless line bracketed at the bottom of a meaningless page.

The word was *Memom*, followed by a telephone number; and despite the fact that the *Tribune* was printed in English, the French in her switchable French-thinking brain absently translated the word as *Maymohm*. She was about to turn the page when a signal from another part of her brain screamed *Stop!*

Memom . . . *mommy*—turned around by a child struggling with his earliest attempts at language. *Meemom!* Jamie—their *Jamie*! The funny inverted name he had called her for several weeks! David had joked about it while she, frightened, had wondered if their son had dyslexia.

"He could also just be confused, *memom*," David had laughed.

David! She snapped up the page; it was the financial section of the paper, the section she instinctively gravitated to every morning over coffee. David was sending her a message! She pushed back her chair, crashing it to the floor as she grabbed the paper and rushed to the telephone on the desk. Her hands trembling, she dialed the number. There was no answer, and thinking that in her panic she had made an error or had not used the local Paris digit, she dialed again, now slowly, precisely.

No answer. But it *was* David, she felt it, she *knew* it! He had been looking for her at the Trocadéro and now he was using a briefly employed nickname only the two of them would know! My love, my *love*, I've found you! . . . She also knew she could not stay in the confining quarters of the small hotel suite, pacing up and down and dialing every other minute, driving herself crazy with every unanswered ring. *When you're stressed out and spinning until you think you'll blow apart, find someplace where you can keep moving without being noticed. Keep moving! That's vital. You can't let your head explode.* One of the lessons from Jason Bourne. Her head spinning, Marie dressed more rapidly than she had ever done in her life. She tore out the message from the *Tribune* and left the oppressive suite, trying not to run to the bank of elevators but needing the crowds of the Paris streets, where she could keep moving without being noticed. From one telephone kiosk to another.

The ride down to the lobby was both interminable and insufferable, the latter because of an American couple—he laden with camera equipment, she with purple eyelids and a peroxide bouffant apparently set in concrete—who kept complaining that not enough people in Paris, France, spoke English. The elevator doors thankfully opened and Marie walked out rapidly into the crowded Meurice lobby.

As she crossed the marble floor toward the large glass doors of the ornate filigreed entrance, she suddenly, involuntarily stopped as an elderly man in a dark pin-striped suit gasped, his slender body lurching forward in a heavy leather chair below on her right. The old man stared at her, his thin lips parted in astonishment, his eyes in shock.

"Marie St. Jacques!" he whispered. "My *God*, get *out* of here!"

"I beg your . . . *What?*"

The aged Frenchman quickly, with difficulty, rose to his feet, his head subtly, swiftly, jerking in short movements as he scanned the lobby. "You cannot be seen here, Mrs. Webb," he said, his voice still a whisper but no less harsh and commanding. "Don't look at me! Look at your watch. Keep your head down." The Deuxième veteran glanced away, nodding aimlessly at several people in nearby chairs as he continued, his lips barely moving. "Go out the door on the far left, the one used for luggage. *Hurry!*"

"*No!*" replied Marie, her head down, her eyes on her watch. "You know me but I don't know you! Who *are* you?"

"A friend of your husband."

"My God, is he *here*?"

"The question is why are *you* here?"

"I stayed at this hotel once before. I thought he might remember it."

"He did but in the wrong context, I'm afraid. *Mon Dieu,* he never would have chosen it otherwise. Now, *leave.*"

"I won't! I have to find him. Where *is* he?"

"You *will* leave or you may find only his corpse. There's a message for you in the Paris *Tribune*—"

"It's in my purse. The financial page. '*Memom*—'"

"Call in several hours."

"You can't *do* this to me."

"You cannot do this to *him*. You'll kill him! Get out of here. *Now!*"

Her eyes half blinded with fury and fear and

tears, Marie started toward the left side of the lobby, desperately wanting to look back, but just as desperately knowing she could not do so. She reached the narrow set of glass double doors, colliding with a uniformed bellhop carrying suitcases inside.

"Pardon, madame!"

"De rien," she stammered, maneuvering again blindly around the luggage and out to the pavement. What could she do—what *should* she do? David was somewhere in the hotel—*in* the hotel! And a strange man recognized her and warned her and told her to get out—*get away*! What was happening? . . . My God, someone's trying to kill David! The old Frenchman had said as much—who *was* it . . . who were *they*? *Where* were they?

Help me! For God's sake, Jason, tell me what to do. *Jason?* . . . Yes, Jason . . . *help* me! She stood, frozen, as taxis and limousines broke off from the noonday traffic and pulled up to the Meurice's curb, where a gold-braided doorman under the huge canopy greeted newcomers and old faces and sent bellboys scurrying in all directions. A large black limousine with a small discreet religious insignia on its passenger door, the cruciform standard of some high office of the Church, inched its way to the canopied area. Marie stared at the small emblem; it was circular and no more than six inches in diameter, a globe of royal purple surrounding an elongated crucifix of gold. She winced and held her breath; her panic now had a disturbing new dimension. She had seen that insignia before, and all she remembered was that it had filled her with horror.

The limousine stopped; both curbside doors were opened by the smiling, bowing doorman as five priests emerged, one from the front seat, four from the spacious rear section. Those from the back immediately, oddly, threaded their way into the noonday crowds of strollers on the pavement, two forward in front of the vehicle, two behind it, one of the priests whipping past Marie, his black coat making contact with her, his face so close she could see the blazing unpriestly eyes of a man who was no part of a religious order. . . . Then the association with the emblem, the religious insignia, came back to her!

Years ago, when David—when *Jason*—was in maximum therapy with Panov, Mo had him sketch, draw, doodle whatever images came to him. Time and again that terrible circle with the thin crucifix appeared . . . invariably torn apart or stabbed repeatedly with the pencil point. *The Jackal!*

Suddenly, Marie's eyes were drawn to a figure crossing the rue de Rivoli. It was a tall man in dark clothes—a dark sweater and trousers—and he was limping, dodging the traffic, a hand shielding his face from the drizzle that soon would turn into rain. The limp was *false*! The leg straightened if only for an instant and the swing of the shoulder that compensated was a defiant gesture she knew only too well. It was David!

Another, no more than eight feet from her, also saw what she saw. A miniature radio was instantly brought to the man's lips. Marie rushed forward, her extended hands the claws of a tigress as she lunged at the killer in priest's clothing.

"David!" she screamed, drawing blood from the face of the Jackal's man.

Gunshots filled the rue de Rivoli. The crowds panicked, many running into the hotel, many more racing away from the canopied entrance, all shrieking, yelling, seeking safety from the murderous insanity that had suddenly exploded in the civilized street. In the violent struggle with the man who would kill her husband, the strong Canadian ranch girl ripped the automatic out of his belt and fired it into his head; blood and membranes were blown into the air.

"Jason!" she screamed again as the killer fell, instantly realizing that she stood alone with only the corpse beneath her—she was a *target!* Then from certain death there was the sudden possibility of life. The old aristocratic French-man who had recognized her in the lobby came crashing out of the front entrance, his automatic weapon on repeat fire as he sprayed the black limousine, stopping for an instant to switch his aim and shattering the legs of a "priest" whose weapon was leveled at him.

"Mon ami!" roared Bernardine.

"Here!" shouted Bourne. "Where *is* she?"

"A votre droite! Près de—" A single gunshot exploded from the glass double doors of the Meurice. As he fell the Deuxième veteran cried out, *"Les Capucines, mon ami. Les Capucines!"* Bernardine slumped to the pavement; a second gunshot ended his life.

Marie was paralyzed, she could not *move!* Everything was a blizzard, a hurricane of iced particles crashing with such force against her face she could neither think nor find meaning. Weeping out of control, she fell to her knees, then collapsed in the street, her screams of despair clear to the man who suddenly was above her. "My children . . . oh *God*, my *children*!"

"*Our* children," said Jason Bourne, his voice not the voice of David Webb. "We're getting out of here, can you understand that?"

"Yes . . . *yes*!" Marie awkwardly, painfully, swung her legs behind her and lurched to her feet, held by the husband she either knew or did not know. *"David?"*

"Of course I'm David. Come on!"

"You frighten me—"

"I frighten myself. Let's *go*! Bernardine gave us our exit. Run with me; hold my hand!"

They raced down the rue de Rivoli, swinging east into the boulevard St.-Michel until the Parisian strollers in their *nonchalance de jour* made it clear that the fugitives were safe from the horrors of the Meurice. They stopped in an alleyway and held each other.

"Why did you *do* it?" asked Marie, cupping his face. "Why did you run away from us?"

"Because I'm better without you, you know that."

"You weren't before, David—or should I say Jason?"

"Names don't matter, we have to move!"

"Where to?"

"I'm not sure. But we *can* move, that's the important thing. There's a way out. Bernardine gave it to us."

"He was the old Frenchman?"

"Let's not talk about him, okay? At least not for a while. I'm shredded enough."

"All right, we won't talk about him. Still, he mentioned Les Capucines—what did he mean?"

"It's our way out. There's a car waiting for me in the boulevard des Capucines. That's what he was telling me. Let's *go*!"

They raced south out of Paris in the nondescript Peugeot, taking the Barbizon highway to Villeneuve-St.-Georges. Marie sat close to her husband, their bodies touching, her hand clutching his arm. She was, however, sickeningly aware that the warmth she intended was not returned in equal measure. Only a part of the intense man behind the wheel was her David; the rest of him was Jason Bourne and he was now in command.

"For God's sake, talk to me!" she cried.

"I'm thinking. . . . Why did you come to Paris?"

"Good *Christ*!" exploded Marie. "To find you, to *help* you!"

"I'm sure you thought it was right. . . . It wasn't, you know."

"That voice again," protested Marie. "That goddamned disembodied tone of voice! Who the hell do you think you are to make that judgment? *God?* To put it bluntly—no, not bluntly, but brutally—there are things you have trouble remembering, my darling."

"Not about Paris," objected Jason. "I remember everything about Paris. Everything."

"Your friend Bernardine didn't think so! He told me you never would have chosen the Meurice if you did."

"What?" Bourne briefly, harshly glanced at his wife.

"Think. Why did you choose—and you *did* choose—the Meurice?"

"I don't know . . . I'm not sure. It's a hotel; the name just came to me."

"*Think.* What happened years ago at the Meurice—right outside the Meurice?"

"I—I know something happened. . . . *You?*"

"Yes, my love, *me.* I stayed there under a false name and you came to meet me, and we walked to the newsstand on the corner, where in one horrible moment we both knew my life could never be the same again—with you or without you."

"Oh, Jesus, I forgot! The newspapers—your photograph on all the front pages. You were the Canadian government official—"

"The *escaped* Canadian economist," broke in Marie, "hunted by the authorities all over Europe for multiple killings in Zurich in tandem with the theft of millions from Swiss banks! Those kinds of headlines never leave a person, do they? They can be refuted, proved to be totally false, yet still there is that lingering doubt. 'Where there's smoke there must be fire,' I believe is the bromide. My own colleagues in Ottawa . . . dear, dear friends I'd worked with for years . . . were afraid to *talk* to me!"

"*Wait* a minute!" shouted Bourne, his eyes again flashing at David's wife. "They *were* false—it was a Treadstone ploy to pull me in—you were the one who understood it, *I* didn't!"

"Of course I did, because you were so stretched you couldn't see it. It didn't matter to me then because I'd made up my mind, my very precise analytical mind, a mind I'd match against yours any day of the week, my sweet scholar."

"*What?*"

"Watch the *road*! You missed the turn, just the way you missed the one to our cabin only days ago—or was it years ago?"

"What the hell are you talking about?"

"That small inn we stayed at outside the Bar-bizon. You politely asked them to please light the fire in the dining room—we were the only people there. It was the third time I saw through the mask of Jason Bourne to someone else, someone I was falling deeply in love with."

"Don't do this to me."

"I have to, David. If only for myself now. I have to know you're there."

Silence. A U-turn on the *grand-route* and the driver pressed the accelerator to the floor. "I'm here," whispered the husband, lifting his right arm and pulling his wife to him. "I don't know for how long, but I'm here."

"Hurry, my darling."

"I will. I just want to hold you in my arms."

"And I want to call the children."

"Now I know I'm here."

28

"You'll tell us everything we want to know voluntarily or we'll send you up into a chemical orbit your hacks never dreamed of with Dr. Panov," said Peter Holland, director of the Central Intelligence Agency, his quiet monotone as hard and as smooth as polished granite. "Furthermore, I should elaborate on the extremes to which I'm perfectly willing to go because I'm from the old school, *paisan*. I don't give a shit for rules that favor garbage. You play cipher with me, I'll deep-six you still breathing a hundred miles off Hatteras in a torpedo casing. Am I clear?"

The capo subordinato, thick plaster casts around his left arm and right leg, lay on the bed in Langley's deserted infirmary room, deserted since the DCI ordered the medical staff to get out of hearing range for their own good. The mafioso's naturally puffed face was additionally enlarged by swellings around both eyes as well as his generous lips, the result of his head having smashed into the dashboard when Mo Panov sent the car into a Maryland oak. He looked up at Holland, his heavy-lidded gaze traveling over to Alexander Conklin seated in a chair, the ever-present cane gripped in anxious hands.

"You got no right, Mr. Big Shot," said the capo gruffly. " 'Cause *I* got rights, you know what I mean?"

"So did the doctor, and you violated them—*Jesus*, did you violate them!"

"I don't gotta talk without my lawyer."

"Where the hell was *Panov's* lawyer?" shouted Alex, thumping his cane on the floor.

"That's not the way the system works," protested the patient, attempting to raise his eyebrows in indignation. "Besides, I was good to the doc. He took advantage of my goodness, s'help me God!"

"You're a cartoon," said Holland. "You're a hot sketch but you're not remotely amusing.

There are no lawyers here, linguine, just the three of us, and a torpedo casing is very much in your future."

"Whaddaya *want* from me?" cried the mafioso. "What do *I* know? I just do what I'm told, like my older brother did—may he rest in peace—and my father—may he also rest in peace—and probably *his* father, which I don't know nothin' about."

"It's like succeeding generations on welfare, isn't it?" observed Conklin. "The parasites never get off the dole."

"Hey, that's my family you're talkin' about—whatever the fuck you're talkin' about."

"My apologies to your heraldry," added Alex.

"And it's that family of yours we're interested in, Augie," broke in the DCI. "It *is* Augie, isn't it? That was the name on one of the five driver's licenses and we thought it seemed most authentic."

"Well, you're not so authentically bright, Mr. Big Shot!" spat out the immobilized patient through his painfully swollen lips. "I got none of them names."

"We have to call you something," said Holland. "If only to burn it into the casing down at Hatteras so that some scale-headed archaeologist several thousand years from now can give an identity to the teeth he's measuring."

"How about Chauncy?" asked Conklin.

"Too ethnic," replied Peter. "I like Asshole because that's what he is. He's going to be strapped into a tube and dropped over the continental shelf into six miles of seawater for crimes other people committed. I mean, that's being an asshole."

"Cut it out!" roared the asshole. "Awright, my name's Nicolo . . . Nicholas Dellacroce, and for even giving you that you gotta get me protection! Like with Valachi, that's part of the deal."

"It is?" Holland frowned. "I don't remember mentioning it."

"Then you don't get *nuthin'!*"

"You're wrong, Nicky," broke in Alex from across the small room. "We're going to get everything we want, the only drawback being that it's a one-time shot. We won't be able to cross-examine you, or bring you into a federal court, or even have you sign a deposition."

"Huh?"

"You'll come out a vegetable with a refried brain. Of course, I suppose it's a blessing in a way. You'll hardly know it when you're packed into that shell casing in Hatteras."

"Hey, waddaya *talkin'*?"

"Simple logic," answered the former naval commando and present head of the Central Intelligence Agency. "After our medical team gets finished with you, you can't expect us to keep you around, can you? An autopsy would railroad us to a rock pile for thirty years and, frankly, I haven't got that kind of time. . . . What'll it be, Nicky? You want to talk to us or do you want a priest?"

"I gotta think—"

"Let's go, Alex," said Holland curtly, walking away from the bed toward the door. "I'll send for a priest. This poor son of a bitch is going to need all the comfort he can get."

"It's times like this," added Conklin, planting his cane on the floor and rising, "when I seriously ponder man's inhumanity to man. Then I rationalize. It's not brutality, for that's only a descriptive abstraction; it's merely the custom of the trade we're all in. Still, there's the individual—his mind and his flesh and his all too sensitive nerve endings. It's the excruciating pain. Thank heavens I've always been in the background, out of reach—like Nicky's associates. They dine in elegant restaurants and he goes over in a tube beyond the continental shelf, six miles down in the sea, his body imploding into itself."

"Awright, *awright!*" screamed Nicolo Dellacroce, twisting on the bed, his obese frame tangling the sheets. "Ask your fuckin' questions, but you give me protection, *capisce?*"

"That depends on the truthfulness of your answers," said Holland, returning to the bed.

"I'd be very truthful, Nicky," observed Alex, limping back to the chair. "One misstatement and you sleep with the fishes—I believe that's the customary phrase."

"I don't need no coaching, I know where it's at."

"Let's begin, Mr. Dellacroce," said the CIA chief, taking a small tape recorder out of his pocket, checking the charge and placing it on the high white table by the patient's bed. He drew up a chair and continued speaking, addressing his opening remarks to the thin silver recorder. "My name is Admiral Peter Holland, currently director of the Central Intelligence Agency, voice confirmation to be verified if necessary. This is an interview with an informer we'll call John Smith, voice distortion to follow on interagency master tape, identification in the DCI's classified files. . . . All right, Mr. Smith, we're going to cut through the bullshit to the essential questions. I'll generalize them as much as possible for your protection, but you'll know exactly what I'm referring to and I expect specific answers. . . . Whom do you work for, Mr. Smith?"

"Atlas Coin Vending Machines, Long Island City," replied Dellacroce, his words slurred and spoken gruffly.

"Who owns it?"

"I dunno who owns it. Most of us work from home—some fifteen, maybe twenty guys, you know what I mean? We service the machines and send in our reports."

Holland glanced over at Conklin; both men smiled. With one answer the mafioso had placed himself within a large circle of potential informers. Nicolo was not new to the game. "Who signs your paychecks, Mr. Smith?"

"A Mr. Louis DeFazio, a very legitimate businessman, to d'best of my knowledge. He gives us our assignments."

"Do you know where he lives?"

"Brooklyn Heights. On the river, I think someone told me."

"What was your destination when our personnel intercepted you?"

Dellacroce winced, briefly closing his swollen eyes before answering. "One of those drunk-and-dope tanks somewhere south of Philly— which you already know, Mr. Big Shot, 'cause you found the map in the car."

Holland angrily reached for the recorder, snapping it off. "You're on your way to Hatteras, you son of a bitch!"

"*Hey*, you get your info your way, I give it mine, okay? There *was* a map—there's *always* a map—and each of us has to take those cock-amamy back roads to the joint like we were driving the president or even a don superiore to an Appalachian meet. . . . You gimme that message pad and the pencil, I'll give you the location right down to the brass plate on the stone gate." The mafioso raised his uncased right arm and jabbed his index finger at the DCI. "It'll be accurate, Mr. Big Shot, because I don't wanna sleep with no fishes, *capisce*?"

"But you won't put it on tape," said Holland, a disturbed inflection in his voice. "Why not?"

"Tape, shit! What did you call it? An inter-agency *master* bullshit? What do you think . . . our people can't tap into this place? Hoo-*hah*! That fuckin' doctor of yours could be one of us!"

"He's not, but we're going to get to an army doctor who is." Peter Holland picked up the message pad and pencil from the bedside table, handing both to Dellacroce. He did not bother to switch on the tape recorder. They were beyond props and into hardball.

In New York City, on 138th Street between Broadway and Amsterdam Avenue, the hard core of Harlem, a large disheveled black man in his mid-thirties staggered up the sidewalk. He bounced off the chipped brick wall of a run-down apartment building and slumped down on the pavement, his legs extended, his unshaven face angled into the right collar of his torn army-surplus shirt.

"With the looks I'm getting," he said quietly into the miniaturized microphone under the cloth, "you'd think I'd invaded the high colonic white shopping district of Palm Springs."

"You're doing beautifully," came the metallic voice over the tiny speaker sewn into the back of the agent's collar. "We've got the place covered; we'll give you plenty of notice. That answering machine's so jammed it's sending out whistling smoke."

"How did you two lily boys get into that trap over there?"

"Very early this morning, so early no one noticed what we looked like."

"I can't wait to watch you get out; it's a needle condo if I ever saw one. Speaking of which, which we are in a way, are the cops on this beat alerted? I'd hate like hell to get hauled in after growing this bristle on my face. It itches like crazy and my new wife of three weeks doesn't dig it."

"You should have stayed with the first one, buddy."

"Funny little white boy. She didn't like the hours or the geography. Like in being away for weeks at a time playing games in Zimbabwe. Answer me, please?"

"The blue coats have your description and the scenario. You're part of a federal bust, so they'll leave you alone. . . . *Hold* it! Conversation's over. This has to be our man; he's got a telephone satchel strapped to his belt. . . . It *is.* He's heading for the doorway. It's all yours, Emperor Jones."

"Funny little white boy. . . . I've got him and I can tell you now he's a soft chocolate mousse. He's scared shitless to go into this palace."

"Which means he's legitimate," said the metallic voice in the collar. "That's good."

"That's bad, junior," countered the black agent instantly. "If you're right, he doesn't know anything, and the layers between him and the source will be as thick as Southern molasses."

"Oh? Then how do you read it?"

"On-scene tech. I have to see the numbers when he programs them into his trouble-shooter."

"What the hell does that mean?"

"He may be legit, but he's also been frightened and not by the premises."

"What does *that* mean?"

"It's all over his face, man. He could enter in false numbers if he thinks he's being followed or watched."

"You've lost me, buddy."

"He has to duplicate the digits that correspond to the remote so the beeps can be relayed—"

"Forget it," said the voice from the back of the collar. "That high-tech I'm not. Besides, we got a man down at that company, Reco-something-or-other, now. He's waiting for you."

"Then I've got work to do. Out, but keep me monitored." The agent rose from the pavement and unsteadily made his way into the dilapidated building. The telephone repairman had reached the second floor, where he turned right in the narrow, filthy corridor; he had obviously been there before, as there was no hesitation, no checking the barely legible numbers on the doors. Things were going to be a little easier, considered the CIA man, grateful because his assignment was beyond the purview of the Agency. Purview, shit, it was illegal.

The agent took the steps three at a time, his soft double-soled rubber shoes reducing the noise to the inevitable creaks of an old staircase. His back against the wall, he peered around the corner of the trash-filled hallway and watched the repairman insert three separate keys into three vertical locks, turning each in succession and entering the last door on the left. Things, reconsidered the agent, might not be so easy after all. The instant the man closed the door, he ran silently down the corridor and stood motionless, listening. Not wonderful, but not the worst, he thought as he heard the sound of only one lock being latched; the repairman was in a hurry. He placed his ear against the peeling paint of the door and held his breath, no echo from his lungs disturbing his hearing. Thirty seconds later he turned his head, exhaled, then took a deep breath and went back to the door. Although muffled, he heard the words clearly enough to piece together the meaning.

"Central, this is Mike up on a Hundred Thirty-eighth Street, section twelve, machine sixteen. Is there another unit in this building, which I wouldn't believe if you said there was." The following silence lasted perhaps twenty additional seconds. ". . . We don't, huh? Well, we got a frequency interference and it don't make no sense to me. . . . The what? Cable TV? Ain't no one in this neighborhood got the bread for that. . . . Oh, I gotcha, brother. *Area* cable. The drug boys live high, don't they? Their addresses may be shit, but inside them homes they got they-selves a pile of fancy crap. . . . So clear the line and reroute it. I'll stay here until I get a clean signal, okay, brother?"

The agent again turned away from the door and again breathed, now in relief. He could leave without a confrontation; he had all he needed. One Hundred Thirty-eighth Street, sec-tion *twelve*, machine *sixteen*, and they knew the firm that installed the equipment. The Reco-Metropolitan Company, Sheridan Square, New York. The lily-whites could handle it from there.

He walked back to the questionable staircase and lifted the collar of his army-surplus shirt. "In case I get run over by a truck, here's the input. Are you reading me?"

"Loud and clear, Emperor Jones."

"It's machine sixteen in what they call section twelve."

"Got it! You've earned your paycheck."

"You might at least say, 'Outstanding, old chap.' "

"Hey, you're the guy who went to college over there, not me."

"Some of us are overachievers. . . . *Hold* it! I've got *company*!"

Below on the bottom of the staircase a small compact black man appeared, his dark eyes bulging, staring up at the agent, a gun in his hand. The CIA man spun behind the edge of the wall as four successive gunshots shattered the corridor. Lunging across the open space, his revolver ripped from its holster, the agent fired twice, but once was enough. His assailant fell to the floor of the soiled lobby.

"I caught a ricochet in my leg!" cried the agent. "But he's down—deep dead or not I can't tell. Sweep up the vehicle and get us both out. *Pronto.*"

"On its way. Stay put!"

It was shortly past eight o'clock the next morning when Alex Conklin limped into Peter Holland's office. The guards at the CIA gates were impressed with his immediate access to the director.

"Anything?" asked the DCI, looking up from the papers on his desk.

"Nothing," answered the retired field officer angrily, heading for the couch against the wall rather than a chair. "Not a goddamned thing. Jesus, what a fucked-up day and it hasn't even begun! Casset and Valentino are down in the cellars sending out queries all over the Paris sewers but so far *nothing*. . . . Christ, look at the scenario and find me a thread! Swayne, Armbruster, DeSole—our mute son of a bitch, the *mole*. Then for God's sake, *Teagarten* with Bourne's calling card, when we know damned well it's a trap for Jason set by the Jackal. But there's no logic anywhere that ties Carlos to Teagarten and by extension to *Medusa*. Nothing makes sense, Peter. We've lost the spine—everything's gone off the wire!"

"Calm down," said Holland gently.

"How the hell *can* I? Bourne's disappeared—I mean really disappeared, if he isn't dead. And there's no trace of Marie, no word from her, and then we learn that Bernardine was killed in a shoot-out only hours ago on the Rivoli—*Christ,* shot in broad daylight! And that means Jason was there—he had to be *there*!"

"But since none of the dead or wounded fits his description, we can assume he got away, can't we?"

"We can hope, yes."

"You asked for a thread," mused the DCI. "I'm not sure I can actually provide one, but I can give you something like it."

"New York?" Conklin sat forward on the couch. "The answering machine? That DeFazio hood in Brooklyn Heights?"

"We'll get to New York, to all of that—them. Right now let's concentrate on that thread of yours, that spine you mentioned."

"I'm not the slowest kid on the block, but where is it?"

Holland leaned back in his chair, gazing first at the papers on his desk and then up at Alex. "Seventy-two hours ago, when you decided to come clean with me about everything, you said that the idea behind Bourne's strategy was to persuade the Jackal and this latter-day Medusa to join forces, with Bourne as the common target, one feeding the other. Wasn't that basically the premise? Both sides wanted him killed. Carlos had two reasons—revenge and the fact that he believes Bourne could identify him; the Medusans because Bourne had pieced together so much about them?"

"That was the premise, yes," agreed Conklin, nodding. "It's why I dug around and made those phone calls, never expecting to find what I did. *Jesus,* a global cartel born twenty years ago in Saigon, peopled by some of the biggest fish in and out of the government and the military. It was the kind of pay dirt I didn't want and wasn't looking for. I thought I might dig up maybe ten or twelve hotshot millionaires with post-Saigon bank accounts that couldn't bear scrutiny, but not this, not *this* Medusa."

"To put it as simply as possible," continued Holland, frowning, his eyes again straying down to the papers in front of him, then up at Alex. "Once the connection was made between Medusa and Carlos, word would be passed to the Jackal that there was a man Medusa wanted eliminated, and cost was no object. So far, yes?"

"The key here was the caliber and the status of those reaching Carlos," explained Conklin.

"They had to be as close to bona fide Olympians as we could find, the kind of clients the Jackal doesn't get and never got."

"Then the name of the target is revealed—say, in a way such as 'John Smith, once known years ago as Jason Bourne'—and the Jackal is hooked. Bourne, the one man he wants dead above all others."

"Yes. That's why the Medusans reaching Carlos had to be so solid, so above questioning that Carlos accepts them and dismisses any sort of a trap."

"Because," added the CIA's director, "Jason Bourne came out of Saigon's Medusa—a fact known to Carlos—but he never shared in the riches of the later, postwar Medusa. That's the background scenario, isn't it?"

"The logic's as clean as it can be. For three years he was used and damn near killed in a black operation, and along the way he supposedly discovered that more than a few undistinguished Saigon pricks were driving Jaguars and were sailing yachts and pulling down six-figure retainers while he went on a government pension. That could try the patience of John the Baptist, to say nothing of Barabbas."

"It's a terrific libretto," allowed Holland, a

slow smile breaking across his face. "I can hear the tenors soaring in triumph and the Machiavellian bassos slinking offstage in defeat. . . . Don't *scowl* at me, Alex, I mean it! It's really ingenious. It's so inevitable it became a self-fulfilling prophecy."

"What the hell are you talking about?"

"Your Bourne was right from the beginning. It all took place the way he saw it, but not in *any* way he could have imagined. Because it was inevitable; somewhere there had to be a cross-pollinator."

"Please come down from Mars and explain to an earthling, Peter."

"Medusa's *using* the Jackal! *Now.* Teagarten's assassination proves it unless you want to concede that Bourne actually blew up that car outside of Brussels."

"Of course not."

"Then Carlos's name had to surface for someone in Medusa who already knew about Jason Bourne. It couldn't be otherwise. You didn't mention either one to Armbruster, or Swayne, or Atkinson in London, did you?"

"Again, of course not. The time wasn't right; we weren't ready to pull those triggers."

"Who's left?" asked Holland.

Alex stared at the DCI. "Good Lord," he said softly. "DeSole?"

"Yes, DeSole, the grossly underpaid specialist who complained amusingly but incessantly that there was no way a man could properly educate his children and grandchildren on government pay. He was brought in on everything we discussed, starting with your assault on us in the conference room."

"He certainly was, but that was limited to Bourne and the Jackal. There was no mention of Armbruster or Swayne, no Teagarten or Atkinson—the new Medusa wasn't even in the picture. Hell, Peter, *you* didn't know about it until seventy-two hours ago."

"Yes, but DeSole did because he'd sold out; he was part of it. He had to have been alerted. '. . . *Watch* it. We've been penetrated. Some maniac says he's going to expose us, blow us apart.' . . . You told me yourself that panic buttons were punched from the Trade Commission to Pentagon Procurements to the embassy in London."

"They were punched," agreed Conklin. "So hard that two of them had to be taken out along with Teagarten and our disgruntled Mole. Snake Lady's elders quickly decided who their vulnerable people were. But where does Carlos or Bourne fit in? There's no attribution."

"I thought we agreed that there was."

"DeSole?" Conklin shook his head. "It's a provocative thought, but it doesn't wash. He couldn't have presumed that I knew about Medusa's penetration because we hadn't even started it."

"But when you did, the sequence had to bother him if only in the sense that although they were poles apart, one crisis followed too quickly upon another. What was it? A matter of hours?"

"Less than twenty-four . . . Still, they *were* poles apart."

"Not for an analyst's analyst," countered Holland. "If it walks like an odd duck and sounds like an odd duck, look for an odd duck. I submit that somewhere along the line DeSole made the connection between Jason Bourne and the madman who had infiltrated Medusa—the new Medusa."

"For Christ's sake, *how*?"

"I don't know. Maybe because you told us Bourne came out of the old *Saigon* Medusa— that's one hell of a connection to begin with."

"My God, you may be right," said Alex, falling back on the couch. "The driving force we gave our unnamed madman was that he'd been cut *off* from the new Medusa. I used the words myself with every phone call. 'He's spent years putting it together. . . .' 'He's got names and ranks and banks in Zurich. . . .' Jesus, I'm *blind*! I said those things to total strangers on a telephone fishing expedition and never even thought about having mentioned Bourne's origins in Medusa at that meeting when DeSole was *here*."

"Why should you have thought about it? You and your man decided to play a separate game all by yourselves."

"The reasons were goddamned valid," broke in Conklin. "For all I knew, *you* were a Medusan."

"Thanks a bunch."

"Come on, don't give me that shit. 'We've got a top max out at Langley' . . . those were the words I heard from London. What would you have thought, what would you have done?"

"Exactly what you did," answered Holland, a tight grin on his lips. "But you're supposed to be so bright, so much smarter than I'm supposed to be."

"Thanks a bunch."

"Don't be hard on yourself; you did what any of us would have done in your place."

"For that I do thank you. And you're right, of course. It had to be DeSole; how he did it, I don't know, but it had to be him. It probably went back years inside his head—he never really forgot anything, you know. His mind was a sponge that absorbed everything and never let a recollection drip away. He could remember words and phrases, even spontaneous grunts of approval or disapproval the rest of us forgot. . . . And I gave him the whole Bourne-Jackal history—and then someone from Medusa used it in Brussels."

"They did more than that, Alex," said Holland, leaning forward in his chair and picking up several papers from his desk. "They stole your scenario, usurped your strategy. They've pitted Jason Bourne against Carlos the Jackal, but instead of the controls being in your hands, Medusa has them. Bourne's back where he was in Europe thirteen years ago, maybe with his wife, maybe not, the only difference being that in addition to Carlos and Interpol and every other police authority on the continent ready to waste him on sight, he's got another lethal monkey on his back."

"That's what's in those pages you're holding, isn't it? The information from New York?"

"I can't guarantee it, but I think so. It's the

cross-pollinator I spoke about before, the bee that went from one rotten flower to another carrying poison."

"Deliver, please."

"Nicolo Dellacroce and the higher-ups above him."

"Mafia?"

"It's consistent, if not socially acceptable. Medusa grew out of Saigon's officer corps and it still relegates its dirty work to the hungry grunts and corrupt NCOs. Check out Nicky D. and men like Sergeant Flannagan. When it comes to killing or kidnapping or using drugs on prisoners, the starched-shirt boys stay far in the background; they're nowhere to be found."

"But I gather you found them," said the impatient Conklin.

"Again, we think so—we being our people in quiet consultation with New York's anticrime division, especially a unit called the U.S. platoon."

"Never heard of it."

"They're mostly Italian Americans; they gave themselves the name Untouchable Sicilians. Thus the U.S. initials with a dual connotation."

"Nice touch."

"Unnice work. . . . According to the Reco-Metropolitan's billing files—"

"The *who*?"

"The company that installed the answering machine on One Hundred Thirty-eighth Street in Manhattan."

"Sorry. Go on."

"According to the files, the machine was leased to a small importing firm on Eleventh Avenue several blocks from the piers. An hour ago we got the telephone records for the past two months for the company, and guess what we found?"

"I'd rather not wait," said Alex emphatically.

"Nine calls to a reasonably acceptable number in Brooklyn Heights, and three in the space of an hour to an extremely unlikely telephone on Wall Street."

"Someone was excited—"

"That's what we thought—we in this case being our own unit. We asked the Sicilians to give us what they had on Brooklyn Heights."

"DeFazio?"

"Let's put it this way. He lives there, but the phone is registered to the Atlas Coin Vending Machine Company in Long Island City."

"It fits. Dumb, but it fits. What about DeFazio?"

"He's a middle-level but ambitious capo in the

Giancavallo family. He's very close, very underground, very vicious . . . and very gay."

"Holy Christ . . . !"

"The Untouchables swore us to secrecy.
They intend to spring it themselves."

"Bullshit," said Conklin softly. "One of the
first things we learn in this business is to lie to
anyone and everyone, especially anyone who's
foolish enough to trust us. We'll use it anytime
it gets us a square forward. . . . What's the other
telephone number, the unlikely one?"

"Just about the most powerful law firm on
Wall Street."

"Medusa," concluded Alex firmly.

"That's the way I read it. They've got seventy-
six lawyers on two floors of the building. Which
one is it—or who among them are they?"

"I don't *give* a goddamn! We go after DeFazio
and whatever controls he's sending over to
Paris. To Europe to feed the Jackal. They're the
guns after Jason and that's all I care about. Go
to work on *DeFazio*. He's the one under contract!"

Peter Holland leaned back in his chair, rigid,
intense. "It had to come to this, didn't it, Alex?"
he asked quietly. "We both have our priorities.
. . . I'd do anything within my sworn capacity to

save the lives of Jason Bourne and his wife, but I will not violate my oath to defend this country first. I can't do it and I suspect you know that. My priority is Medusa, in your words a global cartel that intends to become a government within our government over here. That's whom I have to go after. First and immediately and without regard to casualties. To put it plainly, my friend— and I hope you're my friend—the Bournes, or whoever they are, are expendable. I'm sorry, Alex."

"That's really why you asked me to come over here this morning, isn't it?" said Conklin, planting his cane on the floor and awkwardly getting to his feet.

"Yes, it is."

"You've got your own game plan against Medusa—and we can't be a part of it."

"No, you can't. It's a fundamental conflict of interest."

"I'll grant you that. We'd louse you up in a minute if it'd help Jason and Marie. Naturally, my personal and professional opinion is that if the whole fucking United States government can't rip out a Medusa without sacrificing a man and a woman who've given so much, I'm not sure it's *worth* a damn!"

"Neither am I," said Holland, standing up behind the desk. "But I swore an oath to try—in order of my sworn priorities."

"Have I got any perks left?"

"Anything I can get you that doesn't compromise our going after Medusa."

"How about two seats on a military aircraft, Agency-cleared, to Paris."

"*Two* seats?"

"Panov and me. We went to Hong Kong together, why not Paris?"

"*Alex,* you're out of your goddamned *mind*!"

"I don't think you understand, Peter. Mo's wife died ten years after they were married, and I never had the courage to give it a try. So you see, 'Jason Bourne' and Marie are the only family we have. She makes a hell of a meat loaf, let me tell you."

"Two tickets to Paris," said Holland, his face ashen.

29

Marie watched her husband as he walked back and forth, the pacing deliberate, energized. He tramped angrily between the writing table and the sunlit curtains of the two windows overlooking the front lawn of the Auberge des Artistes in Barbizon. The country inn was the one Marie remembered, but it was not part of David Webb's memory; and when he said as much, his wife briefly closed her eyes, hearing another voice from years ago.

"Above everything, he's got to avoid extreme stress, the kind of tension that goes with survival under life-threatening circumstances. If you see him regressing into that state of mind—and

you'll know it when you see it—stop him. Se-
duce him, slap him, cry, get angry . . . anything,
just stop him." *Morris Panov, dear friend, doctor
and the guiding force behind her husband's
therapy.*

She had tried seduction within minutes after
they were alone together. It was a mistake, even
a touch farcical, awkward for both of them. Neither was remotely aroused. Yet there was no
embarrassment; they held each other on the
bed, both understanding.

"We're a couple of real sexpots, aren't we?"
said Marie.

"We've been there before," replied David
Webb gently, "and I've no doubt we'll be there
again." Then Jason Bourne rolled away and
stood up. "I have to make a list," he said urgently, heading for the quaint country table
against the wall that served as a desk and a
place for the telephone. "We have to know
where we are and where we're going."

"And I have to call Johnny on the island,"
added Marie, rising to her feet and smoothing
her skirt. "After I talk to him I'll speak to Jamie.
I'll reassure him and tell him we'll be back
soon." The wife crossed to the table; she
stopped, blocked by her husband—her husband
yet not her husband.

"No," said Bourne quietly, shaking his head.

"Don't *say* that to me," protested the mother, anger flashing in her eyes.

"Three hours ago in the Rivoli changed everything. Nothing's the same now. Don't you understand that?"

"I understand that my children are several thousand miles away from me and I intend to reach them. Don't you understand *that*?"

"Of course I do, I just can't allow it," answered Jason.

"*Goddamn* you, Mr. Bourne!"

"Will you listen to me? . . . You'll talk to Johnny and to Jamie—we'll both talk to them—but not from here and not while they're on the island."

"What . . . ?"

"I'm calling Alex in a few minutes and telling him to get all of them out of there, including Mrs. Cooper, of course."

Marie had stared at her husband, suddenly understanding. "Oh, my God, *Carlos*!"

"Yes. As of this noon he's got only one place to zero in on—Tranquility. If he doesn't know now, he'll learn soon enough that Jamie and Alison are with Johnny. I trust your brother and his personal Tonton Macoute, but I still want them away from there before it's night in the islands. I also don't know if Carlos has sources in the island's trunk lines that could trace a call between there and here, but I do know that Alex's phone is sterile. That's why you can't call now. From here to there."

"Then, for God's sake, call Alex! What the hell are you *waiting* for?"

"I'm not sure." For a moment there was a blank, panicked look in her husband's eyes— they were the eyes of David Webb, not Jason Bourne. "I have to decide—where do I send the kids?"

"Alex will know, *Jason*," said Marie, her own eyes leveled steadily on his. "Now."

"Yes . . . yes, of course. Now." The veiled, vacuous look passed and Bourne reached for the phone.

Alexander Conklin was not in Vienna, Virginia, U.S.A. Instead, there was the monotonic voice of a recorded operator that had the effect of crashing thunder. "The telephone number you have called is no longer in service."

He had placed the call twice again, believing in desperate hope that an error had been made by the French telephone service. Then bolts of lightning followed: "The telephone number you have called is no longer in service." For a third time.

The pacing had begun; from the table to the windows and back again. Over and over, the curtains were pulled aside, anxious eyes nervously peering out, then seconds later poring over a growing list of names and places. Marie suggested lunch; he did not hear her, so she watched him in silence from across the room.

The quick, abrupt movements of her husband were like those of a large disquieted cat, smooth, fluid, alert for the unexpected. They were the movements of Jason Bourne and, before him, Medusa's Delta, not David Webb. She remembered the medical records compiled by Mo Panov in the early days of David's therapy. Many were filled with wildly divergent descriptions from people who claimed to have seen the man known as the Chameleon, but among the most reliable was a common reference to the catlike mobility of the "assassin." Panov had been looking for clues to Jason Bourne's identity then, for all they had at the time were a first name and fragmented images of painful death in Cambodia. Mo often wondered aloud if there was more to his patient's physical dexterity than mere athleticism; oddly enough, there was not.

As Marie looked back the subtle physical differences between the two men who were her husband both fascinated and repelled her. Each was muscular and graceful, each capable of performing difficult tasks requiring physical co-ordination; but where David's strength and mo-bility came from an easy sense of accomplishment, Jason's was filled with an inner malice, no pleasure in the accomplish-ment, only a hostile purpose. When she had mentioned this to Panov, his reply was succinct: "David couldn't kill. Bourne can; he was trained to."

Still, Mo was pleased that she had spotted the different "physical manifestations," as he called her observation. "It's another signpost for you. When you see Bourne, bring David back as fast as you can. If you can't, call me."

She could not bring David back now, she thought. For the sake of the children and herself *and* David, she dared not try.

"I'm going out for a while," announced Jason by the window.

"You can't!" cried Marie. "For God's sake, don't leave me alone."

Bourne frowned, lowering his voice, some-where an undefined conflict within him. "I'm just driving out on the highway to find a phone, that's all."

"Take me with you. *Please.* I can't stay by myself any longer."

"All right. . . . As a matter of fact, we'll need a few things. We'll find one of those malls and buy some clothes—toothbrushes, a razor . . . whatever else we can think of."

"You mean we can't go back to Paris."

"We can and probably will go back to Paris, but not to our hotels. Do you have your passport?"

"Passport, money, credit cards, everything. They were all in my purse, which I *didn't* know I had until you gave it to me in the car."

"I didn't think it was such a good idea to leave it at the Meurice. Come on. A phone first."

"Who are you calling?"

"Alex."

"You just tried him."

"At his apartment; he was thrown out of his security tent in Virginia. Then I'll reach Mo Panov. Let's go."

They drove south again to the small city of Corbeil-Essonnes, where there was a relatively new shopping center several miles west of the highway. The crowded merchandising complex was a blight on the French countryside but a welcome sight for the fugitives. Jason parked the car, and like any husband and wife out for late-afternoon shopping, they strolled down the central mall, all the while frantically looking for a public telephone.

"Not a goddamned one on the highway!" said Bourne through clenched teeth. "What do they think people are supposed to do if they have an accident or a flat tire?"

"Wait for the police," answered Marie, "and there *was* a phone, only it was broken into. Maybe that's why there aren't more— *There's* one."

Once again Jason went through the irritating process of placing an overseas call with local operators who found it irritating to ring through to the international branch of the system. And then the thunder returned, distant but implacable.

"This is Alex," said the recorded voice over the line. "I'll be away for a while, visiting a place where a grave error was made. Call me in five or six hours. It's now nine-thirty in the morning, Eastern Standard Time. Out, Juneau."

Stunned, his mind spinning, Bourne hung up the phone and stared at Marie. "Something's happened and I have to make sense out of it. His last words were—'Out, Juneau.' "

"*Juneau?*" Marie squinted, her eyes blocking out the light, then she opened them and looked at her husband. "Alpha, Bravo, Charlie," she began softly, adding, "Alternating military alphabets?" Then she spoke rapidly. "Foxtrot, Gold . . . India, *Juneau*! Juneau's for J and J is for *Jason*! . . . What was the rest?"

"He's visiting someplace—"

"Come on, let's walk," she broke in, noticing the curious faces of two men waiting to use the phone; she grabbed his arm and pulled him away from the booth. "He couldn't be clearer?" she asked as they entered the flow of the crowds.

"It was a recording. '. . . where a grave error was made.' "

"The *what*?"

"He said to call him in five or six hours—he was visiting a place where a grave error—grave?—my God, it's *Rambouillet*!"

"The cemetery . . . ?"

"Where he tried to kill me thirteen years ago. That's *it*! Rambouillet!"

"Not in five or six hours," objected Marie. "No matter when he left the message he couldn't fly to Paris and then drive to Rambouillet in five hours. He was in Washington."

"Of course he could; we've both done it

before. An army jet out of Andrews Air Force Base under diplomatic cover to Paris. Peter Holland threw him out, but he gave him a going-away present. Immediate separation, but a bonus for bringing him Medusa." Bourne suddenly whipped his wrist up and looked at his watch. "It's still only around noon in the islands. Let's find another phone."

"Johnny? Tranquility? You really think—"

"I can't *stop* thinking!" interrupted Jason, rushing ahead, holding Marie's hand as she stumblingly kept up with him. *"Glace,"* he said, looking up to his right.

"Ice cream?"

"There's a phone inside, over there," he answered, slowing them both down and approaching the huge windows of a *pâtisserie* that had a red banner over its door announcing an ice cream counter with several dozen flavors. "Get me a vanilla," he said, ushering them both into the crowded store.

"Vanilla what?"

"Whatever."

"You won't be able to hear—"

"He'll hear *me*, that's all that matters. Take your time, give *me* time." Bourne crossed to the phone, instantly understanding why it was not

used; the noise of the store was nearly unbeara-
ble. *"Mademoiselle, s'il vous plaît, c'est urgent!"*
Three minutes later, holding his palm against his
left ear, Jason had the unexpected comfort of
hearing Tranquility Inn's most irritating employee over the phone.

"This is Mr. Pritchard, Tranquility Inn's associate manager. My switchboard informs me that
you have an emergency, sir. May I inquire as to
the nature of your—"

"You can shut *up!*" shouted Jason from the
cacophonous ice cream parlor in Corbeil-Essonnes in France. "Get Jay St. Jay on the
phone, *now*. This is his brother-in-law."

"Oh, it is such a pleasure to hear from you, sir!
Much has happened since you left. Your lovely
children are with us and the handsome young
boy plays on the beach—with *me*, sir—and all
is—"

"Mr. St. Jacques, please. *Now!*"

"Of course, sir. He is upstairs. . . ."

"Johnny?"

"David, where *are* you?"

"That doesn't matter. Get out of there. Take
the kids and Mrs. Cooper and get *out!*"

"We know all about it, Dave. Alex Conklin
called several hours ago and said somebody

named Holland would reach us. . . . I gather he's the chief honcho of your intelligence service."

"He is. Did he?"

"Yeah, about twenty minutes after I talked to Alex. He told us we were being choppered out around two o'clock this afternoon. He needed the time to clear a military aircraft in here. Mrs. Cooper was my idea; your backward son says he doesn't know how to change diapers, sport. . . . David, what the hell is going on? Where's *Marie*?"

"She's all right—I'll explain everything later. Just do as Holland says. Did he say where you were being taken?"

"He didn't want to, I'll tell you that. But no fucking American's going to order me and your kids around—my *Canadian* sister's kids—and I told him that in a seven spade flush."

"That's nice, Johnny. Make friends with the director of the CIA."

"I don't give a shit on that score. In my country we figure those initials mean Caught In the Act, and I told him so!"

"That's even nicer. . . . What did he say?"

"He said we were going to a safe house in Virginia, and I said mine's pretty goddamned safe right here and we had a restaurant and room service and a beach and ten guards who could shoot his balls off at two hundred yards."

"You're full of tact. And what did he say to that?"

"Actually, he laughed. Then he explained that his place had twenty guards who could take out one of my balls at four hundred yards, along with a kitchen and room service and television for the kids that I couldn't match."

"That's pretty persuasive."

"Well, he said something else that was even more persuasive that I *really* couldn't match. He told me there was no public access to the place, that it was an old estate in Fairfax turned over to the government by a rich ambassador who had more money than Ottawa, with its own airfield and an entrance road four miles from the highway."

"I know the place," said Bourne, wincing at the noise of the *pâtisserie.* "It's the Tannenbaum estate. He's right; it's the best of the sterile houses. He likes us."

"I asked you before—where's *Marie*?"

"She's with me."

"She *found* you!"

"Later, Johnny. I'll reach you in Fairfax." Jason hung up the phone as his wife awkwardly made her way through the crowd and handed him a pink plastic cup with a blue plastic spoon plunged into a mound of dark brown.

"The *children*?" she asked, raising her voice to be heard, her eyes on fire.

"Everything's fine, better than we might have expected. Alex reached the same conclusion about the Jackal as I did. Peter Holland's flying them all up to a safe house in Virginia, Mrs. Cooper included."

"Thank God!"

"Thank Alex." Bourne looked at the pink plastic cup with the thin blue spoon. "What the hell is this? They didn't have vanilla?"

"It's a hot fudge sundae. It was meant for the man beside me but he was yelling at his wife, so I took it."

"I don't *like* hot fudge."

"So yell at your wife. Come on, we've got to buy clothes."

The early afternoon Caribbean sun burned down on Tranquility Inn as John St. Jacques descended the staircase into the lobby carrying a LeSport duffel bag in his right hand. He nodded to Mr. Pritchard, whom he had spoken to

over the phone only moments ago, explaining
that he was leaving for several days and would
be in touch within hours after he reached
Toronto. What remained of the staff had been
apprised of his sudden, quite necessary departure, and he had full confidence in the executive
manager and his valuable assistant, Mr. Pritchard. He assumed that no problems would arise
beyond their combined expertise. Tranquility
Inn, for all intents and purposes, was virtually
shut down. However, Sir Henry Sykes at Government House on the big island should be contacted in the event of difficulties.

"There shall be none beyond *my* expertise!"
Pritchard had replied. "The repair and maintenance crews will work every bit as hard in your
absence."

St. Jacques walked out the glass doors of the
circular building toward the first villa on the right,
the one nearest the stone steps to the pier and
the two beaches. Mrs. Cooper and the two children waited inside for the arrival of the United
States Navy long-range seagoing helicopter
that would take them to Puerto Rico, where they
would board a military jet to Andrews Air Force
Base outside Washington.

Through the huge glass windows, Mr. Pritchard watched his employer disappear through the doors of Villa One. At that same moment he heard the growing sounds of a large helicopter's rotors thumping in the air above the inn. In minutes it would circle the water beyond the pier and descend, awaiting its passengers. Apparently, those passengers heard what he had heard, thought Mr. Pritchard as he saw St. Jacques, gripping his young nephew's hand, and the insufferably arrogant Mrs. Cooper, who was holding a blanketed infant in her arms, come out of the villa, followed by the two favorite guards carrying their luggage. Pritchard reached below the counter for the telephone that bypassed the switchboard. He dialed.

"This is the office of the deputy director of immigration, himself speaking."

"Esteemed Uncle—"

"It is you?" broke in the official from Blackburne Airport, abruptly lowering his voice. "What have you learned?"

"Everything is of immense value, I assure you. I heard it all on the telephone!"

"We shall both be greatly rewarded, I have that on the highest authority. They may all be undercover terrorists, you know, St. Jacques himself the leader. It is said they may even fool

Washington. What can I pass on, brilliant Nephew?"

"They are being taken to what is called a 'safe' house in Virginia. It is known as the Tannenbaum estate and has its own airport, can you *believe* such a thing?"

"I can believe anything where these animals are concerned."

"Be sure to include my name and position, esteemed Uncle."

"Would I do otherwise, *could* I do otherwise? We shall be the heroes of Montserrat! . . . But remember, my intelligent Nephew, everything must be kept in utmost secrecy. We are both sworn to silence, never forget that. Just think! We've been selected to render service to a great international organization. Leaders the world over will know of our contributions."

"My heart bursts with pride. . . . May I know what this august organization is called?"

"*Shhh!* It has no name; that is part of the secrecy. The money was wired through a bank computer transfer directly from Switzerland; that is the proof."

"A sacred trust," added Mr. Pritchard.

"Also well paid, trusted Nephew, and it is only the beginning. I myself am monitoring all aircraft arriving here and sending the manifests on to Martinique, to a famous surgeon, no less! Of course, at the moment all flights are on hold, orders from Government House."

"The American military helicopter?" asked the awed Pritchard.

"Shhh! It, too, is a secret, *everything* is secret."

"Then it is a very loud and apparent secret, my esteemed Uncle. People are on the beach watching it now."

"What?"

"It's here. Mr. Saint Jay and the children are boarding as we speak. Also that dreadful Mrs. Cooper—"

"I must call Paris at once," interrupted the immigration officer, disconnecting the line.

"Paris?" repeated Mr. Pritchard. "How inspiring! How privileged we are!"

"I didn't tell him everything," said Peter Holland quietly, shaking his head as he spoke. "I wanted to—I intended to—but it was in his eyes, in his own words actually. He said that he'd louse us up in a minute if it would help Bourne and his wife."

"He would, too." Charles Casset nodded; he

sat in the chair in front of the director's desk, a computer printout of a long-buried classified file in his hand. "When you read this you'll understand. Alex really did try to kill Bourne in Paris years ago—his closest friend and he tried to put a bullet in his head for all the wrong reasons."

"Conklin's on his way to Paris now. He and Morris Panov."

"That's on *your* head, Peter. I wouldn't have done it, not without strings."

"I couldn't refuse him."

"Of course you could. You didn't want to."

"We owed him. He brought us Medusa—and from here on, Charlie, that's *all* that concerns us."

"I understand, Director Holland," said Casset coldly. "And I assume that due to foreign entanglements you're working backwards into a domestic conspiracy that should be incontestably established before you alert the guardians of domestic accord, namely, the Federal Bureau."

"Are you threatening me, you lowlife?"

"I certainly am, Peter." Casset dropped the ice from his expression, replacing it with a calm, thin smile. "You're breaking the law, Mr. Director. . . . That's regrettable, old boy, as my predecessors might have said."

"What the hell do you *want* from me?" cried Holland.

"Cover one of our own, one of the best we ever had. I not only want it, I insist upon it."

"If you think I'm going to give him everything, including the name of Medusa's law firm on Wall Street, you're out of your fucking mind. It's our *keystone*!"

"For God's sake, go back into the navy, Admiral," said the deputy director, his voice level, again cold, without emphasis. "If you think that's what I'm suggesting, you haven't learned very much in that chair."

"Hey, come on, smart ass, that's pretty close to insubordination."

"Of course it is, because I'm insubordinate—but this isn't the navy. You can't keelhaul me, or hang me from the yardarm, or withhold my ration of rum. All you can do is fire me, and if you do, a lot of people will wonder why, which wouldn't do the Agency any good. But that's not necessary."

"What the *hell* are you talking about, Charlie?"

"Well, to begin with, I'm *not* talking about that law firm in New York because you're right, it is our keystone, and Alex with his infinite imagination would probe and threaten to the point where the shredding begins and our paper trail here and abroad ends."

"I had something like that in mind—"

"Then again you were right," interrupted Casset, nodding. "So we keep Alex away from our keystone, as far away from *us* as possible, but we give him our marker. Something tangible he can plug into, knowing its value."

Silence. Then Holland spoke. "I don't understand a word you're saying."

"You would if you knew Conklin better. He knows now that there's a connection between Medusa and the Jackal. What did you call it? A self-fulfilling prophecy?"

"I said the strategy was so perfect it was inevitable and therefore self-fulfilling. DeSole was the unexpected catalyst who moved everything ahead of schedule—him and whatever the hell happened down in Montserrat. . . . What's this marker of yours, this tangible item of value?"

"The string, Peter. Knowing what he knows, you can't let Alex bounce around Europe like a loose cannon any more than you could give him the name of that law firm in New York. We need a pipeline to him so we have some idea what he's up to—more than an idea, if we can manage it. Someone like his friend Bernardine, only someone who can also be our friend."

"Where do we find such a person?"

"I have a candidate—and I hope we're not being taped."

"Count on it," said Holland with a trace of anger. "I don't believe in that crap and this office is swept every morning. Who's the candidate?"

"A man at the Soviet embassy in Paris," replied Casset calmly. "I think we can deal."

"A mole?"

"Not for a minute. A KGB officer whose first priority never changes. Find Carlos. Kill Carlos. Protect Novgorod."

"Novgorod . . . ? The Americanized village or town where the Jackal was initially trained in Russia?"

"Half trained and escaped from before he could be shot as a maniac. Only, it's not just an American compound—that's a mistake we make so often. There are British and French compounds, too, also Israeli, Dutch, Spanish, West German and God knows how many others. Dozens of square miles cut out of the forests along the Volkhov River, dotted with settlements so that you'd swear you were in a different country with each one you entered—if you could get inside, which you couldn't. Like the Aryan breeding farms, the *Lebensborn* of Nazi Germany, Novgorod is one of Moscow's most closely guarded secrets. They want the Jackal as badly as Jason Bourne does."

"And you think this KGB fellow will cooperate, keep us informed about Conklin if they make contact?"

"I can try. After all, we have a common objective, and I know Alex would accept him because he knows how much the Soviets want Carlos on the dead list."

Holland leaned forward in his chair. "I told Conklin I'd help him any way I could as long as it didn't compromise our going after Medusa. . . . He'll be landing in Paris within the hour. Shall I leave instructions at the diplomatic counter for him to reach you?"

"Tell him to call Charlie Bravo Plus One," said Casset, getting up and dropping the computer printout on the desk. "I don't know how much I can give him in an hour, but I'll go to work. I've got a secure channel to our Russian, thanks to an outstanding 'consultant' of ours in Paris."

"Give him a bonus."

"She's already asked for one—harassed me is more appropriate. She runs the cleanest escort service in the city; the girls are checked weekly.''

"Why not hire them all?" asked the director, smiling.

"I believe seven are already on the payroll, sir," answered the deputy director, his demeanor serious, in contrast to his arched eyebrows.

Dr. Morris Panov, his legs unsteady, was helped down the metal steps of the diplomatically cleared jet by a strapping marine corporal in starched summer khakis carrying his suitcase. "How do you people manage to look so presentable after such a perfectly horrendous trip?" asked the psychiatrist.

"None of us will look this presentable after a couple of hours of liberty in Paris, sir."

"Some things never change, Corporal. Thank God. . . . Where's that crippled delinquent who was with me?"

"He was vehicled off for a diplograph, sir."

"Come again? A noun's a verb leading to the incomprehensible?"

"It's not so hard, Doctor," laughed the marine, leading Panov to a motorized cart complete with a uniformed driver and a stenciled

American flag on the side. "During our descent, the tower radioed the pilot that there was an urgent message for him."

"I thought he went to the bathroom."

"That, too, I believe, sir." The corporal put the suitcase on a rear rack and helped Mo into the cart. "Easy now, Doctor, lift your leg up a little higher."

"That's the other one, not me," protested the psychiatrist. "He's the one without a foot."

"We were told you'd been ill, sir."

"Not in my goddamned legs. . . . Sorry, young men, no offense. I just don't like flying in small tubes a hundred and ten miles up in the sky. Not too many astronauts come from Tremont Avenue in the Bronx."

"Hey, you're kidding, Doc!"

"What?"

"I'm from *Garden* Street, you know, across from the *zoo*! The name's Fleishman, Morris Fleishman. Nice to meet a fellow Bronxite."

"Morris?" said Panov, shaking hands. "Morris the Marine? I should have had a talk with your parents. . . . Stay well, Mo. And thank you for your concern."

"You get better, Doc, and when you see Tremont Avenue again, give it my best, okay?"

"I will, indeed, Morris," replied Morris, raising his hand as the diplomatic cart shot forward.

Four minutes later, escorted by the driver, Panov entered the long gray corridor that was the immigration-free access to France for government functionaries of nations accredited by the Quai d'Orsay. They walked into the large holding lounge where men and women were gathered in small groups, conversing quietly, the sounds of different languages filling the room. Alarmed, Mo saw that Conklin was nowhere in sight; he turned to the driver-escort as a young woman dressed in the neutral uniform of a hostess approached.

"Docteur?" she asked, addressing Panov.

"Yes," replied Mo, surprised. "But I'm afraid my French is pretty rusty if not nonexistent."

"It's of no matter, sir. Your companion requested that you remain here until he returns. It will be no more than a few minutes, he was quite sure. . . . Please, sit down. May I bring you a drink?"

"Bourbon with ice, if you'd be so kind," answered Panov, lowering himself into the armchair.

"Certainly, sir." The hostess retreated as the driver placed Mo's suitcase beside him.

"I have to get back to my vehicle," said the diplomatic escort. "You'll be fine here."

"I wonder where my friend went," mused Panov, glancing at his watch.

"Probably to an outside phone, Doctor. They come in here, get messages at the counters, then go like hell into the terminal to find public pay phones; they don't like the ones in here. The Russkies always walk the fastest; the Arabs, the slowest."

"Must be their respective climates," offered the psychiatrist, smiling.

"Don't bet your stethoscope on it." The driver laughed and brought his hand up for an informal salute. "Take care, sir, and get some rest. You look tired."

"Thank you, young man. Good-bye." *I am tired,* thought Panov as the escort disappeared into the gray corridor. *So tired, but Alex was right. If he'd flown here alone, I would never have forgiven him. . . . David! We've got to find him! The damage to him could be incalculable— none of them understands. With a single act his fragile, damaged mind could regress years— thirteen years—to where he was a functioning killer, and for him nothing else! . . .* A voice. The figure above was talking to him. "I'm sorry, forgive me. . . . Your drink, Doctor," said the hostess pleasantly. "I debated whether to wake you, but then you moved and sounded as though you were in pain—"

"No, not at all, my dear. Just tired."

"I understand, sir. Sudden flights can be so exhausting, and if they are long and uncomfortable, even worse."

"You touched on all three points, miss," agreed Panov, taking his drink. "Thank you."

"You are American, of course."

"How could you tell? I'm not wearing cowboy boots or a Hawaiian shirt."

The woman laughed charmingly. "I know the driver who brought you in here. He's American security, and quite nice, *very* attractive."

"Security? You mean like in 'police'?"

"Oh, very much so, but we never use the word. . . . Oh, here's your companion coming back inside." The hostess lowered her voice. "May I ask quickly, Doctor? Does he require a wheelchair?"

"Good heavens, no. He's walked like that for years."

"Very well. Enjoy your stay in Paris, sir." The woman left as Alex, limping, weaved around several groups of chattering Europeans to the chair next to Panov. He sat down and leaned forward awkwardly in the soft leather. He was obviously disturbed.

"What's the matter?" asked Mo.

"I just talked to Charlie Casset in Washington."

"He's the one you like, the one you trust, isn't he?"

"He's the best there is when he has personal access, or, at least, human intelligence. When he can see and hear and look for himself, and not simply read words on paper or a computer screen without asking questions."

"Are you, perchance, moving into my territory again, *Doctor* Conklin?"

"I accused David of that last week and I'll tell you what he told me. It's a free country, and your training notwithstanding, you don't have a franchise on common sense."

"Mea culpa," agreed Panov, nodding. "I gather your friend did something you don't approve of."

"He did something *he* wouldn't approve of if he had more information on whom he did it with."

"That sounds positively Freudian, even medically imprudent."

"Both are part of it, I guess. He made an outside unsanctioned deal with a man named Dimitri Krupkin at the Russian embassy here in Paris. We'll be working with the local KGB—you, me, Bourne and Marie—if and when we find them. Hopefully, in Rambouillet in an hour or so."

"What are you *saying*?" asked Mo, astonished and barely audible.

"Long story, short time. Moscow wants the Jackal's head, the rest of him separated from it. Washington can't feed us or protect us, so the Soviets will act as our temporary paterfamilias if we find ourselves in a bind."

Panov frowned, then shook his head as though absorbing very strange information, then spoke. "I suppose it's not your run-of-the-mill development, but there's a certain logic, even comfort, to it."

"On paper, Mo," said Conklin. "Not with Dimitri Krupkin. I know him. Charlie doesn't."

"Oh? He's one of the evil people?"

"Kruppie evil? No, not really—"

"Kruppie?"

"We go way back as young hustlers to Istanbul in the late sixties and Athens after that, then Amsterdam later. . . . Krupkin's not malevolent, and he works like a son of a bitch for Moscow with a damn good second-rate mind, better than eighty percent of the clowns in our business, but he's got a problem. He's fundamentally on the wrong side, in the wrong society. His parents should have come over with mine when the Bolsheviks took the throne."

"I forget. Your family was Russian."

"Speaking the language helps with Kruppie. I can nail his nuances. He's the quintessential capitalist. Like the economic ministers in Beijing, he doesn't just like money, he's obsessed with it—and everything that *goes* with it. Out of sight and out of sanction, he could be bought."

"You mean by the Jackal?"

"I saw him bought in Athens by Greek developers selling additional airstrips to Washington when they knew the Communists were going to throw us out. They paid him to shut up. Then I watched him broker diamonds in Amsterdam between the merchants on the Nieuwmarkt and the dacha-elite in Moscow. We had drinks one night in the Kattengat and I asked him, 'Kruppie, what the fuck are you *doing*?' You know what he said? He said in clothes I couldn't afford, 'Aleksei, I'll do everything I can to outsmart you, to help the supreme Soviet to gain world dominance, but in the meantime, if you'd like a holiday, I have a lovely house on the lake in Geneva.' That's what he said, Mo."

"He's remarkable. Of course, you told your friend Casset all this—"

"Of course I didn't," broke in Conklin.

"Good God, why *not*?"

"Because Krupkin obviously never told Charlie that he knew *me.* Casset may have the deal, but I'm dealing."

"With what? How?"

"David—Jason—has over five million in the Caymans. With only a spit of that amount I'll turn Kruppie so he'll be working *only* for us, if we need him or want him to."

"Which means you don't trust Casset."

"Not so," said Alex. "I trust Charlie with my life. It's just that I'm not sure I want it in his hands. He and Peter Holland have their priorities and we have ours. Theirs is Medusa; ours are David and Marie."

"Messieurs?" The hostess returned and addressed Conklin. "Your car has arrived, sir. It is on the south platform."

"You're sure it's for me?" asked Alex.

"Forgive me, monsieur, but the attendant said a Mr. Smith had a difficult leg."

"He's certainly right about that."

"I've called a porter to carry your luggage, messieurs. It's a rather long walk. He'll meet you on the platform."

"Thanks very much." Conklin got to his feet and reached into his pocket, pulling out money.

"Pardon, monsieur," interrupted the hostess. "We are not permitted to accept gratuities."

"That's right. I forgot. . . . My suitcase is behind your counter, isn't it?"

"Where your escort left it, sir. Along with the doctor's, it will be at the platform within minutes."

"Thanks again," said Alex. "Sorry about the tip."

"We are well paid, sir, but thank you for the thought."

As they walked to the door that led into the main terminal of Orly Airport, Conklin turned to Panov. "How did she know you were a doctor?" he asked. "You soliciting couch business?"

"Hardly. The commuting would be a bit strenuous."

"Then how? I never said anything about your being a doctor."

"She knows the security escort who brought me into the lounge. In fact, I think she knows him quite well. She said in that delectable French accent of hers that he was 'verry attractiefe.' "

Looking up at the signs in the crowded terminal, they started toward the south platform.

What neither of them saw was a distinguished-looking olive-skinned man with wavy
black hair and large dark eyes walk quickly out
of the diplomatic lounge, his steady gaze directed at the two Americans. He crossed to the
wall, rushing past the crowds until he was diagonally in front of Conklin and Panov near the taxi
platform. Then, squinting, as if unsure, he
removed a small photograph from his pocket
and kept glancing at it as he raised his eyes and
looked up at the departing passengers from the
United States. The photograph was of Dr. Morris
Panov, dressed in a white hospital gown, a
glazed, unearthly expression on his face.

The Americans went out on the platform; the
dark-haired man did the same. The Americans
looked around for a taxi; the dark-haired man
signaled a private car. A driver got out of a cab;
he approached Conklin and Panov, speaking
quietly, as a porter arrived with their luggage; the
two Americans climbed into the taxi. The stranger who followed them slipped into the private
car two vehicles behind the cab.

"Pazzo!" said the dark-haired man in Italian to

the fashionably dressed middle-aged woman behind the wheel. "I tell you it's crazy! For three days we wait, all incoming American planes watched, and we are about to give up when that fool in New York turns out to be right. It's *them*! . . . Here, I'll drive. You get out and reach our people over there. Tell them to call DeFazio; instruct him to go to his other favorite restaurant and await my call to him. He is not to leave until we speak."

"Is this you, old man?" asked the hostess in the diplomatic lounge, speaking softly into the telephone at her counter.

"It is I," replied the quavering voice at the other end of the line. "And the Angelus rings for eternity in my ears."

"It is you, then."

"I told you that, so get on with it."

"The list we were given last week included a slender middle-aged American with a limp, possibly accompanied by a doctor. Is this correct?"

"Correct! *And?*"

"They have passed through. I used the title 'Doctor' with the cripple's companion and he responded to it."

"Where have they gone? It's vital that I *know*!"

"It was not disclosed, but I will soon learn enough for you to find out, old man. The porter who took their luggage to the south platform will get the description and the license of the car that meets them."

"In the name of *God,* call me back with the information!"

Three thousand miles from Paris, Louis DeFazio sat alone at a rear table in Trafficante's Clam House on Prospect Avenue in Brooklyn, New York. He finished his late afternoon lunch of *vitello tonnato* and dabbed his lips with the bright red napkin, trying to look his usual jovial, if patronizing, self. However, if the truth were known, it was all he could do to stop from gnawing on the napkin rather than caressing his mouth with it. *Maledetto!* He had been at Trafficante's for nearly two hours—*two hours*! And it had taken him forty-five minutes to get there after the call from Garafola's Pasta Palace in Manhattan, so that meant it was actually *over* two hours, almost *three,* since the gumball in Paris, France, spotted two of the targets. How long could it take for two bersaglios to get to a hotel in the city from the airport? Like three *hours*? Not unless the Palermo gumball drove to London, England, which was not out of the question, not if one knew Palermo.

Still, DeFazio knew he had been right! The way the Jew shrink talked under the needle there was no other route he and the ex-spook could take *but* to Paris and their good buddy, the fake hit man. . . . So Nicolo and the shrink disappeared, went *poof-zam,* so what the fuck? The Jew got away and Nicky would do time. But Nicolo wouldn't talk; he understood that bad trouble, like a knife in the kidney, was waiting for him wherever he went if he did. Besides, Nicky didn't know anything so specific the lawyers couldn't wipe away as secondhand horseshit from a fifth-rate horse's ass. And the shrink only knew he was in a room in some farmhouse, if he could even remember that. He never saw anybody but Nicolo when he was "compass mantis," as they say.

But Louis DeFazio knew he was *right.* And because he was right, there were more than seven million big ones waiting for him in Paris. *Seven million! Holy Christ!* He could give the Palermo gumballs in Paris more than they ever expected and still walk away with a bundle.

An old waiter from the old country, an uncle

of Trafficante, approached the table and Louis held his breath. "There's a telephone call for you, Signor DeFazio."

As was usual, the capo supremo went to a pay phone at the end of a narrow dark corridor outside the men's room. "This is New York," said DeFazio.

"This is Paris, Signor New York. This is also *pazzo*!"

"Where've you been? You *pazzo* enough to drive to London, England? I've been waitin' three hours!"

"Where I've *been* is on a number of unlit country roads, which is important only to my nerves. Where I am now is crazy!"

"So where?"

"I'm using a gatekeeper's telephone for which I'm paying roughly a hundred American dollars and the French *buffone* keeps looking through the window to see that I don't steal anything—perhaps his lunch pail, who knows?"

"You don't sound too stupid for a gumball. So what gatekeeper's what? What are you talking about?"

"I'm at a cemetery about twenty-five miles from Paris. I tell you—"

"A *cimitero*?" interrupted Louis. "What the hell *for*?"

"Because your two acquaintances drove here from the airport, you *ignorante*! At the moment there is a burial in progress—a night burial with a candlelight procession which will soon be drowned out by rain—and if your two acquaintances flew over here to attend this barbaric ceremony, then the air in America is filled with brain-damaging pollutants! We did not bargain for this *sciocchezze,* New York. We have our own work to do."

"They went there to meet the big cannoli," said DeFazio quietly, as if to himself. "As to work, gumball, if you ever want to work with us, or Philadelphia, or Chicago, or Los Angeles again, you'll do what I tell you. You'll also be terrifically paid for it, *capisce*?"

"That makes more sense, I admit."

"Stay out of sight, but stay with them. Find out where they go and who they see. I'll get over there as soon as I can, but I gotta go by way of Canada or Mexico, just to make sure no one's watching. I'll be there late tomorrow or early the next day."

"Ciao," said Paris.

"Omerta," said Louis DeFazio.

30

The hand-held candles flickered in the night drizzle as the two parallel lines of mourners walked solemnly behind the white casket borne on the shoulders of six men; several began to slip on the increasingly wet gravel of the cemetery's path. Flanking the procession were four drummers, two on each side, their snare drums snapping out the slow cadence of the death march, erratically out of sequence because of the unexpected rocks and the unseen flat grave markers in the darkness of the bordering grass. Shaking his head slowly in bewilderment, Morris Panov watched the strange nocturnal burial rite, relieved to see Alex Conklin limping, threading his way between the tombstones toward their meeting ground.

"Any sign of them?" asked Alex.

"None," replied Panov. "I gather you didn't do any better."

"Worse. I got stuck with a lunatic."

"How?"

"A light was on in the gatehouse, so I went over thinking David or Marie might have left us a message. There was a clown outside who kept looking into a window and said he was the watchman and did I want to rent his telephone."

"His telephone?"

"He said there were special rates for the night, as the nearest pay phone was ten kilometers down the road."

"A lunatic," agreed Panov.

"I explained that I was looking for a man and a woman I was to meet here and wondered if they'd left a message. There was no message but there *was* the telephone. Two hundred francs—crazy."

"I might do a flourishing business in Paris," said Mo, smiling. "Did he by any chance see a couple wandering around?"

"I asked him that and he nodded affirmative, saying there were dozens. Then he pointed to that candlelight parade over there before going back to his goddamn window.''

"What *is* that parade, incidentally?''

"I asked him that, too. It's a religious cult; they bury their dead only at night. He thinks they may be gypsies. He said *that* while blessing himself.''

"They're going to be wet gypsies,'' observed Panov, pulling up his collar as the drizzle turned into rain.

"Christ, why didn't I *think* of it?'' exclaimed Conklin, looking over his shoulder.

"The rain?'' asked the bewildered psychiatrist.

"No, the large tomb halfway up the hill beyond the gatehouse. It's where it happened!''

"Where you tried to—'' Mo did not finish the question; he did not have to.

"Where he could have killed me but didn't,'' completed Alex. "Come on!''

The two Americans retreated down the gravel path past the gatehouse and into the darkness of the rising hill of grass punctuated by white gravestones now glistening in the rain. *"Easy,"* cried Panov, out of breath. "You're used to that nonexistent foot of yours, but I haven't quite adjusted to my pristine body having been raped by chemicals.''

"Sorry."

"Mo!" shouted a woman's voice from a marble portico above. The figure waved her arms beneath the pillared, overhanging roof of a grave so large it looked like a minor mausoleum.

"Marie?" yelled Panov, rushing ahead of Conklin.

"That's nice!" roared Alex, limping with difficulty up the wet slippery grass. "You hear the sound of a female and suddenly you're *unraped.* You need a shrink, you phony!"

The embraces were meant; a family was together. While Panov and Marie spoke quietly, Jason Bourne took Conklin aside to the edge of the short marble roof, the rain now harsh. The former candlelight procession below, the flickering flames now gone, was half scattered, half holding its position by a gravesite. "I didn't mean to choose this place, Alex," said Jason. "But with that crowd down there I couldn't think of another."

"Remember the gatehouse and that wide path to the parking lot? . . . You'd won. I was out of ammunition and you could have blown my head apart."

"You're wrong, how many times have I told you? I *couldn't* have killed you. It was in your eyes; even though I wasn't able to see them clearly I knew what was there. Anger and confusion, but, above all, confusion."

"That's never been a reason not to kill a man who tries to kill you."

"It is if you can't remember. The memory may be gone but not the fragments, not the—well, for me they were . . . pulsating images. In and out, in and out, but there."

Conklin looked up at Bourne, a sad grin on his face. "The pulsating bit," he said. "That was Mo's term. You stole it."

"Probably," said Jason as both men in unison looked back at Marie and Panov. "She's talking about me, you know that, don't you?"

"Why not? She's concerned and he's concerned."

"I hate to think how many more concerns I'll give them both. You, too, I imagine."

"What are you trying to tell me, David?"

"Just that. *Forget* David. David Webb doesn't exist, not here, not now. He's an act I put on for his wife, and I do it badly. I want her to go back to the States, to her children."

"Her children? She won't do it. She came over to find you and she found you. She remembers Paris thirteen years ago and she won't

leave you. Without her then you wouldn't be alive today."

"She's an impediment. She has to go. I'll find a way."

Alex looked up at the cold eyes of the creation once known as the Chameleon and spoke quietly. "You're a fifty-year-old man, *Jason.* This isn't Paris thirteen years ago or Saigon years before that. It's *now,* and you need all the help you can get. If she thinks she can provide a measure of it, I for one believe her."

Bourne snapped his head down at Conklin. "I'll be the judge of who believes what."

"That's a touch extreme, pal."

"You know what I mean," said Jason, softening his tone. "I don't want to have happen here what happened in Hong Kong. That can't be a problem for you."

"Maybe not. . . . Look, let's get out of here. Our driver knows a little country restaurant in Epernon, about six miles from here, where we can talk. We've got several things to go over."

"Tell me," said Bourne. "Why Panov? Why did you bring Mo with you?"

"Because if I hadn't he would have put strychnine in my flu shot."

"What the hell does that mean?"

"Exactly what it says. He's a part of us, and you know it better than Marie or myself."

"Something happened to him, didn't it? Something happened to him because of me."

"It's over with and he's back, that's all you have to know now."

"It was Medusa, wasn't it?"

"Yes, but I repeat, he's back, and outside of being a little tired, he's okay."

"Little . . . ? Which reminds me. A little country restaurant six miles from here, isn't that what your driver said?"

"Yes, he knows Paris and everything around it thoroughly."

"Who is he?"

"A French Algerian who's worked for the Agency for years. Charlie Casset recruited him for us. He's tough, knowledgeable and very well paid for both. Above all, he can be trusted."

"I suppose that's good enough."

"Don't suppose, accept it."

They sat in a booth at the rear of the small country inn, complete with a worn canopy, hard pine banquettes and perfectly acceptable wine. The owner, an expansive, florid fat man, proclaimed the cuisine to be extraordinary, but since no one could summon hunger, Bourne paid for four entrées just to keep the proprietor happy. It did. The owner sent over two large carafes of good *vin ordinaire* along with a bottle of mineral water, and stayed away from the table.

"All right, Mo," said Jason, "you won't tell me what happened, or who did it, but you're still the same functioning, overbearing, verbose medicine man with a chicken in his mouth we've known for thirteen years, am I correct?"

"Correct, you schizophrenic escapee from Bellevue. And in case you think I'm being heroic, let me make it absolutely clear that I'm here only to protect my nonmedical civil rights. My paramount interest is with my adorable Marie, who I trust you'll notice is sitting beside me, not you. I positively salivate thinking about her meat loaf."

"Oh, how I do love you, Mo," said David Webb's wife, squeezing Panov's arm.

"Let me count the ways," responded the doctor, kissing her cheek.

"I'm here," said Conklin. "My name is Alex and I have a couple of things to talk about and they don't include meat loaf. . . . Although I should tell you, Marie, I told Peter Holland yesterday that it was terrific."

"What's with my damned meat loaf?"

"It's the red sauce," interjected Panov.

"May we get to what we're here for," said Jason Bourne, his voice a monotone.

"Sorry, darling."

"We'll be working with the Soviets." Conklin spoke quickly, his rush of words countering the immediate reaction from Bourne and Marie. "It's all right, I know the contact, I've known him for years, but Washington doesn't know I know him. His name is Krupkin, Dimitri Krupkin, and as I told Mo, he can be bought for five pieces of silver."

"Give him thirty-one," interrupted Bourne, "to make sure he's on our side."

"I figured you'd say that. Do you have a ceiling?"

"None."

"Not so fast," said Marie. "What's a negotiable starting point?"

"Our economist speaks," proclaimed Panov, drinking his wine.

"Considering his position in the Paris KGB, I'd say around fifty thousand, American."

"Offer him thirty-five and escalate to seventy-five under pressure. Up to a hundred, if necessary, of course."

"For Christ's *sake,*" cried Jason, controlling his voice. "We're talking about *us,* about the *Jackal.* Give him anything he wants!"

"Too easily bought, too easily turned to another source. To a counteroffer."

"Is she right?" asked Bourne, staring at Conklin.

"Normally, of course, but in this case it would have to be the equivalent of a workable diamond mine. No one wants Carlos in the dead file more than the Soviets, and the man who brings in his corpse will be the hero of the Kremlin. Remember, he was trained at Novgorod. Moscow never forgets that."

"Then do as she says, only *buy* him," said Jason.

"I understand." Conklin leaned forward, turning his glass of water. "I'll call him tonight, pay phone to pay phone, and get it settled. Then I'll arrange a meeting tomorrow, maybe lunch somewhere outside of Paris. Very early, before the regulars come in."

"Why not here?" asked Bourne. "You can't get much more remote and I'll know the way."

"Why not?" agreed Alex. "I'll talk to the

owner. But not the four of us, just—Jason and me."

"I assumed that," said Bourne coldly. "Marie's not to be involved. She's not to be seen or heard, is that clear?"

"David, really—"

"Yes, *really.*"

"I'll go over and stay with her," interrupted Panov quickly. "Meat loaf?" he added, obviously to lessen the tension.

"I don't have a kitchen, but there's a lovely restaurant that serves fresh trout."

"One sacrifices," sighed the psychiatrist.

"I think you should eat in the room." Bourne's voice was now adamant.

"I will *not* be a prisoner," said Marie quietly, her gaze fixed on her husband. "Nobody knows who we are or where we are, and I submit that someone who locks herself in her room and is never seen draws far more attention than a perfectly normal Frenchwoman who goes about her normal business of living."

"She's got a point," observed Alex. "If Carlos has his network calling around, someone behaving abnormally could be picked up. Besides, Panov's from left field—pretend you're a doctor or something, Mo. Nobody'll believe it, but it'll add a touch of class. For reasons that escape me, doctors are usually above suspicion."

"Psychopathic ingrate," mumbled Panov.

"May we get back to business?" said Bourne curtly.

"You're very rude, David."

"I'm very impatient, do you mind?"

"Okay, cool it," said Conklin. "We're all uptight, but things have got to be clear. Once Krupkin's on board, his first job will be to trace the number Gates gave Prefontaine in Boston."

"Who gave what *where*?" asked the bewildered psychiatrist.

"You were out of it, Mo. Prefontaine's an impeached judge who fell into a Jackal contact. To cut it short, the contact gave our judge a number here in Paris to reach the Jackal, but it didn't coincide with the one Jason already had. But there's no question that the contact, a lawyer named Gates, reached Carlos."

"*Randolph* Gates? Boston's gift to the boardrooms of Genghis Khan?"

"That's the one."

"Holy *Christ*—I'm sorry, I shouldn't say that, I'm not a gentile. What the hell, I'm nothing, but you'll admit it's a shock."

"A large one, and we have to know who owns that number here in Paris. Krupkin can find out for us. It's corkscrew, I grant you, but there it is."

"*Corkscrew?*" asked Panov. "Are you now going to produce a Rubik's cube in Arabic? Or, perhaps, a Double-Crostic from the London *Times*? What in heaven's name is a Prefontaine, judge, jury or otherwise? It sounds like a bad early wine."

"It's a late, very good vintage," broke in Marie. "You'd like him, Doctor. You could spend months studying him because he's got more brights than most of us, and that grand intellect of his is still intact despite such inconveniences as alcohol, corruption, loss of family and prison. He's an original, Mo, and where the majority of felons in his league blame everyone but themselves, he doesn't. He retains a gloriously ironic sense of humor. If the American judiciary had any brains—which on the surface the Justice Department would seem to refute—they'd put him back on the bench. . . . He went after the Jackal's people on principle first, because they wanted to kill me and my children. If, on the second round, he makes a dollar, he deserves every penny and I'll see that he gets it."

"You're succinct. You like him."

"I *adore* him, as I adore you and Alex. You've all taken such risks for us—"

"May we get back to what we're here for?" said the Chameleon angrily. "The past doesn't interest me, tomorrow does."

"You're not only rude, my dear, you're terribly ungrateful."

"So be it. Where were we?"

"At the moment with Prefontaine," replied Alex sharply, looking at Bourne. "But he may not matter because he probably won't survive Boston. . . . I'll call you at the inn at Barbizon tomorrow and set up a time for lunch. Out here. Clock yourself on the drive back so we're not hanging around like mateless snow geese. Also, if that fat guy's right about his 'cuisine,' Kruppie will love it and tell everybody he discovered it."

"Kruppie?"

"Relax. I told you, we go back a long time."

"And don't go into it," added Panov. "You really don't want to hear about Istanbul and Amsterdam. They're both a couple of thieves."

"We pass," said Marie. "Go on, Alex, what about tomorrow?"

"Mo and I will take a taxi out to your place, and your husband and I will drive back here. We'll call you after lunch."

"What about that driver of yours, the one Casset got you?" asked the Chameleon, his eyes cold, inquiring.

"What about him? He'll be paid double what he can make in a month with his taxi for tonight, and after he drops us off at a hotel, he'll disappear. We won't see him again."

"Will he see anyone else?"

"Not if he wants to live and send money to his relatives in Algeria. I told you, Casset cleared him. He's granite."

"Tomorrow, then," said Bourne grimly, looking across the table at Marie and Morris Panov. "After we leave for Paris, you're to stay out at Barbizon, and you're not to leave the inn. Do you both understand that?"

"You know, David," answered Marie, bristling and rigid on the pine banquette. "I'm going to tell you something. Mo and Alex are as much a part of our family as the children, so I'll say it in front of them. We all, *all* of us, humor you and in some ways pamper you because of the horrible things you went through. But you cannot and you will not order us around as if we were inferior beings in your august presence. Do *you* understand *that*?"

"Loud and clear, lady. Then maybe you

should go back to the States so you won't have to put up with my *august* presence." Jason Bourne rose from the table, pushing the chair behind him. "Tomorrow's going to be a busy day, so I have to get some sleep—I haven't had much lately—and a better man than any of us here once told me that rest was a weapon. I believe that. . . . I'll be in the car for two minutes. Take your choice. I'm sure Alex can get you out of France."

"You *bastard,*" whispered Marie.

"So be it," said the Chameleon, walking away.

"Go to him," interjected Panov quickly. "You know what's happening."

"I can't *handle* it, Mo!"

"Don't handle it, just be with him. You're the only rope he's got. You don't even have to talk, just be there. With him."

"He's become the killer again."

"He'd never harm you—"

"Of course not, I know that."

"Then provide him with that link to David Webb. It *has* to be there, Marie."

"Oh, *God,* I love him so!" cried the wife, rushing to her feet and racing after her husband— yet not her husband.

"Was that the right advice, Mo?" asked Conklin.

"I don't know, Alex. I just don't think he should be alone with his nightmares, none of us should. That's not psychiatry, it's just common sense."

"Sometimes you sound like a real doctor, you know that?"

The Algerian section of Paris lies between the tenth and eleventh arrondissements, barely three blocks, where the low buildings are Parisian but the sounds and the smells are Arabic. The insignia of the high church small but emblazoned in gold on its doors, a long black limousine entered this ethnic enclave. It stopped in front of a wood-framed, three-story house, where an old priest got out and walked to the door. He selected a name on the mail plate and pressed the button that rang a bell on the second floor.

"Oui?" said the metallic voice on the primitive intercom.

"I am a messenger from the American embassy," answered the visitor in religious garb, his French partially ungrammatical as was all too frequent with Americans. "I can't leave my vehicle, but we have an urgent message for you."

"I'll be right down," said the French Algerian driver recruited by Charles Casset in Washington. Three minutes later the man emerged from the building and walked out on the short narrow pavement. "What are you dressed like that for?" he asked the messenger who stood by the large automobile, covering the insignia on the rear door.

"I'm the Catholic chaplain, my son. Our military chargé d'affaires would like a word with you." He opened the door.

"I'll do many things for you people," laughed the driver as he bent down to look inside the limousine, "but being drafted into your army isn't one of them. . . . Yes, sir, what can I do for you?"

"Where did you take our people?" asked the shadowed figure in the backseat, his features in darkness.

"What people?" said the Algerian, sudden concern in his voice.

"The two you picked up at the airport several hours ago. The cripple and his friend."

"If you're from the embassy and they want you to know, they'll call and tell you, won't they?"

"You'll tell me!" A third, powerfully built man in a chauffeur's uniform appeared from behind the trunk of the car. He walked rapidly forward, raising his arm and crashing a thick ugly black-jack down on the Algerian's skull. He shoved his victim inside; the old man in the guise of a chaplain climbed in behind him, pulling the door shut as the chauffeur ran around the hood to the front seat. The limousine raced away down the street.

An hour later on the deserted rue Houdon, a block from Place Pigalle, the Algerian's bruised and bleeding corpse was disgorged from the large automobile. Inside, the figure in shadows addressed his aged, personally ordained priest.

"Get your car and remain outside the cripple's hotel. Stay awake, for you'll be relieved in the morning and can rest all day. Report any movements and go where he goes. Don't fail me."

"Never, monseigneur."

Dimitri Krupkin was not a tall man but he appeared taller than he was, nor was he particularly heavy yet he seemed to possess a much fuller figure than he carried. He had a pleasant if somewhat fleshy face and a generous head held erect; his full eyebrows and well-groomed pepper-and-salt hair and chin beard combined attractively with alert blue eyes and a seemingly perpetual smile, defining a man who enjoyed his life and his work, an intellect behind both. At the moment he was seated in a booth, facing the rear wall, in the all but empty country restaurant in Epernon staring across the table at Alex Conklin, who sat beside the unidentified Bourne and had just explained that he no longer drank alcohol.

"The world is coming to an end!" exclaimed the Russian in heavily accented English. "You see what happens to a good man in the self-indulgent West? Shame on your parents. They should have stayed with us."

"I don't think you want to compare the rates of alcoholism in our two countries."

"Not for a wager of money," said Krupkin, grinning. "Speaking of money, my dear old enemy, how and where am I to be paid according to our agreement last night on the telephone?"

"How and where do you want to be paid?" asked Jason.

"Ah ha, you are my benefactor, sir?"

"I'll be paying you, yes."

"Hold it!" whispered Conklin, his attention drawn to the restaurant's entrance. He leaned

toward the open side of the booth, his hand on his forehead, then quickly moved back as a couple were shown to a table in the corner to the left of the door.

"What is it?" asked Bourne.

"I don't know . . . I'm not sure."

"Who came in, Aleksei?"

"That's just it, I think I should know him but I don't."

"Where is he seated? In a booth?"

"No, a table. In the corner beyond the bar. He's with a woman."

Krupkin moved to the edge of his seat, took out his billfold and removed from its recess a small mirror the size and thickness of a credit card. Cupping it in both hands, he cautiously angled the glass in front of him. "You must be addicted to the society pages of the Paris tabloids," said the Russian, chuckling as he replaced the mirror and returned the billfold to his jacket pocket. "He's with the Italian embassy; that's his wife. Paolo and Davinia something-or-other, with pretensions to nobility, I believe. Strictly *corpo diplomatico* on the protocol level. They dress up a party quite nicely and they're obviously stinking rich."

"I don't travel in those circles, but I've seen him somewhere before."

"Of course you have. He looks like every middle-aged Italian screen star or any one of those vineyard owners who extol the virtues of the Chianti Classico on television commercials."

"Maybe you're right."

"I am." Krupkin turned to Bourne. "I shall write out the name of a bank and the number of an account in Geneva." The Soviet reached into his pocket for a pen as he pulled a paper napkin in front of him. He was not able to use either, for a man in his early thirties, dressed in a tight-fitting suit, walked rapidly up to the table.

"What is it, Sergei?" asked Krupkin.

"Not you, sir," replied the Soviet aide. *"Him,"* he added, nodding at Bourne.

"What is it?" repeated Jason.

"You have been followed. At first we were not sure, for it is an old man with a urinary problem. He rapidly left the car twice to relieve himself, but once settled he used the car telephone and squinted through the windscreen to read the name of the restaurant. That was barely minutes ago."

"How do you know he was following me?"

"Because he arrived shortly after you did, and we were here a half hour before that securing the area."

"Securing the area!" erupted Conklin, looking

at Krupkin. "I thought this conference was strictly between us."

"Dear Aleksei, benevolent Aleksei, who would save me from myself. Can you really believe I'd meet with you without considering my own protection. Not you personally, old friend, but your aggressors in Washington. Can you imagine? A deputy director of the CIA negotiates with me over a man he pretends to think I do not *know.* A rank amateur ploy."

"Goddamn you, I never *told* him!"

"Oh, dear me, then the error's mine. I apologize, Aleksei."

"Don't," interrupted Jason firmly. "That old man's from the Jackal—"

"Carlos!" cried Krupkin, his face flushed, his alert blue eyes now intense, angry. "The Jackal's after *you,* Aleksei?"

"No, him," answered Conklin. "Your benefactor."

"Good God! With what we've picked up, it's all falling into place. So I have the distinct honor to meet the infamous Jason Bourne. A great *pleasure,* sir! We have the same objective where Carlos is concerned, do we not?"

"If your men are any good, we may reach that objective before the next hour's up. Come *on!*

Let's get out of here and use the back way, the kitchen, a window, whatever. He's found me and you can bet your ass he's coming out here for me. Only he doesn't know we know that. Let's *go*!"

As the three men rose from the table Krupkin gave instructions to his aide. "Have the car brought around to the rear, the service entrance, if there is one, but do it *casually,* Sergei. No sense of urgency, you understand me?"

"We can drive half a mile down the road and turn into a pasture that will lead to the rear of the building. We will not be seen by the old man in his car."

"Very good, Sergei. And have our backup remain in place but be prepared."

"Of course, comrade." The aide hurried back to the front entrance.

"A backup?" exploded Alex. "You had a *backup*?"

"Please, Aleksei, why quibble? It's your own fault, after all. Even last night on the phone you did not tell me about your conspiracy against your own deputy director."

"It wasn't a conspiracy, for Christ's sake!"

"It wasn't exactly a pure rapport between the home office and the field, was it? No, Aleksei

Nikolae Konsolikov, you knew you could—shall we say—use me and you did. Never forget, my fine old adversary, you *are* Russian.''

''Will you two shut up and get *out* of here?''

They waited in Krupkin's armor-plated Citroën on the edge of an overgrown field a hundred feet behind the old man's car, the front of the restaurant in clear sight. To Bourne's annoyance, Conklin and the KGB officer reminisced like two aging professionals dissecting each other's strategies in past intelligence operations, pointing out the deficiencies each held to be with the other's. The Soviet backup was a nondescript sedan on the far shoulder of the road diagonally across from the restaurant. Two armed men were ready to leap out, their automatic weapons prepared to fire.

Suddenly, a Renault station wagon pulled up to the curb in front of the inn. Three couples were inside; all but the driver got out, all laughing, playfully entwining their arms. They walked with abandon toward the entrance as their companion drove the car into the small side parking lot.

''*Stop* them,'' said Jason. ''They could be killed.''

''Yes, they could be, Mr. Bourne, but if we stop them we will lose the Jackal.''

Jason stared at the Russian, unable to speak, the harsh winds of anger and confusion clouding his thoughts. He started to utter a protest but could not do so; the words would not come. Then it was too late for words. A dark brown van shot up the road from the highway to Paris and Bourne found his voice.

"It's the one from the boulevard Lefebvre, the one that got away!"

"The one from *where*?" asked Conklin.

"There was trouble on Lefebvre several days ago," said Krupkin. "An automobile or a truck was blown up. Do you refer to that?"

"It was a trap. For me. . . . A van, then a limo, and a double for Carlos—a trap. That's the second one; it raced out of a dark side street, I think, and tried to cut us down with firepower."

"Us?" Alex watched Jason; he saw the undisguised fury in the Chameleon's eyes, the tight, rigid set of his mouth, the slow spreading and contraction of his strong fingers.

"Bernardine and me," whispered Bourne in reply, suddenly raising his voice. "I want a *weapon*," he cried. "The gun in my pocket isn't a goddamned weapon!"

The driver was Krupkin's powerfully built Soviet aide Sergei; he reached across his seat and pulled up a Russian AK-47. He held it over his shoulder as Jason grabbed it.

A dark brown limousine, its tires skidding on the backcountry road, screamed to a stop in front of the faded, worn canopy; and like trained commandos, two men leaped out of the side door, their faces encased in stocking masks, their hands holding automatic weapons. They raced to the entrance, each spinning his body to either side of the double doors. A third man emerged from the squared vehicle, a balding man in a priest's black clothing. With a gesture of his weapon, the two assault troops spun back toward the doors, their hands on the thick brass knobs. The driver of the van gunned his engine in place.

"Go!" yelled Bourne. "It's him! It's *Carlos*!"

"No!" roared Krupkin. "Wait. It's our trap now, and he must be trapped—*inside.*"

"For Christ's sake, there are people in there!" countered Jason.

"All wars have casualties, Mr. Bourne, and in case you don't realize it, this is war. Yours and mine. Yours is far more personal than mine, incidentally."

Suddenly, there was an earsplitting scream of vengeance from the Jackal as the double doors were crashed back and the terrorists rushed inside, their weapons on automatic fire.

"Now!" cried Sergei, the ignition started, the accelerator on the floor. The Citroën swung out on the road, rushing toward the van, but in a split half second its progress was derailed. A massive explosion took place on the right. The old man and the nondescript gray car in which he sat was blown apart, sending the Citroën swerving to the left into the ancient post-and-rail fence that bordered the sunken parking lot on the side of the inn. The instant it happened the Jackal's dark brown van, instead of racing forward, lurched backward, jerking to a halt as the driver jumped out of the cab, concealing himself behind it; he had spotted the Soviet backup. As the two Russians ran toward the restaurant the Jackal's driver killed one with a burst from his weapon. The other threw himself into the bordering, sloping grass, watching helplessly as Carlos's driver shot out the tires and the windows of the Soviet vehicle.

"Get *out*!" yelled Sergei, pulling Bourne from the seat onto the dirt by the fence, as his stunned superior and Alex Conklin crawled out behind him.

"Let's *go*!" cried Jason, gripping the AK-47

and getting to his feet. "That son of a bitch blew up the car by remote."

"I'll go first!" said the Soviet.

"Why?"

"Frankly, I'm younger and stronger—"

"Shut up!" Bourne raced ahead, zigzagging to draw fire, then plummeting to the ground when it came from the driver of Carlos's van. He raised his weapon in the grass, knowing that the Jackal's man believed his fusillade had been accurate; the head appeared and then was no more as Jason squeezed the trigger.

The second Russian backup, hearing the death cry from behind the van, rose from the sloping grass and continued toward the restaurant's entrance. From inside came the sound of erratic gunfire, sudden bursts accompanied by screams of panic, followed by additional bursts. A living nightmare of terror and blood was taking place within the confines of a once bucolic country inn. Bourne got to his feet, Sergei at his side; running, they joined the other surviving Soviet aide. At Jason's nod, the Russians pulled back the doors and as one they burst inside.

The next sixty seconds were as terrifying as the shrieking hell depicted by Munch. A waiter and two of the men who were among the three couples were dead, the waiter and one man sprawled on the floor, their skulls shattered, what was left of their faces lying in blood; the third man was splayed back in the banquette, his eyes wide and glass-dead, his clothes riddled with bullets, rivulets of blood rolling down the fabric. The women were in total shock, alternately moaning and screaming as they kept trying to crawl over the pine walls of the booth. The well-dressed man and wife from the Italian embassy were nowhere in sight.

Sergei suddenly rushed forward, his weapon on auto fire; in a rear corner of the room he had spotted a figure whom Bourne had not seen. The stocking-faced killer sprang out of the shadows, his machine swinging into position, but before he could exercise his advantage, the Soviet cut him down. . . . *Another!* A body lurching behind the short counter that served as a bar. Was it the *Jackal?* Jason pivoted into the diagonal wall, crouching, his eyes darting into every recess in the vicinity of the wine racks. He lunged to the base of the bar as the second Russian backup, assessing the situation, ran to the hysterical women, spinning around, his gun swinging back and forth protecting them. The stocking-faced head shot up from behind the counter, his weapon surging out over the wood. Bourne sprang to his feet, gripping the hot barrel with his left hand, his right commanding the AK-47; he fired point-blank into the terrorist's contorted face beyond the silk. It was *not* Carlos. Where was the *Jackal*?

"In *there*!" shouted Sergei as if he had heard Jason's furious question.

"Where?"

"Those doors!"

It was the country restaurant's kitchen. Both men converged on the swinging doors. Again Bourne nodded, the signal for them to crash inside, but before they could move, both were partially blown back by an explosion from within; a grenade had been set off, with fragments of metal and glass embedded in the doors. The smoke billowed, wafting out into the dining room; the smell was acrid, sickening.

Silence.

Jason and Sergei once more approached the kitchen's entrance, and once again they were stopped by a second sudden explosion followed by staccato gunfire, the bullets piercing the thin, louvered panels of the swinging doors.

Silence.

Standoff.

Silence.

It was too much for the furious, impassioned Chameleon. He cracked the bolt of his AK-47, pulled the selective lever and then the trigger for auto fire, and crashed the doors open, lunging for the floor.

Silence.

Another scene from another hell. A section of the outside wall had been blown away, the obese owner and his chef, still wearing his toque, were dead, corpses pinned against the lower shelves of the kitchen, blood streaming across and down the wood.

Bourne slowly rose to his feet, his legs in agony, every nerve in his body frayed, the edge of hysteria not far away. As if in a trance, he looked around through the smoke and the debris, his eyes finally settling on a large, ominous fragment of brown butcher's paper nailed to the wall with a heavy cleaver. He approached it and, yanking out the cleaver, read the words printed in a black butcher's pencil:

The trees of Tannenbaum will burn and children will be the kindling. Sleep well, Jason Bourne.

The mirrors of his life were shattered into a thousand pieces of glass. There was nothing else to do but scream.

31

"Stop it, David!"

"My God, he's insane, Aleksei. Sergei, grab him, hold him. . . . *You,* help Sergei! Put him on the ground so I can talk to him. We must leave here quickly!"

It was all the two Russian aides could do to wrestle the screaming Bourne to the grass. He had raced out through the exploded hole in the wall, running into the high grass in a futile attempt to find the Jackal, firing his AK-47 into the field beyond until his magazine was empty. Sergei and the surviving backup had rushed in after him, the former ripping the weapon out of Jason's hands, together leading the hysterical man back to the rear of the mutilated country inn, where Alex and Krupkin were waiting for them. Forcibly, their charge in a sweating, erratically breathing trance, the five men walked rapidly to the front of the restaurant; there the uncontrollable hysteria again seized the Chameleon.

The Jackal's van was gone. Carlos had reversed his line of flight and escaped and Jason Bourne had gone mad.

"Hold him!" roared Krupkin, kneeling beside Jason as the two aides pinned Bourne to the ground. The KGB officer reached down and spread his hand across the American's face, gouging his cheeks with thumb and forefinger, forcing Treadstone Seventy-one to look at him. "I'll say this *once,* Mr. Bourne, and if it doesn't sink in, you may stay here by yourself and take the consequences! But we must leave. If you get hold of yourself, we'll be in touch with the proper officials of your government within the hour from Paris. I've read the warning to you and I can assure you your own people are capable of protecting your family—as your family was explained to me by Aleksei. But you, *yourself,* must be part of that communication. You can become rational, Mr. Bourne, or you can go to hell. Which will it be?"

The Chameleon, straining against the knees

pinning him to the ground, exhaled as if it were his final breath. His eyes came into focus and he said, "Get these bastards off me."

"One of those bastards saved your life," said Conklin.

"And I saved one of theirs. So be it."

The armor-plated Citroën sped down the country road toward the Paris highway. On the scrambled cellular telephone, Krupkin ordered a team to Epernon for the immediate removal of what was left of the Russian backup vehicle. The body of the slain man had been placed carefully in the Citroën's trunk, and the official Soviet comment, if asked for, was one of noninvolvement: Two lower-level diplomatic staff had gone out for a country lunch when the massacre occurred. Several killers were in stocking masks, the others barely seen as the staff members escaped through a back door, running for their lives. When it was over they returned to the restaurant, covering the victims, trying to calm the hysterical women and the lone surviving man. They had called their superiors to report the hideous incident and were instructed to inform the local police and return at once to the embassy. Soviet interests could not be jeopardized by the accidental presence at the scene of an act of French criminality.

"It sounds so *Russian,*" Krupkin said.

"Will anyone believe it?" Alex wondered.

"It doesn't matter," answered the Soviet. "Epernon reeks of a Jackal reprisal. The blown-apart old man, two subordinate terrorists in stocking masks—the Sûreté knows the signs. If we were involved, we were on the correct side, so they won't pursue our presence."

Bourne sat silently by the window. Krupkin was beside him with Conklin in the jump seat in front of the Russian. Jason broke his angry silence, taking his eyes off the rushing scenery and slamming his fist on the armrest. "Oh, Christ, the *kids!*" he shouted. "How could that *bastard* have *learned* about the Tannenbaum house?"

"Forgive me, Mr. Bourne," broke in Krupkin gently. "I realize it's far easier for me to say than for you to accept, but very soon now you'll be in touch with Washington. I know something about the Agency's ability to protect its own, and I guarantee you it's maddeningly effective."

"It can't be so goddamned great if Carlos can penetrate this far!"

"Perhaps he didn't," said the Soviet. "Perhaps he had another source."

"There weren't any."

"One never knows, sir."

They sped through the streets of Paris in the blinding afternoon sun as the pedestrians sweltered in the summer heat. Finally they reached the Soviet embassy on the boulevard Lannes and raced through the gates, the guards waving them on, instantly recognizing Krupkin's gray Citroën. They swung around the cobblestone courtyard, stopping in front of the imposing marble steps and the sculptured arch that formed the entrance.

"Stay available, Sergei," ordered the KGB officer. "If there's to be any contact with the Sûreté, you're selected." Then, as if it were an afterthought, Krupkin addressed the aide sitting next to Sergei in the front seat. "No offense, young man," he added, "but over the years my old friend and driver has become highly resourceful in these situations. However, you also have work to do. Process the body of our loyal deceased comrade for cremation. Internal Operations will explain the paperwork." With a nod of his head, Dimitri Krupkin instructed Bourne and Alex Conklin to get out of the car.

Once inside, Dimitri explained to the army

guard that he did not care for his guests to be subjected to the metal detecting trellises through which all visitors to the Soviet embassy were expected to pass. As an aside, he whispered in English to his guests. "Can you imagine the alarms that would go off? Two armed Americans from the savage CIA roaming the halls of this bastion of the proletariat? Good heavens, I can feel the cold of Siberia in my testicles."

They walked through the ornate, richly decorated nineteenth-century lobby to a typical brass-grilled French elevator; they entered and proceeded to the third floor. The grille opened and Krupkin continued as he led the way down a wide corridor. "We'll use an in-house conference room," he said. "You'll be the only Americans who have ever seen it or will ever see it, as it's one of the few offices without listening devices."

"You wouldn't want to submit that statement to a polygraph, would you?" asked Conklin, chuckling.

"Like you, Aleksei, I learned long ago how to fool those idiot machines; but even if that were not so, in this case I would willingly submit it, for it's true. In all honesty, it's to protect ourselves from ourselves. Come along now."

The conference room was the size of an average suburban dining room but with a long heavy table and dark masculine furniture, the chairs thick, unwieldy and quite comfortable. The walls were covered with deep brown paneling, the inevitable portrait of Lenin centered ostentatiously behind the head chair, beside which was a low table designed for the telephone console within easy reach. "I know you're anxious," said Krupkin, going to the console, "so I'll authorize an international line for you." Lifting the phone, touching a button, and speaking rapidly in Russian, Dimitri did so, then hung up and turned to the Americans. "You're assigned number twenty-six; it's the last button on the right, second row."

"Thanks." Conklin nodded and reached into his pocket, pulling out a scrap of paper and handing it to the KGB officer. "I need another favor, Kruppie. That's a telephone number here in Paris. It's supposed to be a direct line to the Jackal, but it didn't match the one Bourne was given that *did* reach him. We don't know where it fits in, but wherever it is, it's tied to Carlos."

"And you don't want to call it for fear of exposing your possession of the number—initial codes, that sort of thing. I understand, of course. Why send out an alert when it's unnecessary? I'll take care of it." Krupkin looked at Jason, his

expression that of an older, understanding colleague. "Be of good and firm heart, Mr. Bourne,
as the czarists would say facing no discernible
harm whatsoever. Despite your apprehensions,
I have enormous faith in Langley's abilities.
They've harmed my not insignificant operations
more than I care to dwell upon."

"I'm sure you've done your share of damage
to them," said Jason impatiently, glancing at the
telephone console.

"That knowledge keeps me going."

"Thanks, Kruppie," said Alex. "In your words,
you're a fine old enemy."

"Again, shame on your parents! If they had
stayed in Mother Russia, just think. By now you
and I would be running the Komitet."

"And have two lakefront houses?"

"Are you crazy, Aleksei? We would own the
entire Lake Geneva!" Krupkin turned and
walked to the door, letting himself out with quiet
laughter.

"It's all a damned game with you people, isn't
it?" said Bourne.

"Up to a point," agreed Alex, "but not when
stolen information can lead to the loss of life—
on both sides, incidentally. That's when the
weapons come out and the games are over."

"Reach Langley," said Jason abruptly, nodding at the console. "Holland's got some explaining to do."

"Reaching Langley wouldn't help—"

"What?"

"It's too early; it's barely seven o'clock in the States, but not to worry, I can bypass." Conklin again reached into a pocket and withdrew a small notebook.

"Bypass?" cried Bourne. "What kind of double talk is *that*? I'm close to the edge, Alex, those are my *children* over there!"

"Relax, all it means is that I've got his unlisted home number." Conklin sat down and picked up the phone; he dialed.

" 'Bypass,' for Christ's sake. You relics of outmoded ciphers can't use the English language. *Bypass!*"

"Sorry, Professor, it's habit. . . . *Peter?* It's Alex. Open your eyes and wake up, sailor. We've got complications."

"I don't have to wake up," said the voice from Fairfax, Virginia. "I just got back from a five-mile jog."

"Oh, you people with feet think you're so smart."

"Jesus, I'm sorry, Alex. . . . I didn't mean—"

"Of course you didn't, Ensign Holland, but we've got a problem."

"Which means at least you've made contact. You reached Bourne."

"He's standing over my shoulder and we're calling from the Soviet embassy in Paris."

"What? Holy *shit!"*

"Not holy, just Casset, remember?"

"Oh, yes, I forgot. . . . What about his wife?"

"Mo Panov's with her. The good doctor's covering the medical bases, for which I'm grateful."

"So am I. Any other progress?"

"Nothing you want to hear, but you're going to hear it loud and clear."

"What are you talking about?"

"The Jackal knows about the Tannenbaum estate."

"You're *nuts!"* shouted the director of the Central Intelligence Agency so loudly that there was a metallic ring on the transoceanic line. *"Nobody* knows! Only Charlie Casset and myself. We built up a chrono with false names and Central American bios so far removed from Paris that *no* one could make a connection. Also, there was no *mention* of the Tannenbaum place in the orders! S' help me, Alex, it was airtight because we wouldn't let anyone else *handle* it!"

"Facts are facts, Peter. My friend got a note

saying the trees of Tannenbaum would burn, the children with them."

"Son of a *bitch*!" yelled Holland. "Stay on the line," he ordered. "I'll call St. Jacques over there, then max-security and have them moved this morning. Stay on the line!" Conklin looked up at Bourne, the telephone between them, the words heard by both men.

"If there's a leak, and there *is* a leak, it can't come from Langley," said Alex.

"It *has* to! He hasn't looked deep enough."

"Where does he look?"

"Christ, *you're* the experts. The helicopter that flew them out; the crew, the people who cleared an American aircraft flying into UK territory. My God! Carlos bought the lousy Crown governor of Montserrat and his head drug chief. What's to prevent him from owning the communications between our military and Plymouth?"

"But you *heard* him," insisted Conklin. "The names were fake, the chronologies oriented to Central America, and above all, no one on the relay flights knew about the Tannenbaum estate. *No* one. . . . We've got a gap."

"Please spare me that crypto-jargon."

"It's not cryptic at all. A gap's a space that hasn't been filled—"

"Alex?" The angry voice of Peter Holland was back on the line.

"Yes, Peter?"

"We're moving them out, and I won't even tell *you* where they're going. St. Jacques's pissed off because Mrs. Cooper and the kids are settled, but I told him he's got an hour."

"I want to talk to Johnny," said Bourne, bending over and speaking loud enough to be heard.

"Nice to meet you, if only on the phone," broke in Holland.

"Thanks for all you're doing for us," managed Jason quietly, sincerely. "I mean that."

"Quid pro quo, Bourne. In your hunt for the Jackal you pulled a big ugly rabbit out of a filthy hat nobody knew was there."

"What?"

"Medusa, the new one."

"How's it going?" interrupted Conklin.

"We're doing our own cross-pollinating between the Sicilians and a number of European banks. It's dirtying up everything it touches, but we've now got more wires into that high-powered law firm in New York than in a NASA lift-off. We're closing in."

"Good hunting," said Jason. "May I have the

number at Tannenbaum's so I can reach John St. Jacques?"

Holland gave it to him; Alex wrote it down and hung up. "The horn's all yours," said Conklin, awkwardly getting out of the chair by the console and moving to the one at the right corner of the table.

Bourne sat down and concentrated on the myriad buttons below him. He picked up the telephone and, reading the numbers Alex had recorded in his notebook, touched the appropriate digits on the console.

The greetings were abrupt, Jason's questions harsh, his voice demanding. "Who did you talk to about the Tannenbaum house?"

"Back up, David," said St. Jacques, instinctively defensive. "What do you mean who did I talk to?"

"Just that. From Tranquility to Washington, who did you speak to about Tannenbaum's?"

"You mean after Holland told me about it?"

"For Christ's sake, Johnny, it couldn't be before, could it?"

"No, it couldn't, Sherlock Holmes."

"Then *who*?"

"You. Only you, esteemed Brother-in-law."

"What?"

"You heard me. Everything was happening so fast I probably forgot Tannenbaum's name anyway, and if I remembered it, I certainly wasn't going to advertise it."

"You *must* have. There was a leak and it didn't come from Langley."

"It didn't come from me, either. Look, Dr. Academic, I may not have an alphabet after my name, but I'm not exactly an idiot. That's my niece and nephew in the other room and I fully expect to watch them grow up. . . . The leak's why we're being moved, isn't it?"

"Yes."

"How severe?"

"Maximum. The Jackal."

"Jesus!" exploded St. Jacques. "That bastard shows up in the neighborhood, he's *mine*!"

"Easy, Canada," said Jason, his voice now softer, conveying thought, not anger. "You say, and I believe you, that you described the Tannenbaum place only to me and, if I recall, *I* was the one who identified it."

"That's right. I remember because when Pritchard told me you were on the phone, I was on the other line with Henry Sykes in 'Serrat. Remember Henry, the CG's aide?"

"Of course."

"I was asking him to keep half an eye on Tranquility because I had to leave for a few days. Naturally, he knew that because he had to clear the U.S. aircraft in here, and I distinctly recall his asking me where I was going and all I said was Washington. It never even occurred to me to say anything about Tannenbaum's place, and Sykes didn't press me because he obviously figured it had something to do with the horrible things that had happened. I suppose you could say he's a professional in these matters." St. Jacques paused, but before Bourne could speak he uttered hoarsely, "Oh, my *God*!"

"Pritchard," supplied Jason. "He stayed on the line."

"Why? Why would he *do* it?"

"You forget," explained Bourne. "Carlos bought your Crown governor and his Savonarola drug chief. They had to cost heavy money; he could have bought Pritchard for a lot less."

"No, you're wrong, David. Pritchard may be a deluded, self-inflated jackass but he wouldn't turn on me for money. It's not that important in the islands—prestige is. And except when he drives me up the wall, I feed it to him; actually he does a pretty damn good job."

"There's no one else, Bro."

"There's also one way to find out. I'm here, not there, and I'm not about to leave here."

"What's your point?"

"I want to bring in Henry Sykes. Is that all right with you?"

"Do it."

"How's Marie?"

"As well as can be expected under the circumstances. . . . And, Johnny, I don't want her to know a thing about any of this, do you understand me? When she reaches you, and she will, just tell her you're settled in and everything's okay, nothing about the move or Carlos."

"I understand."

"Everything *is* all right, isn't it? How are the kids—how's Jamie taking everything?"

"You may resent this, but he's having a grand time, and Mrs. Cooper won't even let me touch Alison."

"I don't resent either piece of information."

"Thanks. What about you? Any progress?"

"I'll be in touch," said Bourne, hanging up and turning to Alex. "It doesn't make sense, and Carlos always makes sense if you look hard enough. He leaves me a warning that drives me crazy with fear, but he has no means of carrying out his threat. What do you make of it?"

"The sense is in driving you crazy," replied

Conklin. "The Jackal's not going to take on an installation like Tannenbaum's sterile house long-distance. That message was meant to panic you and it did. He wants to throw you off so you'll make mistakes. He wants the controls in his hands."

"It's another reason for Marie to fly back to the States as soon as possible. She's *got* to. I want her inside a fortress, not having lunch out in the open in Barbizon."

"I'm more sympathetic to that view than I was last night." Alex was interrupted by the sound of the door opening. Krupkin walked into the room carrying several computer printouts.

"The number you gave me is disconnected," he said, a slight hesitancy in his voice.

"Who *was* it connected to?" asked Jason.

"You will not like this any more than I do, and I'd lie to you if I could invent a plausible alternate, but I cannot and I undoubtedly should not. . . . As of five days ago it was transferred from an obviously false organization to the name of Webb. David Webb."

Conklin and Bourne stared in silence at the Soviet intelligence officer, but in that silence were the unheard static cracks of high-voltage electricity. "Why are you so certain we won't like the information?" asked Alex quietly.

"My fine old enemy," began Krupkin, his gentle voice no louder than Conklin's. "When Mr. Bourne came out of that café of horror with the brown paper clasped in his hand, he was hysterical. In trying to calm him, to bring him under control, you called him David. . . . I now have a name I sincerely wish I did not possess."

"Forget it," said Bourne.

"I shall do my best to, but there are ways—"

"That's not what I mean," broke in Jason. "I have to live with the fact that you know it and I'll manage. Where was that phone installed, the *address*?"

"According to the billing computers, it's a mission home run by an organization called the Magdalen Sisters of Charity. Again obviously false."

"Obviously not," corrected Bourne. "It exists. They exist. It's legitimate down to their religious helmets, and it's also a usable drop. Or was."

"Fascinating," mused Krupkin. "So much of the Jackal's various façades is tied to the Church. A brilliant if overdone modus operandi. It's said that he once studied for the priesthood."

"Then the Church is one up on you," said Alex, angling his head in a humorously mocking rebuke. "They threw him out before you did."

"I never underestimate the Vatican," laughed Dimitri. "It ultimately proved that our mad Joseph Stalin misunderstood priorities when he asked how many battalions the Pope had. His Holiness doesn't need them; he achieves more than Stalin ever did with all his purges. Power goes to the one who instills the greatest fear, not so, Aleksei? All the princes of this earth use it with brutal effectiveness. And it all revolves around death—the fear of it, before and after. When will we grow up and tell them all to go to the devil?"

"Death," whispered Jason, frowning. "Death on the Rivoli, at the Meurice, the Magdalen Sisters . . . my *God,* I completely forgot! Dominique Lavier! She was at the Meurice—she may still be *there.* She said she'd work with me!"

"Why would she?" asked Krupkin sharply.

"Because Carlos killed her sister and she had no choice but to join him or be killed herself." Bourne turned to the console. "I need the telephone number of the Meurice—"

"Four two six zero, three eight six zero," offered Krupkin as Jason grabbed a pencil and wrote down the numbers on Alex's notepad. "A lovely place, once known as the hotel of kings. I especially like the grill."

Bourne touched the buttons, holding up his hand for quiet. Remembering, he asked for Madame Brielle's room, the name they had agreed upon, and when the hotel operator said *"Mais oui,"* he nodded rapidly in relief to Alex and Dimitri Krupkin. Lavier answered.

"Yes?"

"It is *I,* madame," said Jason, his French just slightly coarse, ever so minimally Anglicized; the Chameleon was in charge. "Your housekeeper suggested we might reach you here. Madame's dress is ready. We apologize for the delay."

"It was to have been brought to me yesterday—by *noon*—you ass! I intended to wear it last evening at Le Grand Véfour. I was mortified!"

"A thousand apologies. We can deliver it to the hotel immediately."

"You are again an ass! I'm sure my maid also told you I was here for only two days. Take it to my flat on the Montaigne and it had better be there by four o'clock or your bill will not be paid for six months!" The conversation was believably terminated by a loud crack at the other end of the line.

Bourne replaced the phone; perspiration had formed at his slightly graying hairline. "I've been out of this too long," he said, breathing deeply. "She has a flat on the Montaigne and she'll be there after four o'clock."

"Who the *hell* is Dominique whatever her name is?" fairly yelled the frustrated Conklin.

"Lavier," answered Krupkin, "only, she uses her dead sister's name, Jacqueline. She's been posing as her sister for years."

"You *know* about that?" asked Jason, impressed.

"Yes, but it never did us much good. It was an understandable ruse—look-alikes, several months' absence, minor surgery and programming—all quite normal in the abnormal world of haute couture. Who looks or listens to anyone in that superficial orbit? We watch her, but she's never led us to the Jackal, she wouldn't know how. She has no direct access; everything she reports to Carlos is filtered, stone walls at every relay. That's the way of the Jackal."

"It's not always the way," said Bourne. "There was a man named Santos who managed a run-down café in Argenteuil called Le Coeur du Soldat. He had access. He gave it to me and it was very special."

"*Was?*" Krupkin raised his eyebrows. "*Had? You employ the past tense?*"

"He's dead."

"And that run-down café in Argenteuil, is it still flourishing?"

"It's cleaned out and closed down," admitted Jason, no defeat in his admission.

"So the access is terminated, no?"

"Sure, but I believe what he told me because he was killed for telling it to me. You see, he was getting out, just as this Lavier woman wants to get out—only, *his* association went back to the beginning. To Cuba, where Carlos saved a misfit like himself from execution. He knew he could use that man, that huge imposing giant who could operate inside the world of the dregs of humanity and be his primary relay. Santos *had* direct access. He proved it because he gave me an alternate number that did reach the Jackal. Only a very few men could do that."

"Fascinating," said Krupkin, his eyes firmly focused on Bourne. "But as my fine old enemy, Aleksei, who is now looking at you as I look at you, might inquire, what are you leading up to, Mr. Bourne? Your words are ambiguous but your implied accusations appear dangerous."

"To you. Not to us."

"I beg your pardon?"

"Santos told me that only four men in the

world have direct access to the Jackal. One of them is in Dzerzhinsky Square. 'Very high in the Komitet' were Santos's words, and believe me, he didn't think much of your superior.''

It was as if Dimitri Krupkin had been struck in the face by a director of the Politburo in the middle of Red Square during a May Day parade. The blood drained from his head, his skin taking on the pallor of ash, his eyes steady, unblinking. "What else did this Santos tell you? I have to *know*!''

"Only that Carlos had a thing about Moscow, that he was making contact with people in high places. It was an obsession with him. . . . If you can find that contact in Dzerzhinsky Square, it would be a big leap forward. In the meantime, all we've got is Dominique Lavier—''

"Damn, *damn*!'' roared Krupkin, cutting off Jason. "How *insane,* yet how perfectly logical! You've answered several questions, Mr. Bourne, and how they've burned into my mind. So many times I've come so close—so many, so close—and always *nothing.* Well, let me tell you, gentlemen, the games of the devil are not restricted to those confined to hell. Others can play them. My *God,* I've been a pearl to be flushed from one oyster to another, always the bigger fool! . . . Make no more calls from that telephone!"

It was 3:30 in the afternoon, Moscow time, and the elderly man in the uniform of a Soviet army officer walked as rapidly as his age permitted down the hallway on the fifth floor of KGB head-quarters in Dzerzhinsky Square. It was a hot day, and as usual the air conditioning was only barely and erratically adequate, so General Grigorie Rodchenko permitted himself a privilege of rank: his collar was open. It did not stop the occasional rivulet of sweat from sliding in and out of the crevices of his deeply lined face on its way down to his neck, but the absence of the tight, red-bordered band of cloth around his throat was a minor relief.

He reached the bank of elevators, pressed the button and waited, gripping a key in his hand. The doors to his right opened, and he was pleased to see that there was no one inside. It was easier than having to order everyone out— at least, far less awkward. He entered, inserted the key in the uppermost lock-release above the panel, and again waited while the mechanism performed its function. It did so quickly, and the

elevator shot directly down to the lowest underground levels of the building.

The doors opened and the general walked
out, instantly aware of the pervasive silence that
filled the corridors both left and right. In moments, that would change, he thought. He proceeded down the left hallway to a large steel
door with a metal sign riveted in the center.

ENTRANCE FORBIDDEN

AUTHORIZED PERSONNEL ONLY

It was a foolish admonition, he thought, as he
took out a thin plastic card from his pocket and
shoved it slowly, carefully, into a slot on the
right. Without the pass card—and sometimes
even with it if inserted too quickly—the door
would not open. There were two clicks, and
Rodchenko removed his card as the heavy,
knobless door swung back, a television monitor
recording his entry.

The hum of activity was pronounced from
dozens of lighted cubicles within the huge, dark
low-ceilinged complex the size of a czar's grand
ballroom but without the slightest attempt at
decor. A thousand pieces of equipment in black
and gray, several hundred personnel in pristine
white coveralls within white-walled cubicles.
And, thankfully, the air was cool, almost cold, in
fact. The machinery demanded it, for this was

the KGB's communications center. Information poured in twenty-four hours a day from all over the world.

The old soldier trudged up a familiar path to the farthest aisle on the right, then left to the last cubicle at the far end of the enormous room. It was a long walk, and the general's breath was short, his legs were tired. He entered the small enclosure, nodding at the middle-aged operator who looked up at his visitor and removed the cushioned headset from his ears. On the white counter in front of him was a large electronic console with myriad switches, dials and a keyboard. Rodchenko sat down in a steel chair next to the man; catching his breath, he spoke.

"You have word from Colonel Krupkin in Paris?"

"I have words *concerning* Colonel Krupkin, General. In line with your instructions to monitor the colonel's telephone conversations, including those international lines authorized by him, I received a tape from Paris several minutes ago that I thought you should listen to."

"As usual, you are most efficient and I am most grateful; and as always, I'm sure Colonel Krupkin will inform us of events, but as you know, he's so terribly busy."

"No explanations are necessary, sir. The conversations you are about to hear were recorded within the past half hour. The earphones, please?"

Rodchenko slipped on the headset and nodded. The operator placed a pad and a container of sharpened pencils in front of the general; he touched a number on the keyboard and sat back as the powerful third *direktor* of the Komitet leaned forward listening. In moments the general began taking notes; minutes later he was writing furiously. The tape came to an end and Rodchenko removed the headset. He looked sternly at the operator, his narrow Slavic eyes rigid between the folds of lined flesh, the crevices in his face seemingly more pronounced than before.

"Erase the tape, then destroy the reel," he ordered, getting out of the chair. "As usual, you have heard nothing."

"As usual, General."

"And, as usual, you will be rewarded."

It was 4:17 when Rodchenko returned to his office and sat down at his desk, studying his notes. It was *incredible*! It was beyond *belief,* yet there it was—he had heard for himself the words and the voices saying those words! . . . Not those concerning the monseigneur in Paris;

he was secondary now and could be reached in minutes, if it was necessary. That could wait, but the other could not wait, not an instant longer! The general picked up his phone and rang his secretary.

"I want an immediate satellite transmission to our consulate in New York. All maximum scramblers in place and operational."

How could it happen?

Medusa!

32

Frowning, Marie listened to her husband's voice over the telephone, nodding at Mo Panov across the hotel room. "Where are you now?" she asked.

"At a pay phone in the Plaza-Athénée," answered Bourne. "I'll be back in a couple of hours."

"What's happening?"

"Complications, but also some progress."

"That doesn't tell me anything."

"There's not that much to tell."

"What's this Krupkin like?"

"He's an original. He brought us to the Soviet embassy and I talked to your brother on one of their lines."

"What? . . . How are the *children?"*

"Fine. Everything's fine. Jamie's thoroughly enjoying himself and Mrs. Cooper won't let Johnny touch Alison."

"Which means Bro doesn't want to touch Alison."

"So be it."

"What's the number? I want to call."

"Holland's setting up a secure line. We'll know in an hour or so."

"Which means you're lying."

"So be it. You should be with them. If I'm delayed, I'll call you."

"Wait a minute. Mo wants to talk to you—"

The line went dead. Across the room, Panov slowly shook his head as he watched Marie's reaction to the suddenly terminated conversation. "Forget it," he said. "I'm the last person he wants to talk to."

"He's back there, Mo. He's not David any longer."

"He has a different calling now," added Panov softly. "David can't handle it."

"I think that's the most frightening thing I've ever heard you say."

The psychiatrist nodded. "It may well be."

The gray Citroën was parked several hundred feet diagonally across from the canopied entrance of Dominique Lavier's apartment building on the fashionable avenue Montaigne. Krupkin, Alex and Bourne sat in the back, Conklin again in the jump seat, his size and disabled leg making the position more feasible. Conversation was at a minimum as the three men anxiously kept glancing over at the glass doors of the apartment.

"Are you sure this is going to work?" asked Jason.

"I am only sure that Sergei is an immensely talented professional," replied Krupkin. "He was trained in Novgorod, you know, and his French is impeccable. He also carries on him a variety of identifications that would fool the Division of Documents at the Deuxiéme Bureau."

"What about the other two?" pressed Bourne.

"Silent subordinates, controlled by and subservient to their superior. They're also experts at their craft. . . . Here he comes!"

Sergei could be seen walking out of the glass doors; he turned left, and within moments crossed the wide boulevard toward the Citroën. He reached the car, went around the hood and climbed in behind the wheel. "Everything is in order," he said, angling his head over the front seat. "Madame has not returned and the flat is number twenty-one, second floor, right front side. It has been swept thoroughly; there are no intercepts."

"Are you *certain*?" asked Conklin. "There's no room for error here, Sergei."

"Our instruments are the best, sir," answered the KGB aide, smiling. "It pains me to say it, but they were developed by the General Electronics Corporation under contract to Langley."

"Two points for our side," said Alex.

"Minus twelve for permitting the technology to be stolen," concluded Krupkin. "Besides, I'm sure a number of years ago our Madame Lavier might have had bugs sewn into her mattress—"

"Checked," broke in Sergei.

"Thank you, but my point is that the Jackal could hardly have monitoring personnel all over Paris. It all gets so complicated."

"Where are your other two men?" asked Bourne.

"In the lobby corridors, sir. I'll join them shortly, and we have a support vehicle down the street, all in radio contact, of course. . . . I'll drive you over now."

"Wait a minute," interrupted Conklin. "How do we get in? What do we say?"

"It's been said, sir, you need say nothing. You

are authorized covert personnel from the French SEDCE—"

"The what?" broke in Jason.

"The Service of External Documentation and Counterespionage," answered Alex. "It's the nearest thing here to Langley."

"What about the Deuxième?"

"Special Branch," said Conklin offhandedly, his mind elsewhere. "Some say it's an elite corps, others say otherwise. . . . Sergei, won't they check?"

"They already have, sir. After showing the concierge and his assistant my identification, I gave them an unlisted telephone number that confirmed the Service and my status. I subsequently described the three of you and requested no conversation, merely access to Madame Lavier's flat. . . . I'll drive over now. It will make a better impression on the doorman."

"Sometimes simplicity backed by authority is best in deception," observed Krupkin as the Citroën was maneuvered between the sparse, erratic traffic across the wide avenue to the entrance of the white-stone apartment complex. "Take the car around the corner out of sight, Sergei," ordered the KGB officer, reaching for the door handle. "And my radio, if you please?"

"Yes, sir," replied the aide, handing Krupkin a miniaturized electronic intercom over the seat. "I'll signal you when I'm in position."

"I can reach all of you with this?"

"Yes, comrade. Beyond a hundred and fifty meters the frequency is undetectable."

"Come along, gentlemen."

Inside the marble lobby, Krupkin nodded at the formally dressed concierge behind the counter, Jason and Alex on the Soviet's right. *"La porte est ouverte,"* said the concierge, his gaze downward, avoiding direct eye contact. "I shall not be in evidence when madame arrives," he continued in French. "How you got in is unknown to me; however, there is a service entrance at the rear of the building."

"But for official courtesy it is the one we would have used," said Krupkin, looking straight ahead as he and his companions walked to the elevator.

Lavier's flat was a testament to the world of haute couture chic. The walls were dotted with photographs of fashion notables attending important showings and events, as well as with framed original sketches by celebrated designers. Like a Mondrian, the furniture was stark in its simplicity, the colors bold and predominantly red, black and deep green; the chairs, sofas and tables only vaguely resembled chairs, sofas and tables—they seemed more suitable for use in spacecraft.

As if by rote, both Conklin and the Russian immediately began examining the tables, ferreting out handwritten notes, a number of which were beside a mother-of-pearl telephone on top of a curved, thick dark green table of sorts.

"If this is a desk," said Alex, "where the hell are the drawers or the handles?"

"It's the newest thing from Leconte," replied Krupkin.

"The tennis player?" interrupted Conklin.

"No, Aleksei, the furniture designer. You press in and they shoot out."

"You're kidding."

"Try it."

Conklin did so and a barely discernible drawer sprang loose from an all but invisible crack. "I'll be damned—"

Krupkin's miniaturized radio suddenly erupted with two sharp beeps from inside his breast pocket. "It must be Sergei checking in," said Dimitri, removing the instrument. "You're in place, comrade?" he continued, speaking into the base of the radio.

"More than that," came the aide's quiet voice accompanied by minor static. "The Lavier woman has just entered the building."

"The concierge?"

"Nowhere in sight."

"Good. Out. . . . Aleksei, get away from there. Lavier is on her way up."

"You want to hide?" asked Conklin facetiously, turning the pages of a telephone notebook.

"I'd rather not start off with instant hostility, which will be the case if she sees you riffling through her personal effects."

"All right, all right." Alex returned the notebook to the drawer and closed it. "But if she isn't going to cooperate, I'm taking that little black book."

"She'll cooperate," said Bourne. "I told you, she wants out, and the only way out for her is with a dead Jackal. The money's secondary— not inconsequential, but getting out comes first."

"Money?" asked Krupkin. "What money?"

"I offered to pay her and I will."

"And I can assure you, money is not secondary to Madame Lavier," added the Russian.

The sound of a key being inserted into a latch

echoed throughout the living room. The three men turned to the door as a startled Dominique Lavier walked inside. Her astonishment, however, was so brief as to be fleeting; there were no cracks whatsoever in her composure. Brows arched in the manner of a regal mannequin, she calmly replaced the key in her beaded purse, looked over at the intruders and spoke in English.

"Well, Kruppie, I might have known you were somewhere in this bouillabaisse."

"Ah, the charming Jacqueline, or may we drop the pretense, Domie?"

"Kruppie?" cried Alex. "Domie? . . . Is this old home week?"

"Comrade Krupkin is one of the more advertised KGB officers in Paris," said Lavier, walking to the long, cubed red table behind the white silk sofa and putting down her purse. "Knowing him is de rigueur in certain circles."

"It has its advantages, dear Domie. You can't imagine the disinformation I'm fed in those circles by the Quai d'Orsay, and once having tasted it, knowing it's false. By the way, I understand you've met our tall American friend and even had certain negotiations with him, so I think it's only proper I introduce you to his colleague. . . . Madame, Monsieur Aleksei Konsolikov."

"I don't believe you. He's no Soviet. One's nostrils become attuned to the approach of the unwashed bear."

"Ah, you *destroy* me, Domie! But you're right, it was a parental error of judgment. He may therefore introduce himself, if he cares to."

"The name's Conklin, Alex Conklin, Miss Lavier, and I'm American. However, our mutual acquaintance 'Kruppie' is right in one sense. My parents were Russian and I speak it fluently, so he's at a loss to mislead me when we're in Soviet company."

"I think that's delicious."

"Well, it's at least appetizing, if you know Kruppie."

"I'm wounded, fatally wounded!" exclaimed Krupkin. "But my injuries are not essential to this meeting. You will work with us, Domie?"

"I'll work with you, Kruppie. My *God,* will I work with you! I ask only that Jason Bourne clarifies his offer to me. With Carlos I'm a caged animal, but without him I'm a near-destitute aging courtesan. I want him to pay for my sister's death and for everything he's done to me, but I don't care to sleep in the gutter."

"Name your price," said Jason.

"*Write* it down," clarified Conklin, glancing at Krupkin.

"Let me see," said Lavier, walking around the sofa and crossing to the Leconte desk. "I'm within a few years of sixty—from one direction or another, it's immaterial—and without the Jackal, and the absence of some other fatal disease, I will have perhaps fifteen to twenty years." She bent down over the desk and wrote a figure on a notepad, tore it off, then stood up and looked at the tall American. "For you, Mr. Bourne, and I'd rather not argue. I believe it's fair."

Jason took the paper and read the amount: *$1,000,000.00, American.* "It's fair," said Bourne, handing the note back to Lavier. "Add how and where you want it paid and I'll make the arrangements when we leave here. The money will be there in the morning."

The aging courtesan looked into Bourne's eyes. "I believe you," she said, again bending over the desk and writing out her instructions. She rose and gave the paper back to Jason. "The deal is made, monsieur, and may God grant us the kill. If he does not, we are dead."

"You're speaking as a Magdalen sister?"

"I'm speaking as a sister who's terrified, no more and certainly no less."

Bourne nodded. "I've several questions," he said. "Do you want to sit down?"

"*Oui.* With a cigarette." Lavier crossed to the sofa and, sinking into the cushions, reached for her purse on the red table. She took out a pack of cigarettes, extracted one and picked up a gold lighter from the coffee table. "Such a filthy habit but at times so damned necessary," she said, snapping the flame and inhaling deeply. "Your questions, monsieur?"

"What happened at the Meurice? *How* did it happen?"

"The woman happened—I assume it was *your* woman—that was my understanding. As we agreed, you and your friend from Deuxième were positioned so that when Carlos arrived to trap you, you would kill him. For reasons no one can fathom, your woman screamed as you crossed the Rivoli—the rest you saw for your-self. . . . How *could* you have told me to take a room at the Meurice knowing she was there?"

"That's easy to answer. I didn't know she was there. Where do we stand now?"

"Carlos still trusts me. He blames everything on the woman, your wife, I'm told, and has no reason to hold me responsible. After all, you were there, which proves my allegiance. Were it not for the Deuxième officer, you'd be dead."

Again Bourne nodded. "How can you reach him?"

"I cannot myself. I never have, nor have I cared to. He prefers it that way, and as I told you, the checks arrive on time, so I have no reason to."

"But you send him messages," pressed Jason. "I heard you."

"Yes, I do, but never directly. I call several old men at cheap cafés—the names and numbers vary weekly and quite a few have no idea what I'm talking about, but for those that do, they call others immediately, and *they* call others beyond themselves. Somehow the messages get through. Very quickly, I might add."

"What did I tell you?" said Krupkin emphatically. "All the relays end with false names and filthy cafés. Stone walls!"

"Still, the messages get through," said Alex Conklin, repeating Lavier's words.

"Yet Kruppie's correct." The aging but still striking woman dragged heavily, nervously on her cigarette. "The routings are convoluted to the point of being untraceable."

"I don't care about that," said Alex, squinting at nothing the others could see. "They also reach Carlos quickly, you made that clear."

"It's true."

Conklin widened his eyes and fixed them on Lavier. "I want you to send the most urgent message you've ever relayed to the Jackal. You *must* talk to him directly. It's an emergency that you can entrust to no one but Carlos himself."

"About *what*?" erupted Krupkin. "What could be so urgent that the Jackal will comply? Like our Mr. Bourne, he is obsessed with traps, and under the circumstances, any direct communication smells of one!"

Alex shook his head and limped to a side window, squinting again, deep in thought, his intense eyes reflecting his concentration. Then gradually, slowly, his eyes opened. He gazed at the street below. "My God, it could *work*," he whispered to himself.

"What could work?" asked Bourne.

"Dimitri, hurry! Call the embassy and have them send over the biggest, fanciest diplomatic limousine you proletarians own."

"What?"

"Just do as I say! Quickly!"

"Aleksei . . . ?"

"Now!"

The force and urgency of Conklin's command had its effect. The Russian walked rapidly to the mother-of-pearl telephone and dialed, his questioning eyes on Alex, who kept staring down at the street. Lavier looked at Jason; he shook his head in bewilderment as Krupkin spoke into the phone, his Russian a short series of clipped phrases.

"It's done," said the KGB officer, hanging up. "And now I think you should give me an extremely convincing reason for doing it."

"Moscow," replied Conklin, still looking out the window.

"Alex, for Christ's sake—"

"What are you *saying*?" roared Krupkin.

"We've got to get Carlos out of Paris," said Conklin, turning. "Where better than Moscow?" Before the astonished men could respond, Alex looked at Lavier. "You say he still trusts you?"

"He has no reason not to."

"Then two words should do it. 'Moscow, emergency,' that's the basic message you're sending him. Put it any way you like, but add that the crisis is of such a nature that you must speak only with him."

"But I never *have.* I know men who have spoken with him, who in drunken moments have tried to describe him, but to me he is a complete stranger."

"All the stronger for it," broke in Conklin, turning to Bourne and Krupkin. "In this city he's got all the cards, *all* of them. He's got firepower, an untraceable network of gunslingers and couriers, and for every crevice he can crawl into and burst out from, there are dozens more available to him. Paris is his territory, his protection—we could run blindly all over the city for days, weeks, even months, getting nowhere until the moment comes when he's got you and Marie in his gun sights . . . you can also add Mo and me to that scenario. London, Amsterdam, Brussels, Rome—they'd all be better for us than Paris, but the best is Moscow. Oddly enough, it's the one place in the world that has a hypnotic hold on him—and also the one that's the least hospitable."

"Aleksei, *Aleksei,*" cried Dimitri Krupkin. "I really think you should reconsider alcohol, for it's obvious you've lost your senses! Say Domie actually reaches Carlos and tells him what you say. Do you really believe that on the basis of an 'emergency' in Moscow he'll up and take the next plane there? Insanity!"

"You can bet your last black-market ruble I do," replied Conklin. "That message is only to convince him to get in touch with her. Once he does, she explodes the bomb. . . . She's just heard an extraordinary piece of information that she knew should only be conveyed to him, not sent through the message tunnels."

"And what in God's name might *that* be?" asked Lavier, extracting another cigarette and instantly lighting it.

"The KGB in Moscow is closing in on the Jackal's man in Dzerzhinsky Square. They've narrowed it down to, say, ten or fifteen officers in the highest ranks. Once they find him, Carlos is neutralized in the Komitet—worse, he's about to lose an informer who knows far too much about him to the Lubyanka interrogators."

"But how would *she* know that?" said Jason.

"Who would *tell* her?" added Krupkin.

"It's the truth, isn't it?"

"So are your very secret substations in Beijing, Kabul and—forgive my impertinence—Canada's Prince Edward Island, but you don't advertise them," said Krupkin.

"I didn't know about Prince Edward," admitted Alex. "Regardless, there are times when advertisements aren't necessary, only the means to convey the information credibly. A few minutes ago I didn't have any means, only authenticity, but that gap has just been filled. . . . Come over here, Kruppie—just you for the moment, and stay away from the window. Look between the corner of the drapes." The Soviet did as he was told, going to Conklin's side and parting the fold of lace fabric from the wall. "What do you see?" asked Alex, gesturing at a shabby, nondescript brown car below on the avenue Montaigne. "Doesn't do much for the neighborhood, does it?"

Krupkin did not bother to reply. Instead, he whipped the miniaturized radio from his pocket and pressed the transmitter button. "Sergei, there's a brown automobile roughly eighty meters down the street from the building's entrance—"

"We know, sir," interrupted the aide. "We've got it covered, and if you'll notice, our backup is parked across the way. It's an old man who barely moves except to look out the window."

"Does he have a car telephone?"

"No, comrade, and should he leave the automobile he'll be followed, so there can be no outside calls unless you direct otherwise."

"I shall not direct otherwise. Thank you, Sergei. Out." The Russian looked at Conklin. "The old man," he said. "You saw him."

"Bald head and all," affirmed Alex. "He's not a fool; he's done this before and knows he's being watched. He can't leave for fear of missing something, and if he had a phone there'd be others down in the Montaigne."

"The Jackal," said Bourne, stepping forward, then stopping, remembering Conklin's order to stay away from the window.

"Now, do you understand?" asked Alex, addressing the question to Krupkin.

"Of course," conceded the KGB official, smiling. "It's why you wanted an ostentatious limousine from our embassy. After we leave, Carlos is told that a Soviet diplomatic vehicle was sent to pick us up, and for what other reason would we be here but to interrogate Madame Lavier? Naturally, in my well-advertised presence was a tall man who might or might not be Jason Bourne, and another shorter individual with a disabled leg—thus confirming that it *was* Jason Bourne. . . . Our unholy alliance is therefore established and observed, and again, naturally, during our harsh questioning of Madame Lavier, tempers flared and references were made to the Jackal's informer in Dzerzhinsky Square."

"Which only I'd known about through my dealing with Santos at Le Coeur du Soldat," said Jason quietly. "So Dominique has a credible observer—an old man from Carlos's army of old men—to back up the information she delivers. . . . I've got to say it, Saint Alex, that serpentine brain of yours hasn't lost its cunning."

"I hear a professor I once knew. . . . I thought he'd left us."

"He has."

"Only for a while, I hope."

"Well done, Aleksei. You still have the touch; you may remain abstemious if you must, much as it pains me. . . . It's always the nuances, isn't it?"

"Not always by any means," disagreed Conklin simply, shaking his head. "Most of the time it's foolish mistakes. For instance, our new colleague here, 'Domie,' as you affectionately call her, was told she was still trusted, but she wasn't, not completely. So an old man was dispatched to watch her apartment—no big deal, just a little insurance in a car that doesn't belong in a street with Jaguars and Rolls-Royces. So we pay off on the small policy, and with luck cash in on the big one. Moscow."

"Let me intellectualize," said Krupkin. "Although you were always far better in that department than I, Aleksei. I prefer the best wine to the most penetrating thoughts, although the latter—in both our countries—invariably leads to the former.''

"Merde!" yelled Dominique Lavier, crushing out her cigarette. "What are you two idiots talking about?''

"They'll tell us, believe me,'' answered Bourne.

"As has been reported and repeated in secure circles too often for comfort,'' continued the Soviet, "years ago we trained a madman in Novgorod, and years ago we would have put a bullet in his head had he not escaped. His methods, if sanctioned by any legitimate government, especially the two superpowers, would lead to confrontations neither of us can ever permit. Yet, withal, in the beginning he was a true revolutionary with a capital *R*, and we, the world's *truest* revolutionaries, disinherited him. . . . By his lights, it was a great injustice and he never forgets it. He will always yearn to come back to the mother's breast, for that's where he was born. . . . Good *God*, the people he's killed in the name of 'aggressors' while he made fortunes is positively *revolting!*''

"But you denied him," said Jason flatly, "and he wants that denial reversed. He has to be acknowledged as the master killer you trained. That psychopathic ego of his is the basis for everything Alex and I mounted. . . . Santos said he continuously bragged about the cadre he was building in Moscow—'Always Moscow, it's an obsession with him'—those were Santos's words. The only specific person he knew about, and not by name, was Carlos's mole high up in the KGB, but he said Carlos claimed to have others in key positions at various powerful departments, that as the monseigneur he'd been sending them money for years."

"So the Jackal thinks he forms a core of supporters within our government," observed Krupkin. "Despite everything, he still believes he can come back. He is, indeed, an egomaniac but he's never understood the Russian mind. He may temporarily corrupt a few cynical opportunists, but these will cover themselves and turn on him. No one looks forward to a stay at the Lubyanka or a Siberian gulag. The Jackal's Potemkin village will burn to the ground."

"All the more reason for him to race to Moscow and put out the brushfires," said Alex.

"What do you mean?" asked Bourne.

"The burning will start with the exposure of Carlos's man in Dzerzhinsky Square; he'll know that. The only way to prevent it is for him to reach Moscow and make a determination. Either his informer will elude internal security or the Jackal will have to kill him."

"I forgot," interrupted Bourne. "Something else Santos said . . . most of the Russians on Carlos's payroll spoke French. Look for a man high up in the Komitet who speaks French."

Krupkin's radio again intruded, the two piercing beeps barely muffled by his jacket. He pulled it out and spoke. "Yes?"

"I don't know how or why, comrade," said the tense voice of Sergei, "but the ambassador's limousine has just arrived at the building. I *swear* to you I have no idea what happened!"

"I do. I called for it."

"But the embassy flags will be seen by everyone!"

"Including, I trust, an alert old man in a brown automobile. We'll be down shortly. Out." Krupkin turned to the others. "The car's here, gentlemen. Where shall we meet, Domie? And when?"

"Tonight," replied Lavier. "There's a showing at La Galerie d'Or in the rue de Paradis. The artist's a young upstart who wants to be a rock star or something, but he's the rage and everyone will be there."

"Tonight, then. . . . Come, gentlemen. Against our instincts, we must be very observable outside on the pavement."

The crowds moved in and out of the shafts of light while the music was provided by an ear-shattering rock band mercifully placed in a side room away from the main viewing area. Were it not for the paintings on the walls and the beams of the small spotlights illuminating them, a person might think he was in a discotheque rather than in one of Paris's elegant art galleries.

Through a series of nods, Dominique Lavier maneuvered Krupkin to a corner of the large room. Their graceful smiles, arched brows and intermittently mimed laughter covered their quiet conversation.

"The word passed among the old men is that the monseigneur will be away for a few days. However, they are all to continue searching for the tall American and his crippled friend and list wherever they are seen."

"You must have done your job well."

"As I relayed the information he was utterly silent. In his breathing, however, there was utter loathing. I felt my bones grow cold."

"He's on his way to Moscow," said the Russian. "No doubt through Prague."

"What will you do now?"

Krupkin arched his neck and raised his eyes to the ceiling in false, silent laughter. Leveling his gaze on her, he answered, smiling. "Moscow," he said.

33

Bryce Ogilvie, managing partner of Ogilvie, Spofford, Crawford and Cohen, prided himself on his self-discipline. That was to say, not merely the outward appearance of composure, but the cold calm he forced upon his deepest fears in times of crisis. However, when he arrived at his office barely fifty minutes ago and found his concealed private telephone ringing, he had experienced a twinge of apprehension at such an early morning call over that particular line. Then when he heard the heavily accented voice of the Soviet consul general of New York demanding an immediate conference, he had to acknowledge a sudden void in his chest . . . and when the Russian instructed him—*ordered* him—to be at the Carlyle Hotel, Suite 4-C, in one hour, rather than their usual meeting place at the apartment on Thirty-second and Madison, Bryce felt a searing-hot pain filling that void in his chest. *And* when he had mildly objected to the suddenness of the proposed, unscheduled conference, the pain in his chest had burst into fire, the flames traveling up to his throat at the Soviet's reply: "What I have to show you will make you devoutly wish we never knew each other, much less had any occasion to meet this morning. *Be* there!"

Ogilvie sat back in his limousine, as far back as the upholstery could be pressed, his legs stretched, rigid on the carpeted floor. Abstract, swirling thoughts of personal wealth, power and influence kept circling in his mind; he had to get hold of himself! After all, he was Bryce Ogilvie, *the* Bryce Ogilvie, perhaps the most successful corporate attorney in New York, and arguably second only to Boston's Randolph Gates in the fast track of corporate and antitrust law.

Gates! The mere thought of that son of a bitch was a welcome diversion. Medusa had asked a minor favor of the celebrated Gates, an in-consequential, perfectly acceptable staff appointment on an ad hoc government-oriented commission, and he had not even answered their phone calls! Calls put through by another perfectly acceptable source, the supposedly irreproachable, impartial head of Pentagon procurements, an asshole named General Norman Swayne, who only wanted the best information. Well, perhaps more than information, but Gates could not have known about that. . . . Gates? There was something in the *Times* the other morning about his bowing out of a hostile take-over proceeding. What was it?

The limousine pulled up to the curb in front of the Carlyle Hotel, once the Kennedy family's favored New York City address, now the temporary clandestine favorite of the Soviets. Ogilvie waited until the uniformed doorman opened the left rear door of the car before he stepped out onto the pavement. He normally would not have done so, believing the delay was an unnecessary affectation, but this morning he did; he *had* to get hold of himself. He had to be the Ice-Cold Ogilvie his legal adversaries feared.

The elevator's ascent to the fourth floor was swift, the walk over the blue-carpeted hallway to Suite 4-C far slower, the distance much closer. *The* Bryce Ogilvie breathed deeply, calmly, and stood erect as he pressed the bell. Twenty-eight seconds later, irritatingly clocked by the attorney as he silently counted "one one-thousand, two one-thousand," ad nauseam, the door was opened by the Soviet consul general, a slender man of medium height whose aquiline face had taut white skin and large brown eyes.

Vladimir Sulikov was a wiry seventy-three-year-old full of nervous energy, a scholar and former professor of history at Moscow University, a committed Marxist, yet oddly enough, considering his position, not a member of the Communist Party. In truth, he was not a member of any political orthodoxy, preferring the passive role of the unorthodox individual within a collectivist society. That, and his singularly acute intellect, had served him well; he was sent to posts where more conformist men would not have been half so effective. The combination of these attributes, along with a dedication to physical exercise, made Sulikov appear ten to fifteen years younger than his age. His was an unsettling presence for those negotiating with him, for somehow he radiated the wisdom acquired over the years and the vitality of youth to implement it.

The greetings were abrupt. Sulikov offered

nothing but a stiff, cold handshake and a stiffly upholstered armchair. He stood in front of the suite's narrow mantel of white marble as though it were a classroom blackboard, his hands clasped behind him, an agitated professor about to question and lecture simultaneously an annoying, disputatious graduate student.

"To our business," said the Russian curtly. "You are aware of Admiral Peter Holland?"

"Yes, of course. He's the director of the Central Intelligence Agency. Why do you ask?"

"Is he one of you?"

"No."

"Are you quite sure?"

"Of course I am."

"Is it possible he became one of you without your knowledge?"

"Certainly not, I don't even know the man. And if this is some kind of amateurish interrogatory, Soviet style, practice on someone else."

"Ohh, the fine expensive American attorney objects to being asked simple questions?"

"I object to being insulted. You made an astonishing statement over the phone. I'd like it explained, so please get to it."

"I'll get to it, Counselor, believe me, I'll get to it, but in my own fashion. We Russians protect our flanks; it's a lesson we learned from the tragedy and the triumph of Stalingrad—an experience you Americans never had to endure."

"I came from another war, as you well know," said Ogilvie coolly, "but if the history books are accurate, you had some help from your Russian winter."

"That's difficult to explain to thousands upon thousands of frozen Russian corpses."

"Granted, and you have both my condolences and my congratulations, but it's not the explanation—or even the lack of one—that I requested."

"I'm only trying to explain a truism, young man. As has been said, it's the painful lessons of history we don't know about that we are bound to repeat. . . . You see, we *do* protect our flanks, and if some of us in the diplomatic arena suspect that we have been duped into international embarrassment, we reinforce those flanks. It's a simple lesson for one so erudite as yourself, Counselor."

"And so obvious, it's trivial. What about Admiral Holland?"

"In a moment. . . . First, let me ask you about a man named Alexander Conklin."

Bryce Ogilvie bolted forward in the chair,

stunned. "Where did you *get* that name?" he asked, barely audible.

"There's more. . . . Someone called Panov, Mortimer or Moishe Panov, a Jewish physician, we believe. And finally, Counselor, a man and a woman we assume are the assassin Jason Bourne and his wife."

"My *God*!" exclaimed Ogilvie, his body angled and tense, his eyes wide. "What have these people got to do with *us*?"

"That's what we have to know," answered Sulikov, staring at the Wall Street lawyer. "You're obviously aware of each one, aren't you?"

"Well, yes—*no*!" protested Ogilvie, his face flushed, his words spilling over one another. "It's an entirely different situation. It has nothing to do with *our* business—a business we've poured millions into, developed for twenty years!"

"And made millions in return, Counselor, may I be permitted to remind you of that?"

"Venture capital in the international markets!" cried the attorney. "That's no crime in this country. Money flows across the oceans with the touch of a computer button. *No* crime!"

"Really?" The Soviet consul general arched

his brows. "I thought you were a better attorney than that statement suggests. You've been buying up companies all over Europe through mergers and acquisitions using surrogate and misleading corporate entities. The firms you acquire represent sources of supply, often in the same markets, and you subsequently determine prices between former competitors. I believe that's called collusion and restraint of trade, legal terms that we in the Soviet Union have no problems with, as the state sets prices."

"There's no evidence *whatsoever* to support such charges!" declared Ogilvie.

"Of course not, as long as there are liars and unscrupulous lawyers to bribe and advise the liars. It's a labyrinthine enterprise, brilliantly executed, and we've both profited from it. You've sold us anything we've wanted or needed for years, including every major item on your government's restricted lists under so many names our computers broke down trying to keep track of them."

"No *proof*!" insisted the Wall Street attorney emphatically.

"I'm not interested in such proof, Counselor. I'm only interested in the names I mentioned to you. In order, they are Admiral Holland, Alexander Conklin, Dr. Panov and, lastly, Jason Bourne and his wife. Please tell me about them."

"Why?" pleaded Ogilvie. "I've just explained they have nothing to *do* with you and me, nothing to do with our arrangements!"

"We think they might have, so why not start with Admiral Holland?"

"Oh, for God's sake . . . !" The agitated lawyer shook his head back and forth, stammered several times and let the words rush out. "Holland—all right, you'll see. . . . We recruited a man at the CIA, an analyst named DeSole who panicked and wanted to sever his relations with us. Naturally, we couldn't permit that, so we had him eliminated—*professionally* eliminated—as we were forced to do with several others who we believed were dangerously unstable. Holland may have had his suspicions and probably speculated on foul play, but he couldn't do any more than speculate—the professionals we employed left no traces; they never do."

"Very well," said Sulikov, holding his place by the mantel and gazing down at the nervous Ogilvie. "Next, Alexander Conklin."

"He's a former CIA station chief and tied in with Panov, a psychiatrist—they're both connected to the man they call Jason Bourne and his wife. They go back years, to Saigon, in fact. You see, we had been penetrated, several of our people were reached and threatened, and DeSole came to the conclusion that this Bourne, with Conklin's help, was the one responsible for the penetration."

"How could he do that?"

"I don't know. I only know that he has to be eliminated and our professionals have accepted the contract—contracts. They all have to go."

"You mentioned Saigon."

"Bourne was part of the old Medusa," admitted Ogilvie quietly. "And like most of that crowd in the field, a thieving misfit. . . . It could be something as simple as his having recognized someone from twenty years ago. The story DeSole heard was that this trash Bourne— that's not his real name, incidentally—was actually trained by the Agency to pose as an international assassin for the purpose of drawing out a killer they call the Jackal. Ultimately, the strategy failed and Bourne was pensioned off—gold-watch time. 'Thanks for trying, old sport, but it's over now.' Obviously, he wanted a great deal more than that, so he came after us. . . . You can see now, can't you? The two issues are completely separate; there's no linkage. One has nothing to do with the other."

The Russian unclasped his hands and took a step forward away from the mantel. His expression was more one of concern than of alarm. "Can you really be so blind, or is your vision so tunneled that you see nothing but your enterprise?"

"I reject your insult out of hand. What the hell are you talking about?"

"The connection is there because it was engineered, created for one purpose only. You were merely a by-product, a side issue that suddenly became immensely important to the authorities."

"I don't . . . understand," whispered Ogilvie, his face growing pale.

"You just said '*a* killer they call the Jackal,' and before that you alluded to Bourne as a relatively insignificant rogue agent trained to pose as an assassin, a strategy that failed, so he was pensioned off—'gold-watch time,' I believe you said."

"It's what I was told—"

"And what else were you told about Carlos the Jackal? About the man who uses the name Jason Bourne? What do you *know* about them?"

"Very little, frankly. Two aging killers, scum who've been stalking each other for years.

Again, frankly, who gives a damn? My only concern is the complete confidentiality of our organization—which you've seen fit to question."

"You still don't see, do you?"

"See *what*, for God's sake?"

"Bourne may not be the lowly scum you think he is, not when you consider his associates."

"Please be clearer," said Ogilvie in a flat monotone.

"He's using Medusa to hunt the Jackal."

"Impossible! *That* Medusa was destroyed years ago in Saigon!"

"Obviously he thought otherwise. Would you care to remove your well-tailored jacket, roll up your sleeve, and display the small tattoo on your inner forearm?"

"No relevance! A mark of honor in a war no one supported, but *we* had to fight!"

"Oh, come, Counselor. From the piers and the supply depots in Saigon? Stealing your forces blind and routing couriers to the banks in Switzerland. Medals aren't issued for those heroics."

"Pure speculation without foundation!" exclaimed Ogilvie.

"Tell that to Jason Bourne, a graduate of the original Snake Lady. . . . Oh, yes, Counselor, he looked for you and he found you and he's using you to go after the Jackal."

"For Christ's sake, *how*?"

"I honestly don't know, but you'd better read these." The consul general crossed rapidly to the hotel desk, picked up a sheaf of stapled typewritten pages, and brought them over to Bryce Ogilvie. "These are decoded telephone conversations that took place four hours ago at our embassy in Paris. The identities are established, the destinations as well. Read them carefully, Counselor, then render me your legal opinion."

The celebrated attorney, *the* Ice-Cold Ogilvie, grabbed the papers and with swift, practiced eyes began reading. As he flipped from one page to another, the blood drained from his face to the pallor of death. "My *God*, they know it all. My offices are *wired*! How? *Why?* It's insane! We're *impenetrable*!"

"Again, I suggest you tell that to Jason Bourne and his old friend and station chief from Saigon, Alexander Conklin. They found you."

"They couldn't have!" roared Ogilvie. "We paid off or eliminated everyone in Snake Lady who even suspected the extent of our activities. *Jesus,* there weren't that many and goddamned few in the field! I told you, they were scum and we knew better—they were the thieves of the world and wanted for crimes all over Australia and the Far East. The ones in combat we knew and we *reached*!''

"You missed a couple, I believe,'' observed Sulikov.

The lawyer returned to the typed pages, beads of sweat rolling down his temples. "God in heaven, I'm *ruined,*'' he whispered, choking.

"The thought occurred to me,'' said the Soviet consul general of New York, "but then, there are always options, aren't there? . . . Naturally, there's only one course of action for us. Like much of the continent, we were taken in by ruthless capitalist privateers. Lambs led to the slaughter on the altars of greed as this American cartel of financial plunderers cornered markets, selling inferior goods and services at inflated prices, claiming by way of false documents to have Washington's approval to deliver thousands of restricted items to us and our satellites.''

"You son of a *bitch*!'' exploded Ogilvie. "You—*all* of you—cooperated every step of the way. You brokered millions for us out of the bloc countries, rerouted, renamed—Christ, *repainted*—ships throughout the Mediterranean, the Aegean, up the Bosporus and into Marmara, to say nothing about ports in the Baltic!"

"Prove it, Counselor," said Sulikov, laughing quietly. "If you wish, I could make a laudable case for your defection. Moscow would welcome your expertise."

"What?" cried the attorney as panic spread across his face.

"Well, you certainly can't stay here an hour longer than absolutely necessary. Read those words, Mr. Ogilvie. You're in the last stages of electronic surveillance before being picked up by the authorities."

"Oh, my *God—*"

"You might try to operate from Hong Kong or Macao—they'd welcome your money, but with the problems they currently have with the Mainland's markets and the Sino-British Treaty of '97, they'd probably frown on your indictments. I'd say Switzerland's out; the reciprocal laws are so narrow these days, as Vesco found out. Ahh, Vesco. You could join him in Cuba."

"Stop it!" yelled Ogilvie.

"Then again you could turn state's evidence; there's so much to unravel. They might even take, say, ten years off your thirty-year sentence."

"Goddamn it, I'll *kill* you!"

The bedroom door suddenly opened as a consulate guard appeared, his hand menacingly under his jacket. The attorney had lurched to his feet; trembling helplessly, he returned to the chair and leaned forward, his head in his hands.

"Such behavior would not be looked upon favorably," said Sulikov. "Come, Counselor, it's a time for cool heads, not emotional outbursts."

"How the hell can you say that?" asked Ogilvie, a catch in his voice, a prelude to tears. "I'm *finished*."

"That's a harsh judgment from such a resourceful man as you. I mean it. It's true you can't remain here, but still your resources *are* immense. Act from that position of strength. Force concessions; it's the art of survival. Eventually the authorities will see the value of your contributions as they did with Boesky, Levine and several dozen others who endure their minimal sentences playing tennis and backgammon while still possessing fortunes. Try it."

"How?" said the lawyer, looking up at the Russian, his eyes red, pleading.

"The where comes first," explained Sulikov. "Find a neutral country that has no extradition treaty with Washington, one where there are officials who can be persuaded to grant you temporary residence so you can carry on your business activities—the term 'temporary' is extremely elastic, of course. Bahrain, the Emirates, Morocco, Turkey, Greece—there's no lack of attractive possibilities. All with rich English-speaking settlements. . . . We might even be able to help you, very quietly."

"Why would you?"

"Your blindness returns, Mr. Ogilvie. For a price, naturally. . . . You have an extraordinary operation in Europe. It's in place and functioning, and under our control we could derive considerable benefits from it."

"Oh . . . my . . . *God*," said the leader of Medusa, his voice trailing off as he stared at the consul general.

"Do you really have a choice, Counselor? . . . Come now, we must hurry. Arrangements have to be made. Fortunately, it's still early in the day."

It was 3:25 in the afternoon when Charles Casset walked into Peter Holland's office at the Central Intelligence Agency. "Breakthrough," said the deputy director, then added less enthusiastically, "Of sorts."

"The Ogilvie firm?" asked the DCI.

"From left field," replied Casset, nodding and placing several stock photographs on Holland's desk. "These were faxed down from Kennedy Airport an hour ago. Believe me, it's been a heavy sixty minutes since then."

"From Kennedy?" Frowning, Peter studied the facsimiled duplicates. They comprised a sequence of photographs showing a crowd of people passing through metal detectors in one of the airport's international terminals. The head of a single man was circled in red in each photo. "What is it? Who is it?"

"They're passengers heading for the Aeroflot lounge, Moscow bound, Soviet carrier, of course. Security routinely photographs U.S. nationals taking those flights."

"So? Who is he?"

"Ogilvie himself."

"What?"

"He's on the two o'clock nonstop to Moscow. . . . Only he's not supposed to be."

"Come again?"

"Three separate calls to his office came up with the same information. He was out of the country, in London, at the Dorchester, which we know he isn't. However, the Dorchester desk confirmed that he was booked but hadn't arrived, so they were taking messages."

"I don't understand, Charlie."

"It's a smoke screen and pretty hastily contrived. In the first place, why would someone as rich as Ogilvie settle for Aeroflot when he could be on the Concorde to Paris and Air France to Moscow? Also, why would his office volunteer that he was either in or on his way to London when he was *heading* for Moscow?"

"The Aeroflot flight's obvious," said Holland. "It's the state airline and he's under Soviet protection. The London-Dorchester bit isn't too hard, either. It's to throw people off—my God, to throw *us* off!"

"Right on, master. So Valentino did some checking with all that fancy equipment in the cellars and guess what? . . . Mrs. Ogilvie and their two teenage children are on a Royal Air Maroc flight to Casablanca with connections to Marrakesh."

"Marrakesh? . . . Air Maroc—Morocco, *Marrakesh.* Wait a minute. In those computer sheets Conklin had us work up on the Mayflower hotel's registers, there was a woman—one of three people he tied to Medusa—who had been in Marrakesh."

"I commend your memory, Peter. That woman and Ogilvie's wife were roommates at Bennington in the early seventies. Fine old families; their pedigrees ensure a large degree of sticking together and giving advice to one another."

"Charlie, what the *hell* is going on?"

"The Ogilvies were tipped off and have gotten out. Also, if I'm not mistaken and if we could sort out several hundred accounts, we'd learn that millions have been transferred from New York to God knows where beyond these shores."

"*And?*"

"Medusa's now in Moscow, Mr. Director."

34

Louis DeFazio wearily dragged his small frame out of the taxi in the boulevard Masséna, followed by his larger, heavier, far more muscular cousin Mario from Larchmont, New York. They stood on the pavement in front of a restaurant, its name in red-tubed script across a green-tinted window: *Tetrazzini's*.

"This is the place," said Louis. "They'll be in a private room in the back."

"It's pretty late." Mario looked at his watch under the wash of a street lamp. "I set the time for Paris; it's almost midnight here."

"They'll wait."

"You still haven't told me their names, Lou. What do we call them?"

"You don't," answered DeFazio, starting for the entrance. "No names—they wouldn't mean anything anyway. All you gotta do is be respectful, you know what I mean?"

"I don't have to be told that, Lou, I really don't," reprimanded Mario in his soft-spoken voice. "But for my own information, why do you even bring it up?"

"He's a high-class *diplomatico*," explained the capo supremo, stopping briefly on the pavement and looking up at the man who had nearly killed Jason Bourne in Manassas, Virginia. "He operates out of Rome from fancy government circles, but he's the direct contact with the dons in Sicily. He and his wife are very, *very* highly regarded, you understand what I'm saying?"

"I do and I don't," admitted the cousin. "If he's so grand, why would he accept such a menial assignment as following our targets?"

"Because he *can*. He can go places some of our *pagliacci* can't get near, you know what I mean? Also, I happen to let our people in New York know who our clients were, especially one, *capisce*? The dons all the way from Manhattan to the estates south of Palermo have a language they use exclusively between themselves, did you know that, *cugino*? . . . It comes down to a couple of orders: 'Do it' and 'Don't do it.' "

"I think I understand, Lou. We render respect."

"Respect, *yes,* my fancy rendering cousin, but not no weakness, *capisce*? No weakness! The word's got to go up and down the line that this is an operation Lou DeFazio took control of and ran from beginning to end. You *got* that?"

"If that's the case, maybe I can go home to Angie and the kids," said Mario, grinning.

"What? . . . You shut up, *cugino*! With this one job you got annuities for your whole passel of bambinos."

"Not a passel, Lou, just five."

"Let's go. Remember, respect, but we don't take no shit."

The small private dining room was a miniature version of Tetrazzini's decor. The ambience was Italian in all things. The walls were papered with dated, now faded murals of Venice, Rome and Florence; the softly piped-in music was predominantly operatic arias and tarantellas, and the lighting indirect with pockets of shadows. If a patron did not know he was in Paris, he might think he was dining on Rome's Via Frascati, at one of the many commercialized family *ristoranti* lining that ancient street.

There was a large round table in the center covered by a deep red tablecloth, with a generous overhang, and four chairs equidistant from one another. Additional chairs were against the walls, allowing for an expanded conference of principals or for the proper location of secondary subalterns, usually armed. Seated at the far end of the table was a distinguished-looking olive-skinned man with wavy dark hair; on his left was a fashionably dressed, well-coiffed middle-aged woman. A bottle of Chianti Classico was between them, the crude thick-stemmed wineglasses in front of them not the sort one would associate with such aristocratic diners. On a chair behind the *diplomatico* was a black leather suitcase.

"I'm DeFazio," said the capo supremo from New York, closing the door. "This is my cousin Mario, of who you may have heard of—a very talented man who takes precious time away from his family to be with us."

"Yes, of course," said the aristocratic mafioso. "Mario, *il boia, esecuzione garantito*—deadly with any weapon. Sit down, gentlemen."

"I find such descriptions meaningless," responded Mario, approaching a chair. "I'm skilled in my craft, that's all."

"Spoken like a professional, signore," added the woman as DeFazio and his cousin sat down. "May I order you wine, drinks?" she continued.

"Not yet," replied Louis. "Maybe later— maybe. . . . My talented relative on my mother's side, may she rest in the arms of Christ, asked a good question outside. What do we call you, Mr. and Mrs. Paris, France? Which is by way of saying I don't need no real names."

"*Conte* and *Contessa* is what we're known by," answered the husband, smiling, the tight smile more appropriate to a mask than a human face.

"See what I mean, *cugino*? These are people of high regard. . . . So, Mr. Count, bring us up to date, how about it?"

"There's no question about it, Signor DeFazio," replied the Roman, his voice as tight as his previous smile, which had completely disappeared. "I will bring you up to date, and were it in my powers I would leave you in the far distant past."

"Hey, what kind of fuckin' talk is that?"

"Lou, *please*!" intruded Mario, quietly but firmly. "Watch your language."

"What about *his* language? What kind of language is that? He wants to leave me in some kind of *dirt*?"

"You asked me what has happened, Signor DeFazio, and I'm telling you," said the count, his voice as strained as before. "Yesterday at noon my wife and I were nearly killed—*killed,* Signor DeFazio. It's not the sort of experience we're used to or can tolerate. Have you any idea what you've gotten yourself *into*?"

"You . . . ? They *marked* you?"

"If you mean by that, did they know who we were, happily they did not. Had they known, it's doubtful we'd be sitting at this table!"

"Signor DeFazio," interrupted the contessa, glancing at her husband, her look telling him to calm down. "The word we received over here is that you have a contract on this cripple and his friend the doctor. Is that true?"

"Yeah," confirmed the capo supremo cautiously. "As far as that goes, but it goes further, you know what I mean?"

"I haven't the vaguest idea," replied the count icily.

"I tell you this because it's possible I could use your help, for which, like I told you, you'll be paid good, real good."

"How does the contract go 'further'?" asked the wife, again interrupting.

"There's someone else we have to hit. A third party these two came over here to meet."

The count and his countess instantly looked at each other. "A 'third party,'" repeated the man from Rome, raising the wineglass to his lips. "I see. . . . A three-target contract is generally quite profitable. *How* profitable, Signor DeFazio?"

"Hey, come on, do I ask you what you make a week in Paris, France? Let's just say it's a lot and you two personally can count on six figures, if everything goes according to the book."

"Six figures encompass a wide spectrum," observed the countess. "It also indicates that the contract is worth over seven figures."

"Seven . . . ?" DeFazio looked at the woman, his breathing on hold.

"Over a million dollars," concluded the countess.

"Yeah, well, you see, it's important to our clients that these people leave this world," said Louis, breathing again as seven figures had not been equated with seven million. "We don't ask why, we just do the job. In situations like this, our dons are generous; we keep most of the money and 'our thing' keeps its reputation for efficiency. Isn't that right, Mario?"

"I'm sure it is, Lou, but I don't involve myself in those matters."

"You get paid, don't you, *cugino*?"

"I wouldn't be here if I didn't, Lou."

"See what I mean?" said DeFazio, looking at the aristocrats of the European Mafia, who showed no reaction at all except to stare at the capo supremo. "Hey, what's the matter? . . . Oh, this bad thing that happened yesterday, huh? What was it—they saw you, *right*? They spotted you, and some gorilla got off a couple of shots to scare you away, that's it, isn't it? I mean what else could it be, right? They didn't know who you were but you were there—a couple of times too often, maybe—so a little muscle was used, okay? It's an old scam: Scare the shit out of strangers you see more than once."

"Lou, I asked you to temper your language."

"Temper? I'm *losing* my temper. I want to deal!"

"In plain words," said the count, disregarding DeFazio's words with a soft voice and arched brows, "you say you must kill this cripple and his friend the doctor, as well as a third party, is that correct?"

"In plain words, you got it right."

"Do you know who this third party is—outside of a photograph or a detailed description?"

"Sure, he's a government slime who was sent out years ago to make like he was a Mario here, an *esecuzione*, can you believe it? But these three individuals have injured our clients, I mean really *hurt* them. That's why the contract, what else can I tell you?"

"We're not sure," said the countess, gracefully sipping her wine. "Perhaps you don't really know."

"Know what?"

"Know that there is someone else who wants this third party dead far more than you do," explained the count. "Yesterday noon he assaulted a small café in the countryside with murderous gunfire, killing a number of people, because your third party was inside. So were we. . . . We saw them—*him*—warned by a guard and race outside. Certain emergencies are communicated. We left immediately, only minutes before the massacre."

"Condannare!" choked DeFazio. "Who is this bastard who wants the kill? *Tell* me!"

"We've spent yesterday afternoon and all day today trying to find out," began the woman, leaning forward, delicately fingering the indelicate glass as though it were an affront to her sensibilities. "Your targets are never alone. There are always men around them, armed guards, and at first we didn't know where they came from. Then on the avenue Montaigne we saw a Soviet limousine come for them, and your third man in the company of a well-known KGB officer, and now we think we *do* know."

"Only you, however," broke in the count, "can confirm it for us. What is the name of this third man on your contract? Surely we have a right to know."

"Why not? He's a loser named Bourne, Jason Bourne, who's blackmailing our clients."

"*Ecco,*" said the husband quietly.

"*Ultimo,*" added the wife. "What do you know of this Bourne?" she asked.

"What I told you. He went out under cover for the government and got shafted by the big boys in Washington. He gets pissed off, so he ends up shafting our clients. A real slime."

"You've never heard of Carlos the Jackal?" said the count, leaning back in the chair, studying the capo supremo.

"Oh, yeah, sure, I heard of him, and I see what you mean. They say this Jackal character has a big thing against this Bourne and vice versa, but it don't cut no ice with me. You know, I thought that fox-cat was just in books, in the movies, you know what I mean? Then they tell me he's a real hit man, wadda y' know?"

"Very real," agreed the countess.

"But, like I said, him I couldn't care less about. I want the Jew shrink, the cripple, and this rot-gut Bourne, that's all. And I *really* want them."

The diplomat and his wife looked at each other; they shrugged in mild astonishment, then the *contessa* nodded, deferring to her husband. "Your sense of fiction has been shattered by reality," said the count.

"Come again?"

"There *was* a Robin Hood, you know, but he wasn't a noble of Locksley. He was a barbaric Saxon chief who opposed the Normans, a mur-dering, butchering thief, extolled only in legends. And there *was* an Innocent the Third, a pope who was hardly innocent and who followed the savage policies of a predecessor, Saint Gregory the Seventh, who was hardly a saint. Between them they split Europe asunder, into rivers of blood for political power and to enrich the cof-fers of the 'Holy Empire.' Centuries before, there *was* the gentle Quintus Cassius Longinus of

Rome, beloved protector of the Further Spain, yet he tortured and mutilated a hundred thousand Spaniards."

"What the *hell* are you talkin' about?"

"These men were fictionalized, Signor DeFazio, into many different shadings of what they may actually have been, but regardless of the distortions, they were real. Just as the Jackal is real, and is a deadly problem for you. As, unfortunately, he is a problem for us, for he's a complication we cannot accept."

"Huh?" The capo supremo, mouth gaping, stared at the Italian aristocrat.

"The presence of the Soviets was both alarming and enigmatic," continued the count. "Then finally we perceived a possible connection, which you just confirmed. . . . Moscow has been hunting Carlos for years, solely for the purpose of executing him, and all they've gotten for their efforts is one dead hunter after another. Somehow—God *knows* how—Jason Bourne negotiated with the Russians to pursue their common objective."

"For Christ's sake, speak English *or* Italian, but with words that make sense! I didn't exactly go to Harvard City College, gumball. I didn't have to, *capisce*?"

"The Jackal stormed that country inn yesterday. He's the one hunting down Jason Bourne,
who was foolish enough to come back to Paris
and persuade the Soviets to work with him. Both
were stupid, for this *is* Paris and Carlos will win.
He'll kill Bourne and your other targets and
laugh at the Russians. Then he'll proclaim to the
clandestine departments of all governments
that he *has* won, that he's the *padrone*, the *mae-
stro*. You in America have never been exposed
to the whole story, only bits and pieces, for your
interest in Europe stops at the money line. But
we have lived through it, watching in fascination,
and now we are mesmerized. Two aging master
assassins obsessed with hatred, each wanting
only to cut the other's throat."

"Hey, back up, gumball!" shouted DeFazio.
"This slime Bourne's a fake, a *contraffazione*.
He never *was* an executioner!"

"You're quite wrong, signore," said the countess. "He may not have entered the arena with
a gun, but it became his favorite instrument. Ask
the Jackal."

"*Fuck* the Jackal!" cried DeFazio, getting up
from the chair.

"*Lou!*"

"Shut *up*, Mario! This Bourne is *mine*, ours!

We deliver the corpse, *we* take the pictures with me—*us*—standing over all three with a dozen ice picks in their bodies, their heads pulled up by the hair, so nobody can say it ain't our kills!"

"Now you're the one who's *pazzo*," said the Mafia count quietly, in counterpoint to the capo supremo's raucous yelling. "And please keep your voice down."

"Then don't get me excited—"

"He's trying to explain things, Lou," said DeFazio's relative, the killer. "I want to hear what the gentleman has to say because it could be vital to my approach. Sit *down*, Cousin." Louis sat down. "Please continue, Count."

"Thank you, Mario. You don't object to my calling you Mario."

"Not at all, sir."

"Perhaps you should visit Rome—"

"Perhaps we should get back to *Paris*," again choked the capo supremo.

"Very well," agreed the Roman, now dividing his attention between DeFazio and his cousin, but favoring the latter. "You might take out all three targets with a long-range rifle, but you won't get near the bodies. The Soviet guards will be indistinguishable from any other people in the area, and if they see the two of you coming in to the killing ground, they'll open fire, assuming you're from the Jackal."

"Then we must create a diversion where we can isolate the targets," said Mario, his elbows on the table, his intelligent eyes on the count. "Perhaps an emergency in the early hours of the morning. A fire in their lodgings, perhaps, that necessitates their coming outside. I've done it before; in the confusion of fire trucks and police sirens and the general panic, one can pull targets away and complete the assignments."

"It's a fine strategy, Mario, but there are still the Soviet guards."

"We take them out!" cried DeFazio.

"You are only two men," said the diplomat, "and there are at least three in Barbizon, to say nothing of the hotel in Paris where the cripple and the doctor are staying."

"So we outmatch the numbers." The capo supremo pulled the back of his hand over the sweat that had gathered on his forehead. "We hit this Barbizon first, *right*?"

"With only two men?" asked the countess, her cosmeticized eyes wide in surprise.

"*You* got men!" exclaimed DeFazio. "We'll use a few. . . . I'll pay additional."

The count shook his head slowly and spoke

softly. "We will not go to war with the Jackal," he said. "Those are my instructions."

"Fairy *bastards*!"

"An interesting comment coming from you," observed the countess, a thin insulting smile on her lips.

"Perhaps our dons are not as generous as yours," continued the diplomat. "We are willing to cooperate up to a point but no further."

"You'll never make another shipment to New York, *or* Philly, *or* Chicago!"

"We'll let our superiors debate those issues, won't we?"

There was a sudden knocking at the door, four raps in a row, harsh and intrusive. *"Avanti,"* called out the count, instantly reaching under his jacket and ripping an automatic out of his belt; he lowered it beneath the overhang of the red tablecloth and smiled as the manager of Tetrazzini's entered.

"Emergenza," said the grossly overweight man, walking rapidly to the well-tailored mafioso and handing him a note.

"Grazie."

"Prego," replied the manager, crossing back to the door and exiting as quickly as he had arrived.

"The anxious gods of Sicily may be smiling

down on you after all," said the count, reading. "This communication is from the man following your targets. They are outside Paris and they are alone, and for reasons I cannot possibly explain, there are no guards. They have no protection."

"Where?" cried DeFazio, leaping to his feet.

Without answering, the diplomat calmly reached for his gold lighter, ignited it, and fired the small piece of paper, lowering it into an ashtray. Mario sprang up from his chair; the man from Rome dropped the lighter on the table and swiftly retrieved the gun from his lap. "First, let us discuss the fee," he said as the note coiled into flaming black ash. "Our dons in Palermo are definitely not as generous as yours. Please talk quickly, as every minute counts."

"You motherfucking *bastard*!"

"My Oedipal problems are not your concern. How much, Signor DeFazio?"

"I'll go the limit," replied the capo supremo, lowering himself into the chair, staring at the charred remnants of the information. "Three hundred thousand, American. That's it."

"That's *excremento*," said the countess. "Try again. Seconds become minutes and you cannot afford them."

"All right, all *right*! Double it!"

"Plus expenses," added the woman.

"What the fuck can *they* be?"

"Your cousin Mario is right," said the diplomat. "Please watch your language in front of my wife."

"Holy *shit*—"

"I warned you, signore. The expenses are an additional quarter of a million, American."

"What are you, *nuts*?"

"No, you're vulgar. The total is one million one hundred fifty thousand dollars, to be paid as our couriers in New York so instruct you. . . . If not, you will be missed in—what is it?—Brooklyn Heights, Signor DeFazio?"

"Where are the targets?" said the beaten capo supremo, his defeat painful to him.

"At a small private airfield in Pontcarré, about forty-five minutes from Paris. They're waiting for a plane that was grounded in Poitiers because of bad weather. It can't possibly arrive for at least an hour and a quarter."

"Did you bring the equipment we requested?" asked Mario rapidly.

"It's all there," answered the countess, gesturing at the large black suitcase on a chair against the wall.

"A car, a *fast* car!" cried DeFazio as his executioner retrieved the suitcase.

"Outside," replied the count. "The driver will know where to take you. He's been to that field."

"Come on, *cugino*. Tonight we collect and you can settle a score!"

Except for a single clerk behind the counter in the small one-room terminal and an air controller hired to stay the extra hours in the radio tower, the private airport in Pontcarré was deserted. Alex Conklin and Mo Panov stayed discreetly behind as Bourne led Marie outside to the gate area fronting the field beyond a waist-high metal fence. Two strips of receding amber ground lights defined the long runway for the plane from Poitiers; they had been turned on only a short time ago.

"It won't be long now," said Jason.

"This whole damn thing's stupid," retorted Webb's wife. *"Everything."*

"There's no reason for you to stay and every reason for you to leave. For you to be alone here in Paris would be stupid. Alex is right. If Carlos's people found you, you'd be taken hostage, so why risk it?"

"Because I'm capable of staying out of sight

and I don't want to be ten thousand miles away from you. You'll forgive me if I worry about you, Mr. *Bourne*. And care for you."

Jason looked at her in the shadows, grateful for the darkness; she could not clearly see his eyes. "Then be reasonable and use your head," he said coldly, suddenly feeling so old, too old for such a transparently false lack of feeling. "We know Carlos is in Moscow and Krupkin isn't far behind him. Dimitri's flying us there in the morning, and we'll be under the protection of the KGB in the tightest city in the world. What more could we want?"

"You were under the protection of the United States government on a short East Side block in New York thirteen years ago and it didn't do you much good."

"There's a great deal of difference. Back then the Jackal knew exactly where I was going and when I'd be there. Right now he has no idea we even know he's in Moscow. He's got other problems, big ones for him, and he thinks we're here in Paris—he's ordered his people to keep searching for us."

"What will you do in Moscow?"

"We won't know until we get there, but whatever it is, it's better than here in Paris. Krupkin's been busy. Every ranking officer in Dzerzhinsky

Square who speaks French is being watched and is under surveillance. He said the French narrowed down the possibilities and that something should break. . . . Something *will* break; the odds are on our side. And when it does, I can't be worried about you back here."

"That's the nicest thing you've said in the past thirty-six hours."

"So be it. You should be with the children and you know that. You'll be out of reach and safe . . . and the kids need you. Mrs. Cooper's a terrific lady, but she's not their mother. Besides, your brother probably has Jamie smoking his Cuban cigars and playing Monopoly with real money by now."

Marie looked up at her husband, a gentle smile apparent in the darkness as well as in her voice. "Thanks for the laugh. I need it."

"It's probably the truth—your brother, I mean. If there are good-looking women on the staff, it's quite possible our son's lost his virginity."

"David!" Bourne was silent. Marie chuckled briefly, then went on. "I suppose I really can't argue with you."

"And you would if my argument was flawed, Dr. St. Jacques. That's something I've learned over the past thirteen years."

"I still object to this *crazy* trip back to Washington! From here to Marseilles, then to London, *then* on a flight to Dulles. It'd be so much simpler just to get on a plane from Orly to the States."

"It's Peter Holland's idea. He'll meet you himself, so ask him; he doesn't say an awful lot on the phone. I suspect he doesn't want to deal with the French authorities for fear of a leak to Carlos's people. A single woman with a common name on crowded flights is probably best."

"I'll spend more time sitting in airports than in the air."

"Probably, so cover those great legs of yours and carry a Bible."

"That's sweet," said Marie, touching his face. "I suddenly hear you, David."

"What?" Again Bourne did not respond to the warmth.

"Nothing. . . . Do me a favor, will you?"

"What is it?" asked Jason, in a distant monotone.

"Bring that David back to me."

"Let's get an update on the plane," said Bourne, his voice flat and abrupt as he touched her elbow and led her back inside. *I'm getting older—old—and I cannot much longer be what I am not. The Chameleon is slipping away; the imagination isn't there the way it used to be. But*

I cannot stop! Not now! Get away from me, David Webb!

No sooner had they reentered the small terminal than the telephone on the counter began to ring. The lone clerk picked it up. *"Oui?"* He listened for no more than five seconds. *"Merci,"* he said, hanging up and addressing the four interested parties in French. "That was the tower. The plane from Poitiers will be on the ground in approximately four minutes. The pilot requests that you be ready, madame, as he would like to fly ahead of the weather front moving east."

"So would I," agreed Marie, rushing to Alex Conklin and Mo Panov. The farewells were brief, the embraces strong, the words heartfelt. Bourne led his wife back outside. "I just remembered—where are Krupkin's guards?" she asked as Jason unlatched the gate and they walked toward the lighted runway.

"We don't need them or want them," he answered. "The Soviet connection was made in the Montaigne, so we have to assume the embassy's being watched. No guards rushing out into cars, therefore no movement on our part for Carlos's people to report."

"I see." The sound of a small decelerating jet

could be heard as the plane circled the airfield once and made its descent onto the four-thousand-foot runway. "I love you so much, David," said Marie, raising her voice to be heard over the roar of the aircraft, rolling toward them.

"He loves you so much," said Bourne, images colliding in his mind. "*I* love you so much."

The jet loomed clearly into view between the rows of amber lights, a white bulletlike machine with short delta wings sweeping back from the fuselage, giving it the appearance of an angry flying insect. The pilot swung the plane around in a circle, coming to a jarring stop as the automatic passenger door sprang out and up while metal steps slapped down to the ground. Jason and Marie ran toward the jet's entrance.

It happened with the sudden impact of a murderous wind shear, at once unstoppable, enveloping, the swirling winds of death! *Gunfire.* Automatic weapons—two of them; one nearby, one farther away—shattering windows, ripping into wood, a piercing screech of pain erupting from the terminal, announcing a mortal hit.

With both hands Bourne gripped Marie by the waist, heaving her up and propelling her into the plane as he shouted to the pilot. "Shut the door and get *out* of here!"

"*Mon Dieu!*" cried the man from the open

flight deck. *"Allez-vous-en!"* he roared, ordering Jason away from the spring-hinged door
and the metal steps, gunning the jet's engine
as the plane lurched forward. Jason plunged to
the ground and raised his eyes. Marie's face
was pressed against the window; she was
screaming hysterically. The plane thundered
down the runway; it was free.

Bourne was not. He was caught in the wash
of the amber lights, the glowing rows a cy-
clorama of yellowish orange. No matter where
he stood or knelt or crouched he was in silhouette. So he pulled out the automatic from his
belt—the weapon, he reflected, given to him by
Bernardine—and began slithering, snaking his
way across the asphalt toward the bordering
grass outside the fenced-gate area.

The gunfire erupted again, but now they were
three scattered single shots from within the terminal, where the lights had been extinguished.
They had to have come from Conklin's gun, or
possibly the clerk's if he had a weapon; Panov
did not. Then who had been hit? . . . No *time*! A
shattering fusillade burst out of the nearest automatic rifle; it was steady, prolonged and
deadly, spraying the side of the small building
and the gate area.

Then the second automatic weapon commenced firing; from the sound it was on the opposite side of the terminal's waiting room. Moments later there were two single shots, the last one accompanied by a scream . . . again on the other side of the building.

"I've been hit!" The voice was the cry of a man in pain . . . on the *other side* of the *building*. The automatic rifle! Jason slowly rose to a low crouch in the grass and peered into the darkness. A fragment of blacker darkness moved. He raised his automatic and fired into the moving mass, getting to his feet and racing across the gate area, turning and squeezing the trigger until he was both out of bullets and out of sight on the east side of the building, where the runway ended and the amber lights stopped. He crawled cautiously to the section of the waist-high fence that paralleled the corner of the small terminal. The grayish-white gravel of the parking area was a gratifying sight; he was able to make out the figure of a man writhing on the stones. The figure gripped a weapon in his hands, then pushing it into the gravel, raised himself to a half-sitting position.

"Cugino!" he screamed. "Help me!" His answer was another burst of gunfire from the west side of the building, diagonally to the right of the

wounded man. "Holy Christ!" he shrieked. "I'm
hit *bad*!" Again the reply was yet another fusillade from the automatic rifle, these rounds
simultaneous with crashing glass. The killer on
the west side of the building had smashed the
windows and was blowing apart everything inside.

Bourne dropped the useless automatic and
grabbed the top of the fence, vaulting over it, his
left leg landing in agony on the ground. *What's
happened to me? Why do I hurt? Goddamn it!*
He limped to the wood-framed corner of the
building and edged his face to the open space
beyond. The figure on the gravel fell back, unable to support himself on the automatic rifle.
Jason felt the ground, found a large rock, and
threw it with all his strength beyond the
wounded man. It crashed, bouncing into the
gravel, for an instant like the sound of approaching footsteps. The killer spastically rose and
spun his body to the rear, gripping his weapon,
which twice fell out of his grasp.

Now! Bourne raced across the stones of the
parking lot and lunged off his feet down into
the man with the gun. He tore the weapon from
the killer's grip and crashed the metal stock into
his skull. The short, slender man went limp. And,

again, suddenly, there was another crescendo of gunfire from the west exterior of the terminal building, again accompanied by the shattering of glass. The first and nearer killer was narrowing down his targets. *He had to be stopped!* thought Jason, his breath gone, every muscle in his body in pain. *Where was the man from yesterday? Where was Delta from Medusa? The Chameleon from Treadstone Seventy-one?* Where *was* that man?

Bourne grabbed the MAC-10 submachine gun from the unconscious figure on the gravel and raced toward the side door of the terminal.

"Alex!" he roared. "Let me *in*! I've got the weapon!"

The door crashed open. "My God, you're alive!" shouted Conklin in the darkness of the shadows as Jason ran inside. "Mo's in bad shape—he was shot in the chest. The clerk's dead and we can't raise the tower out on the field. They must have reached it first." Alex slammed the door shut. "Get down on the floor!" A fusillade raked the walls. Bourne got to his knees and fired back, then threw himself down beside Conklin.

"What *happened*?" cried Jason, breathless, his voice strained, the sweat dripping down his face and stinging his eyes.

"The Jackal happened."

"How did he *do* it?"

"He fooled us all. You, me, Krupkin and Lavier—worst of all, *me*. He sent the word out that he'd be away, no explanation even with you here in Paris, just that he'd be gone for a while. We thought the trap had worked; everything pointed to Moscow. . . . He sucked us into his own trap. Oh, Christ, did he suck us in! I should have known better, I should have seen through it! It was too clean. . . . I'm sorry, David. Oh, God, I'm sorry!"

"That's *him* out there, isn't it? He wants the kill all to himself—nothing else matters to him."

Suddenly a flashlight, its powerful beam blinding, was thrown through a shattered window. Instantly, Bourne raised the MAC-10 and blew the shiny metal tube away, extinguishing the light. The damage, however, had been done; their bodies had been seen.

"Over *here*!" screamed Alex, grabbing Jason and diving behind the counter as a murderous barrage came from the blurred silhouette in the window. It stopped; there was the crack of a bolt.

"He has to *reload*!" whispered Bourne, with the break in the fire. "*Stay* here!" Jason stood up and raced to the gate doors, crashing through them, his weapon gripped in his right hand, his body prone, tense, prepared to kill—if the years would permit it. They *had* to permit it!

He crawled through the gate he had opened for Marie and spun on the ground to his right, scrambling along the fence. He *was* Delta—of Saigon's *Medusa* . . . he could *do* it! There was no friendly jungle now, but there was everything he could use—*Delta* could use—the darkness, the intermittent blocks of shadows from the myriad clouds intercepting the moonlight. Use *everything*! It was what you were trained to do . . . so many years ago—so many. Forget it, forget time! *Do* it! The animal only yards away wants you dead—your wife dead, your children dead. *Dead!*

It was the quickness born of pure fury that propelled him, obsessed him, and he knew that to win he had to win quickly, with all the speed that was in him. He crept swiftly along the fence that enclosed the airfield, and past the corner of the terminal, prepared for the instant of exposure. The lethal submachine gun was still gripped in his hand, his index finger now on the trigger. There was a cluster of wild shrubbery preceding two thick trees no more than thirty feet away; if he could reach them, the advantage was his. He would have the "high ground," the Jackal in the valley of death, if only because he was behind the assassin and unseen.

He reached the shrubbery. And at the moment he heard a massive smashing of glass followed by yet another fusillade—this time so prolonged that the entire magazine had to have been emptied. He had *not* been seen; the figure by the window had backed away to reload, his concentration on that task, not on the possibility of an escape. Carlos, too, was growing old and losing his finesse, thought Jason Bourne. Where were the flares intrinsic to such an operation? Where were the alert, roving eyes that loaded weapons in total darkness?

Darkness. A cloud cover blocked the yellow rays of the moon; there *was* darkness. He vaulted over the fence, concealing himself behind the shrubbery, then raced to the first of the two trees where he could stand upright, view the scene and consider his options.

Something was wrong. There was a primitiveness he could not associate with the Jackal. The assassin had isolated the terminal, *ad valorem,* and the price was high, but there was an absence of the finer points of the deadly equation. The subtlety was not there; instead, there was a brute force, hardly to be denied, but not when employed against the man they called Jason Bourne who had escaped from the trap.

The figure by the shattered window had spent his ammunition; he reeled back against the building, pulling another magazine out of his pocket. Jason raced out of the cover of the trees, his MAC-10 on automatic fire, exploding the dirt in front of the killer, then circling the bullets around his frame.

"That's *it*!" he shouted, closing in on the assassin. "You're dead, *Carlos,* with one pull of my finger—if you *are* the Jackal!"

The man by the shattered window threw down his weapon. "I am not he, Mr. Bourne," said the executioner from Larchmont, New York. "We've met before, but I am not the person you think I am."

"Hit the ground, you son of a bitch!" The killer did so as Jason approached. "Spread your legs and your arms!" The command was obeyed. "Raise your *head*!"

The man did so, and Bourne stared at the face, vaguely illuminated by the distant glow of the amber lights on the airfield's runway. "You see now?" said Mario. "I'm not who you think I am."

"My *God,*" whispered Jason, his incredulity all too apparent. "You were in the driveway in Manassas, Virginia. You tried to kill Cactus, then *me!*"

"Contracts, Mr. Bourne, nothing more."

"What about the tower? The air controller here in the *tower!*"

"I do not kill indiscriminately. Once the plane from Poitiers was given clearance to land, I told him to leave. . . . Forgive me, but your wife was also on the list. Fortunately, as she is a mother, it was beyond my abilities."

"Who the hell *are* you?"

"I just told you. A contract employee."

"I've seen better."

"I'm not, perhaps, in your league, but I serve my organization well."

"Jesus, you're *Medusa!*"

"I've heard the name, but that's all I can tell you. . . . Let me make one thing clear, Mr. Bourne. I will not leave my wife a widow, or my children orphans for the sake of a contract. That position simply isn't viable. They mean too much to me."

"You'll spend a hundred and fifty years in prison, and that's only if you're prosecuted in a state that doesn't have the death penalty."

"Not with what I know, Mr. Bourne. My family and I will be well taken care of—a new name, perhaps a nice farm in the Dakotas or Wyoming. You see, I knew this moment had to come."

"What's come now, you *bastard*, is that a friend of mine inside there is shot up! You *did* it!"

"A truce, then?" said Mario.

"What the hell do you mean by that?"

"I have a very fast car a half mile away." The killer from Larchmont, New York, pulled a square instrument from his belt. "It can be here in less than a minute. I'm sure the driver knows the nearest hospital."

"*Do* it!"

"It's done, Jason Bourne," said Mario, pressing a button.

Morris Panov had been rolled into the operating room; Louis DeFazio was still on a gurney, as it was determined that his wound was superficial. And through back-channel negotiations between Washington and Quai d'Orsay, the criminal known only as Mario was securely in the custody of the American embassy in Paris.

A white-frocked doctor came out into the hospital's waiting room; both Conklin and Bourne got to their feet, frightened. "I will not pretend to be a bearer of glad tidings," said the physician in French, "for it would be quite wrong. Both lungs of your friend were punctured, as well as the wall of his heart. He has at best a forty-sixty chance of survival—against him, I'm afraid. Still, he is a strong-willed man who wants to live. At times that means more than all the medical negatives. What else can I tell you?"

"Thank you, Doctor." Jason turned away.

"I have to use a telephone," said Alex to the surgeon. "I should go to our embassy, but I haven't the time. Do I have any guarantee that I won't be tapped, overheard?"

"I imagine you have every guarantee," replied the physician. "We wouldn't know how to do it. Use my office, please."

"Peter?"

"*Alex!*" cried Holland from Langley, Virginia. "Everything go all right? Did Marie get off?"

"To answer your first question, no, everything did not go all right; and as far as Marie goes, you can expect a panicked phone call from her the minute she reaches Marseilles. That pilot won't touch his radio."

"What?"

"Tell her we're okay, that David's not hurt—"

"What are you *talking* about?" broke in the director of Central Intelligence.

"We were ambushed while waiting for the plane from Poitiers. I'm afraid Mo Panov's in bad shape, so bad I don't want to think about it right now. We're in a hospital and the doctor's not encouraging."

"Oh, God, Alex, I'm *sorry*."

"In his own way, Mo's a fighter. I'll still bet on him. Incidentally, don't tell Marie. She thinks too much."

"Of course not. Is there anything I can do?"

"Yes, there is, Peter. You can tell me why Medusa's here in Paris."

"In *Paris*? It's not according to everything I know and I know a hell of a lot."

"Our identification's positive. The two guns that hit us an hour ago were sent over by Medusa. We've even got a confession of sorts."

"I don't *understand*!" protested Holland. "Paris never entered into our thinking. There's no linkage in the scenario."

"Sure, there is," contradicted the former station chief. "You said it yourself. You called it a self-fulfilling prophecy, remember? The ultimate logic that Bourne conceived as a theory. Medusa joining up with the Jackal, the target Jason Bourne."

"That's the point, Alex. It *was* only a theory, hypothetically convincing, but still just a theory, the basis for a sound strategy. But it never happened."

"It obviously did."

"Not from this end. As far as we're concerned, Medusa's now in Moscow."

"Moscow?" Conklin nearly dropped the phone on the doctor's desk.

"That's right. We've concentrated on Ogilvie's law firm in New York, tapping everything that could be tapped. Somehow—and we don't know how—Ogilvie was tipped off and got out of the country. He took an Aeroflot to Moscow, and the rest of his family headed to Marrakesh."

"Ogilvie . . . ?" Alex could barely be heard; frowning, his memory peeled away the years. "From Saigon? A legal officer from *Saigon*?"

"That's right. We're convinced he runs Medusa."

"And you withheld that information from me?"

"Only the name of the firm. I told you we had our priorities and you had yours. For us, Medusa came first."

"You simple swab-jockey!" exploded Conklin. "I *know* Ogilvie—more precisely, I *knew* him. Let me tell you what they called him in Saigon: Ice-Cold Ogilvie, the smoothest-talking legal scumball in Vietnam. With a few subpoenas and some research, I could have told you where a few of his courtroom skeletons were buried— you blew it! You could have pulled him in for fixing the army courts in a couple of killings— there are no statutes, civilian or military, on those crimes. Jesus, why didn't you *tell* me?"

"In all honesty, Alex, you never asked. You simply assumed—rightly so—that I wouldn't tell you."

"All right, all right, it's done—to hell with it. By tomorrow or the next day you'll have our two Medusans, so go to work on them. They both want to save their asses—the capo's a slime, but his sharpshooter keeps praying for his family and it's not organizational."

"What are you going to do?" pressed Holland.

"We're on our way to Moscow."

"After *Ogilvie*?"

"No, the Jackal. But if I see Bryce, I'll give him your regards."

35

Buckingham Pritchard sat next to his uniformed uncle, Cyril Sylvester Prichard, deputy director of immigration, in the office of Sir Henry Sykes at Government House in Montserrat. Beside them, on the deputy's right, was their attorney, the finest native solicitor Sykes could persuade to advise the Pritchards in the event that the Crown brought a case against them as accessories to terrorism. Sir Henry sat behind the desk and glanced in partial shock at the lawyer, one Jonathan Lemuel, who raised his head and eyes to the ceiling, not to have the benefit of the tropic fan that stirred the humid air but to show disbelief. Lemuel was a Cambridge-educated attorney, once a "scholarship boy" from the colonies, who years ago had made his money in London and returned in the autumn of his life to his native 'Serrat to enjoy the fruits of his labors. Actually, Sir Henry had persuaded his retired black friend to give assistance to a couple of idiots who might have involved themselves in a serious international matter.

The cause of Sir Henry's shock and Jonathan Lemuel's disbelief cum exasperation came about through the following exchange between Sykes and the deputy director of immigration.

"Mr. Pritchard, we've established that your nephew overheard a telephone conversation between John St. Jacques and his brother-in-law, the American Mr. David Webb. Further, your nephew Buckingham Pritchard here, freely, even enthusiastically, admits calling you with certain information contained in that conversation and that you in turn emphatically stated that you had to reach Paris immediately. Is this true?"

"It is all *completely* true, Sir Henry."

"Whom did you reach in Paris? What's the telephone number?"

"With respect, sir, I am sworn to secrecy."

At that succinct and totally unexpected reply, Jonathan Lemuel had lifted his astonished eyes to the ceiling.

Sykes, regaining his composure, put an end to the brief pause of amazement. "*What* was that, Mr. Pritchard?"

"My nephew and I are part of an international organization involving the great leaders of the world, and we have been sworn to secrecy."

"Good God, he believes it," muttered Sir Henry.

"Oh, for heaven's sake," said Lemuel, lowering his head. "Our telephone service here is not the most sophisticated, especially where pay phones are concerned, which I presume you were instructed to use, but within a day or so that number can be traced. Why not simply give it to Sir Henry now. He obviously needs to know quickly, so where is the harm?"

"The harm, sir, is to our superiors in the organization—that was made explicitly clear to me personally."

"What's the name of this international organization?"

"I don't know, Sir Henry. That is part of the confiden*sheeal*ity, do you not see?"

"I'm afraid *you're* the one who doesn't see,

Mr. Pritchard," said Sykes, his voice clipped, his anger surfacing.

"Oh, but I *do*, Sir Henry, and I shall prove it to you!" interrupted the deputy, looking at each man as if to draw the skeptical Sykes and the astonished attorney, as well as his adoring nephew, into his confidence. "A large sum of money was wired from a private banking institution in Switzerland directly to my own account here in Montserrat. The instructions were clear, if flexible. The funds were to be used liberally in pursuit of the assignments delegated to me. . . . Transportation, entertainment, lodgings—I was told I had complete discretion, but, of course, I keep a record of all expenditures, as I do as the second highest officer of immigration. . . . Who but vastly superior people would put such trust in a man they knew only by an enviable reputation and position?"

Henry Sykes and Jonathan Lemuel again looked at each other, astonishment and disbelief now joined by total fascination. Sir Henry leaned forward over the desk. "Beyond this—shall we say—in-depth observation of John St. Jacques requiring the obvious services of your nephew, have you been given other assignments?"

"Actually not, sir, but I'm sure that as soon as the leaders see how expeditiously I have performed, others will follow."

Lemuel raised his hand calmly a few inches off the arm of his chair to inhibit a red-faced Sykes. "Tell me," he said quickly, gently. "This large sum of money sent from Switzerland, just how large was it? The amount doesn't matter legally, and Sir Henry can always call your bank under the laws of the Crown, so please tell us."

"Three hundred pounds!" replied the elder Pritchard, the pride of his value in his voice.

"Three *hundred* . . . ?" The solicitor's words trailed off.

"Not exactly staggering, eh?" mumbled Sir Henry, leaning back, speechless.

"Roughly," continued Lemuel, "what's been your expenses?"

"Not roughly, but precisely," affirmed the deputy director of immigration, removing a small notebook from the breast pocket of his uniform.

"My brilliant uncle is always precise," offered Buckingham Pritchard.

"Thank you, Nephew."

"How much?" insisted the attorney.

"Precisely twenty-six pounds, five shillings, English, or the equivalent of one hundred thirty-two East Caribbean dollars, the EC's rounded off to the nearest double zero at the latest rate of exchange—in this case I absorbed forty-seven cents, so entered."

"Amazing," intoned Sykes, numbed.

"I've scrupulously kept every receipt," went on the deputy, gathering steam as he continued reading. "They're locked in a strongbox at my flat on Old Road Bay, and include the following: a total of seven dollars and eighteen cents for local calls to Tranquility—I would not use my official phone; twenty-three dollars and sixty-five cents for the long-distance call to Paris; sixty-eight dollars and eighty cents . . . dinner for myself and my nephew at Vue Point, a business conference, naturally—"

"That will do," interrupted Jonathan Lemuel, wiping his perspiring black brow with a handkerchief, although the tropical fan was perfectly adequate for the room.

"I am prepared to submit everything at the proper time—"

"I said that will do, Cyril."

"You should know that I refused a taxi driver when he offered to inflate the price of a receipt and soundly criticized him in my official position."

"Enough!" thundered Sykes, the veins in his neck pronounced. "You both have been damn fools of the first magnitude! To have even considered John St. Jacques a criminal of any sort is preposterous!"

"Sir Henry," broke in the younger Pritchard. "I myself *saw* what happened at Tranquility Inn! It was so *horrible*. Coffins on the dock, the chapel blown up, government boats around our peaceful isle—*gun*shots, sir! It will be months before we're back in full operation."

"Exactly!" roared Sykes. "And do you believe Johnny St. Jay would willingly destroy his own property, his own business?"

"Stranger things have happened in the outside criminal world, Sir Henry," said Cyril Sylvester Pritchard knowingly. "In my official capacity I've heard many, many stories. The incidents my nephew described are called diversionary tactics employed to create the illusion that the scoundrels are victims. It was all thoroughly explained to me."

"Oh, it *was*, was it?" cried the former brigadier of the British army. "Well, let me explain something else, shall I? You've been duped by an international terrorist wanted the world over! Do you know the universal penalty for aiding and abetting such a killer? I'll make it plain, in case it's escaped your attention—in your official capacity, of course. . . . It is death by firing squad or, less charitably, a public hanging! Now, what's that goddamned number in Paris?"

"Under the circumstances," said the deputy, summoning what dignity he could despite the fact that his trembling nephew clutched his left arm and his hand shook as he reached for his notebook. "I'll write it out for you. . . . One asks for a blackbird. In French, Sir Henry. I speak a few words, Sir Henry. In French—Sir Henry."

Summoned by an armed guard dressed casually as a weekend guest in white slacks and a loose, bulky white linen jacket, John St. Jacques walked into the library of their new safe house, an estate on Chesapeake Bay. The guard, a muscular, medium-sized man with clean-cut Hispanic features, stood inside the doorway; he pointed to the telephone on the large cherry-wood desk. "It's for you, Mr. Jones. It's the director."

"Thanks, Hector," said Johnny, pausing briefly. "Is that Mr. Jones stuff really necessary?"

"As necessary as 'Hector.' My real name's Roger . . . or Daniel. Whatever."

"Gotcha." St. Jacques crossed to the desk and picked up the phone. "Holland?"

"That number your friend Sykes got is a blind, but useful."

"As my brother-in-law would say, please speak English."

"It's the number of a café on the Marais waterfront on the Seine. The routine is to ask for a blackbird—*un oiseau noir*—and somebody shouts out. If the blackbird's there, contact is made. If he isn't, you try again."

"Why is it useful?"

"We'll try again—and again and again—with a man inside."

"What's happening otherwise?"

"I can only give you a limited answer."

"Goddamn you!"

"Marie can fill you in—"

"Marie?"

"She's on her way home. She's mad as hell, but she's also one relieved wife and mother."

"Why is she mad?"

"I've booked her low-key on several long flights back—"

"For Christ's sake, *why*?" broke in the brother

angrily. "You send a goddamned *plane* for her! She's been more valuable to you than anyone in your dumb Congress or your corkscrew administration, and you send planes for *them* all over the place. I'm not joking, Holland!"

"*I* don't send those planes," replied the director firmly. "Others do. The ones I send involve too many questions and too much curiosity on foreign soil and that's all I'll say about it. Her safety is more important than her comfort."

"We agree on that, honcho."

The director paused, his irritation apparent. "You know something? You're not really a very pleasant fellow, are you?"

"My sister puts up with me, which more than offsets your opinion. Why is she relieved—as a wife and mother, I think you said?"

Again Holland paused, not in irritation now, but searching for the words. "A disagreeable incident took place, one none of us could predict or even contemplate."

"Oh, I hear those famous fucking words from the American establishment!" roared St. Jacques. "What did you miss *this* time? A truckload of U.S. missiles to the Ayatollah's agents in Paris? What *happened*?"

For a third time, Peter Holland employed a moment of silence, although his heavy breathing was audible. "You know, young man, I could easily hang up the phone and dismiss your existence, which would be quite beneficial for my blood pressure."

"Look, honcho, that's my sister out there, and a guy she's married to who I think is pretty terrific. Five years ago, you bastards—I repeat, you *bastards*—damn near killed them both over in Hong Kong and points east. I don't know all the facts because they're too decent or too dumb to talk about them, but I know enough to know I wouldn't trust you with a waiter's payroll in the islands!"

"Fair enough," said Holland, subdued. "Not that it matters, but I wasn't here then."

"It *doesn't* matter. It's your subterranean system. You would have done the same thing."

"Knowing the circumstances, I might have. So might you, if you knew them. But that doesn't matter, either. It's history."

"And now is now," broke in St. Jacques. "What happened in Paris, this 'disagreeable incident'?"

"According to Conklin, there was an ambush at a private airfield in Pontcarré. It was aborted. Your brother-in-law wasn't hurt and neither was Alex. That's all I can tell you."

"It's all I want to hear."

"I spoke to Marie a little while ago. She's in Marseilles and will be here late tomorrow morning. I'll meet her myself and we'll be driven out to Chesapeake."

"What about David?"

"Who?"

"My brother-in-law!"

"Oh . . . yes, of course. He's on his way to Moscow."

"What?"

The Aeroflot jetliner reversed engines and swung off the runway at Moscow's Sheremetyevo Airport. The pilot taxied down the adjacent exit lane, then stopped a quarter of a mile from the terminal as an announcement was made in both Russian and French.

"There will be a five- to seven-minute delay before disembarkation. Please remain seated."

No explanation accompanied the information, and those passengers on the flight from Paris who were not Soviet citizens returned to their reading material, assuming the delay was caused by a backup of departing aircraft. However, those who *were* citizens, as well as a few others familiar with Soviet arrival procedures, knew better. The curtained-off front section of the huge Ilyushin jet, a small seating area that was reserved for special unseen passengers, was in the process of being evacuated, if not totally, at least in part. The custom was for an elevated platform with a shielded metal staircase to be rolled up to the front exit door. Several hundred feet away there was always a government limousine, and while the backs of those disembarked special passengers were briefly in view on their way to the vehicles, flight attendants roamed through the aircraft making sure no cameras were in evidence. There never were. These travelers were the property of the KGB, and for reasons known only to the Komitet, they were not to be observed in Sheremetyevo's international terminal. It was the case this late afternoon on the outskirts of Moscow.

Alex Conklin limped out of the shielded staircase followed by Bourne, who carried the two outsized flight bags that served as their minimum luggage. Dimitri Krupkin emerged from the limousine and hurried toward them as the steps were rolled away from the aircraft and the noise of the huge jet engines began growing in volume.

"How is your friend the *doctor*?" asked the Soviet intelligence officer, shouting to be heard over the roar.

"Holding his own!" yelled Alex. "He may not make it, but he's fighting like hell!"

"It's your own fault, Aleksei!" The jet rolled away and Krupkin lowered his voice accordingly, still loud but not shouting. "You should have called Sergei at the embassy. His unit was prepared to escort you wherever you wished to go."

"Actually, we thought that if we did, we'd be sending out an alert."

"Better a prohibiting alert than inviting an assault!" countered the Russian. "Carlos's men would never have dared to attack you under our protection."

"It wasn't the *Jackal*—the Jackal," said Conklin, abruptly resuming a conversational tone as the roar of the aircraft became a hum in the distance.

"Of course it wasn't him—he's here. It was his goons following orders."

"Not his goons, not his orders."

"What are you talking about?"

"We'll go into it later. Let's get out of here."

"Wait." Krupkin arched his brows. "We'll talk

first—and first, welcome to Mother Russia. Second, it would be most appreciated if you would refrain from discussing certain aspects of my life-style while in the service of my government in the hostile, war-mongering West with anyone you might meet."

"You know, Kruppie, one of these days they'll catch up with you."

"Never. They adore me, for I feed the Komitet more useful gossip about the upper ranks of the debauched, so-called free world than any other officer in a foreign post. I also entertain my superiors in that same debauched world far better than any other officer *anywhere*. Now, if we corner the Jackal here in Moscow, I'll no doubt be made a member of the Politburo, hero status."

"Then you can really steal."

"Why not? They all do."

"If you don't mind," interrupted Bourne curtly, lowering the two flight bags to the ground. "What's happened? Have you made any progress in Dzerzhinsky Square?"

"It's not inconsiderable for less than thirty hours. We've narrowed down Carlos's mole to thirteen possibles, all of whom speak French fluently. They're under total surveillance, human and electronic; we know exactly where they are every minute, also who they meet and who they talk to over the telephone. . . . I'm working with two ranking commissars, neither of whom can remotely speak French—they can't even speak literate Russian, but that's the way it is sometimes. The point is they're both fail-safe and dedicated; they'd rather be instrumental in capturing the Jackal than re-fight the Nazi. They've been very cooperative in mounting surveillance."

"Your surveillance is rotten and you know it," said Alex. "They fall over toilet seats in the women's room when they're chasing a guy."

"Not this time, for I chose them myself," insisted Krupkin. "Outside of four of our own people, each trained in Novgorod, they're defectors from the UK, America, France and South Africa—all with intelligence backgrounds who could lose their dachas if they screw up, as you Westerners say. I really would like to be appointed to the Presidium, perhaps even the Central Committee. I might be posted to Washington or New York."

"Where you could really steal," said Conklin.

"You're wicked, Aleksei, very, very wicked. Still, after a vodka or six, remind me to tell you about some real estate our chargé d'affaires picked up in Virginia two years ago. For a *song*, and financed by his lover's bank in Richmond. Now a developer wants the property at ten times the price! . . . Come, the car."

"I don't *believe* this conversation," said Bourne, picking up the flight bags.

"Welcome to the real world of high-tech intelligence," explained Conklin, laughing quietly. "At least from one point of view."

"From *all* points of view," continued Krupkin as they started toward the limousine. "However, we will dispense with this conversation while riding in an official vehicle, won't we, gentlemen? Incidentally, you have a two-bedroom suite at the Metropole on the Marx Prospekt. It's convenient and I've personally shut down all listening devices."

"I can understand why, but how did you manage it?"

"Embarrassment, as you well know, is the Komitet's greatest enemy. I explained to internal security that what might be recorded could prove most embarrassing to the wrong people, who would undoubtedly transfer any who overheard the tapes to Kamchatka." They reached the car, the left rear door opened by a driver in a dark brown business suit identical with the one worn by Sergei in Paris. "The fabric's the same," said Krupkin in French, noting his companions' reaction to the similar apparel. "Unfortunately the tailoring is not. I insisted Sergei have his refitted in the Faubourg."

The Hotel Metropole is a renovated, prerevolutionary structure built in the ornate style of architecture favored by the czar who had visited fin-de-siècle Vienna and Paris. The ceilings are high, the marble profuse, and the occasional tapestries priceless. Intrinsic to the elaborate lobby is a defiance aimed at a government that would permit so many shabby citizens to invade the premises. The majestic walls and the glittering, filigreed chandeliers seem to stare at the unworthy trespassers with disdain. These impressions, however, did not apply to Dimitri Krupkin, whose baronial figure was very much at ease and at home in the surroundings.

"Comrade!" cried the manager sotto voce as the KGB officer accompanied his guests to the elevators. "There is an urgent message for you," he continued, walking rapidly up to Dimitri and thrusting a folded note into Krupkin's hand. "I was told to deliver it to you personally."

"You have done so and I thank you." Dimitri watched the man walk away, then opened the paper as Bourne and Conklin stood behind him. "I must reach Dzerzhinsky immediately," he said, turning. "It's the extension of my second commissar. Come, let us hurry."

The suite, like the lobby, belonged to another time, another era, indeed another country, marred only by the faded fabrics and the less than perfect restoration of the original moldings. These imperfections served to accentuate the distance between the past and the present. The doors of the two bedrooms were opposite each other, the space between a large sitting room complete with a copper dry bar and several bottles of spirits rarely seen on Moscow shelves.

"Help yourselves," said Krupkin, heading for a telephone on an ersatz antique desk that appeared to be a cross between Queen Anne and a later Louis. "Oh, I forgot, Aleksei, I'll order some tea or spring water—"

"Forget it," said Conklin, taking his flight bag from Jason and heading into the left bedroom. "I'm going to wash up; that plane was filthy."

"I trust you found the fare agreeable," responded Krupkin, raising his voice and dialing. "Incidentally, you ingrate, you'll find your weapons in your bedside table drawers. Each is a .38 caliber Graz Burya automatic. . . . Come, Mr.

Bourne," he added. "You're not abstemious and it was a long trip—this may be a long conversation. My commissar number two is a windy fellow."

"I think I will," said Jason, dropping his bag by the door to the other bedroom. He crossed to the bar and chose a familiar bottle, pouring himself a drink as Krupkin began talking in Russian. It was not a language he understood, so Bourne walked to a pair of tall cathedral windows overlooking the wide avenue known as the Marx Prospekt.

"*Dobryi dyen. . . . Da, da—pochemu? . . . Sadovaya togda. Dvadtsat minut.*" Krupkin shook his head in weary irritation as he hung up the telephone. The movement caused Jason to turn toward the Soviet. "My second commissar was not talkative on this occasion, Mr. Bourne. Haste and orders took precedent."

"What do you mean?"

"We must leave immediately." Krupkin glanced at the bedroom to the left and raised his voice. "*Aleksei,* come out here! Quickly! . . . I tried to tell him that you'd just this second arrived," continued the KGB man, turning back to Jason, "but he was having none of it. I even went so far as to say that one of you was already taking a shower, and his only comment was 'Tell him to get out and get dressed.' '' Conklin limped through the bedroom door, his shirt unbuttoned and blotting his wet face with a towel. "Sorry, Aleksei, we must go."

"Go where? We just got here."

"We've appropriated a flat on the Sadovaya—that's Moscow's 'Grand Boulevard,' Mr. Bourne. It's not the Champs-Elysées, but neither is it inconsequential. The czars knew how to build."

"What's over there?" pressed Conklin.

"Commissar number one," replied Krupkin. "We'll be using it as our, shall we say, our headquarters. A smaller and rather delightful annex of Dzerzhinsky Square—only nobody knows about it but the five of us. Something's come up and we're to go there immediately."

"That's good enough for me," said Jason, putting his drink down on the copper dry bar.

"Finish it," said Alex, rushing awkwardly back into the bedroom. "I've got to get the soap out of my eyes and restrap my lousy boot."

Bourne picked up the glass, his eyes straying to the Soviet field officer who looked after Conklin, his brow lined, his expression curiously sad. "You knew him before he lost his foot, didn't you?" asked Jason quietly.

"Oh, yes, Mr. Bourne. We go back twenty-

five, twenty-six years. Istanbul, Athens, Rome
. . . Amsterdam. He was a remarkable adversary.
Of course, we were young then, both slender
and quick and so taken with ourselves, wanting
so desperately to live up to the images we envisioned for ourselves. It was all so long ago. We
were both terribly good, you know. He was actually better than me, but don't you ever tell him
I said so. He always saw the broader picture, the
longer road than I saw. It was the Russian in
him, of course."

"Why do you use the word 'adversary'?"
asked Jason. "It's so athletic, as if you'd been
playing a game. Wasn't he your enemy?"

Krupkin's large head snapped toward Bourne,
his eyes glass, not warm at all. "Of course he
was my enemy, Mr. Bourne, and to clarify the
picture for you, he still *is* my enemy. Don't, I beg
you, mistake my indulgences for what they are
not. A man's weaknesses may intrude on his
faith but they do not diminish it. I may not have
the convenience of the Roman confession to
expiate my sins so as to go forth and sin again
despite my belief, but I *do* believe. . . . My grand-
fathers *and* grandmothers were hanged—
hanged, sir—for stealing chickens from a
Romanov prince's estate. Few, if any, of my

ancestors were ever given the privilege of the most rudimentary schooling, forget *education*. The Supreme Soviet revolution of Karl Marx and Vladimir Lenin made possible the *beginning* of all things. Thousands upon thousands of mistakes have been made—many inexcusable, many more brutal—but a beginning *was* made. I, myself, am both the proof and the error of it."

"I'm not sure I understand that."

"Because you and your feeble intellectuals have never understood what we have understood from the start. *Das Kapital,* Mr. Bourne, envisages *stages* toward a just society, economic and political, but it does not and never *did* state what specific form the nuts-and-bolts government will ultimately be. Only that it could not be as it was."

"I'm not a scholar in that department."

"One does not have to be. In a hundred years you may be the socialists, and with luck, we'll be the capitalists, *da*?"

"Tell me something," said Jason, hearing, as Krupkin also did, the water faucets in Conklin's room being turned off. "Could you kill Alex— Aleksei?"

"As surely as he could kill me—with deep regrets—if the value of the information called for it. We are professionals. We understand that, often reluctantly.''

"I can't understand either one of you."

"Don't even try, Mr. Bourne, you're not there yet—you're getting closer, but you're not there."

"Would you explain that, please?''

"You're at the cusp, Jason—may I call you Jason?''

"Please do.''

"You're fifty years of age or thereabouts, give or take a year or two, correct?''

"Correct. I'll be fifty-one in a few months. So what?''

"Aleksei and I are in our sixties—have you any idea what a leap that is?''

"How could I?''

"Let me tell you. You still visualize yourself as the younger man, the postadolescent man who sees himself doing the things you did only moments ago in your mind, and in many ways you are right. The motor controls are there, the will is there; you are still the master of your body. Then suddenly, as strong as the will is and as strong as the body remains, the mind slowly, insidiously begins to reject the necessity to make an immediate decision—both intellectually and physically. Simply put, we care less. Are we to be condemned or congratulated on having survived?"

"I think you just said you couldn't kill Alex."

"Don't count on it, Jason Bourne—or David whoever you are."

Conklin came through the door, his limp pronounced, wincing in pain. "Let's go," he said.

"Did you strap it wrong again?" asked Jason. "Do you want me to—"

"Forget it," broke in Alex irritably. "You have to be a contortionist to get the goddamned thing right all the time."

Bourne understood; he forgot about any attempt on his part to adjust the prosthesis. Krupkin again looked at Alex with that strange admixture of sadness and curiosity, then spoke rapidly. "The car is parked up the street in the Sverdlov. It's less obvious over there, I'll have a lobby steward fetch it."

"Thanks," said Conklin, gratitude in his glance.

The opulent apartment on the busy Sadovaya was one among many in an aged stone building that, like the Metropole, reflected the grand architectural excesses of the old Russian Empire. The flats were primarily used—and bugged—for visiting dignitaries, and the chambermaids, doormen and concierges were all frequently questioned by the KGB when not directly employed by the Komitet. The walls were covered with red velour; the sturdy furniture was reminiscent of the ancien régime. However, to the right of the gargantuan ornate living-room fireplace was an item that stood out like a decorator's nightmare: a large jet-black television console complete with an assortment of tape decks compatible with the various sizes of video cassettes.

The second contradiction to the decor, and undoubtedly an affront to the memory of the elegant Romanovs, was a heavyset man in a rumpled uniform, open at the neck and stained with vestiges of recent meals. His blunt face was full, his grayish hair cut close to his skull, and a missing tooth surrounded by discolored companions bespoke an aversion to dentistry. It was the face of a peasant, the narrow, perpetually squinting eyes conveying a peasant's shrewd intelligence. He was Krupkin's Commissar Number One.

"My English not good," announced the uniformed man, nodding at his visitors, "but is understanding. Also, for you I have no name, no official position. Call me colonel, yes? It is below my rank, but all Americans think all Soviets in Komitet are 'colonel,' *da*? Okay?"

"I speak Russian," replied Alex. "If it's easier for you, use it, and I'll translate for my colleague."

"Hah!" roared the colonel, laughing. "So Krupkin cannot fool you, yes?"

"Yes, he can't fool me, no."

"Is good. He talks too fast, *da*? Even in Russian his words come like stray bullets."

"In French, also, Colonel."

"Speaking of which," intruded Dimitri, "may we get to the issue at hand, comrade? Our associate in the Dzerzhinsky said we were to come over immediately."

"Da! Immediate." The KGB officer walked to the huge ebony console, picked up a remote control, and turned to the others. "I will speak English—is good practice. . . . Come. Watch. Everything is on one cartridge. All material taken by men and women Krupkin select to follow our people who speak the French."

"People who could not be compromised by the Jackal," clarified Krupkin.

"Watch!" insisted the peasant-colonel, pressing a button on the remote control.

The screen came alive on the console, the

opening shots crude and choppy. Most had been taken with hand-held video cameras from car windows. One scene after another showed specific men walking in the Moscow streets or getting into official vehicles, driving or being driven throughout the city and, in several cases, outside the city over country roads. In every case the subjects under surveillance met with other men and women, whereupon the zoom lenses enlarged the faces. A number of shots took place inside buildings, the scenes murky and dark, the result of insufficient light and awkwardly held concealed cameras.

"That one is expensive *whore*!" laughed the colonel as a man in his late sixties escorted a much younger woman into an elevator. "It is the Solnechy Hotel on the Varshavkoye. I will personally check the general's vouchers and find a loyal ally, *da*?"

The choppy, cross-cutting tape continued as Krupkin and the two Americans grew weary of the seemingly endless and pointless visual record. Then, suddenly, there was an exterior shot of a huge cathedral, crowds on the pavement, the light indicating early evening.

"St. Basil's Cathedral in Red Square," said Krupkin. "It's a museum now and a very fine one, but every now and then a zealot—usually foreign—holds a small service. No one interferes, which, of course, the zealots want us to do."

The screen became murky again, the vibrating focus briefly and wildly swaying; the camcorder had moved inside the cathedral as the agent operating it was jostled by the crowds. Then it became steady, held perhaps against a pillar. The focus now was on an elderly man, his hair white in contrast to the lightweight black raincoat he was wearing. He was walking down a side aisle pensively glancing at the succession of icons and the higher majestic stained-glass windows.

"Rodchenko," said the peasant-colonel, his voice guttural. "The *great* Rodchenko."

The man on the screen proceeded into what appeared to be a large stone corner of the cathedral where two thick pedestaled candles threw moving shadows against the walls. The video camera jerkily moved upward, the agent, again perhaps, standing on a portable stool or a hastily obtained box. The picture grew suddenly more detailed, the figures larger as the zoom lens was activated, thrusting through the crowds of tourists. The white-haired subject approached another man, a priest in priestly garb—balding, thin, his complexion dark.

"It's him!" cried Bourne. "It's *Carlos*!"

Then a third man appeared on the screen, joining the other two, and Conklin shouted.

"Jesus!" he roared as all eyes were riveted on the television set. "Hold it there!" The KGB commissar instantly complied with his remote; the picture remained stationary, shaky but constant. "The *other* one! Do you recognize him, David?"

"I know him but I don't know him," replied Bourne in a low voice as images going back years began filling his inner screen. There were explosions, white blinding lights with blurred figures running in a jungle . . . and then a man, an Oriental, being shot repeatedly, screaming as he was hammered into the trunk of a large tree by an automatic weapon. The mists of confusion swelled, dissolving into a barrackslike room with soldiers sitting behind a long table, a wooden chair on the right, a man sitting there, fidgeting, nervous. And without warning, Jason suddenly knew that man—it was himself! A younger, much younger self, and there was another figure, in uniform, pacing like a caged ferret back and forth in front of the chair, savagely berating the man then known as Delta One. . . . Bourne gasped, his eyes frozen on the television screen as he realized he was staring at an older version of that angry, pacing figure in his mind's eye. "A courtroom in a base camp north of Saigon," he whispered.

"It's *Ogilvie*," said Conklin, his voice distant, hollow. "Bryce Ogilvie. . . . My God, they *did* link up. Medusa found the Jackal!"

36

"It was a trial, wasn't it, Alex?" said Bourne, bewildered, the words floating, hesitant. "A *military* trial."

"Yes, it was," agreed Conklin. "But it wasn't *your* trial, you weren't the accused."

"I wasn't?"

"No. You were the one who brought charges, a rare thing for any of your group to do then, in or out of the field. A number of the army people tried to stop you but they couldn't. . . . We'll go into it later, discuss it later."

"I want to discuss it now," said Jason firmly. "That man is with the Jackal, right there in front of our eyes. I want to know who he is and what he is and why he's here in Moscow—*with* the Jackal."

"Later—"

"*Now.* Your friend Krupkin is helping us, which means he's helping Marie and me and I'm grateful for his help. The colonel here is also on our side or we wouldn't be seeing what's on that screen at this moment. I want to know what happened between that man and me, and all of Langley's security measures can go to hell. The more I know about him—now—the better I know what to ask for, what to expect." Bourne suddenly turned to the Soviets. "For your information, there's a period in my life I can't completely remember, and that's all you have to know. Go on, Alex."

"I have trouble remembering last night," said the colonel.

"Tell him what he wants to know, Aleksei. It can have no bearing on our interests. The Saigon chapter is closed, as is Kabul."

"All right." Conklin lowered himself into a chair and massaged his right calf; he tried to speak casually but the attempt was not wholly successful. "In December of 1970 one of your men was killed during a search-and-destroy patrol. It was called an accident of 'friendly fire,' but you knew better. You knew he was marked by some horseshit artists down south at head-quarters; they had it in for him. He was a Cambo-dian and no saint by any means, but he knew all the contraband trails, so he was your point."

"Just images," interrupted Bourne. "All I get are fragments. I see but I can't remember."

"The facts aren't important anymore; they're buried along with several thousand other ques-tionable events. Apparently a large narcotics deal went sour in the Triangle and your scout was held responsible, so a few hotshots in Sai-gon thought a lesson should be taught their gook runners. They flew up to your territory, went into the grass, and took him out like they were a VC advance unit. But you saw them from a piece of high ground and blew all your gas-kets. You tracked them back to the helicopter pad and gave them a choice: Get in and you'd storm the chopper leaving no survivors, or they could come back with you to the base camp. They came back under your men's guns and you forced Field Command to accept your multiple charges of murder. That's when Ice-Cold Ogilvie showed up looking after his Saigon boys."

"Then something happened, didn't it? Some-thing crazy—everything got confused, twisted."

"It certainly did. Bryce got you on the stand and made you look like a maniac, a sullen pathological liar and a killer who, except for the war and your expertise, would be in a maximum security prison. He called you everything in the rotten black book and demanded that you reveal your real name—which you wouldn't do, *couldn't* do, because your first wife's Cambodian family would have been slaughtered. He tried to tie you in verbal knots, and, failing that, threatened the military court with exposing the whole bastard battalion, which it also couldn't allow. . . . Ogilvie's thugs got off for lack of credible testimony, and after the trial you had to be physically restrained in the barracks until Ogilvie was airborne back to Saigon."

"His name was Kwan Soo," said Bourne dreamily, his head moving back and forth as if rejecting a nightmare. "He was a kid, maybe sixteen or seventeen, sending the drug money back to three villages so they could eat. There wasn't any other way . . . oh, *shit*! What would *any* of us have done if our families were *starving*?"

"That wasn't anything you could say at the trial and you knew it. You had to hold your tongue and take Ogilvie's vicious crap. I came up and watched you and I never saw a man exercise such control over his hatred."

"That isn't the way I seem to recall it—what I can recall. Some of it's coming back, not much, but some."

"During that trial you adapted to the necessities of your immediate surroundings—you might say like a chameleon." Their eyes locked, and Jason turned back to the television screen.

"And there he is with Carlos. It's a small rotten world, isn't it? Does he know I'm Jason Bourne?"

"How could he?" asked Conklin, getting out of the chair. "There was no Jason Bourne then. There wasn't even a David, only a guerrilla they called Delta One. No names were used, remember?"

"I keep forgetting; what else is new?" Jason pointed at the screen. "Why is he in Moscow? Why did you say Medusa found the Jackal? *Why?*"

"Because he's the law firm in New York."

"What?" Bourne whipped his head toward Conklin. *"He's* the—"

"The chairman of the board," completed Alex, interrupting. "The Agency closed in and he got out. Two days ago."

"Why the hell didn't you *tell* me?" cried Jason angrily.

"Because I never thought for a moment we'd be standing here looking at that picture on the screen. I still can't understand it, but I can't deny it, either. Also, I saw no reason to bring up a name you might or might not remember, a personally very disturbing occurrence you might or might not remember. Why add an unnecessary complication? There's enough stress."

"All right, Aleksei!" said an agitated Krupkin, stepping forward. "I've heard words and names that evoke certain unpleasant memories for *me*, at any rate, and I think it behooves me to ask a question or two—specifically one. Just who is this Ogilvie that concerns you so? You've told us who he was in Saigon, but who is he now?"

"Why not?" Conklin asked himself quietly. "He's a New York attorney who heads up an organization that's spread throughout Europe and the Mediterranean. Initially, by pushing the right buttons in Washington, they bought up companies through extortion and leveraged buy-outs; they've cornered markets and set prices, and in the bargain they've moved into the killing game, employing some of the best professionals in the business. There's hard evidence that they've contracted for the murder of various officials in the government and the military, the most recent example—with which you're no doubt familiar—is General Teagarten, supreme commander of NATO."

"Unbelievable!" whispered Krupkin.

"Jeez—Chrize!" intoned the peasant-colonel, his eyes bulging.

"Oh, they're very creative, and Ogilvie's the most inventive of all. He's Superspider and he's spun a hell of a web from Washington through every capital in Europe. Unfortunately for him, and thanks to my associate here, he was caught like a fly in his own spinning. He was about to be pounced on by people in Washington he couldn't possibly corrupt, but he was tipped off and got out the day before yesterday. . . . Why he came to Moscow I haven't the vaguest idea."

"I may be able to answer that for you," said Krupkin, glancing at the KGB colonel and nodding, as if to say *It's all right.* "I know nothing—absolutely *nothing*—about any such killing as you speak of, indeed of any killing whatsoever. However, you could be describing an American enterprise in Europe that's been servicing our interests for years."

"In what way?" asked Alex.

"With all manner of restricted American technology, as well as armaments, materiel, spare parts for aircraft and weapons systems—even the aircraft and the weapons systems themselves on various occasions through the bloc countries. I tell you this knowing that *you* know I'd vehemently deny ever having said it."

"Understood," nodded Conklin. "What's the name of this enterprise?"

"There's no single name. Instead, there are fifty or sixty companies apparently under one umbrella but with so many different titles and origins it's impossible to determine the specific relationships."

"There's a name and Ogilvie runs it," said Alex.

"That crossed my mind," said Krupkin, his eyes suddenly glass-cold, his expression that of an unrelenting zealot. "However, what appears to disturb you so about your American attorney, I can assure you is far, *far* outweighed by our own concerns." Dimitri turned to the television set and the shakily stationary picture, his eyes now filled with anger. "The Soviet intelligence officer on that screen is General Rodchenko, second in command of the KGB and close adviser to the premier of the Soviet Union. Many things may be done in the name of Russian interests and without the premier's knowledge, but in this day and age *not* in the areas you describe. My *God,* the supreme commander of *NATO!* And never—*never*—using the services of Carlos the Jackal! These embarrassments are no less than dangerous and frightening catastrophes.''

''Have you got any suggestions?'' asked Conklin.

''A foolish question,'' answered the colonel gruffly. ''Arrest, then the Lubyanka . . . then silence.''

''There's a problem with that solution,'' said Alex. ''The Central Intelligence Agency knows Ogilvie's in Moscow.''

''So where is the problem? We rid us both of an unhealthy person and his crimes and go about our business.''

''It may seem strange to you, but the problem isn't only with the unhealthy person and his crimes, even where the Soviet Union is concerned. It's with the cover-up—where Washington's concerned.''

The Komitet officer looked at Krupkin and spoke in Russian. ''What is this one talking about?''

"It's difficult for us to understand," answered Dimitri in his native language, "still, for them it *is* a problem. Let me try to explain."

"What's he saying?" asked Bourne, annoyed.

"I think he's about to give a civics lesson, U.S. style."

"Such lessons more often than not fall on deaf ears in Washington," interrupted Krupkin in English, then immediately resuming Russian, he addressed his KGB superior. "You see, comrade, no one in America would blame us for taking advantage of this Ogilvie's criminal activities. They have a proverb they repeat so frequently that it covers oceans of guilt: 'One does not look a gift horse in the mouth.'"

"What has a horse's mouth got to do with gifts? From its tail comes manure for the farms; from its mouth, only spittle."

"It loses something in the translation. . . . Nevertheless, this attorney, Ogilvie, obviously had a great many government connections, officials who overlooked his questionable practices for large sums of money, practices that entailed millions upon millions of dollars. Laws were circumvented, men killed, lies accepted as the truth; in essence, there was considerable corruption, and, as we know, the Americans are obsessed with corruption. They even label every progressive accommodation as potentially 'corrupt,' and there's nothing older, more knowledgeable peoples can do about it. They hang out their soiled linen for all the world to see like a badge of honor."

"Because it is," broke in Alex, speaking English. "That's something a lot of people here wouldn't understand because you cover every accommodation you make, every crime you commit, every mouth you shut with a basket of roses. . . . However, considering pots and kettles and odious comparisons, I'll dispense with a lecture. I'm just telling you that Ogilvie has to be sent back and all the accounts settled; that's the 'progressive accommodation' you have to make."

"I'm sure we'll take it under advisement."

"Not good enough," said Conklin. "Let's put it this way. Beyond accountability, there's simply too much known—or will be in a matter of days—about his enterprise, including the connection to Teagarten's death, for you to keep him here. Not only Washington, but the entire European community would dump on you. Talk of embarrassments, this is a beaut, to say nothing about the effects on trade, or your imports and exports—"

"You've made your point, Aleksei," interrupted Krupkin. "Assuming this accommodation can be made, will it be clear that Moscow cooperated fully in bringing this American criminal back to American justice?"

"We obviously couldn't do it without you. As the temporary field officer of record, I'll swear to it before both intelligence committees of Congress, if need be."

"And that we had nothing—absolutely *nothing* to do with the killings you mentioned, specifically the assassination of the supreme commander of NATO."

"Absolutely clear. It was one of the major reasons for your cooperation. Your government was horrified by the assassination."

Krupkin looked hard at Alex, his voice lower but stronger for it. He turned slowly, his eyes briefly on the television screen, then back to Conklin. "General Rodchenko?" he said. "What shall we do with General Rodchenko?"

"What you do with General Rodchenko is your business," replied Alex quietly. "Neither Bourne nor I ever heard the name."

"Da," said Krupkin, nodding, again slowly. "And what you do with the Jackal in Soviet territory is your business, Aleksei. However, be assured we shall cooperate to the fullest degree."

"How do we begin?" asked Jason impatiently.

"First things first." Dimitri looked over at the KGB commissar. "Comrade, have you understood what we've said?"

"Enough so, Krupkin," replied the heavyset peasant-colonel, walking to a telephone on an inlaid marble table against the wall. He picked up the phone and dialed; his call was answered immediately. "It is I," said the commissar in Russian. "The third man in tape seven with Rodchenko and the priest, the one New York identified as the American named Ogilvie. As of now he is to be placed under our surveillance and he is not to leave Moscow." The colonel suddenly arched his thick brows, his face growing red. *"That* order is countermanded! He is no longer the responsibility of Diplomatic Relations, he is now the sole property of the KGB. . . . A *reason*? Use your skull, potato head! Tell them we are convinced he is an American double agent whom those fools did not uncover. Then the usual garbage: harboring enemies of the state due to laxness, their exalted positions once again protected by the Komitet—that sort of thing. Also, you might mention that they should not look a gift horse in the mouth. . . . I don't understand any more than you do, comrade, but those butterflies over there in their tight-fitting suits probably will. Alert the airports." The commissar hung up.

"He did it," said Conklin, turning to Bourne. "Ogilvie stays in Moscow."

"I don't give a *goddamn* about Ogilvie!" exploded Jason, his voice intense, his jaw pulsating. "I'm here for Carlos!"

"The priest?" asked the colonel, walking away from the table.

"That's exactly who I mean."

"Is simple. We put General Rodchenko on a very long rope that he cannot see or feel. You will be at the other end. He will meet his Jackal priest again."

"That's all I ask," said Jason Bourne.

General Grigorie Rodchenko sat at a window table in the Lastochka restaurant by the Krymsky Bridge on the Moskva River. It was his favorite place for a midnight dinner; the lights on the bridge and on the slow-moving boats in the water were relaxing to the eye and therefore to the metabolism. He needed the calming atmosphere, for during the past two days things had been so unsettling. Had he been right or had he been wrong? Had his instincts been correct or far off the mark? He could not know at the moment, but those same instincts had enabled him to survive the mad Stalin as a youth, the blustering Khrushchev in middle age, and the inept Brezhnev a few years later. Now there was yet a new Russia under Gorbachev, a new Soviet Union, in fact, and his old age welcomed it. Perhaps things would relax a bit and long-standing enmities fade into a once hostile horizon. Still, horizons did not really change; they were always horizons, distant, flat, fired with color or darkness, but still distant, flat and unreachable.

He was a survivor, Rodchenko understood that, and a survivor protected himself on as many points of the compass as he could read. He also insinuated himself into as many degrees of that compass as possible. Therefore, he had labored diligently to become a trusted mouth to the chairman; he was an expert at gathering information for the Komitet; he was the initial conduit to the American enterprise known to him alone in Moscow as Medusa, through which extraordinary shipments had been made throughout Russia and the bloc nations. On the other hand, he was also a liaison to the monseigneur in Paris, Carlos the Jackal, whom he had either persuaded or bought off from contracts that might point to the Soviet Union. He had been the ultimate bureaucrat, working behind the scenes on the international stage, seeking neither applause nor celebrity, merely survival. Then why had he done what he did? Was it mere impetuousness born of weariness and fear and the sense of a plague-on-both-your-houses? No, it was a logical extension of events, consistent with the needs of his country and, above all, the absolute necessity that Moscow disassociate itself from both Medusa and the Jackal.

According to the consul general in New York, Bryce Ogilvie was finished in America. The consul's suggestion was to find him asylum somewhere and, in exchange, gradually absorb his myriad assets in Europe. What worried the consul general in New York was not Ogilvie's financial manipulations that broke more laws than there were courts to prosecute, but rather the killings, which as far as the consul could determine were widespread and included the murder of high U.S. government officials and, unless he was grossly mistaken, the assassination of the supreme commander of NATO. Compounding this chain of horrors was New York's opinion that in order to save a number of his companies from confiscation, Ogilvie might have ordered additional killings in Europe, primarily of those few powerful executives in various firms who understood the complex international linkages that led back to a great law firm and the unspoken code name Medusa. Should those contracted murders take place while Ogilvie was in Moscow, questions might arise that Moscow could not tolerate. Therefore, get him in and out of the Soviet Union as fast as possible, a recommendation more easily made than accomplished.

Suddenly, Rodchenko reflected, into this *danse macabre* had come the paranoid monseigneur from Paris. *It was imperative they meet immediately!* Carlos had fairly screamed his demand over the arranged public telephone communication they employed, but every precaution had to be taken. The Jackal, as always, demanded a public place, with crowds, and numerous available exits, where he could circle like a hawk, never showing himself until his professional eyes were satisfied. Two calls later, from two different locations, the rendezvous was set. St. Basil's Cathedral in Red Square during the height of the early evening's summer tourist onslaught. In a darkened corner to the right of the altar where there were outside exits through the curtained walkways to the sacristy. *Done!*

Then, during that third telephone call, like a crack of thunder over the Black Sea, Grigorie Rodchenko was struck by an idea so dramatically bold, yet so patently obvious and simple, that he had momentarily lost his breath. It was the solution that would totally distance the Soviet government from any involvement or complicity with either the Jackal or Medusa's Ogilvie should such distance be necessary in the eyes of the civilized world.

Quite simply, unknown to each other, bring the Jackal and Ogilvie together, if only for an instant, just long enough to get photographic evidence of their being seen within the same frame. It was all that was needed.

He had gone to Diplomatic Relations yesterday afternoon, having requested a short routine meeting with Ogilvie. During the extremely innocuous and very friendly conference, Rodchenko had waited for his opening—an opening he had engineered with precision, having done his research.

"You spend summers on Cape Cod, *da*?" the general had said.

"For me it's weekends mainly. My wife and the children are there for the season."

"When I was posted in Washington, I had two great American friends on Cape Cod. I spent several lovely, as you say, weekends with them. Perhaps you know my friends, the Frosts— Hardleigh and Carol Frost?"

"Of course I do. Like myself, he's an attorney, specializes in maritime law. They live down the shore road in Dennis."

"A very attractive lady, the Frost woman."

"Very."

"Da. Did you ever attempt to recruit her husband for your firm?"

"No. He has his own. Frost, Goldfarb and O'Shaunessy; they cover the waterfront, as it were, in Massachusetts."

"I feel I almost know you, Mr. Ogilvie, if only through mutual friends."

"I'm sorry we never met at the Cape."

"Well, perhaps, I can take advantage of our near meeting—through mutual friends—and ask of you a favor, far less than the convenience I understand my government willingly affords you."

"I've been given to understand the convenience is mutual," said Ogilvie.

"*Ahh,* I know nothing of such diplomatic matters, but it is conceivable that I could intervene on your behalf if you would cooperate with us—with my small, although not insignificant, department."

"What is it?"

"There is a priest, a socially oriented militant priest, who claims to be a Marxist agitator well known to the courts of New York City. He arrived only hours ago and demands a clandestine meeting only hours from now. There is simply no time to verify his claims, but as he insists he has a history of legal 'persecutions' in the courts of New York, as well as many photographs in the newspapers, you might recognize him."

"I probably could, if he is who he says he is."

"*Da!* And one way or another, we will certainly let it be known how you cooperated with us."

It had been arranged. Ogilvie would be in the crowds at St. Basil's Cathedral close to the meeting ground. When he saw Rodchenko approach a priest in the far corner to the right of the altar, he was to "come across" the KGB general casually, as if surprised. Their greeting would be brief to the point of discourtesy, so rapid and blurred as to be meaningless, the sort of encounter civilized but hostile acquaintances cannot avoid when they run into one another in a public place. Close proximity was also required, as the light was so dim and so cluttered with shadows that the attorney might not get a good look at the priest.

Ogilvie had performed with the expertise of an accomplished trial lawyer verbally trapping a prosecution's witness with an objectionable inquiry and then shouting "I withdraw the question," leaving the prosecutor speechless.

The Jackal had instantly turned away furiously but not before an obese elderly female, using a miniature camera that was the handle of her purse, had snapped a series of automatically advanced photographs with ultra high-speed film. That evidence was now in a vault in Rodchenko's office. The file was titled *Surveillance of the American Male B. Ogilvie.*

On the page below the photograph showing the assassin and the American attorney together was the following: *Subject with as yet unidentified contact during covert meeting at St. Basil's Cathedral. Meeting covered eleven minutes and thirty-two seconds. Photographs sent to Paris for any possible verification. It is be-*

lieved that the unidentified contact may be Carlos the Jackal.

Needless to say, Paris was working up a reply that included several photographic composites from the Deuxième Bureau and the Sûreté. The answer: *Confirmed. Definitely the Jackal.*

How shocking! And on Soviet soil.

The assassin, on the other hand, had proved to be less accommodating. After the brief, awkward confrontation with the American, Carlos had resumed his ice-cold inquisition, his burning savage self just below the frozen surface.

"They're closing in on you!" said the Jackal.

"Who is?"

"The Komitet."

"I *am* the Komitet!"

"Perhaps you're mistaken."

"Nothing goes on in the KGB without my knowledge. Where did you get this information?"

"Paris. Krupkin's the source."

"Krupkin will do anything to further himself, including the spreading of false information, even where I am concerned. He's an enigma— one moment an efficient multilingual intelligence officer, the next a gossiping clown in French feathers, still again a pimp for traveling ministers. He can't be taken seriously, not where serious matters are concerned."

"I hope you're right. I'll reach you tomorrow, late in the evening. Will you be at home?"

"Not for a phone call from you. I'll dine alone at the Lastochka, a late supper. What will you be doing tomorrow?"

"Making certain you *are* right." The Jackal had disappeared into the crowds of the cathedral.

That was over twenty-four hours ago and Rodchenko had heard nothing to upset the schedule. Perhaps the psychopath had returned to Paris, somehow convinced that his paranoid suspicions were groundless, his need to keep moving, racing, flying all over Europe superseding his momentary panic. Who knew? Carlos, too, was an enigma. Part of him was a retarded sadist, a savant perhaps in the darkest methods of cruelty and killing, yet another part revealed a sick, twisted romantic, a brain-damaged adolescent reaching for a vision that wanted nothing to do with him. Who knew? The time was approaching when a bullet in his head was the answer.

Rodchenko raised his hand for the waiter; he would order coffee and brandy—the decent

French brandy reserved for the true heroes of the Revolution, especially the survivors. Instead of the waiter, the manager of Lastochka came rushing to the table, carrying a telephone.

"There is an urgent call for you, General," said the man in the loose-fitting black suit, placing the phone on the table and holding out the plastic knob of the extension cord that was to be placed into the walled receptacle.

"Thank you." The manager left and Rodchenko inserted the device. "Yes?"

"You're being watched wherever you go," said the voice of the Jackal.

"By whom?"

"Your own people."

"I don't believe you."

"I've been watching all day. Would you like me to describe the places you've been for the past thirty hours? Starting with drinks at a café on the Kalinin, a kiosk in the Arbat, the Slavyanky for lunch, an afternoon walk along the Luznekaya?"

"Stop it! Where are you?"

"Come outside the Lastochka. Slowly, casually. I'll prove it to you." The line went dead.

Rodchenko hung up and signaled the waiter for his check. The aproned man's instant response was due less to the general's status than to the fact that he was the last diner in the restaurant. Leaving his money on top of the bill, the old soldier said good night, walked through the dimly lit foyer to the entrance and let himself out. It was nearly 1:30 in the morning, and except for a few stragglers with too much vodka in them, the street was deserted. In moments an upright figure, silhouetted in the wash of a streetlamp, emerged from a storefront, perhaps thirty meters away on the right. It was the Jackal, still in the black cloth and the white collar of a priest. He beckoned the general to join him as he walked slowly to a dark brown car parked directly across the street. Rodchenko caught up with the assassin, now standing on the curb side of the vehicle, which faced the direction of the Lastochka restaurant.

Suddenly, the Jackal snapped on a flashlight, its powerful beam shooting through the open window of the car. The old soldier momentarily stopped breathing, his heavy-lidded eyes scanning the horrible scene in front of him. Across the seat, the KGB agent behind the wheel was arched back, his throat cut, a river of blood drenching his clothes. Immediately beyond the window was the second surveillance, his wrists and feet bound by wire, a thick rope strapped around his face, yanked taut against his gaping mouth, gagging him, permitting only a rattling, gasping cough. He was alive, his eyes wide in terror.

"The driver was trained at Novgorod," said the general, no comment in his voice.

"I know," replied Carlos. "I have his papers. That training's not what it was, comrade."

"This other one is Krupkin's liaison here in Moscow. The son of a good friend, I'm told."

"He's mine now."

"What are you going to do?" asked Rodchenko, staring at the Jackal.

"Correct a mistake," answered Carlos as he raised his gun, the silencer in place, and fired three bullets into the general's throat.

37

The night sky was angry, the storm clouds over Moscow swirling, colliding, promising rain and thunder and lightning. The brown sedan sped down the country road, racing past overgrown fields, the driver maniacally gripping the wheel and sporadically glancing at his bound prisoner, a young man who kept straining at his wire-bound hands and feet, his rope-strapped face causing him enormous pain, attested to by his constant grimace and his bulging frightened eyes.

In the rear seat, the upholstery covered with blood, were the corpses of General Grigorie Rodchenko and the KGB Novgorod graduate who headed the old soldier's surveillance team. Suddenly, without slowing down the car or giving any indication of his action, the Jackal saw what he was looking for and swerved off the road. Tires shrieking in the sidewinding turn, the sedan plunged into a field of tall grass and in seconds came to a shatteringly abrupt stop, the bodies in the rear crashing into the back of the front seat. Carlos opened his door and lurched outside; he proceeded to yank the blood-drenched corpses from their upholstered crypts and dragged them into the high grass, leaving the general partially on top of the Komitet officer, their life fluids now mingling as they soiled the ground.

He returned to the car and brutally pulled the young KGB agent out of the front seat with one hand, the glistening blade of a hunting knife in his other.

"We have a lot to talk about, you and I," said the Jackal in Russian. "And you would be foolish to withhold anything. . . . You won't, you're too soft, too young." Carlos whipped the man to the ground, the tall grass bending under the fall. He withdrew his flashlight and knelt beside his captive, the knife going toward the agent's eyes.

The bloodied, lifeless figure below had spoken his last words, and they were words that reverberated like kettledrums in the ears of Ilich Ramirez Sanchez. Jason Bourne was in *Moscow*! It had to be Bourne, for the terrified, youthful KGB surveillant had blurted out the information in a gushing, panicked stream of phrases and half phrases, saying anything and everything that might possibly save his life. *Comrade Krupkin—two Americans, one tall, the other with a limp! We took them to the hotel, then to the Sadovaya for a conference.*

Krupkin and the hated Bourne had turned his people in Paris—in *Paris,* his impenetrable armed camp!—and had traced him to Moscow. How? *Who?* . . . It did not matter now. All that mattered was that the Chameleon himself was at the Metropole; the traitors in Paris could wait. At the *Metropole*! His enemy of enemies was barely an hour away back in Moscow, no doubt sleeping the night away, without any idea that Carlos the Jackal knew he was there. The assassin felt the exhilaration of triumph—over life *and* death. The doctors said he was dying, but doctors were as often wrong as they were right, and at this moment they were wrong! The death of Jason Bourne would *renew* his life.

However, the hour was not right. Three o'-clock in the morning was not the time to be seen prowling the streets or the hotels in search of a kill in Moscow, a city in the grip of permanent suspicion, darkness itself contributing to its wariness. It was common knowledge that the night-floor stewards in the major hotels were armed, selected as much for their marksmanship as for their aptitude for service. Daylight brought a relaxation of the night's concerns; the bustling activity of the early morning was the time to strike—and strike he would.

But the hour *was* right for another kind of strike, at least the prelude to it. The time had come to call together his disciples in the Soviet government and let them know the monseigneur had arrived, that their personal messiah was here to set them free. Before leaving Paris he had collected the dossiers, and the dossiers behind those dossiers, all seemingly innocuous pages of blank paper in file folders until they were exposed to infrared light, the heat waves bringing up the typewritten script. He had selected a small deserted store in the Vavilova for his meeting ground. He would reach each of his people by public telephone and instruct them to be there by 5:30, all taking back streets and alleyways to the rendezvous. By 6:30 his task would be finished, each disciple armed with the information that would elevate him—and her— to the highest ranks of Moscow's elite. It was one more invisible army, far smaller than Paris, but equally effective and as dedicated to Carlos, the unseen monseigneur who made life infinitely more comfortable for his converts. And by 7:30, the mighty Jackal would be in place at the Metropole, ready for the early movements of awakening guests, the time for the rushing trays and tables of room-service waiters and the hectic confusion of a lobby alive with chatter, anxiety and bureaucracy. It was at the Metropole where he would be ready for Jason Bourne.

One by one, like wary stragglers in the early light, the five men and three women arrived at the run-down entrance of the abandoned store in the back street known only as the Vavilova. Their caution was understandable; it was a district to be avoided, although not necessarily because of unsavory inhabitants, for the Moscow police were ruthlessly thorough in such areas, but because of the stretch of decrepit buildings. The area was in the process of renovation; however, like similar projects in urban blights the world over, the progress had two speeds: slow and stop. The only constant, which was at best a dangerous convenience, was the existence of electricity, and Carlos used it to his advantage.

He stood at the far end of the bare concrete room, a lamp on the floor behind him, silhouetting him, leaving his features undefined and further obscured by the upturned collar of his black suit. To his right was a wreck of a low wooden table with file folders spread across the top, and to his left, under a pile of newspapers, unseen by his "disciples," was a cut-down Type 56, AK-47 assault weapon. A forty-round magazine was inserted, a second magazine in the Jackal's belt. The only reason for the weapon was the normal custom of his trade; he expected no difficulty whatsoever. Only adoration.

He surveyed his audience, noting that all eight kept glancing furtively at one another. No one talked; the dank air in the eerily lit abandoned store was tense with apprehension. Carlos understood that he had to dispel that fear, that furtiveness, as rapidly as possible, which was why he had gathered eight distressed chairs from the various deserted office rooms in the rear of the store. Seated, people were less tense; it was a truism. However, none of the chairs was being used.

"Thank you for coming here this morning," said the Jackal in Russian, raising his voice. "Please, each of you take a chair and sit down. Our discussion will not be long, but will require the utmost concentration. . . . Would the comrade nearest the door close it, please. Everyone is here."

The old, heavy door was creaked shut by a stiffly walking bureaucrat as the rest reached for chairs, each distancing his and hers from others that were nearby. Carlos waited until the scraping sounds of wood against cement subsided and all were seated. Then, like a practiced orator-actor, the Jackal paused before formally addressing his captive audience. He looked briefly at each person with his penetrating dark eyes as if conveying to each that he or she was special to him. There were short, successive hand movements, mostly female, as those he gazed at in turn smoothed their respective garments. The clothes they wore were characteristic of the ranks of upper-level government officials—in the main drab and conservative, but well pressed and spotless.

"I am the monseigneur from Paris," began the assassin in priestly garb. "I am he who has spent several years seeking each of you out—with the assistance of comrades here in Moscow and beyond—and sent you large sums of money, asking only that you silently await my arrival and render me the loyalty I have shown to you. . . . By your faces, I can anticipate your questions, so let me amplify. Years ago I was among the elite few selected to be trained at Novgorod." There was a quiet yet audible reaction from the chosen eight. The myth of Novgorod matched its reality; it was, indeed, an advanced indoctrination center for the most gifted of comrades—as they were given to understand, yet none really understood, for Novgorod was rarely spoken about except in whispers. With several nods, Carlos acknowledged the impact of his revelation and continued.

"The years since have been spent in many foreign countries promoting the interests of the great Soviet revolution, an undercover commissar with a flexible portfolio that called for many trips back here to Moscow and extensive research into the specific departments in which each of you holds a responsible position." Again the Jackal paused, then spoke suddenly, sharply. "Positions of responsibility but without the authority that should be *yours.* Your abilities are undervalued and underrewarded, for there is *deadwood* above you."

The small crowd's reaction was now somewhat more audible, definitely less constrained. "Compared to similar departments in the governments of our adversaries," went on Carlos, "we here in Moscow have lagged far behind when we should be ahead, and we are behind because *your* talents have been suppressed by entrenched officeholders who care more for their office privileges than they do for the functions of their departments!"

The response was immediate, even electric, with the three women openly if softly applauding. "It is for that reason, *these* reasons, that I and my associate comrades here in Moscow have sought you out. Further, it is why I have sent you funds—to be used totally at your discretion—for the money you've received is the approximate value of the privileges your superiors enjoy. Why should you not receive them and enjoy them as *they* do?"

The rumble of *why not?* and *he's right* rippled through the audience, now actually looking at one another, eyes locked, and heads nodding firmly. The Jackal then began to reel off the eight major departments in question, and as each was named successively, there was an enthusiastic nodding of heads. "The ministries of Transport, Information, Finance, Import/Export, Legal Procedures, Military Supply, Scientific Research . . . and hardly the least, Presidium Appointments. . . . These are your domains, but you have been *cut out* from all final decisions. That is no longer acceptable—changes must be made!"

The assembled listeners rose almost as one, no longer strangers but, instead, people united in a cause. Then *one,* the obviously cautious bureaucrat who had closed the door, spoke. "You appear to know our situations well, sir, but what can change them?"

"These," announced Carlos, gesturing dramatically at the file folders spread out across the low table. Slowly the small group sat down, singly and in couples, looking at one another when not staring at the folders. "On this table are secretly gathered confidential dossiers of your superiors in each of the departments represented here. They contain such injurious information that when presented by you individually will guarantee your immediate promotions, and

in several cases your succession to those high offices. Your superiors will have no choice, for these files are daggers aimed at their throats—exposure would result in disgrace and execution."

"Sir?" A middle-aged woman in a neat but nondescript plain blue dress cautiously stood up. Her blond-gray hair was swept back into a stern bun; she touched it briefly, self-consciously, as she spoke. "I evaluate personnel files on a daily basis . . . and frequently discover errors . . . how can you be certain these dossiers are accurate? For if they are not accurate, we could be placed in extremely dangerous situations, is that not so?"

"That you should even question their accuracy is an affront, madame," replied the Jackal coldly. "I am the monseigneur from Paris. I have accurately described your individual situations and *accurately* depicted the inferiority of your superiors. Further, and at great expense and risk to myself and my associates here in Moscow, I have covertly funneled monies to you so as to make your lives more comfortable."

"Speaking for myself," interrupted a gaunt man wearing glasses and a brown business suit, "I appreciate the money—I assigned mine to

our collective fund and expect a moderate return—but does one have anything to do with the
other? I am with the Ministry of Finance, of
course, and having admitted that, I absolve myself of complicity for being clear about my status."

"Whatever that means, accountant, you're
about as clear as your paralyzed ministry," interrupted an obese man in a black suit too small for
his girth. "You also cast doubt on your ability to
recognize a decent return! Naturally, I'm with
Military Supply, and you consistently short-
change *us.*"

"As you do *constantly* with Scientific Research!" exclaimed a short, tweedy professorial
member of the audience, the irregularity of his
clipped beard due, no doubt, to poor vision, despite the thick spectacles bridging his nose.
"Returns, indeed! What about *allocations*?"

"More than sufficient for your grade-school
scientists! The money is better spent stealing
from the West!"

"Stop it!" cried the priest-assassin, raising his
arms like a messiah. "We are not here to discuss interdepartmental conflicts, for they will all
be resolved with the emergence of our new
elite. Remember! I am the monseigneur from

Paris, and together we will bring about a new, cleansed order for our great revolution! Complacency is *over.*"

"It is a thrilling concept, sir," said a second woman, a female in her early thirties, her skirt expensively pleated, her compact features obviously recognized by the others as a popular newscaster on television. "However, may we return to the issue of accuracy?"

"It is *settled,*" said the dark-eyed Carlos, staring in turn at each person. "How else would I know all about you?"

"I do not doubt you, sir," continued the newscaster. "But as a journalist I must always seek a second source of verification unless the ministry determines otherwise. Since you are not with the Ministry of Information, sir, and knowing that whatever you say will remain confidential, can you give us a secondary source?"

"Am I to be hounded by manipulated journalists when I speak the *truth*?" The assassin caught his breath in anger. "Everything I've told you *is* the truth and you know it."

"So were the crimes of Stalin, sir, and they were buried along with twenty million corpses for thirty years."

"You want proof, *journalist*? I'll give you

proof. I have the eyes and the ears of the leaders of the *KGB*—namely, the great General Grigorie Rodchenko himself. *He* is *my* eyes and *my* ears, and if you care to know a harsher truth, he is beholden to me! For I am his monseigneur from Paris as well."

There was a rustling among the captive audience, a collective hesitancy, a wave of quiet throat clearing. The television newscaster spoke again, now softly, her wide brown eyes riveted on the man in priest's clothes.

"You may be whatever you say you are, sir," she began, "but you do not listen to Radio Moscow's all-night station. It was reported over an hour ago that General Rodchenko was shot to death this morning by foreign criminals. . . . It was also reported that all high officers of the Komitet have been called into an emergency session to evaluate the circumstances of the general's murder. The speculation is that there had to be extraordinary reasons for a man of General Rodchenko's experience to be lured into a trap by these foreign criminals."

"They will tear apart his files," added the cautious bureaucrat, stiffly getting to his feet. "They will put everything under a KGB microscope, searching for those 'extraordinary reasons.' "

The circumspect public official looked at the killer in priest's clothes. "Perhaps they will find you, sir. And your dossiers."

"No," said the Jackal, perspiration breaking out on his high forehead. *"No!* That is *impossible.* I have the only copies of these dossiers— there are no others!"

"If you believe that, priest," said the obese man from the Ministry of Military Supply, "you do not know the Komitet."

"Know it?" cried Carlos, a tremor developing in his left hand. "I have its *soul!* No secrets are kept from me, for I am the repository of *all* secrets! I have volumes on governments everywhere, on their leaders, their generals, their highest officials—I have sources all over the *world*!"

"You don't have Rodchenko anymore," continued the black-suited man from Military Supply, he, too, getting out of his chair. "And come to think of it, you weren't even surprised."

"What?"

"For most of us, perhaps all of us, the first thing we do upon rising in the morning is to turn on our radios. It's always the same foolishness and I suppose there's comfort in that, but I'd guess most of us knew about Rodchenko's death. . . . But you didn't, priest, and when our television lady told you, you weren't astonished, you weren't shocked—as I say, you weren't even surprised."

"*Certainly* I was!" shouted the Jackal. "What you don't understand is that I have extraordinary *control.* It's why I'm trusted, *needed* by the leaders of world Marxism!"

"That's not even fashionable," mumbled the middle-aged, grayish-blond woman whose expertise was in personnel files; she also stood up.

"What are you *saying*?" Carlos's voice was now a harsh, condemning whisper, rising rapidly in intensity and volume. "I am the monseigneur from Paris. I have made your lives comfortable far beyond your miserable expectations and now you *question* me? How would I know the things I know—how could I have poured my concentration and my resources into you here in this room if I were not among the most privileged in *Moscow*? Remember who I *am*!"

"But we don't know who you are," said another man, rising. Like the other males, his clothes were neat, somber and well pressed, but there was a difference in that they were better tailored, as though he took considerable pains with his appearance. His face, too, was different; it was paler than the others and his eyes were more intense, more focused somehow, giving the impression that when he spoke he weighed his words with great care. "Beyond the clerical title you've appropriated, we have no knowledge as to your identity and you obviously do not care to reveal it. As to what you know, you've recounted blatant weaknesses and subsequent injustices in our departmental systems, but they are rampant throughout the ministries. You might as well have picked a dozen others like us from a dozen other divisions, and I dare say the complaints would have been the same. Nothing new there—"

"How *dare* you?" screamed Carlos the Jackal, the veins in his neck pronounced. "Who are you to say such things to *me*? I am the monseigneur from Paris, a true son of the Revolution!"

"And I am a judge advocate in the Ministry of Legal Procedures, Comrade Monseigneur, and a much younger product of that revolution. I may not know the heads of the KGB, who you claim are your minions, but I know the penalties for taking the legal processes in our own hands and personally—secretly—confronting our superiors rather than reporting directly to the Bureau of Irregularities. They are penalties I'd rather not face without far more thorough evidentiary materials than unsolicited dossiers from unknown sources, conceivably invented by discontented officials below even our levels. . . . Frankly, I don't care to see them, for I will not be compromised by gratuitous pretrial testimony that can be injurious to my position."

"You are an insignificant *lawyer*!" roared the assassin in priest's clothing, now repeatedly clenching his hands into fists, his eyes becoming bloodshot. "You are all twisters of the truth! You are sworn companions of the prevailing winds of *convenience*!"

"Nicely said," said the attorney from Legal Procedures, smiling. "Except, comrade, you stole the phrase from the English Blackstone."

"I will not *tolerate* your insufferable insolence!"

"You don't have to, Comrade *Priest,* for I intend to leave, and my legal advice to all here in this room is to do the same."

"You *dare*?"

"I certainly do," replied the Soviet attorney, granting himself a moment of humor as he looked around the gathering and grinned. "I might have to prosecute myself, and I'm far too good at my job."

"The *money*!" shrieked the Jackal. "I've sent you all *thousands*!"

"Where is it recorded?" asked the lawyer with an air of innocence. "You, yourself, made sure it was untraceable. Paper bags in our mail slots, or in our office drawers—notes attached instructing us to burn them. Who among our citizens would admit to having placed them there? That way lies the Lubyanka. . . . Good-bye, Comrade Monseigneur," said the attorney for the Ministry of Legal Procedures, scraping his chair in place and starting for the door.

One by one, as they had arrived, the assembled group followed the lawyer, each looking back at the strange man who had so exotically, so briefly, interrupted their tedious lives, all knowing instinctively that in his path were disgrace and execution. Death.

Yet none was prepared for what followed. The killer in priest's clothing suddenly snapped; visceral bolts of lightning electrified his madness. His dark eyes burned with a raging fire that could be extinguished only by soul-satisfying violence—relentless, brutal, savage vengeance for all the wrongs done to his pure purpose to kill the unbelievers! The Jackal swept away the dossiers from the table and lurched down to the pile of newspapers; he grabbed the deadly automatic weapon from beneath the scattered pages and roared, *"Stop! All* of you!"

None did, and the outer regions of psychopathic energy became the order of the moment. The killer squeezed the trigger repeatedly and men and women died. Amid screams from the shattered bodies nearest the door, the assassin raced outside, leaping over the corpses, his assault rifle on automatic fire, cutting down the figures in the street, screaming curses, condemning the unbelievers to a hell only he could imagine.

"Traitors! Filth! *Garbage!"* screamed the crazed Jackal as he leaped over the dead bodies, racing to the car he had commandeered from the Komitet and its inadequate surveillance unit. The night had ended; the morning had begun.

The Metropole's telephone did not ring, it erupted. Startled, Alex Conklin snapped open his eyes, instantly shaking the sleep from his head as he clawed for the strident instrument on the bedside table. "Yes?" he announced, won-

dering briefly if he was speaking into the coni-
cally shaped mouthpiece or into the receiver.

"Aleksei, stay put! Admit no one into your
rooms and have your weapons ready!"

"Krupkin? . . . What the hell are you talking
about."

"A crazed dog is loose in Moscow."

"Carlos?"

"He's gone completely mad. He killed Rodchenko and butchered the two agents who were
following him. A farmer found their bodies
around four o'clock this morning—it seems the
dogs woke him up with their barking, downwind
of the blood scents, I imagine."

"Christ, he's gone over the edge. . . . But why
do you think—"

"One of our agents was tortured before being
killed," broke in the KGB officer, fully anticipating Alex's question. "He was our driver from the
airport, a protégé of mine and the son of a class-
mate I roomed with at the university. A fine
young man from a rational family but not trained
for what he was put through."

"You're saying you think he may have told
Carlos about us, aren't you?"

"Yes. . . . There's more, however. Approximately an hour ago in the Vavilova, eight people

were cut down by automatic fire. They were slaughtered; it was a massacre. One of the dying, a woman with the Ministry of Information, a *direktor,* second class, and a television journalist, said the killer was a priest from Paris who called himself the 'monseigneur.' "

"Jesus!" exploded Conklin, whipping his legs over the edge of the bed, absently staring at the stump of flesh where once there had been a foot. "It was his cadre."

"So called and past tense," said Krupkin. "If you remember, I told you such recruits would abandon him at the first sign of peril."

"I'll get Jason—"

"Aleksei, listen to me!"

"What?" Conklin cupped the telephone under his chin as he reached down for the hollowed-out prosthetic boot.

"We've formed a tactical assault squad, men and women in civilian clothes—they're being given instructions now and will be there shortly."

"Good move."

"But we have purposely *not* alerted the hotel staff or the police."

"You'd be idiots if you did," broke in Alex. "We'll settle for taking the son of a bitch here! We'd never do it with uniforms prowling around or clerks in hysterics. The Jackal has eyes in his kneecaps."

"Do as I say," ordered the Soviet. "Admit no one, stay away from the windows and take all precautions."

"Naturally. . . . What do you mean, the windows? He'll need time to find out where we are . . . to question the maids, the stewards."

"Forgive me, old friend," interrupted Krupkin, "but an angelic priest inquiring at the desk about two Americans, one with a pronounced limp, during the early morning rush in the lobby?"

"Good point, even if you're paranoid."

"You're on a high floor, and directly across the Marx Prospekt is the roof of an office building."

"You also think pretty fast."

"Certainly faster than that fool in Dzerzhinsky. I would have reached you long before now, but my commissar *Kartoshki* over there didn't call *me* until two minutes ago."

"I'll wake up Bourne."

"Be *careful.*"

Conklin did not hear the Soviet's final admonition. Instead, he swiftly replaced the telephone and pulled on his boot, carelessly lashing the Velcro straps around his calf. He then opened the bedside table drawer and took out the Graz Burya automatic, a specially designed KGB weapon with three clips of ammunition. The Graz, as it was commonly known, was unique insofar as it was the only automatic known that would accept a silencer. The cylindrical instrument had rolled to the front of the drawer; he removed it and spun it into the short barrel. Unsteadily, he got into his trousers, shoved the weapon into his belt and crossed to the door. He opened it and limped out only to find Jason, fully dressed, standing in front of a window in the ornate Victorian sitting room.

"That had to be Krupkin," said Bourne.

"It was. Get away from the window."

"Carlos?" Bourne instantly stepped back and turned to Alex. "He knows we're in Moscow?" he asked. Then added, "He knows where we *are*?"

"The odds are yes to both questions." In short concise statements, Conklin related Krupkin's information. "Does all this tell you something?" asked Alex when he had finished.

"He's blown apart," answered Jason quietly. "It had to happen. The time bomb in his head finally went off."

"That's what I think. His Moscow cadre

turned out to be a myth. They probably told him to pound sand and he exploded."

"I regret the loss of life and I mean that," said Bourne. "I wish it could have happened another way, but I can't regret his state of mind. What's happened to him is what he wanted for me—to crack wide open."

"Kruppie said it," added Conklin. "He's got a psychopathic death wish to return to the people who first found out he was a maniac. Now, if he knows you're here, and we have to assume that he does, the obsession's compounded, your death replacing his—giving him some kind of symbolic triumph maybe."

"You've been talking to Panov too much. . . . I wonder how Mo is."

"Don't. I called the hospital at three o'clock this morning—five o'clock, Paris time. He may lose the use of his left arm and suffer partial paralysis of his right leg, but they think he'll make it now."

"I don't give a goddamn about his arms or his legs. What about his *head*?"

"Apparently it's intact. The chief nurse on the floor said that for a doctor he's a terrible patient."

"Thank *Christ*!"

"I thought you were an agnostic."

"It's a symbolic phrase, check with Mo." Bourne noticed the gun in Alex's belt; he gestured at the weapon. "That's a little obvious, isn't it?"

"For whom?"

"Room service," replied Jason. "I phoned for whatever gruel they've got and a large pot of coffee."

"No way. Krupkin said we don't let anyone in here and I gave him my word."

"That's a crock of paranoia—"

"Almost my words, but this is his turf, not ours. Just like the windows."

"Wait a minute!" exclaimed Bourne. "Suppose he *is* right?"

"Unlikely, but possible, except that—" Conklin could not finish his statement. Jason reached under the right rear flap of his jacket, yanked out his own Graz Burya and started for the hallway door of the suite. "What are you *doing*?" cried Alex.

"Probably giving your friend 'Kruppie' more credit than he deserves, but it's worth a try. . . . Get over there," ordered Bourne, pointing to the far left corner of the room. "I'll leave the door unlocked, and when the steward gets here, tell him to come in—in Russian."

"What about you?"

"There's an ice machine down the hall; it doesn't work, but it's in a cubicle along with a Pepsi machine. That doesn't work either, but I'll slip inside."

"Thank God for capitalists, no matter how misguided. Go *on*!"

The Medusan once known as Delta unlatched the door, opened it, glanced up and down the Metropole's corridor and rushed outside. He raced down the hallway to the cut-out alcove that housed the two convenience machines and crouched by the right interior wall. He waited, his knees and legs aching—pains he never *felt* only years ago—and then he heard the sounds of rolling wheels. They grew louder and louder as the cart draped with a tablecloth passed and proceeded to the door of the suite. He studied the floor steward; he was a young man in his twenties, blond, short of stature, and with the posture of an obsequious servant; cautiously he knocked on the door. No Carlos he, thought Bourne, getting painfully to his feet. He could hear Conklin's muffled voice telling the steward to enter; and as the young man opened the door, shoving the table inside, Jason calmly inserted his weapon into its concealed place. He bent over and massaged his right calf; he could feel the swelling cluster of a muscle cramp.

It happened with the impact of a single furious wave against a shoal of rock. A figure in black lurched out of an unseen recess in the corridor, racing past the machines. Bourne spun back into the wall. It was the *Jackal*!

38

Madness! At full force Carlos slammed his right shoulder into the blond-haired waiter, propelling the young man across the hallway and crashing the room-service table over on its side; dishes and food splattered the walls and the carpeted floor. Suddenly the waiter lunged to his left, spinning in midair as, astonishingly, he yanked a weapon from his belt. The Jackal either sensed or caught the movement in the corner of his eye. He whipped around, his automatic weapon on rapid fire, savagely pinning the blond Russian into the wall, bullets puncturing the waiter's head and torso. At that prolonged, horrible moment, the enlarged sight line on the barrel of Bourne's Graz Burya caught in the waist-line of his trousers. He tore the fabric as the eyes of Carlos swept up centering on his own, fury and triumph in the assassin's stare.

Jason ripped the gun loose, spinning, crouching back into the wall of the small alcove as the Jackal's fusillade blew apart the gaudy paneling of the soft-drink machine and tore into the sheets of heavy plastic that fronted the broken-down ice maker. On his stomach, Bourne surged across the opening, the Graz Burya raised and firing as fast as he could squeeze the trigger. Simultaneously, there were other gunshots, *not* those of a machine pistol. Alex was firing from inside the suite! They had Carlos in their cross fire! It was possible—it could all end in a hotel corridor in Moscow! Let it happen, let *it happen*!

The Jackal roared; it was a defiant shriek at having been hit. Bourne lunged back across the opening, pivoting once again into the wall, momentarily distracted by the sounds of a now-functioning ice machine. Again he crouched, inching his face toward the corner of the archway when the murderous insanity in the hallway erupted into the fever pitch of close combat. Like an enraged caged animal, the wounded

Carlos kept spinning around in place, continuous bursts from his weapon exploding as if he were firing through unseen walls that were closing in on him. Two piercing, hysterical screams came from the far end of the hallway, one male, one female; a couple had been wounded or killed in the panicked fusillade of stray bullets.

"Get *down*!" Conklin's scream from across the corridor was an instant command for what Jason could not know. "Take *cover*! Grab the fucking walls!" Bourne did as he was told, understanding only that the order meant he was to shove himself into as small a place as possible, protecting his head as much as possible. The *corner*. He lunged as the first explosion rocked the walls—somewhere—and then a second, this much nearer, far more thunderous, in the hallway itself. *Grenades!*

Smoke mingled with falling plaster and shattered glass. *Gunshots.* Nine, one after another—a Graz Burya automatic . . . *Alex!* Jason spun up and away from the corner of the recess and lurched for the opening. Conklin stood outside the door of their suite in front of the upturned room-service table; he snapped out his empty clip and furiously searched his trousers pockets. "I haven't got one!" he shouted angrily, referring to the extra clips of ammunition supplied by Krupkin. "He ran around the corner into the other corridor, and I don't have any goddamned *shells!*"

"I do and I'm a lot faster than you," said Jason, removing his spent magazine and inserting a fresh clip from his pocket. "Get back in there and call the lobby. Tell them to clear it."

"Krupkin said—"

"I don't *give* a damn what he said! Tell them to shut down the elevators, barricade all staircase exists, and stay the hell away from this floor!"

"I see what you mean—"

"Do it!" Bourne raced down the hallway, wincing as he approached the couple who lay on the carpet; each moved, groaning. Their clothes were spotted with blood, but they *moved*! He turned and yelled to Alex, who was limping around the room-service table. "Get help up here!" he ordered, pointing at an exit door directly down the corridor. "They're alive! Use that exit and *only* that one!"

The hunt began, compounded and impeded by the fact that the word had been spread throughout these adjacent wings of the Metropole's tenth floor. It took no imagination to realize that behind the closed doors, along both sides of the hallways, panicked calls were being made to the front desk as the sound of nearby gunfire echoed throughout the corridors. Krupkin's strategy for a KGB assault team in civilian clothes had been nullified by the first burst from the Jackal's weapon.

Where *was* he? There was another exit door at the far end of the long hallway Jason had entered, but there were perhaps fifteen to eighteen guest-room doors lining that hallway. Carlos was no fool, and a wounded Carlos would call upon every tactic he could summon from a long life of violence and survival to survive, if only long enough to achieve the kill he wanted more than life itself. . . . Bourne suddenly realized how accurate his analysis was, for he was describing himself. What had old Fontaine said on Tranquility Isle, in that faraway storeroom from which they had stared down at the procession of priests knowing that one had been bought by the Jackal? ". . . Two aging lions stalking each other, not caring who's killed in the cross fire"—those had been Fontaine's words, a man who had sacrificed his life for another he barely knew because his own life was over, for the woman he loved was gone. As

Jason started cautiously, silently down the hall toward the first door on the left, he wondered if he could do the same. He wanted desperately to live—with Marie and their children—but if she was gone . . . if they were gone . . . would life really matter? Could he throw it away if he recognized something in another man that reflected something in himself?

No *time.* Meditate on your *own* time, David Webb! I have no use for you, you weak, soft son of a *bitch.* Get *away* from me! I have to flush out a bird of prey I've wanted for thirteen years. His claws are razor-sharp and he's killed too often, too many, and now he wants to kill my own— *your* own. Get away from me!

Bloodstains. On the dull, dark brown carpet, wet driblets glistening in the dim overhead light. Bourne crouched and felt them; they *were* wet; they were red—bloodred. Unbroken, they passed the first door, then the second, remaining on the left—then they crossed the hall, the pattern now altered, no longer steady, instead zigzagging, as if the wound had been located, the bleeding partially stemmed. The trail passed the sixth door on the right, and the seventh . . . then abruptly the shining red drops stopped—*no,* not entirely. There was a trickle heading left, barely visible, and again, across the hallway—there it *was*! A faint smudge of red just above the knob on the eighth door on the left, no more than twenty feet from the corridor's exit staircase. Carlos was behind that door holding hostage whoever was inside.

Precision was everything now, every movement, every sound concentrated on the capture or the kill. Breathing steadily while imposing a suspension of the muscular spasms he felt everywhere throughout his body, Bourne once more walked silently, now retracing his steps up the hallway. He reached a point roughly thirty paces away from the eighth door on the left and turned around, suddenly aware of a muted chorus of sporadic sobs and cries that came from closed doorways along the hotel corridor. Orders had been given couched in language far removed from Krupkin's instructions: *Stay inside your rooms, please. Admit no one. Our people are investigating.* It was always "our people," never "the police," never "the authorities"; with those names came panic. And panic was precisely what Medusa's Delta One had in mind. Panic and diversion, eternal components for the human snare, lifelong allies in the springing trap.

He raised the Graz Burya automatic, aiming at one of the ornate hallway chandeliers, and fired twice, simultaneously shouting furiously as the earsplitting explosions accompanied the shattered glass that plummeted from the ceiling. "There he *goes*! A black suit!" His feet pounding, Bourne ran with loud emphatic strides down the corridor to the eighth door on the left, then *past* the door, shouting once again. "The exit . . . the *exit*!" He abruptly stopped, firing a third shot into another chandelier, the jarring cacophony covering the absent noise of his pounding feet as he spun around, throwing his back against the opposing wall of the eighth door, then pushing himself away, hurling his body at the door and crashing into it, smashing it off its hinges as he lurched inside, plunging to the floor, his weapon raised, prepared for rapid fire.

He was *wrong*! He knew it instantly—a final reverse trap was in the making! He heard another door opening somewhere outside—he either heard it or he instinctively *knew* it! He rolled furiously to his right, over and over again, his legs crashing into a floor lamp, sending it toward the door, his panicked darting eyes catching a glimpse of an elderly couple clutching each other, crouching in a far corner.

The white-gowned figure burst into the room, his automatic pistol spitting indiscriminately, the staccato reports deafening. Bourne fired repeatedly into the mass of white as he sprang into the left wall, knowing that if for only a split second he was positioned on the killer's blind right flank. It was *enough*!

The Jackal was caught in his shoulder—his right shoulder! The weapon literally snapped out of his grip as he jerked up his forearm, his fingers spastically uncurled under the impact of the Graz Burya's penetration. With no cessation of movement, the Jackal swung around, the bloody long white robe separating, billowing like a sail as he grabbed the massive flesh wound with his left hand and violently kicked the floor lamp into Jason's face.

Bourne fired again, half blinded by the flying shade of the heavy lamp, his weapon deflected by the thick stem. The shot went wild; steadying his hand, he squeezed the trigger again, only to hear the sickening finality of a sharp metallic click—the gun's magazine was empty! Struggling to a crouch, he lunged for the blunt, ugly automatic weapon as the white-robed Carlos raced through the shattered doorway into the corridor. Jason got to his feet, but his knee collapsed! It had buckled under his own weight. Oh, *Christ!* He crawled to the edge of the bed and dived over the pulled-down sheets toward the bedside telephone—it had been demolished, the Jackal had shot it apart! Carlos's demented mind *was* summoning up every tactic, every counteraction he had ever used.

Another sound! This loud and abrupt. The crash bar on the hallway's stairway exit had been slammed into the opening position, the heavy metal door smashed back into the concrete wall of the landing. The Jackal was heading down the flights of steps to the lobby. If the front desk had listened to Conklin, he was *trapped*!

Bourne looked at the elderly couple in the corner, affected by the fact that the old man was covering the woman with his own body. "It's all right," he said, trying to calm them by lowering his voice. "I know you probably don't understand me—I don't speak Russian—but you're safe now."

"We don't speak Russian either," admitted the man, an Englishman, in clipped, guarded tones, straining his neck as he looked at Jason while trying to rise. "Thirty years ago I would have been standing at that door! Eighth Army

with Monty, y'know. Rather grand at El Ala-
mein—all of us, of course. To paraphrase, age
doth wither, as they say."

"I'd rather not hear it, General—"

"No, no, merely a brigadier—"

"Fine!" Bourne crept over the bed, testing his
knee; whatever it was had snapped back. "I
have to get to a phone!"

"Actually, what outraged me was the goddamned robe!" went on the veteran of El Ala-
mein. "Fucking *disgraceful,* I say—forgive me,
darling."

"What are you talking about?"

"The white *robe,* lad! It had to be Binky's—the
couple across the hall we're traveling with—he
must have copped it from that lovely Beau-Riv-
age in Lausanne. The rotten theft is bad
enough, but to have given it to that *swine* is
unforgivable!"

In seconds, Jason had grabbed the Jackal's
weapon and crashed his way into the room
across the hall, immediately knowing that
"Binky" deserved more admiration than the
brigadier afforded him. He lay on the floor bleeding from knife wounds across his stomach and
throat.

"I *can't reach* anyone!" screamed the woman

with thinning gray hair; she was on her knees above the victim, weeping hysterically. "He fought like a madman—somehow he knew that priest wouldn't fire his gun!"

"Hold the skin together wherever you *can,*" yelled Bourne, looking over at the telephone. It was intact! He ran to it, and instead of calling the front desk or the operator, he dialed the numbers for the suite.

"Krupkin?" cried Alex.

"No, me! *First:* Carlos is on the staircase—the hallway I went into! *Second:* a man's cut up, same hallway, seventh door on the right! *Hurry.*"

"As fast as I can. I've got a clear line to the office."

"Where the hell is the KGB team?"

"They just got here. Krupkin called only seconds ago from the lobby—it's why I thought you were—"

"I'm going to the staircase!"

"For God's sake, *why?*"

"Because he's *mine!*"

Jason raced to the door, offering no words of comfort for the hysterical wife; he could not summon them. He crashed his way through the exit door, the Jackal's weapon in his hand. He started down the staircase, suddenly hearing the sound of his own shoes; he stopped on the seventh step and removed both, and then his ankle-length socks. The cool surface of the stone on his feet somehow reminded him of the jungles, flesh against the cold morning under-brush; for some abstract, foolish memory he felt more in command of his fears—the jungles were always the friend of Delta One.

Floor by floor he descended, following the inevitable rivulets of blood, larger now, no lon-ger to be stemmed, for the last wound was too severe to stop by exerting pressure. Twice the Jackal had applied such pressure, once at the fifth-floor and again at the third-floor hallway doors, only to be followed by streaks of dark red, as he could not manipulate the exterior locks without the security keys.

The second floor, then the first, there were *no more*! Carlos *was* trapped! Somewhere in the shadows below was the death of the killer who would set him *free*! Silently, Bourne removed a book of Metropole matches from his pocket; he huddled against the concrete wall, tore out a single match and, cupping his hands, fired the packet. He threw it over the railing, the weapon in his hand ready to explode with continuous rounds of bullets at anything that moved below!

There was nothing—*nothing*! The cement floor was empty—there was no one there! Impossible! Jason raced down the last flight of steps and pounded on the door to the lobby.

"Shto?" yelled a Russian inside. *"Kto tam?"*

"I'm an *American*! I'm working with the KGB! Let me *in*!"

"Shto. . . . ?"

"I understand," shouted another voice. "And, please, you understand that many guns are directed at you when I open the door. It is understand?"

"Understand!" shouted Bourne, at the last second remembering to drop Carlos's weapon on the concrete floor. The door opened.

"Da!" said the Soviet police officer, instantly correcting himself as he spotted the machine pistol at Jason's feet. *"Nyet!"* he yelled.

"Nye za shto?" said a breathless Krupkin, urging his heavyset body forward.

"Pochemu?"

"Komitet!"

"Prekrasno." The policeman nodded obsequiously, but stayed in place.

"What are you *doing*?" demanded Krupkin. "The lobby is cleared and our assault squad is in place!"

"He was *here*!" whispered Bourne, as if his intense quiet voice further obscured his incomprehensible words.

"The *Jackal*?" asked Krupkin, astonished.

"He came down this staircase! He couldn't have gone out on any other floor. Every fire door is dead-bolted from the inside—only the crash bars release them."

"*Skazhi*," said the KGB official to the hotel guard, speaking in Russian. "Has anyone come through this door within the past ten minutes since the orders were given to seal them off?"

"No, sir!" replied the *mititsiya*. "Only a hysterical woman in a soiled bathrobe. In her panic, she fell in the bathroom and cut herself. We thought she might have a heart attack, she was screaming so. We escorted her immediately to the nurse's office."

Krupkin turned to Jason, switching back to English, "Only a woman came through, a woman in panic who had injured herself."

"A *woman*? Is he certain? . . . What color was her hair?"

Dimitri asked the guard; with the man's reply he again looked at Bourne. "He says it was reddish and quite curly."

"*Reddish*?" An image came to Jason, a very unpleasant one. "A house phone—no, the front desk! Come *on,* I may need your help." With Krupkin following, the barefooted Bourne ran across the lobby to a clerk at the reception counter. "Can you speak English?"

"Certainly most good, even many veniculars, mister sir."

"A room plan for the tenth floor. *Quickly."*

"Mister sir?"

Krupkin translated; a large loose-leaf notebook was placed on the counter, the plastic-enclosed page turned to—*"This* room!" said Jason, pointing at a square and doing his best not to alarm the frightened clerk. "Get it on the telephone! If the line's busy, knock off anybody on it."

Again Krupkin translated as a phone was placed in front of Bourne. He picked it up and spoke. "This is the man who came into your room a few minutes ago—"

"Oh, yes, of course, dear fellow. *Thank* you *so* much! The doctor's here and Binky's—"

"I have to know something, and I have to know it right now. . . . Do you carry hairpieces, or wigs, with you when you travel?"

"I'd say that's *rather* impertinent—"

"Lady, I don't have *time* for amenities, I have to *know! Do* you?"

"Well, yes I do. It's no secret, actually, all my

friends know it and they forgive the artifice. You see, dear boy, I have diabetes . . . my gray hair is painfully thin.''

"Is one of those wigs *red*?''

"As a matter of fact, yes. I rather fancy chang-ing—''

Bourne slammed down the phone and looked over at Krupkin. "The son of a bitch lucked out. It was *Carlos*!''

"Come with me!'' said Krupkin as they both raced across the empty lobby to the complex of back-room offices of the Metropole. They reached the nurse's infirmary door and went in-side. They both stopped; both gasped and then winced at what they saw.

There were rolls of torn, unwound gauze and reels of tape in various widths, and broken sy-ringes and tubes of antibiotics scattered about the examining table and the floor, as if all were somehow administered in panic. These, how-ever, the two men barely noticed, for their eyes were riveted on the woman who had tended to her crazed patient. The Metropole's nurse was arched back in her chair, her throat surgically punctured, and over her immaculate white uni-form ran a thin stream of blood. *Madness!*

———

Standing beside the living room table, Dimitri Krupkin spoke on the phone as Alex Conklin sat on the brocaded couch massaging his bootless leg and Bourne stood by the window staring out on the Marx Prospekt. Alex looked over at the KGB officer, a thin smile on his gaunt face as Krupkin nodded, his eyes on Conklin. An acknowledgment was being transmitted between the two of them. They were worthy adversaries in a never-ending, essentially futile war in which only battles were won, the philosophical conflicts never resolved.

"I have your assurance then, comrade," said Krupkin in Russian, "and, frankly, I will hold you to it. . . . Of course I'm taping this conversation! Would you do otherwise? . . . Good! We understand each other as well as our respective responsibilities, so let me recapitulate. The man is seriously wounded, therefore the city taxi service as well as all doctors and all hospitals in the Moscow area have been alerted. The description of the stolen automobile has been circulated and any sightings of man or vehicle are to be reported only to you. The penalty for disregarding these instructions is the Lubyanka, that must be clear. . . . Good! We have a mutual understanding and I expect to hear from you the minute you have any information, yes? . . . Don't have a cardiac arrest, comrade. I am well aware that you are my superior, but then this *is* a proletarian society, yes? Simply follow the advice of an extremely experienced subordinate. Have a pleasant day. . . . No, that is not a threat, it is merely a phrase I picked up in Paris—American origin, I believe." Krupkin hung up the phone and sighed. "There's something to be said for our vanished, educated aristocracy, I'm afraid."

"Don't say it out loud," observed Conklin, nodding at the telephone. "I gather nothing's coming down."

"Nothing to act upon immediately but something rather interesting, even fascinating in a macabre sort of way."

"By which you mean it concerns Carlos, I assume."

"No one else." Krupkin shook his head as Jason looked over at him from the window. "I stopped at my office to join the assault squad and on my desk were eight large manila envelopes, only one of which had been opened. The police found them in the Vavilova and, true to form, having read the contents of only one, wanted nothing to do with them."

"What were they?" asked Alex, chuckling.

"State secrets describing the entire Politburo as gay?"

"You're probably not far off the mark," interrupted Bourne. "That was the Jackal's Moscow cadre in the Vavilova. He was either showing them the dirt he had on them, or giving them the dirt on others."

"The latter in this case," said Krupkin. "A collection of the most preposterous allegations directed at the ranking heads of our major ministries."

"He's got vaults of that garbage. It's standard operating procedure for Carlos; it's how he buys his way into circles he shouldn't be able to penetrate."

"Then I'm not being clear, Jason," continued the KGB officer. "When I say preposterous, I mean exactly that—beyond belief. Lunacy."

"He's almost always on target. Don't take that judgment to the bank."

"If there were such a bank I certainly would, and I'd negotiate a sizable loan on its efficacy as collateral. Most of the information is the stuff of the lowest-grade tabloids—nothing unusual there, of course—but along with such nonsense are outright distortions of times, places, functions and even identities. For example, the Min-

istry of Transport is not where a particular file
says, but a block away, and a certain comrade
direktor is not married to the lady named but to
someone else—the woman mentioned is their
daughter and is not in Moscow but rather in
Cuba, where she's been for six years. Also, the
man listed as head of Radio Moscow and accused of just about everything short of having
intercourse with dogs, died eleven months ago
and was a known closet orthodox Catholic, who
would have been far happier as a truly devout
priest. . . . These blatant falsehoods I picked up
in a matter of minutes, time being at a premium,
but I'm sure there are dozens more."

"You're saying that a scam was pulled on
Carlos?" said Conklin.

"One so garish—albeit compiled with extreme conviction—it would be laughed out of
our most rigidly doctrinaire courts. Whoever fed
him these melodramatic 'exposés' wanted built-
in deniabilities."

"Rodchenko?" asked Bourne.

"I can't think of anyone else. Grigorie—I say
'Grigorie' but I never called him that to his face;
it was always 'General'—was a consummate
strategist, the ultimate survivor, as well as a
deeply committed Marxist. Control was his by-

word, his addiction, really, and if he could control the infamous Jackal for the Motherland's
interests, what a profound exhilaration for the
old man. Yet the Jackal killed him with those
symbolic bullets in his throat. Was it betrayal, or
was it carelessness on Rodchenko's part at
having been discovered? Which? We'll never
know." The telephone rang and Krupkin's hand
shot down, picking it up. *"Da?"* Shifting to Russian, Dimitri gestured for Conklin to restrap the
prosthetic boot as he spoke. "Now listen to me
very carefully, comrade. The police are to make
no moves—above all, they are to remain out of
sight. Call in one of our unmarked vehicles to
replace the patrol car, am I clear? . . . Good.
We'll use the Moray frequency."

"Breakthrough?" asked Bourne, stepping
away from the window as Dimitri slammed down
the phone.

"Maximum!" replied Krupkin. "The car was
spotted on the Nemchinovka road heading toward Odintsovo."

"That doesn't mean anything to me. What's in
Odintsovol, or whatever it's called?"

"I don't know specifically, but I must assume
he does. Remember, he knows Moscow and its
environs. Odintsovo is what you might call an

industrial suburb about thirty-five minutes from the city—"

"*Goddamn* it!" yelled Alex, struggling with the Velcro straps of his boot.

"Let me do that," said Jason, his tone of voice brooking no objection as he knelt down and swiftly manipulated the thick strips of coarse cloth. "Why is Carlos still using the Dzerzhinsky car?" continued Bourne, addressing Krupkin. "It's not like him to take that kind of risk."

"It is if he has no choice. He has to know that all Moscow taxis are a silent arm of the state, and he is, after all, severely wounded and un-doubtedly now without a gun or he would have used it on you. He's in no condition to threaten a driver or steal an automobile. . . . Besides, he reached the Nemchinovka road quickly; that the car was even seen is pure chance. The road is not well traveled, which I assume he also knows."

"Let's get *out* of here!" cried Conklin, an-noyed by both Jason's attention and his own infirmity. He stood up, wavered, angrily rejected Krupkin's hand, and started for the door. "We can talk in the car. We're wasting time."

———

"Moray, come in, please," said Krupkin in Russian, sitting beside the assault squad driver in the front seat, the microphone at his lips, his hand on the frequency dial of the vehicle's radio. "Moray, respond, if I'm reaching you."

"What the hell's he talking about?" asked Bourne, in the backseat with Alex.

"He's trying to make contact with the unmarked KGB patrol following Carlos. He keeps switching from one ultrahigh frequency to another. It's the Moray code."

"The what?"

"It's an eel, Jason," replied Krupkin, glancing over the seat. "Of the Muraenidae family with porelike gills and capable of descending to great depths. Certain species can be quite deadly."

"Thank you, Peter Lorre," said Bourne.

"Very good," laughed the KGB man. "But you'll admit it's aptly descriptive. Very few radios can either send it or receive it."

"When did you steal it from us?"

"Oh, not you, not you at all. From the British, truthfully. As usual, London is very quiet about these things, but they're far ahead of you and the Japanese in certain areas. It's that damned MI-Six. They dine in their clubs in Knightsbridge, smoke their odious pipes, play the innocents, and send us defectors trained at the Old Vic."

"They've had their gaps," said Conklin defensively.

"More so in their high-dudgeon revelations than in reality, Aleksei. You've been away too long. We've both lost more than they have in that department, but they can cope with public embarrassment—we haven't learned that time-honored trait. We bury our 'gaps,' as you put it; we try too hard for that respectability which too often eludes us. Then, I suppose, we're historically young by comparison." Krupkin again switched back into Russian. *"Moray,* come in, please! I'm reaching the end of the spectrum. Where are you, Moray?"

"Stop *there,* comrade!" came the metallic voice over the loudspeaker. "We're in contact. Can you hear me?"

"You sound like a castrato but I can hear you."

"This must be Comrade Krupkin—"

"Were you expecting the pope? Who's this?"

"Orlov."

"Good! You know what you're doing."

"I hope you do, Dimitri."

"Why do you say that?"

"Your insufferable orders to do nothing, *that's* why. We're two kilometers away from the building—I drove up through the grass on a small hill—and we have the vehicle in sight. It's parked in the lot and the suspect's inside."

"What building? What hill? You tell me nothing."

"The Kubinka Armory."

Hearing this, Conklin bolted forward in the seat. "Oh, my God!" he cried.

"What is it?" asked Bourne.

"He reached an armory." Alex saw the frown of confusion on Jason's face. "Over here armories are a hell of a lot more than enclosed parade grounds for legionnaires and reservists. They're serious training quarters and warehouses for weapons."

"He wasn't heading for Odintsovo," broke in Krupkin. "The armory's farther south, on the outskirts of the town, another four or five kilometers. He's been there before."

"Those places must have tight security," said Bourne. "He can't just walk inside."

"He already has," corrected the KGB officer from Paris.

"I mean into restricted areas—like storerooms filled with weapons."

"That's what concerns me," went on Krupkin, fingering the microphone in his hand. "Since he's been there before—and he obviously has—what does he know about the installation . . . *who* does he know?"

"Get on a radio patch, call the place and have him stopped, held!" insisted Jason.

"Suppose I reach the wrong person, or suppose he already has weapons and we set him off? With one phone call, one hostile confrontation or even the appearance of a strange automobile, there could be wholesale slaughter of several dozen men and women. We saw what he did at the Metropole, in the Vavilova. He's lost all control; he's utterly mad."

"Dimitri," came the metallic Soviet voice over the radio speaking Russian. "Something's happening. The man just came out of a side door with a burlap sack and is heading for the car. . . . Comrade, I'm not sure it's the *same* man. It probably is, but there's something different about him."

"What do you mean? The clothes?"

"No, he's wearing a dark suit and his right arm is in a black sling as before . . . yet he's moving more rapidly, his pace firmer, his posture erect."

"You're saying he does not appear to be wounded, yes?"

"I guess that's what I'm saying, yes."

"He could be faking it," said Conklin. "That son of a bitch could be taking his last breath and convince you he's ready for a marathon."

"For what purpose, Aleksei? Why any pretense at all?"

"I don't know, but if your man in that car can see him, he can see the car. Maybe he's just in a hell of a hurry."

"What's going on?" asked Bourne angrily.

"Someone's come outside with a bagful of goodies and going to the car," said Conklin in English.

"For Christ's sake, *stop* him!"

"We're not sure it's the Jackal," interrupted Krupkin. "The clothes are the same, even to the arm sling, but there are physical differences—"

"Then he wants you to think it *isn't* him!" said Jason emphatically.

"*Shto?* . . . What?"

"He's putting himself in your place, thinking like you're thinking now and by doing that *outthinking* you. He may or may not know that he's been spotted, the car picked up, but he has to assume the worst and act accordingly. How long before we get there?"

"The way my outrageously reckless young comrade is driving, I'd say three or four minutes."

"Krupkin!" The voice burst from the radio speaker. "Four other people have come outside—three men and a woman. They're running to the car!"

"What did he say?" asked Bourne. Alex translated and Jason frowned. "Hostages?" he said quietly, as if to himself. "He just *blew* it!" Medusa's Delta leaned forward and touched Krupkin's shoulder. "Tell your man to get out of there the moment that car takes off and he knows where it's heading. Tell him to be obvious, to blow the hell out of his horn while he passes the armory, which he *must* pass from one way or the other."

"My *dear* fellow!" exploded the Soviet intelligence officer. "Would you mind telling *me* why I should issue such an order?"

"Because your colleague was right and I was wrong. The man in the sling isn't Carlos. The Jackal's inside, waiting for the cavalry to pass the fort so he can get away in another car—if there *is* a cavalry."

"In the name of our revered Karl Marx, *do* explain how you reached this contradictory conclusion!"

"Simple. He made a mistake. . . . Even if you could, you wouldn't shoot up that car on the road, would you?"

"Agreed. There are four other people inside, all no doubt innocent Soviet citizens forced to appear otherwise."

"Hostages?"

"Yes, of course."

"When was the last time you heard of people running like hell into a situation where they could *become* hostages? Even if they were under a gun from a doorway, one or two, if not all of them, would try to race behind other cars for protection."

"My *word*—"

"But you were right about one thing. Carlos has a contact inside that armory—the man in the sling. He may only be an innocent Russian with a brother or a sister living in Paris, but the Jackal owns him."

"Dimitri!" shouted the metallic voice in Russian. "The car is speeding out of the parking lot!"

Krupkin pressed the button on his microphone and gave his instructions. Essentially, they were to follow that automobile to the borders of Finland if necessary, but to take it without violence, calling in the police if they had to. The last order was to pass the armory, blowing his horn repeatedly. In the Russian vernacular, the agent named Orlov asked, "What the fuck for?"

"Because I've had a vision from St. Nickolai the Good! Also, I'm your charitable superior. *Do it!*"

"You're not well, Dimitri."

"Do you wish a superb service report or one that will send you to Tashkent?"

"I'm on my way, comrade."

Krupkin replaced the microphone in the dashboard receptacle. "Everything proceeds," he said haltingly, partially over his shoulder. "If I'm to go down with either a crazed assassin or a convoluted lunatic who displays certain decencies, I imagine it's best to choose the latter. Contrary to the most enlightened skeptics, there might be a God, after all. . . . Would you care to buy a house on the lake in Geneva, Aleksei?"

"I might," answered Bourne. "If I live through the day and do what I have to do, give me a price. I won't quibble."

"Hey, David," interjected Conklin. "Marie made that money, *you* didn't."

"She'll listen to me. To him."

"What now, whoever you are?" asked Krupkin.

"Give me all the firepower I need from this trunk of yours and let me off in the grass just before the armory. Give me a couple of minutes to get in place, then pull into the parking lot and obviously—very obviously—see that the car is missing and get out of there fast, gunning your engine."

"And leave you *alone*?" cried Alex.

"It's the only way I can take him. The only way he can be taken."

"Lunacy!" spat out Krupkin, his jowls vibrating.

"No, Kruppie, reality," said Jason Bourne simply. "It's the same as it was in the beginning. One on one, it's the only way."

"That is sophomoric heroics!" roared the Russian, slamming his hand down on the back of the seat. "Worse, it's ridiculous strategy. If you're right, I can surround the armory with a thousand troops!"

"Which is exactly what he'd want—what *I'd* want, if I were Carlos. Don't you see? He could get away in the confusion, in the sheer numbers—that's not a problem for either of us, we've both done it too many times before. Crowds and anxiety are our protection—they're child's play. A knife in a uniform, the uniform ours; toss a grenade into the troops, and after the explosion we're one of the staggering victims—that's amateur night for paid killers. Believe me, I know—I became one in spite of my-self."

"So what do you think you can do by yourself, *Batman*?" asked Conklin, furiously massaging his useless leg.

"Stalk the killer who wants to kill me—and I'll take him."

"You're a fucking megalomaniac!"

"You're absolutely right. It's the only way to be in the killing game. It's the only edge you've got."

"Insanity!" yelled Krupkin.

"So allow me; I'm entitled to a little craziness. If I thought the entire Russian army would en-sure my survival, I'd scream for it. But it wouldn't—it couldn't. There's only this way. . . . Stop the car and let me choose the weap-ons."

39

The dark green KGB sedan rounded the final curve in the sloping road cut out of the country-side. The descent had been gradual. The ground below was flat and summer-green with fields of wild grass bordering the approach to the massive brown building that was the Kubinka Armory. It seemed to rise out of the earth, a huge boxlike intrusion on the pastoral scene, an ugly man-made interruption of heavy brown wood and miserly windows reaching three stories high and covering two acres of land. Like the structure itself, the front entrance was large, square and unadorned except for the dull bas-relief profiles above the door of three

Soviet soldiers rushing into the deadly winds of battle, their rifles at port arms, about to blow one another's heads off.

Armed with an authentic Russian AK-47 and five standard thirty-round magazine clips, Bourne jumped out the far side of the silent coasting government car, using the bulk of the rolling vehicle to conceal himself in the grass directly across the road from the entrance. The armory's huge dirt parking area was to the right of the long building; a single row of unkempt shrubbery fronted the entrance lawn, in the center of which stood a tall white pole, the Soviet flag hanging limp in the breezeless morning air. Jason ran across the road, his body low, and crouched by the hedgerow; he had only moments to peer through the bushes and ascertain the existence or nonexistence of the armory's security procedures. At best, they appeared lax to the point of being informal, if not irrelevant. There was a glass window in the right wall of the entrance similar to that of a theater's box office; behind it sat a uniformed guard reading a magazine, and alongside him, less visible but seen clearly enough, was another, his head on the counter, asleep. Two other soldiers emerged from the immense armory door—double doors—both casual, unconcerned, as one glanced at his watch and the other lighted a cigarette.

So much for Kubinka's security; no sudden assault was anticipated nor had one taken place, at least none that had set off alarms reaching the front patrols, usually the first to be alerted. It was eerie, unnatural, beyond the unexpected. The Jackal was inside this military installation, yet there was no sign that he had penetrated it, no indication that somewhere within the complex he was controlling a minimum of five personnel—a man impersonating him, three other men and a woman.

The parking area itself? He had not understood the exchanges between Alex, Krupkin and the voice over the radio, but now it was clear to him that when they had spoken of people coming outside and running to the stolen car, they were *not* referring to the front entrance! There had to be an exit on the parking area! *Christ,* he had only seconds before the driver of the Komitet car started up the engine and roared into the huge dirt lot, circling it and racing out, both actions announcing the government vehicle's arrival and swift, calamitous departure. If Carlos was going to make his break, it would be then! After waiting for the standard radio backup, every moment of distance he put between himself and the armory would make it more difficult to pick up his trail. And *he,* the efficient killing machine from Medusa, was in the wrong *place*! Further, the sight of a civilian running across a lawn or down a road carrying an automatic weapon within a military compound was to invite disaster. It was a small, stupid omission! Three or four additional words translated *and* a less arrogant, more probing listener would have avoided the error. It was always the little things, the seemingly insignificant that crippled gray to black operations. *Goddamn* it!

Five hundred feet away the KGB sedan suddenly thundered as it swerved into the dirt parking area raising clouds of dry dust while crushing and spitting out pieces of rock from its spinning tires. There was no time to think, time only to act. Bourne held the AK-47 against his right leg, concealing it as much as possible as he rose to his feet, his left hand skimming the top of the low hedgerow—a gardener, perhaps, surveying an anticipated assignment, or an indolent stroller aimlessly touching the roadside shrubbery, nothing remotely threatening, just a sign of the commonplace; to the casual observer, he might have been walking down that road for several minutes without being noticed.

He glanced over at the armory's entrance. The two soldiers were laughing quietly, the one without a cigarette again looking at his watch. Then the object of their minor conspiracy came out of the left front door, an attractive dark-haired girl, barely in her twenties. She humorously clapped both her hands over her ears, made a grotesque face and walked rapidly to the time-conscious man in uniform, kissing him on the lips. The threesome linked arms, the woman in the center, and started to their right, away from the entrance.

A *crash*! Metal colliding with metal, glass shattering glass, the loud harsh sound coming from the distant parking area. Something had happened to the Komitet car with Alex and Krupkin; the young driver from the assault squad had either smashed or skidded into another vehicle in the dry dirt of the lot. Using the sound as an excuse, Jason started down the road, the image of Conklin coming instantly to his mind, producing a limp in his own rapid strides the better to keep his weapon in minimum view. He turned his head, expecting to see the two soldiers and

the woman running down the armory path toward the accident, only to realize that the three
of them were running the *other* way, removing
themselves from any involvement. Obviously,
precious breaks in a military schedule were jealously protected.

Bourne abandoned the limp, crashed through
the hedgerow and raced to the concrete path
that stretched to the corner of the huge building,
gathering speed and breathing heavily with increasing frequency. Jason's weapon was now in
plain sight, slashing the air as he gripped it in the
hand of his swinging right arm. He reached the
end of the path, his chest heaving, the veins in
his neck seemingly prepared to burst as the
sweat ran down his skin, drenching his face, his
collar and his shirt. Gasping, he steadied the
AK-47, his back pressed against the wall of
the building, then spun around the corner into
the parking area, stunned by what he saw. His
pounding feet, coupled with the anxiety that
caused his hair-soaked temples to throb, had
blocked out all sound up ahead. What he observed now, what sickened him now, he knew
had to be the result of multiple gunshots muted
by a weapon equipped with a silencer. Dispas-
sionately, Medusa's Delta understood; he had

been there many times many years before. There were circumstances under which kills had to be made quietly—utter silence was the unreachable goal, but at least minimal noise was crucial.

The young KGB driver from the assault squad was sprawled on the ground by the trunk of the dark green sedan, the wounds in his head certifying death. The car had swerved into the side of a government bus, the sort used to haul workers to and from their places of employment. How or why the accident had happened, Bourne could not know. Neither could he know whether Alex or Krupkin had survived; the car's windows had been pierced repeatedly and there was no sign of movement inside, both facts suggesting the worst but nothing conclusive. Above all, at this moment, the Chameleon also understood that he could not be affected by what he saw— emotions were *out*! If the worst had happened, mourning the dead would come later, vengeance and taking the killer came now.

Think! How? *Quickly!*

Krupkin had said there were "several dozen men and women" working at the armory. If so, where the hell were they? The Jackal was not acting in a vacuum; it was impossible! Yet a collision had occurred, its violent crash heard over a hundred yards away—well over the distance of a football field—and a man had been shot dead at the site of that crash, his lifeless body bleeding in the dirt, yet no one—*no one*—had appeared, either accidentally or intentionally. With the exception of Carlos and five unknown people, was the entire armory operating in a vacuum? Nothing made sense!

And then he heard the muffled but emphatic strains of music from deep inside the building. Martial music, drums and trumpets predominating, swelling to crescendos that Bourne could only imagine were deafening within the echoing confines of the huge structure. The image of the young woman emerging from the front entrance returned; she had playfully clapped her hands over her ears and grimaced, and Jason had not understood. He did now. She had come from the armory's inner staging area, where the decibel level of the music was overpowering. An event was taking place at the Kubinka, a decently attended affair, which accounted for the profusion of automobiles, small vans and buses in the vast parking area—profusion at any rate in the Soviet Union, where such vehicles were not in oversupply. Altogether there were perhaps twenty

conveyances in the dirt lot, parked in a semicircle. The activity inside was both the Jackal's
diversion and his protection; he knew how to
orchestrate both to his advantage. So did his
enemy. Checkmate.

Why didn't Carlos come out? Why *hadn't* he
come out? What was he waiting for? The circumstances were optimal; they couldn't be better. Had his wounds slowed him to the point that
he had lost the advantages he had created? It
was possible, but not likely. The assassin had
gotten this far, and if escape was in the offing,
it was in him to go further, much further. Then
why? Irreversible logic, a killer's *survival* logic
demanded that after taking out the backup the
Jackal had to race away as fast as humanly
possible. It was his only chance! Then why was
he still *inside*? Why hadn't his escape car fled
from the area, speeding him to freedom?

His back once again pressed against the wall,
Jason sidestepped to his left, closely observing
everything he could see. Like most armories the
world over, Kubinka had no windows on the first
floor, at least not for the first fifteen feet from the
ground; he presumed it was because the occasional wildly galloping horses and glass did not
go together. He could see a window frame on

what appeared to be the second floor but close enough to the slain driver to afford maximum accuracy for a silenced high-powered weapon. Another frame on ground level had a knob protruding; it was the rear exit no one had bothered to mention. *The little things, the insignificant things! Goddamn!*

The muted music inside swelled again, but now the swelling was different, the drums louder, the trumpets more sustained, more piercing. It was the unmistakable ending of a symphonic march, martial music at its most intense. . . . That was it! The end of the event inside was at hand and the Jackal would use the emerging crowds to cover his escape. He would mingle, and when panic spread through the parking area with the sight of the dead man and the shot-up sedan, he would disappear—with whom and with what vehicle would take hours to determine.

Bourne had to get inside; he had to stop him, *take* him! Krupkin had worried about the lives of ''several dozen men and women''—he had no idea that in reality there were several hundred! Carlos would use whatever firepower he had stolen, including grenades, to create mass hysteria so that he could escape. Lives meant nothing; if further killing was required to save his own, *nothing.* Abandoning caution, Delta raced to the door, gripping his AK-47 laterally in his arm, the safety unlatched, his index finger on the trigger. He grabbed the knob and twisted it—it would not turn. He fired his weapon into the plated metal around the lock, then a second fusillade into the opposing frame, and as he reached for the smoking knob, his personal world went mad!

Out of the line of vehicles a heavy truck suddenly shot forward, coming straight toward him, wildly accelerating as it approached. Simultaneously, successive bursts of automatic gunfire erupted, the bullets thumping into the wood to his right. He lunged to his left, rolling on the ground, the dust and dirt filling his eyes as he kept rolling, his body a tube spinning away.

And then it happened! The massive explosion tore apart the door, blowing away a large section of the wall above, and through the black smoke and settling debris, he could see a figure lurching awkwardly toward the semicircle of vehicles. His killer was getting away after all. But *he* was alive! And the reason for it was obvious—the Jackal had made a mistake. Not in the trap, *that* was extraordinary; Carlos *knew* his enemy was with Krupkin and the KGB and so he *had* gone outside and waited for him. Instead, his error was in the placement of the explosives. He had wired the bomb or bombs to the top of the truck's engine, not *underneath.* Explosive compounds seek release through the least re- sistant barriers; the relatively thin hood of a vehi- cle is far less solid than the iron beneath it. The bomb actually blew *up;* it did not blow *out* on ground level, sending death-inducing metal fragments along the surface.

No *time*! Bourne struggled to his feet and staggered to the Komitet sedan, a horrible fear coming into focus. He looked through the shat- tered windows, his eyes suddenly drawn to the front seat as a heavily fleshed hand was raised. He yanked the door open and saw Krupkin, his large body squeezed below the seat under the dashboard, his right shoulder half torn away, bleeding flesh apparent through the fabric of his jacket.

"We are hurt," said the KGB officer weakly but calmly. "Aleksei somewhat more seriously than I am, so attend to him first, if you please."

"The crowd's coming out of the armory—"

"Here!" interrupted Krupkin, painfully reach- ing into his pocket and pulling out his plastic identification case. "Get to the idiot in charge

and bring him to me. We must get a doctor. For *Aleksei,* you damn fool. *Hurry!"*

The two wounded men lay alongside each other on examining tables in the armory's infirmary as Bourne stood across the room, leaning against the wall, watching but not understanding what was being said. Three doctors had been dispatched by helicopter from the roof of the People's Hospital on the Serova Prospekt—two surgeons and an anesthesiologist, the last, however, proving unnecessary. Severe invasive procedures were not called for; local anesthetics were sufficient for the cleansing and suturing, followed by generous injections of antibiotics. The foreign objects had passed through their bodies, explained the chief doctor.

"I presume you mean bullets when you speak so reverently of 'foreign objects,' " said Krupkin in high dudgeon.

"He means bullets," confirmed Alex hoarsely in Russian. The retired CIA station chief was unable to move his head because of his bandaged throat. Wide adhesive straps extended down across his collarbone and upper right shoulder.

"Thank you," said the surgeon. "You were both fortunate, especially you, our American patient for whom we must compile confidential medical records. Incidentally, give our people the name and address of your physician in the United States. You'll need attention for some weeks ahead."

"Right now he's in a hospital in Paris."

"I beg your pardon?"

"Well, whenever something's wrong with me, I tell him and he sends me to the doctor he thinks I should see."

"That's not exactly socialized medicine."

"For me it is. I'll give his name and address to a nurse. With luck he'll be back soon."

"I repeat, you were very fortunate."

"I was very fast, Doctor, and so was your comrade. We saw that son of a bitch running out toward us, so we locked the doors and kept moving in the seats and firing at him as he tried to get close enough to put us away, which he damn near did. . . . I'm sorry about the driver; he was a brave young man."

"He was an angry young man as well, Aleksei," broke in Krupkin from the other table. "Those first shots from the doorway sent him into that bus."

The door of the infirmary burst open, which was to say it was not opened so much as it was invaded, submitting to the august presence of the KGB commissar from the flat in Slavyansky. The blunt-featured, blunt-spoken Komitet officer in the disheveled uniform lived up to his appearance. "You," he said to the doctor, "I've spoken to your associates outside. You are finished here, they say."

"Not entirely, comrade. There are minor items to attend to, such as therapeutical—"

"Later," interrupted the commissar. "We talk privately. Alone."

"The Komitet speaks?" asked the surgeon, his contempt minor but evident.

"It speaks."

"Sometimes too often."

"What?"

"You heard me," replied the doctor, heading for the door. The KGB man shrugged and waited for the infirmary door to close. He then walked to the foot of both examining tables, his squinting flesh-encased eyes darting between the two wounded men, and spat out one word. *"Novgorod!"* he said.

"What?"

"What . . . ?"

The responses were simultaneous; even Bourne snapped himself away from the wall.

"You," he added, switching to his limited English. "Understand I say?"

"If you said what I think you said, I think I do, but only the name."

"I explain good enough. We question the nine men women he locked in weapons storage. He kill two guards who do not stop him, okay? He take automobile keys from four men but uses no automobiles, okay?"

"I saw him head for the cars!"

"Which? Three other people at Kubinka shot dead, automobile papers taken. Which?"

"For Christ's sake, check with your vehicle bureau, or whatever you call it!"

"Take time. Also in Moskva, automobiles under different names, different tag plates—Leningrad, Smolensk, who knows—all to not look for automobile laws broken."

"What the hell is he *talking* about?" shouted Jason.

"Automobile ownership is regulated by the state," explained Krupkin weakly from the table. "Each major center has its own registration and is frequently reluctant to cooperate with another center."

"Why?"

"Individual ownership under different family names—even nonfamily names. It's forbidden. There are only so many vehicles available for purchase."

"So?"

"Local bribery is a fact of life. No one in Leningrad wants a finger pointed at him from a bureaucrat in Moscow. He's telling you that it could take several days to learn what automobile the Jackal's driving."

"That's *crazy*!"

"You said it, Mr. Bourne, I didn't. I'm an upstanding citizen of the Soviet Union, please remember that."

"But what's it all got to do with Novgorod— that *is* what he said, isn't it?"

"Novgorod. Shto eto znachit?" said Krupkin to the KGB official. In rapid, clipped Russian, the peasant commissar gave the pertinent details to his colleague from Paris. Krupkin turned his head on the table and translated in English. "Try to follow this, Jason," he said, his voice intermittently fading, his breathing becoming increasingly more labored. "Apparently there is a walk-around gallery above the armory's arena. He used it and saw you through a window on the

road by the hedges and came back to the weapons room screaming like the maniac he is. He
shouted to his bound hostages that you were *his*
and you were dead. . . . And there was only one
last thing he had to accomplish."

"Novgorod," interrupted Conklin, whispering,
his head rigid, staring at the ceiling.

"Precisely," said Krupkin, his eyes focused
on Alex's profile beside him. "He's going back
to the place of his birth . . . where Ilich Ramirez
Sanchez became Carlos the Jackal because he
was disinherited, marked for execution as a
madman. He held his gun against everyone's
throat, quietly demanding to know the best
roads to Novgorod, threatening to kill whoever
gave him the wrong answer. None did, of
course, and all who knew told him it was five to
six hundred kilometers away, a full day's drive."

"Drive?" interjected Bourne.

"He knows he cannot use any other means of
transportation. The railroads, the airports—
even the small airfields—all will be watched, he
understands that."

"What will he do in Novgorod?" asked Jason
quickly.

"Dear God in heaven, which, of course, there
is neither, who *knows*? He intends to leave his
mark, a highly destructive memorial to himself,

no doubt, in answer to those he believes betrayed him thirty-odd years ago, as well as the
poor souls who fell under his gun this morning
in the Vavilova. . . . He took the papers from our
agent trained at Novgorod; he thinks they'll get
him inside. They won't—we'll stop him."

"Don't even try," said Bourne. "He may or
may not use them, depending upon what he
sees, what he senses. He doesn't need papers
to get in there any more than I do, but if he
senses something wrong, and he will, he'll kill a
number of good men and still get inside."

"What are you driving at?" asked Krupkin
warily, eyeing Bourne, the American with alternate identities and apparently conflicting life-
styles.

"Get me inside ahead of him with a detailed
map of the whole complex and some kind of
document that gives me free access to go wherever I want to go."

"You've lost your *senses*!" cried Dimitri. "A
nondefecting American, an assassin hunted by
every NATO country in Europe, inside *Novgorod*?"

"*Nyet, nyet, nyet!*" roared the Komitet commissar. "I understand good, *okay*? You are lunatic, *okay*?"

"Do you want the Jackal?"

"Naturally, but there are limits to the cost."

"I haven't the slightest interest in Novgorod or in any of the compounds—you should know that by now. Your little infiltrating operations and *our* little infiltrating operations can go on and on and it doesn't matter because none of it means a goddamned thing in the long run. It's all adolescent game playing. We either live together on this planet or there is no planet. . . . My only concern is Carlos. I want him dead so *I* can go on living."

"Of course, I personally agree with much of what you say, although the adolescent games do keep some of us rather gracefully employed. However, there's no way I could convince my more rigid superiors, starting with the one standing above me."

"All right," said Conklin from his table, his eyes still on the ceiling. "Down and dirty—we deal. You get him into Novgorod and you keep Ogilvie."

"We've already got him, Aleksei."

"Not clean, you haven't. Washington knows he's here."

"So?"

"So *I* can say you lost him and they'll believe me. They'll take my word for it that he flew out of your nest and you're mad as hell, but you can't get him back. He's operating from points unknown or unreachable, but obviously under the sovereign protection of a United Nations country. As a matter of conjecture, I suspect that's how you got him over here in the first place."

"You're cryptic, my fine old enemy. To what purpose should I entertain your suggestion?"

"No World Court embarrassments, no charges of harboring an American accused of international crimes. . . . You win the stakes in Europe. You take over the Medusa operation with no complications—in the person of one Dimitri Krupkin, a proven sophisticate from the cosmopolitan world of Paris. Who better to guide the enterprise? . . . The newest hero of the Soviet, a member of the inner economic council of the Presidium. Forget the lousy house in Geneva, Kruppie, how about a mansion on the Black Sea?"

"It is a most intelligent and attractive offer, I grant you," said Krupkin. "I know two or three men on the Central Committee whom I can reach in a matter of minutes—everything confidential, of course."

"Nyet, nyet!" shouted the KGB commissar,

slamming his fist down on Dimitri's table. "I understand some—you talk too fast—but all is lunatic!"

"Oh, for God's sake, *shut up*!" roared Krupkin. "We're discussing things far beyond your grasp!"

"Shto?" Like a young child reprimanded by an adult, the Komitet officer, his puffed eyes widened, was both astonished and frightened by his subordinate's incomprehensible rebuke.

"Give my friend his chance, Kruppie," said Alex. "He's the best there is and he may bring you the Jackal."

"He may also bring about his own death, Aleksei."

"He's been there before. I believe in him."

"Belief," whispered Krupkin, his own eyes now on the ceiling. "Such a luxury it is. . . . Very well, the order will be issued secretly, its origins untraceable, of course. You'll enter your own American compound. It's the one least understood."

"How fast can I get there?" asked Bourne. "There's a lot I have to put together."

"We have an airport in Vnokova under our control, no more than an hour away. First, I must make arrangements. Hand me a telephone.

. . . *You,* my imbecilic *commissar*! I will hear no more from you! A *telefone*!" The once all-powerful, now subdued superior, who had really understood only such words as "Presidium" and "Central Committee," moved with alacrity, bringing an extension phone to Krupkin's table.

"One more thing," said Bourne. "Have Tass put out an immediate bulletin with heavy coverage in the newspapers, radio and television that the assassin known as Jason Bourne died of wounds here in Moscow. Make the details sketchy but have them parallel what happened here this morning."

"That's not difficult. Tass is an obedient instrument of the state."

"I haven't finished," continued Jason. "I want you to include in those sketchy details that among the personal effects found on Bourne's body was a road map of Brussels and its environs. The town of Anderlecht was circled in red—that has to appear."

"The assassination of the supreme commander of NATO—very good, very convincing. However, Mr. Bourne or Webb or whatever your name may be, you should know that this story will splash across the world like a giant tidal wave."

"I understand that."

"Are you prepared for it?"

"Yes, I am."

"What about your wife? Don't you think you should reach her first, before the civilized world learns that Jason Bourne is dead?"

"No. I don't even want the slightest risk of a leak."

"Jesus!" exploded Alex, coughing. "That's *Marie* you're talking about. She'll fall apart!"

"It's a risk I'll accept," said Delta coldly.

"You son of a *bitch*!"

"So be it," agreed the Chameleon.

John St. Jacques, tears welling in his eyes, walked into the bright, sunlit room at the sterile house in the Maryland countryside; in his hand was a page of computer printout. His sister was on the floor in front of the couch playing with an exuberant Jamie, she having put the infant Alison back into the crib upstairs. She looked worn and haggard, her face pale with dark circles under her eyes; she was exhausted from the tension and the jet lag of the long, idiotically routed flights from Paris to Washington. In spite of arriving late last night, she had gotten up early to be with the children—no amount of friendly persuasion on the part of the motherly Mrs. Cooper could dissuade her from doing so. The brother would have given years of his life not to do what had to be done during the next few minutes, but he could not risk the alternatives. He had to be with her when she found out.

"Jamie," said St. Jacques gently. "Go find Mrs. Cooper, will you please? I think she's in the kitchen."

"Why, Uncle John?"

"I want to talk to your mother for a few minutes."

"Johnny, *please*," objected Marie.

"I have to, Sis."

"What . . . ?"

The child left, and as children often do, he obviously sensed something serious that was beyond his understanding; he stared at his uncle before heading to the door. Marie got to her feet and looked hard at her brother, at the tears that began to roll down his cheeks. The terrible message was conveyed. "No . . . !" she whispered, her pallid face growing paler. "Dear God, *no*," she cried, her hands and then her shoulders starting to tremble. "No . . . *no*!" she roared.

"He's gone, Sis. I wanted you to hear it from me, not over a radio or a TV set. I want to be with you."

"You're wrong, *wrong*!" screamed Marie, rushing toward him, grabbing his shirt and clenching the fabric in her fists. "He's protected! . . . He promised me he was *protected*!"

"This just came from Langley," said the younger brother, holding up the page of computer printout. "Holland called me a few minutes ago and said it was on its way over. He knew you had to see it. It was picked up from Radio Moscow during the night and will be on all the broadcasts and in the morning papers."

"Give it to me!" she shouted defiantly. He did so and gently held her shoulders, prepared to take her in his arms and give what comfort he could. She read the copy rapidly, then shook off his hands, frowning, and walked back to the couch and sat down. Her concentration was absolute; she placed the paper on the coffee table and studied it as though it were an archaeological find, a scroll perhaps.

"He's gone, Marie. I don't know what to say— you know how I felt about him."

"Yes, I know, Johnny." Then to St. Jacques's astonishment, his sister looked up at him, a thin, wan smile appearing on her lips. "But it's a little early for our tears, Bro. He's alive. Jason Bourne's alive and up to his tricks and that means David's alive, too."

My God, she can't accept it, thought the brother, walking to the couch and kneeling beside the coffee table in front of Marie, taking her hands in his. "Sis, honey, I don't think you understand. I'll do everything possible to help you, but you've got to understand."

"Bro, you're very sweet but you haven't read this closely—really closely. The impact of the message detracts from the subtext. In economics we call it obfuscation with a cloud of smoke and a couple of mirrors."

"Huh?" St. Jacques released her hands and stood up. "What are you talking about?"

Marie picked up the Langley communiqué and scanned it. "After several confused, even contradictory, accounts of what happened," she said, "described by people on the scene at this armory, or whatever it is, the following is buried in the last paragraph. 'Among the personal effects found on the slain assassin's body was a map of Brussels and the surrounding area with the town of Anderlecht circled in red.' Then it goes on to make the obvious connection with Teagarten's assassination. It's a wash, Johnny, from two points of view. . . . First, David would never carry such a map. Second, and far more telling, the fact that the Soviet media would give such prominence to the story is unbelievable enough, but to include the assassination of General Teagarten is simply too much."

"What do you mean? Why?"

"Because the presumed assassin was *in* Russia, and Moscow wants no conceivable linkage to the killing of a NATO commander. . . . No, Bro, someone bent the rules and persuaded Tass to put out the story, and I suspect heads will roll. I don't know where Jason Bourne is, but I know he's not dead. David made sure I'd know that."

Peter Holland picked up the phone and touched the buttons on his console for Charles Casset's private line.

"Yes?"

"Charlie, it's Peter."

"I'm relieved to hear that."

"Why?"

"Because all I'm getting on this phone is trouble and confusion. I just got off with our source in Dzerzhinsky Square and he told me the KGB's after blood."

"The Tass release on Bourne?"

"Right. Tass and Radio Moscow assumed the story was officially sanctioned because it was faxed by the Ministry of Information using the proper immediate-release codes. When the shit hit the fan, no one owned up, and whoever pro-grammed the codes can't be traced."

"What do you make of it?"

"I'm not sure, but from what I've learned about Dimitri Krupkin, it could be his style. He's now working with Alex and if this isn't something out of the Conklin textbook, I don't know Saint Alex. And I do."

"That dovetails with what Marie thinks."

"Marie?"

"Bourne's wife. I just spoke to her and her argument's pretty strong. She says Moscow's report is a wash for all the right reasons. Her husband's alive."

"I agree. Is that what you called to tell me?"

"No," answered the director, taking a deep breath. "I'm adding to your trouble and confu-sion."

"I'm not relieved to hear that. What is it?"

"The Paris telephone number, the link to the Jackal we got from Henry Sykes in Montserrat that reached a café on the Marais waterfront in Paris."

"Where someone would answer a call for a blackbird. I remember."

"Someone did and we followed him. You're not going to like this."

"Alex Conklin is about to earn the prick-of-the-year award. He put us on to Sykes, didn't he?"

"Yes."

"Do tell."

"The message was delivered to the home of the director of the Deuxieme Bureau."

"My God! We'd better turn that over to the SED branch of French intelligence with a restricted chronology."

"I'm not turning anything over to anybody until we hear from Conklin. We owe him that much—I think."

"What the hell are they *doing*?" shouted a frustrated Casset over the phone. "Putting out false death notices—from *Moscow,* no less! What *for*?"

"Jason Bourne's gone hunting," said Peter Holland. "And when the hunt is over—if it's over and *if* the kill is made—he's going to have to get out of the woods before anyone turns on him. . . . I want every station and listening post on the borders of the Soviet Union on full alert. Code name: Assassin. Get him back."

40

Novgorod. To say it was incredible was to obliquely recognize the existence of credibility and that was nearly impossible. It was the ultimate fantasy, its optical illusions seemingly more real than reality, the phantasmagoria there to be touched, felt, used, entered into and departed from; it was a collective masterpiece of invention cut out of the immense forests along the Volkhov River. From the moment Bourne emerged from the deep underground tunnel below the water with its guards, gates and myriad cameras, he was as close to being in a state of shock while still being able to keep walking, observing, absorbing, thinking.

The American compound, presumably like those of the different countries, was broken up into sections, built on areas anywhere from two to five acres, each distinctly separate from the others. One area, erected on the banks of the river, might be the heart of a Maine waterfront village; another, farther inland, a small Southern town; yet another, a busy metropolitan city street. Each was completely "authentic" with the appropriate vehicular traffic, police, dress codes, shops, grocery and drug stores, gas stations and mock structures of buildings—many of which rose two stories high and were so real they had American hardware on the doors and windows. Obviously, as vital as the physical appearances was language—not merely the fluent use of English but the mastery of linguistic idiosyncrasies, the dialects that were characteristic of specific locations. As Jason wandered from one section to another he heard all around him the distinctive sounds. From New England Down East with its "eeahh" to Texas's drawl and its familiar "you-alls"; from the gentle nasality of the Midwest to the loud abrasiveness of the large Eastern cities with the inevitable "know what I mean?" tacked on to conversational sentences, whether questions or statements. It *was* all incredible. It was not simply beyond belief, it made the true suspension of disbelief frighteningly viable.

He had been briefed on the flight from Vnokova by a late-middle-aged Novgorod graduate who had been urgently summoned from his Moscow apartment by Krupkin. The small, bald man was not only garrulously instructive, but in his own way mesmerizing. If anyone had ever told Jason Bourne that he was going to be briefed in depth by a Soviet espionage agent whose English was so laced with the Deep South that it sonorously floated out of his mouth with the essence of magnolias, he would have deemed the information preposterous.

"Good Lawd, Ah do miss those barbecues, especially the ribs. You know who grilled 'em best? That black fellow who I believed was such a good friend until he exposed me. Can you *imagine*? I thought he was one of those radicals. He turned out to be a boy from Dartmouth workin' for the FBI. A *lawyer,* no less. . . . Hell, the exchange was made at Aeroflot in New York and we still write each other."

"Adolescent games," had mumbled Bourne.

"Games? . . . Oh yes, he was a mighty fine coach."

"Coach?"

"Sure 'nuff. A few of us started a Little League in East Point. That's right outside Atlanta."

Incredible.

"May we concentrate on Novgorod, please?"

"Suttn'ly. Dimitri may have told you, I'm semiretired, but my pension requires that I spend five days a month there as a *tak govorya*—a 'trainer,' as you would say."

"I didn't understand what he meant."

"Ah'll explain." The strange man whose voice belonged to the old Confederacy had been thorough.

Each compound at Novgorod was divided into three classes of personnel: the trainers, the candidates and operations. The last category included the KGB staff, guards and maintenance. The practical implementation of the Novgorod process was simple in structure. A compound's staff created the daily training schedules for each individual section, and the trainers, both permanent and part-time retirees, commandeered all individual and group activities while the candidates carried them out, using only the language of the compound and the dialects of the specific areas in which they were located. No Russian was permitted; the rule was tested frequently by the trainers who would suddenly bark orders or insults in the native language, which the candidates could not acknowledge understanding.

"When you say assignments," Bourne had asked, "what do you mean?"

"Situations, mah friend. Jest about anything you might think of. Like ordering lunch or dinner, or buying clothes, or fillin' the tank of your car, requesting a specific gasoline . . . leaded or unleaded and the degrees of octane—all of which we don't know a thing about here. Then, of course, there are the more dramatic events often *un*scheduled so as to test the candidates' reactions. Say, an automobile accident necessitating conversations with 'American' police and the resulting insurance forms that must be filled out—you can give yourself away if you appear too ignorant."

The little things, the insignificant things—they were vital. A back door at the Kubinka Armory. "What else?"

"So many inconsequential things that a person might not consider significant, but they can be. Say, being mugged in a city street at night— what should you do, what shouldn't you do? Remember, many of our candidates, and all of the younger ones, are trained in self-defense, but depending upon the circumstances, it may not be advisable to use those skills. Questions of background could be raised. Discretion, always discretion. . . . For me, as an experienced part-time *tak govorya,* of course, I've always preferred the more imaginative situations which we are permitted to implement whenever we care to as long as they fall within the guidelines of environmental penetration."

"What does that mean?"

"Learn always, but never appear to be learning. For example, a favorite of mine is to approach several candidates, say, at a bar in some 'location' near a military testing ground. I pretend to be a disgruntled government worker or perhaps an inebriated defense contractor—obviously someone with access to information—and start ladlin' out classified material of recognized value."

"Just for curiosity," Bourne had interrupted, "under those circumstances how should candidates react?"

"Listen carefully and be prepared to write down every salient fact, all the while feigning total lack of interest and offering such remarks as"—here the Novgorod graduate's Southern dialect became so rough-mountain South that the magnolias were replaced by sour mash—" 'Who gives a barrel a' hogshit 'bout that stuff?' and 'They got any of them whoors over there lak people say they got?' or 'Don't understand a fuckin' word you're talkin' about, asshole—all Ah knows is that you're borin' the holy be-Jesus outta me!' . . . that sort of thing."

"Then what?"

"Later, each man is called in and told to list everything he learned—fact by salient fact."

"What about passing along the information? Are there training procedures for that?"

Jason's Soviet instructor had stared at him in silence for several moments from the adjacent seat in the small plane. "I'm sorry you had to ask the question," he said slowly. "I'll have to report it."

"I didn't *have* to ask it, I was simply curious. Forget I asked it."

"I can't do that. I won't do that."

"Do you trust Krupkin?"

"Of course I do. He's brilliant, a multilingual phenomenon. A true hero of the Komitet."

You don't know the half of it, thought Bourne, but he said, with even a trace of reverence, "Then report it only to him. He'll tell you it *was* just curiosity. I owe absolutely nothing to my government; instead, it owes me."

"Very well. . . . Speakin' of yourself, let's get to you. With Dimitri's authority I've made arrangements for your visit to Novgorod—please don't tell me your objective; it's not in my purview any more than the question you asked is in yours."

"Understood. The arrangements?"

"You will make contact with a young trainer named Benjamin in the manner I will describe in a few moments. I'll tell you this much about Benjamin so you'll perhaps understand his attitude. His parents were Komitet officers assigned to the consulate in Los Angeles for nearly twenty years. He's basically American-educated, his freshman and sophomore years at UCLA; in fact, until he and his father were hurriedly recalled to Moscow four years ago—"

"He and his *father*?"

"Yes. His mother was caught in an FBI sting operation at the naval base in San Diego. She has three more years to serve in prison. There is no clemency and no exchanges for a Russian 'momma.'"

"Hey, *wait* a minute. Then it can't be all *our* fault."

"I didn't say it was, Ah'm just relayin' the facts."

"Understood. I make contact with Benjamin."

"He's the only one who knows who you are—not by name, of course, you'll use the name 'Archie'—and he'll furnish you with the necessary clearance to go from one compound to the other."

"Papers?"

"He'll explain. He'll also watch you, be with you at all times, and, frankly, he's been in touch with Comrade Krupkin and knows far more than I do—which is precisely the way this retired Georgia cracker likes it. . . . Good huntin', polecat, if it's huntin' you're after. Don't rape no wooden Indians."

Bourne followed the signs—everything was in English—to the city of *Rockledge, Florida,* fifteen miles southwest of NASA's Cape Canaveral. He was to meet Benjamin at a lunch counter in the local Woolworth store, looking for a man in his mid-twenties wearing a red-checkered shirt, with a Budweiser baseball cap on the stool beside him, saving it. It was the hour, within the time span of minutes: 3:35 in the afternoon.

He saw him. The sandy-haired, California-educated Russian was seated at the far right end of the counter, the baseball cap on the stool to his left. There were half a dozen men and women along the row talking to one another and consuming soft drinks and snacks. Jason approached the empty seat, glanced down at the cap and spoke politely. "Is this taken?" he asked.

"I'm waiting for someone," replied the young KGB trainer, his voice neutral, his gray eyes straying up to Bourne's face.

"I'll find another place."

"She may not get here for another five minutes."

"Hell, I'm just having a quick vanilla Coke. I'll be out of here by then—"

"Sit down," said Benjamin, removing the hat and casually putting it on his head. A gum-chewing counterman came by and Jason ordered; his drink arrived, and the Komitet trainer continued quietly, his eyes now on the foam of his milk shake, which he sipped through a straw. "So you're Archie, like in the comics."

"And you're Benjamin. Nice to know you."

"We'll both find out if that's a fact, won't we?"

"Do we have a problem?"

"I want the ground rules clear so there won't be one," said the West Coast–bred Soviet. "I don't approve of your being permitted in here. Regardless of my former address and the way I may sound, I haven't much use for Americans."

"Listen to me, Ben," interrupted Bourne, his eyes forcing the trainer to look at him. "All things considered, I don't approve of your mother still being in prison, either, but I didn't put her there."

"We free the dissidents and the Jews, but you insist on keeping a fifty-eight-year-old woman who was at best a simple courier!" whispered the Russian, spitting out the words.

"I don't know the facts and I wouldn't be too quick to call Moscow the mercy capital of the world, but if you can help me—*really* help me—maybe I can help your mother."

"Goddamned bullshit promises. What the hell can *you* do?"

"To repeat what I said an hour ago to a bald-headed friend of yours in the plane, I don't owe my government a thing, but it sure as hell owes me. Help me, Benjamin."

"I will because I've been ordered to, not because of your con. But if you try to learn things that have nothing to do with your purpose here—you won't get out. *Clear?*"

"It's not only clear, it's irrelevant and unnecessary. Beyond normal astonishment and curiosity, both of which I will suppress to the best of my ability, I haven't the slightest interest in the objectives of Novgorod. Ultimately, in my opinion, they lead nowhere. . . . Although, I grant you, the whole complex beats the hell out of Disneyland."

Benjamin's involuntary laugh through the straw caused the foam on his milk shake to swell and burst. "Have you been to Anaheim?" he asked mischievously.

"I could never afford it."

"We had diplomatic passes."

"Christ, you're human, after all. Come on, let's take a walk and talk some turkey."

They crossed over a miniature bridge into *New London, Connecticut,* home of America's submarine construction, and strolled down to the Volkhov River, which in this area had been turned into a maximum security naval base—again, all in realistic miniature. High fences and armed "U.S. Marine" guards were stationed at the gates and patrolled the grounds fronting the concrete slips that held enormous mock-ups of the stallions of America's nuclear undersea fleet.

"We have all the stations, all the schedules, every device and every reduced inch of the piers," said Benjamin. "And we've yet to break the security procedures. Isn't that crazy?"

"Not for a minute. We're pretty good."

"Yes, but we're better. Except for minor pockets of discontent, we believe. You merely accept."

"What?"

"Your crap notwithstanding, white America was never in slavery. We were."

"That's not only long-past history, young man, but rather selective history, isn't it?"

"You sound like a professor."

"Suppose I were?"

"I'd argue with you."

"Only if you were in a sufficiently broad-minded environment that allowed you to argue with authority."

"Oh, come on, cut the bullshit, man! The academic-freedom bromide *is* history. Check out our campuses. We've got rock and blue jeans and more grass than you can find the right paper to roll it in."

"That's progress?"

"Would you believe it's a start?"

"I'll have to think about it."

"Can you really help my mother?"

"Can you really help me?"

"Let's try. . . . Okay, this Carlos the Jackal. I've heard of him but he's not large in my vocabulary. *Direktor* Krupkin says he's one very bad dude."

"I hear California checking in."

"It comes back. Forget it. I'm where I want to be and don't for a moment think otherwise."

"I wouldn't dare."

"What?"

"You keep protesting—"

"Shakespeare said it better. My minor at UCLA was English lit."

"What was your major?"

"American history. What else, Grandpa?"

"Thanks, kid."

"This Jackal," said Benjamin, leaning against the New London fence as several guards began to run toward him. *"Prosteetye!"* he yelled. "No, *no*! I mean, excuse me. *Tak govorya!* I'm a trainer! . . . Oh, *shit*!"

"Will you be reported?" asked Jason as they quickly walked away.

"No, they're too damned dumb. They're maintenance personnel in uniforms; they walk their posts but they don't really know what's going on. Only who and what to stop."

"Pavlov's dogs?"

"Who better? Animals don't rationalize; they go for the throats and plug up the holes."

"Which brings us back to the Jackal," said Bourne.

"I don't understand."

"You don't have to, it's symbolic. How could he get in here?"

"He couldn't. Every guard in every tunnel up the line has the name and serial numbers of the Novgorod papers he took from the agent he killed in Moscow. If he shows up, they'll stop him and shoot him on sight."

"I told Krupkin not to do that."

"For Christ's sake, why?"

"Because it won't *be* him and lives could be lost. He'll send in others, maybe two or three or four into different compounds, always testing, confusing, until he finds a way to get through."

"You're nuts. What happens to the men he sends in?"

"It wouldn't matter. If they're shot, he watches and learns something."

"You're really crazy. Where would he find people like that?"

"Anyplace where there are people who think they're making a month's salary for a few minutes' work. He could call each one a routine security check—remember, he's got the papers to prove he's official. Combined with money, people are impressed with such documents and aren't too skeptical."

"And at the first gate he loses those papers," insisted the trainer.

"Not at all. He's driving over five hundred miles through a dozen towns and cities. He could easily have copies made in any number of places. Your business centers have Xerox machines; they're all over the place, and touching up those papers to look like the real items is no sweat." Bourne stopped and looked at the Americanized Soviet. "You're talking details, Ben, and take my word for it, they don't count. Carlos is coming here to leave his mark, and we have one advantage that blows away all his expertise. If Krupkin was able to get the news out properly, the Jackal thinks I'm dead."

"The whole *world* thinks you're dead. . . . Yes, Krupkin told me; it would've been dumb not to. In here, you're a recruit named 'Archie,' but I know who you are, Bourne. Even if I'd never heard of you before, I sure as hell have now. You're all Radio Moscow's been talking about for hours."

"Then we can assume Carlos has heard the news, too."

"No question. Every vehicle in Russia is equipped with a radio; it's standard. In case of an American attack, incidentally."

"That's good marketing."

"Did you really assassinate Teagarten in Brussels?"

"Get off my case—"

"Off-limits, okay. What's your point?"

"Krupkin should have left it to me."

"Left what?"

"The Jackal's penetration."

"What the hell are you talking about?"

"Use Krupkin, if necessary, but send the word up to every tunnel, every entrance to Novgorod, to let in anyone using those papers. My guess is three or four, maybe five. They're to watch them, but they're to let everyone come inside."

"You just got awarded a room made of thick sponge rubber. You're certifiable, Archie."

"No, I'm not. I said that everyone should be watched, followed, that the guards maintain

constant contact with us here in this compound."

"So?"

"One of those men will disappear in a matter
of minutes. No one will know where he is or
where he went. That man will be Carlos."

"And?"

"He'll convince himself he's invulnerable, free
to do whatever he wants to do, because he
thinks I'm dead. That sets him free."

"Why?"

"Because he knows and I know that we're the
only ones who can track each other, whether it's
in the jungles or the cities or a combination of
both. Hatred does that, Benjamin. Or desperation."

"That's pretty emotional, isn't it? Also abstract."

"No way," answered Jason. "I have to think
like he thinks—I was trained to do that years
ago. . . . Let's examine the alternatives. How far
up the Volkhov does Novgorod extend? Thirty,
forty kilometers?"

"Forty-seven, to be exact, and every meter is
impenetrable. There are magnesium pipes
crisscrossing the water, spaced above and
below the surface to permit the free flow of un-

derwater life but capable of setting off alarms. On the east bank are interlocking ground grids, all weight-sensing. Anything over ninety pounds instantly sets off sirens, and television monitors and spotlights zero in on any intruder over that weight. And even if an eighty-nine-pound wonder reached the fence, he'd be electrically rendered unconscious on the first touch; that also goes for the magnesium pipes in the river. Of course, falling trees or floating logs and the heavier animals keep our security forces on the run. It's good discipline, I suppose."

"Then there are only the tunnels," said Bourne, "is that right?"

"You came through one, what can I tell you that you didn't see? Except that iron gates literally crash down at the slightest irregularity, and in emergencies all the tunnels can be flooded."

"All of which Carlos knows. He was trained here."

"Many years ago, Krupkin told me."

"Many years," agreed Jason. "I wonder how much things have changed."

"Technologically you could probably fill a few volumes, especially in communications and security, but not the basics. Not the tunnels or the miles of grids in and out of the water; they're built for a couple of centuries. As far as the compounds go, there're always some minor adjustments, but I don't think they'd tear up the streets or the buildings. It'd be easier to move a dozen cities."

"So whatever the changes, they're essentially internal." They reached a miniature intersection where an argumentative driver of an early-seventies Chevrolet was being given a ticket for a traffic violation by an equally disagreeable policeman. "What's that all about?" asked Bourne.

"The purpose of the assignment is to instill a degree of contentiousness on the part of the one driving the car. In America a person will frequently, often loudly, argue with a police officer. It's not the case here."

"Like in questioning authority, such as a student contradicting his professor? I don't imagine that's too popular, either."

"That's also entirely different."

"I'm glad you think so." Jason heard a distant hum and looked up at the sky. A light, single-engine seaplane was flying south following the Volkhov River. "My God, airborne," he said, as if to himself.

"Forget it," countered Benjamin. "It's ours.

. . . Technology again. One, there's no place to land except patrolled helicopter pads; and two, we're shielded by radar. An unidentified plane coming within thirty miles of here, the air base at Belopol is alerted and it's shot down." Across the street a small crowd had gathered, watching the disagreeable policeman and the argumentative driver, who had slammed his hand down on the roof of the Chevrolet as the crowd vocally encouraged him. "Americans can be very foolish," mumbled the young trainer, his embarrassment showing.

"At least someone's idea of Americans can be," said Bourne, smiling.

"Let's go," said Benjamin, starting to walk away. "I personally pointed out that the assignment wasn't very realistic, but it was explained to me that instilling the attitude was important."

"Like telling a student that he can actually argue with a professor, or a citizen that he can publicly criticize a member of the Politburo? They *are* strange attitudes, aren't they?"

"Pound sand, Archie."

"Relax, young Lenin," said Jason, coming alongside the trainer. "Where's your LA cool?"

"I left it in the La Brea Tar Pits."

"I want to study the maps. All of them."

"It's been arranged. Also the other ground rules."

They sat in a conference room at staff head-quarters, the large rectangular table covered with maps of the entire Novgorod complex. Bourne could not help himself; even after nearly four hours of concentration, he frequently shook his head in sheer astonishment. The series of deep-cover training grounds along the Volkhov were more expansive and more intricate than he had thought possible. Benjamin's remark that it would "be easier to move a dozen cities" rather than drastically alter Novgorod was a simple statement of fact, not too much of an exaggeration. Scaled-down replicas of towns and cities, waterfronts and airports, military and scientific installations from the Mediterranean to the At-lantic, north to the Baltic and up the Gulf of Bothnia, were represented within its boundaries, all in addition to the American acreage. Yet for all the massive detail, suggestion and miniaturi-zation made it possible to place everything within barely thirty miles of riverfront wilderness, at a depth ranging from three to five miles.

"Egypt, Israel, Italy," began Jason, circling

the table, staring down at the maps. "Greece, Portugal, Spain, France, the UK—" He rounded the corner as Benjamin interrupted, leaning wearily back in a chair: "Germany, the Netherlands, and the Scandinavian countries. As I explained, most of the compounds include two separate and distinct countries, usually where there are common boundaries, cultural similarities or just to conserve space. There are basically nine major compounds, representing all the major nations—major to our interests—and therefore nine tunnels, approximately seven kilometers apart starting with the one here and heading north along the river."

"Then the first tunnel next to ours is the UK, right?"

"Yes, followed by France, then Spain—which includes Portugal—then across the Mediterranean, beginning with Egypt along with Israel—"

"It's clear," broke in Jason, sitting down at the end of the table, bringing his clasped hands together in thought. "Did you get word up the line that they're to admit anyone with those papers Carlos has, no matter what he looks like?"

"No."

"*What?*" Bourne snapped his head toward the young trainer.

"I had Comrade Krupkin do that. He's in a Moscow hospital, so they can't lock him up here for training fatigue."

"How can I cross over into another compound? Quickly, if necessary."

"Then you're ready for the rest of the ground rules?"

"I'm ready. There's only so much these maps can tell me."

"Okay." Benjamin reached into his pocket and withdrew a small black object the size of a credit card but somewhat thicker. He tossed it to Jason, who caught it in midair and studied it. "That's your passport," continued the Soviet. "Only the senior staff has them and if one's lost or misplaced for even a few minutes, it's reported immediately."

"There's no ID, no writing or marking at all."

"It's all inside, computerized and coded. Each compound checkpoint has a clearing lock. You insert it and the barriers are raised, admitting you and telling the guards that you're cleared from headquarters—and noted."

"Damned clever, these backward Marxists."

"They had the same little dears for just about every hotel room in Los Angeles, and that was four years ago. . . . Now for the rest."

"The ground rules?"

"Krupkin calls them protective measures—for us as well as you. Frankly, he doesn't think you'll get out of here alive; and if you don't, you're to be deep-fried and lost."

"How nicely realistic."

"He likes you, Bourne . . . Archie."

"Go on."

"As far as the senior staff is concerned, you're undercover personnel from the inspector general's office in Moscow, an American specialist sent in to check on Novgorod leaks to the West. You're to be given whatever you need, including weapons, but no one is to talk to you unless you talk to him first. Considering my own background, I'm your liaison; anything you want you relay through me."

"I'm grateful."

"Maybe not entirely," said Benjamin. "You don't go anywhere without me."

"That's unacceptable."

"That's the way it is."

"No, it's not."

"Why not?"

"Because I won't be impeded . . . and if I do get out of here, I'd like a certain Benjamin's mother to find him alive and well and commuting to Moscow."

The young Russian stared at Bourne, strength mingled with no little pain in his eyes. "You really think you can help my father and me?"

"I *know* I can . . . so help *me.* Play by my rules, Benjamin."

"You're a strange man."

"I'm a hungry man. Can we get some food around here? And maybe a little bandage? I got hit a while back, and after today my neck and shoulders are letting me know it." Jason removed his jacket; his shirt was drenched in blood.

"Jesus *Christ*! I'll call a doctor—"

"No, you won't. Just a medic, that's all. . . . My rules, Ben."

"Okay—Archie. We're staying at the Visiting Commissars Suite; it's on the top floor. We've got room service and I'll ring the infirmary for a nurse."

"I said I'm hungry and uncomfortable, but they're not my major concerns."

"Not to worry," said the Soviet Californian. "The instant anything unusual happens any- where, we'll be reached. I'll roll up the maps."

It happened at precisely 12:02 A.M. directly after the universal changing of the guard, during the darkest darkness of the night. The telephone in the Commissars Suite screamed, propelling Benjamin off the couch. He raced across the room to the jangling, insistent instrument and yanked it off its cradle. "Yes? . . . *Gdye? Kogda? Shto eto znachit? . . . Da!*" He slammed the phone down and turned to Bourne at the dinner table, the maps of Novgorod having replaced the room-service dishes. "It's *unbelievable.* At the Spanish tunnel—across the river two guards are dead, and on this side the officer of the watch was found fifty yards away from his post, a bullet in his throat. They ran the video tapes and all they saw was an unidentified man walking through carrying a *duffel* bag! In a guard's *uniform*!"

"There was something else, wasn't there?" asked Delta coldly.

"Yes, and you may be right. On the other side was a dead farmhand clutching torn papers in his hand. He was lying between the two murdered guards, one of them stripped to his shorts and shoes. . . . How did he *do* it?"

"He was the good guy, I can't think of anything else," mused Bourne, rising quickly, and
reaching, pouncing on the map of the Spanish
compound. "He must have sent in his paid impostor with the rotten mocked-up papers, then
ran in himself, the wounded Komitet officer at
the last moment exposing the fraud and speaking the foreign language which his impostor
couldn't do and couldn't understand. . . . I told
you, Ben. Probe, test, agitate, confuse and find
a way in. Stealing a uniform is standard, and in
the confusion it got him through the tunnel."

"But anyone using those papers was to be
watched, followed. They were your instructions
and Krupkin sent the word up the line!"

"The Kubinka," said Jason, now pensive as
he studied the map.

"The armory? The one mentioned in the news
bulletins from Moscow?"

"Exactly. Just as he had done at the Kubinka,
Carlos has someone inside here. Someone with
enough authority to order an expendable officer
of the guard to bring anyone penetrating the
tunnel to him before sending out alarms and
raising headquarters."

"That's possible," agreed the young trainer
rapidly, firmly. "Involving headquarters with

false alarms can be embarrassing, and as you say, there must have been a lot of confusion."

"In Paris," said Bourne, glancing up from the compound map. "I was told that embarrassment was the KGB's worst enemy. True?"

"On a scale of one to ten, at least eight," replied Benjamin. "But who would he have in here, who *could* he have? He hasn't been here in over thirty years!"

"If we had a couple of hours and a few computers programmed with the records of everyone in Novgorod, we might be able to feed in several hundred names and come up with possibilities, but we don't have hours. We don't even have minutes! Also, if I know the Jackal, it won't matter."

"I think it matters one whole hell of a lot!" cried the Americanized Soviet. "There's a traitor here and we should know who it is."

"My guess is that you'll find out soon enough. . . . *Details,* Ben. The point is, he's *here*! Let's go, and when we get outside we stop somewhere and you get me what I need."

"Okay."

"Everything I need."

"I'm cleared for that."

"And then you disappear. I know what I'm talking about."

"No way, José!"

"California checking in again?"

"You heard me."

"Then young Benjamin's mother may find a corpse for a son when she gets back to Moscow."

"So be it!"

"So *be* . . . ? Why did you have to say that?"

"I don't know. It just seemed right."

"Shut up! Let's get out of here."

41

Ilich Ramirez Sanchez snapped his fingers twice in the shadows as he climbed the short steps of the miniaturized entrance to a small church in "Madrid's" Paseo del Prado, the duffel bag in his left hand. From behind a fluted mock pillar a figure emerged, a heavyset man in his early sixties who walked partially into the dim light of a distant streetlamp. He was dressed in the uniform of a Spanish army officer, a lieutenant general with three rows of ribbons affixed to his tunic. He was carrying a leather suitcase; he raised it slightly and spoke in the compound's language.

"Come inside, to the vestry. You can change

there. That ill-fitting guard's jacket is an invitation for sharpshooters."

"It's good to speak our language again," said Carlos, following the man inside the tiny church and turning stiffly to close the heavy door. "I'm in your debt, Enrique," he added, glancing around at the empty rows of pews and the soft lights playing upon the altar, the gold crucifix gleaming.

"You've been in my debt for over thirty years, Ramirez, and a lot of good it does me," laughed the soldier quietly as they proceeded across to the right aisle and down toward the sacristy.

"Then perhaps you're out of touch with what remains of your family in Baracoa. Fidel's own brothers and sisters don't live half so well."

"Neither does crazy Fidel, but he doesn't care. They say he bathes more frequently now and I suppose that's progress. However, you're talking about my family in Baracoa; what about *me,* my fine international assassin? No yachts, no racing colors, shame on you! Were it not for my warning you, you would have been executed in this very compound thirty-three years ago. Come to think of it, it was right outside this idiotic dollhouse church on the Prado that you made your escape—dressed as a priest, a figure that perpetually bewilders the Russian, like most everyone else."

"Once I was established, did you ever lack for anything?" They entered a small paneled room where supposed prelates prepared the sacraments. "Did I ever refuse you?" Carlos added, placing the heavy duffel bag on the floor.

"I'm joking with you, of course," objected Enrique, smiling good-naturedly and looking at the Jackal. "Where is that lusty humor of yours, my infamous old friend?"

"I have other things on my mind."

"I'm sure you do, and, in truth, you were never less than generous where my family in Cuba was concerned, and I thank you. My father and mother lived out their lives in peace and comfort, bewildered naturally, but so much better off than anyone they knew. . . . It was all so insane. Revolutionaries thrown out by their own revolution's leaders."

"You were threats to Castro, as was Che. It's past."

"A great deal has passed," agreed Enrique, studying Carlos. "You've aged poorly, Ramirez. Where's that once full head of dark hair and the handsome strong face with the clear eyes?"

"We won't talk about it."

"Very well. I grow fat, you grow thin; that tells me something. How badly are you wounded?"

"I can function well enough for what I intend to do—what I must do."

"Ramirez, what else *is* there?" asked the costumed soldier suddenly. "He's *dead*! Moscow takes credit over the radio for his death, but when you reached me I knew the credit was yours, the kill yours. Jason Bourne is dead! Your enemy is gone from this world. You're not well; go back to Paris and heal yourself. I'll get you out the same way I got you in. We'll head into 'France' and I'll clear the way. You will be a courier from the commandant of 'Spain' and 'Portugal' who's sending a confidential message to Dzerzhinsky Square. It's done all the time; no one trusts anyone here, especially his own gates. You won't even have to take the risk of killing a single guard."

"No! A lesson must be *taught.*"

"Then let me phrase it another way. When you called with your emergency codes, I did what you demanded, for by and large you have fulfilled your obligations to me, obligations that go back thirty-three years. But now there is another risk involved—*risks,* to be precise—and I'm not sure I care to take them."

"You speak this way to *me*?" cried the Jackal, removing the dead guard's jacket, his clean white bandages taut, holding his right shoulder firm with no evidence of blood.

"Stop your theatrics," said Enrique softly. "We go back long before that. I'm speaking to a young revolutionary I followed out of Cuba with a great athlete named Santos. . . . How is he, by the way? He was the real threat to Fidel."

"He's well," answered Carlos, his voice flat. "We're moving Le Coeur du Soldat."

"Does he still tend to his gardens—his English gardens?"

"Yes, he does."

"He should have been a landscaper, or a florist, I think. And I should have been a fine agricultural engineer, an agronomist, as they say—that's how Santos and I met, you know. . . . Melodramatic politics changed our lives, didn't they?"

"Political *commitments* changed them. Everywhere the fascists changed them."

"And now we want to be like the fascists, and they want to take what's not so terrible about us Communists and spread a little money around—which doesn't really work, but it's a nice thought."

"What has this to do with me—your monseigneur?"

"Horse droppings, Ramirez. As you may or
may not know, my Russian wife died a number
of years ago and I have three children in the
Moscow University. Without my position they
would not be there and I want them there. They
will be scientists, doctors. . . . You see, those are
the risks you ask of me. I've covered myself up
until this moment—and you deserve this moment—but perhaps no more. In a few months I
will retire, and in recognition of my years of service in southern Europe and the Mediterranean,
I will share a fine dacha on the Black Sea where
my children will come and visit me. I will not
unduly risk what life I have before me. So be
specific, Ramirez, and I'll tell you whether you're
on your own or not. . . . I repeat, your getting in
here cannot be traced to me, and, as I say, you
deserved that much, but this is where I may be
forced to stop."

"I see," said Carlos, approaching the suitcase
Enrique had placed on the sacristy table.

"I hope you do and, further, I hope you understand. Over the years you've been good to my
family in ways that I could never be, but then I've
served you well in ways that I could. I led you to

Rodchenko, fed you names in ministries where rumors abounded, rumors Rodchenko himself investigated for you. So, my old revolutionary comrade, I've not been idle on your behalf either. However, things are different now; we're not young firebrands in search of a cause any longer, for we've lost our appetites for causes— you long before me, of course."

"My cause remains constant," interrupted the Jackal sharply. "It is myself and all those who serve me."

"*I've* served you—"

"You've made that clear, as well as my generosity to you and yours. And now that I'm here, you wonder if I deserve further assistance, that's it, isn't it?"

"I must protect myself. Why *are* you here?"

"I told you. To teach a lesson, to leave a message."

"They are one and the same?"

"Yes." Carlos opened the suitcase; it held a coarse shirt, a Portuguese fisherman's cap with the appropriate rope-belted trousers, and a seaman's shoulder-strapped canvas satchel. "Why these?" asked the Jackal.

"They're loose-fitting and I haven't seen you in years—not since Málaga in the early seventies, I think. I couldn't very well have clothes tailored for you, and I'm glad I didn't try—you are not as I remembered you, Ramirez."

"You're not much larger than I remember you," countered the assassin. "A little thicker around the stomach, perhaps, but we're still the same height, the same basic frame."

"So? What does that mean?"

"In a moment. . . . Have things changed a great deal since we were together here?"

"Constantly. Photographs arrive and construction crews follow a day later. The Prado here in 'Madrid' has new shops, new signs, even a few new sewers as they are changed in that city. Also 'Lisbon' and the piers along the 'Bay' and 'Tagus River' have been altered to conform to the changes that have taken place. We are nothing if not authentic. The candidates who complete the training are literally at home wherever they're initially sent. Sometimes I really believe it's all excessive, then I recall my first assignment at the naval base in Barcelona and realize how comfortable I was. I went right to work because the psychological orientation had already taken place; there were no major surprises."

"You're describing appearances," broke in Carlos.

"Of course, what else is there?"

"More permanent structures that are not so apparent, not so much in evidence."

"Such as?"

"Warehouses, fuel depots, fire stations, that are not part of the duplicated scenery. Are they still where they were?"

"By and large, yes. Certainly the major warehouses and the fuel depots with their underground tanks. Most are still west of the 'San Roque' district, the 'Gibraltar' access."

"What about going from one compound to another?"

"Now that *has* changed." Enrique withdrew a small flat object from the pocket of his tunic. "Each border crossing has a computerized registration release that permits entry when this is inserted."

"No questions are asked?"

"Only at Novgorod's Capital Headquarters, if there are any questions."

"I don't understand."

"If one of these is lost or stolen, it's reported instantly and the internal codes are nullified."

"I see."

"*I* don't! Why these questions? Again, why are you *here*? What is this lesson, this message?"

"The 'San Roque' district . . . ?" said Carlos,

as if remembering. "That's about three or four kilometers south of the tunnel, isn't it? A small waterfront village, no?"

"The 'Gibraltar' access, yes."

"And the next compound is 'France,' of course, and then 'England' and finally the largest, the 'United States.' Yes, it's all clear to me; everything's come back." The Jackal turned away, his right hand awkwardly disappearing beneath his trousers.

"Yet nothing is clear to *me,*" said Enrique, his low voice threatening. "And it must be. Answer me, Ramirez. Why are you here?"

"How dare you question me like this?" continued Carlos, his back to his old associate. "How dare *any* of you question the monseigneur from Paris."

"You listen to me, Priest Piss Ant. You answer me or I walk out of here and you're a dead monseigneur in a matter of minutes!"

"Very well, Enrique," answered Ilich Ramirez Sanchez, addressing the paneled wall of the sacristy. "My message will be triumphantly clear and will shake the very foundations of the Kremlin. Not only did Carlos the Jackal kill the weak pretender Jason Bourne on Soviet soil, he left a reminder to all Russia that the Komitet made a colossal error in not utilizing my extraordinary talents."

"Really now," said Enrique, laughing softly, as if humoring a far less than extraordinary man. "More melodramatics, Ramirez? And how will you convey this reminder, this *message,* this supreme statement of yours?"

"Quite simply," replied the Jackal, turning, a gun in his hand, the silencer intact. "We have to change places."

"What?"

"I'm going to burn Novgorod." Carlos fired a single shot into the upper throat of Enrique. He wanted as little blood as possible on the tunic.

Dressed in combat fatigues with the insignias of an army major on the shoulders of his field jacket, Bourne blended in with the sporadic appearances of military personnel as they crisscrossed the American compound from one sector to another on their night patrols. There were not many, perhaps thirty men, covering the entire acreage of the eight square miles, according to Benjamin. In the "metropolitan" areas they were generally on foot, in pairs; in the "rural" districts they drove military vehicles. The young trainer had requisitioned a jeep.

From the Commissars Suite at U.S. headquarters they had been taken to a military warehouse west of the river where Benjamin's papers gained them entrance and the jeep. Inside, the astonished interior guards watched as the silent Bourne was outfitted with a field uniform complete with a carbine bayonet, a standard .45 automatic and five clips of live ammunition, this last obtained only after an authorization call was placed to Krupkin's unknowing subordinates at Capital HQ. Once again outside, Jason complained: "What about the flares I wanted and at least three or four grenades? You agreed to get me everything I needed, not half of it!"

"They're coming," answered Benjamin, speeding out of the warehouse parking lot. "The flares are over at Motor Vehicles and grenades aren't part of normal ordnance. They're in steel vaults down at the tunnel—all the tunnels—under Emergency Weapons." The young trainer glanced at Bourne, a glimmering of humor seen on his face in the glow of the headlights washing over the roofless jeep. "In anticipation of a NATO assault, most likely."

"That's stupid. We'd come in from the sky."

"Not with the air base ninety seconds' flying time away."

"Hurry up, I want those grenades. Will we have any trouble getting them?"

"Not if Krupkin keeps up the good work." Krupkin had; with the flares in hand, the tunnel was their last supply stop. Four Russian army grenades were counted out and countersigned by Benjamin. "Where to?" he asked as the soldier in an American uniform returned to the concrete guardhouse.

"These aren't exactly U.S. general issue," said Jason, putting the grenades carefully, one by one, into the pockets of his field jacket.

"They're not for training, either. The compounds aren't military-oriented but basically civilian. If those are ever used, it's not for indoctrination purposes. . . . Where do we go now?"

"Check with headquarters first. See if anything's happened at any of the border checkpoints."

"My beeper would have gone off—"

"I don't trust beepers, I like words," interrupted Jason. "Get on the radio."

Benjamin did so, switching to the Russian language and using the codes that only senior staff were assigned. The terse Soviet reply came over the speaker; the young trainer replaced the microphone and turned to Bourne. "No activity at all," he said. "Just some intercompound fuel deliveries."

"What are they?"

"Petrol distribution mainly. Some compounds have larger tanks than others, so logistics call for routine apportionments until the main supplies are shipped downriver."

"They distribute at night?"

"It's far better than those trucks clogging up the streets during the day. Remember, everything's scaled down here. Also, we've been driving through the back roads, but there's a maintenance army in the central locations cleaning up stores and offices and restaurants, getting ready for tomorrow's assignments. Large trucks wouldn't help."

"Christ, it *is* Disneyland. . . . All right, head for the 'Spanish' border, Pedro."

"To get there we have to pass through 'England' and 'France.' I don't suppose it matters much, but I don't speak French. Or Spanish. Do you?"

"French fluently, Spanish acceptably. Anything else?"

"Maybe you'd better drive."

The Jackal braked the huge fuel truck at the "West German" border; it was as far as he intended to go. The remaining northernmost areas of "Scandinavia" and "the Netherlands" were the lesser satellites; the impact of their destruction was not comparable to that of the lower compounds and the time element spared them. Everything was timing now, and "West Germany" would initiate the wholesale conflagrations. He adjusted the coarse Portuguese shirt that covered a Spanish general's tunic beneath, and as the guard came out of the gatehouse Carlos spoke in Russian, using the same words he had used at every other crossing.

"Don't ask me to speak the stupid language you talk here. I deliver petrol, I don't spend time in classrooms! Here's my key."

"I barely speak it myself, comrade," said the guard, laughing as he accepted the small, flat, cardlike object and inserted it into the computerized machine. The heavy iron barrier arced up into the vertical position; the guard returned the key and the Jackal sped through into a miniaturized "West Berlin."

He raced through the narrow replica of the

Kurfürstendamm to the Budapesterstrasse, where he slowed down and pulled out the petcock release. The fuel flowed into the street. He then reached into the open duffel bag on the seat beside him, ripped out the small pretimed plastique explosives and, as he had done throughout the southern compounds to the border of "France," hurled them through the lowered windows on both sides of the truck into the foundations of the wooden buildings he thought most flammable. He sped into the "Munich" sector, then to the port of "Bremerhaven" on the river, and finally into "Bonn" and the scaleddown versions of the embassies in "Bad Godesberg," flooding the streets, distributing the explosives. He looked at his watch; it was time to head back. He had barely fifteen minutes before the first detonations took place in all of "West Germany," followed by the explosions in the combined compounds of "Italy-Greece," "Israel-Egypt" and "Spain-Portugal," each spaced eight minutes apart, timed to create maximum chaos.

There was no way the individual fire brigades could contain the flaming streets and buildings in the disparate sectors of their compounds north of "France." Others would be ordered in from adjacent compounds only to be recalled when the fires erupted on their own grounds. It was a simple formula for cosmic confusion, the cosmos being the false universe of Novgorod. The border gates would be flagged open, frantic traffic unimpeded, and to complete the devastation, the genius that was Ilich Ramirez Sanchez—brought into the world of terror as Carlos the Jackal by the errors of that same Novgorod—had to be in "Paris." Not *his* Paris, but the hated Novgorod's "Paris," and he would burn it to the ground in ways the maniacs of the Third Reich never dreamed of. Then would come "England," and finally, ultimately, the largest compound in the despised, isolated, illusionist Novgorod, where he would leave his triumphant message—the "United States of America," breeder of the apostate assassin Jason Bourne. The statement would be as pure and as clear as Alpine water washing over the blood of a destroyed false universe.

I alone have done this. My enemies are dead and I live.

Carlos checked his duffel bag; what remained were the most lethal instruments of death found in the arsenal of Kubinka. Four layered rows of short-packaged, heat-seeking missiles, twenty in all, each capable of blowing up the entire base of the Washington Monument; and once fused and unshielded, each would seek the sources of fire and do its work. Satisfied, the Jackal shut off the fuel release, turned around and sped back to the border gate.

The sleepy technician at Capital Headquarters blinked his eyes and stared at the green letters on the screen in front of him. What he read did not really make sense, but the clearances went unchallenged. For the fifth time the "commandant" of the "Spanish" compound had crossed and recrossed the north borders up into "Germany" and was now heading back into "France." Twice before, when the codes were transmitted and in accord with the maximum alert that was in force, the technician had phoned the gates of "Israel" and "Italy" and was told that only a fuel truck had passed through. That was the information he had given to a code-cleared trainer named Benjamin, but now he wondered. Why would such a high-ranking official be driving a fuel truck? . . . On the other hand, why not? Novgorod was rife with corruption, everyone suspected that, so perhaps the "commandant" was either seeking out the corrupters or collecting his fees at night. Regardless, since there was no report of a lost or stolen card, and the computers raised no objections, it was better to leave well enough alone. One never knew who his next superior might be.

"Voici ma carte," said Bourne to the guard at the border crossing as he handed the man his computerized card. *"Vite, s'il vous plaît!"*

"Da . . . oui," replied the guard, walking rapidly to the clearance machine as an enormous fuel truck, heading the other way, passed through into "England."

"Don't press the French too much," said Benjamin, in the front seat beside Jason. "These cats do their best, but they're not linguists."

"Cal-if-fornia . . . here I come," sang Bourne softly. "You sure you and your father don't want to join your mother in LA?"

"Shut up!"

The guard returned, saluted, and the iron barrier was raised. Jason accelerated, and saw in a matter of moments, bathed in floodlights, a three-story replica of the Eiffel Tower. In the distance, to the right, was a miniature Champs-Elysées with a wooden reproduction of the Arc de Triomphe, high enough to be unmistakable. Absently, Bourne's mind wandered back to those fitful, terrible hours when he and Marie had raced all over Paris trying desperately to find each other. . . . Marie, oh God, *Marie! I want to come back. I want to be David again. He and I—we're so much older now. He doesn't frighten me any longer and I don't anger him. . . . Who? Which of us? Oh, Christ!*

"Hold it," said Benjamin, touching Jason's arm. "Slow down."

"What is it?"

"Stop," cried the young trainer. "Pull over and shut off the engine."

"What's the matter with you?"

"I'm not sure." Benjamin's neck was arched back, his eyes on the clear night sky and the shimmering lights of the stars. "No clouds," he said cryptically. "No storms."

"It's not raining, either. So what? I want to get up to the Spanish compound!"

"There it goes again—"

"What the *hell* are you talking about?" And then Bourne heard it . . . far away, the sound of distant thunder, yet the night *was* clear. It happened again—and again and again, one deep rumble after another.

"There!" shouted the young Soviet from Los Angeles, standing up in the jeep and pointing to the north. "What *is* it?"

"That's fire, young man," answered Jason softly, hesitantly, as he also stood up and stared at the pulsating yellow glow that lit up the distant sky. "And my guess is that it's the Spanish compound. He was initially trained there and that's what he came back to do—to blow the place *up!* It's his revenge! . . . Get *down,* we've got to get up there!"

"No, you're wrong," broke in Benjamin, quickly lowering himself into the seat as Bourne started the engine and yanked the jeep into gear. " 'Spain's' no more than five or six miles from here. Those fires are a lot farther away."

"Just show me the fastest route," said Jason, pressing the accelerator to the floor.

Under the trainer's swiftly roving eyes accompanied by sudden shouts of "Turn here!" and "Go right!" and "Straight down this road!" they raced through "Paris," and north into successive sectors labeled "Marseilles," "Montbéliard," "Le Havre," "Strasbourg" and so many others, circling town squares and passing quaint streets and miniaturized city blocks, until finally they were in sight of the "Spanish" border. The closer they came, the louder were the booms in the distance, the brighter the yellow night sky. The guards at the gate were furiously manning their telephones and hand-held radios; the two-note blasts of sirens joined the shouting and the screaming as police cars and fire engines appeared seemingly out of nowhere, racing into the streets of "Madrid" on their way to the next northern border crossing.

"What's *happening*?" yelled Benjamin, leaping from the jeep and dropping all pretense of Novgorod training by speaking Russian. "I'm senior staff!" he added, slipping the card into the release equipment, snapping the barrier up. "*Tell* me!"

"*Insanity,* comrade!" shouted an officer from the gatehouse window. "Unbelievable! . . . It's as if the earth went crazy! First 'Germany,' all over there are explosions and fires in the streets and buildings going up in flames. The ground trembles, and we are told it's some kind of massive earthquake. Then it happens in 'Italy'—'Rome' is torched, and in the 'Greek' sector 'Athens' and the port of 'Piraeus' are filled with fires everywhere and still the explosions continue, the streets in flames!"

"What does Capital Headquarters say?"

"They don't know *what* to say! The earthquake nonsense was just that—*nonsense.* Everyone's in panic, issuing orders and then
countermanding them." Another wall phone
rang inside the gatehouse; the officer of the
guard picked it up and listened, then instantly
screamed at the top of his lungs. "Madness, it's
complete *madness*! Are you *certain*?"

"What is it?" roared Benjamin, rushing to the
window.

" 'Egypt!' " he screamed, his ear pressed to
the telephone. *" 'Israel!'* . . . 'Cairo' and 'Tel
Aviv'—fires *everywhere,* bombs everywhere! No
one can keep up with the devastation; the trucks
crash into one another in the narrow streets.
The hydrants are blown up; water flows in the
gutters but the streets are still in flames. . . . And
some idiot just got on the line and asked if the
No Smoking signs were properly placed while
the wooden buildings are on their way to becoming rubble! Idiots. They are all *idiots*!"

"Get back here!" yelled Bourne, having made
the jeep lurch through the gate. "He's *in* here
somewhere! You drive and I'll—" Jason's words
were cut off by a deafening explosion up ahead
in the center of "Madrid's" Paseo del Prado. It
was an enormous detonation, lumber and stone

arcing up into the flaming sky. Then, as if the Paseo itself were a living, throbbing immense wall of fire, the flames rolled forward, swinging to the left out of the "city" into the road that was the approach to the border gate. *"Look!"* shouted Bourne, reaching down out of the jeep, his hand scraping the graveled surface beneath; he brought his fingers to his face, his nostrils. *"Christ,"* he roared. "The whole goddamned road's soaked with *gasoline*!" A burst of fire imploded thirty yards in front of the jeep, sending stones and dirt smashing into the metal grille, and propelling the flames forward with increasing speed. *"Plastics!"* said Jason to himself, then yelled at Benjamin, who was running to the jeep, "Go back there! Get everyone out of here! The son of a bitch has the place ringed with plastics! Head for the river!"

"I'm going with *you*!" shouted the young Soviet, grabbing the edge of the door.

"Sorry, Junior," cried Bourne, gunning the engine and swerving the army vehicle back into the open gate, sending Benjamin sprawling onto the gravel. "This is for grown-ups."

"What are you *doing*?" screamed Benjamin, his voice fading as the jeep sped across the border.

"The fuel truck, that lousy *fuel* truck!" whispered Jason as he raced into "Strasbourg, France."

It happened in "Paris"—where else but *Paris*! The huge duplicate of the Eiffel Tower blew up with such force that the earth shook. Rockets? Missiles? The Jackal had stolen *missiles* from the Kubinka Armory! Seconds later, starting far behind him, the explosions began as the streets burst into flames. *Everywhere.* All "France" was being destroyed in a way that the madman Adolf Hitler could only have envisaged in his most twisted dreams. Panicked men and women ran through the alleyways and the streets, screaming, falling, praying to gods their leaders had forsworn.

"England!" He had to get into "England" and then ultimately into "America," where all his instincts told him the end would come—one way or another. He had to find the truck that was being driven by the Jackal and destroy both. He could do it—he *could do* it! Carlos thought he was dead and that was the key, for the Jackal would do what he had to do, what *he,* Jason Bourne, would do if he were Carlos. When the holocaust he had ignited was at its zenith, the Jackal would abandon the truck and put into

play his means of escape—his escape to Paris, the *real* Paris, where his army of old men would spread the word of their monseigneur's triumph over the ubiquitous, disbelieving Soviets. It would be somewhere near the tunnel; that was a given.

The race through "London," "Coventry" and "Portsmouth" could only be likened to the newsreel footage from World War II depicting the carnage hurled down on Great Britain by the Luftwaffe, compounded by first the screaming and then the silent terror of the V-2 and V-5 rockets. But the residents of Novgorod were not British—forbearance gave way to mass hysteria, concern for all became survival for self alone. As the impressive reproductions of Big Ben and the Houses of Parliament crashed down in flames and the aircraft factories of "Coventry" were reduced to raging fires, the streets swelled with screaming, horrified crowds racing through the roads that led to the Volkhov River and the shipyards of "Portsmouth." There, from the scaled-down piers and slips, scores threw themselves into rushing waters only to be caught in the magnesium grids where sharp, jagged bolts of electricity blazingly zigzagged through the air, leaving limp bodies floating toward the next metal traps above and below the angry surface. In paralyzed fragments, the crowds watched and turned in panic, fighting their way back into the miniaturized city of "Portsea"; the guards had abandoned their posts and chaos ruled the night.

Snapping on the jeep's searchlight, Bourne drove in sudden spurts down alleyways and the less crowded narrow streets—south, always south. He grabbed a flare from the army vehicle's floor, pulled the release string, and proceeded to thrust the spitting, hissing, blinding burst of fire into the hands and faces of the hysterical racing stragglers who tried to climb on board. The sight of the constantly pulsating flame so close to their eyes was enough; each screamed and recoiled in terror, no doubt thinking yet another explosive had detonated in his or her immediate vicinity.

A graveled road! The gates to the American compound were less than a hundred yards away. . . . *The graveled road?* Soaked with fuel! The plastic charges had not gone off—but they would in a matter of moments, creating a wall of fire, enveloping the jeep and its driver! With the accelerator pressed to the floor, Jason raced to the gate. It was deserted—and the iron barrier was *down*! He slammed on the brakes, skidding to a stop, hoping beyond reasonable hope that no sparks would fly out and ignite the gravel. Placing the spewing flare on the metal floor, he swiftly removed two grenades from his pockets—grenades he was loath to part with—pulled the pins, and hurled both toward the gate. The massive explosions blew the barricade away and instantly set the graveled road on fire, the leaping flames immediate—enveloping him! He had no choice; he threw the hot flare away and sped through the tunnel of fire into Novgorod's final largest compound. As he did so the concrete guardhouse at the "English" border exploded; glass, stone and shards of metal shot out and up everywhere.

He had been so filled with anxiety on their way to the crossing into "Spain" that he barely recalled the diminutive replicas of the "American" cities and towns, much less the fastest routes that led to the tunnel. He had merely followed young Benjamin's harsh shouted commands, but he did remember that the California-bred trainer kept referring to the "coast road—like Route One, man, up to Carmel!" It was, of course, those streets closest to the Volkhov, which in turn became, in no order of geographi-

cal sequence, a shoreline in "Maine," the Poto-
mac River of "Washington," and the northern
waters of Long Island Sound that housed the
naval base at "New London."

The madness had reached "America." Police
cars, their sirens wailing, sped through the
streets, men shouting into radios as people in
various stages of dress and undress ran out of
buildings and stores, screaming about the terrible earthquake that had hit this leg of the Volkhov, one even more severe than the
catastrophe in Armenia. Even with the surest
knowledge of devastating infiltration, the leaders of Novgorod could not reveal the truth. It
was as if the seismic geologists of the world
were forgotten, their discoveries unfounded.
The giant forces beneath the earth did not col-
lide and erupt in terrible swift immediacy; instead, they worked in relays, sending a series of
crippling body blows from north to south. Who
questions authority in the panic of survival? Everyone in "America" was being prepared,
primed for what they knew not.

They found out roughly ten minutes after the
destruction of a large part of the diminutive
"Great Britain." Bourne reached the com-
pressed, miniaturized outlines of "Washington,
D.C." when the conflagration began. The first to

plunge into flames, the sound of its detonation delayed only by milliseconds, was the wooden duplicate of the Capitol dome; it blew into the yellowed sky like the thin, hollow replica it was. Moments later—only *moments*—the Washington Monument, centered in its patch of grassy park, crumpled with a distant boom as if its false base had been shoveled away by a thunderous ground-moving machine. In seconds the artificial set piece that was the White House collapsed in flames, the explosions dulled both audibly and visibly, for "Pennsylvania Avenue" was awash in fire.

Bourne *knew* where he was now. The tunnel was between "Washington" and "New London, Connecticut"! It was no more than five minutes away! He drove the jeep down to the street paralleling the river, and again there were frightened, hysterical crowds. The police were shouting through loudspeakers, first in English and then in Russian, explaining the terrible consequences if anyone tried to swim across the water, the searchlights swinging back and forth, picking up the floating bodies of those who had tried in the northern compounds.

"The tunnel, the *tunnel*! *Open the tunnel*!"

The screams from the excited crowds became a chant that could not physically be denied; the underground pipeline was about to be assaulted. Jason leaped out of the surrounded jeep, pocketing the remaining three flares, and propelled his way, arms and shoulders working furiously, often fruitlessly, through the crushing, crashing bodies. There was nothing else for it; he pulled out a flare and ripped the release from its recess. The spewing flame had its effect; heat and fire were catalysts. He ran through the crowd, pummeling everyone in front of him, shoving the blinding, spitting flare into terrified faces, until he reached the front and faced a cordon of guards in the uniforms of the United States Army. It was crazy, *insane*! The world had gone *nuts*!

No! *There!* In the fenced-off parking lot was the fuel truck! He broke through the cordon of guards, holding up his computerized release card, and ran up to the soldier with the highest-ranking insignia on his uniform, a colonel with an AK-47 strapped to his waist who was as panicked as any officer of high rank he had ever seen since Saigon.

"My identification is with the name 'Archie' and you can clear it immediately. Even now I refuse to speak our language, only *English*! Is that understood? Discipline is *discipline*!"

"Togda?" yelled the officer, questioning the moment, then instantly returning to English in a maddeningly Boston accent. "Of course, we know of you," he cried, "but what can I *do*? This is an uncontrollable riot!"

"Has anyone passed through the tunnel in the last, say, half hour?"

"No one, absolutely, *no* one! Our orders are to keep the tunnel closed at all costs!"

"Good. . . . Get on the loudspeakers and disperse the crowds. Tell them the crisis has passed and the danger with it."

"How *can* I? The fires are everywhere, the explosions *everywhere*!"

"They'll stop soon."

"How do you know that?"

"I *know*! Do as I say!"

"Do as he *says*!" roared a voice behind Bourne; it was Benjamin, his face and shirt drenched with sweat. "And I hope to hell you know what you're *talking* about!"

"Where did *you* come from?"

"Where you know; how is another question. Try scaring the shit out of Capital HQ for a chopper ordered by an apoplectic Krupkin from a hospital bed in Moscow."

" 'Apoplectic'—not bad for a Russian—"

"Who *gives* me such orders?" yelled the officer of the guard. "You are only a young man!"

"Check me out, buddy, but do it quick," answered Benjamin, holding out his card. "Otherwise I think I'll have you transferred to Tashkent. Nice scenery, but no private toilets. . . . *Move,* you asshole!"

"Cal—if—fornia, here I—"

"Shut *up!*"

"He's *here!* There's the fuel truck. Over there." Jason pointed to the huge vehicle that dwarfed the scattered cars and vans in the fenced parking area.

"A fuel truck? How did you figure it out?" asked the astonished Benjamin.

"That tank's got to hold close to a hundred thousand pounds. Combined with the plastics, strategically placed, it's enough for the streets and those fake structures of old, dried wood."

"*Slushaytye!*" blared the myriad loudspeakers around the tunnel, demanding attention, as indeed the explosions began to diminish. The colonel climbed on top of the low, concrete gatehouse, a microphone in his hand, his figure outlined in the harsh beams of powerful searchlights. "The earthquake has passed," he cried in Russian, "and although the damage is extensive and the fires will continue throughout the night, the crisis has *passed*! . . . Stay by the banks of the river, and our comrades in the maintenance crews will do their best to provide for your needs. . . . These are orders from our superiors, comrades. Do not give us reason to use force, I *plead* with you!"

"*What* earthquake?" shouted a man in the front ranks of the panicked multitude. "*You* say it's an earthquake and we are all *told* it is an earthquake but your brains are in your bowels! I've lived through an earthquake and this is *no* earthquake. It is an armed attack!"

"Yes, yes! An attack!"

"We are being *attacked*!"

"Invaded! It's an *invasion*!"

"Open the tunnel and let us out or you'll have to shoot us down! Open the *tunnel*!"

The protesting chorus grew from all sections of the desperate crowd as the soldiers held firm, their bayonets unsheathed and affixed to their rifles. The colonel continued, his features contorted, his voice nearly matching the hysteria of his frenzied audience.

"*Listen* to me and ask yourselves a question!" he screamed. "I'm telling you, as I have been told, that this *is* an earthquake and I know it's

true. Further, I will tell you *how* I know it's true!
. . . Have you heard a single gunshot? Yes, that
is the *question*! A single *gunshot*! No, you have
not! . . . Here, as in all the compounds and in
every sector of those compounds, there are police and soldiers and trainers who carry weapons. Their orders are to repel by force any
unwarranted displays of violence, to say *nothing*
of armed invaders! Yet nowhere has there been
any gunfire—"

"What's he shouting about?" asked Jason,
turning to Benjamin.

"He's trying to convince them it is—or *was*—
an earthquake. They don't believe him; they
think it's an invasion. He's telling them it
couldn't be because there's been no gunfire."

"Gunfire?"

"That's his proof. Nobody's shooting at anybody and they sure as hell would be if there was
an armed attack. No gunshots, no attack."

"Gunshots . . . ?" Bourne suddenly grabbed
the young Soviet and spun him around. "Tell
him to stop! For God's sake, *stop* him!"

"What?"

"He's giving the Jackal the opening he
wants—he needs!"

"Now what are *you* talking about?"

"Gunfire . . . gunshots, confusion!"

"Nyet!" screamed a woman, breaking through the crowd and shouting at the officer in the center of the searchlight beams. "The explosions are bombs! They come from bombers above!"

"You are foolish," cried the colonel, replying in Russian. "If it was an air raid, our fighter planes from Belopol would fill the sky! . . . The explosions come out of the earth, the fires out of the earth, from the gases *below*—" These false words were the last words the Soviet officer would ever speak.

A staccato volley of automatic gunfire burst from the shadows of the tunnel's parking area cutting the Russian down, his instantly limp, punctured body collapsing and falling off the roof of the gatehouse, plummeting to the ground out of sight at the rear. The already frantic crowd went rabid; the ranks of uniformed "American" soldiers broke, and if chaos had ruled previously, nihilistic mobocracy now reigned supreme. The narrow, fenced entrance to the tunnel was virtually stormed, racing figures colliding, pummeling, climbing over one another, rushing en masse toward the mouth of the underwater access. Jason pulled his young trainer to the side of the stampeding hordes, never for an instant taking his eyes off the darkened parking area.

"Can you operate the tunnel's machinery?" he shouted.

"Yes! Everyone on the senior staff can, it's part of the job!"

"The iron gates you told me about?"

"Of course."

"Where are the mechanisms?"

"The guardhouse."

"Get in there!" yelled Bourne, taking one of the three remaining flares out of his field-jacket pocket and handing it to Benjamin. "I've got two more of these and two other grenades. . . . When you see one of my flares go over the crowd, lower those gates on *this side—only* this side, understood?"

"What for?"

"*My rules,* Ben! *Do* it! Then ignite this flare and throw it out the window so I'll know it's done."

"Then what?"

"Something you may not want to do, but you *have* to. . . . Take the 'forty-seven' from the colonel's body and force the crowd, *shoot* it back into the street. Rapid fire into the ground in front of them—or above them—do whatever you have to do, even if it means wounding a few. Whatever the cost, it must be *done.* I have to find him, isolate him, above all, cut him off from everyone else trying to get out."

"You're a goddamned *maniac,*" broke in Benjamin, the veins pronounced in his forehead. "I could kill 'a *few*'—*more* than a few! You're crazy!"

"At this moment I'm the most rational man you've ever met," interrupted Jason harshly, rapidly, as the panicked residents of Novgorod kept rushing by. "There's not a sane general in the Soviet army—the *same* army that retook Stalingrad—who wouldn't agree with me. . . . It's called the 'calculated estimate of losses,' and there's a very good reason for that lousy verbiage. It simply means you're paying a lot less for what you're getting now than you'd pay later."

"You're asking too *much*! These people are my comrades, my friends; they're Russians. Would you fire into a crowd of Americans? One recoil of my hands—an inch, two inches with a 'forty-seven'—and I could maim or kill half a dozen people! The risk's too great!"

"You don't have a choice. If the Jackal gets by me—and I'll *know* it if he does—I'll throw in a grenade and kill twenty."

"You son of a bitch!"

"Believe it, Ben. Where Carlos is concerned I'm a son of a bitch. I can't afford him any longer, the world can't afford him. *Move!*"

The trainer named Benjamin spat in Bourne's face, then turned and began fighting his way to the guardhouse and the unseen corpse of the colonel beyond. Almost unconsciously Jason wiped his face with the back of his hand, his concentration solely on the fenced parking area, his eyes darting from one pocket of shadows to another, trying to center in on the origins of the automatic gunfire, yet knowing it was pointless; the Jackal had changed position by then. He counted the other vehicles in addition to the fuel truck; there were nine parked by the fence—two station wagons, four sedans and three suburban vans, all American-made or simulated as such. Carlos was concealed beyond one of them or possibly the fuel truck, the last unlikely as it was the farthest away from the open gate in the fence that permitted access to the guardhouse and thus to the tunnel.

Jason crouched and crawled forward; he reached the waist-high fence, the pandemonium behind him continuous, deafening. Every muscle and joint in his legs and arms pounded with pain; *cramps* were developing everywhere, everywhere! *Don't think about them, don't acknowledge them. You're too close, David! Keep going. Jason Bourne knows what to do. Trust him!*

Aaughh! He spun his body over the fence; the handle of his sheathed bayonet embedded itself in his kidney. *There is no pain! You're too close, David—Jason. Listen to Jason!*

The searchlights—someone had pressed something and they went crazy, spinning around in circles, abrupt, blinding, out of control! Where would Carlos go? Where could he *hide*? The beams were erratically piercing everywhere! Then, from an opening that he could not see from across the fenced-in area, two police cars raced inside, their sirens blaring. Uniformed men leaped out from every door, and contrary to anything he expected to see, each scrambled to the borders of the fence, behind the cars and the vans, one after another dashing from one vehicle to another to the open gate that led to the guardhouse and the tunnel.

There was a break in space, in *time*. In *men*! The last four escapees from the second car were suddenly three—and only moments later did the fourth appear—but he was not the same—the uniform was not the *same*! There were specks of orange and red, and the visored officer's cap was laced with gold ribbing, the visor itself too prominent for the American army, the crown of the cap too pointed. What *was* it? . . . And, suddenly, Bourne understood. Fragments of his memories spiraled back years to Madrid or Casavieja, when he was tracing the Jackal's contracts with the Falangists. It was a *Spanish* uniform! That was it! Carlos had infiltrated through the Spanish compound, and as his Russian was fluent, he was using the high-ranking uniform to make his escape from Novgorod.

Jason lurched to his feet, his automatic drawn, and ran across the graveled lot, his left hand reaching into his field-jacket pocket for his second-to-last flare. He pulled the release and hurled the fired stalk above the cars, beyond the fence. Benjamin would not see it from the guardhouse and mistake it for the signal to close the gates of the tunnel; that signal would come shortly—in seconds, perhaps—but at the moment it was premature, again perhaps by seconds.

"Eto srochno!" roared one of the escaping men, spinning around and panicked at the sight of the hissing, blinding flare.

"Skoryeye!" shouted another, passing three companions and racing toward the open section of the fence. As the whirling searchlights continued their maniacal spinning, Bourne counted the seven figures as one by one they dashed away from the last car and passed through the opening, joining the excited crowds at the mouth of the tunnel. The eighth man did not appear; the high-ranking Spanish uniform was nowhere in sight. The Jackal was trapped!

Now! Jason whipped out his last flare, yanked the release, and threw it with all his strength over the stream of rushing men and women at the guardhouse. *Do it, Ben!* he screamed in silence as he removed the next-to-last grenade from the pocket of his field jacket. *Do it now!*

As if in answer to his fevered plea, a thunderous roar came from the tunnel, round after round of hysterical protestations punctuated by screams and shrieks and wailing chaos. Two rapid, deafening bursts of automatic gunfire preceded unintelligible commands over the speakers, shouted in Russian. . . . Another burst and the same voice continued, louder, even more authoritative, as the crowd momentarily but perceptibly quieted down, only to suddenly resume screaming at full volume. Bourne glanced over, astonished to see through the beams of the spinning searchlights the figure of Benjamin now standing on the roof of the concrete guardhouse. The young trainer was shouting into the microphone, exhorting the crowd to follow his instructions, whatever they were. . . . And whatever they were, they were being obeyed! The multitude gradually, then gathering momentum, began reversing direction—then, as a single unit, started racing back into the street! Benjamin ignited his flare and waved it, pointing to the north. He was sending Jason his own signal. Not only was the tunnel shut down but the crowds were being dispersed without anyone being shot with the AK-47. There had been a better way.

Bourne dropped to the ground, his eyes scanning the undersides of the stationary vehicles, the spewing flame beyond lighting up the open spaces. . . . A pair of legs—in *boots*! Behind the third automobile on the left, no more than twenty yards from the break in the fence that led to the tunnel. Carlos was *his*! The end *was* at last in sight! No *time*! *Do what you have to do and do it quickly!* He dropped his weapon on the gravel, gripped the grenade in his right hand, pulled the pin, grabbed the .45 with his left hand and lurched off the ground, racing forward. Roughly thirty feet from the car he dived back down into the gravel, turned sideways and heaved the grenade under the automobile—only at the last instant, the small bomb having left his hand, realizing that he had made a terrible error! The legs behind the car did not move—the boots remained in place, for they were just that, *boots*! He lunged to his right, rolling furiously over the sharp stones, shielding his face, curling his body into the smallest mass he could manage.

The explosion was deafening, the lethal debris joining the whirling beams of the searchlights in the night sky, fragments of metal and glass stinging Jason's back and legs. Move, *move*! screamed the voice in his mind's ears as he lurched to his knees, then to his feet in the smoke and fire of the burning automobile. As he did so the gravel erupted all around him; he zigzagged wildly toward the protection of the nearest vehicle, a square-shaped van. He was hit twice, in his shoulder and thigh! He spun around the wall of the van at the precise moment when the large windshield was blown away.

"You're no *match* for me, Jason Bourne!" screamed Carlos the Jackal, his automatic weapon on rapid fire. "You never *were*! You are a pretender, a *fraud*!"

"So be it," roared Bourne. "Then come and

get me!'' Jason raced to the driver's door, yanked it open, then ran to the back of the vehicle where he crouched, his face to the edge, his Colt .45 angled straight up next to his cheek. With a final hissing expulsion, the flare beyond the fence burned itself out as the Jackal stopped his continuous fire. Bourne understood. Carlos faced the open door, unsure, indecisive . . . only seconds to go. Metal against metal; a gun barrel was rammed against the door, slamming it shut. *Now!*

Jason spun around the edge of the van, his weapon exploding, firing into the Spanish uniform, blowing the gun out of the Jackal's hands. *One, two, three;* the shells flew in the air—and then they stopped! They *stopped,* the explosions replaced by a sickening, jamming click as the round in the chamber failed to eject. Carlos lurched to the ground for his weapon, his left arm limp and bleeding but his right hand still strong, clutching the gun like the claw of a crazed animal.

Bourne whipped his bayonet out of its scabbard and sprang forward, slicing the blade down toward the Jackal's forearm. He was too *late!* Carlos held the weapon! Jason lunged up, his left hand clasping the hot barrel—hold on, hold on! *You can't let it go! Twist it! Clockwise! Use the bayonet—no, don't! Drop it! Use both hands!* The conflicting commands clashed in his head, *madness.* He had no breath, no strength; his eyes could not focus—the *shoulder.* Like Bourne himself, the Jackal was wounded in his right shoulder!

Hold on! Reach the shoulder but *hold on*! With a last, gasping final surge, Bourne shot up and crashed Carlos back into the side of the van, pummeling the wounded area. The Jackal screamed, dropping the weapon, then kicked it under the vehicle.

Where the blow came from, Jason at first did not know; he only knew that the left side of his skull seemed suddenly split in two. Then he realized that he had done it to himself! He had slipped on the blood-covered gravel, and had crashed into the metal grille of the van. It did not matter—*nothing* mattered!

Carlos the Jackal was racing away! With the rampant confusion everywhere, there were a hundred ways he could get out of Novgorod. It had all been for *nothing*!

Still, there was his last grenade. Why not? Bourne removed it, pulled the pin, and threw it over the van into the center of the parking area.

The explosion followed and Jason got to his feet; perhaps the grenade would tell Benjamin something, warn him to keep his eyes on the area.

Staggering and barely able to walk, Jason started for the break in the fence that led to the guardhouse and the tunnel. *Oh, God, Marie, I failed! I'm so sorry. Nothing! It was for nothing!* And then, as if all Novgorod were having a final laugh at his expense, he saw that someone had opened the iron gates to the tunnel, giving the Jackal his invitation to freedom.

"Archie . . . ?" Benjamin's astonished voice floated over the sounds of the river, followed by the sight of the young Soviet running out of the guardhouse toward Bourne. "Christ almighty, I thought you were *dead*!"

"So you opened the gates and let my executioner walk away," yelled Jason weakly. "Why didn't you send a limousine for him?"

"I suggest you look again, Professor," replied a breathless Benjamin as he stopped in front of Bourne, studying Jason's battered face and bloodstained clothing. "Old age has withered your eyesight."

"What?"

"You want gates, you'll have gates." The

trainer shouted an order toward the guardhouse in Russian. Seconds later the huge iron gates descended, covering the mouth of the tunnel. But something was strange. Bourne had not actually seen the lowered gates before, yet these were not like anything he might have imagined. They appeared to be . . . swollen somehow, distorted perhaps. "Glass," said Benjamin.

"Glass?" asked a bewildered Jason.

"At each end of the tunnel, five-inch-thick walls of glass, locked and sealed."

"What are you talking about?" It was not necessary for the young Russian to explain. Suddenly, like a series of gigantic waves crashing against the walls of a huge aquarium, the tunnel was being filled with the waters of the Volkhov River. Then within the violence of the growing, swirling liquid mass, there was an object . . . a thing, a form, a *body*! Bourne stared in shock, his eyes bulging, his mouth gaped, frozen in place, unable to disgorge the cry that was in him. He summoned what strength he had left, running unsteadily, twice falling to his knees, but gathering speed with each stride, and raced to the massive wall of glass that sealed the entrance beyond it. Breathlessly, his chest heaving, he placed his hands against the glass wall

and leaned into it, bearing witness to the macabre scene barely inches in front of him. The
grotesquely uniformed corpse of Carlos
the Jackal kept crashing back and forth into the
steel bars of the gate, his dark features twisted
in hate, his eyes two glass orbs reviling death as
it overtook him.

The cold eyes of Jason Bourne watched in
satisfaction, his mouth taut, rigid, the face of a
killer, a killer among killers, who had won.
Briefly, however, the softer eyes of David Webb
intruded, his lips parted, forming the face of a
man for whom the weight of a world he loathed
had been removed.

"He's gone, Archie," observed Benjamin at
Jason's side. "That bastard can't come back."

"You flooded the tunnel," said Bourne simply.
"How did you know it was him?"

"You didn't have an automatic weapon, but
he did. Frankly, I thought Krupkin's prophecy
was—shall we say—borne out? You were dead,
and the man who killed you would take the
quickest way out. This was it and the uniform
confirmed it. Everything suddenly made sense
from the 'Spanish' compound down."

"How did you get that crowd away?"

"I told them barges were being sent to take
them across the river—about two miles north.

. . . Speaking of Krupkin, I've got to get you out of here. *Now.* Come on, the helicopter pad's about a half a mile away. We'll use the jeep. Hurry up, for God's sake!''

"Krupkin's instructions?"

"Choked from his hospital bed, in as much anger as in shock."

"What do you mean?"

"You might as well know. Someone up in the rarefied circle—Krupkin doesn't know who—issued the order that you weren't to leave here under any conditions. Put plainly, it was unthinkable, but then no one ever thought that the whole goddamned Novgorod would go up in flames, either, and that's our cover."

"Ours?"

"I'm not your executioner, somebody else is. The word never reached me and in this mess it won't now."

"*Wait* a minute! Where's the chopper taking me?"

"Cross your fingers, Professor, and hope Krupkin and your American friend know what they're doing. The helicopter takes you to Yelsk, and from there a plane to Zomosc across the Polish border, where an ungrateful satellite has apparently permitted a CIA listening post."

"Christ, I'll still be in Soviet bloc territory!"

"The implication was that your people are ready for you. Good luck."

"Ben," said Jason, studying the young man. "Why are you doing this? You're disobeying a direct order—"

"I *received* no order!" broke in the Russian. "And even if I had, I'm no unthinking robot. You had an arrangement and you fulfilled your end. . . . Also, if there's a chance for my mother—"

"There's more than a chance," interrupted Bourne.

"Come on, let's go! We're wasting time. Yelsk and Zomosc are only the beginning for you. You face a long and dangerous journey, Archie."

42

Sundown, and the out islands of Montserrat were growing darker, becoming patches of deep green surrounded by a shimmering blue sea and never-ending sprays of white foam erupting from coral reefs off the shorelines; all were bathed in the diaphanous orange of the Caribbean horizon. On Tranquility Isle, lamps were gradually turned on inside the last four villas in the row above the beach at Tranquility Inn, and figures could be seen, by and large walking slowly between the rooms and out on the balconies where the rays from the setting sun washed over the terraces. The soft breezes carried the scents of hibiscus and poinciana across the tropical foliage as a lone fishing boat weaved its way through the reefs with its late-afternoon catch for the inn's kitchen.

Brendan Patrick Pierre Prefontaine carried his Perrier out to the balcony of Villa Seventeen, where Johnny St. Jacques stood by the railing sipping a rum and tonic. "How long do you think it will take before you reopen?" asked the former judge of the Boston court, sitting down at the white wrought-iron table.

"The structural damage can be repaired in a matter of weeks," replied the owner of Tranquility Inn, "but the aftertaste of what happened here will take longer, a lot longer."

"Again, how long?"

"I'll give it four or five months before I send out the initial brochures—it'll be late for the season's bookings, but Marie agrees. To do anything earlier would not only be tasteless, but the urgency would fuel all the gossip again. . . . Terrorists, drug runners, corrupt island government—we don't need that and we don't deserve it."

"Well, as I mentioned, I can pay my freight," said the once honorable justice of the federal district court in Massachusetts. "Perhaps not to the extent of your highest seasonal prices, dear man, but certainly sufficient to cover the costs of a villa, plus a little for the inn's kitty."

"I told you, forget it. I owe you more than I can ever repay. Tranquility's yours as long as you want to stay." St. Jacques turned from the railing, his eyes lingering on the fishing boat below, and sat down opposite Prefontaine. "I worry about the people down there, in the boats and on the beach. I used to have three or four boats bringing in the freshest fish. Now I've only got one coming in for us and what's left of the staff—all of whom are on half salary."

"Then you need my money."

"Come on, Judge, *what* money? I don't want to appear intrusive, but Washington gave me a pretty complete rundown on you. You've been living off the streets for years."

"Ah, yes, Washington," pronounced Prefontaine, raising his glass to the orange-and-azure sky. "As usual, it is twelve steps behind the crime—twenty steps where its *own* criminality is concerned."

"What are you talking about?"

"Randolph Gates, that's what I'm talking about—*who* I'm talking about."

"That bastard from *Boston*? The one who put the Jackal on David's trail?"

"The touchingly reformed Randolph Gates, Johnny. Reformed in all ways but monetary restitution, I might add. . . . Still, nevertheless, with the mind and the conscience that I knew at Harvard years ago. Not the brightest, not the best, but with the literary and oratorical skills that camouflaged a brilliance that was never really there."

"Now what the *hell* are you talking about?"

"I visited him the other day at his rehabilitation center in Minnesota, or Michigan, I can't actually remember which, for I flew first class and the drinks were delivered on request. Regardless, we met and our arrangement was concluded. He's changing *sides,* Johnny. He's now going to fight—legally—for the people, *not* for the conglomerates who buy and sell on *paper.* He told me he's going after the raiders and the merger brokers who make billions in the markets and cost thousands upon thousands in jobs."

"How can he do that?"

"Because he was there. He did it all; he knows all the tricks and is willing to commit his considerable talents to the cause."

"Why would he do it?"

"Because he's got Edith back."

"Who in God's name is *Edith*?"

"His wife. . . . Actually, I'm still in love with her. I was from the time we first met, but in those days a distinguished judge with a wife and a child, regardless of how repulsive both might be, did not pursue such longings. Randy the Grand never deserved her; perhaps now he'll make up for all the lost years."

"That's very interesting, but what's it got to do with your arrangement?"

"Did I mention that Lord Randolph of Gates made great sums of money during those lost but productive years?"

"Several times. So?"

"Well, in recognition of the services I rendered that undoubtedly contributed to the removal of a life-threatening situation in which he found himself, said threat emanating from Paris, he saw clearly the validity of compensating me. Especially in light of the knowledge I possess. . . . You know, after a number of bloodletting courtroom battles, I think he's going after a judgeship. Far higher than mine, I think."

"So?"

"So, if I keep my own counsel, get out of Boston, and for the sake of a loose tongue stay off the sauce, his bank will forward me fifty thousand dollars a year for the rest of my life."

"Jesus *Christ!*"

"That's what I said to myself when he agreed. I even went to Mass for the first time in thirty-odd years."

"Still, you won't be able to go home again."

"Home?" Prefontaine laughed softly. "Was it really? No matter, I may have found another. Through a gentlemen named Peter Holland at the Central Intelligence Agency, I was given an introduction to your friend Sir Henry Sykes over in Montserrat, who in turn introduced me to a retired London barrister named Jonathan Lemuel, originally a native islander. We're both getting on, but neither of us is ready for a different sort of 'home.' We may open a consulting firm, specialists in American and UK laws where export and import licensing is concerned. Of course, we'll have to do some boning up, but we'll manage. I expect I'll be here for years."

St. Jacques rose quickly from the table to replenish his drink, his eyes warily on the former, disbarred judge.

Morris Panov walked slowly, cautiously out of his bedroom and into the sitting room of Villa

Eighteen, where Alex Conklin sat in a wheel-chair. The bandages across the psychiatrist's chest were visible under the light fabric of his white guayabera; they extended down his exposed left arm below the elbow. "It took me damn near twenty minutes to lift this useless appendage through the sleeve!" he complained angrily but without self-pity.

"You should have called me," said Alex, spinning himself around in the chair, away from the telephone. "I can still roll this thing pretty damned fast. Of course, I had a couple of years' experience prior to my Quasimodo's boot."

"Thank you, but I prefer to dress myself—as I believe you preferred to walk by yourself once the prosthesis was fitted."

"That's the first lesson, Doctor. I expect there's something about it in your head books."

"There is. It's called dumb, or, if you like, obstinate stupidity."

"No, it's not," countered the retired intelligence officer, his eyes leveled with Panov's as the psychiatrist lowered himself slowly into a chair.

"No . . . it's not," agreed Mo, returning Conklin's look. "The first lesson is independence. Take as much as you can handle and keep grabbing for more."

"There's a good side, too," said Alex, smiling and adjusting the bandage around his throat. "It gets easier, not harder. You learn new tricks every day; it's surprising what our little gray cells come up with."

"Do tell? I must explore that field one day. . . . I heard you on the phone, who was it?"

"Holland. The wires have been burning on all the back channels between Moscow and Washington, every covert phone on both sides damn near paralyzed thinking there could be a leak and theirs would be held responsible."

"Medusa?"

"You never heard that name, *I* never heard that name, and nobody we *know* has ever heard it. There's been enough bloodletting in the international marketplace—to say nothing of a few buckets of real blood spilled—to call into question the sanity of both governments' controlling institutions, which were obviously blind or just plain stupid."

"How about just plain guilty?" asked Panov.

"Too few at the top to warrant the destruction of the whole—that's the verdict of Langley and Dzerzhinsky Square. The chief pin-stripers at the State Department in the Kremlin's Council of Ministers agree. Nothing can be served by pur-

suing or exposing the extent of the malfeasance—how do you like that, *malfeasance*? Murder, assassination, kidnapping, extortion and
large-scale corruption using organized crime on
both sides of the Atlantic are now conveniently
slotted as 'malfeasance'! They say it's better to
salvage what we can as quietly and as expeditiously as possible."

"That's obscene."

"That's reality, Doctor. You're about to witness one of the biggest cover-ups in modern
history, certainly among powerful sovereign nations. . . . And the real obscenity is that they're
probably right. If Medusa were exposed to the
fullest—and it would be fully exposed if it was
exposed at all—the people in their righteous indignation would throw the bastards out—many
of them the wrong bastards, tainted only by association. That sort of thing produces vacuums
in high places, and these are not the times for
vacuums of any kind. Better the Satans you
know than the ones you don't who come later."

"So what's going to happen?"

"Trade off," said Conklin pensively. "The
scope of Medusa's operations is so far-ranging
geographically and structurally that it's almost
impossible to unravel. Moscow's sending Ogil-

vie back with a team of financial analysts, and with our own people they'll start the process of dismantling. Eventually Holland foresees a quiet, unannounced economic minisummit, calling together various financial ministers of the NATO and Eastern bloc countries. Wherever Medusa's assets can be self-sustaining or absorbed by their individual economies, that'll be the case with restrictive covenants on all parties. The main point is to prevent financial panics through mass factory closings and wholesale company collapses."

"Thus burying Medusa," offered Panov. "It's again history, unwritten and unacknowledged, the way it was from the beginning."

"Above all, that," conceded Alex. "By omission and commission there's enough sleaze to go around for everybody."

"What about men like Burton on the Joint Chiefs, and Atkinson in London?"

"No more than messengers and fronts; they're out for reasons of health, and believe me, they understand."

Panov winced as he adjusted his uncomfortable wounded body in the chair. "It hardly compensates for his crimes, but the Jackal served a purpose of sorts, didn't he? If you hadn't been hunting him, you wouldn't have found Medusa."

"The coincidence of evil, Mo," said Conklin. "I'm not about to recommend a posthumous medal."

"I'd say it's more than coincidence," interrupted Panov, shaking his head. "In the final analysis, David was right. Whether forced or leaped upon, a connection was there after all. Someone in Medusa had a killer or killers using the name of 'Jason Bourne' assassinate a high-visibility target in the Jackal's own backyard; that someone knew what he was doing."

"You mean Teagarten, of course."

"Yes. Since Bourne was on Medusa's death list, our pathetic turncoat, DeSole, had to tell them about the Treadstone operation, perhaps not by name but its essentials. When they learned that Jason—David—was in Paris, they used the original scenario: Bourne against the Jackal. By killing Teagarten the way they did, they accurately assumed they were enlisting the most deadly partner they could find to hunt down and kill David."

"We know that. So?"

"Don't you see, Alex? When you think about it, Brussels was the beginning of the end, and at the end, David used that false accusation to tell

Marie he was still alive, to tell Peter Holland that he was still alive. The map circling Anderlecht in red."

"He gave hope, that's all. Hope isn't something I put much trust in, Mo."

"He did more than give hope. That message made Holland prepare every station in Europe to expect Jason Bourne, assassin, and to use every extreme to get him back here."

"It worked. Sometimes that kind of thing doesn't."

"It worked because weeks ago a man called Jason Bourne knew that to catch Carlos there had to be a link between himself and the Jackal, a long-forgotten connection that had to be brought to the surface. He *did* it, you did it!"

"In a hell of a roundabout way," admitted Conklin. "We were reaching, that's all. Possibilities, probabilities, abstractions—it's all we had to work with."

"Abstractions?" asked Panov gently. "That's such an erroneously passive term. Have you any idea what thunder in the mind abstractions provoke?"

"I don't even know what you're talking about."

"Those gray cells, Alex. They go crazy, spinning around like infinitesimal Ping-Pong balls trying to find tiny tunnels to explode through, drawn by their own inherent compulsions."

"You've lost me."

"You said it yourself, the coincidence of evil. But I'd suggest another conductor—the *magnet* of evil. That's what you and David created, and within that magnetic field was Medusa."

Conklin spun around in the chair and wheeled himself toward the balcony and the descending orange glow on the horizon beyond the deep-green out islands of Montserrat. "I wish everything was as simple as you put it, Mo," he said rapidly. "I'm afraid it's not."

"You'll have to be clearer."

"Krupkin's a dead man."

"What?"

"I mourn him as a friend and one hell of an enemy. He made everything possible for us, and when it was all over, he did what was right, not what was ordered. He let David live and now he's paying for it."

"What happened to him?"

"According to Holland, he disappeared from the hospital in Moscow five days ago—he simply took his clothes and walked out. No one knows how he did it or where he went, but an hour after he left, the KGB came to arrest him and move him to the Lubyanka."

"Then they haven't caught him—"

"They will. When the Kremlin issues a Black Alert, every road, train station, airport and border crossing is put under a microscope. The incentives are irresistible: whoever lets him out will spend ten years in a gulag. It's just a question of time. *Goddamn it.*"

There was a knock on the front door and Panov called out. "It's open because it's easier! Come in."

The be-blazered, immaculately dressed assistant manager, Mr. Pritchard, entered, preceded by a room-service table that he was capable of pushing while standing completely erect. He smiled broadly and announced his presence as well as his mission. "Buckingham Pritchard at your service, gentlemen. I've brought a few delicacies from the sea for your collegial gathering before the evening meal which I have personally attended to at the side of the chef who has been known to be prone to errors without expert guidance which I was all too happy to provide."

"Collegial?" said Alex. "I got out of college damn near thirty-five years ago."

"It obviously didn't take where the nuances of English are concerned," mumbled Morris Panov. "*Tell* me, Mr. Pritchard, aren't you terribly hot in those clothes? I'd be sweating like a pig."

"No nuances there, only an unproven cliché," muttered Conklin.

"I do not perspire, sir," replied the assistant manager.

"I'll bet my pension you 'perspired' when Mr. St. Jacques came back from Washington," offered Alex. "Christ almighty, Johnny a 'terrorist'!"

"The incident has been forgotten, sir," said Pritchard stoically. "Mr. Saint Jay and Sir Henry understand that my brilliant uncle and I had only the children's interests at heart."

"Savvy, very savvy," observed Conklin.

"I'll set up the canapés, gentlemen, and check the ice. The others should be here in a matter of minutes."

"That's very kind of you," said Panov.

David Webb leaned against the balcony archway watching his wife as she read the last pages of a children's story to their son. The outstanding Mrs. Cooper was dozing in a chair, her magnificent black head, crowned by a fleece of silver and gray, kept nodding above her full chest as if she expected at any moment to hear sounds from the infant Alison beyond the half-closed door that was only feet from where she was sitting. The inflections of Marie's quiet voice matched the words of the story, confirmed by Jamie's wide eyes and parted lips. But for an analytical mind that found music in figures, his wife might have been an actress, mused David. She had the surface attributes of that precarious profession—striking features, a commanding presence, the sine qua non that forced both men and women to fall silent and pensively appraise her when she walked down a street or entered a room.

"You can read to me tomorrow, Daddy!"

The story was over, attested to by his son jumping off the couch and Mrs. Cooper flashing her eyes open. "I wanted to read that one tonight," said Webb defensively, moving away from the arch.

"Well, you still kind of smell," said the boy, frowning.

"Your father doesn't smell, Jamie," explained Marie, smiling. "I told you, it's the medicine the doctor said he had to use on his injuries from the accident.''

"He still smells."

"You can't argue with an analytical mind when it's right, can you?" asked David.

"It's too early to go to bed, Mommy! I might wake up Alison and she'll start crying again."

"I know, dear, but Daddy and I have to go over and see all your uncles—"

"And my new grandfather!" cried the child exuberantly. "Grandpa Brendan said he was going to teach me how to be a judge someday."

"God help the boy," interjected Mrs. Cooper. "That man dresses like a peacock flowering to mate."

"You may go into our room and watch television," overrode Marie quickly. "But only for a half hour—"

"Aww!"

"All right, perhaps an hour, but Mrs. Cooper will select the channels."

"Thanks, Mommy!" cried the child, racing into his parents' bedroom as Mrs. Cooper got out of the chair and followed him.

"Oh, I can start him off," said Marie, getting up from the couch.

"No, Miss Marie," protested Mrs. Cooper.

"You stay with your husband. That man hurts but he won't say anything." She disappeared into the bedroom.

"Is that true, my darling?" asked Marie, walking to David. "Do you hurt?"

"I hate to dispel the myth of a great lady's incontestable perceptions, but she's wrong."

"Why do you have to use a dozen words when one will suffice?"

"Because I'm supposed to be a scholar. We academicians never take a direct route because it doesn't leave us any offshoots to claim if we're wrong. What are you, anti-intellectual?"

"No," answered Marie. "You see, that's a simple, one-word declarative."

"What's a declarative?" asked Webb, taking his wife in his arms and kissing her, their lips enveloping, so meaningful to each, arousing to each.

"It's a shortcut to the truth," said Marie, arching her head back and looking at him. "No off-shoots, no circumlocutions, just fact. As in five and five equals ten, not nine or eleven, but ten."

"You're a ten."

"That's banal, but I'll take it. . . . You *are* more relaxed, I can feel you again. Jason Bourne's leaving you, isn't he?"

"Just about. While you were with Alison, Ed McAllister called me from the National Security Agency. Benjamin's mother is on her way back to Moscow."

"Hey, that's *wonderful,* David!"

"Both Mac and I laughed, and as we laughed I thought to myself I'd never heard McAllister laugh before. It was nice."

"He wore his guilt on his sleeve—no, all over him. He sent us both to Hong Kong and he never forgave himself. Now you're back and alive and free. I'm not sure *I'll* ever forgive him, but at least I won't hang up on him when he calls."

"He'd like that. As a matter of fact, I told him to call. I said you might even ask him to dinner someday."

"I didn't go that far."

"Benjamin's mother? That kid saved my life."

"Maybe a quick brunch."

"Take your hands off me, woman. In another fifteen seconds I'm going to throw Jamie and Mrs. Cooper out of our bedroom and demand my connubials."

"I'm tempted, Attila, but I think Bro's counting on us. Two feisty individuals and an over-imaginative disbarred judge are more than an Ontario ranch boy can handle."

"I love them all."

"So do I. Let's go."

The Caribbean sun had disappeared; only faint sprays of orange barely illuminated the western horizon. The flames of the glass-encased candles were steady, pointed, sending streams of gray smoke through their funnels, their glow producing warm light and comfortable shadows around the terraced balcony of Villa Eighteen. The conversation, too, had been warm and comfortable—survivors relishing their deliverance from a nightmare.

"I emphatically explained to Handy Randy that the doctrine of stare decisis has to be challenged if the times have altered the perceptions that existed when the original decisions were rendered," expounded Prefontaine. "Change, *change*—the inevitable result of the calendar."

"That's so obvious, I can't imagine anyone debating it," said Alex.

"Oh, Flood-the-Gates used it incessantly, confusing juries with his erudition and confounding his peers with multiple decises."

"Mirrors and smoke," added Marie, laughing. "We do the same in economics. Remember, Bro, I told you that?"

"I didn't understand a word. Still don't."

"No mirrors and no smoke where medicine's involved," said Panov. "At least not where the labs are monitored and the pharmaceutical money boys are prohibited. Legitimate advances are validated every day."

"In many ways it's the purposely undefined core of our Constitution," continued the former judge. "It's as though the Founders had read Nostradamus but didn't care to admit their frivolity, or perhaps studied the drawings of Da Vinci, who foresaw aircraft. They understood that they could not legislate the future, for they had no idea what it would hold, or what society would demand for its future liberties. They created brilliant omissions."

"Unaccepted as such by the brilliant Randolph Gates, if memory serves," said Conklin.

"Oh, he'll change quickly now," interrupted Prefontaine, chuckling. "He was always a sworn companion of the wind, and he's smart enough to adjust his sails when he has to buck it."

"I keep wondering whatever happened to the truck driver's wife, the one in the diner who was married to the man they called 'Bronk,'" said the psychiatrist.

"Try to imagine a small house and a white

picket fence, et cetera," offered Alex. "It's easier that way."

"What truck driver's wife?" asked St. Jacques.

"Leave it alone, Bro, I'd rather not find out."

"Or that son-of-a-bitch army doctor who pumped me full of Amytal!" pressed Panov.

"He's running a clinic in Leavenworth," replied Conklin. "I forgot to tell you. . . . So many, so crazy. And Krupkin. Crazy old Kruppie, elegance and all. We owe him, but we can't help him."

There was a moment of silence as each in his and her own way thought of a man who had selflessly opposed a monolithic system that demanded the death of David Webb, who stood by the railing staring out at the darkened sea, somehow separated in mind and body from the others. It would take time, he understood that. Jason Bourne had to vanish; he had to *leave* him. *When?*

Not now! Out of the early night, the madness began again! From the sky the roar of multiple engines broke the silence like approaching sharp cracks of lightning. Three military helicopters swooped down toward the Tranquility dock, fusillades of gunfire chewing up the shoreline as a powerful bullet speedboat swung through the reefs toward the beach. St. Jacques was on his intercom. *"Shore alarm!"* he screamed. "Grab your weapons!"

"Christ, the Jackal's *dead*!" yelled Conklin.

"His goddamned *disciples* aren't!" shouted Jason Bourne—no trace of David Webb—as he shoved Marie to the floor and took a gun out of his belt, a weapon his wife knew nothing about. "They were told he was here!"

"It's insane!"

"That's *Carlos*," replied Jason, racing to the balcony railing. "He *owns* them! They're his for life!"

"Shit!" roared Alex as he wheeled his chair furiously and pushed Panov away from the table and the lighted candles.

Suddenly a deafening loudspeaker from the lead helicopter crackled with static, followed by the words of the pilot. "You saw what we did to the beach, *mon*! We'll cut you in two if you don't stop your engine! . . . That's better, *mon*. Drift into shore—*drift,* no motor at all and both of you come on deck, your hands on the gunwale, leaning forward! Do it *now*!"

The searchlight beams of the two circling helicopters centered on the boat as the lead aircraft dropped to the beach, the rotors swirling up the sand, producing an outline of a threshold for its landing. Four men leaped out, their weapons trained on the drifting speedboat as the inhabitants of Villa Eighteen stood by the railing, staring in astonishment at the unbelievable scene below.

"Pritchard!" yelled St. Jacques. "Bring me the binoculars!"

"They're in my hands, Mr. Saint Jay—oh, there they are." The assistant manager rushed out with the powerful magnifiers and handed them to his employer. "I managed to clean the lenses, sir!"

"What do you *see*?" asked Bourne sharply.

"I don't know. Two men."

"Some *army*!" said Conklin.

"Give them to me," ordered Jason, grabbing the binoculars from his brother-in-law.

"What *is* it, David?" shouted Marie, seeing the shock on her husband's face.

"It's Krupkin," he said.

Dimitri Krupkin sat at the white wrought-iron table, his face pale—and it was his full face, as his chin beard had been removed—and refused to speak to anyone until he had finished his third brandy. Like Panov, Conklin and David Webb, he was clearly a hurt man, a wounded man, a man in considerable physical pain, which, like the others, he did not care to dwell upon, as what lay ahead was infinitely better than what he had left behind. His decidedly inferior clothes seemed to annoy him whenever he glanced down at them, but he shrugged continually in silence, the shrugs conveying the fact that soon he would be back in sartorial splendor. His first words were to the elderly Brendan Prefontaine as he appraised the former judge's intricately laced peach guayabera above the royal-blue trousers. "I like that outfit," he said admiringly. "Very tropical and in good taste for the climate."

"Thank you."

Introductions were made, and the instant they were over, a barrage of questions was hurled at the Soviet. He held up both hands, as a pope might from his balcony in St. Peter's Square, and spoke. "I will not bore you or disturb you with the trivial details of my flight from Mother Russia, other than to say I'm aghast at the high price of corruption and will neither forget nor forgive the filthy accommodations I was forced to endure for the exorbitant sums of money I spent. . . . That said, thank God for Crédit Suisse and those lovely green coupons they issue."

"Just tell us what happened," said Marie.

"You, dear lady, are even lovelier than I had imagined. Had we met in Paris I would have whisked you away from this Dickensian ragamuffin you call a husband. *My,* look at your hair—glorious!"

"He probably couldn't tell you what color it is," said Marie, smiling. "You'll be the threat I hold over his peasant head."

"Still, for his age he's remarkably competent."

"That's because I feed him a lot of pills, all kinds of pills, Dimitri. Now tell us, what happened?"

"What *happened*? They found me out, that's what happened! They confiscated my lovely house in Geneva! It's now an adjunct to the Soviet embassy. The loss is heartbreaking!"

"I think my wife's talking about the peasant *me,"* said Webb. "You were in the hospital in Moscow and you found out what someone intended for me—namely, my execution. Then you told Benjamin to get me out of Novgorod."

"I have sources, Jason, and errors are made in high places and I'll incriminate no one by using names. It was simply wrong. If Nuremberg taught us all nothing else, it was that obscene commands should not be obeyed. That lesson crosses borders and penetrates minds. We in Russia suffered far, far more than anyone in America during the last war. Some of us remember that, and we will not emulate that enemy."

"Well spoken," said Prefontaine, raising his glass of Perrier to the Soviet. "When everything's said and done, we're all part of the same thinking, feeling human race, aren't we?"

"Well," choked Krupkin, swallowing his fourth brandy, "beyond that very attractive if overused observation, there are divisions of commitment, Judge. Not serious, of course, but nevertheless varied. For instance, although my house on the lake in Geneva is no longer mine, my accounts in the Cayman Islands remain intensely personal. Incidentally, how far are those islands from here?"

"Roughly twelve hundred miles due west," replied St. Jacques. "A jet out of Antigua will get you there in three hours plus."

"That's what I thought," said Krupkin. "When we were in the hospital in Moscow, Alex frequently spoke of Tranquility Isle and Montserrat, so I checked the map in the hospital library.

Everything seems to be on course. . . . Incidentally, the man with the boat, he won't be dealt with too harshly, will he? My outrageously expensive ersatz papers are very much in order."

"His crime was in his appearance, not in bringing you over here," answered St. Jacques.

"I was in a hurry, it goes with running for your life."

"I've already explained to Government House that you're an old friend of my brother-in-law."

"Good. Very good."

"What will you do now, Dimitri?" asked Marie.

"My options are limited, I'm afraid. Our Russian bear not only has more claws than a centipede has legs, she's also computerized with a global network. I shall have to remain buried for quite some time while I construct another existence. From birth, of course." Krupkin turned to the owner of Tranquility Inn. "Would it be possible to lease one of these lovely cottages, Mr. St. Jacques?"

"After what you did for David and my sister, don't give it a second thought. This house is your house, Mr. Krupkin, all of it."

"How very kind. First, naturally, there'll be the trip to the Caymans, where, I'm told, there are excellent tailors; then perhaps a clever little yacht and a small charter business that can be substantiated as having been moved from Tierra del Fuego or the Malvinas, some godforsaken place where a little money can produce an identity and a highly credible if obscure past. After these are set in motion, there's a doctor in Buenos Aires who does wonders with fingerprints—quite painlessly, I'm told—and then minor cosmetic surgery—Rio has the best, you know, far better than New York—just enough to alter the profile and perhaps remove a few years. . . . For the past five days and nights, I've had nothing to do but think and plan, enduring situations of passage I would not describe in front of the lovely Mrs. Webb."

"You certainly have been thinking," agreed David's wife, impressed. "And please call me Marie. How can I hold you over the peasant's head if I'm Mrs. Webb?"

"Ah, the adorable Marie!"

"What about these adorable plans of yours?" asked Conklin pointedly. "How long will they take to implement?"

"You of all people should ask that question?" Krupkin's eyes were wide in disbelief.

"I think I'd better," broke in Alex.

"*You,* who were instrumental in building the

dossier of the greatest impersonator the international world of terrorism has ever *known*? The incomparable Jason Bourne?"

"If that includes me," said Webb, "I'm out. I'm heavy into interior decorating."

"How long, Kruppie?"

"For heaven's sake, man, you were training a recruit for an assignment, a single mission. *I'm* altering a life!"

"How *long*?"

"You tell me, Alex. It's my life we're talking about now—as worthless as that life may be in the geopolitical scheme of things—it's still my life."

"Whatever he needs," interrupted David Webb, the unseen image of Jason Bourne looking over his wounded shoulder.

"Two years to do it well, three years to do it better," said Dimitri Krupkin.

"They're yours," said Marie.

"*Pritchard,*" said St. Jacques, angling his head. "Fix my drink, if you please."

They walked along the moonlit beach, alternately touching and not touching, the embarrassment of intimacy intermittently intruding as if a world that had separated them had not let them escape its terrible orbit, constantly pulling them into its fiery nucleus.

"You carried a gun," said Marie softly. "I had no idea you had one. I hate guns."

"So do I. I'm not sure I knew I had one, either. It was just there."

"Reflex? Compulsion?"

"Both, I guess. It didn't matter, I didn't use it."

"But you wanted to, didn't you?"

"Again, I'm not sure. If you and the children

were threatened, of course I would, but I don't think I'd fire indiscriminately.''

"Are you sure, David? Would the appearance of danger to us make you pick up a gun and shoot at shadows?''

"No, I don't shoot at shadows.''

Footsteps. In the sand! Waves lapping over the unmistakable intrusion of a human being, breaks in the flow of the natural rhythm— sounds Jason Bourne knew from a hundred beaches! He spun around, violently propelling Marie off her feet, sending her out of the line of fire as he crouched, his weapon in his hand.

"Please don't kill me, David,'' said Morris Panov, the beam of his flashlight illuminating the area. "It simply wouldn't make sense.''

"*Jesus,* Mo!'' cried Webb. "What were you *doing*?''

"Trying to find you, that's all. . . . Would you please help Marie?''

Webb did so, pulling his wife to her feet, both half blinded by the flashlight. "My *God,* you're the *mole*!'' cried Jason Bourne, raising his weapon. "You knew every move I was making!''

"I'm *what*?'' roared the psychiatrist, throwing down his flashlight. "If you believe that, gun me down, you *son of a bitch*!''

"I don't know, Mo. I don't know anything any-more . . . !" David's head arched back in pain.

"Then cry your heart out, you *bastard*! Cry like you've never cried *before*! Jason Bourne is dead, cremated in Moscow, and that's the way it is! You either accept that or I don't want a goddamned thing to do with you anymore! Have you got that, you arrogant, brilliant *creation*! You *did* it, and it's *over*!"

Webb fell to his knees, the tears welling in his eyes, trembling and trying not to make a sound.

"We're going to be okay, Mo," said Marie, kneeling beside her husband, holding him.

"I know that," acknowledged Panov, nodding in the glow of the grounded flashlight. "Two lives in one mind, none of us can know what it's like. But it's over now. It's really over."

ABOUT THE AUTHOR

ROBERT LUDLUM, whose work has been published in twenty-seven languages and thirty-two countries, is the author of *The Icarus Agenda, The Scarlatti Inheritance, The Osterman Weekend, The Matlock Paper, The Rhinemann Exchange, The Gemini Contenders, The Chancellor Manuscript, The Road to Gandolfo, The Parsifal Mosaic, The Aquitaine Progression, The Bourne Supremacy, The Holcroft Covenant, The Bourne Identity, The Matarese Circle,* and *The Ludlum Triad.* He lives in Florida with his wife, Mary.